PLAYERS

Animals in War
Bella
Class
The Common Years
Emily
Harriet
Imogen
Jolly Marsupial
Jolly Super
Jolly Superlative
Jolly Super Too
Lisa & Co
Octavia
Prudence
Riders
Super Jilly
Super Cooper

PLANETS

PLAYERS

(FORMERLY TITLED RIVALS)

JILLY COOPER

BALLANTINE BOOKS

NEW YORK

All rights reserved under International and Pan-American Copyright Conventions. Published in the United States by Ballantine Books, a division of Random House, Inc., New York.
Originally published in Great Britain as *Rivals* in 1988 by Bantam Press, a division of Transworld Publishers Ltd.

Grateful acknowledgment is made to the following for permission to reprint previously published material:

Almo Music Corp.: Excerpts from the song lyrics "The Lady in Red," lyrics and music by Chris De Burgh. Copyright © 1986 by Rondor Music (London) Ltd. (PRS) All rights administered in the U.S. & Canada by Almo Music Corp. (ASCAP) All rights reserved. International copyright secured.

Macmillan Publishing Company: Excerpt from "The Wild Swans at Coole" from *The Poems of W.B. Yeats: A New Edition*, edited by Richard J. Finneran. Copyright 1919 by Macmillan Publishing Company. Copyright renewed 1947 by Bertha Georgie Yeats. Reprinted by permission of Macmillan Publishing Company. Excerpt from "The White Birds" from *The Poems of W.B. Yeats: A New Edition*, edited by Richard J. Finneran. Courtesy of Macmillan Publishing Company. Rights in the open market administered by A P Watt Limited on behalf of Michael B. Yeats and Macmillan London Ltd. Excerpts from the poems taken from *The Collected Poems of W.B. Yeats*.

Warner/Chappell Music, Inc.: Excerpt from the song lyrics "Last Christmas" by George Michael. Copyright © 1986 by Morrison-Leahy Music Ltd. All rights administered by Chappell & Co. Excerpt from the song lyrics "I Get a Kick Out of You" by Cole Porter. Copyright 1934 by Warner Bros. Inc. (Renewed). All rights reserved. Used by permission.

Library of Congress Catalog Card Number: 88-61365

ISBN: 0-345-35937-2

Text design by Mary A. Wirth
Cover design by James R. Harris
Cover photos by Don Banks

Manufactured in the United States of America
First American Edition: April 1989
10 9 8 7 6 5 4 3 2

TO ANNALISE KAY

WHO IS AS WISE AS SHE IS
GOOD AND BEAUTIFUL.

ACKNOWLEDGMENTS

A very large number of people helped me with this book. Most of them work in television and are exceptionally busy. They still found the time to talk to me and—particularly in the case of those from HTV—to entertain me with lavishness and generosity. All of them are experts in their own field. But as I was writing fiction, I only took their advice so far as it fitted my plot. The accuracy of the book in no way reflects their expertise. They were also all so nice to me that it was impossible to base any of the unpleasant characters in the story on any of them.

They include Georgina Abrahams, William Beloe, Michael Blakstad, Roy Bottomley, James Bredin, Adrian Brenard, Doug Carnegie, Stephen Cole, John Corbett, Mike Davey, Patrick Dromgoole, Geoff Druett, Ron Evans, Su Evans, James Gatward, Stuart Hall, Nick Handel, Tom Hartman, Barbara Hazell, Stan Hazell, Paul Heiney, Bruce Hockin, Alison Holloway, Patricia Houlihan, Brian Izzard, Philip Jones, Barbara Kelly, Susan Kyle, Maurice Leonard, Josephine Lyons, Billy Macqueen, George McWatters, Steve Matthews, Malcolm Morris, Bob Simmons, Tom Walsh, Ann de Winton, Richard Whitely, Ron Wordley, and Richard Wyatt.

Tragically, dear Eamonn Andrews, with whom I was privileged to work for four series on "What's My Line?" died in November. His utter integrity, professionalism, and gentle humor were a constant source of inspiration while I was writing the book.

I should also like to thank the crews, the drivers, the makeup girls, and the wardrobe staff with whom I worked over the years, who came up with endless suggestions.

A special debt of gratitude is owed to the Independent Broadcasting Authority, and in particular to the Head of Television, David Glencross, the Librarian, Barrie MacDonald and his staff, and Jenny Crick, who must be the best and nicest Information Officer in London.

I must thank the people who wrote three books, which were invaluable to me in understanding the extraordinarily complicated process by which television franchises are awarded. They are William Butler, author of *How to Win the Franchise and Influence People*, Michael Leapman, author of *Treachery? The Power Struggle at TV-am*, and Asa Briggs and Joanna Spicer, joint authors of *The Franchise Affair—Greeting Fortunes and Failures in Independent Television*.

I am also eternally grateful to Peter Cadbury, former Chairman of Westward Television for giving me access to his autobiography which unaccountably has never been published, to Robin Currie, of the Fire and Rescue Service HQ, Cheltenham, to Toni Westall, secretary to Captain Brian Walpole, General Manager, Concorde, and to Tim and Primrose Unwin for inviting me to some excellent hunt balls.

In addition I need to thank my Bank Manager, Keith Henderson, my publishers, Paul Scherer, Mark Barty-King and Alan Earney and all their staff at Bantam Press and Corgi, and my agent Desmond Elliott, for their faith and continued encouragement.

Three brave ladies, Beryl Hill, Sue Moore, and Geraldine Kilgannon deserve thanks and praise for deciphering my ghastly handwriting and typing several chapters of the manuscript; so does my cleaner, Ann Mills, for mucking out my study once a fortnight.

Finally once again there are no words adequate to thank Leo, my husband, my children, Felix and Emily, and my secretary Annalise Kay, whom I regard as one of the family, and who typed ninety percent of the manuscript. Their collective good cheer, unselfishness, and comfort over the past eighteen months knew no bounds.

Bisley, Gloucestershire
1987.

CHARACTERS
IN ALPHABETICAL ORDER

JOHNNY ABRAHAMS	Head of News and Current Affairs, the B.B.C.
ANTHONY, SECOND BARON BADDINGHAM	Chairman and Managing Director, Corinium Television.
MONICA BADDINGHAM	His wife.
ARCHIE BADDINGHAM	His elder son.
BASIL BADDINGHAM	Tony's illegitimate brother, ace polo player, and owner of the Bar Sinister in Cotchester High Street.
GEORGE BAINES	Sales Director, Corinium Television.
LADY BARNSLEY	A member of the Independent Broadcasting Authority (IBA), late of the White Fish Authority.
BIRGITTA	A comely but Bolshy nanny working for the Verekers.
HARDY BISSETT	A franchise expert. Late of the IBA.
MR. AND MRS. BODKIN	Rupert Campbell-Black's couple.

SIR CEDRIC BONNINGTON	Chairman of Mid-West Television.
HUBERT BRENTON	Bishop of Cotchester.
SEBASTIAN BURROWS	A news reporter, Corinium Television.
DAYSEE BUTLER	A very beautiful, stupid PA, Corinium Television.
RUPERT CAMPBELL-BLACK	Minister for Sport. Tory MP for Chalford and Bisley. Ex-member of the British Show-jumping team.
MARCUS CAMPBELL-BLACK	His son.
TABITHA CAMPBELL-BLACK	His daughter.
CAMERON COOK	Producer/Director, NBS, New York. Later Head of Drama, Corinium Television.
CHARLES CRAWFORD	Retiring Chairman of the IBA.
JUDGE DAVEY	A member of the IBA.
OWEN DAVIES	Leader of the Opposition.
WESLEY EMERSON	Gloucester and England cricket player.
SUZY ERIKSON	An American ex-girlfriend of Rupert Campbell-Black.
LADY EVESHAM	An early feminist, and non-executive Director, Corinium Television.
CHARLES FAIRBURN	Head of Religious Broadcasting, Corinium Television.
JOHNNY FRIEDLANDER	American actor and Megastar.
GISELA	Another comely nanny working for the Verekers.
MARTI GLUCKSTEIN	A brilliant, crooked accountant.

MALISE GORDON — Ex-chef d'équipe of the British Show-jumping team.

HELEN GORDON — His wife. Ex-wife of Rupert Campbell-Black and mother of Marcus and Tabitha.

LADY GOSLING — Chairman of the IBA.

GRACE — Declan O'Hara's housekeeper.

CRISPIN GRAYSTOCK — Professor of English at Cotchester University and a disgusting lecher.

HENRY HAMPSHIRE — Lord Lieutenant of Gloucestershire—a much less disgusting lecher.

SIMON HARRIS — Controller of Programs, Corinium Television.

GEORGINA HARRISON — An undergraduate.

RONNIE HAVEGAL — Head of Co-Productions, NBS, New York.

RALPHIE HENRIQUES — An undergraduate at Trinity Dublin.

IVOR HICKS — Corporate Development Controller, Corinium Television.

JILLY — Yet another Vereker nanny.

BEATTIE JOHNSON — Fleet Street columnist, ghosting Rupert Campbell-Black's memoirs.

GINGER JOHNSON — Financial Director, Corinium Television. No relation to Beattie.

FREDDIE JONES — A multimillionaire in electronics.

VALERIE JONES — His wife, a nightmare.

SHARON JONES — His overweight daughter.

DEIRDRE KILPATRICK   A researcher at Corinium Television.

LAVINIA   Patrick O'Hara's girlfriend.

BILLY LLOYD-FOXE   Sports Announcer, the B.B.C.

JANEY LLOYD-FOXE   An author and national newspaper columnist. Billy's wife.

DERMOT MACBRIDE   A playwright and Angry Not-So-Young man.

JOYCE MADDEN   Lord Baddingham's secretary, Corinium Television.

MRS. MAKEPIECE   A "treasure" who cleans for Valerie Jones and Lizzie Vereker.

KEVIN MAKEPIECE   Her son.

TRACEY MAKEPIECE   Her daughter.

SALLY MAPLES   Head of Children's Programs, Yorkshire Television.

MIKE MEADOWS   Head of Sports, Corinium Television.

MRS. MENZIES-SCOTT   Ex-head of the Woman's Institute, a member of the IBA.

GERALD MIDDLETON   Parliamentary Private Secretary to Rupert Campbell-Black.

DECLAN O'HARA   A television mega-star.

MAUD O'HARA   His ex-actress wife.

PATRICK O'HARA   His son, an undergraduate at Trinity Dublin.

AGATHA (TAGGIE) O'HARA   His elder daughter.

CAITLIN O'HARA   His younger daughter.

ORTRUD   Yet another of the Verekers' comely nannies.

CYRIL PEACOCK	Lord Baddingham's PA and sometime Press Officer, Corinium Television.
PERCY	Lord Baddingham's chauffeur.
PASCOE RAWLINGS	The most powerful theatrical agent in London.
BARTON SINCLAIR	Director of *The Merry Widow.*
SKIP	An American lawyer.
DAME ENID SPINK	A distinguished composer and Professor of Music at Cotchester University.
PAUL STRATTON	Tory MP for Cotchester. An ex-Cabinet Minister.
SARAH STRATTON	His ravishing second wife and ex-secretary.
SYDNEY	Rupert's driver.
URSULA	Declan O'Hara secretary.
JAMES VEREKER	Anchorman of "Cotswold Round-up," Corinium Television.
LIZZIE VEREKER	His wife, a novelist.
ELEANOR VEREKER	His daughter.
SEBASTIAN VEREKER	His son.
HAROLD WHITE	Director of Programs, London Weekend Television.
MAURICE WOOTON	A crooked Gloucestershire real estate millionaire.

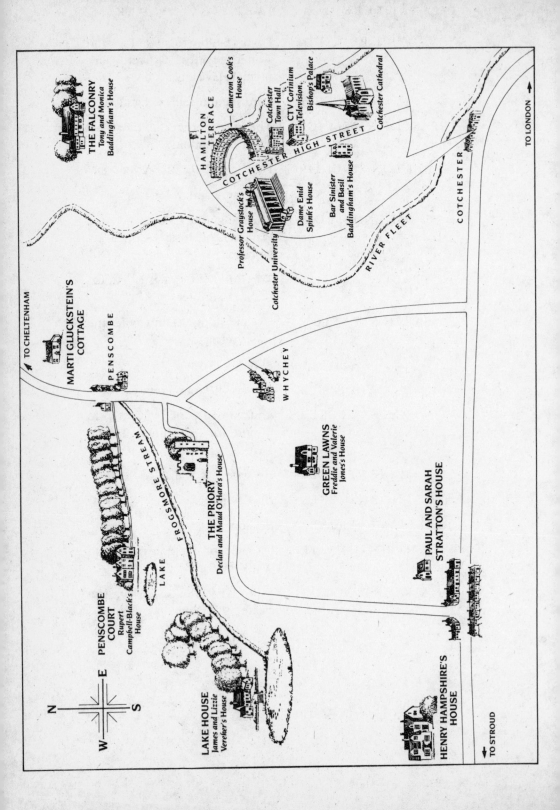

PLAYERS

CHAPTER 1

Sitting in the Concorde departure lounge at Heathrow airport on a perfect blue June morning, Anthony, second Baron Baddingham, Chairman and Managing Director of Corinium Television, should have been perfectly happy. He was blessed with great wealth, a title, a brilliant career, a beautiful flat in Kensington, houses in Gloucestershire and Tuscany, a loyal, much-admired wife, three charming children, and a somewhat demanding mistress, to whom he had just bidden a long farewell on the telephone beside him.

He was about to fly on his favorite airplane, the Concorde, to his favorite city, New York, to indulge in his favorite pastime—selling Corinium's programs to American television and raising American money to make more programs. Tony Baddingham was a great believer in using Other People's Money, or OPM as he called it; then, if a project bombed, someone else picked up the bill.

As a final bonus, neatly folded beside him were the morning papers, which he'd already read in the Post House Hotel, and which all contained glowing reports of Corinium's past six months' ratings announced yesterday.

Just as he was checking out of the Post House an hour earlier, however, Tony's perfect pleasure had been ruined by the sight of his near neighbor and long-term rival, Rupert Campbell-Black, checking in. He was signing the register with one hand and holding firmly onto a rather grubby but ravishing girl with the other.

The girl, who had chipped nail polish, wildly tangled blonde hair, mascara smudges under her eyes, and a deep suntan, had obviously just been pulled out of some other bed and was giggling hysterically.

"Ru-pert," she wailed, "there simply isn't time; you'll miss the plane."

"It'll wait," said Rupert, and, gathering up his keys, started to drag her towards the elevator. As the doors closed, like curtains coming down on the first act of a play, Tony could see the two of them glued together in a passionate embrace.

A deeply competitive man, Tony had felt sick to his stomach. He had seldom had any difficulty attracting women, particularly since he inherited the title and became Chief Executive of Corinium, but he'd never attracted anything so wantonly desirable and desiring as that grubby, vaguely familiar blonde.

"More coffee, Lord Baddingham?" One of the beautiful attendants in the Concorde Lounge interrupted Tony's brooding. He shook his head, comforted by the obvious admiration in her voice.

"Shouldn't we be boarding?" he asked.

"We'll be a few minutes late. There was a slight engineering problem. They're just doing a last minute check."

Tony glanced around the departure lounge, filled with businessmen and American tourists, and noticed a pale, red-headed young man in a gray pinstripe suit, who had stopped his steady flow of writing notes on a pad and was looking apprehensively at his watch.

Boarding the plane twenty minutes later, Tony found himself sitting up at the front on an inside seat with a Jap immersed in a portable computer on his right. Across the aisle next to the window sat the young man in the pinstripe suit. He was even paler now and looking distinctly put out.

"Good morning, Lord Baddingham," said a stewardess, handing Tony today's newly-flown-in copy of *The Wall Street Journal*.

"Engineering fault sorted out?" asked Tony, as the engines started revving up.

Not quite meeting his eyes, the girl nodded brightly; then, looking out of the window, she seemed to relax as a black car raced across the tarmac. Next there was a commotion, as a light, flat, familiar drawl could be heard down the gangway:

"Frightfully sorry to hold you all up; traffic was diabolical."

All the stewardesses seemed to converge on the new arrival, fighting to carry his newspaper and put his hand luggage up in the locker.

"Won't you be needing your briefcase, Minister?" said a steward.

Rupert Campbell-Black shook his head, "No thanks, sweet-heart."

"Have a nice nap then," said the steward, going crimson with pleasure at the endearment.

As the doors slammed shut, Rupert collapsed into the seat across the aisle from Tony. Wearing a crumpled off-white suit, a blue striped shirt, dark glasses and with an eighth of an inch of stubble on his chin, he looked more like a rock star than one of Her Majesty's min-isters.

"Terribly sorry, Gerald," he murmured to the pale young man in the pinstripe suit. "There was a terrible pile-up on the M4."

Smiling thinly, Gerald removed a blonde hair from Rupert's la-pel.

"I really must buy you an alarm clock for Christmas, Minister. If you'd missed that lunchtime speech, we'd have been in real schtuk. Good of them to hold the plane."

"Thank Christ they did." Looking around, Rupert saw Tony Baddingham and grinned. "Why, it's big Baddingham wolf."

"Cutting it a bit fine, aren't you?" said Tony.

Both men needed each other's goodwill. Rupert, as a Member of Parliament within Tony's television company's territory, needed the coverage, whereas Tony needed Rupert's recommendation to the Government that he was running a respectable company. But that didn't make them like each other any better.

"Bloody good ratings you got this morning," said Rupert, fas-tening his seat belt, "I'd better buy some Corinium stock."

Slightly mollified, Tony congratulated Rupert on his recent ap-pointment as Tory Minister of Sport.

Rupert shrugged. "The PM's shit-scared about football vio-lence—seems to think I can come up with some magic formula. I was at Thames Television yesterday," Rupert went on, as the plane taxied toward the runway. "After the program I had a drink with the Home Secretary and the Chairman of the IBA. They were both saying that you'd better watch out. If you don't spend a bit more of that bloody fortune you're coining from advertising on making some de-cent programs, you're going to lose your franchise."

As Rupert leaned forward so Tony could hear him over the en-gines, Tony caught a whiff of the scent the girl had been wearing in the Post House foyer earlier.

"And you ought to spend some time in the area. How the hell can you run a television station in the Cotswolds if you spend all your time in London, hawking your ass around the advertising agencies?"

"The shareholders wouldn't be very pleased if I didn't," said Tony, thoroughly miffed. "Look at our ratings."

Rupert shrugged again. "You're also supposed to make good programs. As your local MP I'm just passing on what's being said."

"As one of your more influential constituents," said Tony furiously, "I don't think you should be checking into the Post House with bimbos half your age."

Rupert laughed. "That was no bimbo, that was Beattie Johnson."

Instantly Tony remembered the girl. Beattie Johnson was one of the most scurrilous and successful women columnists—dubbed by *Private Eye* "the First not-quite-a-lady of Fleet Street."

"She's ghosting my memoirs," added Rupert. "We were doing research. I always believe in laying one's ghost."

As the plane revved up, both men turned to look out the window, and Tony found himself trembling with rage. But not even the splendid, silk-shirted bosom of the stewardess which rose and fell as she showed passengers how to inflate their life jackets, could keep Rupert's eyes open. By the time they were airborne, he was asleep.

Tony accepted a glass of champagne and tried to concentrate on *The Wall Street Journal*. He didn't know which he resented most—Rupert's habitual contempt, his ability to sleep anywhere, his effortless acquisition of women, or the obvious devotion of the palely efficient Gerald, who was now sipping Perrier and polishing the speech Rupert was to deliver to the International Olympic Committee at lunchtime.

There had hardly been a husband in Gloucestershire, indeed in the world, Tony reflected, who hadn't cheered four years ago when Rupert's beautiful wife, Helen, walked out on him in the middle of the Los Angeles Olympics, running off with another rider and causing Rupert the maximum humiliation.

But, infuriatingly, Rupert had appeared outwardly unaffected and had risen to the occasion by winning a show-jumping gold medal despite a pinched shoulder nerve, and had gone on two years later to win the World Championship, the only prize hitherto to elude him. Then, giving up show jumping at the pinnacle of his fame, he had moved effortlessly into politics, winning the Tory seat of Chalford and Bisley with ease. Even worse, he had turned out to be a surprisingly good MP, being very quick on his feet, totally unfazed by the Opposition or the Prime Minister, and prepared to fight very hard for his constituency.

Now, as Minister of Sport, Rupert was free to roam around exuding glamour, raising money for the Olympic team here, defusing a riot against a South African athlete there.

Glancing at Rupert, sprawled out on the pale grey leather seat, taking up most of Gerald's leg room, Tony felt a further stab of jealousy. He couldn't remember a time in his forty-four years when he hadn't envied the Campbell-Blacks. For all their outlandish behavior, they had always been looked up to in Gloucestershire. They had lived in the same beautiful house in Penscombe for generations, while Tony was brought up behind net curtains in a boring suburb of Cheltenham. Tony also had a chip on his shoulder because he'd gone to a local school, where he'd been teased for being fat and short, and because his conventional colorless father (although subsequently ennobled for his work in the war) had been considered far too valuable as a munitions manufacturer to be allowed to go off and fight, unlike Rupert's father, Eddie, who'd had a dazzling military career.

Even when Tony's father had been given his peerage, Eddie Campbell-Black and his cronies had laughed, always referring to him dismissively as Lord Pop-Pop, as they blasted away with his best gun on their large estates.

Growing up near the Campbell-Blacks, Tony had longed to be invited to Penscombe and drawn into that rackety, exciting group. But the privilege had been bestowed on his brother Basil, who was ten years younger and who, because Tony's father had made his pile by then, had been given a pony to ride and sent to Harrow, and had there become a friend of Rupert's.

As a result of such imagined early deprivation, Tony had grown up incredibly competitive. Spurning the family firm when he left school, he'd gone straight into advertising and specialized in buying television air time. From there he moved to the advertising side of television. A brilliant entrepreneur, who felt he was slipping unless he had a dozen calls from Tokyo and New York during Christmas dinner, by changing jobs repeatedly he had gained the plum post of Chief Executive at Corinium Television eight years ago.

Having shot up to five feet ten and lost his puppy fat in his twenties, Tony had in middle age grown very attractive in a brutal sort of way; although with his Roman nose, heavy-lidded charcoal-gray eyes, coarsely modelled mouth and springy close cropped dark hair, he looked more like a Sicilian street kid than an English peer. Considerably adding to Tony's sex appeal was a hunky bull-necked body, kept in shape by self-control and ruthless exercise, and a voice deliberately deep and smooth to eradicate any trace of a Gloucestershire accent. This only slipped when he went into one of his terrifying rages, which flattened the Corinium Television staff against the cream-papered walls of his vast office.

It irritated the hell out of Tony that, despite his success, his fortune and his immense power, Rupert still refused to take him seriously. He would not have been so upset by Rupert's sniping if it had not echoed a warning last night from Charles Crawford, the rotund and retiring Chairman of the Independent Broadcasting Authority (or IBA as they were known). The IBA's job was to grant franchises to the fifteen independent British television companies every eight years or so, monitor their programs, and generally beat them with a big stick if they stepped out of line.

After his program with Rupert and the Home Secretary at Thames Television Network yesterday, Charles Crawford had gone on to Boodles' to dine with Tony.

"As an old friend," said Charles, greedily pouring cream over his strawberries, "I don't see what else we can do but give you a stinking mid-term report. You promised us Corinium would provide at least ten hours of drama a year for the network, and all you've produced is one lousy cops-and-robbers two-parter, totally targeted at the American market. Why can't you provide some decent programs like Patrick Dromgoole does at HTV."

For a second Tony gritted his teeth. He was fed up with having Patrick Dromgoole and HTV held up to him as models of perfection. Then pulling himself together, he filled up Charles Crawford's glass with priceless Barsac.

"Thinks are going to change," he said soothingly, "I've just poached Simon Harris from the B.B.C. as Program Controller. He's very hot on drama, and has dreamed up a terrific idea for a thirteen-week series, a cross between James Herriot and 'Animal House.' "

"Well that's a start," grumbled Charles, "but your regional programs are awful, too. Your territory—which you conveniently seem to have forgotten—stretches from Oxford to Bath, and from Southampton to Stratford. And you're supposed to cover the whole area. That's why we gave you the franchise.

"We also know you've been spending Corinium advertising profits, which should have been spent improving your programs, buying up . . ." Charles ticked the list off with his fat fingers, "a film production company, a publishing firm, a travel agency, a chain of movie houses, a film library, and a safari park, and what's this I hear about plans to buy an American distribution company? American, for Christ's sake."

"That's fallen through," lied Tony. "It was only an idea."

"Well, keep it that way. Finally you've got to spend more time in your area. Many of your staff have absolutely no idea what you look like. I could understand if you had to live in the middle of Birmingham or even Manchester, but Cotchester must be the most delightfully civilized town in England. We awarded you the franchise to reflect the region responsibly, and we've given you a very easy ride up till now."

And I've given you some bloody good dinners, thought Tony sourly.

"But when Lady Gosling takes over from me in the autumn," went on Charles, spooning up the last drop of pink cream, "you're all going to feel the chill cloud of higher education across the industry. Lady G believes in quality programs and lots of women at the helm. Go on producing your usual crap, and you'll be out on your ear."

Having brooded on this conversation and on Rupert Campbell-Black's remarks for the entire flight, the only thing that managed to cheer Tony up was when the limousine that met him at Kennedy turned out to be at least three feet longer than Rupert's and twice as plush.

CHAPTER 2

Tony's rule, once he got to America, was never to check what time it was in England. To compensate for such an unsatisfactory start to the day, he spent the next few hours in a heady spate of wheeling and dealing, selling the format of two sitcoms and a game show for such a large sum that it wouldn't matter even if they bombed. It was only when he got back to the Waldorf and found three messages to call his very demanding mistress, Alicia, and, checking the time, realized that he couldn't because it was long after midnight and she'd be tucked up in bed with her husband, that he suddenly felt tired.

He kicked himself for agreeing to dine with Ronnie Havegal, Head of Co-Production at NBS, particularly as Ronnie had asked if he could bring some producer called Cameron Cook.

"Cameron's a good friend of mine," Ronnie had said in his Harvard drawl. "Very bright, just done a documentary on debutantes, up for a Peabody award, real class; they like that sort of thing in England.''

Tony had often wondered about Ronnie's sexual preferences. He didn't want to spend an evening avoiding buying some lousy program from one of Ronnie's fag friends. Yanks always got class wrong anyway.

Christ, he was tired. Unable to master the taps in the shower, he shot boiling lava straight into his eyes. Then, forgetting to put the shower curtain inside the tub, he drenched the floor and his only pair of black shoes.

Tony spent a lot of money on his clothes and ever since he'd seen Marlon Brando in *Guys and Dolls* as a teenager tended to wear dark shirts with light ties. The new dark blue silk shirt Alicia had given him for his birthday would be wasted on two fags. He would keep it for lunch with Ali MacGraw tomorrow. Dressed, he fortified himself with a large whisky and put the presentation booklet of ''Four Men went to Mow,'' Simon Harris's new idea for a thirteen-part series, on the glass table, together with a video of possible exteriors and interiors to give the Americans a taste of the ravishing Cotswold countryside.

Ronnie phoned from downstairs, but when he came through the door, Tony suddenly didn't feel tired any more, for with him was the sexiest, most truculent girl Tony had ever seen. Around twenty-six, she was wearing a straight linen dress, the color of a New York taxi and earrings like mini satellite dishes. She had a lean, wonderfully rapacious body, long legs, very short dark hair sleeked back from her thin face, and clear olive skin. With her straight black brows, angry, slightly protruding amber eyes, beaky nose and predatory mouth, she looked like a bird of prey—beautiful, intensely ferocious, and tameable only by the few. She gave out an appalling sexual energy.

She was also so rude to Ronnie, who was very much her senior, that at first Tony assumed they must be sleeping together. He soon realized she was rude to everyone.

''This is Cameron Cook,'' said Ronnie.

Nodding in Tony's direction, Cameron began prowling around the huge suite, looking at the large blue urn in the center of the living room holding agapanthus as big as footballs, the leather sofas and arm chairs, the vast double bed next door, and the six telephones, even one in the shower.

''Shit!'' Her voice was low and rasping. ''This place is bigger than Buckingham Palace; no wonder you Brits need American co-production money.''

Tony, who was opening a bottle of Dom Perignon, ignored the jibe, and asked Cameron where she came from.

''Cincinnati.''

''City of the seven hills,'' said Tony smoothly. ''But you must have bought those legs in New York.''

Cameron didn't smile.

''You don't look like a lord, more like a Mafia hood. What do I call you: Your Grace, Sir, my lord, Baron?''

''You can call me Tony.'' He handed her a glass.

Cameron picked up the presentation booklet of ''Four Men went to Mow.'' Kicking off her flat black shoes, she curled up, looking very tiny on the huge pockmarked red leather sofa.

''What's this shit?''

''Cameron!'' remonstrated Ronnie.

''Corinium's latest thirteen-parter,'' explained Tony. ''We aim to start shooting in October.''

''If you get American backing,'' said Cameron sharply.

Tony nodded. ''We'll put it out early in the evening; should appeal to both kids and adults.''

''Dumb title. What the shit does it mean?''

''It's the line of an English song,'' said Tony evenly.

''Thought it was a series about back yards.''

''It's about four agricultural students living in a house.''

''I can read, thank you,'' snapped Cameron, running her eyes down the page. ''And someone finds someone in bed with someone in the first episode. Jesus, you expect this shit to go out as wholesome family entertainment in Middle America, where we haven't seen a nipple on the network for years?''

''Don't listen to Cameron,'' said Ronnie. ''She needs a muzzle.''

''Shut up and let me read it.''

Ronnie then proceeded to update Tony on the recent changes at NBS. ''They fired twenty people last week, good people who've been there fifteen years. The new business guys are running the place like a supermarket.''

But Tony wasn't listening. He was watching Cameron Cook. Christ, he'd like to screw all that smouldering bad temper out of her.

As if aware of his scrutiny, she glanced up.

''There's too much air in this glass,'' she said holding it out for a refill.

"You're too old for TV at twenty-five these days," Ronnie rattled on obsessively. "I work with a guy of fifty. He lives in such constant fear of his age getting out, he keeps having his face lifted."

Ronnie looked desperately tired. Beneath his tan, there were new lines around the eyes. Cameron chucked the presentation booklet back on the glass table.

"Well?" Tony raised his eyebrows.

"Schmaltz, schlock, shit, what d'you want me to say? It's utterly provincial, right, but the dialogue's far too sophisticated. If you're going to appeal to Alabama blacks, Mexican peasants, and Russian Jews in the same program, you can't have a vocab bigger than three hundred words. And I don't know any of the stars. And you've got the wrong hero, Johnny's the guy the American's will identify with. He's got drive, he comes from a poor family, he's going to make it. The Hon Will's got it already. What's an Hon anyway?"

"A peer's son," said Tony.

"Well make him a lord. Americans understand lords. And they're all far too wimpy. Americans hate wimps. You can't wear your sensitivity on your silk shirtsleeve any more."

Tony warmed to this girl.

"Go on," he said.

"As a nation, we're getting behind the family and the strong patriarch again. There's a large segment of the population that want men to reassert themselves, be more aggressive, more accountable, more heterosexual. And you've got a marvelous chance with four guys in a house together to explore friendship between men, I don't mean being gay; I mean comradeship. Today's man shoots first, then gets in touch with his feelings later."

"Is that how you like your men?" said Tony, getting up to put the tape into the machine.

"Shit no, I'm talking about the viewers. You've got one of the guys ironing the woman's ball gown for her; yuk."

Tony filled up her glass yet again.

"Have a look at this."

Up on the screen came a honey-colored Cotswold village, an ancient church, golden cornfields, then a particularly ravishing Queen Anne house.

"We plan to use this as Will's father's house," said Tony.

"Bit artsy fartsy," snapped Cameron, as the camera roved over a lime tree avenue, waterfalls of old roses, and a lake surrounded by yellow irises.

"Beautiful place," said Ronnie in awe.

"Mine," said Tony smugly.

"Don't you have a wife who owns it as well?" asked Cameron.

"Of course, she's a very good gardener."

"Looks like fucking Disneyland," said Cameron.

Switching off the video machine, Tony emptied the bottle into Cameron's glass and said, "Corinium did make more than twelve million pounds last year selling programs to America, so we're not quite amateurs. Some of the points you made are interesting, but we do have to appeal to a slightly more sophisticated audience at home."

"We ought to eat soon," said Ronnie. "You must be exhausted."

"Not at all," said Tony, who was looking at Cameron; "must just have a pee."

Alone in the bathroom, he whipped out his red fountain pen and in the memo page of his diary listed every criticism Cameron had made. Then he brushed his hair and, smiling at his reflection, hastily removed a honey roast peanut from between his teeth. Fortunately he hadn't been smiling much.

Even in a packed restaurant swarming with celebrities, Cameron turned heads. There was something about her combative unsmiling beauty, her refusal to look to left or right, that made even the vainest diners put on their spectacles to have another look.

As soon as they'd ordered, Ronnie went table-hopping. "Nice guy," said Tony, fishing.

"Very Social Register," said Cameron dismissively. "Watch him work the room. He needs a big success. Both series he did last year have bombed."

"Given him an ulcer too."

Cameron looked at Tony speculatively.

"I guess you've never had an ulcer."

"No," said Tony smoothly. "I give them to other people. How do the cutbacks at NBS affect you?"

Cameron shrugged. "I don't mind the cutbacks or the infighting, but now the money men have moved in, I figure I'll have less freedom to make the programs I want."

"How did you get into television?"

"I went to Barnard on a scholarship and got a part-time job to make ends meet. After graduation, I joined *The New York Times*, then moved to the NBS newsroom. Last year I switched over to documentaries, as a writer/producer. At the moment I'm directing drama."

Tony laughed. "What more do you want?"

"Money, power, fame. I want to be the first woman to run a TV station."

"What about marriage and children?"

Cameron shook her head so violently she nearly blacked her own eyes with her satellite dish earrings.

"Gets in the way of a career. I've seen too many women at NBS poised to close a deal, being interrupted by a phone call, and having to rush home because their kid's got a temperature of 104°."

The waiter arrived with their first course. Escargots for Cameron, gulls' eggs for Tony. Ronnie, who hadn't ordered anything, returned to the table, buttered a roll, but didn't eat it.

"Anyway," went on Cameron angrily, "what's the point of getting married? Look at the guys. New York is full of immature, self-indulgent men who won't make a commitment."

"They're all gay," said Tony. He peeled a gull's egg, dipped it in celery salt, and handed it to Cameron.

"Bullshit," she said, accepting it without thanking him. "And what makes it worse is that New York is crawling with successful, talented, women just dying to get laid."

"Give me their telephone numbers," said Tony lightly.

"Don't be fatuous," snarled Cameron. "Men are turned off by bright women; they make them feel inferior. What gets me is why women are so dependent on men. You see them everywhere, with their leather briefcases, and their dress-for-success business suits, mouthing off about independence, yet clinging to a lousy relationship rather than be without a man."

Furiously she gouged the last of the garlic and parsley butter out of her snail shells. The lady, reflected Tony, is protesting too much.

Ronnie was off table-hopping again. The headwaiter was making a great song and dance about cooking Cameron's steak Diane at the table, throwing mushrooms and spring onions into the sizzling butter.

"You're a bit of a puritan at heart." Tony filled her glass yet again. "Your ancestors didn't come over on the *Mayflower* by any chance?"

"No, but my father was British. I've got a British passport."

Better and better, thought Tony.

The headwaiter was pouring Napoleon brandy over the steak now and setting fire to it. The orange purple flames flared upwards, lighting up Cameron's hostile, predatory face. Another waiter served

Tony's red snapper, which was surrounded by tiny zucchini, sweet corn, and carrots.

"They employ one man here to sharpen the turnips," said Cameron, pinching a zucchini from Tony's plate. For a second, she looked at it. "Tiny," she added dismissively. "Like the average New York cock." And with one bite she devoured it.

Tony laughed, encouraging her in her scorn.

"Enjoy your meal," said the head waiter, laying the steak in front of Cameron with a flourish.

CHAPTER 3

As they came out of the restaurant, limos for Ronnie and Tony glided up. Cameron paused between the two.

"I haven't seen your deb program yet," said Tony. "Why don't we go back to the Waldorf and look at it?"

Ronnie shook his head. "You guys go. I'm pooped."

Back in Tony's suite, an almost unbearable tension developed between them. Having poured large brandies, Tony removed his coat. Despite the air-conditioning, he could feel damp patches of sweat forming under his arms and trickling down his spine. In silence they watched Cameron's video. Within five minutes, Tony realized its outstanding quality.

The commentary was cut to a minimum; Cameron had let the debs and their mothers speak for themselves. But you could feel her fierce egalitarian scorn in the way she had highlighted their silliness and pretension, and the compassion she displayed for the *noveau riche* who tried to break in, and for the wallflower who sat unfêted through ball after ball.

"They'll adore it in England," Tony said at the end. "I'll call the Film Purchasing Committee tomorrow and insist they look at it."

"Thanks." Cameron got up to rewind the tape. "I better go. I got up at six this morning, and you must be reeling from Concorde lag."

It'd be like making love to a boy, thought Tony. Putting out a hand to halt her he encountered a huge shoulder pad.

"Sit down. I want to talk to you. You got a regular boyfriend?"

"Until three months ago." She sat down on the far end of the leather sofa. "I don't need a man to look after me. Just someone to make the sparks fly. If I'm not having a good time, I quit. Are you happily married?"

"Not overwhelmingly."

"She a dog?"

"Not at all. It's a marriage of extreme public convenience. We get on very well when we don't see too much of each other."

This girl is exactly what I need to wake them all up at Corinium, he was thinking. She's superbright, ambitious, aggressive. The IBA would adore the deb program; and Cameron would appeal to the incoming chairman, Lady Gosling. She was capable of seeing what was wrong with a program and subtly gearing it toward the American market without making it too bland. And finally, as she had a British passport, there wouldn't be the usual ghastly hassle about work permits.

"How'd you like to work in England?"

"How much?"

"Thirty grand."

"You've got to be joking, I'm making a hundred."

"It's cheaper living in England, and we could pick up a few bills."

"I'd have to have somewhere to live," said Cameron, thinking longingly of the honey-colored houses she'd seen on the video.

"We can arrange that."

"If I'm stuck in the country, I'll need a car."

"Of course."

For a minute she glared at him. "How soon do I get on the board?"

"Cameron," said Tony gently, "I'm the boss of Corinium. I decide that."

"I'll kick it around," she said indifferently. "You'd better sleep with me first."

Not by a flicker did Tony's swarthy face betray his surprise.

"Why? D'you think afterwards I might not want to offer you the job?"

Cameron smiled for the first time that evening. "No, I might not want to take it."

In the bedroom, Tony removed her huge earrings and massaged the reddened lobes.

"D'you get a good satellite picture from these?"

There wasn't much else to take off. Just the yellow dress and a pair of yellow panties. Tony never dreamed that anyone with such a sinewy, well-muscled body could have such smooth skin.

Bearing in mind that it was eight o'clock in the morning in England, Tony thought he acquitted himself with honors.

"Mine eyes have seen the glory of the coming of the lord," sang Cameron as she finally climbed off him.

"Still fighting the American War of Independence," murmured Tony into her shoulder.

Lying on the floor, tangled in each other's arms, they were interrupted much later by the telephone.

It was Corinium's sales director, Georgie Baines.

"I thought you'd like the monthly revenue figures, Tony. I didn't wake you?"

"I've been up for hours."

"You can say that again," said Cameron, wriggling out from under him.

"They're up four million over last year," said Georgie jubilantly.

There was a knock on the door. Tony hung up the telephone and, wrapping a towel around his waist, went to answer it. It was the breakfast he'd ordered before going out last night.

He found Cameron in the bathroom, drying her panties with the hair dryer. She was wearing his dark blue silk birthday shirt, with one of his red paisley ties wound around her waist. Her hair was wet from the shower; she looked sensational.

"Come back to bed."

"Can't. I've got a breakfast meeting. Got to get there early to check the room isn't bugged."

Scooping up the mini-bottles of shampoo, conditioner, bath gel, and cologne, she dropped them into her bag. Then, peeling the shoulder pads out of her yellow dress, she fixed them into the shoulders of Tony's dark blue shirt. As she went into the bedroom, she removed a strawberry as big as a cricket ball from the grapefruit on Tony's breakfast tray.

"What are your plans?" asked Tony.

"I'm in the studio from ten o'clock on. I should be through around eight. And you?"

"I've got people to see: I'm lunching with Ali MacGraw—more my age group, sweetie." He kissed Cameron on the forehead. "And I want that shirt back."

"You can wear my yellow dress. If I wear it, Ronnie'll know I haven't been home." Taking a mirror from her bag, she winced at her reflection in the bright sunlight. "He'll know it anyway."

"I'll call you later," said Tony.

The moment she'd gone, he showered, dressed and, having summoned one of the secretaries from Corinium's American office on Fifth Avenue, dictated a completely new treatment for "Four Men went to Mow." By midday he had a new and beautifully bound presentation booklet containing a character analysis of the new hero, who was now the working-class boy and not the peer's son (who had become a lord), plus a new list of possible stars, suggested locations, story lines, and a couple of pages of simplified dialogue, all based entirely on Cameron's recommendations.

Ronnie called up as Tony was reading it through.

"How d'you like Cameron?"

"Like wasn't the operative word. What's bugging her?"

"More *enfant* than *terrible*," said Ronnie, who wanted to do business with Tony very badly, "but she's too ambitious for her own good, and too outspoken. Don't tell anyone I told you, but the program controller's going to axe her last documentary, and she's been so rude she's being taken off the series. But she's bright," Ronnie sighed. "Sadly they don't give a shit about talent here any more. But that's off the record."

"We haven't spoken," said Tony.

"As a quid pro quo, can we be the first people to see 'Four Men went to Mow?' " asked Ronnie. "I know Cameron carved it up, but it looked great to me."

"Of course," said Tony smoothly.

After an exceptionally affable lunch with Ali MacGraw, who was an old friend, Tony strolled down to USBC, the deadly rival of NBS.

At the plaza of the Seagram building, tourists and office workers sat on the walls, eating sandwiches and pizza, trying to woo the blazing sun down between the buildings onto their bare arms and legs. The flowers in the center strip of Park Avenue wilted in the heat as Tony sauntered past General Motors and the Pan Am buildings with their thousand glittering windows, admiring the colored awnings outside the houses and the beautiful, loping New York girls with their briefcases, who looked back at him with flattering interest. Maybe Cameron was right about the paucity of real New York men.

The Head of Co-Production at USBC and the Daytime Program

Controller were enchanted by the video of the honey-colored houses and the Cotswold countryside.

"This series," Tony told them, his deep, beautiful voice flowing on like vintage port glugging out of a priceless decanter, "will be a cross between James Herriot and 'Animal House,' but in a way it's much, much more. We intend to explore real friendship between men, not homosexuality but comradeship. The hero, a poor boy from a deprived background, doesn't inherit the earth or the girl, but he finds his integrity. The story, despite its depths, is simple enough to appeal to a Mexican peasant or to an Alabama black."

Out of the corner of his eye he noticed that the Vice-President In Charge of Daytime Programming had just entered the room. Tony warmed to his subject.

"In England," he went on, "we are sick of wimps who wear their sensitivity on their silk shirtsleeves. The guys in our story are kind to animals and women, but they shoot from the hip first and get in touch with their feelings later. Nor would they be seen dead in an apron. Let us have men as men again, and bring back dignity and chivalry to our sex."

Thinking he'd gone slightly overboard, Tony switched briskly to finance. "We can do it for three-quarters of a million an hour," he said. "It'll be thirty percent cheaper if we make it in England; we'll put up twenty percent of the cost against Europe and the UK."

Admiring the discreet blue coronet on Tony's dark green shirt, the V.P., who'd just been bawled out on the phone by his wife for forgetting to collect the suit she'd had altered at Ralph Lauren, reflected that Lord B had real class. And he was right—it was high time men were men again.

"Very interesting, Tony," he said. "We'd like to kick the idea around. You in New York for a few days?"

"Yes," said Tony.

"Showing it to other people?"

"Of course."

"We'll get back to you as soon as possible."

Outside it had rained. The trees had taken on a deeper greenness. The city had the warm wet smell of a conservatory. Park Avenue was a solid yellow mass of honking taxis. Quivering with the excitement of wheeler-dealing, Tony knew he ought to call Ronnie and show him the treatment. Let him sweat, he thought, let Cameron sweat. He went back to the Waldorf, checked out and, without leaving a forwarding address, flew to Los Angeles.

* * *

Cameron lived in an eleventh-floor apartment on Riverside Drive with a glorious view of the Hudson River.

The moment she got in, she played back her answering machine, but there was no message from Tony, not even a click to show he'd called and hung up. He hadn't left any messages at NBS either.

Cameron, however, had done her homework. As Tony had learned from Ronnie that she was brilliant but unbalanced, she in turn had discovered that Tony was an unprincipled shit, more interested in making money than good programs, masterly at board-room intrigue, and so smooth he could slide up a hill. Convinced she could handle him, Cameron wasn't at all put off by this information, and had decided to accept the job. She'd always wanted to work in England.

She turned on the light. She would be sad to leave her apartment, which was painted white throughout with yellow curtains and rush matting on the polished floors. Furniture in the living room included a grand piano, a dentist's chair upholstered in red paisley like Tony's tie, a dartboard, and a gold toe, one foot high, which had been surreptitiously chipped from the foot of a cherub in the Metropolitan Museum. Books lined most of one wall, but half a shelf was taken up with videos of the programs she'd made. These were her identity. Cameron only felt she truly existed when she saw her credits coming up on the screen.

And now this English lord had come along and thrown her into complete turmoil because he hadn't called. Cameron was attracted by Tony's utter ruthlessness and, despite her sniping, sexually it had ended up a great night.

Next morning the Hudson River had turned to a sheet of white metal, with the power stations smoking dreamily in the morning mist. Perhaps Tony had only offered her a job as a ruse to get her into bed, but she didn't think he was like that. If he'd just wanted to screw her, he'd have said so. Yet when she phoned the Waldorf to accept, she was outraged to be told that Tony had checked out, leaving no forwarding address.

"This guy's mighty popular," said the operator. "Everyone's been calling him."

Nor would Corinium's New York office tell her where Tony had gone. Even worse, the morning paper had a charming picture of him coming out of the Four Seasons with Ali MacGraw.

* * *

In Los Angeles, when he wasn't spreading the word about "Four Men Went to Mow" or finalizing the deal to buy out the American distributors, which he'd had to acquire through a holding company so as not to upset the IBA, Tony thought about Cameron.

Back in New York two days later, ignoring the increasingly desperate messages from NBS, he went to USBC and, after screwing another quarter million dollars a show out of them on the grounds that Disney was madly interested, he closed the deal.

He returned to the Waldorf, sweating like a pig, had a shower, poured himself an enormous whisky, and called Cameron. He had to hold the telephone at arm's length.

"Where the fuck have you been, you bastard?" she screamed.

"Busy," said Tony and, when she started to give him an earful, very sharply told her to shut up and calm down.

"I've raised the cash for 'Four Men went to Mow.' "

"Who put it up?" demanded Cameron.

"USBC. The lawyers are thrashing out the nuts and bolts at the moment."

"Poor Ronnie. NBS isn't going to be very happy—we didn't even get to see it."

"Well, there you go."

"He probably will, right out the front door, and never come back. Ronnie's right—you are a shit."

"That's no way to address your new boss."

Cameron's heart was hammering so hard, her palms were suddenly so damp, that the receiver nearly slid out of her hand.

"Hello, hello," said Tony. "Have you thought about that job I offered you?"

"You just fuck off like that. How do I know I can trust you?"

"Give me the address. I'll be over in half an hour and we'll talk terms."

Yet when he arrived at Cameron's flat, armed with a bottle of champagne, he was outraged to find an impossibly handsome young man lounging in the dentist's chair, holding a glass that definitely didn't contain mouthwash.

"Who the hell's he?" snarled Tony.

"This is Skip, my lawyer. He dropped by to draw up my contract," said Cameron.

"Why the hell's he wearing my shirt and tie?"

Cameron laughed. "Since I'm moving to England, I figured he deserved a going-away present."

CHAPTER 4

On a cold Friday in February, exactly twenty months after he'd signed up Cameron Cook in New York, Tony Baddingham made an infinitely more dramatic and controversial addition to his staff. Having exchanged contracts in the utmost secrecy in the morning, he popped into the IBA headquarters in Brompton Road for a midday glass of sherry with the new chairman, Lady Gosling, to dazzle her with the secret news of his latest acquisition before setting out on the two-hour drive down to Cotchester.

Even on a raw blustery February afternoon, Cotchester's wide streets and ancient pale gold houses gave off an air of serenity and prosperity. To the north of the town, in the market square, a statue of Charles I on his horse indicated that Cotchester had once been a Royalist stronghold. Round the plinth pigeons peeked among the straw left by the sheep and cattle sold in the market earlier in the day. To the south soared the cathedral, its great bell only muted during rush hour, the shadow of its spire on bright days lying like a benediction over the town.

Dominating the High Street was a fine Queen Anne building, once the Corn Exchange, now the headquarters of Corinium Television. Over the last twenty years, the building had been considerably extended at the back to include studios, dressing rooms, an imposing new conference room, and a suite of splendid offices for the directors. On the roof, the vast dark red letters CTV could be seen for miles around, letters topped by a splendid ram with a Roman nose and curly horns. Originally chosen as a symbol of the wool trade which once characterized the area, according to some of Corinium's more uncharitable employees, the ram could now be used to symbolize Tony Baddingham's sexual excesses.

At the back of the building an entire wall of the conference room consisted of a huge window looking out onto the cathedral close, water meadows, and willows trailing their yellow branches in the River Fleet, a peaceful scene totally at variance with the tensions and feuds within Corinium Television itself.

These tensions had been exacerbated that particular Friday by Tony returning unexpectedly from London and calling a program planning meeting at three o'clock, when he knew most of his staff would be hoping to sneak off early.

Tony had actually returned in an excellent mood. His meeting with Lady Gosling had been decidedly satisfactory. Simon Harris, the ex-B.B.C. Golden Boy, and Cameron Cook had so improved Corinium programs over the last twenty months that he was no longer seriously worried that his franchise would be taken away in mid-term. But, in case there were rival groups who might pitch for the Corinium franchise when it came up for renewal next year, he had made the decision on the way down to clean up Corinium's act well in advance.

Over the next two years, therefore, until Corinium was officially re-selected, he was determined not only to parade some of the most glittering names in television and the arts in front of the IBA, but also to put on some really worthy regional programs.

It was to map out ideas for these programs that he'd called the impromptu meeting. Unfortunately half the staff were away. The Head of News was in Munich on a freebie, the Head of Documentaries was in Rome getting a prize, the male Head of Light Entertainment and the comely female Head of Kids' Programs were both away with gastric flu, which caused a few raised eyebrows, as they had been seen looking perfectly healthy the day before.

Tony took the chair, but was instantly summoned to take an urgent call from Los Angeles. The only people in the room who didn't appear terrified or at least extremely wary of him were Charles Fairburn, Head of Religious Programs, who'd got drunk at lunchtime, and Cameron Cook, now Head of Drama.

Simon Harris, the Controller of Programs, who was principled and intelligent and always saw both sides of every problem, and was therefore labeled indecisive, trembled on Tony's right. He kept his hands under the table to hide a rash he had scratched raw. His thin face twitched. In an attempt to gain some kind of authority he had recently grown a straggly beard. When he took off his coat—Tony always kept the central heating tropical—you could hear the rattle of the Valium bottle, and see the great damp patches under his arms.

Beyond Simon was Tony's PA, Cyril Peacock, an ace pilot in World War II, Corinium's ex-Sales Manager, once a stocky, jolly, assertive fellow, sensational at his job. The point of a Production Assistant, however, is that he should be utterly loyal. Some Chief Executives in television buy this loyalty with money, which is dangerous, because someone else can buy it with more money. Tony bought it with fear. After making Cyril his PA, and sometime publicity officer, Tony had encouraged him to invest his savings in a company that promptly went broke. Now the terror of the Luftwaffe was someone Tony hung his coat on—a poor old dodderer in his early sixties, with loss of job and pension hanging over his head like a sword of Damocles. Tony took great pleasure in making Cyril do his dirty work—he had four people for him to fire on Monday.

On Tony's left was Miss Madden, his secretary, also in her sixties, plain and utterly dedicated, whose chilblains were itching because of the central heating, and who never let anyone into Tony's office without an appointment except Cameron Cook, on whom she had a love-hate crush.

Finally, down the table, opposite Cameron sat James Vereker, the impossibly good-looking, beautifully coiffed anchorman of the six o'clock regional news program, "Cotswold Roundup."

James should have been in the newsroom getting ready for the evening's program, but, hating to miss anything, he had muscled in on the meeting and was now using Tony's absence to rewrite his script.

Glancing across at Cameron, James wondered if she and Tony had rehearsed the whole meeting in bed earlier this week, turning each other on by seeing who could be the most gratuitously hateful to everyone else. He looked at Cameron's dark brown cashmere sweater, snugly fitting the lean body, the pale brown suede skirt, the Charles Jourdan boots and the lascivious unmade-up face, and felt a wave of loathing. Today her short hair had been coaxed upwards in gelled spikes, like a hedgehog who'd rolled in chicken fat.

James pointedly moved the arrangement of Spring flowers left over from Wednesday's board meeting to obscure his view of her and, getting out a package of Lifesavers, offered one to Miss Madden, who went slightly pink as she accepted it.

He knew who to suck up to. Properly courted, Miss Madden would sing his praises to Tony and admit him to the inner sanctum when necessary.

As Tony walked back into the room, everyone stood except Cameron, who pointedly ignored him. Perhaps they've had a fight, thought James Vereker hopefully.

"I'd like to start," said Tony briskly, "by congratulating Cameron on being nominated for a BAFTA award. As you all know, 'Four Men went to Mow' has not only been a huge network success, and sold everywhere overseas, but also because of the exceptional camera work, it's attracted scores of tourists to the area, and last month toppled 'Howard's Way' in the ratings. We're looking for more programs like this that project the area into the network."

"Hear, hear," said Cyril Peacock, his false teeth rattling with nerves.

Tony's conveniently forgotten that "Four Men went to Mow" was my idea in the first place, thought Simon Harris bitterly. Cameron, still ignoring Tony, gazed sourly at the framed photograph on the wall of him smilingly assisting Princess Margaret to plant a cherry tree on the Corinium front lawn.

Christ, they *have* had a fight, thought James.

"I'd like to give the go-ahead for a second series," Tony went on. "We've got the co-production money again from USBC, but I think it would be a good idea, Cameron, if you introduced perhaps a black unmarried mother into the cottage of the agricultural students to appeal to the IBA."

Charles Fairburn suppressed a grin. The IBA were crazy about minority groups. Cameron looked outraged.

"Black unmarried mothers don't become agricultural students," she snarled.

"There's always a first time," said Tony smoothly. "She could be the girlfriend of one of the four boys."

"For Christ's sake, why not have a gay shepherdess with one leg?" said Cameron.

"Why not a deaf, unemployed peasant?" suggested Charles Fairburn with a hiccup. "Or a handicapped harvester?"

"That's enough," snapped Tony.

He then went on to OK plans for an obscure Michael Tippett opera, which Cameron also scowled at, detecting Lady Baddingham's influence (Tony's wife was crazy about opera) and a production of *Midsummer Night's Dream* as a sop to Stratford-on-Avon which was just within the Corinium boundary.

Now it was the turn of James Vereker, who helped himself to a glass of Perrier and then suggested Corinium ought to show its "caring face, Tony" and do a series on poverty and the aged.

"Jesus, how turgid," said Cameron, glaring at him through the screen of fading daffodils. "Of all the boring . . ."

Tony raised his hand for silence, his huge signet ring catching the light.

"Not a bad idea. We could do a very cheap pilot to impress the IBA. We don't have to make the series."

James then suggested they should do something "very strong, Tony" on rioting and drug abuse in the St. Paul's area of Bristol. Swiftly Cameron swooped, the falcon Tony had trained, tearing into James:

"What a crappy awful idea," she screamed. "D'you want to antagonize the entire Tourist Board because everyone's terrified to visit Bristol any more? No one will want to invest money here. We're trying to boost the area for Christ's sake."

Tony then turned to the points made during his talk with Lady Gosling that morning.

"Several viewers," he said, "have complained about field mice copulating too long on our 'Nature at Night' show."

Charles Fairburn, who had a round red face like a Dutch cheese, suppressed another smile. He'd better do his expenses. He hadn't been anywhere this week, but he needed some cash.

"Cloakroom and gratuities £5," wrote Charles. "Drinks with the Archdeacon £15." That was pushing it; the Archdeacon was a teetotaler, but the Accounts Department didn't know that.

"On the kids' shows," went on Tony, "we've had complaints about too much violence in 'Dorothy Dove.' "

"What kind of violence?" asked Simon Harris.

"Pecking Priscilla Pigeon and pulling out all her feathers."

James was tempted to say his children had absolutely adored that particular episode, but decided not to.

"There have also been complaints," went on Tony glaring at Charles, "about insufficient religious content in our religious programs. I'll talk to you after the meeting, Charles, and the IBA are very unhappy about 'Rags to Riches.' "

Simon Harris turned dark red. It was he who had bought the format for "Rags to Riches" from America and adapted it for the British network.

"But the ratings are sensational," he protested.

"I know, but the IBA have pointed out that the contestants are far too glamorous and upmarket. We need a few unemployed frumps to add a touch of reality, and please remember our ethnic minorities."

"You can borrow my black unmarried mother," said Cameron, shooting Tony a venomous look.

"The IBA," went on Tony, squinting down the polished table, "also feel we should have more women on the Corinium Board. After all, Lady Evesham's nearly sixty-five, so we must all wrack our brains for some powerful ladies."

The men in the room exchanged glances of horror. Would Tony use this as an excuse to put the appalling Cameron Cook on the board?

"And," added Tony swiftly, "they feel we still don't have enough directors who live in the area."

That, thought James savagely, also includes Cameron, and her exquisite Regency house on the outskirts of Cotchester.

Now Tony was saying, not without complacency, that Freddie Jones, the electronics multi-millionaire, and Rupert Campbell-Black, the Minister for Sport, who both lived in the area, would be sitting at his table at the West Cotchester Hunt Ball that evening, and he would be sounding them out as possible directors.

"Good names on the stationery. We've got to keep our local MPs happy, with the franchise coming up," said Tony.

Smug in the knowledge that he was the only member of the staff who'd been asked to join Tony's party at the hunt ball that evening, James Vereker couldn't resist saying, as the meeting broke up, how much he and Lizzie, his wife, were looking forward to it, and what time would Tony like them for cocktails.

"About eight," said Tony, gathering up his papers.

James could feel the laser beams of loathing and jealousy directed at him from all around the table, particularly from Cameron. That should rattle the stuck-up bitch, he thought. Since she'd been nominated for a BAFTA, she'd been getting much too big for her Charles Jourdan boots.

As Tony went out of the room, straightening the photograph of himself and Princess Margaret as he passed, James glanced at his watch. Four-thirty. He was on the air in an hour and a half and they would wrap up the program by seven. If he had to drive the eleven miles home, bathe and change, he'd be pushed for time. He'd better have a quick shower and blow dry his hair beforehand; then he could legitimately keep his make-up on—just bronzing gel, and dark brown mascara—for the ball. One got so pale in February.

He considered whether to wear his turquoise evening shirt, which brought out the blue-green in his eyes, or a white one with a turquoise bow tie, then decided on the former. The gel might show up on the white shirt.

Wandering into the newsroom, he selected the secretary who was most in love with him and handed her twenty pages of long-hand, entitled "Poverty and the Aged," a treatment by James Vereker.

"I think you'll have rather fun with this one," he told her. "Could you center the title in caps? I don't need it till first thing Monday morning."

Entirely sobered up now, Charles Fairburn followed Tony into his office. To his amazement, Tony greeted him warmly: "Ratings aren't bad, Charles. Wheel in the Bishop of Cotchester, a few Sikhs and a woman priest next week to talk about the meaning of self-denial and Lent; that should keep Lady Gosling happy. Look, I'm reading the lesson in church on Sunday. Rather tricky phrasing, I want to get the sense right. Could you just run through it with me?"

CHAPTER 5

James Vereker drove home in his Porsche, warmly aware that "my program," as he always referred to it, had gone well. James Vereker's outstanding qualities, apart from his dazzling good looks, were his total egotism and chronic insecurity. In order not to miss himself on television, he had even been known to take a portable television into a restaurant. A huge local celebrity, he disliked going to London, or even worse abroad, because no one recognized him.

At James's house, Birgitta, the children's curvaceous nanny, had just finished ironing both James's white and turquoise evening shirts and was scenting herself and putting on make-up for James's return.

I wish Birgitta would spend slightly more time putting the children to bed, thought James's wife, Lizzie, as they swarmed into her study demanding attention. Lizzie had had two novels published and well reviewed. A third was on the way, but it was causing a great deal of morning sickness.

She and James had been married eight years, and Lizzie had supported James on her publishing salary in the early days when he was trying to break into television. Once very pretty, she had recently put on a lot of weight.

The Verekers lived in a large messy house with a large messy garden two miles down the valley from Rupert Campbell-Black, where the Frogsmore stream hurtled into a large reed-fringed lake. They had bought the Lake House, as it was called, five years ago,

just after James had got the job at Corinium. Viewing it in high summer, they had only seen its romantic aspect, not realizing that for at
least five months of the year it was so low in the valley that it never
saw the sun.

This mattered little to James because he spent so much time at
Corinium. When the house got snowed in, he simply didn't come
home for several days. But it was not good for Lizzie, who wrote
there all day, eating too many cookies to keep out the cold, or for
the children who caught one cold after another, or for the nannies
who found it dank and depressing, except when James was at home.

For Lizzie life turned on the children not getting ill, and nannies
not leaving so that she had time to write. Unfortunately James
couldn't resist screwing the prettier nannies, who invariably walked
out when he moved on to someone else. Lizzie always found out the
score by reading the nannies' diaries when they were shopping in
Cotchester or nearby Stroud. Birgitta, the current nanny, wrote her
diary in Swedish, which Lizzy couldn't understand, but with the aid
of a Swedish dictionary she was beginning to crack the code, and
the word "James" appeared rather too often. Lizzie was used to his
infidelity. She realized he needed little adventures to boost his ego,
but they still upset her. She would have liked an admirer herself, but
felt she was too fat to attract anyone.

Lizzie nearly had a fit when she heard James banging the front
door. She'd stopped writing far too late. Still wrestling mentally with
her plot, she'd spent too long washing her hair and in the bath. Then
she discovered that the long low-cut black silk dress she'd decided
to wear was far too tight, so she had to wear another dress, dark red
velvet to match her distraught face, and calf-length so it wouldn't
conceal her ankles which had swelled up in the bath.

Finally, because she couldn't see out, she'd cut her bangs with
the kitchen scissors, not realizing that Birgitta had just used them to
cut rind off the children's bacon. Now her bangs stuck together and
reeked of bacon. She was about to wash her hair again when James
arrived.

"Have a bath, darling," shouted Lizzie desperately, trying to tone
down her face with green foundation.

"I had a shower at the studio," said James, "so I've only got to
change. We ought to leave in five minutes. How did you think my
program went?"

"Wonderful," lied Lizzie, who hadn't watched it. As it was dark
outside, she couldn't put on her makeup in the car.

"I'll read you an extra story tomorrow, darlings," she told the children as they clung whining to her on the landing. "Or perhaps, Birgitta," she raised her voice hopefully, "will read you one before you go to bed."

But Birgitta was watching James, who had decided on the white shirt after all, putting a pink carnation in his buttonhole. Poor Mr. Vereker, she thought, looking so handsome in his dinner jacket, going out with such a frump.

"You look absolutely lovely, James," said Lizzie dutifully.

Low sepia clouds obscured the moon. As the headlights lit up gray stone walls, acid green tree trunks and long blonde grasses, Lizzie tried abortively to apply eye liner as James described every little triumph of the planning meeting and his program afterwards.

"Anyone interesting in our party tonight?" asked Lizzie as he paused for a breath.

"Rupert Campbell-Black, Beattie Johnson his mistress, Freddie Jones."

"Who's he?"

"Don't you ever read the papers?" said James, appalled, "Mr. Electronics."

Oh God, sighed Lizzie to herself. I daren't ask what electronics are, and I bet I'm sitting next to him at dinner.

"And Paul Stratton and his new wife."

"Oooh," squeaked Lizzie. "That's exciting."

Three years ago, just after the Conservatives won the last election, Paul Stratton, the Tory MP for Cotchester and the very upright Minister for Home Affairs, had rocked his constituency and the entire nation by walking out on Winifred, his solid dependable wife, and running off with his secretary who is half his age.

"Evidently, they've bought a place in Chalford," said James, "Paul and Sarah, I think she's called, are planning to spend weekends down here."

"I wonder if she's as beautiful as her photographs," said Lizzie. "I bet Rupert makes a pass at her. He's always enjoyed bugging Paul."

"Don't be fatuous, they're only just back from their honeymoon," snapped James, steering around a sharp bend and bringing the conversation neatly back to himself.

"I've got a gut feeling tonight is going to mark a turning point in my career," he said importantly. "Tony's been exceptionally nice to me recently. And when I popped into Madden's office later this evening to find out exactly who was in the party, there was a confidential memo on Tony's desk about the Autumn schedules, which I managed to read upside-down. It appears Corinium is committed to a series of prime time interviews for the Network. I didn't dare read any more, in case Madden got suspicious, but I suspect Tony's got me in mind, and that's why he's asked us this evening.''

Tony Baddingham soaked in a boiling Floris-scented bath, admiring his flat stomach. For once the cordless telephone was mute, giving him the chance to savor the prospect of the evening ahead. One of the joys of becoming hugely successful was that it gave you the opportunity to patronize those who, in the past, had patronized you. Paul Stratton, for example. It was going to be so amusing tonight, extending the hand of friendship to Paul and his bimbo wife. How grateful and subservient they'd be.

Then there was Rupert. Tony was not given to fantasy, but more than anything else in the world he longed to be in a position when an abject, penitent, penniless Rupert, who'd somehow lost his looks, was seeking Tony's favor and friendship. In wilder fantasy, Tony dreamed of flaunting an undeniably sexy mistress who would be impervious to Rupert's charms.

''Can't you understand,'' he imagined Cameron screaming at Rupert, ''that Tony's the only man there'll ever be in my life.''

Tony added more boiling water to his bath to steel himself against the arctic climate of the rest of the house. There was a running battle between Tony, who liked the heat, and his wife Monica who regarded central heating as a wanton extravagance.

''I still feel dreadfully guilty not telling Winifred about Paul and Sarah coming tonight,'' said Monica, when later, fully dressed, Tony went into his wife's bedroom and found her sitting at her dressing table vigorously brushing her short fair hair. She was wearing the same emerald green taffeta she'd worn for the last four hunt balls, which went beautifully with Tony's diamonds but did nothing to play down the red veins that mapped her cheeks as a result of gardening and striding large Labrador retrievers across the Gloucestershire valleys in all weather. Yet, in a way, her rather masculine beauty, splendid on the prow of a ship or as a model for a Victorian bust of Duty, needed no enhancement.

Known locally as Monica of the Glen because of her noble appearance and total lack of humor, she was the only woman to whom Tony was always polite. In the icy, high-ceilinged bedroom, opera and gardening books crowded the tables on either side of the ancient crimson-curtained four-poster which Tony visited perhaps once a week. But even after eighteen years of marriage, these visits gave him an incredible sexual frisson.

On the chest of drawers, which contained no new clothes, were silver-framed photographs of their three children. With her sense of fairness, Monica would never let the other two know that she loved her elder son Archie, sixteen last week, the best. Nor that she loved her two yellow Labradors, and her great passions, opera and gardening, a great deal more than she loved her husband.

She was not looking forward to this evening, which would involve talking until three o'clock in the morning to all those people Tony considered so important. Monica was not interested in people individually, or what made them tick or leap into bed with one another, but she was worried about Winifred. When Paul had run off with his secretary, in a scandal that rocked Gloucestershire almost as much as Helen Campbell-Black walking out on Rupert, Winifred had been utterly devastated. And now, Tony had asked Paul and Sarah to join the party tonight, and she, Monica, was expected to smooth over Sarah's first public outing in Gloucestershire.

"I just feel it's revoltingly disloyal to Winifred," said Monica.

She had applied Pond's vanishing cream and face powder, and a dash of bright red lipstick, which was the extent of her daytime makeup, and was now adding her night makeup: brown mascara put on with a little brush.

"I swore to Winifred I'd never have that little tramp"—Monica spat on her mascara—"over the threshold."

Tony's brows drew together like two black caterpillars.

"Paul is still our local MP even if he has been booted out of the Cabinet," he said patiently. "With the franchise coming up next year, I have to entertain whatever wife he chooses. At least I waited until after they were married."

As Tony moved forward to fasten the clasp of her diamond necklace, Monica caught sight of her husband's reflection. The red tailcoat with dove-gray facings made him look taller and thinner, and gave a distinction to his somewhat heavy good looks, but Monica hardly noticed.

"I still ought to telephone Winifred and tell her."

"Let it rest. I better go down; they'll be here in a minute."

Monica glanced at her diamond watch. *Lohengrin* was about to start on the radio. If only she could stay at home and listen to it.

CHAPTER 6

An hour later, downstairs in the huge dark paneled drawing room hung with tapestries, members of the party were beginning to unthaw and retreat from the fierce red glow of the beech logs smouldering and crackling in the vast fireplace. Lizzie Vereker, sustained by at least six glasses of champagne punch, had perked up and forgotten her extra pounds and her straining red dress.

Neither Rupert nor Beattie Johnson had arrived yet, but there was plenty to gaze at. Paul Stratton's new wife, for example, was absolutely gorgeous. She was wearing a yellow silk dress that matched her thick piled-up gold hair and a beautiful tobacco-brown fringed silk shawl covering her shoulders and wound high around her neck.

After replying in shy monosyllables to Tony and Monica's questions, she had allowed herself to be introduced to James and also to Tony's youngest brother, Bas, a playboy with black patent-leather hair, a smooth olive complexion, and a very overdeveloped little finger from twisting women around it. Now a small smile was beginning to play around Sarah's full coral lips at Bas's extravagant compliments, and the shawl was beginning to slip to reveal the most voluptuous golden shoulders and bosom. She and Paul must have been somewhere hot for their honeymoon, decided Lizzie.

Paul didn't seem to have reaped the same benefit. His dark hair, which he'd once brushed straight back, had gone silver gray and been coaxed forward, almost to his eyebrows, and in little commas over his very pink ears. Sarah, being young, had obviously encouraged him into a Paisley bow tie and a wing collar, the points of which kept bending under his new double chin. His once hard angular face seemed to have softened and weakened. He still, however, had the same all-embracing smile that passed over you like a lighthouse beam, and still liked the sound of his own voice. He was talking to Freddie Jones, the electronics multi-millionaire, who was plump and jolly, with rumpled red-gold curls, round, merry gray-blue eyes, a snub nose and an air that life was a tremendous adventure. Lizzie thought he looked much more fun than anyone else.

Across the room, she noticed, James had broken swiftly away from Sarah Stratton, and was now talking to a very slim woman with dimples and short brown curls tied up by a blue bow. She was wearing a pale blue midi dress with a full skirt and a top in which the satin lining was the strapless bodice, and the gauze over it covered her arms down to her wrists and tied in a pussy-cat bow at the neck. It was the most ghastly dress Lizzie had ever seen. But the woman, who Lizzie deduced must be Freddie Jones's wife, was laughing away, rolling her eyes and gazing up at James's beautiful bronzed face.

Apart from Sarah Stratton, Lizzie decided hazily, the men looked much more glamorous than the women this evening, gaudy peacocks in their different tail coats, red with gray-blue facings for the West Cotchester Hunt, red with crimson for the neighboring Gatherham Hunt, dark blue with buff for the Beaufort. If he hadn't been so good-looking, James in a dinner jacket would have been outclassed.

Helping herself to another drink, Lizzie wandered somewhat unsteadily over to the seating plan for dinner at the Town Hall. She was sitting next to Freddie Jones. James was on Monica Baddingham's right. Maybe his predictions about his brilliant future were about to come true.

"I can't think what's happened to Rupert," yelled Monica Baddingham in her raucous voice. "We'll have to leave in a sec, or we'll be late for dinner." She drifted off.

Lizzie glanced across the room to see James beckoning imperiously. Next minute he had crossed the room and seized her wrist. "Do pay attention when I signal," hissed James. "I want you to meet Valerie Jones. She's opening a boutique in Cotchester next month. You must go and buy something."

Never, never, thought Lizzie sulkily, if she sells dresses like that blue thing she's wearing.

"Lizzie writes novels," James told Valerie Jones, as if to explain his wife's scruffy appearance.

"I'd like to write novels if I had the time," said Valerie Jones. "People are always saying: You should write a book, Mrs. Jones, you've had such a fascinating life."

She screwed her face up in what she obviously thought was a fascinating smile.

Close up, Lizzie noticed that Valerie Jones had very clean nails, and the very white eyeballs of the non-reader and non-drinker. She was tiny and very pretty in a doll-like way, but Lizzie suddenly understood the expression: blue with cold. Valerie's china blue eyes were the coldest she'd ever seen.

"I'll leave you girls to get acquainted," said James. "We must have a dance later," he added admiringly to Valerie. "I bet you're as light as thistledown."

"Ninety-eight pounds on the scales this morning," simpered Valerie.

And ninety of that's ego, thought Lizzie. "Where d'you live?" she asked.

"At Whychey," said Valerie.

"Quite near us," said Lizzie. "We're at Penscombe."

But Valerie wasn't remotely interested in where Lizzie lived.

"And only quarter of an hour from the boutique, so I can rush down there, if there's any crisis, or a special client comes in. They always ask for me."

"Which house in Whychey?" asked Lizzie.

"Oh lovely, Elizabethan," said Valerie. "We had to do an awful lot though, ripping out all that horrid dark paneling." Lizzie winced. "And of course we've completely re-landscaped the garden, but it'll be a year or two before Green Lawns is the paradise we want."

Lizzie looked puzzled. "The only Elizabethan house I know in Whychey is Bottom Hollow Court."

"We changed the name," said Valerie. "We thought Green Lawns sounded prettier."

"Where did you live before?"

"Cheam," said Valerie, with the flourish of one saying Windsor Castle.

At that moment Monica came up. "We've decided not to wait for Rupert. Do either of you need a bathroom first?"

Outside it had turned bitterly cold. Valerie came out of the house smothered in an almost floor-length mink. Lizzie watched Freddie open the door and settle Valerie in before going around to the driver's seat.

"Isn't she a sweetie?" said James. "Knew so much about my program."

"Sarah Stratton?" asked Lizzie.

"No, Valerie Jones. I do hope Freddie joins the board. We could do with a few caring wives like Valerie at Corinium."

Lizzie was dumbfounded. Was James such a dreadful judge of character?

"What did you think of Sarah Stratton?" she asked.

"Not a lot. Didn't even know who I was. You'd have thought Paul would have briefed her."

Off they set in convoy, cars skidding all over the road, rattling the cattle grids, lighting up the last gray curls of the traveler's joy and the last red beech leaves. Flakes of snow were drifting down as they arrived at the Town Hall.

* * *

Cotchester Town Hall, a splendid baroque edifice, two hundred yards down on the other side of the High Street from Corinium Television, had been built in 1902. The huge dining rooms on either side of the ballroom were filled with tables, packed with laughing, chattering people. But in a noisy, glamorous gathering easily the most glamourous, scrutinized table belonged to Corinium Television. The Krug was circulating (Tony was always generous when the evening was deductible) and dinner was now well underway, but Rupert Campbell-Black and Beattie Johnson still hadn't turned up and Sarah Stratton, who should have been on Rupert's right, and Tony, who should have had Beattie on his left, were trying to hide their irritation and disappointment.

Lizzie Vereker, however, was having a lovely time sitting next to Freddie Jones. Rattling off remarks in a broad Cockney accent, he was, despite a scarlet cummerbund strained double by his wide girth, curiously attractive.

"I don't know anything about electronics," confessed Lizzie, taking a belt of Krug, "but I know you're very good at them. James says you're one of the most powerful men in England."

"My wife doesn't fink so," said Freddie. "It's a fallacy women are attracted to power. No one's fallen in love wiv me for years. I'd like to be tall like your 'usband. But I got my height from my muvver and my shoulders from my Dad, and the rest 'ad to go somewhere." He roared with laughter.

At the head of the table Monica listened politely to James Vereker talking about his program and his ideas for other programs, and surreptitiously gazed at Sarah Stratton. Her tobacco-brown shawl had slid right off her golden shoulders now. She's so beautiful, thought Monica. What chance could poor Winifred have stood?

She felt jolted and uneasy. She wished she were at home reading gardening books and listening to *Lohengrin*.

Huge oval silver plates of roast beef were now coming around.

"How's Rupert getting on with Beattie Johnson?" asked Lizzie, helping herself.

Freddie shrugged. "Not very well. She keeps 'earing wedding bells, and we all know Rupe's tone-deaf."

Lizzie giggled. "Has she finished ghosting his memoirs yet?"

"Probably providing material for the last chapter at the moment," said Freddie. Digging a serving spoon into a creamy mass of potato dauphinoise, he gave a big helping to Lizzie.

"What's your program about on Monday?" Valerie asked James across the table.

Paul Stratton, on Monica's left, seized his opportunity. Turning to her, he said in a low voice, "It's awfully good of you to take Sarah under your wing this evening. I know how close you were to Winifred."

Monica almost choked on her roast beef. She didn't want to talk about Winifred.

"It meant so much to Sarah," went on Paul. "She was so worried about coming tonight."

She doesn't look worried now, thought Monica.

"I felt guilty at the time," said Paul rather heartily. "But we are all sinners, are we not? I feel I can now walk down Cotchester High Street with my head held high."

Do you indeed, thought Monica furiously.

"But one can't destroy something that's lasted twenty-five years overnight," said Paul, spearing a piece of Yorkshire pudding. "I still miss Win and the girls, particularly when I see old friends like you and Tony."

He wants my sympathy, thought Monica incredulously. He wants me to feel sorry for *him*.

Fortunately, deliverance appeared in the form of one of the hall porters, who whispered a message in Monica's ear.

"Thank you so much," she said, and banging the table with her spoon, yelled down to Tony at the other end. "That was a message from Rupert. He can't make it after all. Something urgent has come up."

"Probably Rupert's cock," said Lizzie idly, earning herself a thunderous look of disapproval from James.

"Pity," said Sarah lightly. "I was *so* looking forward to meeting him."

Tony, for a minute, was unable to disguise his rage.

"Of all the fucking bad manners," he exploded.

Rupert's defection put a considerable dampener on the evening. It was not until the syllabub had been handed around in tall glasses that Bas Baddingham, who was among other things a partner in a local real estate firm, made an attempt to lighten the atmosphere.

"Has anyone else heard a rumor that Declan O'Hara's bought Penscombe Priory?" he asked.

For a second there was a stunned silence.

"I'm going on a crash diet tomorrow," squeaked Lizzie, dropping her spoon with a clatter.

"How much did he pay for it?" asked Valerie Jones.

"Half a million," said Bas.

There was a long pause as everyone did frantic sums to work out how much that now made their houses worth.

"That's an awful lot," grumbled Valerie.

"But it's such a romantic house," sighed Lizzie, "and that lovely wild garden."

"Hellishly cold," shuddered James.

"And faces North," said Valerie.

"So does Declan O'Hara," said Sarah dreamily, earning herself a sharp look from Paul.

"Rather a lot to pay for a weekend retreat," said James, looking put out.

To hell with impressing Rupert with the secret he'd been hugging to himself all day, thought Tony. He had a good enough audience as it was, and it was too late for any of them to leak the story to the press tonight.

"Declan's going to live here," said Tony looking slowly down the table. "He's joining Corinium in September."

There was a gasp of excitement, followed by another stunned silence.

Troublesome, short-tempered, but monumentally talented, Declan O'Hara was the B.B.C.'s hottest property. His weekly interviews with the great and very famous, always seen at prime time, were avidly watched and discussed by the entire nation. Nothing like the normal talk show host, he indulged in no backslapping, nor drinking in the green room, nor bandying of first names before a program. Nor did he bounce around on long pastel sofas, cozily exchanging confidences.

His victims sat facing him, and, once on the air, like a Jesuit priest, he really listened to them, relentlessly probing with the most devastating questions and waiting so unbearably long for an answer that they invariably stumbled into a confession. To the intense disappointment of his armies of female fans, the camera was constantly trained on the person he was interviewing rather than on Declan himself.

Poor James, thought Lizzie, oh poor, poor James. That must be the series of network interviews scheduled for the Autumn.

"How the hell did you persuade Declan?" asked Bas.

"He's fed up with the Beeb," said Tony. "The last straw was when they hacked great chunks out of his interview with Reagan. He wants to broadcast live, so this kind of thing can't happen. He will, when he joins us."

"You'll never get people like Reagan coming down to Cotchester," said Paul Stratton.

"You will for Declan," said Freddie.

The waitresses removed the untouched syllabubs.

"Declan's a bit of a pinko," said Paul.

"That's putting it mildly," said Tony, "but as it looks as though the socialists will be in power next year unless you guys get your act together, we can't afford to be too right wing any more."

Trying, for James's sake, to curb her excitement, Lizzie turned to Monica. "Have you met him?"

"They came to lunch," said Monica. "His wife is charming."

"Beautiful?" asked Lizzie.

"Oh yes, exceptional. And three utterly ravishing children. A boy of twenty at Trinity Dublin and two teenage girls about seventeen and fourteen."

"With Rupert living just across the valley?" said Lizzie, shaking her shaggy head, "Declan'll have to lock his wife and both daughters up in chastity belts."

A group of young waitresses from other tables were now hovering, wondering if it were the right moment to ask James Vereker for his autograph. Tony was also looking at James and experiencing a glow of pure pleasure. Corinium's most popular anchorman was feeling all the pique and disquiet of a big fish who's been basking for years in a rock pool, then suddenly sees the fin of a shark coming over the horizon. James's exquisitely straight nose would be frightfully put out of joint by Declan's arrival. James, Tony decided, had been getting a shade above himself recently. There was nothing Tony loved more than cutting people down to size.

As liqueurs and cigars came around, Tony moved down the table beside Freddie Jones. Now that Rupert had stood him up so summarily, he was even keener to get Freddie onto the Board. With satellite television in the offing, Freddie's millions and electronic expertise would be invaluable.

"When Declan arrives, we'll get him to interview you," said Tony.

Valerie also changed places and sat next to Monica.

"What a lovely meal, Lady Anthony," she said.

"Oh please call me Monica."

"Well thank you, Monica," said Valerie. "You may, if you like, call me Mousie. That's Fred-Fred's pet name for me. I only allow very special friends to become members of the Mousie club.''

The band was playing ''Red Red Wine.'' The brilliantly lit ballroom beckoned. The vast springy floor was now filling up with couples. Like a shaken kaleidoscope, the red coats of the men with their flying tails clashed gloriously with the stinging fuchsia pinks and electric blues of the women's dresses.

''I wouldn't mind if Tony'd given me an inkling beforehand,'' said James Vereker furiously, as, oblivious for once of the admiring glances of most of the young girls in the room, he lugged Lizzie around the floor, ''but I looked like a jerk, knowing nothing about it, and Monica actually admitted never watching my program. What kind of a Chairman's wife is that?''

Lizzie felt terribly sorry for him, but it was such exciting news that Declan was moving to Cotswold, and she was fascinated by what was going on on the floor.

As the tempo speeded up, Valerie took the floor with Freddie.

''What on earth did you find to say to James Vereker's wife?'' she asked as the band paused for a moment. ''What a mess, can't have combed her hair for weeks, and that frightful gown.''

''Nice lady,'' said Freddie firmly. ''I liked her a lot.''

Valerie gazed at Freddie as uncomprehendingly as Lizzie had gazed at James when, earlier, he'd called Valerie ''a sweetie.''

''And that new wife of Paul Stratton's looks like a handful,'' she went on.

Freddie refrained from saying he'd love to have his hands full of Sarah Stratton.

Tony devoted the rest of the evening to wooing Freddie, but he allowed himself the treat of a dance with Sarah. She was really gorgeous, he decided. One could understand exactly why Paul let his heart rule his very swollen head and ditched Winifred, but would he ever hold Sarah? She had obviously fallen in love with Paul because he was powerful and unobtainable. Now that his career had taken a nose dive and he'd been sacked from the Cabinet, he was neither of these things. Nervous of losing his seat at the next election, he kept angling for Tony to offer him an executive directorship on the Corinium Board.

But Paul shouldn't have patronized Tony in the past. How much more amusing, thought Tony, to employ Paul's new wife instead. Holding her dazzlingly full and exciting body, breathing in the scent of her thickly piled up blonde hair, trying not to gaze too openly at the beautiful gold breasts, Tony felt the stirrings of lust. If she was any good, she'd be perfect to anchor the new late night show. That would really put Paul in a tizzy.

"It's terribly exciting about Declan," said Sarah. "I'm such a fan. Did you see him interview Placido Domingo?"

"You must come and meet him as soon as they move in," said Tony. "You're going to be a distinct asset to Gloucestershire."

Suddenly Sarah looked terribly young. Even in the dim light Tony could see she was blushing.

"It was angelic of you to ask us tonight, knowing what friends you were of Winifred's. Paul's friends haven't been exactly friendly. They think I've screwed up Paul's career."

Tony gave a piratical smile. All he needs between his teeth is a cutlass, thought Sarah.

"You've given Paul a cast-iron excuse not to be Prime Minister," he said. "He'd never have made it. He has neither the talent nor the conviction."

"You're speaking of the man I love," said Sarah.

"I'm sorry." Tony didn't sound it. "I'm going to tell James Vereker to interview you for our new 'Behind Every Famous Man' series."

Sarah smiled, showing very small white even teeth.

"You'd do better to interview Valerie. She drives poor Fred-Fred on with a pitchfork."

"Probably spent half the day reading etiquette books on the correct way to hold your pitchfork," said Tony.

Back at the table, the waiter poured more Krug, but Tony put a hand over his glass.

"I'm driving to London after this," he said. "We're announcing Declan's appointment tomorrow, so all hell's going to break loose."

"The Gloucestershire poacher strikes again," said Lizzie, receiving a sharp kick on the ankle from James.

As everyone swarmed out into the High Street, they found a thick layer of snow on the pavement. Down the road, high above them, the Corinium red ram was already wearing a white wig of snow on his curly poll.

"Drive carefully, Tony," called Monica, as Percy the chauffeur held open the door of the Rolls for her. "See you tomorrow evening." Happily she settled back in the gray seat. Soon she'd be home to at least an hour of taped *Lohengrin* before she fell asleep.

"Bet the old ram's making a Cook's detour via Hamilton Terrace," said James Vereker savagely, as Tony set off for London in the BMW, waving goodbye to the last of his guests.

Tony drove toward the highway, but, sure enough, as soon as he'd shaken everyone else off, he did a U-turn and headed back to Cotchester.

CHAPTER 7

It was three o'clock in the morning but Cameron Cook was still working on the first story outline for the new series of "Four Men went to Mow." On Monday she'd start hiring writers. Ones that were talented and bullyable were not easy to find.

Beyond having a shower and brushing her teeth, she made no preparations for Tony, no satin sheets, no black silk negligees, no Fracas—the sharp, dry scent he so adored and which he brought her by the bucket. She was wearing the same brown cashmere sweater she'd worn to the office earlier, tight black trousers and no make-up. After twenty months, the one thing that held Tony was her indifference, her refusal to jump to his ringmaster's whip.

Perhaps he wouldn't turn up at all, to punish her for being so bitchy at the meeting. But she was so pissed off with him going to the Hunt Ball without her, and even worse inviting that jerk James Vereker, that she'd refused to speak to him after the meeting and stormed off home. She mustn't drop her guard like that. Once Tony detected weakness, he stuck the knife in.

All the same, her stint in England had been terrifically exciting. She remembered so well the July day she had arrived. Tony had met her at Heathrow and driven her straight down to Cotchester to the honey-gold house he had bought her. It was the only time she'd ever seen him nervous.

Inside, as they'd gone from room to room, as finely proportioned and delicately colored as the eggs of a bird, primrose and Wedgwood blue, lemon-yellow and cream, pale green and white, with large sash windows and pretty alcoves with shelves for china scooped out of the walls, Cameron hadn't said a word. Apart from a fully equipped kitchen and a television set in the living room, there was no furniture except a huge brass four-poster in the master bed-room, which spread across the whole top floor.

Cameron had opened the window and gazed out at her new backyard with its pale pink roses, and three ancient apple trees at the end. Someone had just mowed the lawn and, as she breathed in the smell of grass cuttings and admired the gray-gold spire of Cot-chester Cathedral rising from its bright green water meadows, she burst into tears.

Tony, who hadn't touched her until then, thinking she hated the house or was feeling homesick, moved forward like lightning and took her in his arms.

"Darling, what's the matter? We'll find something else if you don't like it."

Then Cameron sobbed into his Prussian-blue silk shirt that it was the loveliest house she'd ever seen, and why didn't they christen the bed—and their love-making turned out to be even more rapturous than it had been in New York.

But that was the last time she'd displayed weakness in his pres-ence. From the moment she'd arrived she'd had no time to consider whether she was homesick or not. When she wasn't producing and masterminding every detail of the thirteen episodes of "Four Men went to Mow," battling with directors, designers, actors, and tech-nicians, who weren't at all pleased to have a twenty-seven-year-old American upstart ordering them around, she was furnishing the house, driving from Southampton to Stratford, from Bristol to Ox-ford, picking up antiques, thoroughly acquainting herself with the Cotswold area and seeking new ideas for programs.

Otherwise her life revolved around Tony. He managed to spend several evenings a week with her; people noticed he'd started leaving official dinners and cocktail parties abnormally early. He also took her to all the big events in the television calendar: Edinburgh, Monte Carlo, Cannes, New York, New Orleans, where she'd justified her existence a hundred times over selling Corinium programs and ac-quiring new ones.

But there was still the married side of Tony's life, from which she was so ruthlessly excluded. She had only been once to his beautiful house, The Falconry, when Monica and the children were away, and that, she was sure, was because he wanted to show the place off.

Cameron had only met Monica once or twice at office parties, or at the odd business reception. The galling thing was she never recognized Cameron. In one way, Monica's lack of interest in Tony's job made it much easier for him to deceive her. In another, brooded

Cameron, if you had a rival, you wanted her at least to be aware of your existence.

"Lady Baddingham is a real lady," Miss Madden was fond of saying when she wanted to get under Cameron's skin.

Cameron liked to think Tony only stayed with Monica because the silly old bag gave him respectability, and he didn't want any scandal before the franchise was renewed.

Getting up from her desk, Cameron wandered around the living room. It was the only room in the house she'd redecorated, papering the walls in scarlet with a tiny blue-gray flower pattern and adding scarlet curtains and a blue-gray carpet, sofas, and chairs. She had acquired a new piano in England, lacquered in red, but had brought with her from New York the dentist's chair upholstered in scarlet Paisley, the dartboard, the gold toe from the Metropolitan Museum, and all the videos of her NBS programs. Beside them on the shelf were now stacked the thirteen prize-winning episodes of "Four Men went to Mow" and the two documentaries Cameron had made on All Souls' College, Oxford, and on Anthony Trollope, who'd based Barchester on Winchester, which was, after all, within the Corinium boundary.

On the mantelpiece was a signed photograph of the four young actors who'd starred in "Four Men went to Mow" and a huge phallic cactus, given to her as an end-of-shoot present by the entire cast. *"Darling Cameron,"* said the card, which was still propped against it, *"You're spikey, but you're great."*

After all the screaming matches, it had been a great accolade.

Tony obviously wasn't coming, Cameron decided; she'd blown it once and for all. The weekend stretched ahead, nothing but work until more work on Monday.

For consolation, she picked up the week's copy of *Broadcast*, which fell open at a photograph of her cuddling a dopey looking Jersey cow. "Producer Cameron Cook on location during filming of her BAFTA-nominated series: 'Four Men went to Mow,'" said the caption. "The lucky cow is on the left."

Going over to the window, Cameron realized it was snowing. There was already three inches on top of her car, and soft white dustsheets had been laid over the houses opposite. Snow had also filled up the cups of the winter jasmine that jostled with the Virginia creeper climbing up the front of her house. If you wanted to get to the top you had to jostle, reflected Cameron. Tony had hinted he might put her on the Board, but she knew James Vereker, Simon Harris, and all the Heads of Departments would block her appointment if they could. She had interfered at all levels, criticizing every program and every script she could lay her hands on. She knew she was unpopular with everyone in the building. But she didn't want popularity, she wanted power and the freedom to make the programs she wanted without running to Tony for protection.

She was so deep in thought, she didn't notice the BMW driving up, nor that Tony was outside until he lobbed a snowball against the window. She wished he didn't look so revoltingly handsome in that red coat. Cameron detested hunting, not because she felt sorry for the fox, but because of the bloody-minded arrogance of people like Tony and Rupert Campbell-Black who hunted.

"How was it?" she asked, getting a bottle of champagne from the fridge.

"Great."

Immediately her antagonism came flooding back.

"How was Rupert?" She knew her interest would bug Tony.

"Bastard didn't turn up. But I told everyone Declan was joining Corinium. It was OK," he added, seeing Cameron's look of horror. "It was too late for any of them to call the papers. You should have seen James's face."

Cameron grinned.

"That's an improvement," said Tony. "Why were you so hateful at the meeting?"

"I had a migraine."

They both knew she was lying, but Tony didn't want a row. He soon had Cameron undressed and into the huge brass bed, now curtained with pale gray silk, which he or rather Corinium had paid for, just as they had paid for the whole house. The excuse was that putting up visiting VIPs in Cameron's spare room would be cheaper than the Cotchester Arms, which served awful food and had no airconditioning.

"Do you do this to keep your mind off your work?" asked Tony later, as a naked Cameron straddled him in all her angry, voracious beauty.

Cameron leaned over and took a gulp of champagne.

"Who says it takes my mind off my work? I've got an idea."

"What?" Feeling those muscles gripping his cock, Tony wondered how he ever refused her anything.

"I want to produce Declan when he arrives in September."

* * *

Leaving Cameron at six o'clock, Tony drove up to London. He'd put on a sweater over his evening shirt, and planned to bathe, shave, and eat breakfast at his apartment in Rutland Gate.

Red coat over his arm, Tony let himself into his apartment. For a second he thought he'd been burgled. Clothes littered the hall; bottles, glasses, and unwashed plates covered the kitchen table. Then, going into Monica's bedroom, Tony discovered the naked body of his son Archie fast asleep in the arms of an extremely pretty, very young girl.

Tony's bellow of rage nearly sent them though the ceiling. The girl dived under the flowered sheets. Archie mumbled that he was terribly sorry, but he'd thought his parents were at the Hunt Ball.

"We were," snapped Tony. "Now I'm going to take a bath, and I want her out of here by the time I've finished."

At least Archie had the manners to take the girl home, reflected Tony, as he soaked for the second time in twelve hours in a boiling bath. Pretty little thing too. He'd always been nervous Archie might turn out a bit AC/DC. Having a very dominant but adoring mother didn't help, but he was pleased to see Archie following in his own footsteps. Tony was extremely fond of his elder son. He was frying eggs and bacon when Archie returned, very sheepishly.

"Where the hell does your housemaster think you are?" said Tony.

"In bed, I suppose."

"But not whose. How old is she?"

"Sixteen."

"Over age, thank Christ. If you ever use Mummy's bed again, I'll disinherit you. I hope you took precautions."

"We did," mumbled Archie. "I'm really sorry. We were going to change the sheets."

"Think how upset Mummy would have been."

"We don't have to tell her, do we?" Archie's round face turned pale.

Thinking he would also have some very fast explaining to do if Monica discovered he hadn't got here until eight o'clock in the morning, Tony agreed that they didn't.

"But don't let it happen again. You've got to pass your exams. You know how important grades are. Now I suppose you expect me to give you breakfast?"

CHAPTER 8

Six months later, on the wettest August day in fifty years, Declan O'Hara moved into Penscombe Priory to the feverish excitement of the entire county. It rained so hard that on "Cotswold Roundup" James Vereker warned his viewers about flooding on the Cotchester-Penscombe road. But perhaps being Irish, reflected Lizzie Vereker the next morning, the rain made Declan and his family feel more at home.

Lizzie's children had gone out for the day; her cleaning woman Mrs. Makepiece was due later; Ortrud the Nanny, who had replaced Birgitta in April, was upstairs, no doubt writing about James in her diary. Lizzie had a rare clear day to work. But she was halfway through and very bored with her novel. Outside the downpour had given way to brilliant sunshine and delphinium-blue skies. From her study Lizzie could see the keys on the sycamore already turning coral and yellow leaves flecking the huge weeping willow which blocked her view of the lake. There wouldn't be many more beautiful days this year, reflected Lizzie. Overcome by restlessness and curiosity, she decided to walk up the valley and drop in on the O'Haras. As a moving-in present she would take them some bantam's eggs and the bottle of champagne an adoring fan had given James yesterday.

The trees in the wood that marked the beginning of Rupert's land were so blackly bowed down with rain that it was like walking through a dripping tunnel. Emerging, Lizzie wandered up the meadows closely cropped by Rupert's horses. In the opposite direction thundered the Frogsmore stream, which ran along the bottom of the valley, hurtling over mossy stones, twisting around fallen logs, shrugging off the caress of hanging forget-me-nots and pink campion, and occasionally disappearing altogether in to a cavern of bramble and briar.

Lizzie wandered on. Having had no lunch because she was on a diet, she kept stopping to eat blackberries, which didn't count. Up on the left, dominating the valley, Rupert's beautiful tawny house dozed in the sunshine. The garden wasn't as good as it had been when Rupert's ex-wife Helen had lived there. The beeches she'd planted around the tennis court were nearly eight feet tall now. Rupert should fly a flag when he was in residence, thought Lizzie. One couldn't help feeling excited when he was at home.

Half a mile upstream the village of Penscombe, with its church spire and ancient ash-blond houses, lay in a cleavage of green hills like a retirement poster promising a happy future. Lizzie, however, turned right, clambering over a mossy gate into a beech wood, whose smooth gray trunks soared like the pipes of a vast organ. Following a zigzagging path upwards, she finally stumbled and panted her way to the top.

Across a hundred-yard sweep of lawn which was now almost a hayfield rose the confusion of medieval chimneys, pointed gables, gothic turrets, and crenellated battlements that made up Penscombe Priory. On either side, with the sun behind them like a funeral cortege, towered great black yew trees, cedars, and wellingtonias. To the left of the lawn, where once, before the dissolution of the monasteries, the nuns must have strolled and prayed, grew a tangled rose walk.

Poor O'Haras, thought Lizzie, as she hurried along it. After divorce and death, moving is supposed to be the most traumatic experience. But, as she skirted a large pond overgrown with water lilies, around to the front of the house which faced into the hillside for shelter, she was suddenly deafened by rock music booming out of two of the upstairs turrets, and opera, she thought it was *Rheingold*, pouring out of the other two.

The old oak front door, studded with nails, was open. On the sweep of gravel outside, a moving van was being unloaded. Peering inside, Lizzie noticed some very smeary furniture, a grand piano whose yellow keys seemed to be leering at her, and several cartons full of books.

Lizzie called "Hullo-oo, hullo-oo," in a high voice, and a very plain, self-important black and white mongrel appeared, barking furiously and wagging a tightly curled tail.

Turning right down the hall into the kitchen, which was situated in the oldest, thirteenth-century part of the house, Lizzie found a woman, whom she assumed must be Declan's wife, Maud. Ravishing, but inappropriately dressed in a pink sequinned T-shirt and lime-green sweat pants, with a jeweled comb in her long red hair, she was very slowly unpacking china, stopping to smooth out and read each bit of paper it was wrapped in, and drinking whisky out of a tea cup.

On the window seat, training a pair of binoculars on Rupert Campbell-Black's house, knelt a teenage girl with spiky short pink hair, braces on her teeth, and a pale, clever charming face. In her black clumpy shoes, wrinkled socks, and black woolly cardigan, she looked like a tramp who'd just changed into his old clothes. Neither of them took any notice when Lizzie came in. But a very tall girl in jeans and a dark green sweater with a cloud of thick black hair, strange silver gray eyes, and a smudge on her cheek, looked up and smiled.

"I live down the valley," announced Lizzie. "I've brought you some eggs and a bottle. Don't open it now. It's a bit shaken up. Put it in the fridge."

"Oh how kind of you," said the dark girl. She had a soft deep voice, like a teddy bear's growl. She looked very tired.

Maud, having finished reading her piece of newspaper, glanced up and gave Lizzie the benefit of her amazing eyes which were almond-shaped, sleepy, fringed with very thick dark red lashes, and as brilliantly green as Bristol glass. Deciding Lizzie was worthy of interest, she introduced her daughters Taggie, short for Agatha, the tall dark one, and Caitlin, the little redhead.

The sink was crammed with bouquets still in cellophane. Sidling over, Lizzie noticed one was from Tony and Monica Baddingham.

"All the nation's press tramped through here yesterday in the mud trying to interview Declan," grumbled Maud. "*TV Times* has been here all morning photographing us moving in. Two local papers are due this afternoon, and a man from the Electricity Board says the whole place will have to be rewired. Have a drink."

She extracted a mug wrapped in a page of *New Statesman*, splashed some whisky into it for Lizzie and filled up her own tea cup.

"It's a glorious house," said Lizzie, raising her mug to them. "Welcome. We're all wildly excited you've come to live here."

"After yesterday's deluge, we've discovered it leaks in half a dozen places," said Maud, "so we shall probably have to have a new roof as well."

"We're thinking of renting our pastures to some cows," said Caitlin, putting down her binoculars and helping herself to a chocolate cookie which she proceeded to share with the black and white mongrel.

"Moving's very disorientating," she went on. "Daddy's trying to work upstairs, and he's frantic because he's lost his telephone book. Taggie's lost her bra."

"Caitlin!" The tall girl blushed.

"And I've lost my heart," continued Caitlin, training her binoculars back on Rupert Campbell-Black's house. "Will you introduce me?"

"He's not here that much," said Lizzie. "But when he is, I'm sure he'll introduce himself."

"It's not fair," moaned Caitlin. "I'm going to boarding school next week, and I won't get first crack at him. He's bound to fall for Taggie—or even Mummy."

There was a knock on the door and a moving man came in with a yellowing dress in a plastic bag: where did Mrs. O'Hara want this put?

"My wedding dress," said Maud theatrically, rising to her feet and holding it against her. "Just think, twenty-one years ago."

"Ugh," said Caitlin. "It's gross. How did you get Daddy in that? But I suppose he didn't see you till he came up the aisle, and then it was too late."

"Caitlin, hush," chided Taggie, as Maud's face tightened with anger. "Mummy looked beautiful; you've seen the photos."

There was a knock on the door from another moving man who wanted to know where the piano was to go.

"On the right of the front door," said Maud.

"Not there," shrieked Caitlin. "Wandering Aengus is shut in there. Daddy's let him out twice already."

"Aengus is our cat. He's a bit unsettled," said Taggie, smiling apologetically at Lizzie.

"Oh look," sighed Maud, unwrapping a baby's bottle. "That was Patrick's when he was a baby."

Caitlin tapped the fast-emptying whisky bottle with a finger. "And this was Daddy's when he was forty-two," she said accusingly.

"Oh, go away," said Maud, shooting her another dirty look.

Peering at a pile of books in the corner, Lizzie was highly gratified to see a copy of her first novel.

"I wrote that," she blurted out.

"Did you?" said Maud in amazement, picking up the book and examining the photograph on the inside flap.

"When I was thinner," said Lizzie.

"It was really good," said Maud. "I thoroughly enjoyed it."

At that moment a punk Lord Byron wandered into the room. He had flawless cheek bones, short dark glossy vertical hair, and an inch of violet shadow under his eyes, which were like Maud's, only darker and much more direct; obviously, the son.

"Patrick darling," said Maud in excitement, "this is Lizzie Vereker. She wrote this marvelous novel, and she lives down the valley, so perhaps Penscombe won't be such a cultural desert after all."

Patrick said, "Hullo, Lizzie," and announced that he'd liked the book too, and where did his mother want the piano?

Maud's reply was drowned by a bellow of rage from outside and Declan stormed in, holding a piece of paper in one hand and the cordless telephone in the other. Lizzie caught her breath. She'd never expected him to be so tall and broad in the shoulders, or quite so heroic looking. He had very thick dark hair streaked with gray, and worry and hard work had dug deep lines on either sides of his mouth and around his eyes, which were as somber and dark as the rain-soaked yew trees outside. But even with half-moon spectacles fallen down over his broken nose, a quarter of an inch of stubble and odd socks, one had to admit his force.

"This is Lizzie Vereker," announced Maud. "She's brought us some eggs and a bottle of champagne, and she writes lovely books."

Declan glared at Lizzie as though she didn't exist.

"I can't find the fucking A–D directory." His Irish accent was much more pronounced than the rest of the family's. "I can't find my fucking telephone book. I can't get through to Claridge's. I can't get any answer from the operator in London. I've been trying for the last half-hour."

He dialed the number again, then held out the receiver, so they could all hear the busy signal.

"Shall I try?" said Lizzie. "You have to dial 192 for London operators in the country, and then 01 before the number."

Two minutes later she got through to Claridge's and handed the telephone to an amazed and grateful Declan, who asked to be put through to Johnny Friedlander.

Lizzie almost fainted. Johnny Friedlander was a brilliant, madly desirable American actor, with a well-known cocaine habit and a penchant for under-age school girls.

"*The* Johnny Friedlander," she mouthed at Taggie.

Taggie nodded and smiled.

Declan was put straight through, and invited Johnny on to his first program for Corinium next month.

"I'd ask you to stay with us," Declan went on in his world-famous husky infinitely sexy smoker's voice, "but we're in shit order this end, and you'd do better in a hotel. We can have dinner after the program. I'll get our contract people to talk to your people. Thanks, Johnny, I can't think of a better person to kick off the series."

"But he's never given an interview *ever*," said Lizzie as Declan hung up the telephone.

"I know. Isn't it great?" Declan suddenly smiled, a wide, slightly gap-toothed grin, which made him look much more like Taggie, and made Lizzie feel utterly weak in the knees. "And all because you know how to use a telephone," he went on. "I'll certainly read your book."

He turned to Maud. "D'you hear that, darling? Johnny's coming on the program."

"That's nice," said Maud, without interest.

Lizzie turned to Declan: "What are you writing at the moment?"

"Checks mostly," said Declan.

Gazing out the window, toward the pond, he suddenly started, and grabbed the binoculars from Caitlin.

"Grasshopper warbler," he said a second later. "Pretty rare for this part of the world. There are some marvelous birds around here. I'm off to the public library, darling," he said, attempting to kiss Maud on the cheek.

"But you haven't had any breakfast or lunch," said Taggie in distress.

"Trust you to push off leaving us to do all the work," grumbled Maud.

"Leaving Taggie to do all the work," said Declan with a slight edge to his voice.

After he'd gone, and Maud and Lizzie had had some more whisky, the doorbell rang.

It was another bouquet of flowers, brought in by Caitlin.

"Who are they for?" asked Taggie, hope flaring then dying in her eyes, when Caitlin opened the envelope and read: " *'To Declan and Maura.'* That's a new one, Mum."

Seeing the flash of irritation on Maud's face, Lizzie wondered quite how much fun it must be to be married to such a famous man. It must be awful, looking like that, and having people getting your name wrong.

"Where's Grace?" said Maud fretfully.

"Not up yet," said Caitlin. "Said she couldn't sleep because of the quiet. Grace is our so-called housekeeper," she explained to Lizzie.

"I must go," said Lizzie regretfully.

"Have another drink," said Maud, not looking up.

"Have some lunch," said Taggie. "I was just going to make some omelettes."

"I must work," said Lizzie. "Thanks awfully. The children'll be home soon, it must be nearly four."

"I'll walk some of the way with you," said Caitlin. "Gertrude needs a walk. Do you want to come with us, Mummy?"

"No thanks," said Maud vaguely. "I must measure some windows for curtains."

"Curtains, indeed," muttered Caitlin as she and Lizzie left the room. "The only thing my mother measures with any efficiency is her length after parties." Then, noticing Lizzie's raised eyebrows, "I'm afraid I'm at the age when one tends to criticize one's parents a lot. Sadly one can't sever the umbilical cord gently. It has to be done with a razor blade and without an anesthetic."

Out in the sunshine Lizzie noticed how pale and thin Caitlin was and thought a few terms at a vigorous girls' boarding school would do her no harm. Gertrude bounced ahead, plunging into the beech wood after rabbits.

"Is Rupert Campbell-Black as attractive as everyone says?" asked Caitlin.

"Yes," sighed Lizzie. "He seems to get more so."

"They say he was very wild in his youth."

"Well he's had a rather extended youth."

"And brainy."

"Well, street smart, and very sharp with money."

"My brother Patrick is like that. I have brains. Taggie has beauty. Patrick has both."

"Oh you're going to be very beautiful," said Lizzie.

"I may blossom," said Caitlin. "But at present I am undernourished, and my teeth leave a lot to be desired. I had to make the dentist put this brace on. My mother only believes in going to the dentist when your teeth hurt."

"And Taggie seems very efficient in the kitchen," said Lizzie. "Isn't she bright?"

"Not at all. She's dyslexic, poor darling, she has trouble with cook books, which is a pity, as she wants to be a cook. Patrick said it was ghastly when she was small, everyone thought she was retarded because she couldn't read. Mummy shouted at her all the time, never thought of taking her to an educational psychologist."

The wall at the bottom of the beech wood marked the end of Declan's land. Caitlin scrambled over it and held out a hand to help Lizzie.

"How beautiful," she said, gazing at the flat water meadows and the bustling little stream. "I can imagine knights jousting here in the old days." She whistled to Gertrude who rushed back, splashing and drinking in the stream.

"The ghastly thing about having brilliant famous parents," Caitlin went on, "is you never feel the center of the universe, because they're so obsessed with their own lives. And if you do brilliantly at school, everyone nods sagely and says Declan's daughter, it's in the genes, and if you do badly like poor Tag, they just assume you're lazy. Tag's self-confidence was in tatters when she left school."

"But she's so beautiful," protested Lizzie.

"I know, but she doesn't realize it. She's madly in love with Ralphie Henriques, one of Patrick's even more brilliant friends. After months of pestering, he seduced Tag at a May Ball at Trinity this year. God, look at those blackberries!" Caitlin started tearing them off the bushes with both hands and cramming them into her mouth.

"I hoped Tag would tell me *exactly* what it was like. One can't obtain one's entire sexual education from the pages of Jackie Collins, but she just clammed up, and he never called her again. Just one postcard from Cork, and nothing since. Can you imagine doing that to Tag? Patrick says Ralphie's got someone else, some pert little blonde who reads Sophocles in the original. Poor Tag can't even read English in the original."

"What about Patrick?" asked Lizzie. "Does he like Trinity?"

"He feels right there. He thinks my father has betrayed his roots working in England, and he also rather despises Daddy for being in television. God, these blackberries are good. Perhaps Rupert smiled at them."

"But your father's a genius," said Lizzie, shocked. "Those interviews are works of art."

"I know, but Patrick thinks Daddy ought to write books. He's been working on a biography of Yeats for years, and he used to write wonderful plays."

"What's Patrick going to do when he leaves Trinity?"

"He'll write. He's much more together than Daddy. I know Daddy makes pots of money, but it all gets spent, and he's always having frightful rows at work. Patrick's calmer. He's a prose version of Daddy, really. And for someone with such high principles, he thinks nothing of running up the most enormous debts, which of course Mummy settles out of Daddy's despised television earnings."

They had crossed the stream now, to the same side as Rupert's house. Despite the lack of wind, thistledown was drifting everywhere as though a pillow had just burst. Panting up the slope, and turning in their tracks, they could just see the creepered battlements and turrets of The Priory above its ruff of beech trees, now warmed by the late afternoon sun. Climbing had given Caitlin's pale freckled face a tinge of color.

"Think of all those nuns living there in the Middle Ages," she sighed ecstatically, "gazing across the valley, yearning for Rupert Campbell-Black's ancestors."

Lizzie decided not to spoil such a romantic concept by pointing out that Rupert's house hadn't been built until the seventeenth century.

"It *is* a romantic house, isn't it?" said Caitlin still gazing at The Priory. "Exciting things must happen to us all—even Tag—in a place like that."

"I'm sure they will," said Lizzie.

"I'd better go home now," said Caitlin. "Can I come and see you next time I'm back for the weekend?"

Lizzie floated home. What richness, what a fascinating afternoon. The prospect of new friends excited her these days almost as much as new boyfriends had when she was young. She was still bubbling over when James got home, later than usual.

"What did you think of my program?" he asked.

Lizzie had to confess she'd forgotten to watch it, because she'd dropped in and had a drink with the O'Haras.

"Did Declan say anything about me?" demanded James.

"No," said Lizzie.

"Didn't you tell them you were married to me?" said James, utterly scandalized.

CHAPTER 9

Declan O'Hara had two obsessions in life: his work and his wife.

He was born in a thatched cottage on a green hillside. When Declan was ten, his father broke his back falling from a tractor when drunk, so the family moved back to Cork, his Protestant mother's hometown. Here his mother proceeded to bring up Declan and his three brothers by taking endless cleaning and secretarial jobs. Her one joy in an exhausting life was Declan, who fulfilled his promise at school by winning a history scholarship to Trinity, Dublin. Soon he was writing poetry and plays, working freelance for the *Irish Times* and sending money home.

One evening in his second year at Trinity, he dropped into the theater to see *The Playboy of the Western World*. Maud, with her red hair and her amazing green eyes, was the toast of Dublin as Pegeen Mike. Declan went around in a daze for days, then sat down, wrote a play for her in a month, and mailed it off. Impressed by the play, Maud asked him backstage and was even more impressed by this roaring black-eyed boy with his volcanic moods and his gift for words. The theater put on the play for a three-month run. It was an instant success, with Maud's extra radiance being noted by all the critics. By the sixth week she was pregnant and married Declan as soon as the play closed. Although stunned with amazement and joy that this glorious creature was his, Declan soon realized there was no way he could support her and a baby by writing plays, so he junked his academic career and got a full-time job on the *Irish Times*.

There was talk of Maud returning to the stage when Patrick grew older, but then Taggie came along, and then Caitlin. Habitually strapped for cash, Declan moved to television, where, although his family in Cork thought he was joining the circus, he soon became a star. Snapped up by the B.B.C. in London, in a year he was writing his own programs, culminating in a series of interviews which had promptly climbed to the top of the ratings and remained there for two years.

For not only was Declan the most natural thing ever seen on television, but, unlike other talk show hosts, he never showed off or talked about himself, and he always did his homework. To get public figures, as a result of this quiet, sympathetic, utterly relentless probing, to reveal facts of their character never seen before made for spellbinding television.

These revelations, however, did not always please the B.B.C., who got rattled if a Sinn Fein leader appeared too attractive or a politician too unpleasant. Known as the terror of Lime Grove because of his black moods and his sporadic bouts of heavy drinking, Declan bitterly resented interference from above. He finally walked out when Tony Baddingham offered to triple his salary and Declan couldn't see any other way of paying his tax bill or ever clearing his overdraft.

Also Declan yearned to live in the country. He truly believed it would be cheaper than London, and he would have more time to spend with his family, particularly Maud, and to finish his biography of Yeats.

Maud herself was lazy, egotistical, and selfish. She idled her time away reading novels, spending money, and talking. There was a tremendously strong erotic pull between her and Declan, but even after twenty-one years, Declan still felt he hadn't really won her. He was

also in a Catch-22 situation. In order to support Maud's wanton extravagance he was forced to work all hours, which meant she got
bored and spent more, and, to goad him, toyed with other men.
Another reason Declan had moved to the country was that last year
one of her toyings had got out of hand.

A week after the O'Haras moved into The Priory, Declan started
work at Corinium. He didn't sleep at all the night before. His friends
at the B.B.C. had not been backward in telling him that Tony Baddingham was a shit, or that ITV, notoriously more reactionary and
restrictive than the B.B.C., would be far harder to work for. In the
end, too, as he had been desolate to leave Ireland, he was sad to
leave the B.B.C. The staff had held a succession of riotous and tearful
goodbye parties, finally chipping in to give him the *Complete Oxford
Dictionary of National Biography*. But all his life Declan had walked
away from the safe thing—that was his instinct.

As he lay in the huge double bed, smoking one cigarette after
another, watching dawn creep through the curtainless windows,
Maud slept peacefully beside him. Her red hair spilled over the rose-
pink pillow case, the whole of the dark blue duvet was wrapped
around her hips, and her breasts fell sideways onto a pale green bottom sheet. Nothing ever matched in their house, reflected Declan.

He longed to make love to her to ease the panic and tension,
but there was no way she'd wake before ten o'clock. She was as
obsessive about sleep as he was about work. Tony had told him to
roll up at eleven, but knowing work was the only way out of his
black panic, Declan decided to go in early. He was expecting a pile
of Johnny Friedlander's clippings from America.

Thank God for Taggie, he thought, as he put on a beautifully
ironed black and green check shirt. Grace the housekeeper, who also
never rose before ten, had an ability to singe or iron buttons off
everything she touched.

As he went into the kitchen to pick up his car keys, Taggie came
barefoot and hollow-eyed down the back stairs in her nightgown.

"Daddy, you shouldn't be up yet."

"Couldn't sleep. Thought I might as well go in."

"You must have some breakfast, or at least a cup of coffee."

When he shook his head, she put her arms round him.

"It'll be OK, I know it will. Remember you're the best in the
world."

Declan reached the Corinium Television building at a quarter to
eight, just as the night security man was about to go off.

Walking through the revolving front door, absolutely sick with nerves, Declan found the place deserted except for a cleaner morosely pushing a mop, and a young man in pink trousers arranging roses on the marble-topped reception desk.

Aware that every other girl who worked in the building was at home washing her hair, putting on her prettiest clothes, and emptying perfume bottles over herself in anticipation of Declan's arrival, the receptionist had just nipped down to Makeup to redo her eyes before the hordes started arriving at nine.

Declan therefore waited a few minutes, admired the framed awards on the wall, which seemed all to have been won by Cameron Cook, then, still finding no one at Reception, took the elevator to the fifth floor, where he eventually discovered a coffee machine and an office with his name on it.

It was a splendid office with a thick blue carpet, a huge bare desk with empty drawers, two empty filing cabinets, a radio cassette, two television sets, a video machine and a large bouquet of red roses, which had obviously been arranged by the pink-trousered youth. Out of the window was a marvelous view of the water meadows still white with dew. But even more marvelous, on the virgin sheet of pink blotting paper lay a pile of mail including two fat airmail envelopes. Lighting a cigarette, sitting down at his desk, Declan was soon totally immersed in Johnny Friedlander's press clips—most of them highly speculative and fictitious because Johnny never gave interviews.

The great bell of Cotchester Cathedral had tolled the hour three times when suddenly a red-faced middle-aged lady, reeking of Devon Violets, and with tightly permed hair, barged into his office, gave a squawk of amazed relief, and shot out again, shrieking down the corridor, "He's here, Lord B, he's here."

Next minute Tony Baddingham erupted into the room, purple with rage. "Where the fuck have you been?"

Declan sat back in his chair. "Sitting here, since about eight o'clock."

"Why the hell didn't you tell anyone?"

"There was no one here to tell."

With a colossal effort Tony gained control of himself and shook Declan's hand. "Well, welcome anyway. Look, I've got most of the national press outside waiting to witness your arrival. We nearly had the police out."

"They said you'd left home at seven-thirty," said the lady reeking of Devon Violets, who was Tony's secretary Miss Madden. "We thought you might have had a car crash."

"Or second thoughts," said Charles Fairburn, Head of Religious Programs. "First days in an office are like birthdays. No one's allowed to be mean to you."

"Fuck off, Charles," snarled Tony.

"See you later, darling," said Charles, whisking out again, nearly colliding with an ashen Cyril Peacock.

"They're getting awfully fed up, Tony. Where the hell can the stupid fucker have got to?"

"He's been here all the time," said Tony nastily. "You just didn't look, Cyril. Another classical Peacock-up."

"Oh, hello Declan. Welcome to Corinium," said Cyril, his false teeth rattling violently. "Marvelous to see you. They're all waiting for you in the parking lot."

"Uh-uh," Declan shook his head, looking mutinous. "I've got nothing to say to them."

"Well for a start you might like to refute that piece in the *Guardian* claiming you joined Corinium merely to clear your overdraft and not as a vocational choice," said Tony with a cold smile.

"I interview people, I don't give interviews," said Declan, not budging.

Tony tried a different tack. "It'll be a thrill for the staff," he said suavely. "All we want is pictures of you driving in for the first time and having a glass of champagne in the conference room afterward. Then we can all get down to work."

Declan suddenly decided he needed a drink.

"All right, I'll go get my car."

"You can't do that. They'll see you," said Tony. "Give Cyril your keys. He'll drive it around to the front, then you can drive in again."

"It's a Mini, parked in the far corner," said Declan.

As Declan drove his absolutely filthy Mini into the parking place with his name on it, which was between Tony's maroon Rolls-Royce with the silver Corinium ram on the hood and Cameron's green Lotus, there was absolutely no reaction from the crowd of reporters and cameramen. The next minute, however, there was a furious banging on the roof. Declan wound down the window half an inch. He could see a beaky nose, and a predatory mouth.

"Yes?" he said.

"You can't park here, asshole," said an enraged female voice.

"Why not?"

"Can't you read, you fucking dumbass? This slot's reserved for Declan O'Hara."

"Is it indeed?" said Declan softly. "Then I've come to the right place."

Winding up the window, he got out, towering over Cameron Cook, who gasped and stepped back as she instantly recognized the tousled black curls, the brooding dark eyes and the familiar face as battered as the Irish coastline. Shock made her even more hostile.

"Where the fuck have you been? You should have been here at eleven. It's nearly twenty past."

"So I was, crosspatch, in my office. Nobody thought to look."

There was a shout as the press recognized Declan and surged forward, their cameras clicking away like weaving looms. From every window female staff, their clean hair flopping, screamed and cheered with excitement. Declan grinned up at them and waved.

Inside the building everyone surged forward to say hello to Declan. The corridor was swarming with *Midsummer Night's Dream* fairies coming back from their mid-morning coffee break. As Declan fought his way through them, shaking hands, Bottom took off his ass's head to have a better look. Next minute, Titania struggled to Declan's side, her crown askew, and kissed him on both cheeks.

"Darling, marvelous you've arrived. We must lunch later in the week. Love to Maud."

"Wish we'd never started this fucking production," said Tony, punching more fairies out of the way.

Mercifully he kept the press conference short: "We are all absolutely delighted Declan's joined Corinium," he said, when everyone had been given a glass of champagne. "We feel he has a tremendous contribution to make, and has just the right kind of incandescent talent to revitalize our current affairs schedule."

Declan surpressed a yawn.

The press conference was affability itself compared with the meeting that followed in Tony's office.

As Tony, Declan, and Cameron trooped past the tiny outer office where Cyril Peacock waited, gray and sweating, for Tony's reprisals after the disaster of Declan's arrival, they found Simon Harris, Controller of Programs, lurking apprehensively in Miss Madden's office.

"I'm terribly sorry I wasn't here when Declan arrived," said Simon, following Tony into his office. "Fiona's had to go into hospital, so I had to take the kids to school."

"Couldn't the Nanny have done it?" snapped Tony.

"She's had to take the baby to the clinic." Simon scratched at his eczema.

"I'm so sorry," Declan turned to Simon. "Is your wife OK?"

"Multiple sclerosis," said Simon helplessly. "She's in for new tests."

"I'm so sorry," said Declan again. He held out his hand.

The hand that limply gripped his was wet and trembling. Christ he's aged, thought Declan, appalled. Simon looked awful. His eyes were unbecomingly frightened, the shoulders of the gray suit were coated in dandruff.

"Well, sit down," said Tony irritably, deliberately waving Cameron and Declan towards the dark green leather sofa which lined two walls of his vast office. Simon Harris had to make do with a hard straight-backed chair right in front of Tony. Despite the room's size, the plethora of television sets, video machines, and huge shiny green tropical plants plus Tony's massive empty desk and huge carved chair made it seem unpleasantly overcrowded. A bowl of flesh-colored orchids on Tony's desk and central heating turned up like the tropical house at the zoo increased the jungle atmosphere. Any moment Declan expected a leopard to pad out from behind the filing cabinet. As he'd already downed a couple of glasses of champagne, he wanted to go on drinking, but it was at least half an hour until lunchtime.

"After lunch, Declan," said Tony, "I'll hand you over to Cameron, but I thought I'd like to be in at the kickoff."

Declan looked at Cameron in her sleeveless orange T-shirt and her short black leather skirt. Her hair was greased back, her eyes fierce. She looks like a vulture who's spent the morning at Vidal Sassoon, thought Declan. He loathed meetings; he wanted to get back to his Johnny Friedlander clippings.

Furious at having made an idiot of herself in the parking lot, Cameron was determined to regain the upper hand. "My goal is to give your program more pizazz," she said. "We've chosen several possible theme songs. Once we've decided on the right one, we can go ahead and cut a disc, which should go straight to the top of the charts with a nice profit for Corinium. But we ought to get it recorded at once. Could you listen to them this afternoon?"

Declan's eyes, which never left the face of the person he was listening to, seemed to darken.

"I know what tune I'm having," he said flatly, "the opening of the first movement of Schubert's Fifth Symphony."

"Too up-market."

"The program's up-market. It's a great melody, and it's in the public domain, so we won't have to pay copyright. All we have to do is to record a jazzed-up version and pay the arranger."

Cameron was spitting, but she didn't want to lose face in front of Tony and Simon, so she tried another tack which would certainly have worked with James Vereker.

"I keep hearing the same complaint about your programs."

"What?" said Declan softly.

"The viewers don't see enough of you. We want to feature you much more in the interview, that's why we've designed a terrific set with book shelves and some really good abstract paintings, and this jade green sofa."

"No," interrupted Declan sharply. "I only interview people face-to-face."

"Confrontational TV's kinda dated," taunted Cameron.

Simon Harris opened his mouth to protest and shut it again.

"I'm not using a sofa," said Declan firmly.

"Well, we'll argue about that later," said Cameron.

"We will not. We'll decide now. I want two Charles Rennie Mackintosh chairs, facing each other six feet apart on pale steely blue circular rostra."

"Steely blue?" screeched Cameron.

"Steely blue," said Declan firmly, "so they rise like islands from a floor of dark blue gloss. Then carrying on the dark blue up the bottom of the cyke into a limitless white horizon."

"This is insane!" Outraged, Cameron swung around to Tony for help. "Well?"

But Tony was calmly doing his expense account.

"It's Declan's program," he said smoothly. "He knows by now how to get the best out of people."

"How does he know until he's tried a sofa?"

"Sofas make it look like any other talk show," mumbled Simon.

"No one's asking you, dumbass," hissed Cameron.

She's like a hawk, not a vulture, decided Declan. She prefers her victims alive. He imagined her cruising the hillside, scanning the ground for prey.

Squaring her shoulders, Cameron turned back to Declan. "And we're scrapping the lead-in," she said. "We want you talking to the camera for two or three minutes about the guest, to replace all those dreary stills and clips with a voice-over.''

"The point of those dreary stills and clips with a VO," said Declan, dangerously quietly, "is that they concentrate the viewers' minds on the guest and set the tone of the interview."

"I *must* disagree on this one," said Tony, putting down his red fountain pen. "The point is, Declan, that you have immense presence. It's you the viewers turn on for. You should open the program talking to the camera in a really decent suit," he added, raising a disapproving eyebrow at Declan's scuffed leather jacket, check shirt, and ancient jeans.

"We've got to be different from the B.B.C.," snarled Cameron, "or they'll just say we're serving up the same old garbage."

"Anyway we've got three weeks to kick the idea around," said Tony, "I know Cameron's had a great time dreaming up people for you to interview."

"I decide who I'm going to interview," said Declan harshly.

Cameron stopped in her tracks, glaring at him: "They may not be hot enough."

Declan then stunned the three of them. He was kicking off with Johnny Friedlander on September 21, he announced, followed by Jackie Kennedy the week after.

Frantic now to keep her end up, Cameron snarled that Jackie Kennedy would just drone on about her boring publishing job.

"She may indeed," said Declan, "but she's also going to talk about her marriages and her life as a single woman in New York."

"Isn't it going to overextend your budget, flying her over?" Cameron demanded.

Declan suddenly relaxed and gave Cameron the benefit of the wicked gap-toothed schoolboy grin: "She's coming over on a private visit, and she'll probably stay with us," he said.

Fifteen love to Declan, thought Simon Harris joyfully. Then it was game and first set when Declan announced that in subsequent weeks he'd be doing the French Foreign Secretary who was in the middle of a gloriously seamy sex scandal, followed by Mick Jagger, and the most controversial of the royal princesses.

Desperately fighting a rear-guard action, Cameron said she had lined up a couple of ace researchers, who'd better get started on Johnny Friedlander and Jackie Kennedy at once.

There was a long pause. Very slowly Declan got out a cigarette, lit it, inhaled deeply, and only just avoided blowing smoke in Cameron's face.

"I do my own research," he said softly.

"For Christ's sake," screamed Cameron, "you can't cover subjects like this single-handed!"

"I have done so for the past ten years. For better or worse, what you've bought is not my face, but my vision—what I can get out of people."

"It's a team effort," hissed Cameron.

"Good," said Declan amiably. "Then I suggest we put your researchers onto finding some decent footage and stills."

"We've got an excellent library," said Simon, tugging his beard.

"Shut up!" howled Cameron.

Noticing the disapproval on Declan's face, Tony looked at his watch.

"That was a very stimulating exchange of views," he said, getting to his feet, "but I, for one, need some lunch." Then, deliberately excluding Simon, he added, "Cameron and I've booked a table at a little French restaurant a couple of miles outside Cotchester. We hope you'll join us, Declan, and we can carry on the—er—discussion." He smiled expansively.

Declan didn't smile back. "Thanks, but I'm lunching with Charles Fairburn."

Tony was about to order Declan to cancel, then decided there would be oodles of time later to get heavy. Besides, the clash of wills had turned him on; he had a sudden craving to take Cameron back to Hamilton Terrace for a quickie.

"What are your plans for the afternoon?" Cameron asked Declan.

"I'm going home," said Declan. "I've got Johnny's clippings and all my reference books are there."

"I trust you'll do most of your research in the building and report regularly to me and Tony," she said. "This is a group effort. OK? We want to be fully briefed at all times. Problems arise at Corinium when no one knows what anyone else is doing."

As she flopped down again on the green leather sofa, Declan immediately got up.

"I have to be left alone," he said, speaking only to her. "It's the only way I can operate."

"I'm producing this program," she said furiously.

"Yes, but it's *my* program you're producing."

For a second they glared at each other, then a knock on the door made them start. Round it, like the rising sun, came Charles Fairburn's red beaming face.

"Are you through, sweeties?" he said blithely. "Because I've come to take Declan to din-dins."

They lunched in a very pretty pink and white restaurant off the High Street. Pretty waiters in pink and white striped bow ties converged on Charles.

"We've got your usual table," they said, sweeping him and Declan off into a dark corner.

"Good boys," said Charles. "You know how I detest windows, they show up my red veins. Now get your little asses into gear and bring me a colossal dry Martini, and my friend here would like? Whisky is it still, Declan?"

"Bad as that, is it?" asked Declan three minutes later, as Charles drained his dry Martini and asked the waiter for another one.

"Well I don't want to badmouth the company on your first day, dear boy, but things are a shade tense."

"Cameron Cook," said Declan, tearing his roll apart.

"Got it in one."

"What's her position in the company?"

"Usually prostrate. She's Tony's bit of crumpet. Officially she's Head of Drama—particularly appropriate, as she's always making scenes, but she's also got a finger up to the elbow in every other pie. That's how she talked Tony into letting her produce your program. The food is utterly wonderful here," Charles went on, smiling at the waiter. "I'll have liver and marmalade and radicchio salad."

Declan, who liked his food plain, ordered steak, fried potatoes, and some french beans.

"And we'd like a bottle of '32, and bring us another whisky and a dry Martini while you're about it," said Charles.

As soon as the waiter had disappeared to the bar, however, Charles returned to the subject of Corinium. "The entire staff are in a state of revolt. They've all been denied raises and they're forced to make utterly tedious programs in order to retain the franchise. James Vereker's ghastly 'Roundup' is just a showcase for local politicians and Tony's business chums; and the reason *Midsummer Night's Dream* is taking so long is that you can't get a carpenter to build a set—they're all up at The Falconry building an indoor swimming pool and a conservatory for Tony, when they're not installing a Jacuzzi for Cameron."

Declan grinned. Charles, he remembered from the B.B.C., had always had the ability to make things seem less awful.

"Nor," added Charles, draining his third dry Martini and beckoning to the waiter to pour out the claret, "are the staff overjoyed that you've been brought in at a vast salary to wow the IBA."

Declan stubbed out his cigarette. Suddenly he didn't feel remotely hungry any more.

"Anyway," said Charles, cheering up as the Martinis began to take effect, "the staff like the idea of you, Declan. Christ, this liver is ambrosial. I've told them you're a good egg."

"Thanks," said Declan.

"They all admire your work, and they can't wait to see the fireworks when you tangle with Ms. Cook."

"I already have," said Declan, watching the blood run out as he plunged the knife into his steak. "Tell me about Tony."

"Complete shit, but extremely complex. One never knows which way he's going to jump. Believes in deride and rule, plants his spies at all levels, so really we're all spying on each other. But he does have alarming charm, when it suits him. Because he's so tough most of the time, when he's nice it's like a dentist stopping drilling on a raw nerve."

"What's the best way to handle him?"

"Well, he claims to like people who shout back at him like Cameron does; but, unfortunately, after a row, you and I can't make it up with him in bed, which I bet is where he and Cameron are now. Things were so much more peaceful when he spent all his time in London, but the IBA's warning him to spend more time in the area neatly coincided with his falling in love (though that's hardly the word) with Ms. Cook, so he's down here making a nuisance of himself most of the time now."

Charles suddenly looked contrite.

"You're not eating a thing, dear boy. Have I upset you?"

"Yes, but I'd rather know the score. Will Tony leave Monica?"

"I doubt it. Any scandal, even a piece in *Private Eye* is the last thing he wants with the franchise coming up. The pity of it, Iago, is that Ms. Cook is very good at her job. But if she gets on the Board, we're all in trouble. We have great hopes you're going to rout her, Declan; now let's have another bottle and you can tell me all about poor bored Maud and that ravishing son of yours."

Back at Corinium, James Vereker fingered the prettiest secretary from the Newsroom with one hand as he reread today's fan mail for comfort with the other.

"I do really think," he said petulantly, "Tony might have had the manners to introduce me to Declan."

CHAPTER 10

A fortnight after Declan started at Corinium his younger daughter, Caitlin, went back to her new boarding school in Oxfordshire, and his elder daughter, Taggie, disgraced herself by being the only member of the family to cry.

Caitlin's last week at home coincided with her mother discovering the novels of P. D. James. Maud spent her days curled up on the sitting-room sofa, holding P. D. James on top of a pile of tee shirts, shorts, and navy blue sweat pants. When anyone came into the room, she would hastily whip the clothes over her book and pretend to be sewing on name tapes. The same week Grace, the housekeeper, discovered the local pub.

As well as getting the house straight, therefore, and feeding everyone, and coping with Grace grumbling about the incessant quiet and imagined ghosts and having to drag trash cans to the end of a long drive, the task of getting Caitlin ready for school fell on Taggie.

It was not just the buying of lacrosse sticks, laundry bags, and the New English Bible (which Declan hurled out of the window, because it was a literary abomination, and which had to be retrieved from a rose bush) and the packing of trunks which got Taggie down. Worst of all was scurrying from shop to shop in Gloucester, Cheltenham, Cotchester, Stroud, and finally Bath, trying to find casual shoes and a wool dress for chapel which Caitlin didn't think gross and the school quite unsuitable.

Caitlin spent the morning of her departure peeling Day-Glo stars off her bedroom ceiling, sticking large photographs of Gertrude the mongrel, Wandering Aengus the cat, Rupert Campbell-Black, and smaller ones of her family into a photograph album, and dressing for school. On the first day back girls were allowed to wear regular clothes. By two o'clock she was ready.

"Are you auditioning for *Waiting for Godot*?" asked Declan, as she walked in wearing slashed jeans and an old dark blue sweater she'd extracted from Gertrude's basket.

By two-thirty the car was loaded. Only then did Maud decide to wash her hair and dress herself up to impress the other parents. They finally left at four by which time Caitlin was in a frenzy they were going to be late.

"Goodbye, my demon lover," she cried, blowing a kiss to Rupert Campbell-Black's house as the rusty Mini staggered down the drive. "Keep yourself on ice until I come home again."

No one spoke on the trip. Declan, with his first interview in a week's time, could think of nothing but Johnny Friedlander. Maud was deep in P. D. James. Taggie and Caitlin sat in the back under a pile of lacrosse sticks, radios, records, and teddy bears.

After three-quarters of an hour they reached the undulating leafy tunnels of Oxfordshire, and there, high on the hill surrounded by regiments of pine trees, rose the red-brick walls of Upland House, Caitlin's new school.

"My head ought to be filled with noble thoughts about comradeship," grumbled Caitlin to herself, as they were overtaken by gleaming BMWs and Volvos bearing other girls and their belongings, but all she could think was how embarrassing it was to turn up with such famous parents in such a tatty car.

As they arrived so late, all the beds near the window in Caitlin's dormitory had been grabbed and Caitlin had to be content with the one by the door, which meant she'd be the first to be caught reading with the huge flashlight her mother had given her as a going away present.

While Taggie, her fingers still sore from sewing on name tapes, unpacked the trunk, Maud drifted about, wafting scent and being admired by passing fathers. Declan sat on Caitlin's bed gazing gloomily at all those Lucite cubes full of photographs of black Labradors, ponies, and double-barrelled mothers looking twenty years younger than those in the dormitory. He wondered if he'd been mad to let Maud persuade him to send Caitlin away.

As they left, with all the girls surreptitiously gazing out of the window to catch a glimpse of Declan, Maud did nothing to endear herself to Caitlin's housemistress by calling out, "Don't worry, Caitlin darling, you can always leave if you don't like it."

"Bye Tag," said Caitlin cheerfully. "Don't cry, Duckie. I'll be OK. Keep your eyes skinned for Rupert. I won't look while you drive away. It's unlucky."

"She'll be all right, sweetheart," said Declan, reaching back and patting Taggie's heaving shoulders, until he had to put both hands on the wheel to negotiate the leafy undulating tunnels and was soon deep in thought again.

"Don't be silly, Taggie," snapped Maud. "I'm Caitlin's mother. I'm the one who minds most about losing my darling baby, but I'm able to control myself," and she went back to P. D. James.

Going to bed that night, Taggie felt even worse. In Caitlin's bedroom, she found a moth bashing against a window pane and the needle stuck in the middle of a *Wham* record, and she realized there was no one to leave the light on in the hall for any more to ward off the ghosts and hobgoblins.

Up in her turret bedroom, which was like sleeping in a tree top, and which creaked and leaked and swayed in the high winds like an old ship, she looked across the valley and saw at long last a light on in Rupert's house. Caitlin would have been so excited.

"Oh please God," she prayed, "look after her, and don't let boarding school curb her lovely merry nature."

The O'Hara children, having been raised by a lot of housekeepers and frequently neglected by their parents, were absolutely devoted to one another.

Taggie, in particular, had never enjoyed an easy relationship with her mother, whom she adored but who intimidated her. Ten days late when she was born, Taggie had been a very large baby. Labor had been so long and agonizing Maud had nearly died. Declan, insane with worry, thanked God he was a Protestant, and not faced with the agonizing Catholic preference for saving the baby rather than the mother. Both survived, but the doctors thought later that Taggie's dyslexia might be due to slight brain damage sustained at birth.

Maud, shattered and weakened, never took to Taggie the same way she had to Patrick who'd been born with such ease. As a child Taggie developed normally except that she walked and spoke very late, and even when she was four was only able to manage single syllables and might have been talking Japanese.

At school in Dublin, the staff, eagerly awaiting another dazzlingly bright pupil like Patrick, were disappointed to find that Taggie couldn't read or write. She was also very clumsy and hopeless at dressing herself, putting shoes on the wrong foot, clothes backwards, doing up the wrong buttons and quite unable to tie her shoe laces. Because she couldn't tell time and had no sense of direction, she always ended up in the wrong classroom, bringing the wrong books, and because she was so tall, people automatically assumed she was older than her age, and dismissed her as even more lazy and stupid.

Patrick, two and a half years older, was constantly fighting her battles, but he couldn't help her in class, when the other children teased her and the teachers shouted at her, nor during those agonizing sessions at home when Maud lost her temper and screamed, but in the end got so bored that she sometimes ended up doing Taggie's homework for her.

Patrick never forgot those pieces of homework, smudged with tears of frustration, sweaty from effort, and later peppered with red writing and crossings-out from the teachers.

It was Patrick who got a scholarship to Westminster with ease and who, acquiring a friend there with a dyslexic older sister, persuaded his parents to have Taggie tested by an educational psychologist. He pronounced Taggie severely dyslexic and said she should be sent immediately to a special school.

Maud never told anyone what the psychologist said to her in that brief bitter exchange after he'd seen Taggie, nor was there any way, once the condition was diagnosed, that Maud would ever have the patience to spend each evening helping Taggie with her reading and learning of the alphabet. Declan was always too busy. So it was Patrick, and later Caitlin, who came to her rescue.

Five years of special teaching produced dramatic improvements. At sixteen Taggie wrote her first essay. She still wasn't confident in the order of the alphabet, she still read slowly and hesitantly, following the text with her finger. She had never really mastered penmanship, and punctuation was a closed book. Her spelling was atrocious and she still didn't automatically know her left from her right, and had to think back to the kitchen and Patrick saying: "Window on the right, Tag, stove on the left."

It still took her ages to write letters or recipes, and when they moved to The Priory it took her much longer than the others to find her way around all the rooms. She also always double-checked telephone numbers, asking people to repeat them, ever since the nightmarish day when one of Maud's lovers had called from America and asked if Maud could call him back. Taggie had taken the number down wrong, and he'd never called again. Occasionally, when she was drunk, Maud would bring this incident up, how Taggie had lost her the one great love of her life.

But at the end of her school career, although Taggie only managed "O" levels in cooking and needlework, she left with an excellent final report: "Taggie is a dear girl," wrote her headmaster. "Kind, hardworking, responsible, she deserves to do very well in life."

Offered a place at a catering college, she preferred to learn the hard way, and worked in a restaurant belonging to a friend of her father's. After two years, coinciding with the family's move to Penscombe, he regretfully told Taggie that although he would do anything to keep her, there was nothing else he could teach her.

She cooked, he said, by instinct, a pinch of this here, a pinch of that there. Given a barrel of self-confidence, he told Declan, Taggie could be another Escoffier.

Taggie longed to start her own cooking business. There must be hundreds of people in Gloucestershire who needed someone to do dinner parties, or fill up their freezers at Christmas or at the beginning of the school holidays. But so much of her time lately had been spent looking after the family, or crying herself to sleep at night over Ralphie Henriques. Maybe now that Caitlin had gone back and Patrick was on his way to Trinity, via three weeks in France, she could get started.

The following morning did little to raise Taggie's spirits. She missed Caitlin dreadfully; the morning mail brought no letter from Ralphie, and when Patrick called from France, where he was staying with Ralphie's family, to report he had arrived safely, he made no mention of him. When Taggie finally steeled herself to ask how he was, Patrick had replied that he was fine.

"Doing a lot of waterskiing and drinking. But honestly, duck, I think you'd do better to cut your losses and find yourself a nice rosy-cheeked Gloucestershire farmer."

As the alternatives that afternoon included picking apples, making green tomato chutney, or getting on Maud's nerves, Taggie decided to take Gertrude for a walk and explore the village. In an attempt to beat her dyslexia she tried to learn a new word every day and use it. Today's word was "abhorrent." There was certainly nothing abhorrent about Penscombe that afternoon: the wind that shook her turret bedroom last night had dropped, while the little Beatrix Potter cottages, covered in velvety purple clematis, were white in the afternoon light. A lot of boys on motorbikes by the war memorial eyed Taggie with great interest. A nice farmer who lived down the valley asked her how they were all getting on and said they must come and have supper when the long nights began. At the village shop Mrs. Banks gave her a mutton bone for Gertrude and the new *TV Times* with Declan's picture on the cover, and an old lady with a blue greyhound stopped outside and exhorted her to watch out for the badgers who lived in the Priory woods.

Cheered up by their friendliness, Taggie set out for home. She could feel the heat of the road through her espadrilles, thistledown drifted idly, and the sky was brilliant blue except for a few little violet clouds on the horizon. If only Ralphie were here with his hand in hers. Turning down the drive of yews, hollies, and laurels which almost hid The Priory from the top road, she remembered her promise to keep her eyes skinned for Rupert. She glanced across the valley, then gasped with horror as she saw a huge mushroom of brown smoke rising into the sky and realized that two of Rupert's fields on the far side of the house were on fire.

She ran down the drive to The Priory, dashed into the kitchen and unearthed the Gloucestershire telephone directory. Oh God, she must keep calm. When she panicked, her reading went to pieces, and she had even more difficulty with the alphabet.

Callan, Calvay, Cam Auto Repairs, Camamile—with agonizing slowness her finger moved down the column. There were two Campbells, one in Gloucester, another in Nailsworth, then the list moved on to Cambridge and Campden. No Campbell-Blacks. Rupert must be unlisted like her father.

Great clouds of smoke were belching from Rupert's red-hot flickering fields, the flames spreading even nearer to the house. Taggie dialed 999. All the fire engines were out, explained the man at the other end, but they'd try Cotchester. "Don't worry, my love, we'll get one over as soon as possible."

All the same, thought Taggie, she'd better rush over and warn Rupert. He might not be able to see the fire from the house, although he'd probably be able to smell it. It would be so awful if any of the horses got trapped in their stalls. . . .

She raced across the lawn with Gertrude, slithered down the beech wood, bumping on her bottom most of the way, and ran across the water meadows; she leapt the bustling Frogsmore before starting the steep climb up the other side. Ripping her clothes on barbed wire, oblivious of stinging nettles and brambles tearing at her bare arms and legs, losing an espadrille on the way, she panted on, past surprised horses knee deep in lush grass, past ancient oaks and beeches, skirting the lake, tearing across Rupert's lawn, in through the French doors into a beautiful pale-yellow drawing room, by which time she was so winded she couldn't even shout "Fire."

Although the front door was open, no one was around. Returning to the garden through the French doors, her breath coming in great painful gasps, Taggie was about to run toward the stables when she heard shrieks of laughter coming from the tennis court on the left of the house, which was completely hidden by a thick beech hedge. As she raced down a gravel walk she heard another shriek of laughter.

"I can't hit a bloody thing. I should never have had so much to drink at lunch," said a girl's voice.

"Tit-fault. Your tits were at least six inches over the line," said a man's voice, a clipped, very distinctive drawl.

"Cock fault then," said the girl, giggling hysterically. "You must be at least ten inches over the line."

"You flatter me," said the man. "I wouldn't be if you didn't excite me so much."

"Fire," gasped Taggie to the beech hedge, but no sound came out.

The man was laughing now. "We'll finish this set, and then I'll finish you off upstairs."

Taggie raced around the beech hedge until she came to a gap.

"Fire," she croaked.

Then, very slowly, she realized to her utter horror that a tall, blond, lean, very suntanned man, and a beautiful girl with wispy blonde hair tied up in a pink ribbon, and a golden body like distilled sunflowers, were playing tennis with no clothes on.

The man was serving. His body rippled with muscle as the ball scorched across the net. Dropping her racket, the girl gave a shriek and rushed to the side of the court, breasts flopping, and covered herself with a pale pink shirt. The man proceeded to serve the second ball very hard into the far court, then sauntered almost insolently toward the net over which was hanging a dark blue towel.

"Fire," mumbled Taggie, clapping her hands over her eyes.

"What did you say?" shouted the man. "It's OK. You can look now."

Very gingerly, Taggie lowered her hands. He had wrapped the dark blue towel round his loins. With his sleek blond hair, broad brown shoulders, and long, wickedly mocking eyes, as cornflower blue as the great expanse of sky behind him, he was quite unmistakable, from Caitlin's photographs, as Rupert Campbell-Black.

Acutely aware of her heaving breasts and sweating red face, Taggie muttered, "Your fields are on fire."

"They're meant to be," said Rupert.

"Whatever for?"

"Quickest way to get rid of the stubble after the harvest."

"But it's the most a-a-abhorrent thing I've ever heard," whispered Taggie, utterly appalled. "What about the r-rabbits and voles and field mice, and moles and all the poor birds?"

Rupert shrugged. "They've got legs; they can run away."

"Not that quickly," said Taggie furiously. "You're a murderer."

"I suppose," snapped Rupert, "that you want me to stop

ploughing my fields because it's cruel to worms, earwigs, beetles, woodlice and all the poor bugs." He was mimicking Taggie now. "Do you want me to give them a state funeral?"

The blonde girl giggled. She was very young, only a few years older than Taggie.

"Oh shut up," screamed Taggie, losing her temper. "How would you like someone to set fire to you when you were in bed?"

Rupert nodded at the blonde. "She frequently does."

"Don't be disgusting. You're utterly abhorrent, the sort of person who always has to be killing something: hunting, fishing, shooting."

At that moment, a lot of dogs, back from their walk with one of Rupert's grooms, swarmed barking onto the court. There were Jack Russells, spaniels, a black Labrador, and a beautiful shaggy blue lurcher, which bounded joyfully up to Gertrude, who bridled and curled her tail up even tighter.

"Why don't you take that ugly brute back to its pigsty," said Rupert, picking up a green tennis ball and hurling it at Gertrude, "and stop interrupting other people's innocent afternoon pleasures."

"Don't you d-dare be beastly to Gertrude."

Reaching for his racket, Rupert let his towel drop: "Forty love wasn't it, darling?"

The blonde girl giggled again. But next moment the pussy-cat smile was wiped off her face as, with a manic jangling of bells, three fire engines roared up the drive.

"Fucking hell," screamed Rupert.

Taggie gave a sob and fled back across the valley, her face flaming as much as her poor torn stung legs. Beastly, horrible, abhorrent man. Looking up in front of her she could see The Priory. Except for Declan's twelve acres, all the land in the valley belonged to Rupert. Now, thought Taggie with a shudder, it seemed to curl around The Priory like a man trapping a woman at a party, putting his hands on the wall on either side of her, so she couldn't escape.

Back home she found Maud sitting outside, wearing a big black hat to protect her white skin from the early evening sun. She was drinking a vodka and tonic and immersed in P. D. James.

"I've just met Rupert Campbell-Black," said Taggie.

Maud glanced up and saw Taggie was scarlet in the face, with her black cloudy hair standing up on end in a tangled mess, her red dress ripped and her long legs and arms scratched and bleeding and covered with white nettle stings.

"My God," said Maud, roused out of her usual languor, "I know he's got a fearful reputation, but surely you didn't let him get that far?"

CHAPTER **11**

The following Sunday Monica Baddingham gave a lunch party at The Falconry to welcome Maud and Declan to Gloucestershire and launch the new conservatory built by Corinium's studio carpenters. Accustomed to going out to lunch in London where people seldom ate before two o'clock or even two-thirty, Maud and Declan didn't leave home until half past one. Declan tried to persuade Taggie to come too, but she blushingly refused when she heard Rupert might be there.

"I'm sure Monica said left at The Dog and Trumpet," said Maud, applying a second layer of coral gloss to a pouting bottom lip.

Declan was in a vile temper. Not only had Maud made him late yet again by washing her hair at the last moment, but he had spent all morning trying to cut their hayfield of a lawn with a mower that kept choking on Gertrude's shredded mutton bone. Now they seemed to be driving half way around Gloucestershire.

"Why the hell can't you take directions down properly?" he snarled.

"He's your boss. You should have taken down the directions. Anyway, it was you who wanted to move to the bloody country. Let's go home."

"They're giving the fucking party for us. Why the hell don't they put names on their houses in the country?"

"You don't."

"That's because I don't want anyone to come and see me."

Declan was also aware that, although his wife was looking gorgeous in a very low-cut black silk dress, a green shawl which matched her eyes, black stockings and black high heels, with her shiny red hair piled under the big black hat, she was quite unsuitably dressed for Sunday lunch.

"There it is," said Declan at last, as he drove through two lichened gate posts topped with stone rams. "Christ, people are leaving already."

As a dark green BMW passed them coming the other way, the woman who was driving wound down the window:

"Love your program. Welcome to Gloucestershire; you must come to dinner. Better hurry or there won't be any booze left."

"Jesus," muttered Declan.

The Baddingham's splendid Queen Anne house lay in a hollow surrounded by lush parkland. The stable clock was always kept twenty minutes fast so that people might worry they were late, and be encouraged to leave early.

In huge gold letters against a black background above the door of the porch was written the Baddingham motto *Peaceful is the Country that is strongly armed*. In the hall, stuffed heads of deer, tiger, stag, and buffalo gazed down glassily.

"My head'll be up there next," muttered Declan as Tony came out of the drawing room, plainly in a snit.

"Can't you ever get the time right, Declan? We've been trying to have lunch for three-quarters of an hour."

"I'm terribly sorry," said Maud in her most caressing tones. "Declan and I are used to London hours."

"Well, you'd better acquire a few rural habits. The Pimms has run out; what d'you want to drink?"

"Oh there you are." Monica swept in wearing a blue cotton shirtwaist dress and open-toed sandals on her big bare feet. "Taggie said you were on your way; pity you didn't bring her, I've got so many spare men. Have a quick drink, and then we'll have lunch. It's probably the last time we'll be able to eat outside this year," she added wistfully, thinking how much she'd prefer to be dividing the regale lilies.

Having given Maud a drink, she led her through the vast tapestried drawing room out to the new conservatory, which stretched the entire length of the house at ground floor level and was crammed with statues of goddesses, iron benches painted white, lilies, palms, aspidistras, and plants still wrapped, which people had brought as conservatory-warming presents.

"Beautiful," murmured Maud, taking a huge slug of whisky.

Everyone, gathered on the lawn, turned around and stared.

"Come into the garden, Maud," bellowed Charles Fairburn, who was already tight. Mistiming his kiss, his round red shiny face cannoned off Maud's like a billiard ball.

"Looking beautiful as usual," he said, drawing her aside.

"You're not to monopolize her, Charles," said Monica bossily.

"I promise I'll introduce her to everyone," said Charles. "Your husband's certainly been stirring things up at Corinium,'' he added, lowering his voice.

"Really,'' said Maud, only mildly interested.

"Is that very good-looking man over there Rupert Campbell-Black?'' she asked.

"Unfair to Rupert,'' said Charles. "That's James Vereker, Corinium's most popular newscaster, drinking Perrier and working the room. He's fearfully put out by your husband joining Corinium.''

James was, in fact, absolutely furious. He'd arrived as late as he dared in order to make an entrance, then Declan had swanned in even later. Now he was trapped by three of Monica's friends who did an enormous amount for charity, silly old bags who all wanted him to open their autumn bazaars and Christmas fairs for nothing. To look at Monica's toenails, thought James in disgust, you'd have reckoned she weeded the garden with her feet; and Paul Stratton, who'd put on a hell of a lot of weight, looked ludicrous in those tight new jeans, and a denim shirt undone to the waist to reveal scanty gray chest hair. James, who'd nearly worn jeans and an unbuttoned blue shirt, was glad he'd instead put on a new gray sweater with a pink elephant on the front, knitted by one of his adoring fans.

"Come and meet Maud O'Hara, James,'' yelled Charles Fairburn.

James extracted himself from the old bags and wandered over. Maud O'Hara was certainly extraordinarily beautiful.

"Hullo,'' said Lizzie Vereker, coming over and hugging Maud, "lovely to see you, I'm so pleased you've met James. Thank you for all that lovely whisky the other day. Are you sober yet?''

"Don't ever ask *me* that question,'' said Charles with a shudder. "What's all this about five fire engines rolling up at Rupert's house and catching him playing nude tennis with a blonde?''

"The *on dit* is that she's the girl playing Mustard Seed in *Midsummer Night's Dream*,'' said James.

"Have you heard that Titania's so petrified of getting AIDS, she's refusing to kiss Bottom until he's had a blood test?'' said Charles.

"Is Rupert here?'' asked Maud, who was not interested in Corinium gossip.

"Somewhere. Probably wandered off down one of those garden glades in which everyone except Monica behaves badly,'' said Lizzie.

"Speak for yourself,'' said James disapprovingly.

It was certainly a beautiful garden. Rising out of a sea of lavender, roses coming up for a second pale pink inning rampaged up the walls of the house. Pastel drifts of delphiniums, Japanese anemones, and Michaelmas daisies were sheltered from the bitter winds by yew hedges nine feet high. Two plump Labradors panted on lawns as smooth as an Oxford quad. Beyond was a fish pond and a water garden, fed by the same winding River Fleet that flowed through Cotchester.

"What are you going to do about The Priory garden?" asked Lizzie.

"Get a donkey to keep down the lawn," said Maud.

"I hope to God we eat soon," said a harassed looking man with a moth-eaten yellow beard and a sleeping baby hanging from a baby sling. He was also hanging onto two frantically struggling children by the scruffs of their necks.

"There is a limited amount of time one can entertain one's kids feeding Tony's fish," he added helplessly.

Lizzie introduced Simon Harris. All his skin seemed to be flaking in the open air, thought Maud.

"How's Fiona?" asked Lizzie.

"Still in hospital for another three weeks. It's the nanny's day off, or I'd never have brought this bunch," said Simon, as the two hyperactive horrors strained at their collars like bull terriers after a cat. "I just couldn't resist a square meal."

The panting Labradors struggled to their feet waving their tails as Monica appeared at the conservatory door.

"Lunch," she said. "You stay outside with the children," she added firmly to Simon. "I'll get someone to bring you something out."

As Maud walked into the dining room, Declan came toward her looking really happy for the first time that week: "Darling, you must meet Rupert. He knows Johnny very well. He's given me some great stuff about him. It's added a totally new dimension to his character."

Maud caught her breath. How could I ever have mistaken James Vereker for *that*, she wondered.

Rupert and Declan were both tall and broad in the shoulder, but there the resemblance ended. Declan, with his heavily lined, broken-nosed, shaggy-haired splendor, was like a battle-scarred charger returning from the wars. Rupert was like a sleek capricious thorough-bred, rippling with muscle and breeding, about to win the Derby.

"Welcome to Penscombe." Rupert kissed Maud on the cheek. "I'm sorry I wasn't at home when you moved in, but I've been frantically busy."

"So we hear, Rupert," said Charles archly. "What's this about fire engines and a burning bush?"

"Fuck off, Fairburn," said Rupert, grinning.

"Come on, don't hold up the line," said Monica beckoning from behind a long white table. "You're getting Coronation chicken again, I'm afraid."

Maud stood in front of Declan and Rupert, gulping down her third glass of wine and feeling totally unnerved.

"I know your house very well," Rupert told her. "I remember pursuing something that wasn't a fox across your haha at one party. Ended up ripping the front of my trousers off on the barbed wire. How's the garden?"

"The nettles are on the warpath," said Declan.

"Better get those tackled professionally," said Rupert, "or you'll never get rid of them. I've got a man who'll do it for you."

"How wonderfully positive you are," murmured Maud. "Perhaps you can give me advice on redecorating our bedroom?"

"Redecorating's never been a priority of mine. Not in bedrooms," said Rupert.

"Tuck in, Maud," said Monica impatiently. "And you haven't met my brother-in-law, Bas. He's dying to meet you."

Bas was about five inches taller than Tony and decidedly attractive in a sleek, wicked, Latin way. He kissed Maud's hand, then turned it over and buried his lips in her wrist.

"Calèche," he murmured. "I adore it. Do you wear it all over?"

Maud laughed. "Are you local?"

"Near enough as the helicopter flies. I can land on the palm of your hand. I've got a wine bar in Cotchester High Street," he went on. "Most of my evil brother's staff gather there to plot against him. No doubt your famous husband will shortly join them. You must get him to bring you in one day."

"Don't be silly, Bas," said Monica briskly. "You haven't met Paul Stratton, Maud, our MP for Cotchester, nor his wife Sarah."

She looks more like his daughter, thought Maud. With his anxious, lined, somewhat petulant face, and his brushed-forward blue-gray hair, Paul looked like one of those once-famous television personalities who eke out a middle-aged existence advising housewives to buy soap powder in television commercials.

"Ah, the newlyweds," said Bas, kissing Sarah on the mouth.

"*Basil,*" snapped Monica. "Do stop holding up the line. And you haven't met Freddie Jones, our electronic whiz kid have you, Maud?"

"Oh my goodness, you are smashing," said Freddie in wonder.

Maud felt marvelous. It was such a long time since she'd been admired by so many attractive men, so much more macho than all those wimps in London, and for once people were paying more attention to her than Declan. This dress always worked.

"Come along, Mrs. O'Hara," said Rupert, who had loaded up two plates, acquired a bottle of white wine and two glasses, and put them on a tray. "D'you want to be indoors or out?"

"Indoors," said Maud joyfully. "I freckle so easily."

Rupert found them a window seat in the conservatory.

"Monica's done this rather well," he said, looking around. "I gather it's cost Corinium even more than your husband's first week's salary. You want to avoid this house in winter; it's the sort of place Eskimos send their children as punishment."

Simon Harris's two monsters roared past, sending an aspidistra flying. Ten seconds later they were followed by Simon Harris with Coronation chicken all over his beard. The baby in the sling was bawling its head off.

"Did they go this way?" asked Simon frantically.

There was a crash from the drawing room.

"I'm afraid so," said Rupert.

Rushing almost as fast in the opposite direction came Paul Stratton searching for Sarah, who was sitting on a wall giggling with Bas.

"Paul's jeans appear to be castrating him even more than his new wife," said Rupert, forking up chicken at great speed. "If he bends over, his eyes will pop out."

Maud admired the length of Rupert's pale brown corduroyed thighs. After four large glasses of wine, she suddenly had an irresistible urge to touch one of them.

"She's beautiful, his wife," said Maud.

"She's a tramp," said Rupert, "and Paul's living in Cloud Cuckold land."

"What's Bas like?" asked Maud, putting her chicken down on the floor untouched.

"Divine," said Rupert. "Runs a phenomenally successful wine bar, dabbles in real estate, hunts four days a week in winter, plays polo all summer, and screws all the prettiest girls in four counties. Can't be bad."

"He doesn't look like Tony," said Maud.

"They had different fathers. After twenty-three years of utter fidelity to Lord Pop-Pop, Tony's mother fell for an Argentinian polo player. The result to everyone's amazement was Bas. Hence the name of the Wine Bar—the Bar Sinister."

Maud laughed. Many men had told her that her laugh was beautiful—low, musical, joyous.

"Tell me about Freddie Jones," she said.

"He's a saint."

"Because he buys your horses?"

"Not entirely. I've offered Declan a horse if ever he wants a day's hunting."

"Declan rides very well," said Maud. "He grew up on a farm. Who's that little woman who's bending his ear at the moment, who keeps making silly faces? He looks as though he needs rescuing."

Rupert glanced round. "Not by me, he doesn't. That's Freddie's wife, Valerie, the Lady of the Mannerism; won't rest till she's Queen of England. Freddie unfortunately thinks she is already. Keeping down with the Joneses is an eternal problem around here."

"You're very black and white, aren't you?" said Maud, noticing his long fingers and wishing they were unbuttoning her silk dress.

"I like people or I don't."

Looking up, Maud gave Rupert the benefit of her most bewitching smile. The great expanse of white eyeball and the beautiful teeth (unfairly even and white after so few visits to the dentist) really did light up her face. At the same time her hair escaped from its jeweled comb and cascaded down her back.

"I hope you like me," she murmured.

"I don't know yet," said Rupert slowly, looking at her mouth and then her breasts. "I like your husband very much, but you're certainly too disturbing to be living across the valley."

Glancing through the conservatory window at Maud's pale, rapt face, Declan thought she looked far more exotic than any of Monica's orchids and felt a sick churning jealousy. Rupert had his back turned. Maud was weaving her spells again.

"You need but lift a pearl-pale hand," Declan quoted to himself despairingly, "and bind up your long hair and sigh, And all men's hearts must burn and beat."

Oh Christ, if only he could get away from this party, and spend a few hours on his Yeats book. He'd done his duty at this party. He'd talked to the appallingly pompous Paul Stratton, and asked Simon Harris about his wife, and answered questions from bone-headed locals about the famous people he'd interviewed, and listened to at least three women who had daughters majoring in English at University, who wanted to go into television, and now he was trapped by this monstrous dwarf.

"It's so wonderful to be able to stand at the bottom of one's drive," said Valerie Jones, "and not be able to see one's house. We couldn't be happier with Green Lawns," she went on smugly. "We looked at The Priory, you know. It was on the market for ages, but it's awfully cold, and I really couldn't live in a place that didn't get sun until the evening. I must have sunshine."

She held her silly face up to the sun. Declan could see Maud running her hand through her hair now, shaking it out. Her body was arched towards Rupert. Unnoticed by either of them, the fatter of Monica's Labradors was busy gobbling up Maud's chicken.

"Even Freddie was nervous about meetin' you," Valerie was saying. "I said, don't be silly, Fred-Fred. Famous folk are just like everyone else. Most of them are on drugs, and very lonely, because all their friends have deserted them."

"I wish some of ours would desert us," said Declan grimly. "That's why we moved to the country."

In the hall Tony was throwing out Simon Harris. The elder monster had just smashed a Ming bowl.

"Was it very old?" stammered Simon, white-lipped.

"Only just over six hundred years," hissed Tony. "Out, OUT."

"I'll pay for it."

"It would take you two years' salary, which I don't think you'd like from the way you're always whining about money. Now, bugger off, before those little bastards break the whole place up."

"I must go," said Rupert.

"Oh," said Maud, put out. She wanted the afternoon to go on forever. It was as though the sun had gone in.

"I've got to pick up my children from my ex."

"How old are they?"

"Eight and ten."

"You must bring them over to see us. Taggie, my daughter, dotes on children. She'd keep them out of your hair. Has your ex-wife married again?"

"Yes," said Rupert getting to his feet, "to my old chef d'équipe, Malise Gordon. He used to manage the British team when I was show jumping. Bit of a tartar, so I feel their twin rays of disapproval if I roll up late."

Lizzie Vereker took Valerie's place beside Declan: "D'you need rescuing?"

"I did," said Declan. "I don't any more. How's the book going?"

"Backwards," said Lizzie. "Are you nervous about your first program?"

"Yes. I shouldn't be allowed out before a series starts. I get so wound up, I can't talk to anyone."

"Good luck with Johnny," said Rupert, pausing on his way out.

"Come and have dinner with us after the program," said Declan.

"Can't. I'm off to Ireland. I know we're both hellishly pushed, but let's get together soon. I'll come and look at your nettles. 'Bye, darling." He gave Lizzie a kiss.

As he crossed the deserted hall, Sarah Stratton came out of the downstairs bathroom, reeking of Anaïs Anaïs.

"Come and feed the fish," said Rupert, taking Sarah's hand.

He led her down a grassy path, flanked on either side by yew hedges, to the fish pond. Stuffed to bursting by Simon Harris's monsters, the carp didn't even bother to ruffle the surface of the water lilies.

"Any repercussions?" asked Rupert.

Sarah shook her head. "It seems funny, belting away from your tennis court with a pink dress over my head. The entire Gloucestershire fire brigade will recognize my bush, but not my face."

Rupert grinned, and pulled her inside the thick curtain of a weeping ash. After he'd kissed her, he said: "When are we going to finish the set?"

"Very soon, please."

Her smooth golden face was green in the gloom; she looked like a water nymph.

"How was Maud O'Hara?" she asked.

"Seemed pretty unmoored to me," said Rupert.

"Looks as though she'd like to tie herself to you."

"Were you jealous?"

Sarah nodded.

"Pity your husband's summer recess coincides with mine."

"He's never away," moaned Sarah, as Rupert's fingers moved between her legs. "Why don't we nip into the gazebo?"

"Got to pick up the children. I'm late already."

"When am I going to see you?" gasped Sarah, as Rupert's other hand slid down underneath her panties at the back.

"Come to Ireland with me. I'm leaving on Wednesday afternoon."

"I can't. My ghastly stepchildren are coming for a couple of weeks on a trial visit. Paul's going to Gatwick on Tuesday to meet them."

"That'll give us at least five hours. Ring me at home the minute he leaves."

* * *

Back in the conservatory, Maud was being lectured by Monica, who was busily dead-heading a pale blue plumbago growing up a white-washed trellis.

"You must do something for charity," she was saying. "It's such a good way of meeting new people, and it's awfully easy to get bored in the country."

"I never get bored," lied Maud. "There's so much to do to the house. I can't pass a traffic light at the moment without wondering whether yellow would go with red in one of the children's bed-rooms."

Driving home, Maud put a hand on Declan's thigh, edging it upwards. Pixillated by Rupert's interest, and Bas's extravagant com-pliments, hazy with drink, she felt wildly desirable and alive again.

"Let's go straight to bed."

"What about Taggie?" said Declan.

"Say we're both tired."

Declan curled a hand into the front of her black dress.

"They all wanted you."

"Did you like that?" whispered Maud.

"I know how hard I've got to fight to keep you," he said harshly and felt her nipples hardening.

Back in their bedroom at The Priory, he undressed her slowly down to her garter belt and stockings, so black against the soft white skin.

"When did you get those bruises?" she said sharply, as he took off his shirt.

"This morning. The fucking mowing machine kept stopping and I didn't."

CHAPTER 12

Gertrude, the mongrel, was walked off her feet in the next three days. When Maud wasn't drifting up and down the valley in a new lilac T-shirt and matching flowing skirt, hoping to bump into Rupert, Declan was striding through the woods, trying to work out what questions he would ask Johnny Friedlander and driving Cam-eron Cook crackers because he was never in when she wanted to talk to him.

Cameron's patience was further taxed by her PA getting chicken-pox, and having to be replaced by Daysee Butler, easily the prettiest girl working at Corinium but also the stupidest.

"Why d'you spell Daisy that ludicrous way?" snarled Cameron.

"Because it shows up more on credits," said Daysee simply.

Like all PAs that autumn, Daysee wandered around clutching a clipboard and a stopwatch, wearing loose trousers tucked into suede boots and sweaters with pictures on the front.

"It's just like the Tit Gallery with all these pictures floating past," grumbled Charles Fairburn.

Program day dawned at The Priory with Declan roaring around the house.

"Whatever's the matter?" asked Taggie in alarm.

"I have absolutely no socks. No, don't tell me. I've looked in all my drawers, and in the dirty clothes basket. Utterly bloody Patrick and utterly bloody Caitlin swiped all my socks, so I have none to wear."

"I'll drive into Cotchester and get you some," said Taggie sooth-ingly.

"Indeed you will not," said Declan. "I'm driving into Cotches-ter, and I'm buying thirty pairs of socks in such a disgusting color that none of you will ever wish to steal them again."

He was very tired. He hadn't slept, panicking Johnny might turn up stoned or not at all. And yesterday he and Cameron had been closeted together for twelve hours in the edit suite, putting together the introductory package, arguing constantly over what clips and stills they should use. Daysee Butler's inanities hadn't helped either. Nor had Declan's dismissing as pretentious crap an alternative script Cameron pretended one of the researchers had written, but which she in fact had toiled over all weekend. She got her revenge while Declan was recording his own beautifully lyrical script, by making him do bits over and over again because of imagined mispronuncia-tions or technical faults or bangings outside. They parted at the end of the day not friends.

Having bought his socks, Declan arrived at the studios around five. A game show was underway in Studio 2; the Floor Manager was flapping his hands above his head like a demented seal as a sign to the audience to applaud. *Midsummer Night's Dream* had ground to a halt in Studio 1, because Cameron, unsatisfied with the rushes, had tried to impose an "out-of-house lighting cameraperson" on the crew, who had promptly downed tools.

Deferential, glad-to-be-of-use, Deirdre Kilpatrick, the researcher on "Cotswold Roundup," as dingy as Daysee Butler was radiant, was taking a famous romantic novelist to tea before her interview with James Vereker.

"James will ask you your idea of the perfect romantic hero, Ashley," Deirdre was saying earnestly. "And it'd be very nice if you could say: 'You are, James.'"

"I only go on TV because my agent says it sells books," said the romantic novelist. "Oooh, isn't that Declan O'Hara? Now, he *is* the perfect romantic hero."

Declan slid into his dressing room and locked the door. A pile of good luck cards and telexes awaited him. He was particularly touched by one from his old department at the B.B.C. saying, "Sock it to them."

"Day-Glo yellow sock it to them," said Declan, chucking thirty pairs of socks in luminous cat-sick yellow on the bed.

There was a knock on the door. It was Wardrobe.

"D'you want anything ironed?"

Declan peered gloomily in the mirror: "Only my face."

He gave her his suit, pale gray and very lightweight, as he was going to be under the hot lights for an hour. She hung up his shirt and tie, then squealed with horror at the yellow socks.

"You can't wear those."

"They won't show," said Declan.

In Studio 3 two technicians were sitting in Declan's and Johnny's chairs, while the crew sorted out lighting and camera angles. Crispin, the set designer, whisked about in a lavender flying suit. The set was exactly as Declan had wanted, except the Charles Rennie Mackintosh chairs had been replaced by wooden Celtic chairs, with the conic back of Declan's rising a foot above his head like a wizard's chair: a symbol of authority and magic.

As a gesture of defiance, on the steel blue tables which rose like mushrooms at the side of each rostrum Crispin, the designer, had placed blue- and red-striped glasses and carafes.

"I want plain glasses," snapped Declan.

"Oh, they're so dreary." Crispin pouted.

"I want them—and get rid of those fucking flowers."

"Cameron ordered them specially."

Declan picked up the bouquet threateningly.

"Are you trying to bury me?"

"All right, no flowers," said Crispin sulkily.

Declan went off and shook in the men's room for half an hour.

When he returned to the studio the crew were lining up their four cameras before the meal break.

"Have you heard the latest Irish joke?" the Senior Cameraman was saying. "There was this Paddy who went into a chemist for his heroin fix."

The crew gathered around grinning at the prospect of more Hibernian idiocy. Halfway though the story the Senior Cameraman realized he'd lost his audience. Next moment, he was grabbed by the scruff of the neck.

"You may be the best fucking camerman in ITV," roared Declan, "but you'll not work on my program if you're going to tell Irish jokes. You don't dare tell jokes about Jews and blacks or cripples any more; why pick on the poor bloody Irish?"

With a final shake, which threw the Senior Cameraman halfway across the studio, he stalked out.

"I'll report you to my shop steward," screamed the Senior Cameraman, rubbing his neck.

In the bar they were gathering to catch a glimpse of Johnny Friedlander and to support Declan by watching his program. There was still a latent *esprit de corps* at Corinium. Someone had deliberately changed the color on the bar television, so James Vereker's face looked like a Jaffa orange.

"What's your idea of a romantic hero, Ashley?" he was saying.

"You are, James."

"That's very sweet of you, Ashley." James smoothed his streaks. "What's romantic about me?"

"Well you're so caring, James, and you've got an inner strength like Leslie Howard."

"Anyone seen Declan?" asked Daysee Butler, putting her top half, which had Goofy on the bosom, around the door to a chorus of wolf whistles. It was getting perilously close to transmission time.

"In the can," said Charles Fairburn. "I'm surprised he doesn't move his dressing room in there. Can't even keep down a brandy."

"Declan," shouted the Senior Cameraman. "You can stop worrying. Daysee's too embarrassed to come in 'ere, but Johnny Friedlander's people have just phoned to say they've come off the M4 and they'll be wiv us in twenty minutes."

"Thank Christ for that," groaned Declan.

"And 'ere's a letter for you." A piece of writing paper appeared under the door.

"Dear Declan," it said. *"We're sorry we was telling Paddy jokes. We won't any more, you was quite right."*

All the crew had signed it.

"P.S. Have you heard the one about the Englishman, the Welshman, and the Scotsman?"

Declan grinned, then he glanced at his watch, and nearly threw up again. He'd be on the air in less than an hour.

Johnny Friedlander arrived in a black limo which seemed to stretch the length of Cotchester High Street. He was accompanied by a publicity girl and four security men. In a second limo were four lawyers. Looking at the bulges in the security men's suits, the Press allowed Johnny to be smuggled into the building without too much hassle.

From the start Johnny's visit to Corinium went off with a bang. Taking one look at the ravishing Daysee, he pulled her into his dressing room and locked the door. The four security men stood outside with folded arms.

"Who's she?" asked Johnny's publicity girl in horror.

"A piece of ass," said one of the security men.

"Are you quite sure she's not a reporter?"

"Couldn't report a burglary," said Charles Fairburn, whisking past, thoroughly overexcited by so much security muscle.

In his dressing room a pretty makeup girl with a picture of sheep in a field on her bosom fussed around Declan. He wished he could lie down in her field and go to sleep.

"At least let me paint out the dark rings and give you a bit of base; you're so pale," she murmured. "And we'll have to do something about the beard area. You really ought to shave."

"I'm shaking so much I'll cut myself."

"I'll shave you."

Next moment Cameron stormed in.

"Johnny Friedlander's barricaded himself in his dressing room with Daysee."

"Best place for him," said Declan. "At least if he's having a bang, he's not snorting coke."

In his fifth-floor office, Tony Baddingham, even more nervous than Declan, was dispensing Krug to his special guests, who included several big advertising clients, the Mayor and Mayoress of Cotchester and Freddie and Valerie Jones.

In a corner of the conference room sat Johnny's four lawyers, sipping Perrier and fingering calculators at the prospect of litigation.

"Why the fuck d'you ask so many press?" Tony hissed to Cyril Peacock, who knew he'd have been equally roasted if only a handful had turned up.

Nor did the fact that Tony had been entirely responsible for hiring Declan stop him now blaming everything on Simon Harris. "You ought to be able to control Declan, Simon. That's what you're here for. He hasn't even given Cameron a running order."

"All she needs now is a prayer sheet," said Charles.

"Declan's my favorite telly star," the Lady Mayoress was saying excitedly to Valerie. "I can't wait to meet him later."

"Oh we know him quite well," said Valerie Jones, on the strength of last Sunday's lunch party.

A curious tension was building up through the building.

"Declan's just cut me dead," complained James Vereker, going into the bar. "Awfully uncool to get so uptight."

Daysee came out of Johnny's dressing room, looking as though she'd found the Holy Grail.

"He's having a quick shower," she said. "Then he wants Make-up."

It was five minutes to blast off. The four security men had taken up their positions in the studio. In the control room the production team sat at a desk like a vast dashboard, gazing at two rows of monitor screens. On four of the monitors which came direct from the studio, Cameron could see Johnny Friedlander's carved, beautiful degenerate face with its hollow cheek bones and California suntan. His fair hair was the red-gold of willows in winter, the irises of the deep-set Oxford Blue eyes were almost as dark as the pupils. Thin almost to the point of emaciation, he lounged easily in his three-thousand-dollar suit, with the sleeves rolled up to the elbow. But the air of relaxation was false.

"Why the hell did I agree to do this shit?" he drawled.

"I'm sorry," said Declan, meaning it.

"Aw that's OK. I just don't feel I've got proper lines when they're my own. Rupert called, by the way. He said: 'You can trust this guy, he's one of us.' "

In his earpiece Declan could hear Daysee saying: "The pink strapless is more dressy, but my holiday tan's nearly gone."

"Can we have some level?" asked the Floor Manager. "What did you have for breakfast, Johnny?"

Johnny laughed. "You want to get me arrested?"

On Cameron's left Daysee was checking different stopwatches. The moment they were on air she would forget pink strapless dresses, and become as cool as a computer, timing the program to the second.

On the right sat the vision-mixer in a red T-shirt, hands at the ready over regiments of square buttons, lit up like spangles, ready to punch up the right picture when Cameron demanded it.

"Good luck, everyone," said Cameron, crossing her fingers. "Stand by Studio, stand by Opening Titles, stand by Music."

"One minute to air," said Daysee, clenching her stopwatch and glaring at the leaping red numbers of the clock. "Twenty seconds, ten, five, four, three, two, one, and in."

Schubert's Fifth Symphony started on its jolly jazzed-up course. On the screen a rocket exploded in colored stars above a night-lit Cotchester, and then cascaded down to form the word Declan. A great cheer went up in the bar. Tony puffed on his cigar.

"I want another gin and tonic," said an already drunk reporter from the *Mail on Sunday*.

"Shut up," said Johnny's four lawyers in unison, who were listening like hawks, in the hope of finding something defamatory.

As Daysee cued Declan in, as a concession to Cameron, he swung round to talk directly to camera. For a moment his throat went dry. He's forgotten his first question, thought Cameron in anguish. Then he said: "I welcome my first guest in this new series with the greatest humility. He is simply the best actor to come out of America in the last fifteen years. But this is the first interview you've ever given." He turned to Johnny. "Why?"

"I hate publicity," drawled Johnny. "If all journalists were exterminated life would be just fine."

Up in the board room a howl of protest went up from the press, who stopped filling up their drinks and started listening.

"The Press detest success," went on Johnny, "and they screw up your sex life. However much you try not to get fed up, it pisses you off when you read lies that your latest girlfriend's been two-timing you with some Greek masseur. Every day, my exes are offered millions to tell all."

"How d'you cope?" said Declan.

"I don't read press clippings any more. I just weigh them; if they're light I start worrying."

"By deliberately avoiding publicity, aren't you actually courting it?"

"Don't give me that crap," grinned Johnny.

And they were off, sparring, laughing, fooling about almost like two old friends discussing someone they knew and liked, but frequently disapproved of. Johnny was being absolutely outrageous now about his exploits with his leading ladies, but he drawled out his

answers so honestly and engagingly that the press quickly forgave
him for his earlier sniping. The lawyers were clutching their heads,
but they were laughing.

It's going to be all right, thought Cameron. "Ten minutes to the
commercial break, Declan," she said into his earpiece. Following a
tip-off from Rupert, Declan then said, "And you're about to face your
greatest acting challenge . . ."

Johnny raised an eyebrow.

". . . playing Hamlet at Stratford next year," said Declan.

Johnny looked startled. Upstairs the conference room was in an
uproar.

"No one knows that," screamed the lawyers. "The goddamned
contracts haven't been fucking signed yet."

"I figured I ought to have a crack at it," said Johnny. "Women
don't get taken seriously as actresses until they allow themselves to
look ugly and sweaty and get raped on screen. Guys still have to play
Hamlet. And I like the guy. I mean he had a stepfather problem. I
don't figure Claudius bumped off Hamlet's father at all. That was
Hamlet's fantasy; he hated his stepfather. I hated mine."

"Why?"

"He married my mother. I was jealous. He was a bass-tard."

"Why?"

Tony drew on his cigar; the lawyers fingered their calculators;
even the press were still.

Declan paused, waiting unbearably long. On his pale blue island
in a sea of dark blue, Johnny suddenly seemed terribly vulnerable.

"He abused my baby sister," he said. "So I split. My stepfather
called to say my mother was dying of cancer. I didn't believe him,
so I didn't go home." Johnny put his head in his hands. "But she
did die the next day. She killed herself. I never told anyone that."

"Why did she commit suicide?" asked Declan quietly.

Johnny looked up, his eyes cavernous. "She was jealous because
my stepfather preferred my sister. Christ, what a mess."

"Are you worried, being American, you won't be taken seriously
as Hamlet?" asked Declan.

Relieved at a change of subject, Johnny fast recovered his poise.
"He was a Dane, for Christ's sake. He didn't speak like Leslie Howard."

In the bar James and the lady novelist exchanged caring smiles.

"It's the acting that matters," went on Johnny. "I could play
him like JR."

He launched into To Be or Not To Be in broad Texan; it was

so funny, the cameramen could hardly keep their cameras still. Half-way through Johnny slid into Prince Charles's accent, which was even funnier; then for the last ten lines, he played it straight and was so good that Declan felt his hair standing on end. At the end, Johnny said, "That'll be five hundred pounds, please," in a camp Cockney accent.

"You'll be taken seriously," said Declan.

"I can switch moods, that's why I'm a good movie actor," said Johnny. "But to be on stage four hours, that's something else. But then I've always lived dangerously. . . ."

Declan took a deep breath. "Is that why you went back to America to face trial?"

"That is definitely out of order," screamed the lawyers, positively orgasmic now at the prospect of lucrative litigation. "We agreed he wouldn't talk about that."

"I went back because I missed the States," said Johnny. He still appeared relaxed, but his knuckles were white points as he gripped the arms of his chair.

"Have you always fancied very young girls?"

"Sure, if they're pretty. Most men do. This one was very pretty."

"Did you know she was only fourteen?"

"Sure, I guess it was wrong, but she was so sweet, I really cared for her. I screwed her, but I don't figure I screwed her up. She's very happily married with a baby now."

"How'd you get on in prison?"

Johnny's eyes were cavernous again. "It's not a very nice place to be. But if you're a famous movie star you're trapped anyway; going to jail is just exchanging one kind of captivity for another. And I learned a lot. I could burglarize your place tonight, while you were in it. And I'm hot shit at insider trading."

Declan stretched out his legs.

"Extraordinary colored socks," said the girl from the *Mail on Sunday*, pouring herself another gin.

"Did they give you a hard time inside?" Declan asked Johnny.

"Not really. One guy who couldn't count—he thought the girl was four not fourteen—worked me over a bit, but I made some good friends."

"Have you never fancied older women?"

Johnny thought for a minute, then he smiled wickedly.

"No, they have droopy asses. Droopy asses are so cold in bed."

The telephone rang in the control room.

"For Christ's sake, get him off sex," yelled Tony. "The lawyers are going to take us to the cleaners. We'll lose the franchise if you don't shut him up."

"It's a fucking good program," said Cameron, and hung up.

Then she took the telephone off the hook.

"Five seconds to the cue dot," intoned Daysee. "Five, four, three, two, one." She flicked the cue switch to warn people all over the network to get ready in sixty seconds to roll in the commercials.

As the End-of-Part-One caption came up, Johnny shot out of the studio, saying he must take a leak.

"You stay here," Cameron screamed at Daysee. "Well done, Declan."

Johnny may not have been able to have Daysee in the break, but he had certainly taken something. In the second half he was even more outrageous, but utterly relaxed. Declan, in his wizard's chair, had only to prompt him here, jog his memory there, and curb his amazing honesty when he looked like going over the top.

The floor manager was waving a couple of fingers at Declan for two minutes more.

"Now you're going to play Hamlet, have you got any ambitions left?"

"I guess I'd like to make a happy marriage," said Johnny seriously. "I went to see my grandma the other day, she's been married sixty years. Now that is achievement—like building a cathedral brick by brick, a real life's work. I guess I won't achieve it, but that's what I'd like."

"Aaaaah," said Daysee Butler, so moved that she flicked the cue switch too early.

Now Declan was smiling and thanking Johnny for coming on the program.

On came Schubert, jauntier than ever, up rolled the credits, but alas because of Daysee's early cue, just as Cameron Cook's name was about to come up at the end, the screen went royal blue and the Corinium television logo appeared, with the little red ram seeming to hold his horned head even higher than usual. A second later they were into the commercials.

Another great roar went up in the bar and the conference room. Even the crew broke into rare spontaneous applause and crowded around Declan and Johnny. Upstairs, the press raced for the telephones.

"I must talk to Declan about those yellow socks. I'm definitely going to do a fashion piece," said the girl from the *Mail on Sunday*, pouring herself another gin.

"Great," said Freddie Jones, "really great, congratulations."

The lawyers came up and pumped Tony's hand. "We were shitting bricks at the end, but Johnny came across great, a really nice guy, an attractive guy."

Five minutes later, Tony got off the telephone in his office and ran down to Declan. "Lady Gosling thought it was terrific."

"Thanks," said Declan. "D'you mind if we don't join you? Johnny doesn't want to see anyone. He's reached a stage when he might go right over the top. I'm taking him home for a quiet dinner."

Through the door Tony could see the press and even the lawyers getting drunk. Corinium had walked a tightrope that evening and got away with it.

"Understood," he told Declan. "I'll talk to you tomorrow, but congratulations anyway."

As Cameron went into the conference room, everyone cheered. Tony even forgot himself sufficiently to march over and hug her. His eyes were blazing with triumph.

"Lady Gosling called to say how much she liked it. She sent special congratulations to you."

But Cameron felt utterly drained and despairing. Not just because of her lost credit, but because she had produced and directed a program in which she'd had no part. It had lived, and fortunately not died, with Declan.

CHAPTER 13

Declan's first programs for Corinium were a colossal success. The press agreed that Johnny Friedlander was the best interview he'd ever done, that the ones with Jackie Kennedy and the princess were even better, and the ones with Mick Jagger and Harold Pinter even better than that. The program sold everywhere abroad, and there was even talk at the network meetings of moving the series to seven-thirty on Thursday in an attempt to knock out "EastEnders." Declan sweatshirts, mugs, and posters were selling faster than bikinis in June and Schubert must have looked down from heaven and been surprised but delighted to see his Fifth Symphony galloping up the charts.

Once the first program was over Declan was much less aggressive and uptight and even drank in the bar with the crew, but he was no less intransigent about wanting his own way. Cameron smouldered and bided her time. Tony was besotted with Declan at the moment, but, knowing the nature of the two men, Cameron realized it wouldn't last.

Meanwhile, although the flood of resignations at Corinium had been arrested by Declan's arrival, Simon Harris was getting nearer his nervous breakdown and the staff were muttering even more mutinously into their glasses of Sancerre at the Bar Sinister that Cameron was about to be put on the Board.

But, to stop Cameron getting smug, Tony, ever the bubble-pricker, finally invited the ravishing Sarah Stratton to lunch, and arranged for James Vereker to interview her in the "Behind Every Famous Man" series early in November. Cameron was livid and vented her rage on the rest of the staff.

The same week Sarah was due to be interviewed, Tony summoned Declan to his office.

"How's your cold?" Declan asked Miss Madden as he walked through the outer office.

"Much better," said Miss Madden flushing. "How amazing of you to remember. Better hurry. Cameron's in there already."

Cameron was lounging menacingly by the window, wearing a black turtleneck, black leather trousers, and spiky high heels. Declan wondered if she walked all over Tony in bed in them. The room was full of cigar smoke. Tony was drinking a brandy, but didn't offer Declan one.

"Sit down. Congratulations to both of you," he said briskly. "I've just heard off the record that we got our highest local rating ever for your interview with the princess."

Declan sank into one of the low squashy sofas, which, with his long legs, were desperately uncomfortable unless one was lying down.

Tony leaned back in his chair: "Cameron and I have decided it's time you spread your wings, Declan."

Declan looked wary.

"We'd like you to interview Maurice Wooton this week."

"He's not big enough," said Declan flatly. Lord Wooton was a high profile Cotchester developer, but of little interest nationally. "And I'm already doing Graham Greene this week."

"That's OK," said Cameron. "Do Lord Wooton as a special after the ten o'clock news on Friday night."

"Why can't James do him?"

"James is already doing Sarah Stratton in the Famous Man slot on 'Cotswold Roundup.' Besides, we want you."

"I'm only contracted to do one interview a week."

"Don't worry," said Tony. "We'll pay you extra. We just want you to get really involved in the station."

"I don't have the time." It was so hot in Tony's office that Declan could feel his shirt drenched in sweat.

"That's what researchers are for," said Cameron, as though she was explaining to a two-year-old. "Deirdre Kilpatrick's been working on Maurice Wooton all week. She's come up with some terrific stuff."

Like a dog struggling out of a weed-clogged pond, Declan heaved himself up from the squashy sofa. "I do my own research," he said coldly, and walked out.

Hooray, thought Cameron, it's begun to work.

On Thursday morning Cameron called Declan at home. It was his official day off. He'd stayed up until four in the morning reading Graham Greene. He was determined to spend the next two days on his Yeats biography, and here was Cameron's horrible rasp ordering him to come into a meeting tomorrow at eleven o'clock.

"So we can kick some ideas around about the line you might take with Maurice Wooton."

Declan hung up on her. When he hadn't shown up by eleven-thirty the following morning, Cameron called The Priory in a fury. She got Maud, who said she was sorry but Declan was in bed.

"At this hour? Is he ill?"

"Not at all," said Maud. "He's reading."

"Put him on."

Declan told Cameron to go and jump in the River Fleet and that he'd no intention of coming in for any meeting. Tony then called Declan and ordered him to come in that evening and interview Maurice Wooton. Declan, having just received an eighty-thousand-pound tax bill, which he had no way of ever paying unless he went on working at Corinium, said he'd be in later, but wouldn't submit questions beforehand.

He slid into Corinium around two o'clock, when he knew Cameron and Tony would still be at lunch, and went down to the newsroom to talk to Sebastian Burrows, the youngest, brightest, and therefore most frustrated of the reporters.

"Deirdre Kilpatrick's been working like mad on your Maurice Wooton interview," said Seb.

"Any dirt on him?" asked Declan.

"He's one of Tony's best friends, isn't that enough?"

"Not quite—anything concrete?"

Sebastian's thin face lit up. "I've got enough to send him down for ten years, but I daren't use it."

"Give it to me," said Declan. "I'm going out."

On the same Friday Rupert Campbell-Black, having spent all week in meetings with the FA and the Club Managers trying to thrash out some suitable compromise on football violence, decided he needed a day off, and went hunting with Basil Baddingham.

Scent was very bad, however. It rained all day and the foxes sensibly decided to stay in their earths. Rupert and Bas got back to Rupert's dark blue Aston-Martin to find the windshield covered with leaves like parking tickets. They drove home through the yellow gloom.

"Who shall we do this evening?" said Bas, who was feeling randy.

"No one," sighed Rupert. "I've got to look in at some fund-raising cocktail party."

"Pity," said Bas slyly, "I was going to show you the most amazing girl."

"That's different," said Rupert. "Where does she live?"

"Penscombe Priory."

Thinking Bas meant Maud, Rupert said, "Isn't she a bit long in the tooth for you?"

"No, I'm talking about the daughter," said Bas. "She's absolutely stunning."

Back at The Priory, Grace, the housekeeper, who was making ridiculously slow progress sorting out the attic, stumbled on a trunk of Maud's old clothes. Maud, who had just finished her last P. D. James and was suffering withdrawal symptoms, wandered upstairs and started trying them on. Now she was parading around in a black-and-red-striped mini which fell just below her groin and showed off her still beautiful legs.

"I remember walking down Dublin High Street in 1968 in this," she said, "and an American clapping his hands over his eyes, and screaming: 'Oh my Gard, can they go any higher?' My hair was down like this." Maud pulled out the combs so it cascaded down her back. "I was only twenty-four."

"You don't look a day more than that now. Amizing," said Grace.

"Oh, I adored this dress too." Maud tugged a sapphire blue mini with a pie-frill collar out of the trunk. "I wore it to Patrick's christening. I wonder if I can still get into it."

"Fits you like a glove," said Grace, who was trying on a maxi-coat. "Amizing."

As Maud admired herself in an ancient full-length mirror propped against the rafters, she heard Gertrude barking. Not displeased with her appearance, she went downstairs, then paused halfway. Below her in the hall, she could see two heads: one very dark, the other gleaming blond. Her heart missed a beat.

"Maud," yelled Bas, "are you in?"

"I'm up here," said Maud with the light behind her.

Bas looked up. "Caitlin," he said. "I thought you'd gone back."

"It's me." Maud came slowly down the stairs. "Grace and I were being silly trying on my old clothes."

"How old were you when you first wore that?"

"About twenty-one."

"You look about sixteen today," said Bas, kissing her.

"Flattery will get you an enormous drink. I assume that's what you've come for. Grace," Maud yelled up the stairs, "can you come down and fix some drinks? I'll go and change."

"Don't," said Rupert. "I bet Declan fell in love with you in that dress."

"Where's Declan?" asked Bas, as they went into the kitchen.

"Ordered in to do an extra program," said Maud, getting a bottle of whisky out of the cupboard.

"Have you got anything to eat?" asked Bas. "I'm absolutely starving."

"There's some chocolate cake and a quiche," said Maud, splashing whisky into three glasses. "Have a look and see what you can find."

Rupert prowled around the room. There was a huge scrubbed table in the center of the room, with chairs down either side. Poetry and cook books crammed the shelves. A rocking horse towered over Gertrude's basket in the corner. Aengus the cat snored on some newly ironed shirts. On the walls were drawings of Maud in *Juno and the Paycock*, and a corkboard covered with recipes and photographs of animals, cut by Taggie out of newspapers. Apart from a television set on a chest of drawers, every other available surface seemed to be littered with letters, bills, color swatches, photographs waiting to be stuck in, dog and cat worming tablets, pens that didn't work, newspapers and magazines.

"Nice kitchen," said Rupert.

Valerie Jones, who dropped in half an hour later, didn't think it was a nice kitchen at all. She was shocked to find Maud showing at least six inches of bare thigh, and Rupert and Basil with their long booted legs up on the table, all getting tanked upon Declan's whisky. Rupert was eating bread and bramble jelly and Bas was finishing up the remains of a mackerel mousse with a spoon.

Valerie herself, natty in a tweed suit and a deerstalker, said she had just been to a Distressed Gentlefolk's Committee Meeting with Lady Baddingham, and had dropped in to see if Maud had any old clothes for the Christmas Bazaar next month.

"Having just moved, you must have lots of old junk to throw out."

"Only her husband," said Bas, starting on the quiche.

"I never throw clothes away," said Maud. "Have a drink."

"I'm driving. Have you got anything soft?" said Valerie.

"Not around here, with Maud wearing that dress," said Rupert, cutting himself a piece of chocolate cake.

"I'll have a tea then," said Valerie, "and I'd love a piece of that gateau, and those bramble preserves look quite delicious."

"Taggie picked the blackberries down your valley; we ought to give you a pot," Maud said to Rupert, as she put the kettle on. She felt wildly happy.

At that moment Grace walked in, wearing Maud's red and black mini.

"This is Amizing Grice," said Maud.

"Amizing," said Grace, gazing at Rupert in wonder. "I'm just off to that lecture on glass blowing at the Women's Institute, Maud," she went on. "See you later."

"I didn't know there was a WI meeting tonight," said Valerie, perplexed.

"Straight up to the pub," explained Maud, as the front door banged.

"It's not a very good idea to be on a first name basis with one's help," said Valerie reprovingly. "We don't really do it in Gloucestershire, you know."

" 'Bye Grace! Have a good evening," yelled Rupert.

Valerie's small mouth tightened. Watching Maud pouring boiling water over a teabag, she hoped the mug was clean.

"This quiche is seriously good," said Bas. "And for Christ's sake leave some of that chocolate cake, Rupert."

"Did Grace make it?" enquired Valerie. Maybe Grace was more of a treasure than she had at first appeared.

"Grace can't cook a thing," said Maud. "Taggie made all this. She wants to break into catering and do people's dinner parties."

"She better come and work at the Bar Sinister," said Bas. "Darling, I wondered where you'd got to." He swung his feet off the table and stood up as Taggie came in.

She was very pale, with her hair in a thick black braid down her back, and wearing one of Declan's red shirts above long, long bare legs.

"Hullo," she said in delight to Bas. Then, embarrassed that he aimed straight at her mouth, turned her head slightly so he ended up kissing her hair. At that moment over his shoulder she saw Rupert. She gave a gasp of horror and turned as red as her shirt.

To Valerie's equal horror, Maud removed the teabag from Valerie's tea with her fingers. Then she introduced Taggie to everyone.

Smiling at Valerie, but totally ignoring Rupert, Taggie took a tin of baked beans out of the fridge and started to eat them with a spoon.

"I'm sure we've met before," said Rupert, puzzled. "You're not a Young Conservative are you?" Then, suddenly he started to laugh. "I remember now. It was at a tennis party."

Taggie blushed even deeper.

"Brilliant quiche, stunning mousse, marvelous chocolate cake," said Bas with his mouth full.

"Oh, it was for Daddy's supper," began Taggie, distressed, then stopped herself. Sometimes she could murder her mother. She was about to go upstairs when Bas grabbed her hand and, sitting her down beside him, tried to persuade her to work for him at the Bar Sinister.

"It's really kind of you," mumbled Taggie, "but I worked in a restaurant for two years. I want to branch out on my own."

"You can come and cook my breakfast any day of the week," said Rupert. She looked so different from the angry child who'd screamed at him about his stubble. "You were quite right," he added to Basil.

Taggie was totally thrown. She was only conscious of this horrible monster, who'd haunted her nightmares for weeks, whom she'd last seen oiled, brown-skinned, erect in every sense of the word and as totally unself-conscious of his nakedness as a Zulu chief, and who was now drinking her father's whisky and laughing at her across the table. Out of sheer nervousness, she leapt up and turned on the television.

"Creep," yelled Rupert, as James Vereker appeared on the screen.

Over at Corinium Television Sarah Stratton sat in Hospitality going greener (perhaps that was why it was called a green room), and wishing she'd never agreed to go on James's program.

Ushered into the studio during the commercial break, Sarah was now sitting on the famous pale pink sofa beside him. On rushed the makeup girl to tone down her flushed face.

"Remember to look at me, not the camera, Sarah," said James. She was desperately nervous, which didn't help.

A burst of "Cotswold Roundup" theme music signified the end of the commercial break.

"Sarah Stratton," said James, "you've been married to Paul Stratton, our member for Cotchester for nearly nine months now. How do you see your role as the wife of an MP, Sarah?"

Sarah straightened her face: "To support my husband in every possible way," she said, gazing straight at the camera.

In the O'Haras' kitchen, Rupert turned up the sound.

"Isn't that Lizzie Vereker's husband?" said Maud. "I like Lizzie."

"She's lovely," said Rupert. "If she lost 30 pounds, I'd marry her."

"James is hell," said Basil. "Put him in front of a camera, you can't get him down with a gun."

"Some viewers may find the following scenes disturbing," said Rupert. "Sarah's nervous. Look at the way her eyes are darting, and she's licking her lips. Looks bloody good, though."

Sarah was now saying how hard it was, falling in love with a married man.

"I put no pressure on Paul to leave his first wife," she said demurely.

"Balls," howled Bas. "She carried a chisel around in her bag for years, trying to chip Paul off like a barnacle."

"But because he did eventually leave her for me," went on Sarah, "and *he* made the decision, I'm branded a scarlet woman."

"With some justification," said Rupert. "And her husband is as mean as the grave. It's so hard to get a drink in his house, the PM ought to make him the Minister for Drought. Which is not something anyone could accuse *you* of, Maud darling," he added, as Maud splashed the last of the whisky into his glass.

Taggie, who was ironing sheets, was as perplexed as Rupert had been earlier. "I'm sure I've seen her somewhere before," she muttered, then once again went absolutely scarlet as she realized that Sarah was the beautiful blonde who'd been playing nude tennis with Rupert.

"She's quite excellent at ball play," said Rupert, reading Taggie's thoughts. "And *you're* going to burn that sheet."

Furiously, Taggie went on ironing.

"Taggie," said Maud, "watches too much television."

"Sharon's only allowed to watch occasionally on weekends," said Valerie smugly. "When I was young, my sister and I made our own amusements."

"So did I," agreed Rupert, "until Nanny told me it would make me go blind."

James, winding up Sarah's interview, asked her if she had any plans for a career.

"You must know—as a very famous man yourself," Sarah answered admiringly, "that wives of famous men have to take second place."

"It is possible to be famous and caring, Sarah?" asked James huskily.

"Of course," said Sarah. "I'm just saying if you marry someone who's been married before, you're just that little bit more anxious to make the marriage work, to *not* put your own career first—to prove everyone wrong who said it wouldn't last. So you just try harder."

Taggie was shocked. How *could* Sarah say that, when she was busy having an affair with Rupert? It was only after a few minutes Taggie realized that Valerie was telling her all about the boutique.

"You must pop in some time," said Valerie. "I know it's difficult, dressing when you're so tall, but I'm sure I could find something lovely for you."

"That's really kind," said Taggie gratefully.

Rupert, watching Taggie, decided she really was very beautiful. It was as though someone had taken a fine black pen and drawn lines along her lashes and round the irises of those amazing silver-gray eyes. Her nose was too large, but the curve of the soft pink mouth emphasized by the very short upper lip was adorable, and he'd like to see all that lustrous black hair spilling over a pillow. She must be nearly five foot ten, he reckoned, and most of it legs, and she had the gentle, apologetic clumsiness of an Irish wolfhound, who can't help knocking off teacups with its tail.

Noticing Rupert observing Taggie with such lazy, almost lustful affection, Maud felt a stab of jealousy.

"Go and get another bottle of whisky, Tag," she said sharply, "and clear away all these plates."

"But it's Daddy's last bottle," protested Taggie.

Furious, Maud turned on her. "As if your father would deny a guest a drink in his own house."

Taggie switched off the iron, fetched the bottle, and dumped it on the table with a crash. Gertrude was whining by the back door.

"I'll take you out, darling," said Taggie, pulling on a pair of black gumboots.

"Do wrap up warm," said Valerie. "And if you want to get on in the country, you should wear green wellies," she added kindly.

"If you really want to get on in the country," drawled Rupert, "you should get that dog's tail straightened."

It was the final straw. Giving him a filthy look, Taggie went out, slamming the back door behind her.

"What's up with her?" asked Bas.

"In love," said Maud, unscrewing the bottle of whisky. "Some friend of Patrick's who hardly knows she exists. You know how moody teenagers are."

Outside it was deliciously mild. The wind was shepherding parties of orange leaves across the lawn and sighing in the wood. The stream after the recent rain was hurtling down the garden. Above, russet clouds like stretched cotton wool didn't quite cover the sky. Every so often through a chink glittered a brilliant star. Still shaking, Taggie tramped down the rose walk that so often in the past must have been paced by nuns, like her, praying for deliverance.

"Oh please God, get that horrible man out of the house."

She couldn't stop thinking of Rupert's lean oiled body. It was obvious her mother was wildly attracted to him; she'd seen the rapt expression, the flushed cheeks, the wild drinking so often before. And Rupert was leading her mother on, making those beastly salacious (there, at last she'd used her word for the day) remarks, and drinking all her father's whisky and eating all his supper.

Despite the mildness of the night, she shivered as she contemplated the rows ahead if Maud started one of her things. She, Taggie, would get dragged in to provide alibis. Well, she wouldn't cover up for her mother this time, she wouldn't, she wouldn't.

Her father didn't want hassle at the moment; he needed keeping calm. Turning toward the house, its great battlements and turrets
confronting the shadowy garden with a timeless strength, she felt
slightly comforted. Surely the house would look after them.

Soon after Taggie took Gertrude out, Valerie went home. Maud, Basil,
and Rupert carried on carousing. Going into the kitchen much later,
Taggie was relieved to find only Bas and Maud.

"Daddy's interviewing Lord Wooton in a few minutes," she said.

"My husband," Maud told Basil, "always becomes the person
he's interviewing. When he did Margaret Thatcher he spent the week
wearing power suits, talking about 'circum-starnces', and calling me
Denis in bed."

Noticing Taggie's look of disapproval, Basil patted the chair beside him and said the interview should be interesting as Tony was
pulling out every stop to get Maurice Wooton to join the Corinium
Board.

Rupert returned from the bathroom waving the *New Statesman*.
"Don't tell me Declan reads this," he said in outrage.

Maud nodded. "And actually believes it."

"But he can't be a socialist when he earns such a vast salary."

"I know," sighed Maud. "He's utterly inconsistent."

"I expect he'd like to give some of it away," protested Taggie
angrily, "if everyone didn't spend it all."

"If you can't keep a civil tongue in your head," snapped Maud,
"you better go to bed." She'd never known Taggie to answer back
like this.

Over in Studio 3 Declan always went into himself before a program,
but he nodded when Tony came into the studio, reeking of brandy
and waving a huge cigar. Tony was in an excellent mood; two of
Corinium's news stories had been used with a byline by ITN; he'd
just had an excellent dinner with Maurice Wooton, and now he'd
got his way about Declan doing this interview. It was the thin end
of the wedge. Declan couldn't refuse to do other specials—Freddie
Jones next week, perhaps.

"Maurice is just having a pee. He's been made-up," he said to
Declan. "Give him a nice easy ride. He may have a reputation as a
hatchet man, but he runs a huge empire, he's devoted to his grandchildren and does an enormous amount for charity. He's also delightful if you get him onto opera or his cats."

"Just show his caring face, Declan," said Cameron from the

control room. "And Camera 2, can you try to avoid Lord Wooton's bald patch?"

Lord Wooton was now being ushered in by the floor manager. He had plainly had too much to drink with Tony, but Make-up had toned him down with green foundation, and blacked out his graying sideburns. His revoltingly sensual face with the big red pouting lower lip was just like one of Tony's orchids, thought Declan, as he rose to his feet to welcome him.

"Very warm night," said Lord Wooton.

"Very," said Declan.

The introductory scene, which Cameron had written, was full of nice stills and clips of Lord Wooton romping with cats, visiting children in hospitals, playing cricket with grandsons, watching the first bricks of various buildings being laid, and collecting an OBE at the Palace. He was plainly delighted.

Surreptitiously Declan removed his earpiece and put it in his pocket. His first question was sycophancy itself.

"As the leading real estate developer in Gloucestershire, probably the whole of the West Country, you must be proud of your achievement."

Maurice Wooton put his hands together happily.

"One is only as good as the people who work for one, Declan," he said smoothly. "You must know that. I have first-rate people, hand-picked of course."

"Pity you don't take better care of them," said Declan amiably.

He then proceeded to carve Maurice Wooton up, starting with one of his managers who'd been fired while he was in the hospital recovering from open heart surgery, then proceeding to another who'd been given no compensation when he broke his back falling off some scaffolding.

Tony rang Cameron in the control box.

"What the fuck's going on?" he roared. "Tell him to ask Maurice about his fucking grandchildren."

"I can't get through to him," yelled Cameron. "He's taken out his earpiece."

"Well, tell the floor manager to tell him to fucking put it back in again."

Ignoring all Maurice Wooton's spluttering denials, Declan moved onto illegal takeovers, shady deals, and then produced a just-published secret Town Hall report, which claimed that, despite a huge grant from the Council, his firm had built a block of cheap flats to faulty specifications.

Temporarily speechless now, Maurice Wooton was mouthing like a great purple bull frog.

"Another even more unattractive aspect of your business career," went on Declan relentlessly, "was the way you bribed three Labor councillors in the housing department at Cotchester Town Hall to give you the contract for the tower block development on Bankside."

"This is preposterous," exploded Maurice Wooton.

"You deny it?"

"Of course I do."

Out of the corner of his eye, Declan could see the floor manager making frantic signals for him to replace his earpiece.

Ignoring them, he said: "Why, then, do Councillor Bridie, Councillor Yallop, and Councillor Rogers have five thousand pounds entered on their bank statements, paid in by you from a Swiss bank account? Here are the photostats of the bank statements, the checks, and your letters to them." Declan brandished them under Maurice Wooton's hairy expanding crimson nostrils, then threw them down on the table. "Thank God there are some Town Hall officials with integrity."

Cameron was insane with rage.

Maurice Wooton was standing up and shouting at Declan that the whole thing was a trumped-up pack of lies, and he was going home to call his lawyers. Next moment he'd stormed out, leaving the studio in an uproar. Declan sat turned to stone in his chair.

To their great disappointment, Corinium's viewers were then treated to soothing music and a film showing close-ups of Cotchester's wild flowers, so they missed Tony roaring into the studio, so angry he could hardly get the words out.

"I've spent five years courting that man," he spluttered. "He was just about to join the Board and put fifteen million into our satellite project."

Declan rose to his feet, towering over Tony.

"You should have given me time to research him properly," he said coldly. "I might have found something nice to ask him, but I doubt it." And with that, he walked out of the studio.

Back at The Priory, Rupert, wiping his eyes, turned to Maud: "That was the best television program I've seen for years. After Tony Baddingham, Maurice Wooton is without doubt the biggest shit in England, and your husband is the first socialist I've ever really admired.

The Corinium switchboard must be absolutely jammed, or 'preserved', as dear Valerie would say, with congratulatory calls.''

At that moment the telephone rang. Rupert picked it up.

"Brilliant program," said a voice. "It's the *Western Daily Press*. Is Declan in?''

"What did I tell you?" said Rupert, handing the receiver to Maud. "Don't look so cross," he added to Taggie. "I'll nip home in a minute and get your father another bottle."

After Rupert had returned with the whisky, and he and Bas had left, Taggie watched her mother go to the hall mirror, fluff up her hair on top and smooth the dress over her hips before sitting down at the drawing room piano. She must be very drunk, thought Taggie, judging by the number of wrong notes.

What on earth could she give her father for supper? she wondered wearily, as she started to load up the dishwasher. Perhaps she ought to accept Bas's offer of a job, and get out and meet people. She couldn't eat her heart out for Ralphie forever. She heard the front door bang. Going into the hall, she saw Declan gazing into the drawing room at Maud playing Schumann in the dress she'd worn when they were first married, living blissfully on no money in Ireland. Her hair almost touched the piano stool.

Putting his hands on her shoulder, he said, "Why did you put that on?''

"Grace and I were tidying away some of my old clothes.''

"You look beautiful.''

Schumann halted abruptly, as Declan's hands slid under the piefrill collar. "Let's go to bed.''

As Maud walked upstairs in front of him, his hands slid up between her bare thighs:

"Christ you're wet.''

Maud smiled sleepily. "I've been thinking all evening about your coming home.''

C H A P T E R 14

Tony would have fired any other member of his staff for savaging Maurice Wooton like that. As it was, he spent the weekend poring over Declan's contract. Unfortunately there was no clause about not presenting his victims with unpalatable truths. So in the end Tony merely wrote Declan a sharp note accusing him of misconduct and warning him that if he stepped out of line a second and third time he'd be out on his ear.

Tony's guns were further spiked by the Government immediately ordering an investigation into Cotchester Town Hall's Housing policy, and by the very favorable press coverage of the program and Corinium in particular.

"Corinium shows its teeth at last," wrote the *Western Daily Press*.

"Corinium proves it's no longer a Tory poodle," wrote the *Guardian*.

Hardest for Tony to take was an enthusiastic telephone call from the IBA: "Splendid stuff, Tony. No one can accuse you of political bias now."

The following Wednesday there was a Corinium Board Meeting. Tony's temper was not improved when one of the non-executive directors, old Lady Evesham, Vice Chancellor of the local university, arrived on her bicycle in the pouring rain, just as Tony rolled up in the Rolls. Why did the stupid old bag always arrive an hour early and go nosing round the office, talking to staff and stirring up trouble? Hoping she'd go away, Tony cringed behind the *Financial Times*. Next minute she was tapping on the window. Grudgingly, Tony lowered it a few inches.

"Congratulations," said Lady Evesham, thrusting her wrinkled, whiskery muzzle towards him. "That interview with Maurice Wooton's the sort of thing we should be doing all the time. Routing out injustice. Man's a rogue. I shall seek out Declan and tell him so in person."

Tony, however, had other things on his mind. In the same telephone call praising Declan's interview, the IBA had complained that Corinium still wasn't giving sufficient attention to the Southampton end of the area.

"Charles Fairburn has just finished a program on Isaac Watts," Tony had countered swiftly.

"Who's he?" asked the IBA's Head of Television.

"Famous philosopher, poet, teacher." Tony hastily consulted the advance program notes. Wrote "Oh God, our help in ages past."

"That's not much help in ages present," said the IBA. "People in Southampton will hardly regard one hour on the Sunday Godslot as good enough. We're talking about news coverage."

As a result of this conversation, Tony summoned his two most valuable executive directors, who usually worked in London but who had come down for the board meeting, into his office beforehand. Known as "Beauty and the Beast," Georgie Baines and Ginger Johnson looked after sales and finance respectively.

Gorgeous Georgie, who had big brown eyes and even bigger expenses, was up to every single fiddle and lived in the big advertising agencies' pockets, which he lined as effectively as his own. He also made vast sums of money for Corinium. Ginger Johnson, the Beast, was a thug, with carroty hair and a beetroot face, like a particularly unappetizing winter salad. As Financial Director, he saw that the vast sums netted by Georgie were administered as remuneratively as possible. All the most important business on the agenda was always done by the three men before the board meeting.

Going into Tony's office that Wednesday, Georgie and Ginger found him looking at a map of the area.

"If we're going to hang onto the franchise," said Tony, "we've got to be properly represented."

"So?" said Georgie, who'd heard this all before.

"We're going to build a studio here." Tony jabbed the red dot of Southampton with his finger.

"Cost a fortune," said Ginger, aghast. "Even a small studio'll set us back five million. We don't need a studio there."

"The IBA will love the idea," said Tony happily. "More programs, more employment, better coverage. We don't have to actually build the fucking thing. But if we have Board sanction and some provisional architect's plans under the IBA's nose, it'll keep them quiet until the franchise is in the bag."

"I'm sure the Board won't approve it, when we're slashing budgets everywhere else," said Ginger.

"Leave it to me," said Tony.

There was great excitement at Corinium the following Wednesday, when Dame Nellie Finegold, a friend of Lady Evesham, and one of the last surviving suffragettes, who'd agreed to come on Declan's program that evening, dropped dead from a heart attack.

Even greater excitement was caused when the Prime Minister, who was in Gloucestershire opening a new hospital and later dining with the Cotchester Regiment, graciously agreed to step into Dame Nellie's shoes to balance Declan's extremely favorable interview with the Leader of the Opposition the previous week. The Prime Minister, appreciating the value of preaching to eighteen million viewers, thought she could handle Declan. Her one condition, which Tony leaped at, was that Declan should submit questions first, and agree not to depart from them.

"This is our chance to nail him," Tony told Cameron gleefully. "If he submits questions today, we can insist he does the same for all future interviews. Then we can manipulate him to our own advantage. You've seen how lethal he can be, just think what havoc he could cause in an election year."

Declan looked tired and tense as he walked into Tony's office waving a sheaf of the Prime Minister's clippings. Tipping back his chair, Tony stretched his legs and gazed consideringly at him for a moment.

"This is a big day for you, Declan."

Declan grunted. "I'm very much looking forward to shaking her by—" he paused—"the neck."

"Now, now," said Tony, "let's keep it all sweetness and light."

"The PM's only coming on the program if she knows exactly what you're going to ask her, and no funny business," said Cameron.

"Don't be ridiculous," snapped Declan. "Why should she be treated differently from anyone else?"

"Because she's the PM, dumbass, and the IBA is ultimately answerable to her, so she's got to be kept happy."

"Not by me she hasn't."

"Don't be so fucking pigheaded," screeched Cameron.

An almighty row followed, ending in Declan flatly refusing to do the interview and walking out.

Cameron and Tony exchanged glances of joy and horror—what the hell were they going to do? The Prime Minister was already in the area. She was due at the studios at seven-forty to go on air at eight. The network had been trailing Declan's dramatic change of guest since lunchtime.

"James will have to do it," said Tony. "But we won't announce the change of plan until just before transmission, or we'll lose the audience."

In his office, James switched off the radio because he was fed up with hearing Declan's theme song. Turning to his fan mail, he found a letter from Sarah Stratton thanking him for his standard letter thanking her for coming on the program. Nice bold handwriting, thought James; he was sure those huge loops to the Ls meant something. During their drink at the bar, he'd decided she was very attractive, and wondered by what ruse he could see her again. But a second later, as Cameron burst into his office, his thoughts were only for one woman: the Prime Minister.

"Here's a brief of what the PM's been up to in the last two months, but you're pretty well briefed anyway, aren't you?" said Cameron.

James blushed. It was the first compliment she had ever paid him. "I thought Declan was doing this interview."

"Declan's sick," said Cameron.

"Seriously?" said James.

"Not nearly seriously enough," said Cameron viciously.

As soon as she'd gone, thanking God he'd had his hair streaked last week, James called Lizzie: "I'll be late. I've got to interview the PM."

"My God! Ask her when she last got laid."

"Don't be silly, this is for real. I'm sending a driver over for my blue suit, and could you put in my jade green silk shirt, and the sapphire blue tie. And could you phone the Strattons and ask them to record the program." He wanted Sarah to witness his hour of glory. "I don't trust our machine one hundred percent."

You mean you don't trust me to remember, thought Lizzie.

Cameron, popping into the studio later on her way to the control room, was nearly knocked sideways by Aramis.

"She's arrived. Tony'll bring her through in a minute. Are you nervous?"

"Not yet," said James, replumping cushions on the pastel pink sofa.

"Nice change from Declan," said Cameron. "Good luck."

Perhaps he'd maligned Cameron, thought James, as he combed his hair for the hundredth time and removed the shine on his nose with a Nouveau Beige creme puff. He used to use Gay Whisper, but had decided the name had rather unfortunate connotations.

The Prime Minister, like most women, had a weakness for charming handsome men. Seeing her appearing through the black curtain, radiant in dark blue taffeta, being guided over the cables and uneven surfaces by Tony, James leaped to his feet. For a second Diorella fought with Aramis. Aramis won easily.

"Welcome to Cotchester, Prime Minister. I can't tell you how privileged I feel to meet you," said James, giving her the benefit of his beautiful aquamarine eyes, now subtly enhanced by the jade green shirt and the sapphire blue tie. Then, when she offered him her hand, he bowed his streaked head and kissed it reverently.

"Silly cunt," muttered the Senior Cameraman.

"Come and sit down," said James.

Down came the famous bottom on the pastel pink sofa.

"I'll leave you in good hands, Prime Minister," said Tony.

"Indeed, Lord Baddingham," said the PM in her low voice.

The interview was pure Barbara Cartland. Aware no difficult questions would be forthcoming, the PM was at her most relaxed and charming, and unbent to James as she'd never done before on television.

"Prepared only to see the steely side of your character, Prime Minister, some people make the ridiculous mistake of thinking you don't care about the unemployed or the old and poverty-stricken."

"Mr. Vereker—" the Prime Minister's voice dropped an octave— "if only you could realize the sleepless nights we spend worrying about hyperthermia, particularly with another winter coming on."

"How many more times is the stupid asshole going to use the word 'caring,' " snarled Cameron to Tony, who'd stayed with her in the Control Room.

"Hush, she's really unbuttoning," purred Tony.

During the commercial break, the PM became positively skittish. At the end of the second half she even shed tears as she talked of her worries as a mother.

"But you are a mother to all of us," said James, handing her his Aramis-scented handkerchief.

"Pass me the motion sickness bag," groaned Cameron.

"It's good," said Tony. "Should win her a lot of votes."

"Ten seconds to out, James," said Cameron, flicking on the key switch. "Close the program."

"Thank you, Prime Minister, for showing us your caring face," said James, "and please come back to Cotchester again soon."

As the credits went up, they could be seen laughing and joking together.

"I'm going to frow up," said the Senior Cameraman.

"Come back, Declan," muttered the Floor Manager, "nothing needed to be forgiven."

"I would love a tape of that program, Mr. Vereker," said the Prime Minister.

Outside, a second Corinium camera crew filmed her departure, lethargically cheered by a hand-picked crowd of Corinium staff.

"I hope we get overtime for this," said Charles Fairburn, waving a British flag, as a jubilant James, Cameron, and Tony accompanied the PM down the steps. Settled in her car, ready to depart to a late dinner with the Cotchester Regiment, the PM wound down her window.

"I hope Mr. O'Hara feels better soon," she said earnestly.

"What a caring lady," sighed James.

He woke next morning to find himself temporarily famous. Both the B.B.C. and ITN picked up the interview, which was fulsomely praised the next day by the Tory press. Only the *Mirror* and the *Guardian* grumbled that James had let the PM get away with murder.

By Friday the story had got out that Declan hadn't been ill at all, but had simply refused to do the interview with the Prime Minister.

"The Rows Begin Again," said a huge headline in the *Sun*.

At the B.B.C. and around the network, people smirked knowingly. They'd known the honeymoon wouldn't last.

CHAPTER 15

Declan was having a row about money with Maud in the kitchen when the telephone rang:

"Yes," he snapped.

"This is Valerie Jones," said an ultra-refined, vaguely familiar voice.

"Yes," said Declan, who was no wiser.

"We met at Lady Monica's buffet luncheon. Fred-Fred and I were wondering if you could come and dine on December 7th, that's tomorrow week, just a few close friends. Tony and Monica Baddingham. . . ."

Declan had heard enough. He was sorry, he said, but they had a previous engagement.

Maud was absolutely furious. "We never go out," she stormed. "How dare you refuse for me. I might have wanted to go."

"It was that horrendous dwarf we met at the Baddingham's; bound to have been hell."

"There might have been other amusing people there. How can we ever meet anyone if you turn down everything?"

Maud's sulk lasted all day. Declan was trying to come to grips with the volatile, volcanic personality of John McEnroe, who was coming on the program on Wednesday. Maud's black mood permeated the whole house and totally sabotaged his concentration. At dusk, unable to bear it any longer, he went downstairs and apologized.

"I'm sorry; it was selfish of me. I must work, but you go on your own. I hate it, but I've got to get used to it. Are you lonely?" he went on as Maud clung to him. "D'you want to go back to London?"

She shook her head violently. "I just miss my friends. I was wondering if we could give a tiny party for Patrick's birthday on New Year's Eve."

Declan's heart sank. "Not really, not this Christmas. We simply can't afford it."

"It's his twenty-first," pleaded Maud. "He's always had such lousy birthdays, having them so near Christmas. Just the tiniest party, half a dozen couples. Taggie can do the food; it'll be good training for her. She's not getting any response from those cards."

Declan was about to say no when the telephone rang again. Taggie picked it up in the kitchen. Five minutes later she rushed, pink-faced with excitement, into the drawing room.

"The most p-p-prodigious—" her word for the day—"thing has happened. Valerie Jones got one of my cards and she's asked me to do her dinner party next Friday. Isn't it prodigious?"

"It is, indeed," said Declan, disentangling himself from Maud and hugging her.

"She asked us," said Maud fretfully. "What are you going to cook for her that we won't get?"

"I've got to go over tomorrow and discuss menus," said Taggie.

Maud seized her chance. "Daddy's agreed we can have a little party for Patrick on New Year's Eve," said Maud, ignoring Declan's look of horror, "so you can start thinking up some nice food for that."

Taggie's already euphoric face lit up even further: "What a prodigious idea."

Upstairs in her turret bedroom, she clutched herself, pressing her face against one of the thin, cool ecclesiastical windows. If Patrick was having a party, how could Patrick's best friend not be there? She was going to see Ralphie again.

Cooking for Valerie's dinner party was Taggie's first big job, but her nerves were nothing to Valerie's. Valerie was livid with Freddie for asking Rupert, who was coming down to Gloucestershire for a constituency meeting and to present the cup at the Cotchester–Bristol football Derby. Originally he was supposed to be bringing some French actress, but she'd got stuck on location in Scotland. So Valerie'd had to find a spare woman at the last moment. She settled for Cameron Cook who had just won an American award for a documentary about arranged marriages which she'd produced last spring. Valerie had no idea she was Tony's mistress.

And now Valerie wouldn't stop flapping around the kitchen tasting and criticizing everything Taggie was making—"A soupçon more cayenne in the cucumber sauce, Agatha—" or fretting whether they should have cheese before dessert, or who should sit next to whom.

"It says," she announced, poring over the etiquette book, "that the most important man should sit on my right."

"That's me," said Freddie, roaring with laughter.

"Don't be silly, Fred-Fred," snapped Valerie, "and don't pick."

"That fish pâté's champion," said Freddie, who'd only been allowed a small salad at lunch.

"Are you going to be all day with that dessert, Agatha?" said Valerie, beadily looking at the huge ice cream and meringue castle, around which Taggie was curling whipped cream to simulate pounding waves. "The place is a frightful mess."

"I promise I'll clear up in time. Everything's done but this."

People were due at eight to eight-thirty to dine at nine. The pheasants, simmered with cranberries and ginger, had to go in at six forty-five.

"You've still got the menus to write out, one for each end of the table," said Valerie. "It would be nice to have them in French."

Taggie went pale. She couldn't even spell them properly in English; she'd always had trouble with pheasant. She started to shake.

"I'm going to check the rest of the house," said Valerie.

The house looked beautiful. She'd got florists in to provide two beautiful pink arrangements. The dining room was also a symphony in pink, with a centerpiece of roses. Valerie adored pink; it was so feminine and went so well with her mauve velvet evening gown with the flowing skirt and the trumpet sleeves. She was glad they weren't having soup—Freddie drank it so noisily. She'd worked out where everyone was going to sit. Now standing at the end of the table, Valerie practiced her commands:

"Bring in the appetizer, please, Agatha. Take away the entrée, Agatha. Bring in the dessert."

Then there was the tricky bit, catching all the women's eyes. She glanced at alternate chairs. "Shall we go upstairs?"

What happened if that awful Rupert read the message wrong and followed her upstairs too? He was quite capable. For safety, she better say: "Shall we *ladies* go upstairs?"

"What am I to do about this menu?" said Taggie helplessly.

"I'll help you. I'm doing French for '0' levels," said Sharon, the daughter of the house, who'd inherited her father's bulk and his sweet nature. "I'm sure the French for pheasant is *payson*."

In the kitchen, Taggie finished the dessert and put the pheasants into the oven. She must remember to add chopped dill to the prawn sauce. She wished Valerie hadn't wanted things quite so elaborate. Everything was going swimmingly until Valerie came down dressed, and insisted Taggie put on a maid's black uniform and a white apron which came miles above her black stockinged knees, and then made her put her hair up. Even Taggie balked at the white maid's cap.

"I expect you to answer the door," said Valerie, "supervise everything in the kitchen and wait on table."

"Will you come and watch 'Dynasty' with me?" Sharon asked Taggie.

"You're not watching rubbish like that, Sharon. You're to hand around hors d'oeuvres and make yourself pleasant," snapped Valerie nearly jumping out of her skin, as music blared out from the speakers all over the house.

"It's Daddy's theme song," said Taggie in delight.

"Turn that horrible din down, Fred-Fred," screamed Valerie.

"Monica loves classical music," said Freddie.

"Oh well, leave it on, then."

The doorbell rang. "Go and answer it, Agatha. Put the men's coats in the downstairs toilet, and the ladies' coats upstairs in the master bedroom, and then direct them toward the living room, where Mr. Jones and I will receive them."

It was Paul and Sarah Stratton. For a second Taggie and Sarah stared at each other, remembering their previous encounter on Rupert's tennis court. Then, with a wicked little smile, Sarah took off her red velvet cloak. Her tan had gone, but a black taffeta dress, off-the-shoulders and with a bustle, showed off her beautiful, opulent figure. Never having seen Paul before, Taggie thought he looked dreadfully old and careworn to be married to such a glowing overexcited young girl.

The next arrival was Cameron Cook, who Taggie recognized from Declan's description and tried not to hate. Declan had omitted to say she was so beautiful, and wonderfully dressed this evening in a dark red velvet jacket and black tie with a wing collar, her hair sleeked back to show off her smooth white forehead and thick black brows. She looked straight through Taggie, and, having no coat to take, stalked past her into the living room.

She was shortly followed by Tony and Monica. Tony'd been away at a conference, and for once, because he was cleaning up Corinium's act, hadn't taken Cameron with him. Now he was unflatteringly unpleased to see her. The big smile he switched on like a light bulb switched off as though there'd been a power failure. He always felt twitchy when Cameron and Monica were in the same room, and, even worse, Cameron, it seemed, had been invited for Rupert, his old rival. And there was Declan's bloody theme song blaring out.

"This music is wonderful," exclaimed Monica.

"Come and see it in action," said Freddie, bearing her off to witness the electronic wizardry in his study.

"Have you got any Wagner?" said Monica.

Next moment, to Valerie's horror, Siegfried's funeral march pounded deafeningly through the house.

"What the hell are you doing here?" hissed Tony to Cameron.

"I was invited," said Cameron coldly.

"We must be very careful."

"Of course," said Cameron, holding her glass out to Reg, the hired butler, for an instant refill. "We mustn't jeopardize the franchise."

Valerie was telling Paul about the house: "We replaced those dreary old mullioned windows with picture windows."

"Please God don't let the sauce curdle," prayed Taggie in the kitchen as she added egg yolks and vinegar.

"Door, love," said Reg, giving her a pinch on the bottom. "You look much the sexiest of the lot."

It was Lizzie and James, who'd plainly had a row because of Lizzie's catastrophic navigations. James immediately gravitated towards Sarah and thought how nice it was to see Cameron out of her depth socially, and for once rather insecure.

Lizzie, who looked awful (she'd worked too late on her novel again and had not had time to wash her hair), had brought some bantams' eggs for Freddie and Valerie, and was thrilled to see Taggie: "I know it'll all be delicious; don't worry."

Valerie looked at her watch yet again: quarter past nine and no Rupert.

"Doesn't matter," said Freddie, filling up everyone's glasses. "Nice to relax on a Friday."

"Freddie's equipment is quite staggering," said Monica returning from the study.

Sarah caught Lizzie's eye and giggled.

Mashing the potatoes in the kitchen, Taggie was getting frantic. Everything would be ruined unless they ate soon.

"Off you go," said Reg, as the doorbell rang.

Crimson with rage and embarrassment, bending her legs to make her maid's dress look longer, Taggie answered the door. Grinning, Rupert walked into the hall. "Called any good fire engines lately?"

"Would you like to take off your coat?" said Taggie stiffly.

"I'd much rather take off your dress," said Rupert. "You look like the object of all red-blooded men's fantasies. I'm late. I better go and make my peace."

Cameron choked on her champagne. Having never actually met Rupert and having been poisoned by Tony's almost pathological jealousy, she'd expected him to just be another loud-mouthed, upper-class English shit. In the flesh he was glorious, and much more American-looking than English.

Having apologized to Valerie, Rupert turned to kiss Monica.

"You haven't met Cavendish Cook have you, Rupert?" said Monica.

"How do you do, sir," said Rupert, admiring Cameron's jacket.

"Cavendish works for Tony," went on Monica. "I gather you won another prize last week, Cavendish; jolly good show."

Seeing Sharon sneaking through the hall toward the kitchen, Valerie gave a screech.

"Sharon, Sharon, come in here and give Auntie Monica some goodies. She keeps slipping off to watch 'Dynasty,' " she added to Monica. "I won't have my kids watching soaps."

"Oh I love 'Dynasty,' " said Monica, smiling at Sharon. "Do tell me whether Blake and Krystle have made up."

Rupert walked over to James, who was still talking to Sarah.

"That was a bloody good interview you did with the PM," he said. "And she thought you were marvelous. Asked me for your address so she could write to you."

James, who'd always hated Rupert, melted faster than a snowball in the microwave. Then Rupert turned to Sarah, kissing her white shoulder.

"Evening, my darling, that's an incredibly sexy dress, I don't

know why you bother to wear any clothes at all. Bloody cold outside. I think it's going to snow.''

Sitting next to Rupert at dinner, Sarah found herself talking gib-
berish. The awful thing about adultery, she thought, was that one
had to remember in public that one hadn't heard things that one's
lover had told one in private.

"I saw your 'Behind Every Famous Man' interview with James,"
said Rupert, as he unfolded his napkin. "Very good. Were you nervous?"

"Desperately," said Sarah, blushing.

As they had discussed the whole thing at length in bed yesterday
afternoon, and because, under the table, Rupert's hand was already
creeping up between the slit in her skirt, Sarah found it impossible
not to giggle.

Fortunately, distraction was provided by Taggie bringing around
the fish mousse. Not remembering her left from her right, having
served Monica, she moved backwards to serve James.

"Clockwise," screeched Valerie.

There was another awful moment for Taggie when she saw Rupert and Lizzie having hysterics over the menu.

"Gingered French peasant, cravat sauce and desert chateau,"
translated Rupert.

"Crusty bread anyone?" Valerie cried, waving the basket. "I will
not have white bread in this house."

"I love it," said Freddie wistfully.

"So do I," said Rupert. "I'll send you a loaf for Christmas."

Sitting opposite Tony, trying desperately not to catch his eye, Cameron longed to be able to sparkle and scintillate.

"How's your series on caring for the elderly doing?" she asked
James.

James brightened. "We think we've found a moderator at last—
a Mrs. Didbody. She's a seventy-five-year-old colored lady, a widow
with a daughter of fifty. Which makes her a single parent," added
James triumphantly.

"A real franchise grabber," said Cameron, turning to Rupert. He
was easily the most attractive man she'd seen since she came to England, probably ever. It was a combination of elegance, deadpan
arrogance, and a total inability to resist stirring things up. He was
plainly sleeping with Sarah Stratton.

"What exactly are electronics?" Monica was saying to Freddie
in her piercing voice. "What exactly d'you do?"

Cameron saw a look of fury on Tony's face, but Freddie seemed delighted by her interest.

"I make everything really: videos, televisions, synthesizers, compact disks, floppy disks, silicon chips."

"I always muddle up silicon with cellulite," said Monica.

"With my computers," went on Freddie proudly, "scientists on the ground can place satellites in orbit. All satellites now carry my computers on board."

"Good heavens," said Monica. She could see now how useful Freddie'd be to Tony.

Tony was not enjoying himself. It was one of life's ironies, he thought, that at dinners like this Monica always sat next to all the brilliant achieving men, who usually didn't interest her at all (although she did seem to be having fun with Freddie), and he got stuck with their unachieving wives. Lizzie Vereker on his left looked a complete mess.

"That was delicious," she said, taking another piece of bread to wipe up the last vestiges of prawn sauce. "Did you make it?" she asked Valerie slyly.

"Yes," said Valerie, as Taggie was out of the room.

"How's Archie?" Lizzie asked Tony.

"Doing Business Studies for 'A' levels," said Tony with a grin, "which he thinks allows him to tell me exactly where I'm going wrong in running Corinium."

The only time he's nice, thought Lizzie, is when he talks about his children.

Taggie, who was chopping parsley for the zucchini, heard the bell ring. She threw down the knife and ran into the dining room, tugging down her horribly short dress.

"Can you clear away the appetizer, Agatha," said Valerie.

Returning to the kitchen with the plates, Taggie found Reg the butler, very drunk now, carving the pheasants. She wished he wouldn't cut quite such huge slices, there might not be enough to go around.

"Tender as a woman's kiss," said Reg, helping himself to a slice. "You're another Mrs. Beeton, Agatha."

"Oh, it does look yummy. Can I have a bit?" said fat Sharon.

"Have some later," said Taggie, as she poured the sauce over it and scattered parsley over the zucchini. "I must take it in."

"I'll serve the zucchini," said Sharon, who wanted to gaze at Rupert.

Taggie served the pheasant the right way this time. She noticed Rupert still had his hand inside Sarah's slit skirt, the revolting man, but had to remove it to help himself to pheasant. Was she imagining it or was he deliberately rubbing his black elbow against her breast as he did so? When she served the potatoes, she stood as far away as possible, arching over him like a streetlight. As she moved down the other side of the table, his wicked dissipated blue eyes seemed to follow her, making her even more hot and bothered. Reg was serving the Mouton Cadet now, and had reached Valerie.

"That will be all, Reginald and Agatha. I'll ring if anyone wants second helpings."

It was going wonderfully well, reflected Valerie later, as Taggie cleared away the cheese board. Everyone was talking like mad. In five minutes, Taggie would bring on the moated castle.

Turning to Cameron, Rupert thought how different she was from Sarah, as lean and hungry as Sarah was replete and curvaceous.

"I'm dying to have a pee," he murmured, "just for an excuse to prowl around and see what a ghastly mess our hostess has made of a once-ravishing house. I used to come to children's parties here."

"I can't imagine you as a kid."

"I always cheated at doctors and nurses."

He noticed Sarah deliberately flirting with James, to make him jealous perhaps or to put Paul off the scent.

To Valerie's disapproval Cameron got out a cigarette. Picking up a pink candle, Rupert lit it for her.

"You hunt with the same pack as Tony?" she asked.

"Sometimes," said Rupert softly. "Sometimes after the same quarry."

Looking at his suddenly predatory, unsmiling face, she felt a quivering between her legs. Christ, she wanted him.

"D'you want a ride home?" he said.

"No." She could have wept. "I brought my own car."

"The Lotus?" said Rupert.

She nodded.

"Nice Corinium perk," said Rupert, instantly returning to his former flippant mood. "I see James has finally got himself a Porsche, I'll have to get rid of mine."

* * *

There was a chorus of oohs and aahs as Taggie came in with the moated ice cream castle. It was the last lap. Once she'd served this, and cleared away, she could relax.

"What d'you do at Corinium?" Rupert asked Cameron, as he idly watched Taggie moving around the table. She was bright pink in the face, her tongue clenched between her teeth in her efforts to hold the dessert steady. Any makeup had sweated off. Her dark hair was fighting the pins that held it up. But nothing could disguise the length of leg, or the long dark eyelashes, or the voluptuous swell of her breasts. She was going anti-clockwise again, but most people were too plastered to notice.

"I produce Declan," said Cameron. "Why don't you come on the show?"

"What?" said Rupert, dragging his thoughts back from Taggie.

"Come on the show. I'm sure you and Declan would strike sparks off each other."

"I don't want to," said Rupert flatly. "I don't need that kind of grief, and you'd never hear any chat above the rattle of skeletons tumbling out of closets."

Having just served Valerie, Taggie was moving slowly around toward him.

"How d'you get on with Declan?" he asked Cameron wickedly.

"Utterly obnoxious," said Cameron. "He really pisses me off."

Rupert watched Taggie. "Very pretty," he said examining the dessert. "Feel I ought to get a building permit before I dig into this. Thanks angel," he added, helping himself to a piece of battlement and a dollop of cream.

Ignoring him, Taggie moved around to his other side to serve Cameron.

"How on earth does Declan's wife put up with him?" asked Cameron.

"You better ask Taggie," said Rupert. "Maud's her mother."

Cameron paled visibly. Noticing Taggie for the first time, she tried to remember what ghastly things she'd said about Declan.

"I'm sorry. I didn't realize."

In embarrassment she helped herself to too much dessert. The whole thing swayed. Rupert could smell Taggie's body, he could feel how hot, and nervous and trembling she was. Her skirt was so short. Almost without thinking, he put a leisurely hand between her thighs.

Taggie gave a shriek and dropped the very considerable remains of the dessert all over Cameron's beautiful red jacket and black satin trousers.

"You stupid bitch," screamed Cameron, forgetting herself. "What the fuck d'you think you're doing?"

In tears Taggie fled to the kitchen.

Remembering one must behave with dignity at all times, Valerie swept an almost hysterical Cameron upstairs.

Lizzie turned on Rupert: "You bastard," she yelled. "Don't you realize this was her first job? She's been trying to break into catering for months. She cooked like an angel and you had to fuck it up."

"With looks like that," said Rupert, retrieving pieces of broken plate from the floor, "I wouldn't have thought a career was that important."

"Don't be so fucking insensitive. Didn't you know poor darling Taggie's dyslexic? Can't you imagine how ghastly it is being the only unbright one in such a brilliant family?"

"Oh Christ," said Rupert, truly appalled. "I simply didn't know. It was entirely my fault, Freddie. I couldn't resist goosing your cook, but really you shouldn't have dressed her in such sexy clothes. I'd better go and apologize."

"Leave her bloody alone," said Lizzie, rushing out to the kitchen to comfort a sobbing Taggie, who was being ineffectually patted by a swaying Reg.

"Go and get a cloth and clear up the mess," Lizzie told him, "and give everyone another drink."

"There there, duck." She hugged Taggie.

"I'm so sorry. I wanted everything to be perfect for Mrs. Jones," sobbed Taggie.

"You mustn't worry. It was the most marvelous food anyone's had in years." Lizzie pulled off a piece of paper towel to dry Taggie's eyes. "Rupert's a bastard. He just can't resist a beautiful girl."

"Cameron is changing into one of my gowns," said Valerie sweeping in.

"I'm so sorry, Mrs. Jones," said Taggie in a choked voice.

"I was just telling her how brilliantly she cooked," said Lizzie.

Valerie was livid. She'd been shown up as not doing the cooking at all.

"Pull yourself together, Agatha," she said sharply. "Go and collect the rest of the plates, and see if Lord Baddingham and Miss Cook would like some fresh fruit, as they didn't get any dessert."

"Cameron got her just dessert," giggled Lizzie.

"I can't go back in there," said Taggie aghast.

"You will," said Valerie, "if you want to work for me again."

In the dining room James was furious with Lizzie for making such a fuss over Declan's idiot daughter, and Sarah was furious with Rupert for so openly groping Taggie. She'd tried to be laid back about her affair with him, but now all she could feel was a red hot lava of jealousy pouring over her.

Tony, on the other hand, was delighted by the turn of events. "Child's clearly over-emotional and unbalanced like her father," he kept saying.

"Bloody good cook," said Freddie.

And when Taggie, very tearstained and head hanging, brought in a bowl of peaches and grapes, Monica leaned out and squeezed her hand.

"Delicious dinner, my dear. I've got a ladies' lunch next week. Perhaps you'd like to help me out with that? Nothing elaborate, very cozy. I'll call you tomorrow."

Gulping gratefully, Taggie said she'd love to.

Attention was then taken off her by the return of Cameron, wearing one of Valerie's black gowns. It was perfectly frightful with a bow on the bum, and much too tight.

"I'm desperately sorry," mumbled Taggie, as she passed Cameron, "I'll pay for it."

"You couldn't begin to," hissed Cameron.

"Don't be a bitch," said Rupert sharply. Putting a hand on Taggie's arm, he said, "I'm really sorry, angel, it was all my fault."

Taggie didn't say anything, but seemed to shrink away.

James sidled up to Valerie.

"One of my programs is on in a minute. Would anyone mind if I slipped upstairs and watched it?"

"Of course," said Valerie. "In fact I think, ladies, we'll all go upstairs."

Cameron got her own back by flatly refusing to go and staying to drink port with the men. Little good it did her. Tony got Freddie in a corner and persuaded him to have lunch immediately after Christmas to discuss his joining the Corinium Board, and, leaving Cameron with the frightful Paul, Rupert went off to the kitchen. Here he found Taggie loading up the dishwasher and making coffee.

"Go away!" she sobbed. "You're the most m-m-m-malefic man I've ever met."

" 'ere, 'ere," groaned Reg from underneath the kitchen table.

CHAPTER 16

The following Monday Declan stormed into Cameron's office without knocking. "You were at Valerie Jones's dinner party."

"Right," said Cameron coolly. Inside she quailed, wondering if Taggie had told Declan how she'd screamed and sworn at her, and how earlier she'd bitched about Declan to Rupert.

"I gather Taggie tipped the dessert over you. I'm sorry," said Declan. "If you can't get the spots out, I'll be happy to repay you."

"It was no big deal," said Cameron, absolutely weak with relief. "I took the stuff to the cleaners on Saturday, they'll be just fine."

"Then we'll pick up your cleaning bill."

"Rupert can bloody well do that."

Declan's face hardened. "The bastard—poor little Tag. She was distraught."

"She did really well," protested Cameron, feeling she could afford to be generous. "The food was terrific, and Monica asked her to do a lunch for her."

"I know. Monica called on Saturday. That cheered Taggie up."

"It was all Rupert's fault," said Cameron.

"Wait till I get my hands on the bastard."

"Why don't I ask him on your program?" said Cameron idly. "That'd be a much more subtle way of burying him."

Declan paused in his prowling and thought for a minute. It was violently against all his principles to ask someone deliberately on to the program in order to do a hatchet job.

"He really screwed her up," insisted Cameron, who wanted an excuse to call Rupert.

"All right," said Declan.

Even Tony was temporarily roused out of his anti-Declan mood. "Bloody good idea. If Declan does a Maurice Wooton on Rupert, I'll double his salary."

Cameron called Rupert. "I'm just checking out your availability over the next few months."

"You should have come home with me on Friday," said Rupert.

Because he was horrendously busy and not given to introspection and would much rather spend any spare second in Gloucestershire on constituency work, or with his children or his horses, or in bed with Sarah Stratton, Rupert then told Cameron he had no intention of going on Declan's program.

Cameron played her trump card. "I'll tell Declan you're chicken."

That nettled Rupert: "Don't be silly. All right, I'll think about it."

And with that Cameron had to be content.

As Christmas approached Declan grew more depressed. He was totally disillusioned with Tony. Not a day passed without some loaded request to open Monica's Christmas bazaar for the Distressed Gentlefolk, or draw the raffle at the NSPCC Ball (tickets seventy-five pounds each), or take part in Corinium's Pantomime to Help the Aged, or turn on the Christmas lights in Cotchester. Declan refused them all, which increased Tony's animosity and enabled James Vereker to step caringly into his shoes. The implication was the same: if you bothered to make use of our excellent research team, you could pull your weight as a member of the Corinium team.

Sapped by endless rows, Declan was aware his program was losing its edge. He was still very high in the ratings, but he knew people were beginning to tune in in the hope he'd be better this week.

Desperate for some kind of intellectual satisfaction, he was getting up at five every day to spend three or four hours on his Yeats biography, but was too drained to make any real progress. He was also grimly aware that he wasn't paying enough attention to Maud. After a long bout of lethargy, excited about Caitlin and Patrick coming home for Christmas, she was having one of her spates of frantic energy, which invariably involved spending money. She came to the office Christmas party and charmed absolutely everyone.

Patrick arrived the next day, walking through the door slightly drunk with four suitcases of dirty clothes.

"Is this the Priory laundry?"

"Why did you come by taxi?" asked Maud, flinging her arms around his neck.

"Because I totalled the Golf yesterday."

At that moment Caitlin called from school.

"Patrick's home," said Maud in ecstasy.

Christmas Eve saw scenes of frantic revelry at Corinium. The whole building thrummed with lust. Seb Burrows from the newsroom scaled the front of the building when drunk, and placed Charles Fairburn's Russian hat on one of the red horns of the Corinium ram. Another

joker put rainbow condoms on the horns and tail of the bronze Corinium ram in the conference room, just before Tony ushered in the
local representative from the IBA for a Christmas drink. Secretaries
with tinsel in their hair ran shrieking down the hall blowing party
horns. Just as James Vereker passed the conference room door, carrying a pile of Christmas presents from caring fans out to his car,
four shrieking secretaries converged on him and unzipped his fly.
His trousers dropped, to reveal seasonal boxer shorts covered with
Santas, just as Tony was ushering the IBA man out. Tony was absolutely livid, but not so livid as Cameron, who'd opted to work over
Christmas for want of anything better to do, when she discovered
Tony had dispatched Miss Madden to choose Christmas presents for
both her and Monica.

"I bought two diamond bracelets," whispered Miss Madden con-
spiratorially. "I thought you might like to choose first."

"I'll take the bigger one," said Cameron grimly.

James was even more annoyed to find that Declan had ten times
more Christmas cards than he had, and that the Christmas tree in
Reception completely obscured James's framed photograph. Declan's photograph had been deliberately left unhidden for all to admire.

Despite being horribly broke, Declan sold a first edition of Trol-
lope and took everyone who worked on his program, including
Cameron, out to a splendid lunch at The Dog and Trumpet outside
Cotchester, whose manager subsequently banished anyone from
Corinium Television from ever crossing the threshold again.

As the Senior Cameraman pointed out, "You don't need directions to go to one of Corinium's Christmas parties—just follow the
blue flashing lights."

Afterwards they all conga-ed down Cotchester High Street back
to the office, where Declan found Charles Fairburn, who was meant
to be organizing the live transmission of Midnight Mass from Cotchester Cathedral that evening, drinking Cointreau and doing his expense account.

In the newsroom the Corinium weatherman leaned out of the
window at sunset, just to check that the forecast he was about to
give on air of a very fine evening was correct. Next moment he
received a bucket of cold water over his newly washed hair.

"It's raining, you jerk," shouted a voice from above.

Cotchester by midnight, with the golden houses and the great Cathedral floodlit, was at its most beautiful.

The church, which was lit by candles, white lights on the Christmas tree, and television lights, was absolutely packed with people hoping both to appear on television and to catch a glimpse of Declan O'Hara.

Tony read the first lesson and stumbled twice, to his entire staff's delight. Rupert read the second in his flat drawl, and hardly a girl in the congregation, except Taggie, didn't long to have him in her stocking the following morning.

"Please God, if you think it's right, give me Ralphie," prayed Taggie.

"I wonder if Aengus and Gertrude knelt down at midnight to honor the birth of Christ," said Patrick, as they drove home. Far from honoring anyone's birth, sulking at being left behind, Aengus had knocked off and smashed several balls from the Christmas tree and Gertrude had opened three presents from underneath and also chewed the label off a small parcel for Taggie. Inside was the most beautiful silver pendant inlaid with amethysts on a silver chain. She gasped as she slowly read the note:

"Darling Taggie, I'm sorry I've been such a sod. Have a lovely Christmas. See you on New Year's Eve. All Love R."

"Oh it's beautiful," she said with a sob, and fled upstairs, clutching herself in ecstasy.

Outside the stars and the new moon seemed to be shining just for her. Ralphie had remembered after all, and in seven days she'd see him again.

C H A P T E R 17

By New Year's Eve the Christmas decorations at The Priory were sagging, and Wandering Aengus, having smashed every ornament on the Christmas tree, had taken up crash-landing in the Christmas cards.

Outside, a raging gale, Hurricane Fiona, as Patrick had called her, was rampaging up the valley, rattling the windows, and howling down the chimneys. On the lawn a huge pink-and-white-striped tent, heated by gas burners, wrestled with its moorings.

"Perhaps we could enter it for the Americas Cup," said Caitlin.

"We can line all the drunks around the bottom to hold it down," said Patrick, taking another slug of Moet.

"You'll be one of them if you don't stop knocking back that stuff," said Caitlin.

"It's my birthday. Everyone is entitled to behave appallingly on their birthday. Oh, I've got the Key-hee-hee of the door, never been twenty-one before." He was extremely happy because, unknown to his father, his mother had given him a new Golf for his birthday.

As Maud had gone off to the hairdressers and to pick up a new dress that was being altered, Patrick and Caitlin carried on doing the seating plan she had started. Taggie had tried to write names on some of the cards, but was in such a state of excitement about Ralphie's arrival that her spelling had gone totally to pot. Worried about the tent coming down, she had gone off to ring the firm who'd put it up. Her arms ached from mashing the potatoes for a dozen enormous shepherd's pies. She seemed to have peeled a billion grapes for the fruit salad. The garlic bread lay like a pile of silver slugs in its aluminium foil. The turkey soup only needed heating up. The kedgeree for breakfast was in four huge dishes on top of the deep freeze, with cucumber, prawns, and hard-boiled eggs, ready chopped to add at the last moment. Patrick's birthday cake, in the shape of a shamrock, rested in the fridge.

An extension cord still had to be found for the disco, a bulb was needed for the outside light, and Caitlin still hadn't written out large cards to show people where the bathrooms were and where to hang their coats.

But things were gradually getting under control. Taggie had never felt so tired in her life. She had cooked herself into the ground, but she kept telling herself that if she got through everything and didn't grumble, God would reward her with Ralphie.

Back in the tent, Caitlin was hastily rewriting new place cards for people Taggie had seriously misspelled.

"Monknicker Baddingham," she giggled. "Do let's leave that one. Put Monknicker on Daddy's right. Look," she screeched. "Utterly bloody Mummy's put Rupert Campbell-Black next to her. I'm bloody sitting next to him."

Removing the card from Maud's right, she bore it off and placed it reverently beside hers, three tables away and behind a huge flower arrangement, so her mother couldn't spy.

"In fact—" she scribbled Rupert's name onto a second card— "I'm going to put him on both sides of me so there's no slipup."

Looking at his place, Patrick noted that he was sitting next to Lavinia, his current girlfriend, and someone called Sarah Stratton.

"I've put Tag next to Ralphie," said Caitlin.

Patrick shook his head: "I wouldn't. He and Georgina Harrison have been inseparable all term. He's bringing her tonight."

"Well, why did he send Tag that amethyst pendant then, and apologize for being such a sod?"

"Sounds *most* unlikely. Last week he couldn't afford to buy his mother a box of handkerchiefs for Christmas, and he still owes me fifty pounds. Are you sure it was Ralphie?"

"Quite sure, the two-timing shit."

Maud came back from the hairdressers, with her hair set in a mass of snaky curls.

"It looks lovely, Mummy," said Taggie.

"It looks gross," muttered Caitlin.

The telephone rang. It was Bas Baddingham.

"Darling Maud, may I bring my new lady?"

"Of course," said Maud. "More the merrier."

"How many d'you reckon are coming?" said Patrick.

"About two to three hundred," said Maud airily.

"But we haven't rented nearly enough plates or knives or forks or anything," said Taggie aghast, "or got anywhere to seat them."

Maud turned to Patrick. "Pop across the valley to Rupert's and borrow some," she said.

"I didn't know he was coming too," whispered Taggie, even more horrified. "I thought he was away skiing."

"He's come back specially for the party," said Maud dreamily. "It was too windy for him to land the helicopter but I've just seen him driving through Penscombe. Well, if there's nothing else for me to do, I'm going upstairs to paint my nails. As she went out, running her eyes over the table seating, she caught sight of Rupert's cards on both sides of Caitlin.

Tearing one up in a rage, she put the other back on her right. "You will not sit next to Rupert, Caitlin, you're going to sit next to Archie Baddingham and like it." She turned back to Taggie.

"Has Grace made up the beds for all Patrick's friends?"

"Someone insulted her in the pub at lunchtime," said Taggie. "She's gone to bed in a huff."

"Well, get her up," snapped Maud. "You better make up some more beds."

"They can all sleep in armchairs," said Patrick soothingly as he gathered up his new car keys. "I'll go and borrow those plates from Rupert."

"I've made up a bed for Ralphie in the spare room," said Taggie, blushing.

At six-thirty Declan returned home having recorded an interview with the Bishop of Cotchester, which he was aware was totally lacking in sparkle. He had been wracked with increasing foreboding during the day, as one person after another—Charles Fairburn, James Vereker, Simon Harris, Daysee Butler and then, horrors, Cameron Cook and Tony Baddingham—said they'd see him this evening. Maud had obviously got chummier than he'd realized at the Corinium Christmas party. But he never expected the frantically billowing pink and white tent on the lawn or the tables laid for two hundred people, or the disco boys checking acoustics, or the three hundred bottles of Moët on ice in various bathtubs around the house.

Roaring upstairs, he found Maud lying on the bed naked except for a face pack and an eyepad.

"What the fuck is going on? Do you want to ruin me?" He slammed the door behind him.

In the drawing room below a group of Patrick's glamorous friends, who'd just arrived and were having a drink, could see the mistletoe hanging from the chandelier trembling beneath Declan's demented pacing. Then they heard Maud screaming.

"Oh dear," sighed Caitlin, "Daddy doesn't seem in a party mood."

Upstairs Taggie was frantically making up beds for Patrick's friends.

The din was increasing in her parents' room.

"Peace on earth, and mercy mild, God and sinners reconciled,"—sang Caitlin outside the door. "Shut up you two, you're upsetting Gertrude."

Downstairs Taggie could hear more of Patrick's friends arriving. Running to the banisters, she could see Patrick's exquisite girlfriend, Lavinia, giving him a present. She was followed by a beautiful dark girl and behind her—Taggie caught her breath—just under the mistletoe in the hall, stood Ralphie. He seemed to have got even more beautiful with his big blue eyes and blond curls.

In a panic she rushed back into the spare room and, putting another log on the fire, rearranged the Christmas roses in the blue jug beside the bed. At least they had curtains in this room, and a really comfortable bed for Ralphie—and perhaps her. There was a knock on the door.

"Come in," croaked Taggie, hanging on to the mantelpiece for support.

The beautiful dark girl she'd seen in the hall came through the door. She was very slim and tiny, not more than five foot one.

"Oh what a lovely room," she said, dumping a squashy bag and a black ruched dress on the bed, "and a fire too. You are kind. Will I be able to have a bath?"

"Of course," stammered Taggie, "but it may not be a hot one."

"You must be Taggie," said the girl. "You look just like Patrick. Oh, look at the lovely Christmas roses! You shouldn't have bothered."

Taggie, blushing so hard she felt she could fry an egg on her face, said, "Actually this is Ralphie's room."

"And mine," said the girl happily. "I'm Georgina Harrison, Ralphie's girlfriend."

Patrick had never seen such grief. Taggie seemed almost deranged, her whole body shuddering and shuddering with sobs.

"I can't bear it, I can't bear it, I love him so much."

"Angel, I know you do. But he's frightfully shallow, and you're simply not his type. It's not anything you've done, you're just too large for him. It's like expecting a chihuahua to mate with a wolf-hound. Well, not quite, but, being small, he feels daunted by tall girls. He said to me last summer, 'Your sister'd be absolutely heart-breaking if only she were tiny.' "

"I can't shrink."

"Go off and nibble a mushroom."

"Don't make jokes," sobbed Taggie.

"Sweetheart, you've got to pull yourself together and get dressed. Mum and Dad have stopped rowing, but there's no way they can organize the grub. Mrs. Makepiece has arrived with two frightful teenage children, and Grace and Reg the butler and his friends are all getting stuck into the Moët. You must go down and supervise them. Now be a good girl and dry your eyes. I'm not twenty-one every day."

Maud had the ability to make houses look beautiful. There were no curtains on the windows, but huge fires crackled in all the downstairs rooms, which were lit by hundreds of red candles and decorated by huge banks of holly, yew, and laurel. She was also totally unfazed by being a hostess, or by the frightful row she'd just had with Declan. She had certainly never looked more beautiful. The Medusa curls had dropped a little after her bath, and framed her pale face to which the heat from the fires had given a touch of color. She was wearing a very low-cut ivy-green taffeta dress with a bustle, which brought out the witchy green of her eyes and clung to her figure. She'd lost seven pounds, hardly eating a thing over Christmas. Pearls gleamed at her wrists, her ears, and her throat. If she couldn't ensnare Rupert tonight, she never would.

"New dress," snarled Declan, tying his black tie in the drawing room mirror.

"Oh, this old thing," said Maud mockingly.

"The old thing's in the dress," said Caitlin sourly.

Pinching some of her mother's scent, she had seen the bill for the dress, and really thought her mother had overdone it this time. Why did she need to spend that much money on clothes when she'd already got a man? Caitlin was worried that her father was deliberately setting out to get drunk, and even more worried about poor old Taggie. But at least at a ball with hundreds of people, Taggie might meet someone new.

"Pretend it's a job, pretend it's a job," Taggie told herself through gritted teeth, as she stirred the great vats of turkey soup.

"Could you possibly ask Caitlin to make sure Aengus is locked in one of the bedrooms? I'm afraid he might get under a car," she said to Mrs. Makepiece's daughter, Tracey, who, dressed in the tightest of black skirts and a white polyester shirt and pearls, was upwardly mobilizing her spiky hair in the kitchen mirror. Tracey was plainly avid to have a crack at one of Patrick's friends.

Outside Mrs. Makepiece's punk son Kevin was directing cars into a nearby field, and coming in frequently to fortify himself against the cold with slugs of wine. Reg and his two friends were doing sterling work drinking and serving drinks. Grace was already pissed. "Goodness you look tired," she said to Taggie. "What 'ave you been up to?"

Gertrude grew hoarse with barking as more and more people poured in. The party was plainly a success. Maud had produced a splendid mix: lots of London friends, who were knocked out by the beauty of the house and how good Maud was looking. Many of them had brought teenage children. Then there were Patrick's friends from Trinity, a large contingent from Corinium Television, and all Maud and Declan's new friends from Gloucestershire. With two hours' hard drinking before dinner, most people were soon absolutely plastered.

Tony, to his amazement, was thoroughly enjoying the party. Shrewd enough to appreciate his vanity, Maud was treating him as the guest of honor, keeping him constantly plied with beautiful women and introducing him to them as: "Declan's gorgeous boss." Tony was soon purring like a great leopard let loose in a goat farm.

Archie, Tony's beloved son, was getting plastered upstairs with Caitlin's friends. Poor fat Sharon Jones was desperately shy. Caitlin had introduced her to boy after boy, ordering them to look after her, but within seconds Sharon had waddled back to her increasingly irritated mother.

"I told you, go and make some friends of your own age," hissed Valerie furiously.

Mrs. Makepiece sidled up to Maud. "Miss Taggie says we ought to eat; everything's ready."

At that moment, Rupert sauntered through the open door with snow on his dinner jacket and in his hair.

"Rupert," said Maud joyfully, "you made it."

She looked so beautiful, glowing under the hall mistletoe, that Rupert kissed her on the mouth. "You look sensational," he said.

"Not nearly as sensational as you," whispered Maud. "You must have had wonderful weather."

"I can feel the temperature dropping here," said Rupert, as Declan turned on his heel and stalked off toward the kitchen.

Maud turned to the passing Reg. "Bring Mr. Campbell-Black a bucket of whisky."

Going back to the kitchen via the tent, Caitlin put her place card back on Rupert's right and removed Wandering Aengus who was sitting on Valerie's plate.

"Wonderful party," she said to Taggie who was grimly pouring turkey soup into bowls on trays. "Rupert's arrived looking like a red Indian, so Mummy says we can eat now, and Daddy's terribly drunk."

"Daddy's not the only one," said Taggie. "You should see Reg and his friends. Both Tracey and Kev have already buggered off upstairs, and good old Grace is singing 'This Joyful Eastertide.' "

CHAPTER 18

Tony Baddingham was even happier at dinner. It was obvious, he reflected with satisfaction, that Maud and Declan had had the most frightful row—probably about money. There must be at least three hundred people here and by the way the Moët was being splashed about, nothing had been stinted, which was good, because the broker Declan got, the more dependent he'd be on Corinium, and the more Tony could torment and manipulate him.

Then, looking across the room at Maud's enraptured face turned toward Rupert, her elbows pressed together to deepen her cleavage, her turkey soup untouched, he decided it was more likely that Declan was upset because his wife had a thumping great crush on Rupert. This suited Tony even better, because it meant Declan would crucify Rupert even more when he interviewed him.

Sarah Stratton was looking rather bleak as she sat down beside Tony.

"I'm glad we're next to each other," he said. "I wanted to talk to you."

"Have you made any New Year's resolutions?" said Sarah, picking up her soup spoon.

"Yes," said Tony, his swarthy pirate's face suddenly looking as though he was going to fight off a flotilla of rival clipper ships, "to keep the franchise."

"I'll drink to that," said Sarah.

Upstairs in a scene of Petronian debauchery, teenagers smoked, drank, necked, and screamed with laughter as they opened another box of Tampax and shot the cotton wool out like cannons.

Archie was sharing a bottle of Moët with Caitlin, who had briefly abandoned Rupert at dinner to smoke an illicit cigarette.

"What has an Upland House girl in common with a Tampax?" Archie asked her.

"Dunno," said Caitlin.

"They're both stuck-up cunts."

Caitlin screamed with laughter. "Have you got a girlfriend?"

"I did," said Archie, "but she went off me because of my zits."

"You mustn't worry about zits," said Caitlin kindly. "It means you're producing lots of testosterone and will make a wonderfully vigorous lover later.''

"My father said all your family were weirdos," said Archie, "but I think you're cool."

Declan, whom Maud had put deliberately between Monica and Valerie, so he couldn't make a scene, was so drunk he was in danger of seriously jeopardizing his career. He didn't even realize Monica was talking about *Otello* until she got onto Iago.

"He's an even more evil character than Scarpia," she was saying.

"Much more," agreed Declan. "Very like your husband, in fact."

"Garlic bread either of you?" said Valerie, unable to believe her ears.

"Your husband is an absolute shit," said Declan.

"I know," said Monica calmly, as she tore off a piece of garlic bread. "However, I have three children and I don't believe in divorce."

"Nor do I," said Declan, filling up both their glasses.

"You won't try and wind Tony up too much at work will you?" went on Monica. "You're very good for Corinium. They need people with integrity. I'd like you to stay."

"I'm not sure your husband would."

"I think we both better stop discussing Tony," said Monica gently, "or we might become very indiscreet. This is a very good party. Maud's looking so beautiful."

"Has anyone ever told you you're a beautiful woman?" said Declan.

Monica went pink. "That's jolly well overdoing it. You really ought to eat some of this shepherd's pie. It's frightfully good."

But Declan was looking at Maud who was gazing at Rupert. "O heart! O heart!" he murmured, "if she'd but turn her head."

"You'd know the folly of being comforted," said Monica finishing the quotation for him. "Don't worry about Rupert," she went on briskly. "Bertie Berkshire once described him as a 'particularly nasty virus, that one's wife caught sooner or later,' but we all get over it."

Declan looked back at her startled. "Even you?"

Monica sighed. "Even me, although Rupert had no idea. Don Giovanni must have been very like him. He can't resist the conquest, and I think, although he won't admit it, he still misses show jumping desperately, and it's a question of constantly filling the aching void."

"He's usually filling other people's wives' aching voids," said Declan bitterly.

At last Maud had to stop monopolizing Rupert and turn to Declan's old boss at the B.B.C., Johnny Abrahams, who was sitting on her left.

"You can talk to me now," said Caitlin to Rupert.

"How d'you do? I saw you at Midnight Mass," said Rupert.

He liked her merry face and her bright beady eyes.

"Tell me," he went on lowering his voice, "is your sister ever going to forgive me?"

"Ah," said Caitlin, "well, you haven't been very nice to her. I heard about the groping at the dinner party, which was pretty crass, and the row over the stubble burning. Taggie probably overreacted there, she's so soppy about animals, she spends her time prying frozen worms off the paths in this weather. What really pissed her off was that you were so unkind about Gertrude."

"Gertrude?" said Rupert bewildered.

"Our dog. You may think Gertrude is very plain, but we're all devoted to her. Taggie's led such a sheltered life, she's never left home like Patrick and me, and she and Gertrude have never been parted."

Rupert grinned. "Perhaps I should have sent Gertrude a pendant instead."

"Oh my God," said Caitlin in horror, "it was *you*! Because you signed it R, we all assumed it was from Ralphie. Taggie's mad about him, you see."

"Glad I gave her a happy Christmas," said Rupert acidly.

"Caitlin," said Maud very sharply, "go and tell Taggie to clear away the fruit salad plates. We must have Patrick's cake, or we'll be still sitting here at midnight." She turned to Rupert. "We've managed to get tickets for *Phantom of the Opera* the week after next. D'you want to come?"

"Taggie, Taggie," Caitlin squealed, racing into the kitchen, "Mummy wants the plates cleared, then we can have Patrick's cake. And it was Rupert who sent you that pendant, because he was sorry about goosing you at Valerie Jones's."

"There's no way we're going to get 300 slices out of this." Taggie nearly dropped Patrick's cake. "What did you say?"

"Rupert sent you the pendant."

"He couldn't have," whispered Taggie. "I hate him."

"No you don't. He's really nice. Go and sit next to him. I'll try and find Reg and his mates to carry the cake in and people can eat it on their fruit salad plates. Go on, Tag."

"Never, never," gasped Taggie. She was deathly pale now. "I'm going to send it back."

Maud's plans had gone seriously awry. She had wanted them all to be dancing and her and Rupert to be standing under one of Caitlin's hundred bunches of mistletoe at midnight, but they were still sitting at the tables waiting for Patrick to cut his cake. Why on earth couldn't Taggie be more efficient?

At five minutes to midnight Declan got somewhat unsteadily to his feet, and tapped the table with his knife. "I'm very pleased to see you all here tonight," he said, "and I'd just like to drink my son Patrick's health. He's a good boy and he's given us a lot of pleasure over the years."

"And me too," piped up Patrick's girlfriend, Lavinia, and everyone laughed and sang "Happy Birthday" as Reg and his mates staggered in very perilously carrying the cake.

There were more loud cheers. Then, just as Caitlin finished lighting the candles, like the dark stranger coming over the threshold, Cameron Cook walked in. She was wearing an extremely tight-fitting, strapless, black suede dress, which came eight inches above her knees. Three-inch cross-laced gaps on either side from armpit to hem made it quite plain she was wearing nothing but Fracas and Mantan underneath. There was a heavy metal chain around her neck, and among the heavy silver bangles worn over her long black suede gloves gleamed Tony's diamond bracelet.

Anyone else would have looked tarty in that dress, but Cameron, with her marvelously lean, sinuous, rapacious beauty, succeeded in looking both menacing and absolutely staggering.

"Holy shit," said Patrick.

"Blow out your candles," said Caitlin.

Still gazing at Cameron, Patrick blew them out with one puff, then turned to Declan. "Who the hell's that?"

"The biggest bitch in television," said Declan bleakly.

"She may well be your future daughter-in-law," said Patrick.

"Sorry I'm late," said Cameron, fighting her way through the crowd to Maud's side. "We've had a lot of hassle at work."

"Lovely to see you at any time," said Maud. "Caitlin," she added pointedly, terrified that Caitlin might start monopolizing Rupert again, "will get you something to eat."

"She needs a drink," said Patrick.

Goodness, he's pretty, thought Cameron. Like Declan, but purer-looking somehow.

"Aren't you going to cut your cake?" she said to him.

"I've got to wish," said Patrick. Never taking his eyes off her, he slowly plunged the knife into the cake, right up to the hilt.

"I didn't have time to buy you a present," said Cameron.

"You brought yourself," said Patrick, slightly mockingly. "Just what I wanted."

Filling up his glass with champagne, he handed it to her.

"Thanks." Taking it, Cameron drained the glass.

Just at that moment, from speakers all around the tent, Big Ben boomed out the twelve strokes of midnight. As everyone started kissing everyone and cheering, Patrick drew Cameron into his arms and kissed her on and on and on.

At last they broke away.

"The *coup de foudre*," said Patrick softly. "I've waited twenty-one years for this to happen."

"Look at Tony's face," whispered Lizzie Vereker to Charles Fairburn with a shiver.

As the last notes of "Auld Lang Syne" rang out, Declan could be heard saying, "Bloody January again."

Plates were being cleared away, tables pushed back and the tent cleared for dancing, as the women drifted upstairs to do their faces. Telling Cameron he wouldn't be a second, Patrick went off to the kitchen to thank Taggie. Oblivious that Monica might be watching, Tony fought his way over to Cameron and seized her arm: "What the hell are you playing at?"

Cameron winced. "Celebrating Christmas. It hasn't been great so far."

"I couldn't get away."

"I guess not."

"That dress is deliberately provocative," snarled Tony.

"Well, if it deliberately provokes you, it's doing a great job."

Patrick never made it to the kitchen. Declan dragged him into the library.

"For Christ's sake, Cameron's out of bounds."

"Why?"

"She's Tony Baddingham's mistress."

"So. Are you frightened of losing your job?"

For a second Patrick thought Declan was going to hit him.

"It's not that. You've no idea of the evil of both of them."

"He may be, she's not. She just needs someone of her own age to play with for a change."

"He's taught her some very unpleasant habits," said Declan heavily.

"Like arguing with you, I suppose," said Patrick.

"She's out of your league."

"I don't give a fuck," said Patrick, walking out.

Cameron escaped to check her face. After Patrick's kiss, she certainly couldn't have any lipstick left. Upstairs, in the only bedroom that didn't seem to be inhabited by necking teenagers, she found Sarah Stratton brushing her hair.

"Good party," said Sarah.

"It seems so."

"I'm glad I bumped into you," said Sarah. "Tony's offered me a job at Corinium. Ought I to take it?"

"Sure," said Cameron coolly.

"You don't think he's just after my body?"

"No way," said Cameron, who was having difficulty applying lipstick, her hands were trembling so much. "Did Tony make a pass at you?"

"Not exactly—but he was terrifically complimentary," said Sarah. "And I must say for an older man he's not unattractive."

As they came downstairs James Vereker was hovering. Deliberately ignoring Cameron, he asked Sarah to dance. Oh well, thought Sarah, anything to make Rupert jealous.

"How did you get on with Tony's mistress?" asked James.

"Oh my Christ, is she?" gasped Sarah, appalled, and she told James what had happened. "I'd better not take that job at Corinium after all," she said finally.

"I'll kill Tony, I'll absolutely kill him," thought Cameron as, seething with rage, she went into the tent. Both Tony and Patrick were waiting. Patrick was quicker.

"Come and dance," he said, taking her hand. "I'm not going to let you go for the rest of the evening, probably not for the rest of my life."

Taggie, mindlessly washing up in the kitchen, noticed Rupert standing in the doorway. He was as brown as he'd been last summer when he'd had no clothes on. Taggie went scarlet.

"It was the most lovely dinner," said Rupert gently, noticing

Taggie's reddened eyes. "Will you please stop playing Cinderella and come and dance?"

"I've got too much to do, thank you, and thank you for the pendant. I didn't realize." She stumbled on the words.

Feeling Rupert's hand close over hers, she followed him into the tent.

"I'm a very, very bad dancer," she muttered.

"Doesn't matter," said Rupert. "We can sway in a dark corner."

Taggie's hair smelled of shepherd's pie. As he drew her to him, Rupert could feel the substantial softness of her breasts, the incredible slenderness of her waist. Her body was rigid with tension and embarrassment. She had absolutely no sense of rhythm at all.

"Did you have a nice Christmas?" asked Rupert.

"Yes."

"Did you get nice presents?"

"Yes."

"Come on my angel, relax." His hands moved over her back, gentling her as though she was one of his young horses. "Look! Gertrude's followed us. She knows I'm a rotter and she won't let you out of her sight."

Catching Gertrude's disapproving eye, Taggie gave a half laugh, half sob.

Rupert reached down and stroked Gertrude. "Good Gertrude, beautiful Gertrude. See, I am trying."

"Lady in Red, Lady in Red," sang everyone as they swayed around the floor.

Rupert took Taggie's face in his hands. She was so tall her eyes were only just below his.

"Don't be so sad," he murmured. "You'll get over him."

Taggie started. "How d'you know?"

"Caitlin told me. You thought the pendant was from him. I'm sorry."

"It was very kind," said Taggie stiffly. "I just don't accept presents from men."

"I see. Only from boys."

He gripped her waist, knowing she was about to bolt.

"Last Christmas, I gave you my heart," sang George Michael, *"But the very next day you gave it away."*

Across the room Taggie could see Ralphie and Georgina dancing together. He was stroking her cheek with his hand. With a low moan, Taggie tugged herself away from Rupert. Cannoning off startled couples, she fled from the tent upstairs to cry her eyes out once again.

In the kitchen, surrounded by undergraduates and dirty plates and glasses, Declan was declaiming Yeats:

> *"And the flame of the blue star of twilight, hung low*
> *on the rim of the sky,*
> *Has awaked in our hearts, my beloved, a sadness that*
> *may not die."*

Cameron stood listening to him, her hand in Patrick's.

"He recites best when he's drunk," whispered Patrick. "Loses all self-consciousness."

"He should do a program on Yeats," marveled Cameron.

"Hardly of local interest."

"We could do it for Channel Four."

Upstairs Maud was arranging her breasts in the green dress, and putting scent on her hair, and applying coral blusher to her pale cheeks. Her freckles were like a sprinkling of nutmeg tonight.

"I'm not middle-aged," she whispered to herself. "I'm still young and beautiful."

"I get no kick from champagne," sang the disco.

"Pure alcohol doesn't thrill me at all."

The message was all in the music, thought Maud. Go forth and multiply and seek love.

Going downstairs, she could hear Declan declaiming in the kitchen. She was safe for half an hour or so. Screams and shouts were coming from the direction of Caitlin's room.

The berries of the mistletoe gleamed brighter than her pearls under the hall light. It was three in the morning; soon Taggie would be serving kedgeree. As if in answer to her prayer, Maud heard Rupert's voice, "Darling, I was looking for you."

Taking her hand, he led her into the study where Caitlin, taking no chances, had hung more mistletoe. Rupert's hand felt so warm and dry, and the ball of his thumb was so pudgy, noticed Maud. That was the fortune-teller's clue to a passionate highly-sexed nature. It was certainly the only spare flesh on his body. Maud's heart was pounding. She must try and be distant, a little mysterious. As he turned toward her, her eyes were on a level with his black tie. She longed to caress the lovely line of his jaw. It's going to happen, she thought in ecstasy, as Rupert shut the door to blot out the screams and raucous laughter, and coming toward her, gazed deeply into her eyes.

"Angel, I've been wanting to ask you something from the moment we met, certainly from the moment I came over here with Bas after hunting. You won't be cross with me?"

"No, no," whispered Maud. She was having difficulty breathing.

"You probably think I'm the biggest shit in the world."

"I don't. I don't. I just think people misunderstand you."

She could smell the faint lemon tang of his aftershave as he moved nearer.

"I'm absolutely mad," began Rupert.

"Go on," stammered Maud.

"About little Taggie, and she can't stand me. Could you possibly put in a good word for me?"

"Taggie," said Maud in outrage, "TAGGIE! For Christ's sake," she screamed, "Taggie's eighteen, you're thirty-seven. She's dyslexic, which makes her seem even younger. How dare you, you revolting letch, how dare you, how DARE you?" And, bursting into tears, she fled upstairs and locked herself in her bedroom.

She couldn't bear it, she, who'd always got anyone she wanted, being spurned under the mistletoe by the biggest rake in Gloucestershire. And for Taggie, of all people, which made it far, far worse. Almost pathologically jealous of Taggie, there was no one in the world Maud would less like to lose a man to. Was that to be her fate, growing older and less attractive, until no one wanted her?

An hour later in the kitchen Declan was still declaiming to an enraptured group.

"You see why he can't go on doing crappy interviews with the Bishop of Cotchester," said Patrick to Cameron.

Cameron nodded.

"A woman of so shining loveliness," Declan was saying, *"That men threshed corn at midnight by a tress. A little stolen tress."*

He looked up, and saw Maud. *"A little stolen tress,"* he repeated slowly.

For a minute they gazed at each other.

"There is gray in your hair," he began very softly.

"Young men no longer suddenly catch their breath, when you are passing."

Maud turned away, her face stricken.

Declan dropped his cigarette into the sink and, stepping over the enraptured seated undergraduates, caught up with Maud on the stairs. Not having had anything to drink for a couple of hours, he was sobering up.

"What's the matter? Did he turn you down?"

Maud nodded, tears spilling out between her eyelashes.

"I've seen it coming since September. I wanted to warn you."

"Why didn't you then?"

Declan sighed: "Has there even been any point? He's no good for you. It might have lasted a week, a month, then he'd have dumped you."

He put his huge hands round her neck above the pearl choker.

"I'm sorry," she mumbled. "He's just so attractive."

"I know. Hush, hush." He raised his thumbs to still her quivering mouth. "Let's go to bed."

"We can't in the middle of a party."

"What better time?"

"I've spent so much money."

"Doesn't matter," said Declan as they went up the remaining stairs.

"I love you," he said softly, "and I'm the only one of the lot of them who understands you."

"I know," whispered Maud.

Declan shut the bedroom door behind them.

Caitlin, going past, heard the key turn. Removing the sign outside the bathroom on which she had earlier written *Ladies*, Caitlin turned it over, wrote *Do Not Disturb, Sex in Progress*, and hung it on her parents' door.

Downstairs the party showed no signs of winding down.

"I love yew," said Lizzie, looking at a dark clump of greenery in the corner, as she danced round with Freddie.

"I love you," said Freddie, giving her a squeeze. "Honestly, on my life and at least a bottle-and-a-half of Moët."

It was obvious that Tony wasn't going to be able to pry Cameron away from Patrick for even a second.

"We must go," he said bleakly to Monica.

"All right," said Monica reluctantly. "I haven't seen Archie for hours. Where is he?"

"Upstairs, I think," said Caitlin.

Monica swayed up the stairs, hanging onto the banisters. She hadn't drunk so much since she was a deb; it was really rather fun.

Finding several rooms heavily occupied by couples, she finally tracked down her elder and beloved son on a chaise longue on the top floor, absolutely superglued to Tracey Makepiece, his hand burrowing like a ferret inside her shirt.

"Archie," thundered Monica. "Drop!"

Archie dropped.

"We're leaving," said Monica, "at *once*."

Downstairs, she told Tony what Archie had been up to.

"Christ," exploded Tony. "Get him out of this bloody house as fast as possible."

"I don't know where Declan and Maud are. We ought to thank them," said Monica, as Archie shuffled sheepishly down the stairs.

"Are your parents around?" Monica asked Caitlin.

"I'm afraid they've gone to bed," Caitlin said.

"Well if you'd just tell them how very much we all enjoyed it," said Monica.

"You may have enjoyed it," hissed Tony slipping on the icy drive in his haste to get to the Rolls and the frozen chauffeur, "but frankly it was the most bloody party I've ever been to, and that child Caitlin is a minx."

"She's sweet," protested Archie with a hiccup.

"If you have anything more to do with any of the O'Hara children I'll disinherit you."

About five in the morning, having behaved just as badly as everyone else, Rupert came back into the living room looking for the whisky decanter, and saw a black and white tail sticking out from under the piano.

"Gertrude," he said.

The tail quivered. Crouching down, Rupert found both Gertrude and Taggie.

"What on earth are you doing?"

"A drunk's passed out in my bed," said Taggie with a sob. "Every other bedroom in the house is occupied; a bloody great party, including Ralphie and his blonde are in the kitchen, so I can't clean up, the disco people haven't been paid, Mummy and Daddy have gone to bed, and I don't want to be a wallflower and cramp everyone's style."

"You won't cramp mine. Come on." Rupert dragged her out.

An empty champagne bottle rolled out at the same time.

"You drink all that?"

"Nearly."

Rupert threw a couple of logs on the dying fire and then sat Taggie down on the sofa beside him. Gertrude took up her position between them.

"It's been a wonderful party," he said.

"It hasn't," said Taggie despairingly. 'It's been a disaster. Patrick's gone off with Lord Baddingham's m-mistress, which'll make Lord Baddingham even crosser at Daddy. And Mummy's got a terrific crush on someone." She blushed, remembering it was Rupert, and added hastily, "I'm not sure who, and poor Daddy's got to pay for it all. I tried and tried to keep the cost down, but then Mummy went off and ordered all that champagne, and invited hundreds and hundreds of people."

"Your father must earn a good salary from Corinium," said Rupert reasonably.

"He does," Taggie cuddled Gertrude like a terrified child clutching a teddy bear, "but it's not nearly enough. He got another huge tax bill yesterday, and he hasn't paid the last one yet, and Mummy and Caitlin and Patrick won't take it seriously. They think Daddy's a bottomless pit, who'll always provide.

"To produce his best work," she went on, "he's got to be kept calm. That's why we moved to the country for some peace and for him to finish his book. And he loathes Lord Baddingham, he thinks he's dreadfully cor-cor . . ." She blocked on the word.

"Corrupt," said Rupert.

"That's right, and shouldn't be running Corinium at all. Daddy's so headstrong, I'm sure he'll walk out if there are any more rows, and he says the B.B.C. won't have him back."

"Of course the B.B.C. would," said Rupert. "Your father's a genius. He's got everything going for him."

"Except us," said Taggie with a sob. "We're all a drain on him."

"You're not," said Rupert.

"I am. Ralphie doesn't love me. No one will ever love me."

Rupert let her cry for a few minutes, then made her laugh by putting his black tie on Gertrude.

"I'm so sorry," stammered Taggie, wiping her eyes on someone's discarded silk shawl. "I'm being horribly s-s-self-indulgent."

"You're not." Suddenly Rupert felt very avuncular and protective as he did when one of his dogs cut its paw. He wished a visit to the vet and a few stitches could cure Taggie's problems.

"I'm going to get that drunk out of your bed and then you can go to sleep."

"I must pay the disco, but no one seems to want them to stop—

and the Makepieces. I've got the money." She got a large wad of tenners out of the George V Coronation tin on the desk.

"I'll pay them," said Rupert taking the money. "You're going to bed."

Up in Taggie's turret bedroom, with some effort, Rupert lifted Charles Fairburn out of the bed and, lugging him down the winding stairs, put him on the chaise longue recently vacated by Archie and Tracey Makepiece. As Taggie's room was like the North Pole, he returned with a duvet he'd whipped off a fornicating couple in the spare room. Taggie had got into a red flannel nightgown and cleaned her teeth. Lady in Red, thought Rupert. She had huge black circles under her eyes. She looked about twelve.

"Everything'll work out all right," he said, tucking her in.

"You've been so kind," stammered Taggie. "I'm sorry I was so rude to you before, and thank you for the pendant."

But as Rupert put out a hand to touch her cheek, Gertrude, still in his black tie, growled fiercely.

"You may have forgiven me," said Rupert, "but Gertrude hasn't."

CHAPTER 19

At seven-thirty the disco was still pounding. All over the house Patrick's friends had crashed out on arm chairs and sofas. Charles snored happily on his chaise longue. In the small sitting room, watched balefully by Gertrude still in Rupert's black tie, Cameron and Patrick opened Patrick's presents, throwing the wrapping paper into the fire to ignite the dying embers. Cameron had never seen such loot: gold cufflinks, Rolex watches, diamond studs, a Leica camera, a Picasso drawing, a red- and silver-striped silk Turnbull and Asser dressing gown.

Patrick was like the prince in the fairy story, thought Cameron, whom each of the neighboring kings was trying to win over with more and more extravagant presents. She thought bitterly back to her own twenty-first birthday. Neither of her parents had even bothered to send her a card.

"You'll never remember who gave you what. That's neat," she added, as Patrick drew out a copy of *The Shropshire Lad* from some shiny red paper.

"Very," said Patrick. "First edition. What have you got there?"

"Silver hip flask, from someone called All my Love Lavinia. She's had it engraved. Who's she?"

"My Ex," said Patrick, collapsing onto the sofa to read *The Shropshire Lad*.

"How Ex?"

"About two minutes before midnight last night. Listen: *When I was one-and-twenty, I heard a wise man say, Give crowns and pounds and guineas, but not your heart away*. Hope that's not prophetic. I wish Housman hadn't used the word "Lad" so often; so appallingly hearty. Who's that from?"

Cameron pulled a long, dark-brown cashmere scarf from a gold envelope. "Georgie and Ralphie."

"I bet Georgie paid for it—kind of them, though."

He got up and wound the scarf round Cameron's neck, holding on to the two ends and slowly drawing her toward him.

"It's yours. Everything I have is yours," he said, kissing her, only breaking away from her because the telephone rang.

He grinned as he put down the receiver. It was the vicar of Penscombe asking if they could turn the disco down for an hour so he could take early service.

"I must go," said Cameron.

"You must not. I'll tell those disco boys to go and have some breakfast and then you and I are going to watch the sun rise."

Wearing three of Patrick's sweaters, a pair of Taggie's jeans, rolled over four times at the ankle, Caitlin's gumboots, and a very smart dark blue coat with a velvet collar left over the banisters by Bas Baddingham, Cameron set out with Patrick.

"I've shaved so I won't cut your face to ribbons," he said.

"The wind'll do that," grumbled Cameron.

The wind, in fact, had dropped, but a vicious frost had ermined all the fences, roughened the surface of the snow and turned the waterfall in the wood to two foot-long icicles. Gertrude charged ahead leaping into drifts, tunneling the snow with her snout.

"Wow, it's beautiful," said Cameron, as the valley stretched out below them. "How much of it's yours?"

"To the bottom of the wood. The rest of the valley belongs to Rupert Campbell-Black."

Christ, it's a kingdom, thought Cameron, looking across at the white fields, the blanketed tennis court, Rupert's golden house with its snowy roof and the bare beech wood rearing up behind like a huge spiky white hedgehog.

"Nice scent," said Patrick, burrowing his face in her neck. "What is it?"

"Fracas."

"Very appropriate. Who gave it to you?"

"Tony."

"Why hasn't he got a neck?" Patrick hurled a snowball into the woods. Gertrude hurtled after it. "You'd have thought with that much money he could have bought himself a neck."

"Shut up," said Cameron. "Tell me, do your mother and father always sneak off to bed in the middle of their own parties?"

"It's a very odd marriage," said Patrick, pointing his new Leica at her. "Look towards the stream, darling. My father has always seen my mother as Maud Gonne."

"The woman Yeats was hooked on?"

"Right. Yeats fell in love with her at exactly the same age my father fell in love with my mother. Look, badger tracks." Patrick bent down to examine them. "Maud Gonne was a rabid revolutionary. Yeats knew he wouldn't impress her with poetry, so he got caught up in a political movement to unite Ireland. Then she married John MacBride, another revolutionary. Broke Yeats's heart, but it made him write his best poetry. He claimed Maud Gonne was beyond blame, like Helen of Troy."

"But your mother isn't a revolutionary for Christ's sake, and she hasn't married someone else."

"No, but she has Maud Gonne's tremendous beauty, and my father has an almost fatalistic acceptance that she's above blame and will have affairs with other men."

"Doesn't your mother care for him?"

"In her way. I once asked her why she messed him about so much. She said that, with every woman in the world after him, she could only hold him by uncertainty."

Cameron digested this.

"But if he only loves her, and doesn't want all these women, why can't she stop playing games and love him back?"

"That's far too easy. She's convinced that, once he's sure of her, his obsession would evaporate. So the games go on."

"I wish they wouldn't," said Cameron. "It sure makes him cranky to work with."

She sat on a log and watched Patrick write "Patrick loves Cameron" in huge letters in the snow. Then he got out his hip flask, now filled with brandy, and handed it to her.

"You warm enough?"

Cameron nodded, taking a sip.

Hand in hand they watched the huge red sun climbing up behind the black bars of the beech copse.

Patrick turned toward her. "Let me look at you."

Her dark hair, no longer sleeked back with water, was blown forward in black tendrils over her cheek bones, and in a thick fringe which softened the slanting yellow eyes and the beaky nose. Her skin and her full pale lips were amber in the sunshine.

Patrick sighed. "Even the sun's upstaged. You're so dazzling, he'll have to wear dark glasses to look at you."

Cameron laughed. He'd be terribly easy to fall in love with, she was shocked to find herself thinking.

"How many more terms have you got?" she asked as they wandered back.

"Two."

"What do you want to do?"

"To take you to bed when we get home."

"Don't be an asshole! Apart from that?"

"Get a first, then write plays."

"Just like that?"

"Just like that. I've started one already."

"What's it about?"

"Intimidation—by British soldiers in Ulster."

"You're crazy—neither the B.B.C. nor ITV would touch it, particularly in an election year. Nor will the West End."

"Broadway would, and a success there would come here."

"Very self-confident, aren't you?"

"Not particularly. I just know what I want from life."

He moved closer, putting his hands inside the three sweaters, warming them on her small breasts.

"I want you most."

Back at The Priory people were beginning to surface. Bas, having put so many Alka-Seltzers in a glass of water, they'd fizzed over the top, was trying to find his overcoat. Caitlin was eating granola and reading *Lady Chatterley's Lover*.

"I'm going home to call the office and get some sleep," said Cameron.

"No," said Patrick, suddenly frantic. "If we go to sleep it won't be my birthday any more and we'll break the spell."

He took her up the winding stairs to his bedroom in the east turret, which was painted dazzlingly white, as though the snow had fallen inside. There were no carpets or curtains, and the only furniture was a desk, a chair, a green and white sofa piled high with books, and a vast red-curtained oriental four-poster with bells hanging from the tops of the posts. The view, however, was magnificent, straight across the valley and up to Penscombe. You could see the weathercock on top of the church spire glittering in the sunlight.

A volume of Keats lay open on the bed: the pages were covered with penciled notes. Picking it up, Cameron crawled under the duvet and tried to decipher Patrick's writing. Looking up, she saw the ceiling was painted dove grey with little stars picked out in white.

If only she'd had a room like this when she was young, she thought bitterly. Patrick went off to get them some breakfast.

Returning upstairs he found Cameron wearing his new red and silver dressing gown and reading Keats. The sun shining through the stained glass of one of the windows had turned her face emerald, ruby, and violet like a nymph of the rainbow. Patrick felt his heart fail.

He had brought up croissants, Taggie's bramble jelly, a bunch of green grapes, a jug of Buck's Fizz and some very strong black coffee. Cameron, who'd had no dinner the night before, was starving and ate most of it. It was astonishing, thought Patrick, that she looked desirable even with croissant crumbs on her lips. But even the black coffee couldn't keep her awake for long. Patrick didn't sleep. He sat making notes for a paper on Keats but spending more time gazing at her. In sleep her face lost all its aggression.

It was almost dark when she woke up. For a second she looked bewildered and utterly terrified.

"It's all right," said Patrick gently. "You're safe now."

She got up and looked out the window. Orion the swaggering Voyeur was looking in at her. The great yews and cedars were black against the snow. She could hear an unearthly strangulated croaking.

"What's that?"

"Foxes barking. It's a love call. Come here."

"Not till I've brushed my teeth."

Grabbing her bag she went down the landing, terrified of bumping into Declan. Instead, coming out of the bathroom she found Caitlin and Maud having a row.

"I'm nothing like Lady Chatterley," Maud was screaming. "Good evening, Cameron. Nothing at all."

"You're so lucky to have a family," said Cameron as she slid back under the duvet beside Patrick. He was still wearing a sweater and trousers.

"How many times have you been home, since you came over here?" he asked.

"I haven't."

"Why not? One must see one's family occasionally if only to fight with them."

The argument outside was growing more clamorous.

"My parents are divorced. My father's married again. My mother lives with someone. I don't want to talk about it," said Cameron shrilly. Suddenly she was trembling, her teeth chattering, her eyes darting and frightened.

"You must," said Patrick. "How can I love you properly if I don't know everything about you?"

"No!" It was almost a scream.

"Come on. It'll help, I promise."

They argued for some minutes before she gave in.

"My mother walked out on my father when I was fourteen," said Cameron tonelessly. "Decided she wanted to be her own person. She dabbled in a lot of things, peace marches, consciousness raising, but she wasn't sufficiently focused and when the money ran out she moved to a female commune. Took me with her, but left my dog behind, because it was male." Cameron gave a bitter, choked laugh, "I never forgave her for that. My father got married again, and got all tied up with his new wife. Then Mom shacked up with Mike."

"Your stepfather?"

There was a long pause.

"You could call it that. Mike was a lesbian. My mother wrote a piece about coming out in the *Village Voice*. All her friends thought she was real brave. My classmates just sniggered and nudged each other."

"You poor little baby." Patrick took her trembling hands, and drew her to him. He could feel the pouring sweat, the terrible fits of shivering sweeping over her.

"Go on, darling," he whispered.

"One night I was alone in the house with Mike. I was trying to work in my room. I can't tell you. I've never told anyone this." She was suddenly frantic like a cat struggling and clawing to escape. Patrick held onto her. "It's OK. You've got to trust me. Come on, sweetheart, come on."

"Mike yelled for me to come downstairs and fix her some supper." Cameron's voice was toneless again, and so quiet Patrick could hardly hear her.

"I was frying eggs and bacon when suddenly she came up behind me and started ripping my clothes off, trying to kiss me. Ugh. She was terribly strong. I swung the pan around and hit her with it. Then I ran out into the night."

Cameron put her fingers in her hair, rubbing the ball of her hand over and over again against her forehead, as if to blot out the memory. Patrick waited.

"I went to some neighbors. I lied that Mike had tried to beat me up. They said they'd expected it for months. They called Dad in Washington. He came the next day and took me to live with him. He'd been dying to get something on Mom and Mike and the court ruled I should stay with him."

"What happened then?"

"It didn't work," said Cameron wearily. "The honeymoon wore off. My stepmother's a lawyer, my father's a diplomat; they had a young baby. They're Very Civilized People and Very Busy; they couldn't handle a savage like me. I disrupted their lives, I made scenes, stayed out all night. They couldn't see I was crying out for someone to care. I ran away from them too in the end. I got a scholarship to Barnard, worked part-time to support myself, got a job on the *New York Times*, and finally got into television. The rest is hysterics." She gave her bitter mirthless laugh again.

"You poor darling." Patrick pulled her back into his arms again, kissing her forehead. He'd never felt so sorry for anyone in his life.

"Didn't you have a boyfriend to look after you?"

"Oh I screwed around like crazy, just to prove I was heterosexual. Then the AIDS scare started in the States. Then Tony came along."

"Hardly the ideal father figure," said Patrick.

"I'm not dependent on him," snarled Cameron too quickly. "I'm not dependent on anyone. The only time I feel I belong is when my credits come up on the screen."

She was shivering violently now, furious with herself for dropping her guard and revealing so much.

"I guess you'll run to Declan now and tell him the whole thing, so you can have a good laugh."

"Don't be childish," snapped Patrick. "I'm going to look after you. I'll blot out all the bad memories, even if it takes a lifetime."

Never taking his eyes off her face, he started to unbutton his shirt.

"It's too soon," she whispered.

"I'm not going to fuck you," said Patrick. "I'm just going to hold you close. You've got to learn that someone loves you for other things besides your heavenly body and your skills as a career bitch."

Patrick was as good as his word. Gradually the shivering stopped and he soothed all the tension out of her. Exhausted by so much revelation, she even slept again. At midnight she insisted on going back to her house. He was very loath to let her go.

"Let me get dressed. I'll run you home."

"I've got my car."

"I want to see your house."

"That's Tony's territory."

"Not any more. Tony's past history."

Cameron sighed. "It's a bit more complicated than that."

"I feel like Demeter letting Persephone go back to the underworld," said Patrick as he fastened her seat belt. "For Christ's sake, drive carefully. The roads are like glass. I'll call you tomorrow. I love you."

Hell, thought Cameron, as she drove up to the house. I must have left the living room light on. She glanced in the hall mirror. Not a scrap of makeup. Despite the sleep, the circles under her eyes were darker than her eyebrows. Patrick had really seen her in the raw, yet she felt strangely cleansed and at peace. Tomorrow they'd make love. She knew it would be wonderful. The slow lazy smile of anticipation was wiped off her face, when she went into the living room and found Tony.

The cassettes of her programs lay scattered over the floor. The ashtray was filled with cigar butts. The whisky bottle, which had been half-full, was empty now. Tony was a slow drinker; he must have been there for hours. Cameron shut the door and leaned against it, her heart pounding. With a particularly unpleasant smile on his face, Tony picked up some papers lying on the table.

"I've been looking at your contract," he said amiably. "D'you want to leave now or work out your termination?"

It was as though the last twenty-four hours had never existed. Here was reality. Her whole career, her only security, was crashing around her ears in ruins.

"I haven't done anything. You can't fire me," she whispered in terror.

"I don't have to. Your contract runs out in six weeks. Such a pity you blew it." He examined his square, beautifully manicured fingernails. "I came around to tell you that Simon Harris gave in to his nervous breakdown and was carted off to a loony bin this afternoon on extended leave. But you know what I feel about unpunctuality and twenty-four hours is a little late to come home from the ball."

"But I never see you on Sunday," said Cameron illogically. She seemed too stunned to take anything in.

"That doesn't mean I don't expect you to be here."

Smiling, he picked up his glass of whisky.

"You bloody little whore," he said softly. The next moment he'd hurled it in her face.

For a second she was speechless, as the liquid dripped down onto the suede dress.

"How odd," she said in a strained, high voice. "Every time I buy something new and expensive some jerk spills something all over it." Then she lost her temper.

"You bastard," she screamed. "I haven't taken a weekend off in three years. I'm always at your fucking beck and call."

"That's what I pay you for," said Tony. His eyes were sparkling with pleasure now.

"If you paid me time and a half for the hours I put in for you, I'd be Howard Hughes by now. You fuck around doing exactly what you like, expecting me to behave like a fucking nun, except when you require my services. Well, it's not good enough."

She sprang at him, trying to claw his face, but he grabbed her wrists. He was not bull-necked and thick-armed for nothing. As his grip tightened, Cameron gasped with pain.

"I'd put up with it," she said through clenched teeth, "if the relationship was remotely even. You raise hell if I date anyone else, but you're quite free to take Sarah Stratton out to lunch and make passes at her and offer her a job."

Tony's eyes gleamed. "So that's it. Who told you that?"

"She did," yelled Cameron, desperately struggling to get away. "And she said you still sleep with Monica."

Tony grinned. "She must have an excellent spy system."

"And you told me you hadn't laid a finger on her for years."

"It's rather exciting sleeping with Monica. There's a rarity element about it."

"So that's why you sent Madden out on Christmas Eve to buy us both diamond bracelets. Jesus Christ!"

Starting to laugh, Tony let go of her wrists. "You discovered that too, did you? Poor little Cameron, you must have been festering over Christmas. Jealousy is the most destructive of emotions you know. It hurts only oneself.''

"I hate you," screamed Cameron, wrenching off the bracelet and hurling it at him. Missing him, it hit the window, slithering scratchily down the glass like a fingernail on a blackboard.

"Get out! I'll move out tomorrow, but leave me alone now." She collapsed, sobbing, on the sofa. Confessing her past to Patrick had only underlined how terrifying it was to have no security. She was a panic-stricken sixteen-year-old again, racing through the night away from Mike with nowhere to go.

Tony poured two fingers of brandy into a glass, then moved toward her, until she could feel the solidness of his thigh against hers. She resisted the temptation to cling on to it, as a child might fling its arms around a tree for comfort.

"You were jealous, really jealous," purred Tony. "Was that why you led that boy on?"

"Sure."

He caught her hair, yanking her head back. "Did you sleep with him?"

"Yes," she muttered. Then, terrified he was going to hit her or throw the brandy into her face. "But not the way you think, I was so goddamn tired. I hadn't slept for nights worrying about everything. I crashed out on his bed."

"And nothing happened?"

"Nothing, nothing! He's just a kid." Oh please, make him believe her.

"Did Declan know you spent the night there?"

"No, I never saw him. He never came out of the bedroom."

With the franchise coming up this year, Tony decided, he didn't really want to lose her, but he was going to enjoy torturing her a bit more.

"And you promise never to see the boy again?"

"I promise," said Cameron wearily. "But he may try to see me."

"We'll have to put pressure on Declan to stop him then, won't we?" said Tony silkily, as he took off Cameron's jacket.

"That is a very disturbing dress. I'd rather you didn't wear it in public again."

Putting his hand under the skirt, he jabbed two fingers up inside her.

Cameron winced. "I can't, Tony, not tonight. I'm really pooped."

"You can," said Tony softly, "if you want to be Controller of Programs."

Three days after Patrick's party Taggie was gingerly testing her heart and finding that the ache for Ralphie was much less acute than she'd expected it to be when the doorbell rang.

In the doorway stood Rupert. His suntan was already beginning to fade.

"Hullo," he said, gazing into her eyes. "Since your wonderful party, I haven't been able to eat a thing."

"Oh my goodness," stammered Taggie, her heart beginning to thump.

Rupert grinned. "Could I possibly have my knives and forks and plates back?"

Taggie was used to unrequited love. Patrick, however, was not. Hopelessly spoiled by his mother, accustomed to attracting girls effortlessly, he couldn't believe Cameron didn't want to see him any more.

Despite Declan's tirades and Taggie's pleading, he continued to pester her with letters and telephone calls. Then, when these were not answered, he hung around the Corinium studios and outside her house.

Cameron, in fact, had hardly had time to think. As well as producing Declan's program and coping with her new job as Acting Controller of Programs, she had to face a virtual palace revolution from a staff outraged by her appointment.

The afternoon before he was due to go back to Trinity, Patrick called Cameron at the office. Expecting a call from Rupert about coming on Declan's program, Cameron unthinkingly picked up the telephone instead of leaving it to her secretary.

"Can I speak to Cameron?" said Patrick.

Cameron froze. Putting on a cockney accent, she said, "I'm afraid she's not at her desk at the moment."

"Where is she?" snapped Patrick. "Lying with the Managing Director under *his* desk."

Cameron hung up.

The telephone was ringing again as she got home that evening. Running into the hall, she snatched up the receiver. It was Rupert answering her call.

"We were talking about a date for you to come on Declan's

program,'' she said with a confidence she didn't feel. "I was just hoping to confirm it.''

His diary was ridiculously full, but to her amazement he said he could make a Wednesday in February, which turned out to be Valentine's Day.

"That was a good party on New Year's Eve," said Rupert. "I saw you bopping in your suede dress. I hoped you'd jump out of your skin.''

The next moment Cameron nearly did jump out of her skin, as she felt a kiss on the back of her neck. Patrick had walked in through the unlocked door.

"Get out," hissed Cameron, clapping her hand over the receiver.

Shaking his head, Patrick sauntered into the living room. She caught a blast of whisky as he passed.

Furious at having to wind up her conversation with Rupert so precipitously, she said goodbye and went into the living room, where she found Patrick hurling darts at the dart board.

"Nice place you've got here. I can see why you wouldn't want to give it up in a hurry.''

"Get out," screamed Cameron.

"Not until you tell me why you didn't call back.''

He went up to the board, and pulled out the darts. His hands were shaking, his eyes were black hollows in a deathly pale face. He must have lost pounds; he looked terrible.

"There was no reason to call back. We had a fun day.''

"A fun day?" he asked incredulously. "Was that all it meant to you, after the sunrise, and all you told me about your mother and Mike and you falling asleep in my arms.''

"Shut up," hissed Cameron, looking around in terror, expecting Tony to pop up from under the piano.

Patrick picked up a huge bunch of anemones which he'd left on the dentist's chair.

"I bought you these. For Christ's sake, I love you. Can't you understand that?''

In answer Cameron snatched the flowers from him and hurled them into the fireplace. Patrick winced and turned back to the dart board. The first dart missed, crashing into the wall, the second hit the glass in the frame of one of Cameron's awards, the third hit a plate.

"Cut it out," said Cameron more calmly. "If Tony turns up, he'll kill us both.''

"He's a fiend," said Patrick sitting down at the piano. "He's corrupting you too, turning you into his pet Rottweiler to savage any of his staff he wants to reduce to jelly. You'll never get out of the Underworld if you stay with him."

"Tony suits me," said Cameron over the din. "We've been together for three years, OK? My career's the only thing that matters."

"So you agreed to drop me if he made you Controller of Programs?"

"What can you offer me?"

Patrick's hands came down in a jumble of discords. "I, being poor," he said bitterly, "can only offer you my dreams."

"Stop talking like a prime-time soap."

"You should know, you make enough of them. Can I have a drink?"

"You've had enough," snarled Cameron. "Tony'll be here in a minute."

"And he'll settle you in that dentist's chair," said Patrick scornfully, "and say 'open wide', and then it's Wham, Bam, thank you, Mammon. My Christ."

He slammed the piano lid down and got to his feet.

"Don't be obnoxious," hissed Cameron.

On New Year's Day, when she'd sobbed in his arms, he'd seemed so strong. Suddenly now he looked terribly young and frightened. Cameron was too insecure herself to be drawn to frailty.

"I'm truly sorry," he muttered. "It hurts loving you, that's all. Look, I'll do anything. I'll chuck Trinity, get a job. It'll be easy with Pa's connections."

"Always fall back on Daddy, don't you?" taunted Cameron. "You bitch about his philistine program, but you'll bleed him white when it suits you. Well I'm not having you bleeding *me* white. Can't you get it into your Neanderthal skull that I don't want you around?"

Guilt at the way she'd treated him made her even more brutal.

"I can't help myself," said Patrick going toward the door. "La Belle Dame sans merci has me totally in thrall."

He went to the nearest pub and drank until long after closing time. The barmaid felt sorry for the beautiful, obviously desolate young man sitting there quietly gazing into space.

At midnight Patrick parked his car four houses down from Cameron's and got out. It was a punishingly cold night. Cotchester slumbered beneath her eiderdown of snow. In a sky russet from the streetlamps huge stars flickered. Icicles glittered from Cameron's gutters. In front of the house beside Cameron's green Lotus was parked Tony's bloody great dark red Rolls-Royce with the Corinium ram on the hood. There was a light on in the top of the house—Cameron's bedroom, guessed Patrick. He imagined Tony brutally clambering over her lovely body. The Sunday before last she'd lain in his arms, pliant as a child. He wanted to plunge one of the icicles into Tony's heart.

Wearing only a sweater and an old pair of jeans, he was shivering violently now. Then he noticed that Tony's car keys were still in the ignition. Trying the car door he found it open. The lecherous bugger had obviously been in such a hurry to get at Cameron he'd forgotten to lock it.

Easing open the door, pulling out the keys, Patrick chucked them into a nearby flower bed. They landed deep in a lavender bush, hardly scattering the snow.

* * *

At four o'clock in the morning Tony looked at his watch. "I must go."

Cameron didn't dissuade him. She was utterly shattered. To eradicate any memory of Patrick, Tony had recently insisted on indulging in sexual marathons. Four times that night, he thought smugly; no one could accuse him of losing his touch. Cameron daren't complain. She was also twitchy that Patrick might do something insane to rock the boat.

Hearing Tony let himself out, she was just falling asleep when she heard a key turn in the door. For a wild moment of dread and longing she thought it might be Patrick.

"Did I leave my keys here?" shouted Tony.

By the time they'd upended the entire house, the car and the drive, screamed at each other and nearly frozen to death, the lights had come on in the house opposite and curtains were twitching in the houses on either side. There was no way Tony could start the Rolls, or get someone to help push it out of the way. If he rang Percy, his chauffeur, it would be around the entire network in a flash, so he spent the next three hours frantically and abortively calling around, trying to find another set of keys.

In the end he had to order a taxi from the station. His temper was not improved by the driver recognizing him.

Arriving at The Falconry, he had to provide Monica with a ridiculously convoluted explanation that he'd decided to come home that night, but that his car had gone into a skid on the highway and he'd had to abandon it. He then had to keep her in bed in the morning, so she wouldn't drive into Cotchester and see his car parked outside Cameron's house.

As it was, poor, loyal Cyril Peacock tracked down a key and removed the Rolls by midday, but by then almost the entire Corinium staff had seen the car on their way in to work and had had a good laugh. Later in the day, Cameron passed the staff bulletin board. Beneath the card announcing her appointment as Acting Controller of Programs, someone had added the words: "and Mistress of the Rolls."

Later that day, Patrick called Cameron from Birmingham Airport to say goodbye.

"Did you steal Tony's keys?" she shouted.

"Tell him to look under the lavender bush on the left of the front door."

Cameron let Patrick have it. "You stupid asshole. If Monica had come by and seen the car, you'd have landed Tony in divorce court."

"I thought that's what you wanted."

"Don't be so fucking infantile."

"I couldn't help it." Patrick's voice faltered. "I can't bear to think of that great toad in bed with you."

"Get out of my life," screamed Cameron. "You don't know the rules."

"I love you," Patrick was almost crying.

"Well I don't love you. You're a fucking nuisance. Piss off and try and do something worthwhile with your life."

She was dead scared of telling Tony about the keys, but was amazed to find that he was grimly pleased.

"What a very silly little boy to put such a very large nail in his father's coffin."

CHAPTER 20

At the end of January the IBA formally asked for applications for the new franchises. These applications, which had to be provided not only by the fifteen incumbent independent companies, but also by any rival consortium who sought to oust them, often ran to hundreds of beautifully bound pages, giving details of finance, staffing policies, plans for future programs, and proposed boards of management.

After the applications were handed in in early May, the IBA

would study them and then conduct a series of public meetings around the country, attempting to find out whether the public felt well-served by their particular local television company. After private meetings between the IBA and all the individual contenders in October and November, the franchises would finally be awarded in December.

Anticipating a long year of lobbying and hustling, Tony Baddingham's immediate task in the New Year was to strengthen the Corinium Board. Knowing the IBA and particularly Lady Gosling's penchant for women, he intended to make Cameron a director. But he wanted to punish her as long as possible for stepping out of line with Patrick, and, as the staff were still in a state of mutiny over her appointment, he didn't want a strike on his hands in franchise year. The staff, however, had short memories. Cameron had found Simon Harris's affairs in such a shambles that Tony had quite enough excuses to dispense with his services when he came out of hospital, but that would have to be done discreetly too. Then he could appoint Cameron to the Board just before the applications went in.

Tony also had his lunch with Freddie Jones, who, heavily pressured by Valerie, was poised to join the Corinium Board but decided against it. With his electronics empire and his race horses and his hunting, he would not have sufficient time. If he were a director, he wanted to do some directing and that was not in the cards at Corinium.

Tony couldn't blame Declan for Freddie Jones's defection, but he blamed him for everything else: for inciting rebellion in the newsroom with his subversive lefty attitudes, for egging Charles Fairburn to put in larger and larger expenses, for Cameron's bad temper which was no doubt caused by Declan's handsome son Patrick, for Declan's trouncing of Maurice Wooton, which had made Tony so anxious to get Freddie on the Board and waste so much time wooing him, only to be rejected.

It was generally agreed at Corinium that Tony had never sustained a mood of utter bloody-mindedness for quite so long, and the only way Declan could redeem himself would be to crucify Rupert Campbell-Black when he interviewed him on Valentine's Day—a massacre Declan looked forward to with grim relish.

As he researched the program, Declan found himself increasingly fascinated by the complexities of Rupert's character. He was obviously very good at his job. The Ministry of Sport, when Rupert was offered it, had been merely a PR post, answerable to the Ministry of the Environment, with the Home Office dealing with any major disasters like football riots.

Rupert, however, had refused to take on the job unless he was given sole responsibility for all sports in the country and any trouble that ensued. The gamble paid off. He had had spectacular success in curbing football violence, he had raised a vast amount of money for sports, particularly the next Olympics. He had had rows with the Teachers Unions over the decline of competitive sports in schools, with the Football Association, rows with fellow ministers, even rows with the PM. But he got things done and he cut through red tape. Utterly sure of his own judgment, he was sometimes too arrogant, and, having been a great athlete himself, he tended to side with the players rather than the management, but when he went against officials it was always because he'd discovered a weakness in their argument. He was extremely lucky in Gerald Middleton, his private secretary.

Declan noted Rupert's appallingly deprived childhood, not of material things, but of love and stability. His beautiful mother was on her fifth marriage. His father's fourth marriage had just come unstuck. Then there was his taking over of the family home at Penscombe, with its five hundred acres, when he was only twenty-one and just making the big time in show-jumping, and soon having it running at a huge profit. There were the frequent rumblings in the press about his cruelty to his horses, or at least ruthlessly overjumping them. There was the compulsive womanizing that hardly stopped with marriage or divorce. Even today, when he should be setting a good example, far too many women appeared only too anxious to say "Yes Minister."

Declan had spoken to Rupert's best friend, Billy Lloyd-Foxe, now Head of Sport at the B.B.C., who had nothing but praise for the way Rupert had helped him in the past, curing him of alcoholism and virtually saving his marriage. He also talked to Malise Gordon, Rupert's old chef d'équipe, now married to Rupert's ex-wife Helen, who said Rupert's urge to win was the strongest motivating force in his character. "Whatever he does, he'll get to the top." He talked to numerous exes, who all described Rupert as impossible but irresistible, not least because he made them laugh, and to several cabinet ministers, who spoke of him with respect rather than affection.

Everyone cited Rupert's phenomenal energy. After the punishing hours of show jumping he took the grueling work load of Sports Minister in his stride. Accustomed to adulation and easy conquest on the show-jumping circuit, he had been unaffected both by the reverence and sycophancy which surround MPs and the brickbats thrown at them by the Press and in the House. Because he was fearless and not short of money, he made a surprisingly good MP, happy to kick up a fuss on behalf of his constituency whenever necessary. Chalford and Bisley were proud. Once again Rupert had put them on the map.

This, therefore, was the man that Declan read every word written about and became obsessed with as he strode through the frozen Gloucestershire valleys, or tossed and turned in his bed at night. This was the man, he thought, as he worked out his questions with a black, churning, sickening hatred, who could at any moment take Maud or Taggie or even Caitlin away from him.

Valentine's Day dawned, causing the usual flutter of excitement at Corinium Television, and giving hernias to the postmen staggering up Cotchester High Street under sackfuls of colored envelopes.

None of these envelopes, however, were addressed to Cameron. Not that she really noticed. Since she'd taken over Simon Harris's job, she was working herself into the ground.

Not only was she still producing Declan and overseeing the production of a new series of "Four Men went to Mow," but she was now in sole charge of Corinium Programs, and seemed to spend her time scheduling, commissioning, arguing about budgets, or going to meetings with other Program Controllers in London.

Patrick bombarded her with increasingly anguished letters to which she didn't reply. Only that morning he'd sent her a huge Valentine bunch of lilies of the valley at home.

"Darling Cameron," said the accompanying letter,

"I am going into a decline. Decline O'Hara. I've lost so much weight my friends are convinced I've got AIDS. Having been told by you to make something of my life, you will be pleased that I have given up drink (almost) and am writing my play and working hard. The play is no longer about British intimidation in Ireland, but about a young boy in love with an older woman, who can't tear herself away from an absolute bastard. Don't worry about libel, I've given Lord Bullshit red hair. I suppose I ought to thank you for making me experience unhappiness in love. Did you know James Joyce actually encouraged his wife to have affairs, so he could find out what it was like to be a cuckold? Stupid twit, he couldn't have loved her.

My mother says my father is incredibly ratty. Are things go-

ing very badly at Corinium? Before you tear this letter up, re-
member it will be worth something one day, and might well
keep you in lonely old age, when your ancient lover, Badding-
ham, has croaked. I love you and remain in darkness, Patrick."

As she left for the office, Cameron put the lilies of the valley
outside the back door in case Tony came home with her after Declan's program. Not that that was likely. Their relationship had de-
teriorated. They fought less, but when Tony made love to her there
was a brutality and coldness never there before.

To make matters worse, Sarah Stratton, in all her radiant beauty,
had joined Corinium as a prospective anchorwoman, and her pussy-
cat smile, her blonde halo of hair, her soft angora bosom and her
wafts of Anaïs Anaïs, knocked the male staff sideways. James
Vereker, wearing a different pastel turtleneck every day and behaving like a lovesick schoolboy, had been nicknamed Hanker-man by
the newsroom. The Head of News was taking the task of initiating
Sarah very seriously indeed. Even Tony chose every opportunity to
see if she was all right, summoning her to drinks in his office after
work.

James got so many Valentines he decided to do a little item on
"Cotswold Roundup" to thank his fans and conduct a studio discussion as to whether men were more romantic and caring than they
used to be. Sarah received one Valentine, postmarked Penscombe,
with no writing inside. Having never had a letter from Rupert, she
couldn't be sure the flashy blue scrawl on the envelope was his, but
she was almost certain. Declan's Valentines arrived by the bagful, but
he was too preoccupied with Rupert to open them.

Taggie had a trying day. No one sent her any Valentines. She was
doing dinner for the Lord-Lieutenant that evening and had made a
huge ratatouille and left it to cool overnight in the larder, only to
find that Declan had put it out on the lawn for the badgers, who'd
refused to touch it. Declan's only distraction these days, apart from
bird-watching, was putting food out at night and crouching in a
dimly lit kitchen waiting for the foxes and badgers to turn up.

Now he was roaring around the house in bare feet, complaining
once again that his children had swiped every single one of the Day-
Glo cat-sick yellow socks that he had made so fashionable. Looking
for a pair under Caitlin's bed, he found a vodka bottle, empty except
for a cockroach, and said once again that they really must fire Grace.

"Absolutely not," said Maud firmly. "I need my Greek chorus."

Declan was just leaving for the studios, weighed down with poisoned rapiers to stick into Rupert, when Taggie came rushing into the kitchen, speechless with excitement and brandishing a vast Valentine covered in hearts, which had just arrived by special delivery, and which played "The White Cliffs of Dover" on the xylophone when you opened it.

"What the hell's that?"

"It's from Rupert. He's sent Gertrude a Valentine."

"Whatever for?" snapped Maud.

"He once said she was ugly. He must have changed his mind. How gratuitously"—Taggie brought out her word for the day in triumph—"kind of him."

Bloody hell, thought Declan as he went out into the dank February drizzle. Not content with ensnaring Taggie and Maud, he's now trying to seduce my dog.

Taggie ran after him. "You won't give Rupert too hard a time, will you?"

Declan's interview with Rupert was the talk of the hour on the hour all during the day. Make-up had drawn lots as to who was to attend to him. Declan tried to snatch a quiet couple of hours in his office sharpening his poisoned rapiers, but was interrupted by one member of the staff after another trooping in to grumble about Tony.

Sarah Stratton, wearing a clinging pale gray angora dress, sat in the Newsroom with the Head of News.

"Of course, 'Cotswold Roundup' is the company's flagship," he told her. "We lose or retain the franchise according to whether or not the program truly represents local news and views. We have to be consistent, questioning, responsible, and entertaining. It's the one area where interference from Cameron or Tony isn't tolerated. The autonomy of the newsroom is undisputed."

Beside him the internal telephone rang. Taking his hand off Sarah's knee, the Head of News picked up the receiver and turned pale.

"Of course, Lord B. I quite understand. I'll put someone on the story right away."

Sarah smiled into her paper cup and said nothing.

On the air now, James Vereker, having thanked all his fans ver' ver' much for their caring Valentines, was interviewing a local witch who'd just made a record. She was wearing a black mini and crinkled black boots, and had huge bare mottled thighs which she kept crossing and recrossing so James could see everything.

"I'm sure you're a very caring person, Tamzin," said James, averting his eyes, "but don't you think the general public has a rather more sinister idea of witches?"

"Turn him into a toad," screamed Seb Burrows in the newsroom, throwing a paper dart at the screen.

"Wish she'd make an effigy of Tony and stick pins into it," said Charles Fairburn.

"We could market a Baddingham pin cushion," said Seb. "It'd sell even better than Declan T-shirts."

Sarah wasn't listening. Rupert will be here soon, she thought. She'd warned Paul she might be late, because Tony wanted her to help at some PR party. Tony, in fact, had asked her up to the conference room to watch Rupert's interview and impress a couple of big advertisers. Rupert was bound to pop in after the program.

I know he sent me the Valentine, thought Sarah, wriggling in ecstasy. He must want to come back.

Rupert, in fact, had had a very tough day. He had had an acrimonious meeting with the UEFA Committee, who were still refusing to let English soccer teams play in Europe next season. He'd had to smooth over the scandal of a Chinese Ping-Pong player caught shoplifting. He'd tried to persuade the Advertising Institute that there was no very good reason why a large condom manufacturer shouldn't sponsor the Rugby League Cup final next year, and coped with the Health Authority up in arms because a famous racing driver had appeared on TV in a Marlboro T-shirt. Because all these meetings ran late, he had only had half an hour to harangue a group of headmasters on the decline of competitive sports in schools, which had been exacerbated by the teachers' strike.

Finally, just as he was leaving for Cotchester, the PM had summoned him, wanting him to lean on the British Lions to cancel their tour of South Africa to encourage the athletes to boycott the European games next month.

Rupert lost his temper. "Politics shouldn't be brought into sports," he snapped. "I'm not going to pressure anyone to boycott anything. You've absolutely no idea what it's like to be an athlete. How would you have liked it if the day you became Prime Minister, someone had ordered you to refuse the job, and you'd been almost certain you'd never get another chance? You can't force people to abide by principles you wouldn't dream of sticking to yourself."

And the Prime Minister had dismissed Rupert very frostily, saying she hoped he'd have second thoughts on the matter.

"I feel like a football at the end of the Cup Final," said Rupert as he collapsed into the black Government car beside Sydney, his official driver. "Everyone's having a go at me today. Who won the three-thirty?"

They discussed racing until the Heathrow exit, then Rupert fell asleep. Sydney liked working for Rupert. He enjoyed the glamour and Rupert's erratic hours brought him spectacular overtime.

Gerald Middleton, Rupert's private secretary, sat in the back seat with the light on, going through Rupert's calendar, streamlining as much as possible, penciling in little notes. He looked at his watch. They were cutting it very fine. Just as well—Rupert wouldn't have time for too many whiskys in Hospitality beforehand.

Cameron went to the control room early. She liked to have half an hour before the program to take a deep breath and think about what she had to do. As she closed the door, the *Jaws* theme belted out from the sound room next door. This joke had been going on ever since she was made Controller of Programs. She found it very unfunny, but, it obviously cracked everyone else up.

Rupert's cool unsmiling face stared out at her from every single monitor screen, except those that would feed in stills and movie clips to illustrate aspects of Rupert's life. On the studio floor they were checking the order of the stills. Up on the monitor came pictures of Rupert winning the World Cup and standing on the Olympic rostrum with his arm in a sling, of his beautiful ex-wife Helen, of Beattie Johnson, Nathalie Perrault, the glamorous French actress, and Amanda Hamilton, wife of the Foreign Secretary. There was Jake Lovell, Rupert's arch-rival on the show-jumping circuit, and his chef d'équipe, Malise Gordon, who'd ended up with Helen. They looked like characters in some glamorous Hollywood miniseries. Declan was clearly hell bent on carnage.

The rest of the crew drifted into the studio after their dinner break. Daysee Butler, weighed down with stop watches and blue mascara and wearing a new pale pink sweatshirt with a large gray cat on the front, took up her position on Cameron's left.

"Rupert'll be here in five minutes. Go and meet him, Daysee, and take him straight to make-up," said Cameron.

On the monitor she could already see Declan slumped in his wizard's chair. Flicking the key switch, she warned him of Rupert's arrival.

"Are you going to have a drink with him beforehand?"

"I am not."

He looks shattered, thought Cameron. He'd lost a lot of weight recently. His black hair was even more threaded with gray. The violet shadows under his eyes reminded her of Patrick. But she mustn't think of Patrick.

"Just do a Maurice Wooton on him, Dee, and Tony'll die happy."

"As long as he dies," growled Declan, "I don't care if he's happy or not."

Rupert, Sydney, and Gerald waited in Reception, looking at photographs of Declan, Charles Fairburn, and James Vereker, who was no longer obscured by the Christmas tree.

"Fuckin' 'ell, it's Farrah Fawcett Majors," said Sydney, as Daysee swayed down the royal blue steel staircase, giving them the benefit of her bouncing strawberry-blonde hair and undulating figure.

"Can I take you straight to makeup, Minister?" said Daysee.

"Can't you and I go to the Cotchester Arms instead?" said Rupert.

Daysee looked at her watch. "I don't think there's time," she said seriously. "You're on in fifteen minutes."

"You're lovely and brown," said the makeup girl, applying a touch of Nouveau Beige to the shine on Rupert's nose and forehead.

"Skiing last weekend," said Rupert.

He wondered for the millionth time why the hell he'd agreed to do this interview. Partly, he knew, it was Cameron taunting him about being afraid of Declan. But, in between frantic hard work and cavorting in bed and on the ski slopes with Nathalie Perrault, he had kept remembering Taggie in tears at Patrick's party over her father's catastrophic finances.

Daysee brought Rupert a dark mahogany whisky, which Gerald immediately took to the makeup department wash basin and diluted with water.

"You haven't eaten all day, Minister."

"Yes, Nanny," said Rupert.

"I'd better take you down," said Daysee.

Gerald straightened Rupert's blue spotted tie.

"For Christ's sake be careful. If he asks you anything you don't like, just say you didn't come on the program to discuss personal matters. Don't bitch up other ministers. Try not to lose your temper."

Rupert grinned. "Anyone would think I was off to my first term at prep school."

Gerald didn't smile. "You behave like it sometimes."

CHAPTER 21

Large orange letters outside the studio said: No Entry when flashing.

"I should think not," said Rupert, draining his whisky and giving the glass to Daysee. "Do they want me to expose myself on air?"

"Christ, he's photogenic," said Cameron in the gallery, as she watched Rupert sit down opposite a tense, unsmiling Declan. "Look at that jawline, and the way his eyes lengthen when he smiles."

"Declan's nervous," said the Vision Mixer, as the sound man tested both men for level. "Listen to the quiver in his voice."

In his earpiece, Declan could now hear Daysee discussing a boyfriend who was coming to dinner tomorrow.

"The recipe says lots of garlic, but I think I'll leave it out. That Rupert's dead attractive, isn't he?"

Declan looked at Rupert, lounging, so relaxed, radiating élitism and privilege with his Red Indian suntan, his beautifully cut suit and his blue silk shirt matching his insolent blue eyes. He thought of Maud sobbing in his arms the night of Patrick's twenty-first, and his resolve hardened.

"Either of you need a touch-up?" asked the makeup girl whisking on with her steel basket.

"I'd love to give you one," said Rupert.

The makeup girl blushed. Rupert leaned forward and looked at the name-tape on one of Declan's odd socks. It said Charlotte Webster-Lee.

"She's a friend of Caitlin's," snapped Declan.

"I think I used to know her mother very well," said Rupert. "Is Charlotte blonde with blue eyes?"

Can't he let up for a second? thought Declan savagely.

Trouble ahead, decided Rupert, as he chatted idly with the crew about Cotchester's chances against Wandsworth United on Saturday. This man's out to bury me.

"One minute to air, Declan," said the Floor Manager.

"Good luck," said Cameron.

"Stand by tape," said Daysee.

The floor manager raised his hand to cue Declan, the red light flashed on, and he was off.

"My guest tonight needs no introduction. He has been described as the greatest show jumper in the world, the handsomest man in England, the icing on the cake of the Tory party. He is, of course, the Minister of Sport, and the MP for Chalford and Bisley, Rupert Campbell-Black.''

Declan waded straight in: "Do you mind being described as the handsomest man in England?''

"Why should I?''

"You're not frightened of being dismissed just as a pretty face?''

"No.''

"Of being dragged into the Tory party just to add an element of much-needed glamour?''

"No, because it's not true.''

"For what other reason could you possibly have been brought in?'' said Declan dismissively.

"I know more about sports than anyone else in the party,'' said Rupert simply. "Having lasted in show jumping for sixteen years on what must be the most grueling circuits in the world, I can cope with the pressures. One day you're king of the castle in show jumping, next day you're bottom of the heap. It's helped me to be resilient about the ups and downs of politics.''

"Do you find politics as satisfying as show jumping?''

"Of course not, but it has its compensations.''

"What are they?''

"The Olympic Fund has just passed four million and we've still got eighteen months to go. Soccer violence is down by seventy percent. Comprehensive schools are gradually upping competitive sports and''—Rupert grinned nastily—"England trounced Ireland at Rugger last Saturday.''

Gerald, sipping Perrier in the conference room, winced. That was a cheap point. Rupert shouldn't have made it.

"The Government makes two hundred million pounds a year from tax on football pools,'' accused Declan, "and yet you're asking the clubs to spend two million this year tightening up their security to reduce football violence. Why don't you give them some help?''

"With footballers earning one hundred thousand pounds a year I think the football clubs can put their own houses in order.''

"Some people feel you're taking a strong line on soccer violence because it's electorally attractive.''

"Do they?'' said Rupert politely.

Shit, thought Declan, I walked right into that one.

Rupert relented: "Just because something is electorally attractive doesn't make it wrong. I want to clean up the stadiums and make them safe places for fathers to take their families again—or the game'll be drained of its support and future talent."

Declan changed tack: "I see from the evening paper that you're backing the British Lions tour of South Africa, thereby giving your blessing to a corrupt and evil regime."

"Rubbish," said Rupert, wondering if the PM was listening. "Sport's outside politics. Athletes are so briefly at their peak, they should be allowed to compete where and against whom they like. It's bloody easy to have principles when you're not making the sacrifices."

And so the program went on, with nice bitchy repartee flashing back and forth, but on the whole Rupert deflected Declan's needling easily.

Then Declan said: "You've been described as the Prime Minister's blue-eyed boy."

"Boy's pushing it. I'm thirty-seven," said Rupert, "but as I've got blue eyes, I don't see how I could be anything else."

"She seems to prefer good-looking men."

"She'd need her head examined if she didn't," said Rupert coldly. "Do you prefer dogs yourself?"

"You've always got on well with women," said Declan. "Wasn't it Amanda Hamilton," a large glamorous picture of the Foreign Secretary's wife appeared on the screen, "who drew you into politics?"

"And her husband Rollo," said Rupert quickly. "They both encouraged me."

Despite repeated probing from Declan, Rupert refused to give an inch on the subject of Amanda Hamilton.

"It was Mrs. Hamilton," said Declan pointedly, "who drove you down to your first meeting with your constituency. Do you find a conflict between your ministerial and constituency duties?"

"Of course," snapped Rupert. "I don't have enough time to devote to my constituency. They come first; they're the people who voted me in. I've lived in the area all my life, and I don't want a four-lane highway half a mile from Penscombe any more than they do."

Gerald put his head in his hands.

Tony, purring with pleasure, was pacing up and down the conference room carpet. "Rupert is beginning to lose his temper," he said softly.

I can't help it, thought Sarah, I still love him.

"Was it merely lust for power that drove you into politics?" asked Declan dismissively.

"It certainly wasn't the money, or the free time," snapped Rupert. "Most ministers are hopelessly overworked. The civil service want control and pile work on to keep us quiet. Sometimes you get home at three in the morning after a session in the House, then still have to go through your notes. That's when the trouble starts. You're so zonked you OK a nuclear power station in your constituency and six months later you realize to your horror what you've done. I'm very lucky. I have an exceptional private secretary in Gerald Middleton. He does all my donkey work, and raps my knuckles if I go too far. I'm also lucky," went on Rupert, yawning ostentatiously, "because on the circuit I learned to grab sleep at any time."

"With anyone?" said Declan. He was taunting Rupert now.

"No," drawled Rupert. "I've always been selective."

"That's not what your press clippings say."

A still of Samantha Freebody, the starlet who'd told all about sleeping with Rupert while he was married, appeared on the screen, followed by a succession of beauties including Amanda Hamilton's daughter, Georgina, Beattie Johnson, and Nathalie Perrault.

"Coming to 2. We must catch Rupert's reaction," said Cameron. "Take 2."

But Rupert's face was expressionless.

Declan picked up a clipping from the table: "One Gloucestershire peer has described you as 'rather a nasty virus, that everyone's wife caught sooner or later.' "

"If you'd seen his wife, it's definitely later," said Rupert lightly, but there was a muscle going in his cheek.

"With the advent of AIDS, don't you feel you should mend your ways?"

"Sure," said Rupert. "I'm giving up casual sex for Lent."

Tony was getting restless, and, picking up a telephone, dialed the control room:

"Tell Declan to stop farting around,"

"Tony says sink your claws in, Declan," Cameron told Declan. "Get him on to cruelty."

Declan squared his shoulders. "Over the past two years you've expressed sympathy for the football rioters."

Rupert stared at his shoes. "Most of them probably led appallingly dull lives during the week. Many are out of work, or just turning lathes in a factory. The stadiums are their stage, their chance to vent the frustrations of the week. They generally riot because they're losing, or there's been a bad penalty at half-time."

"You were a bad loser, weren't you?" said Declan gently.

It was the voice of Torquemada, the pale intent face of the Jesuit priest.

Rupert looked wary: "What's the point of competing—except to win?"

"Even to the extent of beating up your horses?"

Rupert's eyes narrowed, but he just stared back at Declan.

"Look at this picture," said Declan, showing a still of a horse so thin it was almost a skeleton.

"This was one of your horses, Macaulay. You beat him up so badly he wouldn't jump for you and then sold him off to be starved in the Middle East. And your deadly enemy Jake Lovell nursed the horse back to health, and entered it in the World Championship."

"Coming to 2, take 2," screamed Cameron, frantic once again to get the reaction on Rupert's face. But once again it was completely blank. Only his long fingers clenched around the glass of water on the table betrayed any emotion.

"He's going to walk out," said Tony happily.

"Have you got any regrets you treated your horses so badly?"

"I didn't treat them all badly or they wouldn't have jumped so well. Of course I regret it, but it helped me understand the football rioters; out of work, their fathers out of work, often their grandfathers too. Out of sheer frustration at not winning, they resort to violence."

"You were in work."

"I know. There was really no excuse."

"You treated women very badly in the past."

Rupert shrugged helplessly. "I liked winning there too."

"Jake Lovell," went on Declan remorselessly, "was your arch rival because you bullied him at school. He finally got his revenge by running off with your wife, Helen, in the middle of the 1980 Olympics. How did you feel at the time?"

Rupert'll kill Declan in a minute, thought Gerald in panic. No one's ever dared ask him these questions.

"I was principally outraged that she should distract me and Jake, when we should have been concentrating on a team gold," said Rupert.

"But you still got your medal, despite dislocating your shoulder, and riding with one arm."

"That was just to show them that, even riding one man short and one man injured, we could beat the whole world."

Prompted by Declan, Rupert went on to talk about the Olympics and Rocky, the horse he'd won a gold medal on, who still lived at Penscombe.

"I'm so cruel to Rocky," drawled Rupert, "that he has the entire run of my garden, and spends his time trampling over the flower beds and peering in at the drawing-room window."

I like this man. Why I am trying to crucify him? thought Declan.

I like this man, even though he's trying to crucify me, thought Rupert.

Tony went into the next-door office to call Cameron, so the sponsors wouldn't hear him.

"Declan's gone soft, for Christ's sake. Tell him to fucking nail him."

"What did you feel," Declan was asking now, "when Helen split up with Jake and married your old team manager?"

"Well, I didn't let off fireworks. It was like one's childhood sweetheart marrying one's headmaster."

"Do you mind her being happy now?"

"Not at all," said Rupert in surprise. "It's better for the children. Anyway she deserved it; she had a rough time with me."

"In what way?"

"Show jumping and marriage don't mix. I was never there when she needed me. When she was having Marcus I was stuck on an Alpine pass. Then the dogs were always getting in the bed."

"Yes," said Declan. "People say you were fonder of your black Labrador, Badger, than of Helen."

"I had him first," said Rupert flatly. "He lived with me six years after she left me. *He* never criticized or tried to improve me."

"Is that what you want from women, uncritical adulation?"

Rupert grinned. "Probably."

The questions were still barbed, but the animosity had gone.

"Your name's been linked since your divorce with some dazzling women. Have you ever thought of marrying again?"

"Just because I enjoy flying on Concorde doesn't mean I want to buy the plane."

Out of the corner of his eye, Declan could see the Floor Manager holding up his hand for three minutes.

"When you get any free time, what's the thing you like doing best?"

Rupert put his head on one side: "I thought this was supposed to be a family program."

"You must have some hobbies," said Declan hastily.

"Hunting, shooting, fishing," said Rupert.

"All the blood sports." Declan's lip was curling.

"Not all. I didn't include being interviewed by you on television."

"Touché," said Declan laughing. "Who are your heroes? If you could choose, who would you like to meet in an afterlife?"

For a second Rupert seemed to have difficulty in speaking: "I'd like to see Badger again," he muttered.

"Oh, how sweet," said Daysee, who was now revving up for her most important moment: pressing the cue switch. The Floor Manager was making wind-up signals to Declan.

"Looking back on your sixteen years in show jumping, can you remember the hardest thing you had to do? Was it getting the first bronze, winning the Kings Cup three years running, clinching the team gold in 1980, or finally winning the World Championship?"

There was another long pause.

"What was the hardest thing?" Declan urged him.

Just for a second the despair showed through on Rupert's face.

"The thing that nearly killed me," he said bleakly, "was giving it up."

As Schubert's Fifth Symphony pounded out and the credits came up, Declan most uncharacteristically could be seen getting out of his chair and shaking Rupert by the hand. As soon as they were off the air, Cameron came down onto the studio floor. Maybe it was because she was blinking in the unaccustomed light after the darkness of the control room, but for once her yellow eyes seemed to have lost all their aggression.

"Great program, Declan. Best you've done for us—and you were marvelous." Flushing slightly she turned to Rupert. "Declan threw you some really tough questions and you handled them so well."

"I hope my boss thinks so," said Rupert. "Coming on your program's rather like being interrogated by the IRA. I was expecting electrodes any minute."

Cameron had amazing legs, he noticed, as she walked upstairs in front of them.

Up in Hospitality, Tony Baddingham was feeling far from hospitable, but had to restrain himself in front of his two big sponsors, who were terrific fans both of Declan and Rupert, and who felt they had just witnessed a great gladiatorial contest. With a shaking hand, the normally teetotal Gerald helped himself to a triple whisky.

"Wasn't it wonderful?" said Sarah, busily powdering her nose and undoing another pearl button of her little gray dress. "Declan brought out a really vulnerable side of Rupert. I'm sure he just needs the love of a good woman."

And the attention of a whole harem of mistresses as well, thought Gerald. He had disapproved very strongly of Rupert's affair with Sarah, regarding it as political dynamite. He hoped it wasn't going to start again.

But, as Rupert walked in with Declan and Cameron, Sarah rushed up and flung her arms round his neck, giving him the benefit of unsupported breasts and half a bucket of Anaïs Anaïs. "Darling, you were wonderful, so honest."

"Not much else I could do without walking off the set."

"When am I going to see you?" murmured Sarah. "Thank you so much for your Valentine."

But before Rupert had time to answer her, bloody Gerald muscled in.

"I'm sorry, Minister, I never dreamed Declan'd go that far."

Rupert raised an eyebrow at Gerald's glass of whisky.

"Are we in trouble?"

"I don't know," said Gerald. "The Press are going beserk already. I told the switchboard to say you'd left. We'll have to smuggle you out by a side door."

Tony, having introduced the big sponsors to Rupert, went and vented his fury on Declan.

"I thought I told you to fucking well crucify him."

"I tried to," said Declan coldly, "but he was too good for me," and, turning on his heel, he headed toward the bar.

Seeing Tony coming to give her an earful, Cameron grabbed a plate of quiche and took it over to Rupert who, to Sarah's fury, turned away from the group to talk to her. After the tension of the interview, he was gripped by the lust that always used to overwhelm him after a big show-jumping class. In the old days he would have screwed a groom or a show-jumping groupie in the back of his horse trailer. Tonight he was sure he could choose among Daysee, Sarah or Cameron. Daysee was too thick, Sarah too possessive, Cameron on the other hand had a reckless, scrawny nymphomania and screwing her would have the added charm of irritating the hell out of Tony.

"Well," he said icily, "I had to box bloody clever to get out of that one. I suppose Tony put Declan up to it."

"I'm sorry," said Cameron.

Glancing up, she found she couldn't tear her eyes away.

"Being sorry isn't enough," said Rupert softly. "I'm going to get my own back."

Cameron gasped. She could see Tony bearing down on them.

"I was wondering if you'd like to come on another program? It's the third Thursday in March," she stammered.

"And have open-heart surgery all over again without an anaesthetic? No thanks. Besides it's Cheltenham."

"It's not until the evening," said Cameron quickly. "All we'd want you to do is judge Miss Corinium Television with Declan. There are some beautiful girls entered."

"I might just be able to drag myself away," said Rupert, "as long as you promise me a night in the Cotchester Arms with the winner as second prize."

"What's the first prize?" said Cameron, knowing the answer.

"A night in the Cotchester Arms with you," said Rupert, "and my God I'd make you walk differently in the morning."

It was several seconds before they both realized that a tense-looking Gerald was tapping Rupert on the arm.

"Telephone. It's the PM."

"Oh Christ," said Rupert.

"Well done," said the Prime Minister in her rich deep voice that always sounded like Carnation Milk pouring out of a can. "We were very proud of you."

"You were?" said Rupert in amazement.

"Well what else could you have done, faced with that spiteful little pinko? You handled him very well. That interview will do us a lot of good in the opinion polls."

"Good God," said Rupert putting down the telephone, "she actually liked it."

"Was that really the PM?" said one of the big sponsors in awe.

"Did she mention me?" said James, who'd rolled up from a Save-the-Aged fund-raising party.

"I've booked a table for us at the Horn of Plenty at nine-thirty," said Cameron casually to Rupert. "The cars are waiting downstairs."

Despite her off-hand manner, Rupert noticed she was quivering with expectancy, like a greyhound ordered to sit when the woolly rabbit sets off around the track. Then he caught a glimpse of Declan, looking gray and utterly shattered. He remembered Taggie's tears on New Year's Eve.

"Sweet of you," he said to Cameron, "but Declan and I are going back to Penscombe. We've got things to discuss."

Aware of Tony watching her, Cameron hid her bitter disappointment. Being very young, Sarah had no such reserve. "You can't go," she wailed. "We'll be far too many girls."

"James can come instead," said Tony smoothly. "That's if he hasn't got to rush home to Lizzie."

"Of course not," said James.

"That's rather uncaring of you," said Sarah sulkily.

"Work comes first," said James sanctimoniously. "And you haven't told me what you thought of my Valentine, Sarah. I thought it was rather nice that it was sold to raise money for the Cat's Protection League."

Back at Penscombe, two Jack Russells, a young black Labrador, two springer spaniels, and a blue lurcher threw themselves on Rupert in ecstasy. Once inside, Rupert whisked Gerald and Declan past tapestried hunting scenes and portraits of ancestors, only pausing to point out a huge oil painting of Badger, into the kitchen, which was low-beamed with a flagstone floor, and a window looking over the valley. As Gerald found a bottle of whisky and three glasses and Rupert investigated the fridge and the pantry, Declan looked at the pictures on the wall. They were mostly paintings of dogs and horses and framed photographs of two incredibly beautiful children.

"That's Tabitha," said Rupert, pointing to a little girl on a pony festooned with ribbons.

"She's magic," said Declan.

"She's doing bloody well in junior classes already."

"Does the boy ride?" said Declan, looking at the sensitive, nervous face and the huge eyes.

"No. He gets asthma, but he skis well, and he's extremely clever." There was a slight edge to Rupert's voice.

"Can I have a look around?" asked Declan.

"Go ahead," said Rupert.

As he wandered through beautiful pastel room after pastel room admiring the incredible pictures: a Romney, a Gainsborough, a Lely, a Thomas Lawrence, and two Stubbs for starters, and the lovingly polished furniture, he thought the whole house was like a museum, beautiful but crying out for someone to live in it, or like a horse, constantly bridled, saddled, and groomed to perfection, but with no one to ride it.

Finding the library, Declan was lost in admiration. He'd never seen such books in a private house—first editions of Scott, Dickens, Trollope, Wordsworth, Keats, and Shelley, and a whole set of Oscar

Wilde, and other books so rare there couldn't be more than half-a-dozen copies in the country.

Half an hour later Rupert found him, oblivious of time, immersed in a first edition of *Middlemarch*.

"Supper. Christ, you can't read in this light!"

"Can I come and live here?" said Declan, shaking his head in bewildered reverence.

"Borrow anything you like whenever you want to. No one else reads them. Helen pretended to, but never seemed to get beyond the first chapter."

Laid out on the kitchen table was smoked salmon, brown bread, gulls' eggs, and half a heated-up chicken pie. Gerald had also made a tomato salad and fried some potatoes.

"It's very good of you," mumbled Declan. "I couldn't have faced dinner with Tony."

"Not up to Taggie's standard, I'm afraid," said Rupert, adding casually, "How is she?"

"Very pleased with Gertrude's Valentine."

"Oh, she got it?" said Rupert. "Ironic that the first Valentine I ever sent in my life should be to a dog."

They talked about politics, horses, and sports, and then Rupert filled Declan in on local gossip, and some of the early history of Penscombe. It was not until they'd both got pretty drunk, and Gerald had gone to bed, that Rupert asked how things were at Corinium.

"Bloody awful," said Declan.

"Tony?"

Declan nodded wearily. "I seem to go from Baddingham to worse."

"He didn't look very happy after the program."

"He wasn't. He wanted me to carve you up."

Rupert grinned. "You had a bloody good try. I know why Tony was out for my blood, but why you? Just because I'm a Tory?"

"No, for screwing up Tag at Valerie Jones's dinner party."

"Ah."

"And I thought you were after her at Patrick's birthday party."

Suddenly Declan didn't want to mention Maud.

Rupert inhaled deeply on his cigar. "Would that have been so bad?"

"She's eighteen and desperately insecure," said Declan roughly. "She's simply not equipped to cope. You'd break her like a moth caught in the typewriter keys."

"Ouch," said Rupert wincing.

"I saw them all slavering this evening," went on Declan. "Sarah, Cameron, that imbecile Daysee. You could have had any of them. Just spare Taggie."

Rupert, however, was reluctant to drop the subject.

"But she seems incredibly competent. She cooked brilliantly for Valerie and she coped with your party on New Year's Eve virtually single-handed."

"Oh she's competent enough," said Declan. "You mustn't assume people with dyslexia are thick, just because they have difficulty reading and writing. Albert Einstein, Leonardo da Vinci, and Thomas Edison were all dyslexic. So was Gerald Patton. He could never learn the alphabet or his tables by heart."

"Good God," said Rupert in alarm. "So we can expect to see Taggie commanding the Third Army at any minute."

Declan grinned.

Rupert filled up their glasses with brandy.

"Is Tony really giving you a hard time?"

"Septic tankwise, I'm up to here." Declan drew a finger across his throat.

He got up and wandered slightly unsteadily toward the window.

"Beautiful house this. Where's The Priory from here?"

Rupert pointed to the left, where, through a spiky fuzz of trees, a light was burning. "Taggie's still awake, that's her bedroom," he added without thinking. Then, when Declan instantly looked alarmed, "It's all right. I had to bodily remove some drunk from her room the night of your party because Taggie wanted to go to bed— alone."

As Rupert joined Declan beside the window, dogs, sprawled all over the floor, sleepily thumped their tails.

"D'you know what I've always wanted to do?" said Rupert idly. "Buy those woods below your house."

"Pretty useless piece of land," said Declan.

"Fifty yards to the right of the stream you could make the most perfect dry ski slope. You wouldn't see it from the road. It'd be hidden by trees on both sides."

"How much d'you reckon it's worth?"

"About thirty-five grand," lied Rupert.

"Seems a helluva lot," said Declan, stroking Jack Russells with both hands.

"You could still walk through the rest of the woods if you wanted to," said Rupert.

But Declan wasn't listening. Thirty-five grand would get me off the hook for the moment with the tax man, he thought, and pay the electricity bill and Caitlin's tuition.

"Think about it, anyway," said Rupert. "You also need a day off. Come out hunting on Saturday. I'll lend you a horse."

When Declan finally got back to The Priory, he left all the car lights on, flattened several purple crocuses on the edge of the lawn, and drove slap through a flower bed.

Waiting for him on the stairs, both looking equally disapproving, were Taggie and Gertrude.

"Why," said Taggie, "were you so g-g-gratuitously beastly to Rupert?"

CHAPTER 22

On the third Monday in March Cameron Cook had the sadistic idea of summoning the entire Corinium staff to a power breakfast in Studio 1 at eight o'clock in the morning. While they blearily consumed croissants and orange juice, Tony gave them a rousing pep talk on how each one of them could personally help retain the franchise.

"This is a very exciting time," said Tony heartily. "Dorothy Dove" and "Four Men went to Mow" have yet again been nominated for BAFTA Awards. Our new series on the elderly, "Young as You Feel," starts next week. And we're delighted to announce that our new anchor is going to be Naomi Hargreaves, who, as you know, climbed Everest last year at the age of sixty-five.

"Our new syndicated quiz, 'Master Dog,' to find the canine brain of Britain, starts taping on Wednesday. The new series of 'Four Men went to Mow' starts at the end of April and a performance of Michael Tippett's *Midsummer Marriage* will be recorded in Cotchester Park in early June. James Vereker's and Sarah Stratton's new afternoon program starts a week from Monday." Tony smiled warmly at Sarah, and received a black look from Cameron. "And we all wish them the best of luck.

"Finally, *Midsummer Night's Dream*," Tony added with a sigh of relief, "is virtually in the can. We anticipate two days reshooting, tomorrow and Wednesday, leaving Studio 1 free for Miss Corinium Television on Thursday."

To put Declan down, Tony had deliberately not mentioned his program, but now, looking around the packed studio, he discovered to his fury that Declan didn't appear to be present.

Declan, in fact, was at home, having got up at five to wrestle with his Yeats biography. Looking at the pile of scribbled notes and typed pages on his desk, he felt like Vidal Sassoon confronted by the wild woman of the West with fifty years of burrs and tangles in her hair. He wished he had Vidal Sassoon's skills. He was so tired, he hadn't had an original thought for weeks. Matters had not been helped by Grace finally walking out because Declan had bawled her out for drinking all his whisky. Maud, furious at losing her ally and sparring partner, blamed Declan for the whole thing and was refusing to talk to him.

His black gloom was interrupted by his secretary, Ursula, calling to say she had flu.

"Poor thing. Stay in bed," said Declan. "Can I bring you anything?"

"No, but I'm terribly sorry, I forgot to remind you about Cameron's power breakfast," said Ursula.

At Corinium Tony was winding up his peroration: "I have no doubt that Corinium will retain the franchise, but I cannot remind you too strongly that this year we are on display. The IBA will not only be monitoring our program more closely, and examining our finances and our staff relations, but they will be looking to see how we conduct ourselves both as individuals and as a company. Any complaints from a local body, pressure group or a restaurateur will count as the blackest mark. Seb Burrows' birthday party last week, for example, completely broke up the Beaufort room at the Cotchester Arms. If you ever have another birthday Seb—" Tony's big smile flashed on— "you'll be fired."

Realizing some sort of joke had been made, the staff tittered feebly.

"And remember above all, appearance does matter."

Exactly on cue, Declan walked in, deathly pale, hair unbrushed, stubble blacking his jaw, and his sweater inside out.

"I'm sorry, Tony," he said, "I forgot."

"We've just finished," said Tony coolly. "I'm afraid you've missed the boat, but that's nothing unusual."

"Where are you going?" shouted Cameron, as Declan turned towards the exit.

"Home," snapped Declan, "I've got a lot of lying down to do."

* * *

The next day, March 21st, was the first day of Spring. The Head of
News sent a crew off to photograph lambs playing in a field. James
wore a new primrose yellow tracksuit to urge viewers to join his
new sponsored Slim-for-Spring campaign to raise money for heart
research, and Declan came in to interview Guilini. The program, for
once, was being recorded as Guilini was flying to New York for a
concert straight afterwards.

As he was intending to take Thursday off to go to the Gold Cup with
Rupert, Declan went into the office on Wednesday to wade through
a mountain of mail. After the row with Maud about the telephone
and liquor bills she'd hidden behind the recipe books in the kitchen,
Corinium, with all its crises, seemed the quieter place. The tax man
had also called the day before to collect twenty thousand pounds,
and, being told Declan was out, said he would call again next day,
which was another reason for not hanging around at home. He was
beginning to think there was no alternative except to sell Rupert the
woods. The only thought that sustained him was that he was due for
a two-month break at the end of April, but, as things were going,
he'd have to spend the time off doing programs in America to raise
some cash.

He was also aware that his interviews had been very lackluster
recently. The one on Rupert had attracted huge ratings and newspaper coverage, but Declan in retrospect was bitterly ashamed of it,
knowing that initially he'd let personal animosity overwhelm his
detachment. Since then, the program had had the bite of a rubber
duck.

God, he was tired. He looked at the mountain of mail, a lot of
it probably bills. Ursula was still out sick. He could smell today's
special, boeuf bourguignon, drifting down from the cafeteria, as could
the contestants of "Master Dog" who were barking hungrily in Studio 2.

He picked up the first memo. *"The Gay and Lesbian Sub-Committee of the ACTT has been re-named the Sexuality Sub-Committee."*

On cue, Charles Fairburn drifted in, having just collected his
expenses.

"Come and have a drink at the Bar Sinister."

Declan shook his head. "Got to deal with all this."

"Never grumble about fan mail," chided Charles. "Think of poor
me going off to Southampton first thing tomorrow to supervise Holy
Communion for the Deaf. Have you been asked to Tony's bash for

Badminton? He's put the little red ram logo on the corner of all the invitations so he can put the whole thing on his expense account."

"He won't ask me," said Declan grimly.

"No, you are a bit out of favor, poor dear," said Charles sympathetically, "and you work harder than any of us. I'm expecting to get the Old Queen's Award for Lack of Industry any minute. That's better; at least you're smiling. And I'll tell you something else to cheer you up even more. In Studio 2 you'll find a lot of lovable mongrels rummaging for chocolates which have all melted under the lights, on caring James's pastel sofa. James is going to be livid when he gets back from another three-hour lunch with Mrs. Stratton."

The telephone rang. "Corinium Waifs and Strays," said Charles, picking it up. "Oh, hi, Madden dear. All right, I'll send him along. Tony's leaving for London in twenty minutes, thank God," he told Declan, "but he wants a word with you first. I'd take the slow elevator. He's in a vile mood."

Tony, in fact, seemed in an excellent mood, purring away like a great cat about to enjoy an extended game of mouse-taunting.

"Ah, Declan. Shut the door behind you and sit down."

As usual the central heating was turned up so high Declan felt he was having a hot flash.

"I wonder if you'd explain this."

Tony threw Declan a picture postcard of a huge crocodile with gaping jaws. On the other side was scrawled in huge black writing: "Here's a picture of your boss. Bloody hot here. If I don't talk to you before, I'll pick you up at The Priory at eleven o'clock. Rupert."

There was no address or stamp.

"Who the fuck opened this?" asked Declan.

"We open all mail during franchise year," said Tony smoothly. "Just to check whether any of our staff are being propositioned by other franchise contenders."

"This place gets more like the KGB every minute." Declan made no attempt to hide his rage.

"I also see you've taken up élitist sports," went on Tony, happily handing Declan the *Daily Express*, which was folded back at a picture of Rupert and Declan out fox hunting.

"Burying the hatchet after their recent encounter on 'Declan,'" said the caption.

Tony shook his head. "You're not keeping very good company, Declan."

"Then why has Rupert been asked to judge Miss Corinium tomorrow?"

"That's a slipup of Cameron's. It won't happen again. There's also a piece in yesterday's *Standard* quoting you as saying you've given up hope for Lent. Not a very positive attitude. Be a bit more careful when you talk to the Press in the future."

Tony got up and wandered toward the bar.

"Like a drink?"

Declan shook his head.

"Just as well," said Tony, pouring himself one. "I gather you were plastered when you interviewed Guilini yesterday. I am very worried about your ratings. Only ten million for the first week in March. Cameron was at a network meeting yesterday and they're now considering what was unthinkable a few months ago, shifting your program from prime time to perhaps a ten-thirty or even an eleven o'clock slot."

"That's insane," said Declan. "We only got ten million because the B.B.C. have moved 'Dallas' opposite us. We'll get it back."

"I doubt it," said Tony brutally. "Quite honestly you've lost your authority, Declan. There was a time when every interview made the front page of every newspaper."

"I will next week. Bob Geldof's coming on."

"Bit old hat—all that famine stuff."

Tony tipped back his chair, stretched his legs, and gazed at Declan considerately. "I'm so sorry," he said. "I know how depressing it is for stars when they drop down from Number One. I do hope you're not overdoing things. Why are your hands shaking?" He looked complacently down at his own beautifully manicured hands. "Mine don't shake."

Declan stood up. "That's because you don't have to work with people like you," he snarled.

Out of the window he could see a posse of lovable mongrels scampering across the water meadows, pursued by a panting camera crew.

Tony also rose to his feet: "I'm trying to be sympathetic," he said in a voice that froze even Declan's blood, "and all I get is abuse."

He pressed the button. Miss Madden appeared so quickly she must have been listening at the door.

"Declan's leaving," said Tony imperiously.

Back in his office, trembling from head to foot, Declan got a bottle of whisky from the desk drawer and, pouring two inches into a paper cup, drained it. The first thing that really registered in his mail was a typescript and a letter from Patrick. He had finished his play and sent it to Declan to read:

"*Dearest Pa,*
I've been poisonous enough about your stuff in the past,
now I'm going to get a taste of my own medicine (as Cameron
would say). Please read it and tell me the truth. Give my love
to Cameron, if you're still speaking. See you next week.
Love Patrick"

Patrick, Declan reflected, was a lot better at getting down to things than he was. He was about to start reading when there was a knock on the door. It was Miss Madden, red as a beet, bringing him a cup of coffee and two roast beef sandwiches.

"You don't eat enough."

"You mean I'm drinking too much. That's terribly sweet of you, darling. How much do I owe you?"

"It's a present," said Miss Madden, blushing even more deeply. "As Lord B's gone to town and Ursula's sick, I thought you might like some help with your mail. I can polish that off in no time. I expect it's mostly from fans."

"I doubt it."

"Don't take Lord B's remarks too much to heart. He's only try-ing to goad you. Please don't walk out. We need you here."

Declan was touched, and dutifully sat down and went through his mail. When Miss Madden had taken it away, he felt unable to settle down to Bob Geldof's clippings. Wandering down the corri-dor, he found James and Sarah recording their first afternoon pro-gram in front of a small geriatric audience. James was interviewing a large woman in a pin-striped suit and a monocle. Insufficiently briefed, having spent far too long lunching with Sarah, he was fran-tically leafing through his notes to find out something about her. At last he turned up Deirdre's list of questions. Christ, she was a fucking composer. James was tone-deaf.

"A very good afternoon and welcome to Dame Edith Spink," he said.

The audience clapped lethargically.

"May I call you Edith?"

"You may, but my name's actually Enid," said the lady composer.

Flustered, James consulted his notes. He'd kill Deirdre after the show.

"I'd like to say, Enid, how much I personally have enjoyed all your symphonies."

"I've only written one," snapped Dame Enid.

From the darkness by the door, Declan was beginning to enjoy himself. Dame Enid Spink was an extremely distinguished musician, probably only second to Michael Tippett as a composer in Britain. A notorious lesbian and a feminist, she was already furious that Corinium was doing Michael Tippett's opera this year rather than one of hers.

"You've just visited the States, Enid," ploughed on James, "to conduct your newest opera. Er, what do the Americans think of your work?"

"Bloody stupid question," said Dame Enid. "I didn't ask them all. There are thirty-five million, you know."

Bitch, thought James furiously. I'll fix her.

"Many critics," he read from Deirdre's notes, "say this latest opera of yours isn't up to standard."

Crash came Dame Enid's hands down on her wide-apart pin-striped thighs. "Name four," she thundered.

"Pardon?" stammered James.

"Name four of those critics," persisted Dame Enid.

James couldn't. Dame Enid stalked off the set.

James mopped his brow, thanking Christ the program wasn't live. He was lucky that it was not until ten minutes later that Cameron put in an appearance and therefore entirely missed the encounter.

Now it was Sarah's turn. Her task was to interview some female soccer players and a group of lady buyers in suits with pussy-cat bows on whether it was still a man's world, followed by a studio discussion in which James would whiz around the audience with a roving mike.

Although there was already an extremely competent director, Cameron, in her role as Program Controller, couldn't resist putting her oar in, making an already nervous Sarah fluff her introductory patter over and over again.

"Thank you so much for spending March with us," she told the tittering audience after the tenth take.

Sarah fluffed her patter again.

"This is an elaborate way to tell us you're quitting, Sarah," taunted Cameron to more titters. Sarah looked imploringly at James, who, sitting on the yellow sofa, suddenly seemed very interested in his cuticles. Sarah fluffed the patter again.

"You'd better shape up," Cameron told her.

Declan had seen enough. "Stop being a fucking bitch," he yelled, marching up to Cameron.

The crew, grinning broadly, gave him a round of applause. The audience, wildly excited to see such a megastar and thinking it was part of the show, started to clap and cheer too.

"How dare you!" screamed Cameron over the din. "I'm going home."

"Put the kettle on," the Floor Manager shouted after her. "We'll all be around for tea in half an hour."

Down the steps swarmed the audience, crowding around Declan, clamoring for his autograph.

"You're very like yourself," said one lady.

"Thank you so much, Declan," said Sarah tearfully.

"Now you can get on with the show," said Declan, beating a hasty retreat.

Utterly dispirited after his outburst, Declan returned to his office and, getting out the whisky bottle, settled down to read Patrick's play. As he finished it, he was equally consumed with pleasure and despair, because the play was quite simply marvelous: incredibly original, funny, very moving, slightly overdone, but possessing all the vigor and fearlessness of youth. Reading it made Declan realize once again what an utter fuckup he'd made of his own career.

Emptying the bottle, very drunk now, he wandered into the corridor, ending up in the big studio where they were shooting the last retake of *Midsummer Night's Dream*.

Even the cardboard trees seemed to pulsate with midsummer heat and enchantment. Declan stood in the shadows, tears pouring down his face, impossibly moved by the poetry. Would *he* ever write anything good again?

Feeling a tap on his shoulder, he jumped violently. It was Cameron. Rubbing his eyes frantically, he followed her out into the corridor.

"I'm sorry I came on strong this afternoon," she said. " 'Four Men went to Mow' starts again next month. I guess I'm uptight."

"I guess you are," said Declan ungraciously. "Pick someone your own weight next time. Sarah could be very good if you don't frighten her off too soon."

He stalked into his office, gathered up the pages of Patrick's play, and chucked the whisky bottle into the wastebasket with a clang.

"As Tony's opening people's mail, I suppose he's frisking wastebaskets as well," he snarled at Cameron. "That should really convince him I'm drinking too much. I imagine it was you who told him I was drunk on the program last night."

Cameron blushed. "No way."

"Well, I wasn't." He went on gathering papers together.

"What's that?" said Cameron anxious to change the subject.

"Patrick's play."

"Any good?"

"Exceptional. You'll be sorry one day you passed him up."

"I'm sure you won't be," snapped Cameron.

"No." Declan's brooding eyes looked at her contemptuously. "I can't imagine anything that would have filled me with more horror. He sent his love by the way."

Cameron tried again: "Look, I know it's screwing you up working here."

"I'm surprised you talk in the present tense," growled Declan, going toward the door.

"Don't forget you're judging Miss Corinium Television tomorrow? We want you and Rupert here by seven," said Cameron.

"About all I'm fit for," said Declan wearily, and walked out.

Declan was not a vain man, but if anything could have boosted his self-confidence it was that day at Cheltenham. Whenever he put his nose out of Freddie's tent to have a bet, he was mobbed, and the combination of him and Rupert together among that horse-loving, strongly Irish crowd, caused almost as much excitement as the returning winner of the Gold Cup. To add to everyone's high spirits, Freddie's horse danced home an effortless winner in the second race. Nor was it anyone's fault that, as a result of a freak snowstorm, the Gold Cup was postponed for an hour, or that Rupert had bet across the board on the winner. Consequently Rupert and Declan got unbelievably drunk and didn't reach Cotchester until seven forty-five.

"Is this the forest of Hard-On?" said Rupert, as he tripped over a lot of stacked-up cardboard trees outside Studio 1.

Cameron, Tony, and James, who was emceeing the program in a midnight-blue dinner jacket with a dinky rose-pink bow tie, were all absolutely livid they were so late.

"It's a disgrace," stormed Cameron. "There's no time to brief you. Go into my office and you'll have a chance to meet the other judges and the fifteen finalists before we go on the air."

The other judges were a male pop star called Big Lil, the Mayor of Cotchester, the head of the local tourist board, and a naval officer called Ron, who'd just returned from sailing around the world single-handed.

"After a girl-less ten months," whispered Rupert, "he'll have to be lashed to his chair."

"We're now selecting the last seven," Cameron told the judges. "You should look for the kind of girl you can take anywhere."

"In the broom closet, under the mulberry tree," said Rupert.

As each girl sidled in, Tony and Cameron fired questions at them. Miss Bisley came from Cotchester. Miss Painswick from Bisley. Miss Chipping Sodbury was so well stacked she could have won a National Front award.

When Miss Wooton-under-Edge said her ambition was to run a home for homeless pussies, Rupert and Declan got serious giggles. Fortunately the room was ill-lit.

"They all talk like Valerie Jones," said Rupert.

Having selected the last seven, they all adjourned to Studio 1, which was now organized with tables, at which sat the so-called invited audience, and the contest was on the air.

The fifteen contestants then teetered on in bathing suits and four-inch heels. Although the judges had already preselected their last seven, as far as the audience, the contestants, and the viewers were concerned, they were picking them now. Seeing the girls in bathing suits for the first time, however, Declan and Rupert realized some of the ones they *hadn't* chosen had much better figures and legs, and noisily tried to change their minds.

"You're supposed to be picking the first three now," hissed Cameron.

As Declan and Rupert rushed out to have a pee in the commercial break, Rupert grabbed a bottle of champagne from one of the tables, shoving it under his coat. Cameron, waiting in the corridor as they came out of the men's room, shoved them into an empty dressing room. "Big Lil's going to sing his new single while the last seven change. You two stay in here and behave yourselves."

Rupert put on Bottom's head, which was hanging on a hook, and read out a notice on the wall: "We apologize to all performers for any inconvenience caused by accommodating them in a temporary dressing room."

Declan took a swig from Rupert's bottle. Totally forgetting they were wearing mikes, they starting discussing the contest.

"Why's James Vereker wearing red shoes?" asked Rupert.

"Must be the blood running down from all the people sticking knives in his back," said Declan.

"What d'you think of Miss Bisley's bottom?" asked Rupert from the furry depths of his ass's head.

"Terrific," said Declan. "What d'you think of Miss Chipping Sodbury's tits?"

"Wonderful, but not as good as Miss Wooton-under-Edge's crotch."

"Which one d'you think Tony Baddingham's fucking?" said Declan.

"The whole bunch," said Rupert, collapsing on the bed with laughter.

Declan leaned against the wall, shaking.

Next minute a chalk-white sound man erupted through the door to tell them they were being overheard by everyone in the control room, including Cameron and Tony. After that, Declan found, events became slightly hazy. Miss Bisley was crowned Miss Corinium Television and even wept a few tears, but not enough to streak her waterproof mascara.

"I'll see you in my office in half an hour," hissed Tony to Declan, as he ushered the Mayor and a lot of visiting VIPs upstairs.

"I won't be long," Declan told Rupert. "Wait in the car."

He got his contract out of the filing cabinet in his office and took the elevator to the fifth floor. He felt curiously elated.

As he stood in the doorway of the conference room he heard Miss Bisley saying to Miss Painswick that Miss Cotchester's trouble was that she had an unphotogenic crotch.

Tony was talking to his VIPs, who were all ogling the girls. Declan went up and tapped Tony on the shoulder.

"I'd like a word now."

"Piss off."

"Now—in your office," said Declan, "unless you want me to tell these creeps exactly what I think of you."

"Do be careful," said Miss Madden, who was sitting at her typewriter in a mauve satin dress.

Sauntering after Tony, Declan blew her a kiss.

"You look beautiful," he told her.

"How dare you?" thundered Tony, as Declan slammed the door behind them.

"Because you're rotten," said Declan. "So rotten, even maggots throw you up."

Tony went purple. "You've flouted my authority on every opportunity," he spluttered.

Slowly Declan walked towards him, huge, cavernous-eyed and menacing. "Violence isn't the answer," he said softly, "but it's a bloody good start."

Tony backed up against the wall, licking his lips, eyes darting, hand edging toward the intercom button.

"Don't touch me," he croaked.

As Declan raised his hand, Tony cringed away until his head crashed against the framed photograph of himself and the Queen. Then he realized that Declan was holding a folded-up piece of paper.

"This is my contract," said Declan grimly. Slowly and with great relish he tore it into tiny pieces and sprinkled it over Tony's head. Then he turned toward the door.

For a second Tony was struck dumb, but, as Declan's hand touched the door handle, he said, "Can I take it you've quit?"

"Indeed you can," said Declan. "I've prostituted myself for—" he counted up on his fingers—"seven months too long, and tonight I'm going to have the first night's sleep since I started working for you."

"Has it occurred to you that you're breaking your contract?"

"I don't give a fuck," said Declan, opening the door. "I'm not staying here till you break me, like you broke Cyril and Simon and half the poor mentally crippled sods in this building."

The moment he'd gone Tony pressed the rewind button on the tape recorder and poured himself a huge glass of brandy.

"Miss Madden," he shouted, extracting the tape from the cassette, "can you transcribe this at once? Make a dozen copies. Then sweep up these bits of paper and put them in an envelope marked Declan O'Hara's contract. What the fuck are you crying for?"

"He was a nice man," sobbed Miss Madden. "He always asked me about my life as though it mattered to him."

Outside in the parking lot the wind had dropped and the moon was shining dimly through the clouds like a ten-watt bulb.

Rupert had finished the bottle of champagne.

"Sorry to keep you," said Declan, getting into the car.

"How did it go?"

"I'm out."

"Christ! I thought you had a water-tight contract?"

"Unfortunately it wasn't whisky-tight," said Declan. "Let's go and get seriously drunk."

CHAPTER 23

Taggie slept fitfully, worried about her father, disturbed by a restless Gertrude, who imagined every creak and rattle of creeper blown against the turret windows was Declan returning. Waking at five, Taggie glanced out across the valley, as she always seemed to be doing these days, and saw that Rupert's lights were on. She tried not to envy her father spending a whole day with him; he'd had such a ghastly time at work lately, he deserved a break. Going downstairs to check if the car was back she froze with horror to see it once more parked across a flowerbed with all the lights on. Rushing outside, she found it empty and stealthily started to search the house. Declan was not in the bedroom—her mother, sprawled diagonally across the bed as though denying him access—nor in the spare room. He wasn't in Patrick's room, or the kitchen, or either of the living rooms or the dining room.

She was beginning to panic that he'd gone for a walk in the woods and fallen down the ravine when she heard an excited squeak from the library. Gertrude had found him, still dressed, passed out cold over his desk. In his hand he still held the pen with which he had been writing his Yeats biography. He had knocked over a glass of whisky which had spilled over the open page of the notebook, blurring the drunken scrawl.

Taggie wrapped a couple of blankets around him, and put a cushion under his head, but he didn't stir.

He woke six hours later with a terrible hangover and an even worse sense of foreboding. Staggering groaning into the kitchen, he found Maud reading Anthony Powell upside down and looking boot-faced. Without being asked, Taggie dropped four Alka-Selzters into a glass. Declan took a gulp, retched, and fled from the room.

"Well," said Maud, when he came back, even more white and shaking, "what kept you?"

"I don't remember," growled Declan.

The telephone rang and he clutched his head, groaning. It was the *Scorpion*, the most seamy of the tabloids. Could they speak to Declan?

"He's not here," said Taggie quickly.

"I gather he's resigned from Corinium. D'you know where I can get hold of him?"

Taggie went pale. "Are you sure?"

"Quite. The press office confirmed it."

"No. He's definitely not here." Taggie slammed down the telephone.

Declan glared at her with bloodshot eyes, sensing trouble. "What am I supposed to have done?"

Taggie looked nervously at her mother.

"Come on," said Declan.

"Qu-Quit."

"Kerist! Did I really?"

"You bloody idiot," hissed Maud. "Call Tony at once and apologize. Say you were drunk."

At that moment Ursula arrived, looking pale from her flu, but very overexcited by events. Joyce Madden had called her in tears in the middle of the night and told her what had happened.

"I was just telling Declan to call Tony and say he's sorry," said Maud. "They're bound to take him back. He's such a big star." The contempt was undeniable.

"I'm not sure they will," sighed Ursula.

"Sit down," said Taggie, pulling out a chair. "I'll make you a cup of tea."

"Declan's got a contract," said Maud, "and he was far too plastered to put anything in writing last night."

Ursula turned to Declan who was sitting with his head in his hands.

"Don't you remember anything?"

"I remember a lot of girls in bathing suits, who were rather ugly, and Rupert dressed up as a horse, and I think I remember having a fight with Tony," he muttered.

"You did," said Ursula. "You gave him an earful. Then you tore up your contract and scattered it all over him and quit."

"Oh Jesus!" Declan opened a bloodshot eye. "Did I really?"

"And Tony taped the entire conversation, and Joyce Madden transcribed it at once, and no doubt copies are winging their way to the IBA and the ICTA and God knows who else at this moment."

"You stupid idiot," whispered Maud.

Fear is the parent of cruelty. Having found Declan impossible to live with for the past few months, she had considerable sympathy for Tony. Declan's career, albeit meteoric, had always been peppered with rows. She was totally unable to appreciate the pressure he'd been under.

"Well, I'm not going back," said Declan.

"You have no choice. The B.B.C. wouldn't touch you with a ten-foot pole. You'll have to crawl for once."

"Oh Mummy," protested Taggie, putting heavily sweetened, very strong cups of tea in front of Declan and Ursula.

Declan warmed his shaking hands around the mug that had a picture of a girl whose bikini disappeared when the mug was filled with boiling liquid. Like my career, thought Declan.

"It's all your fault," went on Maud, "taking days off to go hunting, getting plastered with Rupert before a program. You're like a couple of schoolboys."

All the animosity she harbored after Rupert had rejected her and embraced Declan seemed to pour forth like scalding lava.

"I rang up Personnel and resigned too," said Ursula importantly. "I'm not working for a police state any more."

Oh Christ, thought Declan, that means I'll have to pay her salary myself until she gets another job. But he put a hand on her arm.

"Thanks, darling. That was very loyal of you."

Everyone jumped as the telephone rang. Maud picked it up. It was the *Star*. Maud could never resist journalists.

"We're a bit hazy this end," she said. "Declan hasn't told us anything. What happened?"

The reporter, enchanted by Maud's soft, caressing tones, told her.

"I see," said Maud grimly. "Where's Rupert?"

"Well, he arrived in London ten minutes late to chair a seminar on 'Alcoholism in the ex-Athlete.' "

"Thanks," said Maud. "We'll call you back when he comes in. How could you?" she rounded on Declan. "Badmouthing Tony when you were wearing a microphone. I thought you were supposed to be a professional."

Declan hardly heard her. "We'll have to sell the house," he said bleakly.

The telephone rang again. Declan got up and seized the receiver. "Will you fucking go away?" he screamed.

"Charming," said a shrill voice. "This is Caitlin, your daughter, if you hadn't forgotten, and why hasn't someone come to pick me up?"

"Oh God," said Taggie in anguish, catching the gist. "I thought she was supposed to come tomorrow."

"Well, you'd better go and get her," snapped Maud, who had forgotten to pass on the message.

"I'm going out," said Declan.

"Whatever for?" screamed Maud.

"To do some thinking."

"Well, you'd better come up with something pretty quickly. I have no intention of selling this house."

With four Extra Strength Anacin, four Alka-Seltzers, a cup of strong tea and the remains of last night's whisky churning uneasily inside him, Declan set out. A mild and sunny day with a gentle breeze had followed yesterday's torrential rain, freak snow storms and razor-sharp winds. Everything sparkled. For the first time in months the birds were singing and courting in the trees.

Down the Frogsmore, in one day, spring seemed to have arrived. Primroses nestled on the bank. Coltsfoot exploded sulphur yellow beneath his feet, celandines arched back their shiny yellow petals in the sunshine; even the most uncompromising spiked red blackberry cable was putting out tiny pale green leaves.

In the fields above, he could see Rupert's horses pounding around in their New Zealand rugs, tails held high, like children let out of school. In the woods, he found the first anemones and blue and white violets. Far above him the woodpecker was rattling away at a tree trunk. He could almost hear the buds bursting open.

Why the hell had he blown it all in his fucking intellectual arrogance? All he'd had to do was to hack on working at Corinium until the end of April, then in the break look around for another job. Now that he'd left in a blaze of drunken publicity with plummeting ratings, no one would want him.

He crushed a wild garlic leaf between his fingers. The smell reminded him of lunches in Soho and endlessly plotting with his cronies to make a better world at the B.B.C. He'd loved London, but he didn't want to go back.

It was so hot that, on the way home, he took off his coat and sat down on the bank of the stream for a long time, watching the water as it glittered and squirmed with pleasure in the sunshine. Gertrude splashed about, and, picking up a stick, bounced up to Declan hoping he'd pull the other end; then, when he wouldn't, dropped it and licked his face.

An old man, walking his ancient Jack Russell back from Penscombe, stopped for a chat. His grandfather used to be the gamekeeper at The Priory, he said, a hundred years ago, when the land stretched for three hundred acres across the north side of the

Penscombe-Chalford Road. He'd kept the place like a new pin. It was
sad to see the state it had fallen into, the rotting trees and collapsing
walls everywhere. Declan felt ashamed.

"You can tell spring's come at last," said the old man, "because
all the blackbirds are singing."

But not for me any more, thought Declan in despair.

Then the old man peered closer. "Didn't you used to be Declan
O'Hara?" he said.

By late afternoon Taggie was shattered. Ursula, having parried the
press all day, had gone home. After another terrible row with Maud,
Declan had barricaded himself into the library, refusing to talk to
anyone. Caitlin sat on the kitchen table with her arm around Gertrude, both watching Taggie stuffing a chicken with a mixture of
apricots, sausage meat, breadcrumbs, and garlic.

"I aced the exam on *The Mayor of Casterbridge*," said Caitlin.
Then, seeing Taggie struggling to understand a recipe for potatoes
Lyonnaise, her lips moving slowly as she read, she added kindly,
"but a sixth former told me all the answers beforehand. And two
girls in the upper sixth are having abortions during the vacation."

"That's nice," said Taggie absentmindedly.

"Taggie, you're not listening."

"I'm sorry. I'm so worried about Daddy."

"He'll be OK. Someone will snap him up."

"I don't know. He's lost all his confidence. I've never known
him so down."

"That's hangover," said Caitlin.

Her ability to spread mess everywhere was even greater than
Maud's. Her open trunk lay in the hall and lacrosse sticks, tapes,
posters, rolled-up art work, wet towels, colored files, a teddy bear,
and a laundry bag overflowing with underwear, were scattered in a
trail all the way to the kitchen. She was wearing a very expensive
pink T-shirt, over which all her friends had written messages in magic
marker, a puffball skirt, tights, and black clogs, and was now eating
granola out of a cup with a teaspoon.

"Christ, this house is cold."

The telephone rang again for the hundredth time. The connection was terrible.

"Can I speak to Declan?" said a male voice.

"He can't talk to anyone," said Taggie hysterically.

"Is that Taggie?"

"Yes."

"It's Rupert. How's your father?"

"Not great." Taggie felt herself going very red, and turned her back on Caitlin. "He walked out, you know."

"It was partly my fault. I should have stopped him storming in to see Tony, but he's better out of it; it was killing him. Are you all right, sweetheart?"

The sudden gentleness in his voice made her want to burst into tears.

"I'm fine," she mumbled.

"Well, tell him I'll be over later."

Upstairs, Declan turned on the five forty-five news and found Tony Baddingham, with a red carnation in his buttonhole, giving a press conference.

"The truth of the matter," he was saying, "is that Declan O'Hara tendered his resignation last night, and we accepted it."

Stupid word "tendered," thought Declan. There was nothing tender about it at all.

"Naturally, we're very sad to lose Declan," said Tony, looking absolutely delighted, "but, quite frankly, there have been a series of disagreements and there's a general feeling at Corinium that when people get too big for their boots, we'd prefer them to go off and wear out other people's carpets."

Declan switched off and looked down at the floorboards. He hadn't got any carpets to wear out, and probably now he never would have. The telephone rang again. It was one of the Corinium shop stewards.

"Fuckin' idiot," he chided Declan, "you should've hung in and let him fire you."

"I know," said Declan almost apologetically. "I felt I had to retain some shred of integrity."

"Wish you'd come to us. Look, the lads want to go on strike. You've only got to ask. We'll black out the 'ole network for you, Declan, and get you reinstated."

Declan was so moved he couldn't say anything for a minute. Then he said gruffly that there wouldn't be any point.

"I can't work for Tony any more, but thanks very much all the same, and say goodbye and thanks to all the boys for me."

It was dark outside now, but a robin was singing on the bare honeysuckle outside his window. It had turned up at exactly six-thirty for the last week now, as if to cheer him on.

"Art thou the bird whom man loves best," he murmured to himself, *"The pious bird with the scarlet breast, Our little English robin?"*

Tears filled his eyes. Oh God, what was he going to do?

Taggie knocked on the door and, getting no answer, walked in. She found him looking so haggard and despairing that she ran across the room, stumbling over the piles of papers and books all over the floor, and put her arms around him.

"Please don't be so sad. It doesn't matter if we go back to London. We were all happy there. You've just got to get your confidence back. Rupert rang, by the way. He's coming around."

Going upstairs to her bedroom, she was horrified by how awful she looked. She'd been so busy she hadn't had a moment to wash or even brush her teeth all day. She knew she had no chance with Rupert, that it was appallingly presumptuous, but for once she wanted to look her best when she saw him. Caitlin's welcome-home supper could wait, she decided. She was going to have a bath and wash her hair.

Caitlin wolf-whistled when Taggie came into the kitchen an hour later. She was wearing a red-and-black-striped turtleneck sweater which Patrick had given her for Christmas, tucked into black jeans which were in turn tucked into black boots. As her hair was still damp she'd tied it back with a black ribbon. She wore no make-up except smudged black eyeliner, which made her silver-gray eyes look huge and almost luminous. A hot bath and the hairdryer had given her pale cheeks quite enough color.

"Because you so seldom bother," said Caitlin critically, "one forgets how beautiful you are: much more so than anyone else I know."

"Oh, don't be silly," muttered Taggie in embarrassment, putting the chicken into the oven.

"How soon will it be ready?"

"About nine."

"Good, I can watch 'Dynasty.' Who are you going out with?"

"No one." Taggie busied herself with draining the parsnips. "You like parsnip purée, don't you?"

"Adore it. You haven't answered my question."

"No one."

"Then why are you done up like Gertrude's dinner?"

"I just felt awful," muttered Taggie apologetically, as she threw the parsnips into the blender. "I didn't have time to wash all day."

"Hum," said Caitlin beadily, as she watched Taggie add curry powder, then butter, then cream to the parsnips. "Fee, Fi, fo fumble, I smell the blood of Rupert Campbell."

"Oh shut up," said Taggie, turning on the blender.

Caitlin waited until she had turned it off.

"I am Campbell-Black but comely," said Caitlin giggling. *"Rise up, my love, my fair one, and come away, For lo, the winter is past, the rain is over and gone. The flowers appear on the earth; the time of the singing of birds is come, and the turtle-necked sweater is worn in our land."*

"Oh shut up," screamed Taggie. Picking up Gertrude's rubber bone, she hurled it at Caitlin, missed and nearly hit Rupert, who, finding the door open, had let himself in, followed by Freddie Jones. Taggie stood rooted to the spot with horror. Gertrude went into a frenzy of outraged barking that someone had entered the house without her knowing.

"Hello, Gertrude," said Rupert. "How extraordinarily good you look today. Nice dog, Gertrude, well done, hurrah, what a beautiful curly tail you've got." Bending down, he stroked the bemused Gertrude over and over again.

Taggie giggled.

"That's better," said Rupert. He looked a bit pale after yesterday's excesses, but seemed in excellent spirits.

"Hullo," he said to Caitlin. "How are you?"

"Fine." Caitlin beamed. "I was just quoting the Bible to my sister to keep her on the straight and narrow."

"Cait*lin*," pleaded Taggie in despair, frantically concentrating on spooning the purée out of the blender.

Rupert went over to Taggie and, putting a hand on the back of her neck, drew her toward him. With most women, he would have dropped a kiss on the tops of their heads, but Taggie was so tall, he was able to rest his lips for a second against her temple.

"There, angel, you mustn't worry about your papa. Frederico, the whiz kid, and I will sort him out."

"I'll get you a drink," stammered Taggie. "What would you like? Daddy's in the library."

"I'd like a Bacardi and Coke, love," said Freddie, "and if Rupe 'ere can keep it down, he'd like a whisky and soda."

"If there isn't any Malibu, I'll have a Vod and Ton, Tag," added Caitlin.

Fleeing into the pantry, Taggie paused before she got down the bottles. Unbelievingly she touched her left temple where Rupert had kissed it, then, moving her fingers to her lips, kissed them in ecstasy.

What was happening to her? She wondered if Caitlin's welcome-home chicken would stretch to six.

" 'Ullo, Declan," said Freddie, as they went into the library and found him slumped at his desk. "I've just seen that fucker Tony on the news. You're well shot of the smarmy bastard."

Sitting down on the window seat, Rupert waited until Taggie had brought in the drinks. Then he shut the door behind her and said, "Look, Frederico and I have been talking about you for some time. To put it bluntly, both being hard-nosed businessmen, we hate to see a hot property like you being wasted."

"We've decided to form our own independent production company," said Freddie, "an' employ you to make programs for the network, *Channel 4* and the overseas market."

It took a lot of tough talking to persuade Declan they weren't just being kind. He looked at his untouched glass for a second; then a real gleam of excitement came into his eyes: "I've got a better idea. Why don't we pitch for the Corinium franchise, and boot out Tony."

Freddie and Rupert looked at each other. "Aren't we too late?"

"Not at all," said Declan. "If we step on it. The applications don't have to be in until the beginning of May."

"We know all the right people," said Rupert. "So there won't be any problem getting our board together."

"And we won't have any trouble getting the backing," said Freddie, jumping up and down with excitement. "An' I can provide you wiv all the technical know-how."

"And I know the Corinium Programs backwards," said Declan, "so we can submit better plans standing on our heads."

Taggie popped her head around the door: "Anyone want more drinks."

Declan shook his head. So did Freddie, who'd hardly touched his glass. Only Rupert handed out his. "Please, angel," he said with a grin, "and could I have soda this time?"

"Oh goodness, did I give you Coke? I'm really sorry, and poor Mr. Jones must have had Bacardi and soda."

"I don't think he's noticed," said Rupert.

As Freddie and Declan got more and more excited over their plans, Rupert thought about Taggie, how she'd trembled when he kissed her, and how adorable she'd looked with her long legs in those black boots, and her hair tied back like a boy soldier. But he mustn't think about her, he told himself grimly. She was Declan's kid daughter, totally out of bounds. Wrenching his mind back, he heard Declan saying: "In fact Tony's only trump card with the IBA is Cameron Cook, and the staff are in a state of uproar about her as it is.''

"How would it be if I seduced her onto our side?'' said Rupert idly.

"We don't want *her*!'' Declan exploded. "She's a treacherous evil bitch.''

"Not once I've sorted her out,'' said Rupert. "I was always good with difficult horses. I guarantee to have her eating out of my hand in a few weeks.''

CHAPTER 24

Overwhelmed by the day's vicissitudes, Declan went to bed and didn't emerge for thirty-six hours, waking on Saturday morning to thank God he wouldn't ever have to work for Tony again before falling back to sleep. On Sunday he woke to a glorious day and apologized to his darling Maud for being such a bear. She apologized for being such a bitch and, after he had explained about bidding for the franchise and selling the woods to Rupert to raise some cash, they vowed that things would be better between them and made passionate, ecstatic love. Replete, tranquilized, Maud wondered why she had ever wanted to look at anyone else. Taggie, as she later cooked lunch, listened to her mother singing and playing Schubert lieder. She found these staggering *volte-faces* bewildering, but felt only relief that the row was over.

Rupert, having spent Saturday hunting and on constituency business, rose early on Sunday and tried out several new horses that had arrived from Ireland earlier in the week. One dark bay mare was really exceptional, incredibly quick off the mark with a huge wild jump. In a couple of years he could have made a world-class horse out of her. He felt, as always, that reluctance to sell her, that temptation to have one more crack at show jumping, then put the thought sternly behind him. An election was in the offing this summer and there was the franchise to be won. He was seeing Declan and Freddie that afternoon to work out a campaign. They had arranged to meet at Freddie's house because they wanted to keep their bid secret until the applications went in, and because the Press were still hanging around Penscombe Court and The Priory hoping to get some juicy story about Declan's exit from Corinium.

Handing the mare back to one of the grooms, Rupert mounted his old Olympic gold medal horse, Rocky, for a ride around the estate, as he always did if he was at home on a Sunday. The pack of dogs raced ahead putting up pheasants, chasing rabbits, snuffling down badger sets, and foxes' earths. Rocky loved these outings, and to prove they were both still great, Rupert put the old horse over the occasional wall and any streams or fallen logs in their path. Rupert's eagle eye missed nothing, a loose wire here, a tree blown across a fence there, which would have to be repaired before sheep were moved in, how poor or good the grass was in each field, and how the winter barley was spreading in an emerald-green haze over the rich brown earth.

In the distance he could hear Penscombe church bells ringing, and the rattle of a clay shoot. Across the valley The Priory was in shadow with the sun behind it. The beech trees in front were a crimson blur as the buds thickened. Soon the leaves would be out and he wouldn't be able to see the house any more. Taking the muddy track that wound high above the Frogsmore, he noticed the first primroses blooming happily and safely under wild rose and bramble bushes, the spiky branches keeping the grazing horses and cattle away.

In their sweet pale trusting innocence, the primroses reminded him of Taggie, who, he felt, could only blossom if she were fiercely protected. He suddenly wished he could be those spiky powerful branches keeping away anyone who threatened her. He imagined putting her on his gentlest horse, showing her all over his land, pointing out his favorite places, then making love to her among the wild flowers, as he had done to so many other women before—but with Taggie it would be different. Christ, he must get a grip on himself and get involved with someone else very quickly. Thank goodness Nathalie Perrault was arriving this evening for a few days, and there was still the conquest of Cameron Cook to be orchestrated.

Back at Penscombe, stripped for a bath, Rupert got on the scales and winced. One hundred and seventy pounds: at six feet two, no one could call him fat, but it was a far cry from the honed muscular leanness, the one hundred fifty-five pounds produced by eight hours in the saddle, which he'd trained down to before the Olympic Games and the World Championship. Too many dinners, too much booze, not enough exercise, he was hopelessly unfit. If he was going to seduce Cameron, he'd have to knock off a few pounds first—that meant no alcohol, and just meat, fish, and vegetables for the next month.

* * *

When he rolled up at Freddie's house, Declan, looking ten years younger, had already arrived, and he and Freddie were poring over a book called *How to Win The Franchise.*

"The first thing we gotta do is appoint a chairman," said Freddie.

"Better be you," said Rupert.

"OK," said Freddie, "but we'll need someone respectable like a lord or a bishop or something as deputy chairman."

"We must also remember," said Declan, "that the IBA, despite all their pronouncements about quality, are looking for applicants who won't go broke in the first eighteen months, and who'll be able to produce programs that'll keep the company in the black over the next eight years. That's why we need a very experienced chief executive and a very strong Program Controller."

"You better be chief executive, then," said Rupert.

"But I'm terrible with money."

"You know about television. I'll be Financial Director, and I'll get hold of a hot-shit accountant to keep an eye on you. Sandwiched between him and me and Freddie, you can't go far wrong."

"I've got just the man for Program Controller," said Declan, "Harold White, ex-ITN and B.B.C. Currently Director of Programs at London Weekend. He's bloody good."

"I've been doing some sums," said Freddie. "We'll need at least fifteen million to keep the station going for the first two years, but before that we'll need at least two hundred grand up front as burn money to pay for brokers, bankers, running costs and to launch the publicity campaign."

"Which we'll forfeit if the bid fails," said Declan.

"Right," said Freddie. "Why don't we put that up ourselves? Give us some control."

Rupert was about to agree. Then, catching signs of Declan's twitching face, said, "Let's argue about that later. Now which do we find first, board or backing?"

"Backing's easy," said Freddie. "Let's get the right people first. Apart from the directors, who are actually going to run the station, we need some local millionaires and a liberal sprinkling of the great and the good as nonexecutive directors."

"Before we approach anyone, we better come up with a name," said Rupert.

"I've been thinking. What about Venturer?" said Declan.

"Sounds all right," said Freddie. "What's it say it means in the dictionary?"

"Someone who's daring and willing to take risks, someone who's prepared to brave dangers or embark on a possibly hazardous journey."

In Declan's deep husky voice it sounded wonderfully romantic.

"Perfirck. What we going to use as a logo?"

"I've been thinking about that too," said Declan. "You know that bronze I admired in your sitting room, Rupert?" He turned back to Freddie. "It's a boy in an open-necked shirt and shorts. He's shading his forehead with his hand as he gazes into the distance. It's ravishing and it's got the right mix of strength and grace and vision."

"I've seen it, it's great," said Freddie in excitement. "We'll get someone to draw it; then we can put it on our stationery and on the front of the application."

"We better get T-shirts and ties and bumper stickers printed," said Rupert, "and posters too. Just imagine a poster of Taggie in a Victory for Venturer T-shirt!"

"What about a studio?" said Declan.

"Well if Tony Baddingham's prepared to sell the Corinium building, it would be much cheaper to take over that," said Rupert. "But, in case he turns really nasty, we better make contingency plans."

Valerie Jones was absolutely livid. She never admitted reading the *Scorpion*, but the weekend fish had arrived wrapped in Saturday's edition, and Valerie couldn't miss the huge headline announcing that Declan had resigned from Corinium while getting disgustingly drunk with Rupert, and now they were both closeted together in Fred-Fred's den, and the air was thick with cigar smoke, and she was sure they were up to no good. She'd grumbled so much in the past about Freddie blasting her out with his music that he'd had the room thoroughly soundproofed. Now she couldn't hear a word that was going on inside, even when she went outdoors and pretended to pull non-existent weeds out of the flowerbed under the window. How could they keep the windows closed on such a lovely day?

"Shall I take them in afternoon tea?" said poor fat Sharon, who still cherished a long-range crush on Rupert.

"No," snapped Valerie. "You haven't done your religious study yet. Miss Fidduck said at least one hour a day; nor have you groomed Merrylegs. What is the point of your father buying you an event horse?"

As Sharon waddled upstairs, Valerie could bear it no longer.

"Afternoon tea," she announced ten minutes later, barging into Freddie's den with a tray.

Declan was striding up and down the room scattering cigarette ash. Freddie was whizzing around in his revolving chair. Rupert lounged on the sofa, playing with one of Freddie's executive games, which involved clashing huge ball bearings against each other. All three of them looked up with ill-concealed irritation.

"What a stink," said Valerie, dumping down the tray and throwing open the window, so all Freddie's papers blew around.

"I don't know how you can stay inside. I hope you won't be long, Fred-Fred. We're due at Sir Arthur's for cocktails at six-thirty and you promised to walk around the grounds with me beforehand."

She turned to Rupert and Declan: "We're opening Green Lawns to the public in July. All proceeds to the NSPCC. I'm surprised you're not opening Penscombe Court this year, Rupert," she added, raising her voice to cover the increasing clash of ball bearings.

"You can hardly expect the public to look at a lot of weeds," said Rupert.

"But you've got buckets of time to get it shipshape. It seems so selfish not to raise the money if you can." Valerie gave her little laugh.

"I'm sure the NSPCC would prefer a check," said Rupert evenly.

"I don't expect Maud'll be interested in opening *your* garden," went on Valerie, turning to Declan. "I've just read all about your exploits in the *Sunday Express*. Tony Baddingham is quoted as saying one of the reasons you left Corinium was because you couldn't face being knocked out by 'Dallas.' "

As Freddie gently shooed her out, Rupert and Declan both reflected that not throttling Valerie before December would be infinitely harder than winning the franchise.

The next five weeks were frantic. Many of the bidders for franchises in other parts of England had spent several years perfecting their applications, raising the cash, and getting their boards together. To speed up the operation, Freddie, Declan, and Rupert divided the role of recruiting officer between them.

"There's no point enlisting people who won't contribute anything," said Declan. "We mustn't confuse celebrity with attainment, and they *must* live in the area. Once we land a really big fish, the rest will follow."

Hubert Brenton, Bishop of Cotchester, who was currently furious with Tony for deciding to televise Easter Communion at Gloucester Cathedral rather than Cotchester, was the first to be signed up. Declan invited him to lunch at The Priory the following week, and, as it was Lent and a Friday, Taggie cooked the most succulent Coquille St. Jacques, followed by sole Veronique. Maud, with a cross around her neck and her titian hair drawn back in a bun, gravely asked the Bishop to say Grace.

Rupert, who, as part of his getting-fit-for-Cameron-Cook campaign, was off the booze, provided the most exquisite white wine. Caitlin, who, unlike poor Sharon Jones, had passed her religious studies "O" level, was able to converse with the Bishop at length about St. Luke, and particularly the Prodigal Son.

There was a dicey moment when she dropped her bread, butter-side down, and said "Shit," but by then the Bishop was fortunately talking to Maud about his recent trip to the Holy Land. Fortunately, too, he'd been wandering around the Sea of Galilee last weekend and missed the newspaper reports of Declan's exit from Corinium. Over the lemon sorbet, Declan and the Bishop discussed how thrilling it would be to dramatize Lytton Strachey's brilliant essay about Cardinal Newman and Cardinal Manning, who had both lived in Oxford, which was, after all, within the franchise area.

After lunch Maud, Taggie, and Caitlin discreetly withdrew, and Declan produced Rupert's venerable port.

"Not drinking?" asked the Bishop, as Rupert passed the decanter on.

"No, My Lord," said Rupert gravely. "I've given it up for Lent."

The Bishop had always thoroughly disapproved of Rupert and was pleased that at long last, after such a turbulent past, he was trying to shed his jetset playboy image and forge a more satisfying way of life.

Declan and Freddie steered the conversation around to Corinium Television and the appalling poverty of their religious programs, and then raised the subject of their rival bid. They very much hoped the Bishop would join Venturer and become their Deputy Chairman.

"Television today," said the Bishop warmly, "is a key factor for the quality of life and for establishing values."

For the past ten years, he went on, he had had special responsibilities for communication in the diocese and he saw joining Venturer as a way of extending a work that interested him greatly.

"We know busy people don't do fings for nuffink," said Freddie, cozily. "If we win the franchise, there'll be a very small director's fee, say ten thousand a year, which could always go to your favorite charity."

Signing up Henry Hampshire, the Lord-Lieutenant, was even easier. Freddie and Rupert wooed him over a very expensive lunch in London. Henry, as it turned out, was absolutely furious with Tony for selling off a field ten miles from The Falconry, but only a quarter of a mile from and in full view of Henry's house, to a developer. He was also a very old friend of Rupert's, having a wife too plain for even Rupert to have had a crack at, and he liked Freddie.

"Any money in it?" he asked, having sold two stone lions last week to pay a tax bill.

"Fucking fortune," said Rupert. "We'd need a bit up front."

"Don't mind that," said Henry. "Suppose I could always sell a Stubbs."

"You needn't go that far," said Rupert, shocked. "We only want about ten grand. What about that minor Pre-Raphaelite, the one over the chimney-piece in the sitting room?"

"Good idea," said Henry. "Never liked it. Silly girl lying in the water, covered in flowers. Someone should have taught her the backstroke."

Doing his homework, Declan investigated the likes and dislikes of Lady Gosling, Chairman of the IBA. He also discovered that her best friend, Dame Enid Spink, was the composer interviewed so disastrously by James Vereker. Declan called on Dame Enid in her rooms at Cotchester University, where she was director of music, and found her ferociously conducting to a phonograph record of her latest opera, *The Persuaders*.

"Worst program I've ever been on," boomed Dame Enid, as she and Declan dipped pieces of stale seed cake into tea the color of mahogany. "In fact Corinium's whole attitude to music is utterly philistine. Last time the franchises came up for grabs, that treacherous little fart, Tony Baddingham, promised to finance a Cotchester Youth Orchestra. Not a penny have we seen."

Declan said truthfully that Venturer wouldn't be prepared to finance anything except television programs until they broke even, but he hoped Dame Enid would advise them on their music programs.

"If you get the franchise," asked Dame Enid, "would you get rid of that little squirt James Vereker?"

"Indeed we would," said Declan.

Once Dame Enid agreed, it was a piece of cake to recruit Professor Crispin Graystock, a rich left-wing English Literature don who had dry, unmanageable hair, wild eyes, and a wet formless face, and who longed to be a television star because he thought it would help sell his slim and unutterably dreary volumes of poetry.

Although he was still smarting over not being included in the new *Oxford Companion to English Literature*, Crispin Graystock was regarded as a considerable heavyweight in the academic world.

Freddie Jones took Lord Smith, the even more left-wing ex-president of the Transport and General Workers Union, out to yet another very expensive lunch, where, with his mouth crammed simultaneously with lobster and Pouilly Fuissé, Lord Smith agreed to join Venturer and provide a substantial cash investment from Union funds.

"Doesn't he feel guilty about getting involved with such a capitalist organ as Venturer?" said Rupert.

"Not at all. Once I told him the money he was likely to make," said Freddie. "He feels television is for the people."

Rupert, seeking a hot-shit money man, rang up Marti Gluckstein, arguably the most brilliant accountant just this side of the law.

"How'd you like to join our bid for the Corinium franchise?"

"I've already turned down four other groups," said Marti in his nasal twang. "I loathe television."

"You'd have to buy a house in the area," said Rupert. He could feel Marti shudder all the way down the telephone wires.

"I loathe the country," said Marti.

"Don't have to live here," said Rupert. "Just buy a place and sell it the moment we clinch the franchise. Prices are going up so fast you'll double your money by the time you sell it. I'll find you one."

The prospect of making a fast buck clinched it.

"Marti Gluckstein's a crook," said Declan in outrage, when Freddie and Rupert jubilantly told him the good news.

"Don't be anti-Semitic," said Rupert primly.

"And he doesn't live in the area."

"He's just bought a cottage in Penscombe," said Rupert blithely. He was quickly learning he had to tread very softly around Declan's integrity.

Bearing in mind the IBA's obsession with minority groups, particularly ethnic ones, Declan, who knew nothing about cricket, recruited Wesley Emerson, a six-foot-five West Indian bowler and the hero of Cotchester Cricket Club, whom he'd met at a Sports Aid cocktail party.

Rupert was as outraged as Declan had been about Marti Gluck-stein. "You're crazy," he yelled. "It was only me and the Government stepping in with some very fast talking that stopped Wesley getting busted in New Zealand this winter. He was snorting coke on the pitch, and he's the biggest letch since Casanova."

"I thought that was your prerogrative," said Declan coldly. "Talk about the kettle calling the Pot Campbell-Black."

It took all Freddie's diplomacy to calm them down.

Basil Baddingham was the easiest of all to recruit.

"D'you really want to infuriate Tony?" asked Rupert.

"How much?" said Bas, after Rupert had explained.

"Ten grand."

"Cheap at the price. You're on," said Bas.

Having assembled their board of the great and the good, Venturer now needed some heavyweight production people. This had to be handled with great delicacy. Anyone worth his salt had already been approached by other consortiums. Two department heads at York-shire had just been fired when it was discovered they'd joined a consortium in the Midlands. Most ITV companies, and the B.B.C. as well, had threatened to kick out anyone found having dealings with any new franchise applicants, even in another area. As Declan was only too aware, Tony was already going through all incoming mail, monitoring telephone calls and checking through desk drawers and wastebaskets after dark.

Declan therefore proceeded with extreme caution. Early in April he called Harold White, program controller at LWT, arguably the most brilliant and innovative brain in television.

"Harold, it's Declan."

"How extraordinary," said Harold. "I've been trying to get your home telephone number all day. We're bidding for Granada. You interested in joining our consortium?"

"Not really, but thanks all the same," said Declan. "We've just moved here, and I couldn't face another move. How about joining ours?"

One of the pledges that Venturer planned to make to the IBA was that, if they won the franchise, they would retain most of the Cori-nium staff, but there were three people Declan was anxious to secure for Venturer in advance, in case they were lured away by another consortium.

"I want Charles Fairburn," he told Rupert. "He knows the area like the back of his handbag and he's very bright. He's just bored out of his skull. I'd move him away from Religious programming and put him in charge of Documentaries."

Declan didn't recognize Charles when he rolled up at The Priory. He was wearing a false nose, a moustache, a green felt hat with a Tyrolean feather and dark glasses.

"Can't be too careful, dear," he said, whisking into the house. "James Vereker spent three hours at lunchtime getting his hair streaked yet again, and Tony's absolutely refusing to believe he didn't go to a job interview."

Declan was glad he was alone with Charles when he asked him to join Venturer as Head of Documentaries, because Charles promptly burst into tears. For an awful moment Declan thought he'd insulted him.

"I'm sorry," he muttered. "I had a feeling you were bored with religion."

"I am, I am," sobbed Charles. "You don't understand! The absolute bliss of the thought of getting away from Corinium! You've no idea how we all miss you."

It was only then that Declan realized, despite the quips and the jokey exterior, the strain Charles must have been under for years.

"Tony demoralizes one so much, one feels one will never be good enough to work for anyone else again. I can't thank you enough, Declan. Do you think there's any chance of us getting it?"

Declan was touched by the "us."

"Well, a station whose record is good," he said, "stands a better chance than a new applicant of unknown potential. But Tony's record isn't exactly good, and we're getting together an incredibly strong team. Now if I tell you who they are, will you promise to keep your trap shut?"

"Mum's the word," said Charles wiping his eyes. "Now, is there anyone else at Corinium you want me to sound out?"

Declan said he was interested in gorgeous Georgie Baines, the Sales Director, and Seb Burrows from the News Room.

"Very good choice," said Charles approvingly. "Both stunningly able. You're not interested in Cameron are you? She's up for a BAFTA this week."

Declan shook his head violently. He hoped that Rupert had forgotten about Cameron.

Rupert called Declan that evening from London.

"We need a really good Head of Sports. How about Billy Lloyd-Foxe?"

"Excellent. I've heard nothing but good about Billy," said Declan. "Will you talk to him?"

The following day Rupert had a drink with his best friend and old show-jumping partner. Billy, who was working for the B.B.C. and very strapped for cash, looked tired and pale. Janey, his journalist wife, had just had another baby; they weren't getting much sleep at night. He absolutely jumped at Rupert's proposition, particularly when Rupert offered to triple his salary.

"You'd have to come back and live in Gloucestershire."

"Try and stop me. You know I hate London. Might there be something in it for Janey?"

" 'Course there would," said Rupert. "How extraordinary we didn't think of her before. The IBA are dotty about women. She could have her own program. Those chat shows she did for Yorkshire were terrific. Tell her not to write anything too outrageous in her column before Christmas. We won't know whether we've got the franchise until December."

"What happens in the meantime?" said Billy, who felt guilty that Rupert was buying him large whiskys, and only drinking Perrier himself. "I'd adore to join Venturer, but until you can pay me a salary, and the franchise is safely in the bag, I can't afford to burn my boats with the B.B.C."

"It's all right," said Rupert. "Georgie Baines, Seb Burrows, Harold White, and Charles Fairburn are all in exactly the same boat. All that happens is we attach a strictly confidential memo to our application saying we've signed up a Head of Sports, a Sales Director, a Program Controller, etc., who are all wildly experienced, but for security reasons we can't reveal their names until we go up to the IBA for the interview in November."

"How very cloak and dagger," said Billy. "I must say it'll be fun working together again."

"We need some more women," said Declan. "Janey Lloyd-Foxe is gorgeous and talented, but a bit lightweight, and Dame Enid's almost a man."

"I'm going to have a crack at Cameron Cook. I'm working on it," said Rupert, who'd already lost twelve pounds.

"Not safe," growled Declan. "She'd rat on us to Tony."

* * *

Together Freddie and Rupert raised the money.

Rupert, in between his punishing work load as Sports Minister, had several meetings with Henriques Bros., the London Merchant Bank. He found it very difficult not drinking and sticking to his diet over those interminably long lunches, but at least it left him with a clear head. By the second week in April he'd organized a potential seven-million-pound loan.

Freddie's methods were more direct. He invited half a dozen rich cronies to lunch in his conference room and got Taggie up to London to do the cooking. With the boeuf en croute he produced a claret of such vintage and venerability that a one-minute silence was preserved as the first glass was drunk.

"Christ, that's good," said the Chief Executive of Oxford Motors.

Freddie tipped back his chair, his red-gold curls on end, his merry gray eyes sparkling: "I can only afford to drink wine like this once a year," he said, "but I'd like to be able to drink it every day, and that's where all you gentlemen come in."

By the end of lunch, having bandied the names of Marti Gluckstein, Rupert, and Declan around the table, Freddie was well on the way to raising the eight million.

Jubilant, he traveled back to Gloucestershire by train and, seeing a plump lady walking down the platform, recognized Lizzie Vereker and whisked her into a first-class carriage. His mood of euphoria, he soon discovered, was matched by Lizzie's. Thanks to a wonderful new nanny, who seemed impervious to James's advances, she'd finished and delivered her new novel and the publishers loved it. It was an excuse for her to buy him an enormous drink, she said, but she didn't know if British Railways stocked Bacardi and Coke.

"Leave it to me," said Freddie, and came back with two half-bottles of Moët.

"How's James?" he asked, as the train whizzed through Slough.

"Frightfully cross," said Lizzie. "People keep calling him up asking for Declan's home number because they want him to join their consortiums. Have you seen Declan?"

"No," lied Freddie, and wished he didn't have to. Looking at Lizzie's round, smiling face and capacious cashmere bosom, Freddie couldn't help thinking how nice it would be if Lizzie joined Venturer. She had just the right soothing quality to keep everyone happy. She had three novels under her belt and lived in the area. He gave her a lift home. Although the trees were still leafless, the wild garlic and the dog mercury were sweeping like a great emerald-green tide over the floor of the woods.

"Oh I love spring," sighed Lizzie. "The bluebells will be out soon. I've only been away two days and it's like missing 'Dynasty'; you suddenly discover nature's moved on another installment without you."

"I know I shouldn't ask," said Freddie as the red Jaguar pulled up outside her house, "but will you have lunch with me one day?"

"I know I shouldn't accept," said Lizzie, "but yes please."

Dropping in at The Priory on the way home, Freddie found Declan and Rupert in the library surrounded by tapes. Declan was busy writing the section of the application which would tear Corinium's programs to shreds.

He and Rupert were now watching a tape of "Cotswold Roundup." Sarah was interviewing some old lady who couldn't pay her gas bill and James was sitting on the pink sofa looking caring.

"Christ, she's pretty," said Declan. "She'd be dazzling if she were properly produced. We do need some more women."

"No, no, no, no," said Rupert. "She really is lightweight."

"What would you feel about Lizzie Vereker?" said Freddie, his voice thickening.

"Good idea," said Declan. "She writes very well."

"And she's so sweet," said Rupert, "and it would infuriate James."

"And she lives in the area," they all chorused.

"Let's recruit her later in the year," said Declan. "She's too near to Tony and I really don't want him to know what we're up to before the applications go in."

CHAPTER 25

On the second Monday in April, Ursula, who was still working for Declan, although he could ill afford her salary, was due to lunch with her old friend Joyce Madden.

"See if you can find out Tony's whereabouts next weekend," Rupert had asked her on the telephone beforehand.

Ursula, who loved conspiracy, came back from lunch and half a bottle of Sauternes, bustling with excitement, and called Rupert.

"Joyce told me in the strictest confidence that Tony and Cameron are off on a naughty to Madrid this weekend. Cameron's flying out on Friday afternoon. Evidently she wants some peace to polish Corinium's application before it goes off to the IBA. Tony's giving a party at The Falconry on Friday night because it's Badminton weekend and a nice excuse to ask all his posh friends paid for by Corinium. Then he's flying to Madrid on Saturday at lunchtime. They're staying at the Ritz and on Sunday night Cameron's picking up some award for 'Four Men went to Mow.' They're flying home on separate planes on Monday."

"Well done, thou good and faithful servant," said Rupert. "Could you bear at this stage not to mention this to Declan?"

Later in the day Rupert went to a reception to welcome some visiting Russian gymnasts, during which they gave a demonstration of their skills. Watching them go into incredibly graceful contortions on parallel bar and rug, Rupert wondered whether Cameron Cook was as supple and agile as that in bed. How the hell was he to get her on her own to launch his attack? Then inspiration struck. The moment the party was over he raced out to his Government car and called his friend the handsome Duke, who lived at Badminton.

"Could you do me a great favor?"

"Depends how great," said the Duke.

"You've got the Princess staying next weekend, haven't you?"

"Yes."

"Could you possibly ask Tony and Monica Baddingham to dinner on Saturday night?"

"Do I have to? I don't mind Monica, but he's such a ghastly snob."

"I'll knock half a grand off that Irish mare."

"Oh, all right then."

"I'm going away this weekend," Rupert told Gerald Middleton next morning as they went through his calendar. "I bumped into the Secretary of State for Scotland last night, who reminded me that Hearts are playing Madrid on Saturday, and it seemed wrong that no one from our department was going."

Gerald raised his eyebrow.

"They're the only British team in the semi-final," said Rupert blandly.

"You're meant to be chairing a meeting opposite the highway

in Gloucester on Friday night," said Gerald, who didn't approve of dates being broken.

"I know. Call them and say I'm terribly sorry. They have my full support, but they'll have to get someone else. And can you get me a couple of presents for the wives of the British Ambassador and the Spanish Minister for Sport?"

Rupert rolled up at The Priory in the highest spirits the following evening to find Declan still surrounded by tapes and Basil Baddingham sitting on the edge of his desk drinking a Bloody Mary and discussing tactics.

"I was just telling Declan that I've found you a possible building in case Tony won't let us buy the existing Corinium studios," said Bas. "Cotchester Hall's coming on to the market in November. Why are you looking so bloody pleased with yourself?"

"I came to tell you," said Rupert, "that I'm going away for the weekend."

"But we've got our first Venturer meeting on Sunday," protested Declan. "Everyone's coming—even Harold White and Marti Gluckstein."

"Christ, he's never been to the country in his life," said Rupert. Then, hurriedly remembering the cottage he was supposed to be buying for Marti, asked, "Where are you having it, at the Bar Sinister?"

"Too close to Tone," said Bas. "Freddie's earmarked a fantastic little pub in the middle of Salisbury Plain which no one knows and which has amazing food. The landlord just runs it for fun."

Declan was still looking disapproving. "You ought to be there. Meetings are essential at this stage to establish some kind of *esprit de corps*. And we'll all be tossing ideas around."

"You know I never have any," said Rupert.

"I thought you were chairing the highway meeting," said Bas.

"Had to cancel it," said Rupert. "If I don't spend more time in my constituency other than on Venturer business, they're going to drop me."

"Where *are* you going?" asked Bas.

"To Madrid to watch some soccer."

"Balls," said Bas. "You're up to something."

"I need a break," said Rupert. "Man cannot live by bread alone; he needs crumpet."

* * *

There is a moment every spring when even the most dedicated workaholic is overwhelmed by restlessness and longs to wander hand in hand with a new love through the burgeoning countryside. Cameron Cook was no exception. The weather had suddenly turned so warm as she packed for Madrid on Friday morning that she was able to wander naked around her bedroom with the smell of newly mown grass drifting in through the wide open windows. The apple trees at the bottom of her backyard were still bare, but the long grass around their gnarled gray trunks was filled with bright blue cillas, polyanthus and narcissi. Beyond the fence two mallard had nested in the rushes on the edge of the water meadows, and in the distance the willows, bowed over the river, were fringed with palest green.

She had spent several hours a week over the last month in the tanning salon, baking her body to that dark smooth gold that Tony loved. She was in great shape too; her coach at the gym last night had told her that, apart from a few professional athletes, her body was the most perfect and finely tuned he had ever handled. She admired it every time she passed the long mirror. Yet only yesterday Tony had shattered her confidence once again.

In order to discuss some change in the running order, she had barged into Sarah Stratton's dressing room and found her sharing a bottle of champagne with Tony. Sarah's gold hair was prosaically in rollers and she was sitting in a dove-gray silk petticoat which showed off her cleavage and a strip of flesh between the hem of her dove-gray silk French panties and her pale gray stockings. Tony was leaning against the wall six feet away from her, but there was something about the way they stopped talking when Cameron came in. Normally Cameron would have bawled Sarah out for drinking before a show, but she couldn't with Tony permitting it. Instead she had a row with Tony after work.

Tony was quite unrepentant.

"Poor darling Sarah, she was a bit nervous about interviewing the head of the Chamber of Commerce, in case it influenced the franchise. She was asking my advice on her best line of questioning. Her great strength," he went on, with a nasty smile, "is that she's not afraid to show a man she's vulnerable, and she is *so* deliciously feminine."

"And I'm not, I suppose?"

Tony shrugged and ruffled her spiky hair.

"No one could call you feminine, darling."

So this morning, in a rage, Cameron, who had never worn baby-

doll nighties or anything underneath her clothes other than the briefest bikini panties, rushed out and spent a fortune on matching underwear and nightgowns and négligées.

In other more subtle ways her self-confidence had been eroded
recently. Ironically, since Tony had made her Program Controller, a
role she'd coveted for so long, she'd become less secure, because
she spent so much time in meetings and was doing less and less of
the thing she was really good at—producing shows. All the prizes
she was winning now were for work done last year. The new series
of "Four Men went to Mow," starting next week, would largely be
produced, directed, and rewritten by other people. Having clawed
her way to the top, she realized, as many men had realized before
her, that the view from there wasn't that great. Finally, she was aware
that by flexing her muscles in the office, in bed, and in the gym, she
was frightening guys off. In the last three years Patrick and Tony
were the only ones who'd fallen in love with her, and Tony was
showing every sign of getting bored.

Out on the water meadows and the cathedral close she could
see office workers in shirt sleeves and cotton dresses, many of them
probably from Corinium, sneaking out to early lunches, wandering
arm in arm, carrying bottles to drink under the willows.

She glanced at the status symbols littered in ludicrously expensive confusion over her bed—the Charles Jourdan shoes, the Hermes
scarves, the Filofax, the Rayban shades, the huge Rolex watch, the backless kingfisher-blue Jasper Conran for Sunday night's presentation—
what was the point of all these trappings if there was no one else to
share them with? Her mood of despair lasted all the way to Madrid.

There, however, the black limo that met her at the airport and
the splendor of her magnificent suite at the Ritz, paid for by the
Spanish television authorities, gradually cheered her up.

There were two bedrooms in the suite, each with two beds, a
huge living room stuffed with antiques and lit by huge chandeliers,
and an enormous bathroom with a hair dryer and two beautiful white
terrycloth robes. There was a bottle of champagne in a bucket of ice
and a huge basket of fruit with pomegranates, persimmons, and apples as big as grapefruit. Pink carnations floated in the finger bowls;
there were flowers in every room to match the pale pink walls, and
silver trays of chocolates. There were also telephones everywhere,
even in the shower. And this was just her suite. Tony's suite next
door was identical.

She strolled out on to the balcony and saw that there was a little garden restaurant below, with a summer house and floodlit lemon trees and a lawn with a fountain. The tables were filled with handsome, hawklike men with sleek black hair, and beautiful women in suits with very padded shoulders, all talking their heads off and having a wonderful time.

Going back into the living room to attack a pomegranate, she noticed an etching of the Judgment of Paris on the wall. Juno and Athena, both fully dressed, were looking furious as Venus, who was flashing an ankle and a bare boob, was awarded the apple. Venus looked just like Sarah Stratton. Cameron turned the picture to the wall. It must be tiredness that suddenly made her feel so unbelievably down again. She couldn't be bothered with supper; taking two Valium, she crashed out.

She got up early, spent two hours working out camera angles for the first part of "Four Men went to Mow," then spent the rest of the morning working on Corinium's application. God it was turgid, longer than *Gone With the Wind* and infinitely less readable: all those Brownie points being notched up with promises to employ independent production companies and set up audio-visual workshops, or subsidize roving repertory companies and youth orchestras. There was also a lot of guff about grass-roots involvement and worker participation schemes. A few figures had been provided, but there was very little talk of profits.

Unable to face tinkering with it any more, Cameron lunched at the hotel, wandered round Madrid, which seemed to be packed with Scottish football supporters, then spent two hours restoring her sanity looking at the Goyas and El Grecos in the Prado. The telephone was ringing as she let herself into her suite. It was Joyce Madden.

"Lord B's terribly sorry." Cameron could tell Madden wasn't. "He's been trying to get you all afternoon. He's sorry but he won't be able to fly out for the awards. Something's cropped up. The Duke's asked him to dine at Badminton tonight. He says he can't refuse, particularly in franchise year. Hullo, hullo . . ." but Cameron had hung up.

She was so angry she ate all the chocolates on the silver tray. How dare he, the bastard! Standing her up for a fucking dinner party. Asshole star-fucker.

Absolutely on cue there was a knock on the door and in came a valet bringing a huge bunch of roses.

"Sorry I can't make it, Darling," said the card. *"Good luck tomorrow, all love Tony."*

Cameron was so furious she went out and hurled the roses over the balcony, watching them whiz around and around until they landed on a mob of cheering fans.

"Bastard, fucker, asshole," screamed Cameron at the top of her voice, then let out an enormous fart, which seemed the only way she could demonstrate her utter contempt for Tony.

"Hush," drawled a voice, "you'll frighten the pigeons."

Cameron swung around and gave a gasp of appalled embarrassment.

For there, laughing his handsome head off on the next-door balcony, his face as brown as the glass of whisky in his hand, lounged Rupert.

"What are you doing here?" muttered Cameron.

"Watching Hearts win a football match. Never thought I'd get in here, but they had a last-minute cancellation, a Mr. Smith." He grinned wickedly. "What an extraordinary coincidence to find you here. Why are you looking so bad-tempered?"

"I am bad-tempered. The TV doesn't speak English."

"You expecting guests?"

"Not any more."

"So that bouquet you were bombing the masses with was a peace offering from the Oily Baron?"

"You're *so* fucking perceptive," said Cameron sulkily. Then rage overcame pride. "Madden just called to say he can't make it. He's been summoned to dine at Badminton."

"Probably has," said Rupert. "I know there's a dinner party there tonight and the Princess is going. Let's have a drink. Your place or mine?"

"Mine," said Cameron. "Give me half an hour while I take a bath and dress."

"I wouldn't bother," said Rupert. "You're overdressed as it is."

It was all going too fast for her. What the hell was Rupert doing here? It could hardly be coincidence. He was the biggest rake in the world. No one emerged unscathed. So why was she feeling so wildly elated, washing her ears when she'd washed them that morning, and trimming her bush, and rubbing Fracas into her belly and inner thighs? As she slid into her new peach satin underwear it seemed to be caressing her in anticipation. Finally, she put on a pale apricot tunic, very demure and clinging with all the buttons done up, but with the hemline six inches above the knee, making her legs seem endless.

All powerful men are attractive. Men who are powerful and kind are irresistible. For once Rupert seemed to have abandoned his flip cracks and his sexual innuendoes. He appeared to be really, really interested in her career, in Corinium's program plans and how they were approaching their application for the franchise. He was also incredibly well informed. She'd always thought he was only interested in sports and screwing.

Cameron was enjoying herself so much she didn't notice she'd drunk almost an entire bottle of champagne and Rupert had hardly touched his glass of whisky. As the boat race is usually won in the first two minutes by one crew surging ahead and taking advantage of smoother water, so the conquest of Cameron was really achieved in that first hour when she was off guard and feeling bruised and vulnerable because Tony had stood her up. As Rupert got up to fill her glass yet again, he pointed to the mound of paper on her desk.

"What are you doing?"

"Working on the final application."

"Anyone bidding against you?" asked Rupert, idly.

"A group of Bristol businessmen calling themselves Mid-West. They claim we're too Cotchester-oriented. But I don't think they're much competition."

That's three of us pitching, thought Rupert. "Is Tony worried?" he asked.

"No way, but we can't afford to be complacent. Southern lost their franchise last time, and they didn't appear to have done anything wrong. The IBA have to make some changes to make it look like they're doing their job."

"What about Declan? Tony lost a network slot there. How's he going to replace him?"

"I'm not sure. Declan cost Tony so much dough, and he really freaked him out. Tony can't stand not being able to bully people. I guess he'll poach some top on-camera person in the next few weeks, just to distract people from Declan's departure. The media are still sniffing around."

"Any idea who it might be?" said Rupert.

"No. Tony loves to surround himself in mystery."

"How are you enjoying being Program Controller?"

Cameron shrugged. "Not as much as I expected. There's so much hassle. I had to fire four people last week. You ever done that?"

"Frequently," said Rupert. "You should get out. Any of the network companies would snap you up."

Cameron looked at the bulky application on the desk. "I'd like to see Corinium retain the franchise. I'll probably look around in the fall. Although why I hang in with that bastard, I can't think. Is it usual to be asked to dine with Royalty at the last moment?''

''No,'' said Rupert.

''So Tony must have known about the dinner party for ages, and didn't have the guts to tell me he wouldn't be coming.''

''Probably didn't want you to make other arrangements,'' said Rupert, emptying the bottle into her glass.

He was shrewd enough to realize that, having existed on a diet of Tony for three years, what Cameron was missing was a legitimate social life. He got to his feet.

''Well, thanks for the drink. I'm going out to dinner.''

Cameron's happiness drained away. ''Goodbye,'' she said coldly, gazing at the plane trees in the square which were turning pink in the setting sun.

Back in his own suite, Rupert extracted a tape recorder the width and size of half a pencil from his shirt pocket, removed the tape, and put it in a secret compartment in his brief case.

Alone in her seven rooms, Cameron nearly went into orbit with frustration. In the mirror she could see her eyes glittering feverishly, her breath coming in great gasps, her nipples sticking through the apricot dress like thimbles. She half expected to see a pulse jumping between her legs.

She was nearly thirty. Perhaps she was losing her touch and Rupert really didn't want to sleep with her. She couldn't stand it. Ripping off the dress and the temptress's satin underwear he hadn't even seen, she went into the bathroom and turned on the cold shower, letting the icy jet blast away all the Fracas and the body lotion and the gel, and, hopefully, the desire. She turned it on so hard that it was a few seconds before she realized the telephone was ringing. No doubt it was Tony, establishing his ascendancy, so she let it ring just to worry him. After two minutes she picked it up.

''Cameron.'' Cameron leaned against the wall, feeling giddy with relief.

''Yes.''

''Am I going to have to swing across the balcony like Tarzan or are you going to let me in?''

Rupert had brushed his teeth and was still wearing his blue striped shirt and suit trousers. Without the camouflage of his jacket, Cameron could see how divinely proportioned he was, hunky on the shoulders, and lean and streamlined everywhere else. The golden meanie, she thought. As he came toward her, she clutched the towel around her, looking very young and vulnerable with her hair flat and wet from the shower, like a guard dog who's been uncharacteristically caught with its hackles down.

Very gently Rupert took off the huge Rolex watch she'd forgotten to remove in the shower. "I want to see if you've got a designer cunt."

He stopped her reply by kissing her; the towel slid to the floor.

It was a very good thing, he reflected later, that he'd lost all that weight and been jogging for an hour every morning, or he'd never have coped with the pace. Cameron was like an electric eel, knew every sexual permutation in the book, could twist herself into any position, and ordered him around like a sergeant-major.

"You are incredible," he murmured into the back of her head, "you'd make a matchstick feel like a cigar."

After two hours' fairly sustained screwing in both bedrooms, on the sofa in the drawing room, under the shower, and admiring themselves in every mirror, they collapsed onto the carpet and Rupert came for the fourth and, from his point of view, final time.

"I haven't come yet," said Cameron in his ear.

Rupert was astounded. "What was wrong, for Christ's sake?"

"Nothing. It was the best first fuck I've ever had, I'm too uptight I guess."

"Well, I'm not jumping ship till you do, so you may as well relax and stop fighting."

Wriggling downwards, he parted her sodden bush.

Waking first, Cameron reached out and realized she wasn't with Tony. Rupert had an enormous erection. Getting up, she drew back the curtain an inch. Rupert was certainly the best-looking man she'd ever been to bed with, and, despite her sniping, the best lay. Once she'd let him take over last night, everything had been perfect. She knew too that, in the space of fourteen hours, she was a different person. She'd been dependent on Tony for security but never happiness. For the first time in her life, she was in love, and it terrified her.

The ring of the telephone woke Rupert up. It was Tony, all smarm, calling from his car, so the line wasn't very good. This was a good thing as Rupert started kissing Cameron all over in the middle, and so distracted her she couldn't remember anything practical, like what time the awards were or when she flew in tomorrow, or concentrate on the witty remarks Tony had made to the Princess.

"It's Tony," she wrote frantically on the telephone message pad.

"So?" wrote Rupert.

"I'm so sorry," gasped Cameron. "I was working very late on the application."

"How's it shaping?"

"Very well," shrieked Cameron, as Rupert, grinning broadly, lunged into her. "Look I've got to go, I'm off to Toledo. I'll call you before I leave tomorrow morning. You're insupportable," she howled at Rupert, as she slammed down the telephone.

"How was the dinner party?"

Cameron grimaced. "Said he only accepted because he felt the Duke needed his support and it was always a bit nerve-racking entertaining royalty."

Rupert had to bury his face in her neck to stop himself laughing.

They made love again, with less energy but more tenderness.

"Can I get down?" said Cameron finally as she straddled him.

"You are *able* to get down," said Rupert, quoting his old nanny, "but whether you *may* is another matter."

Cameron caressed his cheek. "Are you coming with me tonight?"

Rupert shook his head. "Not safe. There'll be too many Press."

Cameron looked so seductive in her new kingfisher-blue backless that Rupert nearly dragged her back to bed again.

"Uh, uh." Cameron skipped out of the way. "I'll stagger onto the podium like John Wayne as it is. I hope I don't fall asleep during the speeches."

As soon as she walked into the Reception she realized that it was a very good thing she'd come by herself. There was Ivor Hicks, Corinium's corporate development controller, chatting up a tough-looking Spanish woman. She also recognized people from Granada and TVS, and one of Robert Maxwell's henchmen.

"What the hell are you doing here?" she whispered to Ivor.

"Tony's after a stake in Spanish television," said Ivor. "The Government here's creating three new channels. Tony wants twenty-five per cent of one of them. Maxwell, Granada, and TVS are after the same thing."

Cameron sighed. "That means less money for programs."

"But more security for Tony, in case he loses the franchise," said Ivor. "Diversification is the name of the game."

* * *

Rupert gave Cameron half an hour. Then, watching her going into dinner on television, he went systematically through her Filofax, dictating her future appointments into his tape recorder—and a lot of Tony's that she'd listed. Then he opened her briefcase and removed the Corinium Application. It was very bulky, like smuggling in *Lady Chatterley's Lover* when he was at Prep School.

At first the pretty girl at the reception desk told Rupert the office was closed and there was no way the application could be copied. But Spanish guests at the hotel seldom had such blond hair, or such blue eyes, or such good teeth, or waved so many thousands and thousands of pesetas in front of her. She would see what she could do, she said. She'd have to sneak the application into the office, it might take a little time, as the manager was on duty. She'd call Rupert's room as soon as it was done. Sweating, he went back upstairs and paced up and down, drinking whisky. On television the awards were well underway. Stars were tottering up onto the platform wiping their eyes and thanking every member of the crew, and every madre and padre, for the help they had given. What if Cameron had been on already and, overcome with lust, was on her way back to him?

Going downstairs again, he met the receptionist, very flustered, but with the completed copy. It was only when he got back to his room that he realized the silly cow had put it back out of order; the sections on "Master Dog" and "Dorothy Dove" were in the wrong place and James Vereker's afternoon program was in the middle of Engineering specifications. It was a long and laborious task to get them in the right order, and even then Rupert wasn't sure he'd done it right. He rushed downstairs to get the various chapters stapled together.

He was just getting back into the elevator when he saw Cameron coming through the revolving door. Pressing the button, he creaked up to the seventh floor, rushed to her room, which he'd rashly left open because he didn't have a key, and double-locked it on the inside.

With trembling hands he shoved the original back in her briefcase, hoping it was the right way up, snapped the clasp and shoved the copied pages inside his jacket under his arm. The next minute there was a knock on the door.

"Rupert, open up," said Cameron.

Pretending to rub the sleep out of his eyes, he opened the door. "Sorry, sweetheart, I didn't want to be disturbed by maids replacing chocolates and turning down beds. How was it?"

"Scary," said Cameron. "I'll never, never be mean to any on-camera people again. Wasn't it awful when I cried?"

"You were sweet," lied Rupert, "and they were all so touched you tried to speak Spanish."

Fortunately Cameron was a bit tight. "Have you eaten?" she asked.

"I wasn't hungry," said Rupert, edging toward the door. "In fact I've got a bloody awful headache."

"I've got some aspirin," said Cameron, going to her briefcase.

"I've got something even stronger next door," said Rupert hastily. "I'll be back in a minute."

Back in his suite, he nearly died. He'd never had nerves like this when he was show jumping and screwing everyone else's wives. With shaking, sweating hands, he stuffed the copied application in the secret compartment of his briefcase.

Cameron had kicked off her shoes and was lying on the bed drinking white wine when he got back.

"Good thing you didn't come," she said. "There were so many people who'd have recognized you. I picked up a *Sunday Times*."

"Thanks."

Rupert turned immediately to the sports page, she noticed, then the smile was wiped off his face.

"Fucking hell!" He turned to the front page.

"What's the matter?"

"Riots after both semi-finals of the FA Cup," he howled. "Two policemen stabbed, cars overturned and burned, shop windows smashed, twenty people taken to the hospital, forty-five arrests. Fucking, fucking hell! I play hookey for one weekend and this happens."

In a second he was on the phone to Gerald in London.

"I've been trying to get you since yesterday, Minister."

There were obviously other people in the room or Gerald would never have been so formal.

"Is it very serious?"

"Yes—four people are still in intensive care."

"I'll fly back tonight."

"I'm sorry, Minister. After all your hard work, it's a most tragic setback."

By one o'clock, Rupert managed to get onto a private jet, arranged by the British Ambassador. He seemed to have forgotten Cameron's existence until he was leaving.

"I'm sorry to walk out on you, angel. I'm just so pissed off. I was so certain I'd pegged the violence." He took her face in his hands. "Look it's been great. I won't call you in case I get Tony. You call me. Here's Gerald's number; he'll know where to find me."

And he was gone.

It's a beginning, thought Cameron, hanging over the balcony to see if she could catch a glimpse of him getting into his car. It was still warm. Breathing in the scent of the lemon trees from the little garden, she had a sudden vision of Rupert's beautiful house in Gloucestershire and all that wonderful sweep of land, and decided the only status symbol she really wanted was a Cartier wedding ring with R C-B and CC engraved inside.

CHAPTER 26

Rupert went back to England slap into a political storm. The dramatic drop in football rioting had been a high spot of the Tory administration. Now, after a sickening day of violence, their claims were looking very dubious. With an election in the offing, the opposition were roaring for blood and, in an emergency debate on Monday night, tabled a motion of no confidence in the Minister of Sport and howled for Rupert's resignation. Although Rupert was certain left-wing militants were behind the riots and hinted as much in the House, he couldn't prove it yet and the Government won the debate by the narrowest majority. Some of his own side were not displeased by events; Rupert had been the PM's darling for too long. The Cup Final was not until May 15th, but all Rupert's energies were now channelled into seeing that the violence wasn't repeated.

He spent most of the next week trying not to lose his temper with the pack of reporters snarling at his heels as he visited the two devastated football clubs, and comforted those who'd been hurt in the riots. As a result, he didn't get down to Penscombe until late Wednesday afternoon, landing the helicopter on the lawn.

He had only been away a week, but already bluebells were flaming like Bunsen burners in his woods, and the crimson glow of the beeches had turned to a rusty terra-cotta as green leaves burst out of their narrow brown buds. Although brilliant sunshine and blue skies welcomed him, across the valley he could see an April shower tumbling darkly out of a huge purple cloud onto The Priory.

However angry he was, returning to Penscombe always soothed him. He was greeted by messages from Gerald that the two stabbed policemen were now off the danger list and that Cameron Cook had called three times, leaving a number. Instead of calling her, he had a quick shower and drove over to The Priory where the rain had almost stopped, leaving a heady smell of wet earth and nettles. As he walked through the door, he was greeted by an even headier smell of frying garlic and onions. Taggie must be home, which unconsciously soothed him even more. He'd go and see her when he'd reported in. In the library he found Freddie, Bas, and Charles giving a slightly unreceptive Declan tips on how to write the application.

"What a fucking awful week you're having," said Declan. "You poor bastard. You must feel like Sisyphus."

"I don't know who he is," said Rupert, "but I'm sure I do."

"Get him a drink, Bas," said Declan.

"Only Perrier," said Rupert. "I've got to fly back and vote after this. How did the first Venturer meeting go?"

The others looked at each other. Was the sun shining through the stained glass window or was Freddie blushing?"

"It was somewhat hazardous," said Declan. "You tell him, Freddie."

"Well, we all went down to this pub on Salisbury Plain," said Freddie sheepishly, "which I could've sworn was always deserted, and we'd just settled into prelunch drinks and managed to stop Wesley Emerson offering the Bishop a joint when the entire nation's press arrived in three buses to 'ave a bite before witnessing the launching of a new tank at some army base down the road."

"Christ," Rupert started to laugh. "Did any of them see you?"

"Billy the Kid couldn't have emptied a saloon bar faster," said Freddie.

"It was seriously funny," said Bas. "We all hotfooted it back to The Priory for a Chinese takeout, and the whole thing seemed to bring us closer together. I must say I'd forgotten how stunningly attractive Janey Lloyd-Foxe is."

"And belongs to Billy," said Rupert firmly.

Through the window he could see Taggie, who'd gone out into the garden to pick some thyme from the herb garden, gazing in rapture at a rainbow. She had the most adorable bottom, he decided, which became even more adorable when she bent over the flower bed in her jeans.

"Rupert," said Bas, "are you still with us?"

"Looking at the rainbow," said Rupert, hastily opening his briefcase. "I've got a stunning bit of news to cheer you all up. I've brought you an Easter present, Declan."

Triumphantly he chucked the two tapes and the photostat of the Corinium application down on Declan's desk.

"What's this?" said Declan, putting on his spectacles.

"Two extraordinarily informative conversations with Cameron Cook, and a copy of the corrected final draft of Corinium's application."

Freddie, Bas, and Charles were so excited, none of them noticed Declan's look of thunderous disapproval, or that he'd dropped the application as though it was a wasp-infested pear.

"Where did you get that?" asked Freddie in awe.

"I spent the weekend in Madrid, in bed with Cameron."

Basil's jaw clanged. "Does my brother know?"

"Tony was due out there," said Rupert, "but I arranged for a chum to offer Tony an invite for Saturday night he couldn't refuse."

Basil started to laugh. "To meet HRH at Badminton?"

"My God, was that your doing?" said Charles in amazement. "Tony was boasting about it to everyone."

"So he stood up Ms. Cook," said Rupert wandering over to the bar table and splashing more Perrier into his glass, "who was not overly delighted until I suddenly appeared on the adjacent balcony like *Private Lives* and took Tony's place."

"What was she like?" asked Bas, fascinated.

"Fucks like a stoat," said Rupert. "In fact the end-away definitely justified the means."

"You ought to join the CIA," said Bas.

"She'll be after your blood when she finds out," said Charles delightedly.

"She won't," said Rupert. "She hadn't a clue. Well?" He turned to Declan for approval.

But Declan was looking infinitely more thunderous than the cloud that drenched The Priory earlier.

"You can't fucking do that," he exploded.

"Why ever not?"

"Because it's bloody dishonest."

"I must be dreaming," said Rupert incredulously. "Declan dear, we're pitching for a business with a hundred-and-twenty-five million pound turnover, not playing fucking tiddlywinks. Have a read. You can find out exactly what Tony's up to and pre-empt it. It's the most turgid stuff, Tony seems to be promising an unchecked flow of good causes and Elizabethan drama for the next ten years!"

"I'm not going to read it," said Declan roughly. "We're playing this thing straight."

"Now come on, Declan," protested Freddie. "Think of the clout it'll give us."

Declan was now absolutely shaking with rage. "I repeat, we're playing it straight."

"Tony is evil," hissed Rupert. "Don't you think he'd do the same thing to you, given the chance? I thought you were out to get him."

"Not by sinking to his methods," said Declan coldly.

"Then what are you doing asking the Bishop to lunch, dressing Maud up like a nun and asking him to say Grace?"

"That's different."

"It is NOT!" Rupert was furiously pacing up and down the floor-boards now. "And what are you doing poaching half Tony's staff? I'm amazed you didn't call Tony first and ask his permission."

"That's entirely different," yelled Declan. "What you've done is stolen Corinium's property. It's a criminal offence."

"Isn't Charles Corinium's property?" yelled back Rupert.

"Ooo," said Charles, looking excited. "They're fighting over me."

"Shut up," screamed Rupert and Declan, both turning on him.

"Charles came of his own volition," said Declan, "but Cameron had no idea what you were up to."

"She certainly enjoyed it," snarled Rupert. "Don't you go feel-ing sorry for her, and Jesus, the hassle I went to, getting that thing copied. I practically had to bang the receptionist."

"Never been a hardship for you," said Declan icily, and, picking up the application and the two tapes, he chucked them into the wastepaper basket. Bas, Freddie, and Charles winced. Rupert went very still.

"And if any of you try and retrieve them, I'll put them in the furnace," added Declan.

"All my life I've been accused of lacking application," drawled Rupert, "then when I actually get hold of one."

"It's not a joke," roared Declan.

"I'm not laughing," said Rupert bleakly. "Fuck you, Declan, and screw your bloody franchise."

"Now, wite a minute," said Freddie, leaping to his feet.

But Rupert had walked out. In the hall he nearly sent Taggie flying. She was carrying a pile of Airtex shirts and green skirts up-stairs. Caitlin was going back to school next week.

"What on earth's the matter?" she said in alarm.

"Your fucking father."

"What's he done? Come into the kitchen."

"It's what he won't do." For a second Rupert debated whether to walk out, but he was so angry with Declan he had to tell someone, so he followed her into the kitchen.

"I'll get you a drink."

"I'm not drinking. And I'll never touch a drop of your father's liquor again."

"What's happened?" said Taggie, bewildered. Then, realizing the steak and kidney she was cooking was burning, she ran across the kitchen to give it a stir.

"I've just spent all last weekend in Madrid screwing Cameron Cook," said Rupert furiously, "to get her on our side, and to get information about Corinium's application, and by Sunday night I not only had her eating out of my hand, but had secretly copied the entire application."

He was so angry, he didn't notice that Taggie's wooden spoon had stopped moving.

"What's Daddy objecting to?" said Taggie in a strangely high voice.

"He won't read it. He thinks it's taking unfair advantage. Jesus, no wonder he's broke."

At that moment Freddie appeared in the doorway. But, seeing Rupert was talking to Taggie, he decided she'd be better at calming him down than any of them and tiptoed back to the library.

"Let me make you a cup of tea," said Taggie.

By the time the kettle had boiled and the tea had brewed for three minutes, and Rupert had told her the whole story, she'd recovered her composure. After all, Rupert was entitled to go to bed with whom he chose, and perhaps he just did it with Cameron because he wanted to get hold of the application document, she thought hopefully, although Cameron was terribly beautiful and Patrick would be absolutely heartbroken if he found out. Oh God, what a terrible muddle.

Rupert leaned against the stove, looking moodily at a huge vase of bluebells.

"From our woods," said Taggie, trying to lift the conversation. "Aren't they lovely?"

Rupert was about to snap that they were from his woods now.

"Don't try to placate me," he said coldly.

Taggie handed him a cup of tea. Then she took a deep breath. "I think Daddy's right," she stammered.

Rupert looked up. "You what?" he said, unbelievingly. "Not you, too?"

"He wouldn't feel right with himself. It's like cheating in exams. To most people it wouldn't matter, but he's got such utter integ . . ." Taggie stumbled over the word.

"Integrity, and I haven't I suppose."

"Of course you have, but of a different kind. If you won the franchise because he'd spied on Tony Baddingham, he wouldn't be able to live with himself."

"Well, he's not living with me any longer. D'you think Tony won't wheel out every trick in the book, once he finds out we're bidding against him? Your father's trying to fight a nuclear war with a B-B gun."

"It's because he disapproves of Lord Baddingham so much. He couldn't descend to his level. That's why he's bidding against him."

"Not with me, he ain't," said Rupert, putting down his mug. "I'm out."

"Oh please not," pleaded Taggie. "It's so lovely for them having you as part of the consortium. You've got such c-c-charisma."

"Is that your word for the day?" snapped Rupert.

"No, it's my word for always about you," said Taggie, blushing crimson. "Honestly, they think you're marvelous."

"Funny way of showing it," said Rupert, walking toward the door.

Taggie ran after him, her eyes filling with tears.

"Oh, please. Daddy really needs you. You and Freddie were so wonderful when he was down, I know he seems terribly clever but he's not street smart like you."

Gazing at her, Rupert noticed how her tears and the old gray denim shirt of Declan's she was wearing emphasized the strange silver-gray of her eyes.

"Darling Taggie," he said, his face softening, "how can anyone refuse you anything?"

"Then you'll stay?"

Rupert shrugged. "I suppose so . . . but I'm extremely pissed off." He reached into his pocket and rooted out a crimson leather box. "I got you an Easter egg in Madrid. I hope you'll like it better than the present I brought your father."

Inside the box Taggie found a little gold egg, speckled with rubies and diamonds. She gave a gasp.

"Look further," said Rupert.

Opening the egg, she found a tiny gold bird with ruby eyes.

"Poor thing's got conjunctivitis," said Rupert.

"I can't believe it," breathed Taggie. "No one brings me presents like that. Oh thank you so so much. I love it."

Blushing furiously again, she leaned forward and kissed him on the cheek. She's the little sister I never had, Rupert told himself firmly.

"Your steak and kidney's burning," he said.

"Are you staying for supper?"

"No, I've got to go back and vote."

"What on?"

"Capital punishment for terrorists."

Taggie looked horrified.

"They're not going to bring it back, are they? Daddy'd leave the country."

In the library Freddie was giving Declan a piece of his mind. "This is the big league, if you'll excuse me saying so. Rupert's a very clever operator, and we can't afford to lose 'im. You've got to learn to argue wivout rancor, Declan. You can't stick your chest out all the time."

"What do you know about it?" growled Declan.

"I've never 'ad a strike at work," said Freddie, "because I don't judge everyone the same. I cultivate their individual skills. You're always bangin' on about giving creative people the right atmosphere to work in. Then, when Rupert does somefink really creative, you shit on 'im."

Watched in awed amazement by Bas and Charles, Freddie calmly retrieved the application from the wastebasket.

Declan gazed at him appalled: "But, it's dishonest for fuck's sake. You wouldn't have pinched that document, would you?"

"Wouldn't 'ave 'ad the nerve," said Freddie. "But now we've got it, I'm certainly goin' to 'ave a little look. This is war, as Rupert said, not tiddlywinks. You don't want to be too 'igh-minded, Declan."

By the time Sydney his driver had dropped Rupert off at Westminster, the yellow stone of the House was softened by floodlighting and Big Ben shone like a great sugar sifter against an inky blue sky.

"Only one vote," Rupert told Sydney. "But I've got a hell of a lot of work still to do. Can you come back about twelve-thirty?"

Nodding good evening to the policeman on the gate, Rupert went through the Member's entrance, an expression that usually made him laugh. Glancing at the monitor he saw that Owen Davies, the Labor leader, was winding up for the abolitionists. Time for a large drink . . . he was bloody tired, and he'd never had any doubts that stringing up was the answer for terrorists. But as he headed for the bar he thought fleetingly of Taggie's horror of capital punishment, and Declan's passionate disapproval, and decided to listen to the debate instead.

As he entered the chamber the Ministers for Employment and for Health moved slightly apart to make room for him on the green leather front bench.

"Owen's in barnstorming form," whispered the Minister of Health.

Hearing a din behind him, Rupert glanced around to see Paul Stratton, who was violently pro-hanging for everything, particularly wife-pinching, looking excited for the first time in months.

"Rubbish," Paul yelled. "Resign, check your figures. What's the point of having British soldiers out there if we don't support them?"

Owen Davies, a brilliant orator on the dullest subject, was in magnificent form tonight. What about all those people who'd been imprisoned for terrorism, he demanded, who'd later been found innocent? What evidence was there in any country that the death penalty curbed terrorism, and, conversely, didn't hanging make sainted martyrs out of the most vicious thugs?

It was great emotional stuff. But, putting aside the soft cadences, the eloquence, the Welsh voice, Rupert suddenly knew Owen was right. The Prime Minister, who was almost more pro-hanging than Paul Stratton, looked most distressed. Owen Davies sat down to a storm of applause.

Scenting blood, the abolitionists roared for the PM to get up. "On your feet. Don't be bashful."

But the PM wasn't budging. Instead, she let the Home Secretary, who was decidedly ambivalent about the merits of hanging anyway, wind up. Every time he opened his mouth, he was howled down, but he ploughed on bravely with his prepared speech. As Big Ben tolled ten o'clock, the noise subsided and the house divided.

The Ayes, looking tight-lipped and apprehensive, shuffled to the right. The Noes, looking elated, sauntered to the left. Without a moment's deliberation, ignoring the outraged looks of the PM, Rupert joined the Noes. Owen Davies, turning in delighted amazement, tapped Rupert on the shoulder. "I didn't know you were one of us."

"I wasn't until I heard you," said Rupert.

The Minister of Health, a pacific and gentle soul, also joined the Noes.

"We'll be on the carpet tomorrow," he said.

Feeling suddenly shattered and not wanting a lecture from the PM, Rupert beat a quick retreat to his office, a small room on the lower Ministers' floor. Inside, the walls were covered with signed photographs of famous athletes: Pat Eddery, Ian Botham, Maradona, John McEnroe, Pat Cash, Gary Lineker, Dino and Fenella Ferranti, to name only a few. Above the filing cabinet was a picture of Wesley Emerson, the local cricketing hero who had joined the Venturer consortium, and whom Rupert had saved from getting busted.

"Thanks, Rupe, Wesley Emerson," he had scrawled across the blue sky behind him.

I should think so too, reflected Rupert whenever he looked at the photo.

Having taken off his tie, and undone his top button, he poured himself a large whisky and soda. Christ, he was tired. He'd been on the go since five that morning and hadn't had any real sleep for a week. Making him feel even more tired was the envelope on the blotter full of constituency letters to be signed and the even bigger pile of mail to be read, which was probably mostly abusive letters about the football riots.

The admirable Gerald had scribbled a note: *"Gone to* Madam Butterfly. *Back about one-thirty. Call if you need me."*

In the corner of the room was a hard olive-green sofa, where Rupert was supposed to snatch some sleep during late-night sittings. It had never looked more seductive. If he had an hour's nap he might work better. He had another six o'clock start in the morning. The telephone ringing made him jump.

"Rupert, it's Cameron."

Christ, he'd completely forgotten to call her back.

"Angel! You got home safely?"

"Well, I'm not lying in a pile of wreckage at the bottom of the Bay of Biscay." All the insecurity and truculence had returned to her voice.

"I'm sorry I didn't call. It's been frantic, and I didn't want to tread on Tony's bunions. When am I going to see you?" He suppressed a yawn.

"Christ knows," snapped Cameron. "Tony's taking me away for the weekend."

"To Buckingham Palace?"

Cameron didn't laugh. "To LA, to close a couple of deals over Easter. Then we fly straight to Cannes to meet with our various co-production partners and firm up existing relationships. I won't be back till a week from Monday."

Rupert glanced at the calendar. That was April 26th. He'd be away until the 30th and the franchises had to be in on the 3rd. That would give him hardly any time after she got back to persuade her to join Venturer. He ought to establish interim ascendancy over Tony by seeing her this evening.

"Where are you?" he asked.

"At home."

"Alone?"

"Yes."

"I'll drive down."

"Are you crazy? D'you know what time it is?" But it was impossible for her to keep the elation out of her voice.

"I've got at least an hour's work," said Rupert. "The drive at this time of night should take an hour and a half. I can't afford to get caught speeding. I'll be with you about two."

Thank God, he'd had a shower and changed at Penscombe earlier in the evening, it seemed a thousand years ago. He trusted Sydney, but not entirely, so he dismissed him and took the Ferrari, which was parked outside his Westminster flat. Torrential rain on the highway gave way to moonlight as he reached the outskirts of Cotchester. The cathedral clock was tolling the hour; the shadow of the spire lay thick and black across the watermeadows. He was so tired he'd never be able to get it up.

Cameron, however, opened the front door with nothing on.

"I might have been the milkman," said Rupert reprovingly.

"You're not that late," she whispered.

As her warm, oiled and scented body twined around him, she was obviously so delighted to see him that miraculously Rupert woke up.

Bounding upstairs after her, he decided this was one relationship he would have absolutely no difficulty firming up.

CHAPTER 27

Although Cameron was kept ludicrously busy selling herself and Corinium's programs, she was shattered by how much she missed Rupert. LA was bad enough, but Cannes seemed so tantalizingly near. Every minute in the booth, or at the numerous Corinium parties, or in her hotel bedroom, conveniently next to Tony's, she expected Rupert to appear grinning like a Cheshire cat.

On her second Thursday away from him, however, her black mood was caused by rage rather than longing. One of Tony's myriad subsidiary companies, Falconry Films Inc., had made a lousy miniseries called "Stowaway," about an aristocratic orphan who disguised herself as a cabin boy on a clipper ship and had a fling with the pirate captain. And now Tony had actually sailed a real clipper ship, at vast expense, into Cannes Harbor as a publicity stunt and was holding a huge bash on board. Sourly watching all the fatcat international buyers and their bikinied bimbos stuffing their faces with champagne and caviar, Cameron felt they were guzzling all the profits she'd made for Corinium from "Four Men went to Mow."

The Mediterranean suited Tony; his olive skin had already turned mahogany. As he purred around the clipper ship in his dark glasses and discreetly coroneted black shirt, clinching deals and pinching bottoms, he looked more like a pirate king than ever.

Cameron had had plenty of time to compare Tony with Rupert while she was away. Both were reputed to be absolute shits. But, while Tony was coldly sensual, utterly venal, eaten up with envy and sadistically dedicated to putting people down, Rupert, Cameron felt, was only sharp-tongued because he was arrogant and easily bored. She had been so touched that he'd driven all the way down to Cotchester on that last night, and that after he'd made love to her he hadn't fallen asleep as most men would, but stayed awake pestering her with questions about what she and Tony would be doing and selling in LA and Cannes.

It was a relief too that he couldn't call her, so she didn't go through the roof with expectation every time the telephone rang. Instead, at grave risk, she'd phoned him twice from LA and every day from Cannes.

There was no doubt, too, that she was the flavor of the month at the festival. The third series of "Four Men went to Mow" had

already been presold worldwide. The Corinium publicity department had taken a full-page advertisement in *Broadcast* this week,
with a stunning photograph of Cameron holding a baby lamb, with
the caption: *"Cameron Cook works for Corinium, meet her on stand
329"*, then listing all the prizes she'd won in the last year. Everyone
wanted to congratulate her and offer her work.

Back at The Priory, Declan was still working on the Venturer application, only pausing occasionally to pick up the binoculars on the
window seat to check on some newly-arrived migrant bird; swallows, housemartins, whitethroats were all winging in now. Last night
he had even heard the first nightingale in the wood.

"*Our duty,*" wrote Declan, "*is to tell the truth, to be relevant,
entertaining and interesting, to monitor power and expose its abuse,
to be nobody's mouthpiece.*"

Christ, it was difficult not to use clichés, to be concise: *To bring
the balloon of the mind that bellies and drags in the wind,* as Yeats
had so perfectly put it, *into its narrow shed.*

"*We will give the area a nationally recognized television identity,*" he wrote. "*This we feel Corinium has failed to do. In their
last application they promised to provide a new studio, a new youth
orchestra, a trust fund for the arts and sciences, adequate training
schemes and worker participation at board level. This they have
failed to do.*

*They also promised that fifty percent of their profits after tax
would go to shareholders, and the rest would be ploughed back into
making programs. This they have also failed to do.*"

He was about to tackle Venturer's program plans, when Gertrude leapt barking off the sofa, scattering papers, as Rupert and Freddie walked in.

"Christ, you're a slut, Declan," said Rupert, looking around at
the files, tapes, coffee cups, and overflowing ashtrays that covered
every available inch of space. "Why don't you let Taggie tidy up
a bit?"

"I'm superstitious," grumbled Declan. "I never tidy up between
books in case I throw pages away."

Rupert threw a copy of *Broadcast*, open at Cameron's advertisement, down on Declan's desk. "We must have her for Venturer."

"She's riding far too high to be interested in us," said Declan
quickly.

"We need some 'eavy-weight ladies," said Freddie, moving the
binoculars and sitting on the window seat.

"Think how useful Cameron would be for the rest of the year as a mole in the Corinium camp," said Rupert.

"We've got Georgie and Seb and Charles," protested Declan.

"None of them sleep with Tony," persisted Rupert. "Look," he said patiently, "she's Tony's only trump card. If the IBA know from the start she's with us, it'll totally discredit him."

"It's a risk wurf taking," said Freddie. "We needn't tell her too much."

"I've got to tell her anyway," said Rupert flatly. "If she reads that we're pitching for the franchise in the Press on Tuesday morning, there'll be no hope of ever getting her."

Declan shook his head. "I want it to go on record," he said grimly, "that I utterly deplore the idea of using her as a mole. It's unethical and dangerous. Nor is Cameron going to be very pleased when you tell her what you've been up to already."

Freddie scratched his curls. "I 'aven't told Valerie yet," he confessed. "Been putting it off. Don't fink she'll be very pleased either."

Back from Cannes, Cameron plunged into the first five days of shooting "Four Men went to Mow." Rupert was aboard, smoothing the path for the Rugby Union World Cup later in the year and playing in a Pro-Am Tennis tournament to raise money for the Olympic fund, so he and Cameron didn't meet up until late on Friday.

Cameron always drove too fast. Fortunately there was little traffic on the road that Friday night as she scorched around corners and shot crossroads in her frenzy to reach Rupert. Hardly a light was on in Penscombe village, but huge, quivering stars and a full moon lit her path. The chestnuts lining Rupert's drive had reached a perfect pitch of pale greenness to welcome her. And as she screeched to a halt in front of the house, her headlights flood-lit a big white magnolia in full flower on the edge of the lawn—a thing of such unearthly incandescent beauty Cameron just gazed and gazed. I want to marry Rupert, she thought, and be as beautiful a bride as that tree.

The next moment the front door opened and the pack of dogs swarmed around the car, wagging and barking. She didn't even mind their paws scrabbling the paintwork. Rupert followed them, blond hair silver in the moonlight. Wearing a clean pink and white striped shirt, reeking of expensive cologne, he had obviously just bathed and brushed his teeth. Holding his arms out he swept her off the ground above the tidal wave of dogs.

"But they're lovely," she cried as he put her down in the hall, and, kneeling, she hugged the dogs as they surged forward, shoving, nudging, and licking her bare arms and legs in welcome.

"How strange and how nice," said Rupert, leading her into the drawing room. "I never imagined you'd like dogs."

There was a bottle of Dom Perignon on ice, which Rupert immediately opened, and a huge plate of smoked salmon and some buttered whole wheat rolls on the table.

"After a long hard day, I don't believe in screwing on an empty stomach," said Rupert, "and I'm certainly going to give you a long hard night."

Cameron moved up behind him, fingering the powerful shoulders, feeling the thrust of the muscular buttocks against her belly, melting against him with lust.

"How are things at Fort Knocks-off?" asked Rupert.

Cameron shook her head. "I feel like a mole."

Rupert nearly spilled the champagne he was pouring. "How d'you mean?"

"If you'd been stuck in a studio for twelve hours, you'd worry you'd never see the light again."

"Oh, I see," said Rupert, relieved. "And you've got over Cannes?"

"Almost." Cameron took a great slug of champagne. "That's better. D'you know, I was approached by five different groups to join their consortiums?"

"Very flattering," said Rupert, piling smoked salmon onto a roll and handing it to her. "Anyone interesting?"

"Not bad. Unfortunately they're all pitching against companies like Granada and Yorkshire, who are virtually impregnable, and if Tony got a whiff of it, I'd be out on my ear."

"How is he?" Rupert filled up her glass. "Has the Corinium application gone in?" he asked idly.

"Yes, thank God," said Cameron, who was shaking hands with one of the Springer spaniels. "Tony's handing it in to the IBA tomorrow morning."

Rupert heaved a sigh of relief. If Cameron flipped when he told her about Venturer later tomorrow, at least it would be too late for her to alter Corinium's application.

Slowly Cameron was taking in the beauty of the room, registering the Romney, the Gainsborough, the Stubbs, and the Lely on the pale yellow walls. Determined not to be impressed, she asked almost too aggressively. "How can you possibly live all alone in this great barn?"

"I don't," said Rupert. "I've got Mr. and Mrs. Bodkin who look after me, and the children are often here on weekends, and there's—er—usually a house guest."

I asked for that, thought Cameron, biting her lip.

"Don't worry." Rupert read her thoughts. "In order not to besmirch the memory of our last blessed encounter, I've been holding my own ever since. I suppose you've been sating yourself on Lord B?"

"Much less than before," said Cameron quickly.

The grandfather clock struck midnight.

"D'you know what day it is now?" asked Rupert.

"May 1st," said Cameron, glancing at her Rolex.

"D'you know our local poem?" said Rupert, grinning and putting on a Gloucestershire accent:

"First of May, first of May,
Outdoor fucking starts today.
But as usual it do rain.
So we fucks off indoors again."

As he moved toward her he stopped, smiling. "Will it be too cold for you outside?"

"Not if you keep me warm," whispered Cameron.

Outside under the moonlit magnolia he took off her clothes, slowly kissing her all over where each garment had been, until she was squirming and helpless with desire. She could feel the dew-drenched lawn under her back. Rupert's cock was really incredible. As he slid inside her, she felt all the amazed joy of a canal lock suddenly finding it can accommodate the QE2.

When she made love to Tony, she always shut her eyes. She didn't want to see the uncharacteristically untidy hair, the bulging eyes, the clenched teeth, the veins knotting on his forehead as he came. She liked him sleek and in control. With Rupert she kept her eyes open all the time because he was the stuff of fantasy, and because she didn't want to miss a second.

Deciding the ground was too hard for her, he later insisted she get on top.

"You're so beautiful," he said, watching her transported maenad face, ghostly in the moonlight.

As Cameron opened, so did the heavens.

"But as usual it do rain," murmured Rupert, moving in and out of her.

* * *

She woke in Rupert's huge Jacobean four-poster to find him gone and a note beside the bed saying he was doing a morning surgery at his constituency and would be back around lunchtime.

Looking around the beautiful room with its peachy walls, corn-colored carpet, yellow-and-pink-striped silk curtains on the four-poster and at the windows, and rose-pink silk chaise longue, Cameron felt she was waking in the middle of a sunrise. It was an incredibly feminine room for a man. Then she remembered the pale blue hall and the pale yellow drawing room, and decided it must all be Helen's taste. On the dressing table, amid Rupert's clutter of silver backed brushes, cigar wrappers, and loose change, were photographs of his children. The girl, exactly like Rupert, had the same arrogant blue-eyed stare; the boy had very dark red hair and large dark wary eyes. Having met Rupert's pack last night, Cameron felt seven stepdogs might be an easier proposition to take on than two stepchildren. Helen must have been spectacular to produce kids like that.

Outside, through a frame of rampant, budding clematis, lay the valley, pale green except for the occasional wild cherry tree in flower, or the blackthorn breaking in white waves over the hedgerows. From an ash grove by the lake she could hear the haunting, sweet cry of the cuckoo. How could Helen have walked out on such a view and such a man?

Having showered and dressed, Cameron went downstairs. The dogs lying in the hall thumped their tails and followed her into the kitchen. She took some orange juice and coffee out onto the terrace. That must be Declan's house across the valley, still just visible through the thickening beech wood.

She wondered what he'd been up to since his fall from grace. How strange that on January 1st with Patrick, she'd looked across at Rupert's house and thought, What a kingdom, and now, four months later, here she was.

She stopped only briefly to glance at the library and the first editions, then set out with the dogs to explore. There was a wonderful untamed beauty, rather like Maud O'Hara, about the garden. Green leaves were uncurling on the tangled old roses, the peacocks and crowing cocks once clipped out of the yew hedges were looking distinctly shaggy. The swimming pool was full of leaves, the beech hedge around the tennis court was in need of a cut, the lawns dotted with daisies were still lit along the edges by pools of dying daffodils. Rupert and this place need a woman, thought Cameron, to cherish and sort them out.

The ground was still carpeted with bluebells. Only when she pressed her face close could she distinguish their faint sweet hyacinth scent from the rank sexy stench of the wild garlic. The dogs charged ahead, but the shaggy lurcher called Blue kept bounding back solicitously, shoving his wet nose in her hand, giving her a token lick. It was all so beautiful; she had never felt so happy or so right anywhere.

She glanced at her watch. It was half past twelve. She must get back. Gray clouds were creeping over the sun; it had become much cooler. She even felt a spot of rain. As she dropped down the woods toward the house an owl hooted. Surely it shouldn't hoot at midday? Through the trees she could see the lake, gray and blank now as a smudged mirror, and as she reached the big lawn she gave a moan of horror. Last night's deluge had stripped all the petals from the magnolia, scattering them over the grass. Last night's bride was naked now.

The dogs converged, barking, as a car drew up at the front door. Cameron hoped it was Rupert, but it turned out to be a youth delivering some boxes of T-shirts, who gazed at Cameron in admiration.

"This is the first lot. Mr. C-B wanted them in a hurry," he said. "Tell him the stickers, the posters, and the badges'll be ready by Monday."

Cameron couldn't resist having a look. The T-shirts were a beautiful cerulean blue, with a dark bronze drawing of a boy shading his forehead on the front and the words *Support Venturer* on the front and the back. They must be for some sporting event. Taking one upstairs, Cameron stripped and put it on. It fell just below her bush. Suddenly feeling incredibly randy, she hoped Rupert hadn't got anything planned for the afternoon. As it was much colder, she shut the window, trapping a tendril of clematis which was already wilting and bruised from being trapped on previous occasions. Trying to insinuate its way into Rupert's bedroom, like her and every other woman, thought Cameron wryly.

Next minute the front door banged. Very slowly she walked downstairs. Rupert was looking at the boxes in the hall.

"They're great," she said. "Can I keep one?"

Rupert glanced up and froze for a second.

"Hullo, angel. Did you sleep well?"

"So well," murmured Cameron seductively, "that I'm ready to be exhausted again." She lifted the T-shirt to show him her bush. Then, when he didn't react as she'd expected and come bounding up the stairs, she said, "What is Venturer, anyway?"

Rupert's eyes seemed to have gone a darker, more opaque shade of blue and lost all their sparkle. "Come and have a drink," he said.

Disappointed, Cameron followed him into the drawing room. Suddenly he seemed incredibly tense and, when she refused a drink, poured himself two fingers of neat whisky and drank it in one gulp. Then he pulled her down on to the sofa beside him.

"Look, sweetheart, this is a bit difficult, but there's something I've got to tell you."

Cameron went white. Suddenly in that baggy T-shirt, she looked as fragile, pale, and defenceless as once of the anemones that strewed the paths of Rupert's woods.

"You want to stop seeing me?" she whispered.

"No, no, quite the reverse." Very gently he smoothed a tendril of dark hair behind her ear and stroked her rigid, quivering cheek.

"But you may be finished with me. Freddie Jones, Declan, and I are pitching for the Corinium franchise. We've called ourselves Venturer."

At first she was so relieved that he wasn't trying to end the relationship she couldn't think straight.

"You and Declan? How long has this been going on?"

"Since the day after Declan walked out."

"So turning up in Madrid wasn't only to see a football match?"

"No."

"Or showing such interest in my career and the goings on at Corinium?"

"No."

"Did you read the application in my briefcase?"

"I copied it."

She was trembling violently now and her lips were quite white.

"Don't worry," he reassured her. "Declan was so appalled by my skulduggery he refused to read it; so we haven't pinched anything."

"And I suppose you arranged those riots as an excuse to fly straight home once you'd got what you wanted?"

"Uh uh," protested Rupert. "Two stabbed cops, twenty-five people injured and a burned-down stadium is going too far even for me."

"But driving down to see me before I flew out to LA and all those questions you asked me? Did you give that 'Stowaway' story to Dempster?"

Rupert nodded. Truth, however devastating, was the only answer now.

"And, Christ, how much have I already told you this weekend?" whispered Cameron, looking at her watch. "And our application's already gone in."

Rupert had expected rage, tantrums, having his face clawed, but not this numb state of shock.

"I trusted you," she said slowly. "You're the first person I've trusted since I was fourteen. I thought you were so caring, you bloody Judas. This is the worst thing that's ever happened to me."

"It isn't as awful as it seems," said Rupert soothingly. "I thought you were the sexiest thing on two legs the moment I saw you. Didn't I offer you a lift home after Valerie's dinner party? I would have moved in at Declan's party if young Patrick hadn't been making the running, and at Corinium, if Tony hadn't been hanging about. If I hadn't fancied you to death, I'd never have bothered coming to Madrid. I wanted to level with you but I didn't know how you'd react. We couldn't afford to let you rush back to Tony and tell him everything."

Cameron leaped to her feet, tugging down the T-shirt. "And I figured you were really interested in me. What a joke. I know how Declan detests me. He must have cracked up, and I suppose Patrick and that dumb ass Taggie were in on it too. Christ, you must have all been laughing yourselves sick."

She was crying now—angry, agonized rasping tears, and Rupert suddenly appreciated her terrible insecurity, her paranoia, her vulnerability, and her terror; for the first time his heart was truly touched by her. Getting up, he tried to take her in his arms and comfort her.

"Angel, you've got it wrong. No one's laughing at you. I want you, I absolutely adore you. We all want you to join Venturer. We were just picking our moment. We've got an absolutely alpha lineup, but you'd be the jewel in our crown, and you'd be totally free to make the programs you wanted."

"Get out of my way!" screamed Cameron. "I hate you! I never want to see you again!" And, diving under his outstretched arms, she bolted out of the door.

Rupert had never felt like such a shit in his life. She'll have to get her clothes and her suitcase from upstairs, he thought; I can cut her off on her way downstairs. But Cameron shot straight out the front door, and next moment he heard the wheels of the Lotus crunching on the gravel. Tony was probably still on his way down from London. Cameron couldn't rage around to The Falconry in nothing but that T-shirt, but she'd be on the telephone in a flash. The early-warning system had gone off. It was just a matter of time before the H-bomb landed.

CHAPTER 28

All over the country on Sunday, May 2nd the independent companies and those consortiums who sought to oust them were assembling, color-coding, and ring-binding forty copies of their application document, complete with attached confidential material to be delivered to the IBA headquarters in Brompton Road by noon the following day.

Corinium, to be on the safe side, had submitted their application the day before. Venturer, who were pushed for time, spent a wildly exciting Sunday at Freddie's house in Holland Park knocking their final draft into shape.

Everyone agreed that Declan had done a masterly job, but Freddie and Marti Gluckstein, who arrived looking like a costive lizard, were considerably extending the financial section. Freddie and Lord Smith were going through the technical specifications with a fine-tooth comb, while Harold White, Janey Lloyd-Foxe, Charles Fairburn, Dame Enid, and Professor Graystock were having fun jazzing up the program content.

Bas, having provided architects' plans for the conversion of Cotchester House into studios and offices should Tony turn nasty, was now playing checkers with Henry Hampshire, the Lord-Lieutenant, who hadn't spent a Sunday in London for twenty-five years, and with Wesley Emerson, who had nothing really to add to the bid except his illustrious presence. The Bishop was driving up to London immediately after Evensong. Maud, who'd come along for the ride, was playing the piano. Upstairs Ursula and Freddie's secretary were frantically typing and retyping drafts and then running okayed pages off on the word processor.

Taggie was in the kitchen. She had given everyone pâté and cheese for lunch, and was now making Chicken Estragon for the celebration dinner. Four plump boiling chickens, carrots, and onions were already simmering in a huge pan. There was an extremely complicated and hazardous sauce to be made later, involving egg yolks, cream, and lemon juice which might easily curdle. But at least having tramped the length of Notting Hill Gate that morning, she'd found some fresh tarragon.

From the next door room she could hear screams of laughter.

"We must do a series on local studs called 'Dongs of Praise,' " Janey Lloyd-Foxe was saying. "We can start off with Rupert; then we won't have to pay him a fee."

Janey was absolutely gorgeous, thought Taggie. Rupert had said she was nearly forty, but, except for the fine pencilling of lines around her wicked dark brown eyes, you'd never have known it. Poor Billy, her husband, was abroad covering the Paris Tennis Tournament for the B.B.C., and Janey had turned up with the most adorable baby, who was so fat, smiling, and gurgling that even the men wanted to hold her. And Janey was so blonde and beautiful, and had such wonderful brown breasts after a week in Portugal, that no one minded her breast-feeding at all.

"I've got a terrific idea for a game show," Janey was now saying. "You have a panel and they have to guess who the celebrity is by interviewing the cleaning women who work for them. We call it 'Daily Daily.' Mrs. Makepiece can give us some wonderful stories about James Vereker, and Mrs. Bodkin would be riveting about Rupert's goings on. Mrs. Bodkin used to work for us," continued Janey, shifting the baby to her right breast. "The first time we got a cordless telephone she found it in our bed and, assuming it was some auto-erotic device, discreetly hid it in my underwear drawer. Then, when it started ringing, Billy, who was expecting some summons to jump for Britain, went frantic trying to find it."

Everyone screamed with laughter.

"Don't you think it's a brilliant idea, Declan?"

"No," said Declan, who already adored Janey. "The IBA would think it utterly undemocratic."

They were all so bright and clever, thought Taggie wistfully. She had contributed nothing. "An army marches on its stomach," Declan was fond of telling her, but she was sure that everyone would have been just as happy with an Indian takeout this evening and that her father had only suggested she do the food in order to involve her.

She pored over the Estragon recipe in the book, but half the words were in French. Embarrassed at having to resort to a tape recorder she shut the door, so no one could hear.

She was worried about Rupert too. He'd been edgy and refused to eat anything when he'd popped in earlier, then furious because he'd forgotten to bring the T-shirts. He'd also taken an instant dislike to Professor Graystock, whom he hadn't met before. Then he had pushed off, promising he and the T-shirts would be back later. Taggie was sure he didn't look after himself properly. If she made the chicken particularly nice, he might eat something this evening.

At eight o'clock the first bottle of Bollinger was cracked as they waited for the final draft to be ready. Declan had just rewritten the last page to give the whole thing a uniformity of style. Ursula and Freddie's secretary were busy collating everything and Freddie and Declan were folding up the confidential memos listing Harold White, Georgie Baines, Charles, Seb, and Billy as Heads of various departments and putting these memos into envelopes.

"Pity we can't add Cameron Cook," sighed Freddie.

"Rupert would have called by now if he had anything to report," said Declan.

Dame Enid and Maud, both tiddly, were now playing duets. The Lord-Lieutenant had lost so much money to Bas he'd probably have to sell another Pre-Raphaelite, but he couldn't have enjoyed himself more. There were so many pretty women to gaze at.

Janey was breast-feeding again.

"Mother and child—a lovely sight," said the Bishop who'd just arrived.

"I hope all our burn money isn't being squandered on bubbly," said Professor Graystock, who was on his fourth glass.

"It isn't," said Taggie quickly. "Rupert's paid for all of it."

Helped by Seb, she was now putting out big plates of chicken Estragon and rice salad. She'd worried herself sick that the sauce had gone wrong, but mercifully it had thickened as it cooled.

"That looks marvelous, Taggie. I wish you'd marry me when I grow up," said Bas, who was now comfortably ensconced on the sofa with Janey and a full bottle.

"This tomato salad is out of this world," said Seb, carrying the bowl in.

Taggie liked Seb. He had a good body, hunky without being fat, thick light-brown hair, short at the back and long at the front, very direct slate gray eyes and he was very nearly as tall as she was.

Then, as Big Ben struck nine, the applications were ready: forty copies of beautifully typed, ring-bound pages. On the front, beneath the clear plastic cover, was a drawing of a beautiful boy with his hand to his forehead, standing on the capitals T and U of the word Venturer against a clear cerulean background. On the back, also protected by a plastic cover, was an exquisite water-color map of the area, painted by Caitlin, including the towns and villages, with little drawings of the relevant houses, where all the prospective Venturer directors lived, and with pale blue arrows from each of them converging on Cotchester. It had cost a lot to print, but they'd all thought it was worth it.

Everyone went mad with excitement as they sat around reading, and at last holding in their hands, tangible proof that it was all really happening.

"It's very good, Declan," said Harold White. "I'd forgotten how well you write. I love the bit about 'carpets being so thick and offices so soundproofed on the Corinium directors' floor, that all one can hear is the faint rustle of nests being feathered.' "

"I liked that too," said Declan, blushing.

"And I love this bit about Corinium's local news programs being presented by 'pretentious pastel-clad narcissists,' " boomed Dame Enid. "That boring little fart Vereker won't like that one bit."

"I hope that's not actionable," said Professor Graystock primly. "And are you quite sure there was a Roman camp at Whychey?"

"Quite," said Declan.

"I like my cottage," said Marti Gluckstein, examining the map at the back. "I must come and look at it some time. Ouch!" he yelled, as Freddie kicked him sharply on the ankle.

"Sorry, but Declan thinks you spend every weekend there," whispered Freddie.

"I do like your ideas for religious programs," said Janey, smiling up at the Bishop, who went very pink.

Declan saw that everyone's glasses were full, then got to his feet. "I'd just like to thank you all for having the courage to join Venturer, and for all the hard work you've put in already. But I must warn you, this has been the easy bit. Once it's out in the open that we're pitching for Corinium, Tony Baddingham is going to do everything to discredit us and rake up dirt about all of us. Our only hope is to stick together and trust each other." He smiled around at everyone. "This is a very very proud day for me. Let's all raise our glasses."

"Victory to Venturer," said Henry Hampshire, and amazingly unself-consciously, everyone followed suit.

"I shall compose a battle song for Venturer and we'll make a record," said Dame Enid.

"I hope it's better than the song cycle she's just written," muttered Seb to Taggie. "It sounded more like a lot of tom cats being garrotted. This chicken is just as much a work of art as your father's application," he went on. "Can I have some more?"

Everyone jumped as the doorbell rang.

P   L   A   Y   E   R   S

"I can't help thinking it's Tony with a pitchfork," said Georgie Baines nervously.

But it was only the man with the T-shirts and once again every-one went wild and put them on, including the baby and Gertrude. They were baggy enough, having been ordered to Caitlin's specifi-cation, to fit Dame Enid and Charles Fairburn, and even the Bishop wore one over his dog collar. Janey wore hers over just underpants to show off her long brown legs, and, after a lot of persuading, Tag-gie did the same.

"They're much better than Corinium's T-shirts," said Seb in delight. "They're custard yellow with Caring Corinium written across the front. Tony eschewed the symbol of the Corinium ram as being too libidinous."

More champagne was drunk and food eaten. Then the photog-rapher arrived.

"Where the hell's Rupert?" said Declan irritably.

"I think we ought to get on and get this pickie taken without him," said Freddie in an undertone. "Line up for the photograph everyone."

Seb dragged Taggie in from the kitchen. She loathed group pho-tographs. She was always taller than half the men.

"You're as much a part of Venturer as anyone else," said Seb.

Taggie sat on the sofa, Gertrude on her knee, bristling in a child's T-shirt, with Maud on one side and Janey and the baby on the other. Bas stood behind Janey. Taggie suddenly noticed his suntanned fin-gers caressing the back of Janey's neck and hastily looked away.

"Straighten your T-shirt, so I can see all the Venturers," said the photographer. "Look nice and happy please. Can you get the little dog to prick up his ears? Lovely! Smile please."

He was still snapping away two minutes later when Taggie gave a shriek as Gertrude leaped off her bare legs, barking furiously, as Rupert came through the door.

He had that same look of blazing triumph on his face, reflected Janey, that he used to have in the old days when one of his horses won a big class and he used to ride it out of the ring, giving its neck great slaps of joy. He hadn't looked like that for years.

Rupert paused in the doorway.

"Ladies and Gentlemen," he drawled, "may I introduce Ventur-er's Head of Drama."

Taggie gave a gasp of horror; Harold White went white. Seb, Georgie and Charles nearly jumped out of the window in terror, as

Rupert turned around and, putting his arm around Cameron's shoulders very much in a gesture of possession, drew her into the room.

She looked very pale and very shy, but incredibly beautiful, with her face strangely softened by love.

Maud broke the stunned silence. For months, despite Declan's denials, she had suspected Rupert of having a growing preference for Taggie. It was the one thing she couldn't have stood. Joyfully, she welcomed such a public transferring of his affections to Cameron. Rushing forward, she hugged them both.

"Congratulations, darlings. Now I'm convinced Venturer's going to get the franchise."

"Don't look so worried," said Rupert mockingly to the cringing Corinium contingent. "Cameron's on the level. Her name's going to be put forward on the confidential memo like the rest of you, and she's going to stay working for Corinium until December."

Charles decided to make the best of a bad job. "Welcome to Venturer, sweetie," he said, kissing Cameron.

"Fucking hell," muttered Seb to Georgie.

"Look at the way she's looking at Rupert," said Georgie. "He's got her exactly where he wants her."

"As long as he stays wanting her," said Seb, shaking his head.

Soon the champagne was circulating again. Cameron was sitting on the sofa now, flipping through the application document with one hand, clinging onto Rupert's hand with the other.

"Why's Taggie crying in the kitchen?" Dame Enid asked Maud.

"I expect she'd like to be able to read her father's application like everyone else," said Maud airily. "She's dyslexic, you see."

"Poor darling," said Dame Enid. "She's a bloody good cook. I'm going to have thirds."

Seb put his arm round Taggie in the kitchen. "You OK, babes?"

"Fine," she muttered blowing her nose on a dish cloth. "I'm just tired, I guess."

"Your application's dazzling," said Cameron, following Declan over to the bar where he was opening another bottle. "Miles, miles better than ours. Any slight doubts I might have had about joining Venturer have been dispelled by reading it. I do hope Rupert hasn't railroaded you all into accepting me?"

"I don't want any bullying," said Declan, glaring at her. "One's only as good as one's work force and don't you ever forget it."

I'm going to have to put in a lot of spade work to win him over, thought Cameron, but all that really mattered was that Rupert loved her.

Freddie clapped his hands. "Let's get this pickie finished."

"Come on, Cameron," said Charles, brandishing a T-shirt.

"I'm not sure I ought to appear in it," stammered Cameron, suddenly realizing what compromising evidence it would be.

"Put it on," snapped Declan.

Charles slid the T-shirt over her head and once again they all lined up, George and Seb taking up their position on either side of her, with Charles standing behind.

"Straighten your T-shirts, look happy everyone," said the photographer.

"Let's get one thing straight besides T-shirts, Miss Cook," said Georgie out of the corner of his handsome mouth, as he beamed into the camera.

"If you shop us to Tony, we'll shop you," said Seb as he also beamed into the camera.

"And don't forget, there are well over two hundred shopping days to December 15th," said Charles.

As Venturer had called a press conference for the following afternoon, Declan stayed the night at Freddie's house and Taggie drove her mother and Gertrude back to Penscombe just after midnight.

Maud was plastered and went on and on about how nice Janey was and wasn't it a gas, Rupert rolling up with Cameron, and did Taggie think Rupert had offered her marriage or to move into Penscombe or what. Taggie answered in monosyllables and fortunately, as they passed the Reading exit, Maud fell into a drunken sleep.

Taggie then proceeded to give herself a very good talking to. What the hell was she feeling so miserable about? Rupert was as far beyond her as the huge stars daisying the black lawn of sky above, and plainly as impervious to her love. It was the stupid sort of crush teenagers had on rock stars or actors, someone to dream about when you were tucked up in bed or wandering through the woods.

Rupert had probably been kind to her because he missed his own children. The silver necklace, Gertrude's Valentine, the little Easter Egg, were all presents you might give a child, she told herself firmly. And saying that no one could resist her (Taggie wished she could memorize recipes and how to spell words as easily as she remembered every conversation she'd had with Rupert) was just the sort of thing he'd say to any girl. Cameron was beautiful, brilliant, sophisticated, and tough. Maybe she and Rupert were well suited. Taggie was sure she only disliked her because she'd upset Declan and hurt Patrick so much, but Rupert wouldn't stand any nonsense, so perhaps they were well-suited.

Next minute she felt a cold nose nudging her elbow and put out her hand to stroke Gertrude who slid forward along the hand brake until she could climb onto Taggie's knee and settle down with a martyred sigh.

Taggie knew she shouldn't allow Gertrude to lie there, but she needed the comfort. She was not someone who regarded happiness as a right, but the ghastly shock of seeing Cameron and Rupert so obviously in love tonight made her realize how happy, without being conscious of it, she'd been since Valentine's Day, when Rupert began dropping in at The Priory whenever he was at home. Despite the talking to, she didn't think she'd ever felt so unhappy in her life.

CHAPTER 29

At noon the lists closed. The information office at the IBA then had a frantic three and a half hours going through the applications and extracting the names and addresses of those involved for a press release at three-thirty.

Down at Cotchester three of the four Corinium moles made themselves scarce. Charles Fairburn drove to the Forest of Dean to spend two days in a monastery ostensibly interviewing monks. Georgie flew to Manchester to see a big pet-food client. Cameron disappeared to Stow-on-the-Wold on location, leaving strict instructions that she wasn't to be interrupted. Seb Burrows, being a true journalist and hating to miss the fireworks, hung around the newsroom.

Corinium staff not involved with the Venturer bid were also kept busy. James Vereker slipped home with Sarah Stratton for an extended lunch hour. Daysee Butler, who'd been out in the evenings so much recently she hadn't watched any television, was reading the soap updates in the *Mail*, as she soaked up the sun in her bikini in the Cathedral close. Tony Baddingham and Ginger Johnson were having a celebrity conference lunch with the French co-producers of "Stowaway," having just sold it both to NBS and the B.B.C. What a relief, they all agreed, they hadn't killed off the handsome pirate villain, as a sequel was already planned.

How nice it was too, thought Tony, to lunch with Europeans who still appreciated a good feed blow-out and decent claret, compared with the Yanks who seemed totally addicted to rabbit food and Perrier.

By three forty-five Tony was back in his office. In half an hour he would sober up and be wondering who to bully. Now he merely felt lecherous. All those pale green trees and pale half-naked girls stretched out among the buttercups. The first flush and flesh of spring always got him going. Having spent a weekend without Cameron, he decided to drop in and see her after the Chamber of Commerce dinner that night, an event which had to be endured in a franchise year.

Still feeling randy, he was about to summon Sarah Stratton to discuss her posing with a lamb for a Caring Corinium poster when Miss Madden buzzed. "Barney Williams from the *Telegraph*, Lord B. He wants to talk about the franchise."

"Put him on." Tony extracted a cigar from the box on his desk and relaxed in his leather chair, preparing to be generous about Mid-West's pathetic bid.

Barney Williams came straight to the point. "Did you know Declan O'Hara put in a rival bid?"

Tony laughed heartily. "Is this some kind of joke?"

"I'm afraid it isn't."

"Who else is involved?"

"Rupert Campbell-Black, Freddie Jones."

"Whaaaat!"

It sounded like a great oak tree crashing to the ground, even through soundproofed doors. Miss Madden jumped in the next-door office. Then Tony was leaning on the buzzer.

"Madden!" he yelled. "Take these names down. Who else?" he asked Barney.

"Henry Hampshire, the Bishop of Cotchester, Marti Gluckstein."

"He's never been to Gloucestershire."

"Evidently he has a weekend cottage there. Janey Lloyd-Foxe, Dame Enid Spink, Lord Smith."

"He can't join. He's a union member."

"Ex-member—just. Crispin Graystock. Wesley Emerson—he's the only bit of name-plate engineering. They're all pretty heavyweight, in fact, and, oh yes, there's your brother Bas. Bit Jacob and Esau isn't it?"

Tony gave a low hiss that was almost a sigh.

"And you had absolutely no idea?" asked Barney.

"None."

"And they're all friends of yours?"

"They were."

"They're calling a press conference in London at four-thirty. Will you be doing the same, or can I have a quote now?"

"I've nothing to say until I've talked to my board!"

Tony slammed down the telephone. Bastards! Traitors! Every single one of them. The maddened bull's roar could be heard all down the corridor.

"Ginger, Cyril, Georgie, Cameron, Charles! Come in here."

"Georgie's in Manchester," said Miss Madden, "and Cameron's on location."

"Get them back."

Ginger Johnson thought Tony was going to have a coronary. He was magenta in the face, veins bulged like huge snakes on his forehead. He seemed to be popping out of his dark green collar. Ginger wanted Tony's job, but not until the franchise was safely in the bag.

"What on earth's up?"

Tony was so angry as he paced up and down, fists clenched, froth flecking his mouth, he could hardly get the words out to tell him. Once he lit a cigar from the wrong end, then hurled it out of the window. Without taking the top off, he tried to pour himself a stiff whisky, then banged the bottle down.

"What have they called themselves?" asked Cyril Peacock.

"Venturer—adventurers more likely—every bloody one of them! God, I'll crucify them! I'll take them to the cleaners!"

Ginger went to the bar and poured Tony a large brandy.

Madden buzzed: "It's the *Sun*, Lord B, and just hang on a minute . . . Beryl says the *Mirror* are on the other line."

"Tell them Lord B's in conference and to ring back in half an hour," said Ginger, taking the initiative. "Don't talk to them now," he added to Tony. "Get your breath back. The most important thing at this stage is not to show we're rattled. Leave the mud-slinging to Venturer. We've got seven months to put the screws in. The only possible approach now is Olympian. These boring little pygmies are yapping at my heels, but I can't feel it."

"Should we call a press conference?"

"Certainly not. They're not worth it. Why show them we're panicking?"

Downstairs in the newsroom Seb Burrows picked up his telephone. It was ITN: "Hello, Seb. Christ, what a story! Did you know anything about it?"

"What story?" said Seb innocently.

ITN told him. "Did you know anything about it?"

"None of us did. Christ!"

"Can you interview Tony for us for the five-forty-five news?"

"I'll try. I don't imagine he'll be in carnival mood."

But, to Seb's amazement, Tony agreed. By the time the crew got up to Tony's office, every award Corinium had ever won, including the EMMYs and the BAFTAs nicked from Cameron's office, had been put on the bookshelf or hung on the wall behind Tony's head.

The earlier storm had subsided; Tony's rage was ice cold now. He had even extracted a salmon-pink carnation from the vase on the desk to put in his buttonhole.

"What's your reaction to Venturer's bid?" asked Seb.

Tony gave a big, but slightly dismissive smile: "Well, they're good chaps, all jolly good friends of mine. I'm sure there's a lot of merit in their application, but frankly I'm more interested in the things Corinium are doing—like announcing plans for a ten-million-pound studio near Southampton, which'll mean about four hundred extra jobs, and spending two million on new equipment at Cotchester, to enable us to make even better programs, and meet with every confidence the challenge of cable and satellite. We've won a lot of awards over the last few years." He waved airily at the trophies glittering behind him. "We provide an excellent local news service and make jolly good programs, and there we rest our case."

I'm not getting anywhere, thought Seb.

"People are saying that Declan O'Hara and your brother Basil have been deliberately plotting to oust you since Declan walked out of here last March in a blaze of publicity."

Tony examined his nails. "Are they?" he said with another big smile.

Ask a silly question, thought Seb, kicking himself.

"Had you any idea they were engaged in a rival bid?"

"None. I wish them luck. It would be a dull race if there were no other contenders, but it doesn't dent my confidence."

"Which consortium, Mid-Week or Venturer, worries you the most?"

"Neither. I congratulate Venturer on putting an application together on such short notice and with such secrecy. I'll be interested to see what's in it in due course."

"And you feel no bitterness toward Freddie Jones and Rupert Campbell-Black and Henry Hampshire, who have all enjoyed your hospitality?"

"None at all," laughed Tony, as though the idea had never occurred to him. "Nor does Corinium have any desire to get involved in mudslinging. Let 'Dorothy Dove,' who recently won us a BAFTA award, be a symbol of our company, noncombative but victorious.''

The moment the camera stopped rolling the smile was wiped from Tony's face. ''Now bugger off, all of you, but come back the moment 'Cotswold Roundup' is over, Seb, and bring James Vereker with you.''

Cameron ignored Tony's summons to return at once and insisted on carrying on shooting until the four-thirty tea break. It was vital to be as stubborn as usual, or Tony would suspect something. As she drove through the angelic spring greenness with the top down, she heard a flash on the five-thirty news that Declan O'Hara, after a mega-bust-up with Corinium in March, was now getting his revenge on Tony by heading a rival bid for Corinium. Rupert, Freddie, Dame Enid, the Bishop, Wesley, Lord Smith, and Janey were also mentioned. Cameron waited in terror for her name to be tagged on at the end.

She was still in a state of shock after the weekend. When she'd run out on Rupert on Saturday, she'd gone straight home and called Tony at home—something he'd told her never to do—and promptly got Monica. Remembering that Tony had the French co-production people over for the weekend, who were probably *Mon Dieu*-ing over Monica's fading stretch of daffodils at that moment, she'd hung up. For the next twenty-four hours she crouched shuddering in her bed-room, telephone off the hook, all doors locked, not answering the bell, going through every kind of torture at the prospect of life with-out Rupert. The craving had got so bad that when on Sunday after-noon he'd smashed the pane of her French windows at the back and let himself in, pounding up the stairs, and taken her in his arms, telling her he couldn't go on without her, the sheer relief of having him back made her agree to anything. She would join Venturer; she would stay at Corinium and spy on Tony.

Now at last the crunch had come. All day she'd been snapping at the cast for acting badly. Now she had to give a BAFTA perfor-mance herself. At least she'd heard the news bulletin, so she didn't have to simulate complete surprise when she saw Tony.

But as she drove into her slot in the Corinium parking lot and read the words ''Cameron Cook, Controller of Programs'' she felt she should cross out the last three and put Traitor.

She reached Tony's office just before the main B.B.C. news. The commercials, with the sound turned down, were airing on ITV. Tony, Ginger, and Cyril were all watching. Cameron went straight up to Tony and put her arms around him.

"I'm so sorry, I heard it on the radio. They're all traitors, but Freddie and Bas are the worst of all."

"Was Bas mentioned on the radio?" said Cyril, pencil poised. "What station?"

"I don't remember," said Cameron hastily. "I was switching around to see what I could find out."

Christ, that was a near one, she thought, going to the bar and pouring herself a stiff vodka and tonic. She'd have to be careful with the liquor too; she was so tired; other indiscretions might slip out. How the hell had Guy Burgess kept his communist affiliations a secret for so long if he was always plastered?

The B.B.C. led on the story. Beautiful weather apart, there wasn't much news. After some introductory waffle about the contenders now circling in the paddock, they went straight over to the Venturer press conference. Not wanting him to see her face, Cameron took up her position behind Tony, leaning against the wall with her hand on his shoulder. He seemed calm enough, but she could feel the knotted tension of his muscles. A tic was leaping in his jaw and the carnation in his buttonhole had already wilted, as though poisoned by his venom.

The Venturer team looked splendid. Declan had been so hostile last night that she hadn't noticed how well he was looking, already tanned from gardening and sitting outside writing the application. Half the heavy lines seemed to have been ironed out of his face. And there was Rupert laughing with Janey, who looked amazing, bearing in mind the amount she'd drunk yesterday. Rupert had said she was the one person Cameron need never be jealous of, but she removed her hand from Tony's shoulder, in case she clutched it convulsively. Rupert looked marvelous, too. Christ, he was beautiful.

There was also a massive contingent of press there. People were standing on tables, fighting for space.

"Why have you pitched for the Corinium franchise, Declan?" asked the B.B.C.

"We want to create a company that is genuinely local," said Declan. "And we want to make some bloody good programs."

"And a fortune into the bargain?" said the *Mirror*.

Everyone laughed. Declan grinned. "That too. Then we can afford to make even better programs."

Soon, however, the vitriol was flowing freely.

"Corinium has lost touch with the public and their region. They need a good shake-up," said Rupert.

"After eleven years in business," said Freddie, "it seems amazing that Tony B. has only just decided to build a studio near Southampton."

"I appeared on 'Cotswold Roundup' recently," boomed Dame Enid. "I was interviewed by some pastel-clad pansy—" she winked at Declan—"who didn't know what the hell he was talking about. It was the worst program I've ever been on."

"What drew you in, Bishop?" asked the *Catholic Herald*.

"Television today is a key factor in the quality of life, in the community, in the establishment of Christian values," said the Bishop heartily. "I hope to play a part through Venturer in making television more uplifting and more enjoyable." He wagged a finger. "One doesn't exclude the other, y'know."

Realizing the Bishop was all set to deliver a sermon, Rupert cut in, "The Bishop feels as I do, that there's far too much sex and violence on Corinium's programs."

"Fucking hypocrite," thundered Tony.

"Very much so," agreed the Bishop. "On 'Four Men went to Mow' young people are continually going to bed with other young people and shown not to be taking precautions."

"Corinium's drama record as a whole," added Janey, "is abysmal."

"Bitch," hissed Cameron in genuine outrage. "How dare she!"

"There are, of course, good people working at Corinium," said Declan, "but they're hamstrung by a greedy and incompetent management."

Tony puffed on his cigar, the knuckles of his left hand whitening as he made a dagger of the silver paper knife on his desk. Cyril's doodles became more extravagant.

"Having worked at Corinium for seven months," went on Declan. "I know just how bad things are."

"Isn't that actionable?" said Ginger furiously.

But Tony held up his hand for silence as the *Star* asked Declan who Venturer were poaching from other companies.

Declan smiled again. "We have a string of incredibly talented people who will take over as Heads of the various departments the moment we win the franchise," he said, "but as they're all working for ITN or the B.B.C., we can't tell you who they are."

"What d'you feel about your other rival, Mid-Week?" said the *Sun*.

Rupert laughed. "Well, they were advertising for ideas for programs in the local paper last week," he said, "so they must be a bit short on imagination, and as their regional trump card is a geography teacher who's never been to London I can't say we feel very threatened.''

The B.B.C., obviously feeling they'd given Venturer enough coverage, turned to the wonderful weather.

Tony immediately switched over to "Cotswold Roundup" who put out an outwardly impartial report about there being two contenders for the Corinium franchise, then ran Tony's interview with Seb in full.

Next the clip was run in from the program in which Declan quoted the Gloucestershire peer describing Rupert as "a nasty virus everyone's wife caught sooner or later." And Rupert replying: "If you could see his wife, it'd definitely be later."

Finally came Declan's questions as to whether Rupert was going to mend his ways because of AIDS, and Rupert cracking back that he was giving up casual sex for Lent. Without any qualifying comment, the program then switched to a story about playing fields.

"That was offensive," said Cameron furiously. "That clip should *never* have been taken out of context."

"The IBA won't like it one bit," said Ginger, shaking his head.

"I didn't authorize it," lied Tony quickly. "I can't help it if my newsroom gets a little protective and leaps to my defense."

Cameron felt sick. It was going to be much dirtier and more difficult than she'd thought. Things became worse when Seb and James rolled up after "Cotswold Roundup." Tony, utterly businesslike now, said their chief object should be to dig up as much dirt on Venturer as possible and then get other people to leak the stories.

"We've got to appear whiter than white and above it all. Here's the list of their consortium." Tony handed copies to James and Seb. "Declan was desperately pushed for cash when he left Corinium. How's he managed to be in funds again? Investigate any IRA sympathies. His wife's a tart. See if there's any rift there."

"Rupert's a government minister," said Ginger. "That's out of order for a start. He could influence the PM to lean on the IBA to give Venturer the franchise."

"Excellent," said Tony. "Ring up Paul Stratton, Ginger. He detests Rupert. Get him to ask a question in the House about it. And find out who Rupert's sleeping with, Seb. It's bound to be different from yesterday. If anything moves, or rather stays still, he'll fuck it. Sarah Stratton used to sleep with him; she may still be. Talk to her."

Seb didn't dare look at Cameron. Suddenly, he felt desperately sorry for her.

"Lord Smith likes the fleshpots far too much for a socialist," went on Tony. "He's got his own house with five bedrooms and a very nice car. See if he's been using Union funds. Graystock's a pinko too. Investigate any communist sympathies. He's also divorced, got a second house, and definitely sent his second child to a private school. Hang around the University, Seb, and see if he's ever fiddled with one of his students, or knocked one up."

"Ditto Dame Enid," said Ginger with his dry mirthless laugh. "She's probably miffed we're doing a Michael Tippett opera this year and not one of hers."

"That's possible," said Tony. "Good story to leak to the gossip columns. And the Bishop of Cotchester must have had a choirboy in his time."

He ran his finger down the list. "Henry Hamsphire's a terrible letch; keep an eye on him. Janey Lloyd-Foxe is a whore. She left Billy for a bit and went off with one of his sponsors, and they're always broke. There's bound to be some dirt there. And Wesley Emerson's a cinch. He's always stoned or dipping his wick. We've just got to pick our moment to leak a really juicy story."

Ginger shook his head. "Got to be careful, there. Wesley's such a local hero, the public'll forgive him anything. He took five wickets today, only person who did."

"Send Sarah Stratton to interview him," said Tony. "That should do the trick."

James's stomach gave a terrific rumble; his extended lunch with Sarah today had not included food. "I think we should be careful about smirching Corinium's caring face," he said palely.

"I agree," said Cameron, who'd also gone very white. "Can't we just, as you said, stand on our record? We're better than them. It seems so tacky to sink to their level."

"Don't be fucking stupid," snapped Tony. "This is war. I don't believe Marti Gluckstein lives in Penscombe either. Find out his alleged address and go and pump the neighbors."

"I'll do that story," said Seb quickly.

"Charles is a friend of both Rupert's and Declan's," said Tony. "He can find out what they're up to. Where the hell is he, anyway?" He turned furiously on Cyril.

"Gone to a monastery for two days," stammered Cyril. "They're not in the phone book."

"Well, drive over and fetch him back, sunshine," said Tony with exaggerated patience. "If you both value your jobs, see that he calls me at home tonight after eleven o'clock."

He opened his briefcase and took out a clean shirt and a tie. "I've got to go to the Chamber of Commerce dinner. So bugger off, all of you. I want to talk to Cameron."

After they'd gone Cameron couldn't stop shaking. "It's so awful," she kept saying.

"I think it might be rather fun," said Tony softly. "When the right moment comes, I'll press the destruct button on the lot of them. They've no idea what they've taken on."

As he came toward her, his breath was foul, as though all the hatred had churned and rotted inside him. His body stank of stale sweat. Trying not to flinch when he grabbed her, Cameron said, "I thought you were dropping by this evening?"

"I'd like to, but it's not safe. Press'll be hanging round. Venturer might even put a private dick on to me."

He was so mad to get inside her, he broke the elastic of her panties. It was all over in a minute.

"The bastards," he groaned. "They've all betrayed me."

Then he took her throat between his hands. "If you ever betray me, I'll kill you."

Down the High Street at Radio Cotchester the Controller of Programs received an irate telephone call from the Managing Director who'd never been near the station since Princess Michael opened it five years ago.

"I've just heard a very favorable interview with Bas Baddingham," he roared. "I don't want anymore crap like that on Radio Cotchester. Tell all our announcers and DJs we're backing Corinium a hundred percent throughout this campaign. After all, Tony Baddingham owns twenty percent of us."

Up the High Street at the *Cotchester News* the Editor was reading tomorrow's lead story: *"Tony Baddingham's words to Declan O'Hara that people who get too big for their boots should go and wear out other people's carpets must ring hollow in his ears today when the mega-star Irishman and Penscombe resident headed a bid to oust Tony Baddingham and walk on Corinium's carpets himself after 15th December. Venturer, as he's called his consortium, appears to be soundly based financially, rich in talent and determined to grasp the infinite . . ."*

The Editor had read enough and buzzed the writer. "You can't publish this! We own twenty percent of Corinium, and Tony Baddingham owns twenty-five percent of us. Go back and rewrite it."

"Corinium may not be perfect," the writer retyped defiantly. *"What company is? But it has now reached a level of performance far beyond that which any newcomer could achieve in a few years. Corinium has a massive expansion program, it has won countless awards, it has all the expertise it needs, and it has Cameron Cook."*

Then he went out and got drunk.

Cameron finally tracked down Rupert at the House after he'd voted.

"Sweetheart, are you OK?" he said. "How's Sledge-Hammer House of Horror? Has Tony had a seizure?"

"I hate you and I hate myself," stormed Cameron. "How dare Janey Lloyd-Foxe say Corinium drama was abysmal, and that bloody Bishop attacking the morals of 'Four Men went to Mow'!"

"That was tactless. I'm sorry, but if we don't knock you, Tony'll suspect something. How did he take it?"

"Fine," said Cameron. "Very together, very positive."

"That's not what Barney Williams told me. He said he was quite hysterical. All this expansive crip-crap about welcoming competition came much later in the day."

Cameron wasn't interested. "Look, Rupert, I'm not sure I'm going to go any good as a double agent."

"What's happened?"

"Seb's got to trail you to find out who you're sleeping with."

Rupert laughed. "He's going to have a very boring time then. The only person I'm sleeping or likely to stay awake with is you."

"Are you sure?" Cameron's voice broke. "I'm so confused. It all happened so fast. I need to see you, just to talk."

"I need to fuck," said Rupert. "I want you so badly at this moment, but it'd be madness. The Press are still baying around. We've got to be careful."

"I don't think I can handle it."

"Yes, you can. You're very brave and strong, that's what I adore about you. You're very tired too. Take a couple of Valium and sleep in. And sustain yourself with the thought that one day in December we'll be awarded tickets on the one surviving gravy train."

"I thought we were only interested in making good programs," said Cameron.

"Oh well, that, too," said Rupert.

CHAPTER 30

Within a week the IBA had provided the Press with précis of all the applications and placed a copy of each application in their library so that the public could come and look at them.

Immediately, Tony despatched Miss Madden to the IBA to transcribe Venturer's application in her neat shorthand. Going through the revolving doors she met Ursula, Declan's secretary, on a similar mission.

"I'm not supposed to talk to you," said Joyce.

"Nor I you," said Ursula.

Both agreed, however, that much time could be saved if Ursula mailed Joyce a copy of Venturer's application and Joyce sent Ursula a copy of Corinium's. Then they could pretend they had transcribed and typed them themselves, and pop over to Harrods instead for a lunch of breaded plaice, fruit salad, and several glasses of sweet sherry before going to the movies.

"We mustn't discuss the franchise or I'll get fired," said Joyce, "but you've no idea how demented Lord B. was when he heard Declan was bidding against him. He's really out to get him now. It's a shame we're on different sides. I always liked Declan. He was such a nice man."

Having read Venturer's application, Tony launched his counter-offensive.

"It would be foolish to denigrate the competition," he told the press expansively, and then proceeded to do so.

He also spent a lot of time playing his staff off against each other, having them in individually, offering them large drinks and cigars in his most urbane and disarming manner, then telling each one they were the one person he really relied on to spy on the rest. Pinned on the board was a new notice reiterating instant dismissal for any member of the staff found having dealings with any of the Venturer or Mid-Week consortiums.

The Bishop of Cotchester was therefore rather bewildered when, every time he walked down the High Street or around the Cathedral close and tried to pass the time of day with any of the Corinium staff, they bolted like squirrels up the nearest tree.

The following Sunday Declan called a Venturer meeting at The

Priory. Janey and Billy couldn't make it, nor could Wesley Emerson, but Wesley had vindicated himself already by taking twenty-five wickets and wearing the Venturer T-shirt on every possible occasion.

Georgie, Seb, and Charles (who was wearing a hard hat and brandishing a riot shield borrowed from Wardrobe) all turned up giggling hysterically in James Vereker's very distinct pale-blue Porsche.

"The silly bugger left it in the Corinium parking lot and a second set of keys in his office," said Georgie. "We're going to abandon it outside your house later this afternoon, Enid, then ring up Tony and tip him off."

"How's it going?" said Freddie.

"Tony's in a vilely twitchy mood," said Charles, "bugging everyone's telephones. You'd better watch out, Declan. If your chief engineer rolls up in a yellow van heavily disguised as a TV repairman, don't let him in."

It was such a mild day they all sat outside. Apple blossom and lilac were both out and wafting their sweet fragrance. Cow parsley frothed up to meet the trailing young green leaves and white candles of the horse chestnuts around the lawn. The rushing stream was clogged with forget-me-nots and marsh marigolds, and, although the bluebells were fading, the wood was now lit up by the white flowers of the wild garlic. It was definitely a day to be in love. Rupert turned up with Cameron, obviously just out of bed. Their hair was still wet from the shower. She sat on the lawn propped against him, her hand on his thigh. They looked lean, glamourous, and intensely separate.

Great excitement was caused by the arrival of the rest of the Venturer publicity material: buttons, bumper stickers, bookmarks, peaked caps with adjustable straps at the back, which had to be taken in to fit Henry Hampshire's narrow stoat's head but let out for Dame Enid and Declan. The *pièce de résistance* was the poster. It was a blow-up from the group photograph of Taggie with Gertrude on her knee, both wearing Venturer T-shirts.

"It's fuckin' gorgeous," said Freddie. "Every garage mechanic will put it up in the service bay."

"I'll have some for the bar," said Bas.

"And I for the Close," said the Bishop.

Both Dame Enid and Professor Graystock wanted several for the faculty lounge.

"Dirty old letch," muttered Rupert, glaring at the Professor.

"I'll keep mine under my pillow," said Seb, "in case Tony drops in for coffee one evening."

Only Cameron had been scornful when Rupert showed the poster to her earlier.

"It's too fucking kitsch for words," she snapped.

"I thought you might like to have a look at Corinium's rival offering," said Georgie, unrolling a poster of Sarah Stratton cuddling a baby calf with a caption 'Corinium Cares' underneath. Her shirt had rather too many buttons undone.

" 'Corinium Bares,' more likely," said Rupert dismissively. "Venturer have definitely won the battle of the Crumpet. Here, let me carry that, angel," he went on, leaping to his feet as Taggie came out with a huge chocolate cake and a plate of cucumber sandwiches on a tray.

Taggie couldn't meet his eyes, nor did she say anything when she saw the poster. It reminded her too poignantly of when she'd still been happy, when Rupert had not yet rolled up with Cameron.

After tea Declan came to the serious part.

"For the next two months," he told them, "while the IBA are sifting through the applications before the public meetings begin in July, our job is to get Venturer across to the area. We got off to an excellent start. With such a dazzlingly flamboyant panel—" he grinned around at them—"publicity has been no problem. Now we've got to get out and meet the people who matter—in the Town Halls, the Chambers of Commerce, the Rotary Clubs all around the area—and show them we're not just a bunch of dilettantes.

"We've also got to cast our net wide to cover schools, colleges, churches, young farmers, the police, sports clubs, political groups, race relations officers, etc., etc. We must let them know what we intend to do, find out how we can help them, and then sign them up as friends of Venturer. We'll collect a huge petition of names and organizations to send the IBA. But it'll have far more effect if they can also be persuaded to write a private letter to Lady Gosling giving their support.

"We must try to cover the entire area," he went on. "I know you're all busy and it's going to be a long hard slog, and obviously none of the Corinium moles or Billy or Harold can be seen to be doing anything."

"I'll help," pleaded Taggie. "Please let me. I can drive around delivering flyers and telling people how good you are."

"How can she possibly explain to anyone why they should support Venturer," said Cameron too loudly to Rupert, "if she can't read the fucking application?"

Seeing Taggie go crimson with mortification, Seb leaped to her defense. "Put it on tape," he said. "I'll do it for you, Taggie. If I can't go around the area canvassing, it's the least I can do."

Seb was as good as his word. Over the next two days he not only put the most important points of the application on tape for her, but also the answers she should give to any questions.

"If they're a Leftie organization," he explained, "say we've got Professor Graystock, Lord Smith, and your Dad in the consortium. If they're Tory, plug Freddie, Henry, Rupert, and Marti Gluckstein. If they're Social Democrat, bandy Dame Enid's name around.

"If anyone starts grumbling about sex and violence," he went on, "say we've got the Bishop of Cotchester and he's going to oversee all our programs. On the other hand, if anyone says we haven't got enough sex and violence, say we've got Rupert, Bas, and Wesley Emerson."

He coached her until her spiel was word-perfect. Taggie found him incredibly kind and patient.

"I wish I'd been taught by people like you at school," she said wistfully.

And so the hard grind started. But as Rupert was chronically busy, and Freddie was tied up with his electronics empire, and Declan was locked into his biography of Yeats, and both professors were frantically preparing their students for finals, in the end most of the work fell to Taggie. With a car full of stickers, buttons, and posters, she drove around the vast area visiting everyone from Trade Unionists to Youth Leaders, from Mothers' Unions to Arts Councils, taking in every imaginable pressure group, begging them to sign her petition, to write to the IBA and best of all to come along and cheer Venturer at the public meeting in July. Because of her beauty, sweetness, and passionate belief in her father's and Venturer's cause, she had surprising success.

Sometimes she was joined by the Bishop, sometimes by Dame Enid, which was great fun. Dame Enid had a convertible and they drove through the glorious Spring together with the top down, getting brown, sucking lemon sherbets and calling an awful lot of people "boring little farts" after they'd safely got them signed up. Driving around with Professor Graystock was less fun. He had a horrible habit of squeezing Taggie's bare legs when he made a point, so she took to wearing trousers.

The third Saturday in May, however, was a very bad day for Taggie. She was tired because she'd been up very late doing a dinner party for Valerie Jones the night before. As he was scheduled to tour the Winchester area, which she didn't know, she'd put directions to all the places she had to visit on tape, but even so she got terribly lost and flustered.

On one of her calls she'd got the Social Democrats muddled up with the Labor Party and started plugging Dame Enid when she should have been pushing Lord Smith and Professor Graystock. Then she'd called on a vile headmaster who'd made her tremble because he reminded her of school. "How can Venturer help your school personally?" she asked.

"Well, get a pencil, write it down," he said bossily.

"I'll remember it," stammered Taggie.

"Write it down," snapped the headmaster.

"I can't." Taggie hung her head. "I'm dyslexic."

He was incredibly nice after that, giving her a glass of sherry. His eldest son who'd been killed in Northern Ireland had been dyslexic and he got out a lot of photographs to show her.

It was half past nine and getting dark when Taggie left. She got desperately lost on the way home. She couldn't read any of the unfamiliar names on the signposts, and once it got really dark she was frightened to stop the car and ask strangers the way. There were no stars, or moonlight or street lamps to guide her along the country lanes. She seemed to have been going around for hours and hours, until at last she saw a sign she could recognize: *Penscombe two miles.*

Gertrude was noisily delighted to see her, but the trail of clothes in the hall and up the stairs told her that her parents had gone up somewhat precipitously to bed. The débris of their dinner was still on the kitchen table, one of the burners on the stove was on, and Aengus had knocked over a half-full bottle of whisky which was still dripping on to the flagstones.

"Oh God," sighed Taggie. "Can't they ever do anything for themselves?"

The cow parsley she'd picked that morning was already shedding all over the table.

Nothing lasts, she thought in despair.

Across the valley, Rupert's house was almost blotted out by the trees. There were no lights on. He was probably tucked up in bed with Cameron. It was always when she was really tired that the longing became unbearable.

* * *

Rupert, in fact, had spent the day at the Cup Final, making the main speech at the official dinner afterwards. Despite horrific setbacks, he was the first Minister of Sport who'd tackled rioting and violence head on, and when he sat down they cheered him to the rooftops.

After the dinner was over, however, he beat a hasty retreat, taking a bottle of brandy over to that other Wembley stadium, home of the Horse of the Year Show, where he persuaded an obliging groundsman to put on the lights.

Sitting in the competitors' stand, drinking out of his bottle, he proceeded hazily to relive his past glories as a show jumper. And suddenly the huge arena seemed to be filled with colored jumps and with the ghosts of all his great horses: Revenge, Rocky, Belgravia, Mayfair, Arcturus, Snakepit, and even the cussed Macaulay. He could hear the sound of the bell, the screams of the Pony Club, the roar of applause, even the voice of the commentator, Dudley Diplock, who always got the names wrong. Oh Christ, what was he to do?

Putting his head in his hands, he was overwhelmed with despair as he realized, despite his political triumphs and the buzz of pitching for the franchise and stealing Cameron from Tony, how hopelessly empty his life was now. He hadn't got fat when he'd given up show jumping, or taken to drink, except tonight, or to boring other people with endless anecdotes about his sporting glories as so many other great athletes had. But something had died inside him.

It was nearly midnight. The government car was still waiting outside. The groundsman wanted to lock up.

"Probably fallen asleep," said Sydney, Rupert's driver. "He's a devil for dropping off anywhere. I'll go and wake him."

But when Sydney tapped him on the shoulder, the face Rupert raised was so stricken and haggard that Sydney was prompted to ask if there'd been a death in the family.

"Only myself," muttered Rupert, chucking away the empty bottle and stumbling to his feet. "Only myself."

Taggie had just finished cleaning up and feeding Gertrude the corned beef hash which Declan normally loved but had left half-eaten this evening, when the doorbell rang. Gertrude ran out barking as loudly as she could with her mouth full. Taggie followed, hastily kicking her mother's rather grubby bra and French panties under the radiator. For a second she thought she must be dreaming, for there, swaying in a dinner jacket was Rupert.

"Hullo, angel. Thought I'd catch up on the gossip. Is your father in?"

"Yes, but he and Mummy have gone to bed."

"I'm sorry. I saw a light on. Thought he might be working late."

"Do you want a drink?"

Oh God! Suddenly she remembered. Aengus had knocked over the whisky.

"I've had enough," said Rupert. "I'd love a cup of coffee."

His normally sleeked-back blond hair had flopped over his forehead, his black tie was crooked, his blue eyes crossing. Taggie realized he was absolutely plastered.

"You didn't drive down?" she said in horror.

"No, no, Syd dropped me off."

"Where have you been?" said Taggie, putting the kettle on, wondering if by some miracle he might have had a bust-up with Cameron.

"To the Cup Final."

"Of course. You were making a speech. How did it go?"

"All right, I suppose. The speech that the department had written was so ghastly I tore it up and told a lot of dirty stories instead. I hope no one was there from Corinium with a tape recorder."

"And they liked it?"

"They seemed to. They could afford to be kind. It's probably the last one I'll make."

"What d'you mean?" Taggie put three spoonfuls of sugar into the blackest cup of coffee and put it down on the table in front of him.

"Thanks, darling. The PM's announcing the election date on Monday: June 20th. At least I won a bet on it."

"But you'll win," said Taggie, sitting down at the table beside him.

Rupert shrugged. "I'm not sure we will. The awful thing is, I don't give a bugger. I'm fed up with politics."

"You'll feel differently tomorrow," said Taggie.

At that moment Gertrude strolled in, looked beadily at Rupert, then, to Taggie's amazement, jumped onto his knee and gave his face a quick lick, before settling down, leaving white hairs all over his dinner jacket. Rupert stroked her and laughed.

"There are some small victories left to me," he said.

"Was C-C-Cameron with you?"

Taggie felt it would be better if they could talk about her openly.

"No, it was much too public. Every photographer would have picked us up. Anyway, Tony's *in situ* this weekend."

"It must be awfully difficult for you both."

"Worse for her. At least I don't have to sleep with Tony. I wish she wasn't so fucking insecure."

"Patrick said she had a terrible childhood," said Taggie. "He didn't give any details," she added quickly. "Just said she'd really been through it."

What on earth am I doing defending her, she wondered.

"I don't believe all that junk about terrible childhoods," said Rupert. "I've had four stepmothers and five stepfathers. You had Declan and Maud, which is even worse."

Taggie giggled.

"We're not screwed up," said Rupert.

That was debatable, thought Taggie.

Rupert picked up the petition. "Look at all these names!" His eyes ran down page after page. "Christ, you've been working hard."

He yawned without even putting his hand over his mouth, showing a long pink tongue, and teeth without a single filling. Then he said. "Why have you written L and R on the back of your hands?"

Blushing, Taggie shoved her hands under the table.

"I'll drive you home," she said quickly.

As she started up the car, the tape came on. Frantic with embarrassment, she tried to tug it out of the machine, but Rupert's hand closed over hers like a vice.

"Leave it."

"Turn left at the A412," said Taggie's deep breathy voice, "then keep going for two miles, then turn left just before the Old Mill pub, then keep going till you come to a big barn, turn right, then left up a winding road. Winchley Women's Institute is at the top on the right."

Pulling out the tape, Rupert looked up at the windshield, on which a large capital L and R were stuck on opposite sides.

"You poor little duck," he said softly.

The chestnut candles were shedding their white petals along his drive, a couple of horses blinked in the gloom. As Taggie drew up in front of the house, he said again, "You poor little duck."

Taggie hung her head. "I can't map read very well. It takes me so long and signposts are difficult too, because I don't know the words. If I put it on tape it speeds everything up, and we've got so much ground to cover before July."

Rupert couldn't bear it. What was it about Taggie that so often brought a lump to his throat?

"Angel, you can't go around on your own. Particularly not at night."

"I don't always. Dame Enid's come with me, and the Bishop, and Professor Graystock once or twice."

Rupert shuddered. "That's worse than being alone."

Enforced celibacy was not natural to Rupert. It was like asking a man who smoked sixty cigarettes a day only to smoke ten cigarettes one day a week. Denied Cameron, he was certainly not used to sleeping alone. Still very drunk, he only just stopped himself taking Taggie in his arms to comfort her, and Christ knows where that would have led to. Declan would take him apart and Cameron would bolt straight back to Tony.

Getting out of the car, however, a brilliant idea struck him. "I'll be traveling all around the area canvassing over the next month. You can come with me and hand out Venturer posters and stickers, and paddle the Venturer canoe at the same time. We can even use the Tory loudspeaker to plug Venturer when no one from the Party's listening."

"Is that allowed?" said Taggie in awe.

"Politics is a dirty business," said Rupert blandly. "The Socialists paid a lot of actors twenty-five pounds to dress in rags and pretend to be a soup kitchen line for their election poster last time."

C H A P T E R 31

Next morning Caitlin rang up The Priory wild with excitement.

"Gertrude's in the *Daily Mail*! She looks so sweet."

"What's she doing?" asked Taggie.

"Wearing a Venturer T-shirt and an expression of absolute outrage. She sitting on your knee. You look nice, much better than that old tart Sarah Stratton."

"Oh goodness," said Taggie. "What's the piece about?"

"The headline says: '*Rival Beauties weigh in for the Battle of the Box,*'" read Caitlin. "They've used the two posters of you and Sarah. '*Will the blonde or the brunette pack the greater punch?*' it starts. Then there's a lot of guff about Sarah being Paul Stratton's second wife, and Corinium's latest star anchorwoman, who pulls in three hundred fan letters a week.

"Then it goes on: *'The dark horse (or rather beauty) in the race is Agatha O'Hara, 18-year-old daughter of TV megastar Declan O'Hara, who's bidding to oust his ex-boss Lord Baddingham in the Corinium franchise fight. Agatha runs her own business'* . . . get you . . . *'cooking for the great and famous, but sadly she can no longer undertake dinner parties for her favorite client, Tony Baddingham's wife, Monica, in case state secrets slip out over the soufflé.'*"

"Gosh," said Taggie in amazement. "Where did they get all that from? I hope Lady B. isn't cross. How are you anyway?"

"All right. Can you send me some money, and tell bloody Mummy and Daddy to write."

"They've been really busy with the franchise and things," said Taggie.

"Mummy's never busy with anything," said Caitlin bitterly.

The long, hard grind of getting Venturer's message across to the people who mattered continued throughout the long, hot summer. But things were much easier now for Taggie. Several other papers reproduced the poster and, as she toured the area, people began to recognize her, welcome her and even ask her to autograph the poster.

More important, she spent much of May and June driving around with Rupert on his campaign trail. Leaving him to canvass or to rally support for other South West Tory MPs, Taggie nipped off to visit vicars, youth clubs, and Chambers of Commerce.

Rather too often for Tony Baddingham or Central Office's liking, the two campaigns merged. Rupert was not above urging people to support Venturer on the Tory loudspeaker, or sticking Venturer posters up on the van alongside those urging the public to vote Conservative. Everywhere he and Taggie went, they handed out Venturer publicity material and had great fun after dark, driving around plastering the gateposts of Corinium directors, and even the Corinium building itself, with "Support Venturer" stickers.

To add to Tony's apoplexy, Rupert conducted the entire campaign in a blue Venturer T-shirt and twice appeared similarly clad on "Cotswold Roundup," and, even worse, with huge "Support Venturer" posters on the Tory party van behind him.

Tony was quoted as saying the Venturer T-shirts had been chosen entirely by Rupert to match his blue eyes, and that no doubt the boy shading his forehead on the front symbolized all those Gloucestershire husbands trying to see where Rupert had hidden their wives. Rupert cracked back that everyone knew who the Corinium Ram was supposed to symbolize.

And so the mudslinging went on, with the local press and radio stations uniformly backing Corinium, but the National and Trade press, having scrutinized the applications and the candidates, universally agreeing that Venturer had the more exciting program plans. Dame Enid wrote a battle song, sung by Maud, called "Everything Venture," which unfortunately didn't make the charts.

On June 20th Labor won the election by twenty seats, with the Social Democrats holding the balance of power. Paul Stratton lost his seat. Rupert kept his. He had, in fact, fought a brilliant campaign. Taggie's presence seemed to soothe him, so he was far less acerbic with bores and hecklers, and, as he was one of the only Tories reelected with a much increased majority, Central Office had to stop grumbling about him using Tory funds and equipment to promote Venturer.

In an unprecedented move, Owen Davies, the new Labor Prime Minister, asked Rupert whether he would like to stay on as Minister for Sport if the post was made nonpolitical. Rupert was deeply touched, but refused. He was fed up with swimming meets and Ping-Pong matches, and there was a big row brewing about players taking drugs at Wimbledon, which he was only too happy to hand on to his successor. He was also immediately offered a job by the International Olympics Committee, but refused that too for the moment, knowing it would mean more buzzing around the world.

He wanted a breathing space, to spend the rest of the summer at home concentrating on the horses, seeing something of his children, and putting in a lot of spade work with Cameron, who was getting increasingly uptight. Falling more and more in love with Rupert, she found it almost impossible to pander to Tony's sexual needs and cope with the demanding job of Program Controller at Corinium. While Rupert was fighting the election, he'd been constantly hounded by the press, baying for franchise gossip and trying to catch him out in some new affair, so he and Cameron had had to be doubly careful.

"All this secrecy's just like adultery, darling," said Rupert on one of their few meetings. "Very good training for when you're married."

"That is the most cynical remark I've ever heard," stormed Cameron.

"Not at all. The secret of a happy marriage is not getting found out."

"How d'you know? You didn't have a happy marriage."

"That's because I was always getting found out."

As the election was over, and Tony was tied up all day in meet-

ings in London, she and Rupert had arranged to meet at a hotel outside Henley. As they settled down to Bloody Marys and a splendid
view of the Thames, a barge came chugging up stream. Two young
girls in bikinis were sunbathing on deck. Cameron watched Rupert
run an expert eye over them. Now he had free time on his hands,
would she find it increasingly difficult to hold him? All the same, she
was still not prepared to burn her boats with Corinium until Venturer
had safely won the franchise, and, she had to confess, all the secret
meetings with Rupert did give the affair a certain edge.

"Come on," he said, draining his Bloody Mary and picking up
the keys of their hotel bedroom. "I want to indulge in some mole-
molesting."

But she who lives more lives than one, more deaths than one must
die. Next day, in the Corinium cafeteria, Daysee Butler and Deirdre
Kilpatrick took their cottage cheese and kiwi-fruit salads to a corner
table and didn't notice Cameron sitting behind them.

At first there were the usual grumbles about bosses and crews,
but just as Cameron had abandoned her shepherd's pie half-eaten
and started on her yogurt, Deirdre said, "I don't usually read the
Scorpion but did you see that story that Rupert Campbell-Black's
having an affair with a cook?"

"Cameron Cook?" said Daysee in amazement. "Lord B. won't
like that."

"Not Cameron Cook—a cook. Declan O'Hara's daughter. She
does directors' lunches and things. She's seriously pretty. Well, according to the *Scorpion*, she's been canvassing with Rupert and now
they're absolutely inseparable."

Looking down, Cameron saw she had squeezed her yogurt con-
tainer so hard that it had spurted all over the table. Without attempting to clear up the mess, she walked out of the cafeteria into
Cotchester High Street and the nearest telephone booth.

Rupert was trying out one of his new, very young horses over a
row of jumps in the field beyond the stables. When the telephone
suddenly rang in his pocket, the horse nearly took off back to Ireland. Even when he'd pressed the answer button to silence the ringing, it took all his strength to pull up the terrified animal. All Cameron
could hear was a muffled thunder of hooves and expletives.

"Hullo," Rupert said finally.

"Have you seen the *Scorpion*?"

"Yes. So what?"

"All about you and Ms. O'Hara."

"That was yesterday's *Scorpion*. They've linked me with Mary Whitehouse this morning."

"Can't you be fucking serious?" screamed Cameron. "Everyone's talking about it."

"Good," said Rupert. "At least it keeps the heat off us. Then, as Cameron showed no signs of calming down, he added, "Darling, there's nothing in it, I promise you. As Taggie said in today's *Star*, 'Rupert's old enough to be my father. In fact he's a friend of my father's.' "

"Doesn't mean a thing—Augustus John was old enough to be a lot of girls' great-grandfather—that didn't stop him. Oh Christ . . ." she screamed as her money ran out. "I'll call you back in a minute."

"Please don't until you've cooled down," said Rupert. "I don't want both you and the horse having hysterics at the same time."

Next time they met, it took a great deal of sweet-talking to win her over.

The next big event in the franchise battle was the public meeting held in Cotchester Town Hall at the beginning of July. Chaired by members of the IBA board, it was supposed to give the general public the chance to air their grievances about existing program content and quiz the rival applicants about their plans. It also gave the IBA the opportunity to observe the applicants in action and gauge the degree of local support.

Much-needed rain had been bucketing down all day, but it stopped just before the meeting was due to start. Venturer arrived first. As Rupert had given them all a pep talk about being properly dressed, Declan had sulkily put on a suit and a tie.

"And you can get out of jeans," he had snapped in turn at Taggie. "I've hardly seen your legs since you were born."

Taggie, having rifled through her wardrobe in despair, had rushed into Cheltenham and bought a beautiful violet dress with a scooped neckline, a nipped-in waist and flounced gypsy skirt. Newly washed, her dark hair fluffed down to her shoulder blades as though she'd beaten it with an egg whisk.

Declan, in somewhat unflattering amazement, told her she looked absolutely gorgeous. She was glad she did, when she later found that Sarah Stratton, Cameron, Daysee, and Janey had all pulled out the stops. To Taggie's delight she also found the audience packed with people whose support she had sought in her drives around the

area. Local councillors, social workers, ladies from the Women's Institute from as far afield as Southampton, Oxford, and Stratford, had
turned up and now surged forward to shake her hand.

"We've still got your lovely poster up; we've written to the IBA;
we've been following Venturer's program with such interest," they
all said. "We thought we'd come and cheer you on."

"Remember me?" said a gaunt-looking man in a crumpled lightweight suit, which had obviously just been unearthed from a trunk
in the attic.

"Of course," said Taggie, quite overwhelmed. "How wonderful
of you to turn up."

It was the headmaster with the dyslexic son.

A diversion was caused when Marti Gluckstein, who'd never
been to the country before, tried to enter the hall wearing gumboots
and holding an umbrella over his head.

"Don't bring that thing in here. It's unlucky!" boomed Dame
Enid.

"Come on, Marti, I'll buy you a stiff drink before we kick off,"
said Bas, guiding Marti back through the puddles over the road to
the Cotchester Arms.

Sprinting after them, Rupert handed Bas his hip flask. "Can you
fill this up with weak rum for Wes?"

Wesley, having taken another five wickets that afternoon, had
been celebrating and was now busy signing autographs.

A great theatrical hiss went up from the Venturer camp as the
Corinium mafia trooped in. They were led by Tony, very brown
from Ascot. Wearing a new pale pink and blue silk shirt, a pink tie,
and a pink carnation in his buttonhole, he managed to flash his teeth
at everyone in the room except Venturer. He was followed by Ginger
Johnson, Georgie Baines, who'd obviously had a few to steady his
nerves, Mike Meadows, Head of Sport, Charles Fairburn, Seb Burrows, Simon Harris, who'd been allowed back in a consultancy capacity to impress the IBA, and whose straggly beard had turned quite
white, Cyril Peacock, false teeth rattling, sweating through his suit,
and Cameron, truculent in an elongated black T-shirt which came
five inches above her knees. Sarah Stratton, wearing a dress in Virgin
Mary blue, with a white Puritan collar also to impress the IBA,
brought up the rear with James Vereker, whose head was held high
so more people could recognize him.

"Who's chair?" James asked Charles Fairburn as the Corinium
contingent sat down in the front row.

"Dunno. Belongs to the Town Hall, I should think," said Charles.

"No," said James impatiently, "who's Chair?"

"I've just told you."

"I'm asking you, who is chairing the meeting?"

"Oh." Comprehension dawned on Charles's round red face. "Might be Old Mother Goose—" which was everyone's nickname for Lady Gosling—"but I wouldn't have thought she'd have bothered to come this far."

Cameron grabbed a seat at the end of the row by the window, as far away from Tony as possible. All she could see was one of his beautifully polished black shoes, rotating as if he were doing an ankle-slimming exercise—a sign that he was nervous. The company *in situ* always got more flak at public meetings than those seeking to oust it. Tony, frightened of ridicule, knew he was in for a bumpy evening. The entire Corinium contingent studiously ignored Venturer. Henry Hampshire, however, who'd been to a cocktail party, had no such reservations.

"Hello everyone," he beamed as he came through the door. "Hullo, Taggie darling, you're looking beautiful. Hullo, Rupert." Then, turning to the Corinium contingent, boomed, "Oh look, there's Charles, Georgie, and Cameron. Must go and say hello."

"Hen-ree," hissed Rupert, grabbing his arm and whispering in his ear. "You're not supposed to know they're on our side."

"What?" said Henry loudly. "What's that? How d'yer mean, not on our side? 'Course they are."

Fortunately Tony was talking to the Archdeacon and didn't hear. As Rupert tried to explain, Henry looked as deflated as an English setter who's been told he's not going on a walk, then cheered up when he saw Daysee Butler.

"Who's she? She on our side?"

"No, she's with Corinium."

"Damn shame, pretty girl like that, and that's Sarah Stratton next to her, isn't it? She's a damn pretty girl too. Why isn't *she* on our side?"

And next moment Henry had broken away from Rupert's restraining hand and marched across the room to talk to Sarah, who introduced him to Daysee.

"Just saying to Rupert, pretty girls like you should be on our side. What are you both doing afterwards?"

"Bugger off, Henry," snarled Tony.

"Hen-ree," Rupert dragged him off.

Fortunately at that moment a diversion was provided by Basil returning with Marti, quite soberly dressed now, and Janey Lloyd-Foxe in a pink jumpsuit.

"Hullo, Rupert darling." Janey kissed him full on the mouth. "Sorry I'm late."

Rupert tugged up her zipper to the bounds of decency, saying, "For Christ sake go and distract Henry."

Basil took Rupert aside. "I've filled up the hip flask for Wesley." Then, dropping his voice, he whispered, "Those lovely lips just puckered up to meet yours were around my dick at eight o'clock this morning."

"What?" exploded Rupert. "What did you say?"

"You heard," said Basil, grinning.

"How dare you," thundered Rupert. "She's married to my best friend."

" 'Course she is, and very happily. I'm just making sure she doesn't suffer from post-natal depression when Billy's away."

Rupert might well have hit Bas across the room if the IBA—three members of the Board and various members of their staff—hadn't trooped in and taken up their places on the platform.

"We are honored," Charles whispered to James. "Old Mother Goose *is* in the chair. The IBA must regard the outcome as by no means certain then, if she's come all this way to have a look."

"I can't think why you're looking so cheerful," said James fretfully. "Venturer's bound to offer me a job if they get the franchise. I mean I am 'Cotswold Roundup,' but, as they've got the Bishop to handle religious programs, I can't see them wanting you."

"Who are those deadbeats over there?" Janey asked Bas.

"The Mid-West consortium," said Bas. "Can't think they'll bother us much."

Rupert, having at last persuaded Henry to stop flirting with Daysee and sit down, collapsed into a seat between Taggie and Declan.

"How the hell am I going to keep this bunch under control until December?" he said.

Taggie giggled: "Henry's certainly fallen for Daysee."

"Let me not to the marriage of true mindlessness admit impediment," said Declan.

The audience were now occupying every seat in the hall, with Corinium spread out along the front row and Cameron at the far end by the window. Next to her, at right angles, on a single row of chairs, sat the Mid-West consortium, who looked a pretty moth-eaten bunch.

Facing them, also on a single row of chairs, forming a square with the platform, sat Venturer.

Lady Gosling, decided Cameron, looked more like a hedgehog than a goose, a Mrs. Tiggywinkle with small twinkling intelligent eyes, a long thin nose, a pointed chin and rather wild gray hair, held down on either side by tortoise-shell barettes. She wore no makeup and, despite the warmth of the evening, was smothered in several shawls over her olive-green wool dress. The cozy exterior, however, was deceptive and hid a rapier mind. As Head of an Oxford college, Gwendolyn Gosling had taught Russian. Her fellow dons were not altogether joking when they nicknamed her "Khrushchev." There was shrewdness beneath the amiability, and the twinkling eyes, like the stars, gave off little warmth.

For a hideous moment at the beginning of the meeting it looked as though no one was going to ask any questions. Then a man in spectacles got up and grumbled about the bad reception in Glouces-ter. Corinium's Chief Engineer got up to answer him, and the stupor produced by engineers at public meetings allowed everyone time to collect their thoughts.

More straightforward complaints then followed from local poli-ticians who had not yet been interviewed by James on "Cotswold Roundup" that coverage in their area was pitiful.

Mrs. Makepiece, James's cleaning woman, then rose to her feet, and, disclaiming any connection with Corinium, said "Cotswold Roundup" was the best program on telly, and why couldn't it be on seven days a week?

One of the Corinium shop stewards, who'd just squeezed a two-thousand-pound raise out of Tony for all his union members, as well as a fat bribe for himself, shouted from the back that he wouldn't trust Declan O'Hara's mob further than he could throw them. His claim that industrial relations at Corinium were second to none, how-ever, was greeted by cries of 'si-down' from all over the hall.

"As Corinium forks out whatever the unions demand and most of the technicians earn more than the Prime Minister, I should think industrial relations are second to none," yelled Bas, to loud cheers from the Venturer supporters.

A large woman from Chipping Sodbury then rose to her feet and said in a ringing voice that she was sick to the teeth of news about Cotchester and nothing about Chipping Sodbury.

Remembering Miss Corinium Television, Rupert caught Declan's eye. "She's forgotten Miss Chipping Sodbury's tits," he whispered across Taggie.

Both men started to shake with laughter, until quelled by a cold look from Lady Gosling.

Tony rose to reply. "I can assure you, madam," he said smoothly, "that, by an extraordinary coincidence, 'Cotswold Roundup' is due to visit Chipping Sodbury later this week."

"Are we?" said James to Sarah, looking startled.

"In fact," Tony went on warmly, "we have super plans for the entire Corinium area."

"You've been here eight years. Why haven't we seen any of them?" bellowed Taggie's headmaster.

More cheers were counterpointed by snores from Mrs. Makepiece.

"I've studied both Venturer's and Corinium's applications at the public library," went on Taggie's headmaster, "and Venturer's program plans seem infinitely more imaginative. What I would like to ask Lord Baddingham is how much have his grandiose new plans for a multimillion-pound studio, for slots for every possible minority group, for cultural improvement and for spectacular entertainment been spawned by a desire to hang onto his very lucrative franchise?"

Tony was about to rise and shout back over the deafening cheers, but James was too quick for him. "James Vereker, 'Cotswold Roundup,' " he announced, getting to his feet and turning sideways so he could be recognized both by the platform and the floor.

"As anchorman of 'Cotswold Roundup,' " said James, "I know I speak for each and everyone of us at Corinium from Tony Baddingham downward when I say that Corinium's ethos can be summed up in two words."

"Bloody terrible," shouted Bas, to screams of laughter.

"Two little words—" James ploughed on—"Corinium cares."

"The only fing Tony cares about is making a fast buck," shouted Freddie, to more deafening cheers.

Mrs. Makepiece snored so loudly that she woke herself up. "Let's get up a partition," she said loudly.

Cameron knew she ought to stand up and defend Corinium, but she didn't relish getting ripped apart by Declan. She was saved by the Women-in-Broadcasting lobby, who all had moustaches and who complained that there weren't enough women in any of the consortiums. Lady Gosling nodded in agreement, and made notes.

The meeting droned on. Wesley Emerson had had a hard day in the field. No one but Rupert and Bas realized that each time his noble head nodded onto his right buttonhole he was taking a long suck of rum from a straw to Rupert's hip flask in his breast pocket.

Outside in Cotchester Park, the lime trees were in flower; their sweet delicate scent, stronger after the downpour, drifted in through the open window. Cameron watched the house martins swooping after insects, flashing their white bellies. The tennis courts were packed with people playing vigorous post-Wimbledon tennis. In a week or so they'd revert to their usual patball. She glanced surreptitiously across at Rupert, who was sitting next to that drip Taggie, who (whatever Rupert said to the contrary) had a thumping crush on him.

Nothing except for the occasional yawn, not even a glance in her direction, betrayed the fact that Rupert had left her bed at six o'clock that morning. Cameron wondered sometimes if she'd imagined the whole thing. She was so deep in thought, she had to be nudged in the ribs by Seb to answer a question from a pale girl from Gay Lib as to whether the lesbian shepherdess who'd appeared briefly in the last series of "Four Men went to Mow" would appear in the next one.

As Cameron sat down, the large woman from Chipping Sodbury returned to the attack. "Nothing that comes from Corinium TV," she said, "is truly regional. Even Dorothy Dove speaks with a London accent."

Another rabble-rouser, again heavily prompted by Tony, then rose to his feet.

"While we're on the subject of accents," he sneered, "in the first week of July four people were brutally butchered by the IRA. Do we really want an Irishman, namely one Declan O'Hara, bearing in mind his left-wing attitudes and the subversive nature of many of his programs, to be the Chief Executive of an English television company?"

"Out of order," screamed the Venturer contingent.

Declan, who'd gone white, was just about to answer.

"Careful," whispered Rupert.

"I'd like the speaker to withdraw that remark," said Lady Gosling frostily. "Next question please."

The Clean-Up Television Campaign, headed by the Archdeacon, then started slamming sex and violence, followed by the Bishop of Cotchester who said how concerned he was about his flock, and that he would be working with Venturer to reduce not only sex and violence, but the very widespread blasphemy on television. He was just hitting his stride when Henry Hampshire's ancient gardner staggered to his feet.

"I like to go to bed very early," he grumbled. "I do wish Corinium wouldn't pull all those sexy fil-lums on so late at night, because I and the missus can never stay awake to watch them."

Everyone roared with laughter, including Lady Gosling, who then clapped her hands and said it was with great regret that she had to bring this very stimulating meeting to a close as they were running out of time. They would end, she added, with a seven-minute sales pitch from each of the three contenders.

Tony rose first, deliberately turning his back on Venturer and talking half to the platform and half to the audience.

"Good evening," he began suavely. "I am the Chief Executive of—er," he glanced down at his notes and everyone laughed, "Corinium Television. We have noted," he went on, "the very perceptive and instructive points raised tonight, and, although we don't agree with all of them, anyone who would like a further answer to his— or indeed, her," he smiled broadly, "question, please write to me personally."

"Prick," muttered Rupert under his breath. He folded his arms belligerently and, with the hand that was hidden, fought a violent urge to caress the side of Taggie's left breast which swelled so seductively beneath her violet dress. She looked ravishing this evening, and she'd done so well to get all those strange but incredibly influential people to the meeting.

Firmly clenching his hand away from Taggie, he looked across at Cameron, who was gazing moodily into space with a kind of deadpan, terrorist truculence. She reminded him of the girl grooms he used to fuck in the old days. He desperately wanted a fuck now, but he wouldn't get Cameron tonight. Tony, overexcited by the meeting, would no doubt take advantage of that release. Rupert was finding the enforced celibacy more and more trying.

Having finished a rousing spiel about Corinium's long and honorable record, Tony was now paying tribute to "the thriving, creative community" he had the privilege to lead. "We are aware, Ladies and Gentlemen, that there is life west of Harrods, our hearts are not in 'Dallas,' nor in our headquarters in London. Our company is run by people from the region, who have a special place in the Cotswolds and, indeed, in West Country life. We are pledged to serve the whole community. Above all we care."

He sat down to moderate cheers. Then it was Mid-West's turn.

A fat man with straggly white hair staggered to his feet and then took ages to find his notes. "That's obviously the geography teacher who never found his way to London," whispered Rupert to Taggie.

"I am deeply honored," began the fat man.

"Name, name," yelled the audience.

"My name is Cedric Bonnington," he mumbled. "I hope to be Chairman of Mid-West television."

"Well don't be bashful, speak up," shouted Tony's rabble-rouser.

Sadly, Sir Cedric didn't. In a low mumble he laboriously read out that he was very interested in all the fascinating points that had been made by the floor.

"I cannot reveal who our backers are," he droned on, "but very substantial funds will be available should the very talented group, whose names I also cannot divulge at this stage, win the franchise."

"He'll probably get it," said Georgie Baines to Seb Burrows.

"What about women?" yelled the Women-in-Broadcasting lobby.

Sir Cedric consulted his notes. The company's Program Controller, whose name he also couldn't divulge, he said, would be a woman of the widest experience.

The audience waited for more exciting revelations and, when none materialized, egged on by the Corinium consortium, who'd all got to their feet, started to drift away. It was almost dark outside; the pubs beckoned.

"No one's going to stay and listen to Daddy," said Taggie in anguish, and, as Declan got up to speak, people were swarming out into the High Street.

"I'd like first to answer the speaker who questioned the right of an Irishman to run an English television company," he began softly. "As much right perhaps as that great Irishman, the Duke of Wellington, to command a British Army."

He spoke without notes. As people poured back into the hall again, the deep soft husky voice carried easily around the hall.

"I am proud to be Irish," he went on, "and, to echo the words of another great Irish patriot, Irwin Cobb, I too had an ancestor who was out with the pikes in '98. He was captured by the English and tried for treason. They hanged him by the neck until he was dead, but his soul goes marching on, transmitting to his descendants, of whom I am proud to be one, the desire to fight against tyranny whenever I come across it. I also love and honor British television. It is the best in the world. That's why I and so many of my countrymen are over here, learning from it and, I hope, contributing to it.

"But we still go on fighting tyranny and oppression whenever we find it. I found it in the six months I worked for Corinium. That's why I walked out, and why, with my English friends—" he turned and smiled briefly at the Venturer consortium—"I have put in a bid to oust Lord Baddingham."

He then proceeded to carve up Tony and tear Corinium's boring sycophantic programs to shreds. Only at the end did be briefly outline how Venturer would be different, how they would truly both represent the area and foster local talent. "I would like all great artists of the future to be able to say they had their first chance at Venturer."

The audience stood up and cheered him for nearly three minutes. Stony-faced, Tony strode out of the hall. Cameron tried to follow him, but, trapped by the crowd, she watched Rupert, Declan, Taggie and the rest of Venturer, plus their supporters, jubilantly heading for the Bar Sinister for drinks on the house. Rupert never gave her a backward glance. Sick with desire, she wondered how much longer she could go on playing a double game.

Although the *Cotchester News* reported the meeting a rousing success for Corinium and published numerous rigged readers' letters of support, it was generally agreed that Venturer had won that round.

CHAPTER 32

After his humiliation at the public meeting, Tony stepped up his campaign to discredit Venturer. Flipping through a list of their names the following morning, he decided his newsroom had been singularly inept in uncovering any dirt. The Bishop of Cotchester, it seemed, had neither fiddled with the collection plate nor with any of his more cherubic choir boys; Dame Enid had never straddled anything more exciting than her cello; Professor Graystock was recognized as an old goat, but no more so than the averaged don. On the other hand, Henry Hampshire was plainly capable of being led astray by Daysee Butler. Perhaps she ought to be sent off to interview him.

Nothing as yet on Rupert, except an alleged walk-out with Taggie O'Hara, which Tony didn't believe. All the same it might be a good idea to allow her to cook for Monica again. Primed with a few late-night brandies, she might become indiscreet about the moles who were joining Venturer from other companies. He added Taggie's name to the list, but that didn't bring him any nearer Rupert. He made a note to track down Beattie Johnson, who'd been writing Rupert's memoirs when Rupert booted her out last year. There must be some grievances to fan there.

Freddie Jones, Tony decided blackly, was Venturer's greatest asset. He was so solid, so dependable, so popular, so hugely successful after such a lowly start, which appealed to a crusading streak in the IBA. Ha! though Tony, *cherchez la femme*. He buzzed Miss Madden. "Will you tell James Vereker to come up."

James was not happy. Even through his layers of egotism he realized he'd made a fool of himself at the public meeting. He was still miffed because no one had asked him to join their consortium, and, opening a new edition of *Who's Who in Television* that morning, he'd discovered two columns devoted to Declan and not even a reference to himself.

James brushed his hair and put on a tie. He hoped Tony wasn't still miffed about the meeting.

Tony, however, was at his most amiable, steering James toward the squashy beige sofa, telling Madden they didn't want to be disturbed, offering James a large drink.

James normally only drank Perrier at lunchtime, both for his figure and to keep his wits about him for his program, but now he felt it fitting to accept a large scotch, just to show that he and Tony were both males capable of holding their liquor.

"I've got a very special mission for you, James," said Tony.

Half an hour later James returned to his office in a state of euphoria to find Sarah exuding Anaïs Anaïs and expectancy.

"Are we lunching, darling?"

"Probably," said James. "I've got to make a call."

When he rang Valerie Jones, she was absolutely "delighted" to hear from him. "Oh, don't mention that silly franchise. If one can't talk to one's friends," she said. "I was going to phone you and your— er—lovely wife—" she always forgot Lizzie's name—"to remind you that we're opening Green Lawns to the public on Saturday, and we hoped you'd both pop in. It is looking really rather lovely at the moment."

"What an extraordinary coincidence," said James. "I was phoning to say of course we've got your opening in our diary and we were hoping we might come and film it for 'Cotswold Roundup.' We're only covering the best gardens. Tony and Monica's, of course, and the Duchess's at Badminton. Hullo, hullo, are you still here?"

"She's fainted," said Sarah.

"Of course I am," shrieked Valerie.

"Could I come take a look this afternoon? Will Freddie be there?"

"He's away."

"Good," said James wolfishly. "Give me a chance to get you on my own."

Valerie's tinkle of laughter showed she was not displeased.

"What *are* you playing at?" asked Sarah as James hung up.

"Tony wants a spy in the Venturer camp. He's chosen me because he thinks I'm the one guy who can charm secrets out of Valerie."

"The spy who came in from the cold frame," giggled Sarah. "Are you going to stick poison umbrellas into Valerie's garden gnomes?"

It was a muggy, still afternoon, French-gray sky on the horizon deepening to forget-me-not blue overhead. The tall seeding grasses in the hayfields were turning gold against the deep summer greens of the trees. At the bottom of the Jones's drive was a large sign saying: "Garden Open on July 9th, to be televised on 'Cotswold Roundup.' Come and meet James Vereker in person—proceeds to the Red Cross."

Smirking, James drove up a paved black driveway as wide as a highway. Long before he reached the house he was almost blinded by a blaze of color. Every flowerbed was packed with serried clashing ranks of French marigolds, yellow calceolaria, royal blue cineraria, flaming red geraniums, billiard-ball pink zinnias, and mauve asters. As he drew up in front of the house a truck was unloading plants. Having denuded every nursery for miles around, Valerie was now renting four hundred scarlet salvias and three hundred yellow begonias from Rent-a-Garden.

Around the corner came a sweating youth pushing a wheelbarrow crammed with scarlet and mauve petunias. Next moment Valerie came screaming after him, brandishing a small fork.

"What are you doing, Spicer?"

"Putting them on the rubbish heap, ma'am."

"They're meant to be planted in the wheelbarrow, you idiot. Can't you recognize creative gardening when you see it? Take it straight back to the patio."

Then she saw handsome James getting out of his pale blue Porsche and her face softened.

"James," she said holding out both her hands, "it's been too long."

"You're looking lovely, Mousie," said James, taking her hands and holding them, also a little too long. "And so's your garden."

Valerie swept James around to the patio and asked him if he'd rather have iced coffee first or wander around.

James said he'd rather have iced coffee, and sat down very quickly for fear of being concussed by half-a-dozen hanging baskets weighed down by every color of petunia. But although he coyly patted the seat beside him, once Valerie had poured the iced coffee she insisted on prowling the patio, denuding petunias.

"Tony sent his special love, so did Monica," lied James.

"Oh, we miss them both," sighed Valerie. "I do wish Freddie'd never got caught up in this stupid franchise. It's all so pointless."

"D'you get roped into meetings?" asked James.

"No, no," said Valerie, "but the socializing side of it's quite fun. Henry took us to As-Cot."

"With such interesting program plans, Venturer must have roped in some pretty considerable production people," said James idly.

"I hope you like our border of massed glads over there," said Valerie. "Bring your coffee and let's have a wander."

Having admired every petal, every gnome, every plastic Venus de Milo, James still hadn't learned anything about Venturer.

"Freddie used to pop into Corinium a lot," he said as they passed a dolphin regurgitating blue-tinted water into a pond. "Does he still see any of his old friends there? I bet they're knocked-out by this lovely garden."

"It is lovely, isn't it?" said Valerie smugly, "but I wish we could grow rhodos in Gloucestershire."

"Are Venturer recruiting their staff locally?" asked James. "Who else have they signed up?"

But Valerie was off leaping across a stream to tug up some mare's tail.

"I know Tony's keeping an eye out for moles at Corinium," fished James as Valerie joined him again.

"So are we," said Valerie. "Moles are Freddie's biggest worry."

"Perhaps we should compare notes, Mousie," said James.

As they were now hidden from the house by a row of yellow conifers, he slid his hand around her waist. It was nice and trim.

"Well, Freddie's been putting down Mole-Ban everywhere," said Valerie, "but I'm still terrified I'm going to wake up tomorrow and find mole hills all over the lawn."

James gave up. He arranged that he and the crew would arrive at about three-thirty, and asked if she could keep Venturer T-shirts and posters to a minimum.

"Tony feels you're so special and that a lovely garden is above personalities. But we really can't use the footage on 'Roundup' if it's full of plugs of Venturer."

As James was filming gardens all Saturday afternoon, Lizzie had planned to work on her book. Then, feeling rather old and dried-up, she rubbed a lot of collagen anti-aging cream into her face, only to realize she'd forgotten her neck, which is supposed to betray your age most, so she rubbed the excess down into it. Then she remembered you were supposed never to rub downwards, as it made your face droop. Would her life have been different, she wondered, if she'd always remembered to rub upwards? Would James have stayed faithful to her? Unwisely, knowing it would hurt her, she snooped around in James's drawers and found a ravishing photograph of Sarah Stratton under his boxer shorts. Feeling utterly miserable, she thought how nice it would be to see Freddie Jones again. Abandoning any thought of work, she decided to go along to Valerie's opening.

As she drove through Green Lawns's electric gates, she noticed a large "Support Venturer" sticker on the huge sign announcing that James and Corinium Television would be present that afternoon. Lizzie couldn't even be bothered to peel the sticker off. In the turn-around she found Rupert unashamedly sticking more Venturer stickers on everyone's windshields.

"Darling." He kissed her. "Divided as we are by our rival consortiums, we shouldn't consort, but do let's go around together. I need a good laugh. Mrs. Jones's new rockery is like the polar bear pit at the zoo; she's been training gro-lights on her roses all night and twenty-four-hour fluorescent lighting in the greenhouse is forcing out the Christmas roses."

Lizzie laughed. "You can't bring that dog," she said as Rupert let Beaver out of his car. "Particularly if he's not on a leash. Valerie will have a coronary."

"Good," said Rupert locking the car. "Look how well he's trained," he went on as Beaver lifted his leg on a cohort of salmon pink petunias.

"It's just like a park," said Lizzie as they walked toward the house.

"Unfair to parks," said Rupert.

On the edge of the lawn a booth featured clothes from Valerie's boutique, with the mark-up going to the Red Cross. Models, sweating in Valerie's Autumn Line, wandered aimlessly around, fanning themselves with price tags. There was not a Venturer plug in sight.

"What a lot of people," said Rupert. "Judging by the mob on the lawn, your husband's holding court. Let's go the other way."

As they proceeded down the crazy pavement, they could hear Valerie dispensing advice on the other side of the yellow conifer hedge.

"How d'you manage to grow such whopping glads?" asked a neighbor admiringly.

"I feed them with Grow-More," said Valerie.

"She's obviously been feeding her children the same thing," muttered Rupert as poor fat Sharon, blushing at the sight of Rupert, waddled past them.

"Hullo, Bishop," they could now hear Valerie screaming. "How good of you to look in. I'm about to be interviewed on TV, but you'll find Fred-Fred in the grounds."

"It'd be grounds for divorce if I was married to her; the only person not allowed into Valerie's opening is Fred-Fred," said Rupert, grabbing Lizzie's arm. "Come on, buck up, let's look at the pond. I don't want to get trapped with the Bishop any more than she does."

"I thought the Bishop was on your side," said Lizzie, panting after him.

"He is, and a god-awful bore too. He's mad about Taggie, so he keeps dropping in at The Priory unannounced, and finding Maud and Declan having a bang, or hurling plates at one another, which, bearing in mind the Bishop's views on sex and violence, doesn't go down very well."

"I thought it was you having a walk-out with Taggie," said Lizzie slyly as they passed Hybrid Teas, massed in clashing colors above totally weedless beds.

Rupert raised his eyes to heaven. "Would that I were! She's *so* sweet."

"Why aren't you then?"

"Declan would murder me, and she's too young."

"Never deterred you in the past."

"Ah, but it's franchise year." Rupert bent down to press a Venturer sticker on the bare belly of a plastic Venus de Milo. "And we're all having to behave ourselves as I'm sure your husband knows. Why have you got that rash on your hands?" he asked more gently as Lizzie whipped off the sticker.

"The doctor says it's stress-related," said Lizzie bitterly.

"Mistress-related, more likely." Suddenly she could bear it no longer. "James is having an affair with Sarah Stratton. I shouldn't have told you that. You'll leak it to *Private Eye* and discredit Corinium even further."

"Why don't you leave him? He's such a cunt," said Rupert, putting another sticker as a figleaf over a cherub, and dragging Lizzie on before she could remove it.

"Helen didn't leave you." Lizzie paused to examine the pond which was a mass of scarlet and yellow water lilies. "God, isn't this hell?"

"She did in the end," said Rupert. "Besides, I'm not a cunt."

They had reached the end of the garden now; cornfields the color of French mustard and bluey-green woods stretched to the horizon. On the right, a red tractor chugged back and forth, anxious to get the hay baled and away before tonight's promised rain.

"Heaven to see some decent country," said Rupert. "Do you think 'cunt-ricide' means murdering one's mistress?"

Lizzie laughed. "You do cheer me up. I wish someone would murder Sarah."

Leaving the pond, they wandered back to the house and walking under a weeping willow ran slap into Freddie.

He looked very tired, and only nodded at them politely until he realized who they were. Then he jumped up and down with pleasure, giving Lizzie a big hug.

" 'Ullo, Rupe, 'ullo Lizzie. 'Ow are you, love? You look grite. Better not let Valerie see Beaver, Rupe, she's a bit uptight. Been dead-'eading petunias in her sleep all night; fink she's about to dead-'ead me. Let's go inside and 'ave a drink. Val's doing her TV interview. Finks the sun shines out of James Vereker's arse. Oh, sorry, love—" he squeezed Lizzie's arm—"I quite forgot he was your 'usband!"

"James thinks the same," said Rupert, spiking another sticker on a garden gnome's fishing rod. "I'm sure he's only here because he wants to worm secrets out of your wife, Freddie."

Although, watching the way Freddie and Lizzie were looking at each other, Rupert reflected that Lizzie, with all her warmth and sympathy, would be far more skilled at getting Venturer's secrets out of Freddie.

Cameron had expected to spend Friday night with Tony, but he'd decided to fly to France a day early, leaving her with an unexpected free evening. Unable to get in touch with Rupert, she'd slept alone and very well for the first time in months and woke feeling rested and happy. As she wasn't due to meet Rupert until the evening, she decided to wander over and watch James filming gardens. She didn't stay long at The Falconry. The garden was too wonderful, and she didn't like such tangible proof of Monica's skills. She was surprised Tony hadn't stayed at home to crow.

By comparison Valerie's garden was utterly dreadful, but had certainly attracted large crowds, particularly around the television crew. Fighting her way through until she was blocked by a large bed of purple and salmon-pink gladioli, Cameron saw James up at the other end interviewing Valerie and quickly stifled a scream of laughter. Valerie was dressed for Ascot in a yellow and white shirt-waist dress and a huge buttercup-yellow hat trimmed with yellow roses, but was totally unaware that someone had stuck a "Support Venturer" sticker on her bottom.

Looking across the sea of mauve and salmon-pink, Cameron caught her breath in joy, because there, beside Freddie and Lizzie Vereker, also trying very hard not to laugh, was Rupert. As if drawn by her longing, he looked up and gave a brief grin of surprise before instantly resuming his normal deadpan expression.

" 'Cotswold Roundup'/Green Lawns/Take Four," said the second assistant, snapping the clapper board.

"One only has to look at your flower beds, Valerie," said James as the camera panned slowly in on the sea of mauve and salmon-pink, "to appreciate what a truly caring gardener you are. Tell us your secret."

"Well, James," began Valerie; then her little laugh turned to a squawk of rage as the normally well-trained Beaver, suddenly seeing Cameron, who'd spent a great deal of time sharing his master's bed recently, crashed across the bed of gladioli, snapping and flattening most of them, and throwing himself on Cameron in total ecstasy.

Just for a few seconds, to a crescendo of Valerie's squawks, Cameron and Rupert were caught on camera, absolutely collapsing with laughter, before Rupert sharply called Beaver off.

As she drove home rather tight later in the evening with James, Lizzie said, "Cameron's the one you and Tony should be watching. I'm certain she's having an affair with Rupert."

"Don't be ridiculous," snapped James. "Cameron only cares about Corinium."

On Sunday night on his way back from France, where he'd made great strides in acquiring a stake in French television, Tony dropped in at the office to see how The Falconry garden looked on video. The cameraman had left the tape on his desk. Loosening his tie, pouring himself a large drink, Tony put the tape in the machine and lay back on his squashy sofa to watch. He was enchanted with the results. Monica had really come up trumps this year. How right he'd been not to leave her for Cameron. Having played back The Falconry footage twice more, he decided to have a good laugh, and ran the tape of Valerie's garden. He played it back five times, freezing the frame on the last ten seconds.

Then he walked out of the building not even bothering to lock the bar or his office door, and drove straight over to Hamilton Terrace. Cameron was not there. Letting himself in, he searched systematically through the house. In the bedroom wastebasket he found what he was looking for. A pile of tiny torn-up scraps of paper. No one tore paper up that small unless they wanted to hide something. It took him a long time to put the pieces together because his hands were trembling so, but finally he was able to read the words: *Venturer meeting, Henry's house, 12:30 Sunday.*

Cameron got home about midnight. Sated and reeling from Rupert, she hadn't even bothered to shower afterwards as she wanted to keep the sweat and smell of him on and inside her body as long as possible. Dropping her briefcase in the hall, she wandered into the drawing room. The bulb that turned on by the door had blown, so in the faint light from the street lamps she groped her way across the room to turn on the light by her desk. The next minute she leaped in terror as a hand shot out, grabbing her leg just above the knee. Burglars was her first panic-stricken thought; then, as a light flashed on, she saw Tony crouched on the sofa like a venomous toad.

"What are you doing skulking in the dark?" she stammered.

"What are *you* doing," said Tony in a voice that utterly froze her blood, "going to a Venturer meeting at Henry Hampshire's house today?"

Cameron's gasp of horror gave it all away: "I-I-I had a tip-off. I went along to spy. I just hung around outside the gates, trying to see who was going in."

"Who gave you the tip-off?"

Cameron's mind raced. "I overheard people talking in the Bar Sinister—in the next booth."

"You bloody liar," hissed Tony. "And how long has Rupert been stuffing you?"

"He isn't," jibbered Cameron, wincing as his hand tightened on her leg. "He's a bastard. The last person I'd shack up with."

Tony tugged her toward him, burying his nose in her groin.

"You reek of him, you fucking whore. And how come his dog knows you so well? It's all on tape, sweetheart."

And the next moment he'd hit her across the room. She fell with a crash, catching her head on the bookshelf. Then he was on her again, picking her up by her shirt and smashing his left fist into her face. This time she crashed back into a small table, knocking over a vase of buddleia.

He's going to kill me, she thought as he lunged at her again, kicking her in the ribs until she groaned for mercy. Yet, at the same time, another part of her terror-crazed mind was thinking that she had to get out of there before he got his hands on her briefcase which contained all her notes on the meeting, and, even worse, the names of the Corinium moles.

As he dragged her to her feet and hit her again, she managed to grab a chair and, swinging it around, caught him on the side of the head, narrowly missing his eye with one of the legs. It gave her a breathing space. Grabbing the vase of buddleia that was now leaking onto the floor, she hurled it at him and stumbled out of the room, banging the door behind her. Gathering up her briefcase she just managed to put up the double catch on the front door, locking him in as she slammed it. By the time he'd managed to climb out of the drawing room window, she'd started up the Lotus and was on her way to Rupert's.

Putting her hand up to her head where she'd hit the bookcase, she could feel her hair sticky with blood. Looking in the rearview mirror she saw more blood pouring out of her right eye and nearly blacked out. She had got to make it to Rupert's with the briefcase, or Tony would catch up and kill her. Somehow, in a daze of pain and sickness, constantly wiping the blood out of her eyes, she managed to reach Penscombe.

Rupert's front door was unlocked. The hall was dimly lit. Tripping over the dogs she screamed for him.

"Angel, how nice. Have you forgotten someone?" he said, coming down the stairs wearing only a pair of jeans and reading *Horse and Hound*.

Then she found and switched on the main hall light and he saw her properly. Her right eye had closed up now and her upper lip was cut and terribly swollen. Her face, hair, and shirt were drenched in blood.

"My Christ," he said, appalled. "What the fuck happened?"

"Tony found out."

"My poor little baby." He raced down the stairs, drawing her into his arms, feeling the stickiness of her blood-soaked hair and the frantic racing of her heart. "The bastard, where is he? Let's get you a doctor, then I'm going around to kill him."

"I'm OK," mumbled Cameron. "He had provocation. You'd probably have done the same thing." The next moment she passed out.

When she regained consciousness she was in Rupert's double bed, dressed in one of his shirts, with most of the blood washed off. A Dr. Benson, who was rather smooth and glamorous, had rolled up in his dinner jacket, reeking of brandy and, after examining her, assured her that her face wouldn't be marked. Having patched her up, saying she might have to have stitches in her head in the morning, he gave her a shot to sedate her.

"I don't want my head shaved," she muttered when Rupert came back.

"Your hair's so short it's practically shaved already," said Rupert, sitting down on the bed and taking her hands. "I'm so desperately sorry, angel. I got you into it."

It took all Cameron's pleading to stop him going straight around to Hamilton Terrace or even to The Falconry to beat Tony to a pulp.

"Think of the adverse publicity. It'll only trivialize Venturer's bid."

"Nothing trivial about those bruises," said Rupert, touching her swollen lip with his finger. "How did he find out?"

"Saw the video of Valerie's opening and Beaver's crash-landing in the gladioli. And somehow he found out I was at the Venturer meeting yesterday."

Very, very gently Rupert was stroking her cheek. Despite the pain in almost every part of her body, she had never felt safer or closer to him.

"Hell knows no fury like a womanizer scorned," he said lightly. "Well, he had to know some time. You'd better move in here."

Cameron utterly despised women who cried in front of men. It was taking an unfair advantage and outraged her feminist principles. But once the tears started spilling out of her bruised eyes, she found she couldn't stop them.

"Is it such a ghastly thought?" said Rupert, taking her in his arms.

"No, no it's the nicest thought in the world. I guess I don't want to pressure you."

"You're not. You've no idea how I hated letting you go back

every time, particularly to Tony. I'm sick of never seeing you. Don't worry about your brilliant career. I'll look after you. And tomorrow I'm going to chuck that beastly briefcase into the lake."

Cameron managed a weak smile. "You had better take the papers out first, or Tony'll be dropping by, using the truth drug on your duck."

She was drowsy with dope now, so he laid her back on the pillow.

"I'll try not to get under your feet," she muttered. "I d-do love you—so so much."

"I know you do." Rupert got to his feet. "Now go to sleep."

"Please don't go." She was suddenly frantic. "You will sleep here, won't you?"

" 'Course I will. I'll be back in a minute. I'm just going to take the dogs out."

Wandering mindlessly through the garden, Rupert found himself on the edge of the lake, breathing in the soapy smell of the meadowsweet, listening to the frogs croaking. There were no stars, and, glancing across the valley, he saw Taggie's turret was in darkness.

CHAPTER 33

Valerie Jones was absolutely furious when nothing about her opening appeared on "Cotswold Roundup," but not nearly as angry as Declan when Rupert told him what had happened.

"What the fuck were you doing taking a dog you can't control to Valerie's opening? Think of the adverse publicity."

"It was terribly funny. I wish you'd seen Valerie's face."

"It's not funny," thundered Declan. "I suppose you're used to having your character blackened but it won't do Venturer any good. The IBA don't like this kind of thing."

He couldn't understand how Rupert could be so unrattled by such a catastrophe. He supposed he'd always lived in the eye of the storm.

"I don't know who comes out worse," Declan went on, "you setting out coldly and deliberately to seduce Cameron so we had a mole on our side, or Tony who beat her up. A lot of people will feel Tony was justified. He was only acting in the heat of the moment."

"Oh, come off it," snapped Rupert. "Talk about making mountains out of moles. The story we leak is that Cameron and I were attracted to each other when we met, when you interviewed me in February. We resisted it for as long as we could because we were on opposing sides, but now she's moved in with me and Venturer has the best Head of Drama in the country. Christ, we're both free agents. It's Tony who's the adulterer and the mistress-basher. He won't want to make a big thing of it because of Monica and the IBA.''

A story was duly leaked and appeared in the *Mail* the next day that Cameron Cook had changed sides, moved in with Rupert and that Tony was devastated to lose his star producer. No reference was made to Cameron being Tony's mistress, or of her being beaten up.

Tony, once he had cooled down, was absolutely shattered by Cameron's defection. Discovering through his spies that Rupert would be in London opening a new sports stadium on Thursday, Tony drove over to Penscombe to see her. Surrounded by Rupert's pack of dogs, with Mrs. Bodkin in the kitchen and Mr. Bodkin trimming the long grass around the lake, Cameron felt safe to let him in.

Tony followed her out to the pool, which sparkled brilliant turquoise in the sunshine and was no longer filled with leaves. It killed him to see her in this beautiful opulent setting, stretched out oiled on one of Rupert's reclining chairs, guarded by Rupert's lurcher Blue, who lay by her feet panting, but growling every time Tony approached.

Tony begged her to come back, telling her for the first time how much he loved her and, when that had no effect, offering to leave Monica and marry her. He didn't even lose his temper when she told him to fuck off.

"Your job's open for you to come back whenever you want it, and here are the keys to Hamilton Terrace." He threw them on to the table. "The house may belong to Corinium, but it's still yours when you need it. Come and get your clothes whenever you want to. I shouldn't have beaten you up, but I love you and I just saw red."

"Just like you did the last time I came home late after spending the day with Patrick," said Cameron. "Get out."

Tony, predictably, couldn't remain nice for long. "You know it's only a matter of time until Rupert ditches you," was his parting shot. "Five days, five weeks; he may even keep you five months until Venturer finally don't get the franchise; then he'll kick you out like all the rest and you'll come running back to me."

Rupert couldn't have been more angelic those first few days, fussing over her, seeing she didn't get too tired, ensuring Mrs. Bodkin made her delicious food, making love to her with surprising gentleness and subtlety, so he didn't crush her bruised ribs or her battered face.

The weather was beautiful too—long hot days, followed by short sweet nights. Cameron was happy to sleep and read and sunbathe and explore Rupert's woods and fields with the dogs. Gradually, as the black eye and the swelling on her lips disappeared, she felt she was healing inside and out.

The only drawback was Mr. and Mrs. Bodkin, shadowy, polite, running Rupert's life like clockwork, but always there in the background. Cameron wanted Rupert on her own; she was not used to servants. She wanted to wander around the house naked and make love in the kitchen if she felt like it. She was also inclined to treat Mr. and Mrs. Bodkin like Corinium minions, rapping out orders, snapping at slowness and even more at ignorance.

Even Rupert, famous for his caprice and short fuse with staff, had to pull her up repeatedly: "Taggie O'Hara increases her vocabulary by learning a new word everyday. You could start off with: please and thank you."

Any reference to Taggie sent Cameron through the roof, so, the second week after she moved in, determined to prove to Rupert that she could cook and run a house much better than Taggie, she persuaded Rupert to give Mr. and Mrs. Bodkin a few days off.

"I'm better," she insisted. "I want to cook you some decent food. You're getting far too much cholesterol."

"Do I look as though it's harming me?" said Rupert, who was eating white bread with dripping and was immersed in The *Scorpion*.

"No, but it's futile to abuse a magnificent constitution. It'll catch up with you. And why don't you try to read the *Guardian* occasionally instead of that trash?"

"Because it uses much too long words and makes snide remarks about my party," said Rupert.

"But objective criticism's valuable, for Chrissake."

"Not to me. I only like people who think I'm perfect. I'd better get Mr. and Mrs. Bodkin back for the weekend, the children are coming on Saturday. They make a hell of a lot of work."

"Oh, don't," said Cameron, suddenly excited. "Let's look after them ourselves. We'll have picnics and barbecues and be cozy. It'll be so much fun."

Like many insecure people, Cameron was much easier to live with when she was down. After she'd been beaten up, it was her intense vulnerability that had appealed to Rupert. Wanting to protect her, he'd asked her to move in. But as she got better, her natural aggression and stridency started to reassert itself.

The day before the children were due, Cameron decided to make a big paella for dinner; the rest could be heated up for them the following day. Discovering in the middle she'd forgotten to get any saffron or squid, she dispatched Rupert to the village shop.

"I'm sure they won't stock them," grumbled Rupert, who wanted to read *Horse and Hound*.

The kitchen radio was blaring out Dame Enid's latest tone poem; the *New Statesman* and the *Times Literary Supplement* lay on the kitchen table all giving Rupert an unpleasant feeling of *déjà vu*. It was like Helen all over again.

"Well, drive into Stroud then," snapped Cameron.

She'd forgotten what a bitch paella was to make, but she was determined to cook better than Taggie.

"And get some Parmesan as well," she shouted after him.

The village shop had recently been converted into a tiny supermarket with shelves all around the walls, and a partition, also with shelves on both sides, running parallel to the counter. If the ubiquitous Mrs. Makepiece, who cleaned for Lizzie and Valerie and one morning a week for Maud now, hadn't been holding forth so noisily and indignantly at the head of the line, Rupert would never have slid into the shop unobserved. Picking up a red wire basket, he chucked in some cupcakes because the children liked them and a can of corned beef because he liked it; he couldn't find any squid, but he supposed a tin of sardines in tomato sauce would do as well—a squid pro quo.

As he moved around to the spice shelf, Mrs. Makepiece, encouraged by a chorus of clicking tongues, raised her voice. "Declan and 'er ladyship have pushed off on some second honeymoon in the Lake District, leaving her all on her own."

Rupert stiffened, gazing unseeingly at rows of paprika, dill, and cayenne.

"All alone in that 'uge 'ouse," went on Mrs. Makepiece, "and we all know it's 'aunted. Well, 'alf the fuses blew, so Taggie went to the fuse box and read the instructions all wrong—she's disconnected, you know, the poor lamb, and she blew all the fuses, and had to shiver all night in the dark, with only Gertrude, that's her little dog, for company."

Despite the baking heat of the day, Rupert had gone absolutely cold. Taggie might have killed herself fiddling about with that fuse box.

"She was crying her heart out this morning when I come in," said Mrs. Makepiece, egged on by the row of shocked faces. "At first she wouldn't tell me what was the matter. Then I made us a nice cup of tea and it came out—they'd all forgotten her birthday."

Rupert was so enraged he dropped the basket and walked straight out of the shop with the sardines in his hand.

The moment he got home he called Ursula. "Where the fuck are Maud and Declan?"

"Windermere."

"Give me their number."

"I promised not to; they don't want to be disturbed. This is a patch-up operation. Declan's been devoting too much time to his biography."

"They forgot Taggie's birthday."

"Oh, my God."

"And you should have bloody well reminded them. Give me the number."

Declan and Maud were out when he called. He left a message for Declan to call him, saying it was about the franchise and very urgent.

Then he called Taggie. "Happy birthday, darling. Cameron and I are going to take you out to dinner. No, I don't want any 'Buts.' We'll pick you up about eight."

He was still sweating with horror at the thought of the poor little duck all alone in that big house in the dark with all those winding stairs and long passages.

"Bloody Maud and Declan," he howled as he went into the kitchen.

"What on earth have they done now? Don't turn it off, it's Vivaldi," protested Cameron. "Did you get the squid?" Then, as Rupert handed her the sardines, "These won't do, dumbass. And where's the Parmesan and the saffron?"

"They forgot Taggie's birthday," said Rupert bleakly.

"Well, that's not such a big thing." Then, seeing the rage on Rupert's face, "Haven't you forgotten your kids' birthdays?"

"No—yes, I suppose so, but Helen always remembers."

When he told Cameron what had happened, and that they were taking Taggie out to dinner, she hit the roof. "But it was our last night on our own. This was to be a celebration I was cooking specially for us."

"There'll be plenty of time for that in the future."

The telephone rang. It was Declan. Fueled by indignation, and also because Declan had been so censorious about him and Cameron, Rupert let him have it. "You fucking hypocrite, always banging on about tyranny and exploitation. The worst case I've seen is going on under your roof."

"What the fuck are you talking about?"

"Taggie. She works like a slave for the bloody lot of you, and all you can do is leave her alone in a huge house, with the fuses blown, and then forget her fucking birthday."

"Oh, my Christ," said Declan appalled. "Have we really?"

"You get on the telephone the moment I ring off and say how sorry you are."

"We ought to come back."

"No. Cameron and I'll look after her tonight. You come home first thing tomorrow and bring her a decent present, not a crappy book of Wordsworth's poems she can't read."

"God, I feel terrible," said Declan. "Now, what was this urgent thing about the franchise?"

"That was it," said Rupert furiously. "If she hadn't worked her ass off trailing around the area, rounding up names for your bloody franchise, we wouldn't be ahead in the race now."

Crashing down the telephone, he poured himself a huge whisky. He was absolutely shaking with rage.

"Well, well, well," said Cameron, chucking the wooden spoon onto the drying rice and switching off the stove. "What gives with Taggie O'Hara?"

"She doesn't deserve parents like that. She's only a baby."

"Nineteen today, to be exact. Well beyond the age of consent."

She knew it was madness to bitch, but she couldn't help herself. "You've got a very soft spot—or is it a hard spot—for her, haven't you? Are you nurturing some secret passion? What I want to know is where does that put me?"

Rupert looked her up and down. There wasn't a trace of tenderness in his face now.

"You're living here, aren't you?"

"At the moment."

"Let's get one thing straight," he said softly. "If you want to go on living here, stop being such a fucking bitch."

Draining his whisky, he picked up his car keys. "I'm going to get her a present. You can ring up the White Elephant in Painswick and reserve a table for three at nine o'clock."

* * *

Henry Hampshire's Springer spaniel had recently had six puppies. They'd all gone to new homes except the runt whose paw, broken when someone stepped on it, was still in a cast. The puppy had a freckled face, a bright pink mouth, crossed eyes that looked as though he'd been on the booze all night, and a stumpy tail which agitated his whole body.

"He's a great character," said Henry. "You can have him for a hundred pounds."

"With a broken paw? Don't be ridiculous."

"Cast comes off next week. Then he'll be as right as rain."

"Fifty," said Rupert. "He'll always be slightly lame."

"Oh, all right," said Henry. "I had lunch with Daysee Butler today."

"Well, you shouldn't," snapped Rupert. "You're bound to give away trade secrets."

"Daysee said Tony's flown to LA to search for a new Program Controller."

When Rupert got back to Penscombe, Cameron had washed her hair and changed into the clinging kingfisher-blue dress she'd worn to get her award in Madrid. She looked apprehensive, very beautiful, and came straight up and put her arms around Rupert's neck.

"I was jealous. I'm sorry."

He breathed in Fracas, the dry bitter sexy scent she always wore; it made his senses reel.

"I'm sorry too," he said. "I overreacted, but I feel so sorry for her."

Under the blue dress he could feel Cameron's nipples stiffening. Glancing at the kitchen clock he saw that it was a quarter to eight.

"We haven't got time. It'd muss you up."

"*You* have," said Cameron.

Dropping to her knees, she unzipped his fly. This was one skill she knew she was better at than Taggie O'Hara.

A battered dark green GTI was parked outside The Priory as they drove up. The front door was open; the hall was filled with clothes, books, and suitcases.

"Perhaps she won't want to come out to dinner," murmured Cameron hopefully.

" 'Course she will," said Rupert.

It was debatable who got the worse shock, Cameron or Rupert, when they went into the kitchen and found Taggie sobbing in the arms of a tall black-haired, incredibly beautiful young man. The only difference was that Cameron instantly recognized Patrick, whereas Rupert did not. Patrick looked around, still with his arms around Taggie.

"Well?" he said icily.

Taggie glanced up, gave a gasp, then tugging herself away from Patrick, blindly snatched a paper napkin, frantically wiping her eyes and blowing her nose.

"I'm sorry," she mumbled. "Hullo, Rupert, hullo, Cameron. How are you?"

She was amazed to see Rupert glaring at Patrick.

"I don't think you've met my brother Patrick, have you?" she said quickly.

"Your brother!" Instantly the hostility was gone. "It was your party on New Year's Eve, wasn't it? How did your finals go?"

"Perfectly all right," said Patrick shortly.

Turning back to Taggie, Rupert dumped two bottles of Dom Perignon on the table.

"Happy birthday, angel. They're just out of the fridge. Open them," he added to Patrick, totally unaware of the look of utter loathing that Patrick was shooting in his direction.

Oh hell, thought Cameron, poor Patrick. Taggie must have told him about me moving in with Rupert.

Cutting short Taggie's stammering thanks for the champagne, Rupert seized her hand and led her out to the car. "Come and see your proper present."

"You d-don't have to bother," stammered Taggie in the hall. "I'm having a lovely birthday. Mummy and Daddy have just called. They're bringing my present back tomorrow afternoon. They couldn't pick it up until today, and Patrick brought me the most gorgeous sweater. He's just got back. He had so much stuff to bring after three years." She was rattling now, on the verge of tears again.

"Sweetheart, what's the matter?"

"I'm absolutely fine," she said. How could she possibly explain to him that the blown fuses, the night in the dark, and the forgotten birthday, were mere irrelevancies, that it was Cameron moving in with him that had brought the world down around her ears.

Outside, the puppy, with its speckled paws out the car window, was grinning at them.

"Oh, how adorable," breathed Taggie. "What's he done to his paw?"

"It's nearly better. He's your birthday present."

Taggie was in ecstasy. No one had ever given her anything so lovely.

"Gertrude will be very jealous to begin with," warned Rupert, as the puppy rushed off onto the lawn, quartering frantically, pursuing various cat and dog smells. "You'll have to make a lot of fuss over her."

He noticed Taggie was still wearing jeans and an old torn red-and-white striped shirt of Declan's.

"Aren't you going to change? We've booked a table for nine. Patrick can come too. I've never met him properly."

Taggie blushed. "It's terribly kind of you but we're fine on our own."

"Don't be silly, I'm not having you cooking on your birthday."

"Patrick and I haven't seen each other for ages."

"You've got the rest of the summer."

"He's going abroad tomorrow. He—er—he—"

"Yes," said Rupert, pulling her down beside him onto the old bench on the side of the lawn.

Taggie blushed even more deeply. "He adores Cameron, you see, and he's absolutely d-d-devastated about her moving in with you."

"Ah," said Rupert.

Taggie was frantically peeling paint off the bench. As the puppy bounded back to them, she gathered him up, cuddling him for comfort.

"Patrick could accept her having an affair with Tony because he thought she was doing it for her career, b-but you're different."

"Why?" said Rupert, suddenly anxious to know the answer.

Taggie buried her crimson face in the puppy's ears.

"Because one wouldn't need any incentive . . ."

"Is that your word for the day?"

"No." She shook her head frantically. ". . . any incentive to move in with you."

Inside, Cameron was gazing at Patrick. He's grown up, she thought. He's much tougher and more detached and less vulnerable.

"How did you do on your finals?"

"Got a first."

"Have they told you?"

"No, but I know."

He got a pack of Marlboros out of his duty-free bag and lit a cigarette without offering her one. As the match flared she could see the bitterness in his face.

"I gather you've just become our next-door neighbor," he said. "Christ, you've got awful taste in men. Tony was a disgusting thug. This man—" he couldn't bring himself to say Rupert's name—"is like a foxhound. Can't you understand? You can't domesticate him. He'll always be hunting for something new. It's in his blood. He'll get bored with you in a few weeks, and if he doesn't, you'll get bored with him; he's the most ghastly philistine, never read a book in his life."

"You're just jealous."

"Not anymore," said Patrick wearily. "I am ashes where once I was fire. I'm going abroad tomorrow."

"Whereabouts?"

"Australia—to work on a sheep farm. I'm not hanging around for the rest of the year seeing you all scrapping over the franchise and watching your relationship with that bastard self-destruct."

"He isn't all bastard. Look how kind he's been to Taggie." Cameron was fishing now.

"He's totally fucked her up."

Cameron's throat went dry. "Has he tried anything?"

"Nothing according to Tag. Just exercises his bloody *droit de seigneur*, Lord Bountiful fashion, bombarding her with presents—silver necklaces, Fabergé eggs."

"Fabergé eggs?" said Cameron, appalled.

"Oh, Taggie didn't know that it was. He brought her that from Madrid. I don't know what's being offered today. A Monet perhaps, or a Henry Moore!"

"A puppy," said Cameron in a frozen voice. "This is it."

The next moment Aengus shot into the kitchen, tail fluffed out like a lavatory brush, growling ferociously, and took refuge under the kitchen counter. The puppy frolicked after him, then let out a piercing shriek as Aengus caught him with a punishing right hook on his pink nose. Instantly Gertrude bustled in, the personification of outrage. The puppy bounced up to her, then let out another shriek as Gertrude bit him sharply on the ear.

"Oh God," groaned Patrick. "Not content with disrupting humans, Rupert has to disrupt animals as well."

"For Christ's sake open one of those bottles," said Cameron.

"I don't want a drink," said Patrick sulkily.

"You'll need it. We've come to take you out to dinner."

"Well, we're not coming."

A black lock of hair had fallen over his forehead, a muscle was going in the beautiful lean right cheek. His eyes were as dark and forbidding as the depths of the huge cedar outside the window.

"Please don't hate me so much," Cameron was amazed to find herself pleading.

They both jumped as the telephone rang. It was Caitlin who was staying with a friend in Newbury, calling to wish Taggie many happy returns. By the time they had finished talking, Rupert and Cameron had left.

"How did you get rid of them?" asked Taggie.

"I told them to fuck off," said Patrick, opening one of Rupert's bottles. "At least we can now get drunk at their expense!"

CHAPTER 34

Cameron and Rupert had a disastrous dinner at the White Elephant. Rupert was outraged at being thrown out by Patrick. "Arrogant little fucker, just like his father."

"I thought you adored his father."

"Not when he's playing God, or neglecting his children."

"You certainly aren't neglecting one of them—silver necklaces, Fabergé eggs, handicapped puppies—singularly appropriate in a franchise year."

"Oh, shut up."

The row continued until they got to bed, when Rupert maddened Cameron most of all by falling asleep when she was in mid-harangue. She woke next morning, feeling suicidal, to find Rupert gone. Wondering if he were already collecting his children, she went downstairs, found the paella gathering flies on the stove and chucked it out. There was a chicken in the fridge. She supposed she'd better roast it for lunch. Dispiritedly, she peeled some potatoes, put them on to par-boil, then started to make a French dressing. There wasn't any dill. If she sent Rupert off to the village shop he'd come back with nutmeg.

Outside, the sun was shining through the mist like a dog's identity disk. Cameron longed to go out to the pool and swim off her hangover. Until last night, with the Bodkins away, she had at last been able to enjoy a marvelously sybaritic few days with Rupert, swimming and sunbathing naked, brazenly tantalizing him away from whatever he was doing. She had even galloped bareback down the valley at twilight one night with no clothes on, until Rupert had caught up with her, pulled her off the horse and fucked her in the meadowsweet.

But last night's row had ruined all that, and now, with the kids around, there'd be no more nude frolicking this weekend. She jumped as the dogs barked and the front door banged.

"Cameron," yelled Rupert.

As he sauntered into the kitchen, blithe as a skylark, as though there'd been no row at all, Cameron frantically stirred the French dressing.

"We're out of dill," she said.

"I'm sorry I don't give you presents," he said, kissing the back of her neck. "Vainly, I thought my presence was enough. Which hand will you have?"

"Both," said Cameron sulkily.

"Telepathic," said Rupert, uncurling his fingers.

Glittering on each palm was a diamond earring, a two-inch-long chandelier, lit by little diamonds instead of crystals. Cameron was speechless. Incredulously, she ripped out the gold hoops she normally wore and hooked on the diamonds, running to the kitchen mirror, rubbing away the steam with her sleeve to have a look.

The earrings hung halfway down her slender neck, throwing rainbows of light on the lean, tense jawline, illuminating and softening the truculent hostile little face. Next minute Rupert's reflection appeared beside hers.

"Like them?"

In answer, she turned, kissing him with a fury and passion he'd never known in her. Cupping her face with his hands, he felt the tears sliding into his fingers. Very gently he unhooked the earrings.

"Shame to take them off so soon, but I must have you before I pick up the children."

By the time they'd finished, the potatoes were too soft to roast, so Cameron mashed them instead.

Groggy with love, she waited to love Rupert's children. At half past one, trailing barking dogs, Tabitha erupted into the kitchen. Her cheeks were flushed, her eyes bright with excitement. She was clutching a huge box of chocolates.

"Mrs. Bodkin! Mrs. Bodkin!" She slithered to a halt in front of Cameron. "Where's Mrs. B?"

"Away for the weekend."

"Daddy never told us. Are you the temp?"

"Well, not too temporary I hope!" said Cameron, smiling. "You must be Tabitha?"

"Well, I'm not Marcus." At nine, Tabitha was as blonde and as effortlessly elegant as Rupert. She stared at Cameron with the wary blue eyes of a stray kitten.

She was followed by Marcus, who at eleven was very thin, with very dark red hair, huge surprised yellow eyes, and pale delicate freckled features. He looked like a fawn likely to bolt at any minute.

"You must be Marcus, then," said Cameron. "I hope you're both hungry. There's roast chicken for lunch."

"Not yet," said Tabitha, grabbing an apple out of the fruit bowl. "I'm going down to the stables."

Marcus smiled shyly and apologetically. "I've got a letter from my mother for Mrs. Bodkin. I'd better give it to you. The chocolates were for her, perhaps you'd like . . ." His voice trailed off.

"No, no," said Cameron, "leave them for her."

Helen's writing was very Vassar: *"Dear Mrs. B,"* she had written, *"I hope your arthritis is better and the kids won't make too much work. Marcus's medication is in his suitcase. Please see that he takes it, if he gets uptight. I enclose a list of their clothes. Could you check them off before they come home? They lost so much last time, and can you see Tabitha learns her vocabulary, and that both do half an hour's piano practice, and say their prayers at night? I also enclose stats of their reports. Can you give them to Mr. C-B? Yours sincerely, Helen Gordon."*

Christ, she's formal, and a born-again too, thought Cameron. Then she smiled at Marcus. "Is Daddy on the way?"

"He's gone to the stables. Can I do anything?"

"Tell him and Tabitha lunch'll be ready in ten minutes."

Putting on the cabbage and removing the chicken from the baking dish, Cameron started to make the gravy, and at the same time read the kids' reports. Tab's was perfectly frightful except for sports. Marcus's was brilliant. He returned to the kitchen looking apprehensive.

"They're trying out some new pony for Tab. Daddy said would half past two be OK?" Then, quailing at Cameron's expression of fury, he said, "If you don't mind I'll go and unpack."

How, thought Cameron furiously, can I possibly keep up Taggie O'Hara standards when I get fucked over like this? Then she remembered the diamond earrings, and the fact that Rupert hadn't seen the kids for a few weeks, and decided not to make a fuss.

In fact they were back in forty minutes.

"I'm starving," said Tab, heading straight for the pantry. "I thought you said lunch was ready." She came out tearing open a bag of potato chips with her teeth.

"Don't eat that. It'll spoil your lunch," said Cameron. Ignoring her, Tab sat down at the table with *Pony* magazine.

Rupert came in with a large vodka and tonic for Cameron. "Hullo, darling—" Cameron noticed how Tabitha looked up, eyes narrowed at the endearment—"sorry we're late. Geoffrey Gardener brought the pony over specially. I wanted Tab to try him."

"Any good?"

"We're going to keep him over the weekend."

"He's called Biscuit," said Tabitha.

"Here are the kids' reports and a letter from Helen," said Cameron as Rupert started to carve.

"I only eat breast," said Tab, when Rupert handed her a leg.

"Well, give it to Marcus, then," said Rupert, who was reading the reports at the same time.

Cameron opened her mouth and shut it again. She noticed Marcus was very nervous around his father, and that, while Rupert hardly glanced at Marcus's report, he spent ages reading Tabitha's.

" 'Tabitha must learn not to be so competitive at volleyball.' What the fuck do they mean by that?" he said furiously. "You can't be too competitive at games."

"I should be on the team next term," boasted Tab, "and I'm easily the youngest. I don't want any," she added to Cameron, snatching her plate away, so a large dollop of mashed potato fell on the table. Cameron's lips tightened as she scooped it up and put it on Rupert's plate.

"Or any cabbage or salad."

"You must have veggies. I'm sure you do at home."

"This is home." Tabitha's blue-eyed stare was as arrogant as Rupert's. "Isn't it, Daddy? This is home," she repeated to Rupert, who was still reading the headmistress's report.

"Of course it is, angel," he said, kissing her.

Then opening the racing pages of *The Times*, he added, "There's a horse called Venturer in the three-thirty. We must have a bet."

"Put a pound on for me," said Tab. "We're doing a project on snakes next term."

"You could start off by interviewing Tony Baddingham," said Rupert, picking up the telephone.

Now here's a chance to help Tabitha and win her confidence, thought Cameron.

"You could start off with Adam and Eve," she said, helping herself to salad.

"The project's about snakes, not sex," said Tab rudely.

"Eve got tempted by the snake, stupid," said Marcus. "That's why they left the Garden of Eden. It's a jolly good idea," he added, kindly, to Cameron.

"My project's about real snakes," snapped Tab.

Getting up from the table and rummaging in her suitcase, she produced a photograph which she handed to Rupert as he got off the telephone.

"This is the pony Malise bought me. She's brilliant at cross-country."

"You've already got a pony?" asked Cameron, shocked.

"Yes, she's called Dollop the Trollop."

"Then why is Daddy buying you another one?"

Tabitha looked at Cameron as though she were crackers.

"Because I need at least two if I'm going on the junior circuit next summer. I can, can't I, Daddy?"

"Who'd like fruit salad?" said Cameron, as she cleared away the first course.

"Not me," said Tab. "Is there any ice cream in the freezer?"

Cameron had spent a long time that morning peeling grapes. "If you don't like fruit salad, I'm afraid you'll have to go without," she said sharply.

"Then I'll have another bag of potato chips," said Tab. "I can come over every weekend this summer, Daddy, except the last week in August which is Pony Club camp."

"Good," said Rupert.

Oh, please no, thought Cameron. She was sure it was only out of kindness that Marcus had a second helping of fruit salad.

Fortunately, spirits were raised when Venturer won by three lengths, which meant that Rupert and Tabitha were richer by three hundred pounds and eight pounds respectively.

"Can we go into Stroud and spend it?" Tabitha climbed onto Rupert's knee, the kitten again, but this time tactile and adoring.

"Christ, no, not on a Saturday afternoon."

"Can we watch *Amityville I* tonight?"

"No way," said Cameron. "It doesn't start until ten and it'll give you nightmares for months."

"Can we go into Stroud and get a James Bond video then?" persisted Tab.

"I'll take you, if you like," conceded Cameron.

The journey to Stroud was the most successful part of the weekend. The roof of the Lotus was down and, although Marcus went white, Tab thoroughly approved of Cameron's driving.

"This is a nice car, and you go much faster than Mummy. Can I have an ice cream?"

"May I. You may if you promise to eat your supper."

On the way back, however, Tabitha smiled sweetly at Cameron. "You haven't got a husband, have you? Why don't you get one?"

"I'd like to," said Cameron, thinking longingly of Rupert.

"But not my Daddy," hissed Tabitha.

"It is absolutely ludicrous," said Cameron to Rupert as, later, they listened to Tabitha sulkily crucifying Beethoven's Minuet in G on the baby grand. "This is a Saturday during the vacation *and* she's got to learn her vocabulary."

"Helen is petrified the children will inherit my lack of brains."

"Marcus is clearly superbright," said Cameron. "He's such a sweet, sensitive kid."

"Takes after his mother," snapped Rupert. "Tab takes after me. My reports were much worse than hers."

"She doesn't strike me as being dumb," said Cameron, "just unmotivated."

"She looks OK," said Rupert coldly. "And she rides like a dream. What else matters?"

Supper was decidedly scratchy. Tab ostentatiously gave all her shepherd's pie to Beaver. Afterwards Rupert packed both children off upstairs to watch James Bond. Cameron was reading the *Guardian* in the drawing room and feeling absolutely shattered. How the hell did mothers cope day in and day out? The next minute Marcus had run into the room, waving the remote control. He had difficulty breathing.

"I don't think Tab should watch this video. It's called *For Your Eyes Only*, but it's not James Bond."

A second later Tab came storming in and tried to grab the remote control. When Marcus held it above his head she went for him, kicking his shins and giving him a karate chop in the stomach which doubled him up.

"Stop it," shouted Rupert, pulling her off.

"It's a lovely film," screamed Tabitha. "It's all about ladies licking each other."

"I'd better come and have a look," said Rupert.

He returned, grinning. "Marcus was right. It's a blue film about lesbians." He threw the video on the sofa beside Cameron. "We must have a watch later."

She was wearing a sleeveless T-shirt, and he slid his hands inside caressing her armpits, then feeling for her breasts. It was ridiculous the way he could turn her to Jell-O.

More shrieks issued from upstairs, followed by a crash on the terrace outside. Going out through the French doors, Rupert found the remote control with all its entrails spilling out.

Cameron stormed upstairs. "Why did you throw that out the window?" she yelled at Tab. "I know it was you."

"Marcus won't let me watch *Amityville*," sobbed Tab. "I hate him! I hate him!"

Rupert put her to bed screaming. Cameron was relieved at only having to deal with Marcus's asthma attack.

"I'm sorry about Tab," he murmured as she finally tucked him in.

"Surely she doesn't behave like this at home?"

"Of course she doesn't. Both Malise and Mum are quite strict, so when she comes here she sort of runs wild. And she and Daddy love each other so much," he added wistfully.

"He loves you too," said Cameron, giving him a kiss.

Cameron found Rupert talking to Tab, who was tucked up in bed with Paddington Bear, gloomily transvestite in the family christening robes.

"You really ought to be asleep, Tab," she said. "Marcus says Mummy puts your lights out at nine."

"Marcus is a bloody sneak," said Tabitha, yawning.

"Have you said your prayers?"

"OK." Tab rolled out of bed. "Dear God," she prayed loudly, "please bless Daddy, Mummy, Marcus, Dollop, and Beaver. And please give me Biscuit, if you think that's right, God." Then her fingers opened a fraction. She could see Cameron hovering on the landing, hopeful of a mention. "And please God, make Mummy and Daddy get married again, so I can come and live at Penscombe for always; make me a good girl, Amen."

Cameron walked back to Rupert's bedroom, quivering with rage. Rupert thought it was very funny. "Isn't she awful? She asked me earlier why I didn't sell my double bed as I didn't need it anymore."

Things went from bad to worse the next day. Rupert went off to see his constituency secretary. Tab vanished to the stables and didn't return for lunch. Grimly setting out to collect her, Cameron found Tabitha, watched by an idling trio of grooms, jumping the new pony which ground to a halt each time it came up to a large wall.

"This pony don't jump," yelled Tabitha.

"Think of something really nasty before take-off, and then give him a good whack," advised one of the grooms.

Tab rode toward the wall with great determination: "I'm going to think of CAMERON," she howled, bringing her whip down on Biscuit's quarters. The grooms screamed with laughter, and then cheered as Biscuit cleared the wall by a foot. Tabitha leaped off the pony, cuddling him and stuffing him with pony treats. "Good boy, good boy."

"Lunch, Tabitha," said Cameron icily.

Even Tabitha looked faintly sheepish and ran on ahead back to the house. "Where's Daddy?" she demanded as Cameron went into the kitchen.

"Not coming back till later this afternoon."

"I don't want any lunch till he gets back."

"Sit *down*," ordered Cameron.

"Don't speak to us like that," said Tab coldly. "You're not our mother."

Cameron walked out of the kitchen and went and swam twenty lengths in the pool to work off her rage. Going upstairs, she discovered Tabitha must have changed at least four times that day and used the carpet of Rupert's bedroom as a dirty clothes' basket.

"Tab," she bellowed.

"Yes." Tab appeared from the television room, eating a Mars bar.

"Pick up your clothes, OK?"

"Mrs. Bodkin picks them up."

"Mrs. Bodkin is not here. Pick them *up*."

"Bloody shan't."

She shot under Cameron's arm, downstairs and back to the stables.

A blinding headache nudged Cameron's skull. She took a Valium and went down to the kitchen where she found Marcus trying to clean up lunch.

He had put the roasting pan, undrained, in the sink so the grease floated thick and yellow on top of the water.

"I'm sorry about Tab," he mumbled.

"You make up for it," Cameron said, hugging him. "Would you like your parents to get married again?"

Marcus went green. "No, absolutely not."

"Tab would."

"Oh, Tab gets on much better with Daddy than I do," said Marcus bitterly. "And if she was here she could ride all the time."

As Rupert probably wouldn't have eaten at lunchtime, Cameron decided to make him a nice dinner. Just the two of them; the kids could go to bed early. Marcus chatted to her while she cooked and, when she'd finished, offered to play the piano for her. He was just playing a Chopin impromptu quite magically when Tab charged in with Wham full blast on the radio.

"Turn if off," said Cameron sharply.

"Why should I?"

"Turn it *off*," yelled Marcus, but he stopped playing and shut the piano.

Immediately Tab grinned and turned off the radio.

"I've never been so bored in my life," she said moodily. "I'm starving. What's for supper?"

"SpaghettiOs"

"Yuk. What's that cooking in the oven?"

"Boeuf Provençal."

"My favorite thing. And there are kiwi fruits in the fridge. That's also my favorite thing."

"As you haven't eaten anything I've cooked for you yet," said Cameron coolly, "you're going to have SpaghettiOs cooked by Mr. Heinz, and then you're going to bed early. I want to spend some time with your father—alone."

Rupert came home around half past seven, and amazed Cameron by backing her up. "Go up to bed both of you. Cameron's looked after you all day and she needs a break. You can watch 'Howard's Way.' "

"Tab's been hateful all day," Cameron was appalled to find herself saying as soon as the children went out of the room.

Later Rupert went upstairs and Cameron toured wearily around the house, picking up kids' clothes. If she put a load of laundry in tonight she could iron first thing in the morning.

Rupert found Tab curled up in bed in a blue nightie looking through a photograph album of when Helen and Rupert were married: "Wasn't I a sweet little baby? Look at me riding on Badger's back."

Rupert was not to be deflected. "Why have you been so bloody to Cameron?" he asked, sitting down on the bed. "I told you to be nice to her."

"I hate her," said Tab calmly, "and all the grooms hate her, and they say Mr. and Mrs. Bodkin hate her because she's so bossy. Even Beaver and Blue hate her."

"Rubbish! Beaver and Blue adore her."

"Shows how thick they are, then."

"I told you to be nice to her," repeated Rupert sternly.

"It's all God's fault," said Tab, petulantly pulling the duvet up to her chin. "I prayed specially hard to him this morning to make me really nice to Cameron, and he did absolutely nothing about it."

Rupert thought it so funny he had to go straight off and tell Cameron. He found her in the living room, rigid with anger.

"What was this doing on my side of the bed?" She handed Rupert a prayer book bound in ivory. "Look inside," she said shrilly.

"To my own darling Rupert," read Rupert slowly. *"All my love, Helen. All other things to their destruction draw, only our love hath no decay."* He grinned at Cameron. "Well, Helen certainly goofed on that one, didn't she?"

"Tab must have put it there," hissed Cameron.

"What's wrong with that?" protested Rupert. "Most children want their mothers and fathers to love each other. Didn't you?"

"She's spoiled rotten." Cameron could hear the obsessive rattle in her voice. "Can't you see how she fawns all over you and freezes out everyone else? Your whole relationship with her is overly symbiotic."

"I don't know what symbiotic means." Rupert's voice was suddenly brutally icy. "But it's fuck all to do with you how I handle my children. I suggest you read this prayer book yourself. It might teach you a little Christianity."

"Where are you going?" she said as he went toward the door.

"To bed. I don't want any dinner. And you can bloody well sleep in the spare room."

A minute later she heard the front door open and the dogs barking. Terrified Rupert had stormed out, she ran into the hall to find Mr. and Mrs. Bodkin blinking in the light, clutching their suitcases and looking sheepish.

"I hope you didn't mind us coming home a day early," muttered Mrs. Bodkin, "but we wanted to see the children, and I thought you might need a bit of help with their meals and their washing. Mrs. Gordon likes everything back in good order."

Cameron was never so pleased to see anyone. "Sure, it's OK," she said. "We've all missed you. There's some supper in the oven if you're hungry."

The next moment she was sent flying by Tabitha tearing downstairs and throwing herself into Mrs. Bodkin's arms. "Oh, Mrs. B," she said in a choked voice, "I'm so glad you're home. It's so horrid when you're not here."

The next day passed without incident until the afternoon. Cameron, who knew she should have disarmed Tab by being sweet, spent the day sulking, thawing out, then sulking again. The children were due to go back to Warwickshire after tea. Rupert had bought the pony, Biscuit, for Tab, and would drive pony and two children back in the trailer.

Mrs. Bodkin finished the ironing and packed the bags while Rupert and the children watched *High Society* on television. Ecstatic about the new pony, Tabitha sprawled on Rupert's knee, defiantly covering him with kisses. Cameron, determinedly doing the *Guardian* crossword puzzle, sat on the sofa as far away from Rupert as possible. They hadn't spoken since last night. The sight of Cameron's long smooth brown thighs in the shortest of khaki shorts, however, was finally too much for Rupert. As the credits came up at the end he stretched out, putting a hand on her leg.

"Don't touch her," screamed Tab. "It's disgusting," and, bursting into tears, she fled upstairs. Rupert followed her to find out what was the matter. He came down shaking his head. "It's the same old story. She wants me and Helen to get together again like Bing Crosby and Grace Kelly, so she can live here all the time."

The following morning Rupert got a letter from Taggie: *Dear Roopurt,* she had written, *thank you for the luvly puppy. He is sweet we*

called him Clawdeeus becos patrick says it goes with gurtrude. they
love eech other now. thank you for the shampain. Sorry we did not
come out to dinner. I hope you understand. Yours sincearly Taggie
O'Hara.

Rupert wanted to weep.

The weekend left Cameron exhausted and with a numb sense of
failure. What sort of monster was she to detest an innocent little girl
of nine? Desperate for someone to dump on, she was tempted to ask
Seb or even Charles Fairburn out to lunch, but decided it was too
risky. Tony might easily have bugged their telephones.

While Cameron moped around the house, Rupert went over to The
Priory in an attempt to melt the dangerous froideur that seemed to
have developed between him and Declan.

Declan, however, seemed enchanted to see him. Switching off
Brahms' Fourth, and making a heavily gin-laced jug of Pimms—"Just
the kind of fucking English upper-class drink you would like!"—he
took Rupert out into the garden.

"Is that the new puppy's work?" said Rupert, noticing a shredded bedroom slipper on the lawn and the flattened flower beds.

"I'm afraid so. He's been re-christened High Claudius, as he
rolled on unspeakable fox's crap yesterday, and, rushing in, leaped all
over Professor Graystock who'd dropped in to drool over Taggie!
At least he got rid of the Professor double quick—so he does have
his advantages! It's all right," he added hastily, misreading the sudden outraged expression on Rupert's face, "he's a dear little dog—
we all love him. Caitlin's taken him and Gertrude for a walk."

He poured the Pimms into two pint mugs, then put the jug in
the shade under a chestnut tree. It was another glorious afternoon.
Grasshoppers scraped like toy violins in the long grass, a marbled
white butterfly basked on a cushion of thyme. Through the silver
trunks of the beech trees they could just see Rupert's cornfields turning gold. Even the birds were silent, worn out with feeding their
young.

Declan stretched out. "It's days like this that make that terrible
long winter seem worthwhile. D'you know we've been here for
nearly a year?"

"Here's to many more," said Rupert, noticing how tired Declan
was looking again. "How's the book going?"

"All right, except that I'm constantly disturbed by my wife and
daughter screaming at each other."

"Taggie screaming?" said Rupert in surprise.

"Never Taggie. Maud and Caitlin. Maud's menopause appears to be coinciding with Caitlin's adolescence. I'm thinking of calling in the International Peacekeeping Force."

"I could have done with them this weekend," said Rupert, swatting an ant. "My children were staying. Tab and Cameron were like weasels at each other's jugulars. Why can't women get on with each other?"

Declan laughed. "I'd never have cast Cameron as Mary Poppins."

Idly they discussed the franchise. Declan had recruited a very good girl from Yorkshire Television as Head of Children's Programs. Then, heavily prompted by Rupert, he confessed he was desperately strapped again for money.

"Have you spent all that thirty thousand already?" said Rupert disapprovingly. "You shouldn't keep sneaking off to grope Maud in the Lakes."

"I know, but I'd been working flat out and she's so restless. And I've just paid a massive tax bill and Patrick's fare to Australia and Caitlin's tuition for last term. And I've never seen anything like the electricity bill. Talk about electric shock treatment. Poor Tag's the only breadwinner. She's over at Monica's at the moment, filling up her deep freeze."

"Can't she shove Tony in as well?" said Rupert, fishing a piece of cucumber out of his mug.

Declan wasn't listening. His Mini, which was a 1976 model welded together by dog hair, rust, and mud, had finally given up the ghost, he told Rupert.

"You can borrow one of my cars for the moment," said Rupert. "In actual fact, what you need is a massive cash injection. D'you want an advance from the Venturer kitty?"

"We'll need all of that. I've got to earn it. I've spent the last week writing a script for a documentary on Yeats."

"Who?"

"The Irish poet. The man I'm writing the book about," said Declan impatiently.

"Ah," said Rupert. Then, regaining the ascendancy, "Doesn't sound like a money maker to me."

"Will be—if it's good enough. I've sold the idea to Channel Four. And the IBA will be in raptures. Lady Gosling's half-Irish."

Lying on his back, listening to the hum of insects and the idle cooing of the wood pigeons, gazing up at Taggie's bedroom window,

Rupert suddenly had a brainwave. "If Freddie and I put up some more money, you can afford to have Cameron produce and direct it, so we can keep it in the family."

"Indeed you will not," said Declan. "Cameron and I don't get on."

Rupert turned towards Declan, eyes squinting against the sun: "Time you bloody learned. She thinks you're great. She just has a communication problem. And it'll give her something to do. She's like a sheep dog, she needs work."

"To stop her getting in your hair?" snapped Declan.

Rupert, who hadn't had any lunch, had now finished all the fruit in his Pimms and was reduced to eating the mint. "I'm thinking of Venturer, not myself," he said sanctimoniously, as Declan filled up both their mugs. "We just don't want her getting restless and running back to Tony."

"It'd mean several weeks in Ireland," said Declan. "I want to start shooting in early September. Then we'll need another week in the end of November to do the Coole woods in Autumn."

"Perfect," said Rupert. "I'll be popping over to Ireland all the time from now on, buying horses, so Cameron won't suffer too badly from withdrawal symptoms. I promise you, Cameron really, really admires your work."

Declan blushed slightly: "Well she's got to read the script before committing herself. I'm not having her working on something she doesn't like one hundred percent."

Cameron called Declan later that evening trying to keep the excitement out of her voice. "I've just read your script. I love it. The characters are terrific and all the ideas for interviews are great. The text reads so beautifully; it's superb."

Declan was utterly disarmed. Ursula, who'd typed the script, had said she'd loved it, but then she was paid to.

"I'd adore to do it," went on Cameron, "if you really figure I'm the right person?"

"Sure you are," said Declan. "I've just been talking to Jeremy at Channel Four and told him you might be interested. He's mad about the idea."

"You look as though you're floating on Eire," said Rupert as Cameron put down the telephone.

"You won't mind my being away so much?"

"Yes," said Rupert, taking her in his arms, "of course I will, but you've got to have your freedom. I did when I was show jumping. It was the one thing that fuelled me.''

Cameron blushed. ''Do you swear it was Declan's idea I should direct it?''

''Would I lie to you?'' said Rupert blandly. ''He asked me to ask you. He really admires your work. He just has a communication problem.''

''Oh, wow!'' sighed Cameron. ''I feel like the first woman on the moon.''

CHAPTER 35

Deliriously happy to be working again, Cameron threw herself into producing Declan's program. Much of her time was spent in London or over at The Priory and she turned one of Rupert's upstairs bedrooms into a study so she could work there as well. Rupert, who'd been neglecting the horses and his business interests and still had a full calendar as an MP despite the summer recess, was also kept very busy. This suited them both; they still argued a lot, but sex at least was still miraculous. Even the children's visits seemed less of a hassle. Mrs. Bodkin did all the work, and when Tabitha became unbearable, which was most of the time, Cameron retreated upstairs to work.

On the franchise front, the IBA had now sifted through everyone's lengthy applications and fired off letters to all the consortiums containing supplementary questions about program plans, management structure, studios, and general finance.

''We promised them a cross between Camelot and Utopia,'' said Declan, ''and now we've got to justify it.''

The long written answer to this letter was almost as crucial in winning the franchise as the original application. Once again, the Venturer team had to get together to thrash out policy. Meetings at anyone's house were now considered too risky, as Tony had stepped up his espionage.

Rupert, being a practised adulterer, was therefore deputed to find a meeting place where they wouldn't be found out. He chose a seedy room over a nightclub in a back street in Cheltenham.

''If this is where you bring your mistresses,'' grumbled Georgie

Baines when he arrived for the first meeting, "I can see why they get fed up."

Night after night, through the end of July and a long hot August, Declan, Freddie, Bas, Rupert, Cameron, Lord Smith, Harold White, and the Corinium Moles—when they could get away—met to hammer out the answers. Charles Fairburn still turned up every time in a different disguise, which made everyone giggle. They needed to. Declan, deadly serious now, insisted everyone drink only Perrier until the meeting was over. They were nearly halfway through their long ordeal in the franchise fight and nervous tension was mounting.

At least they were spared the Bishop, who was spending a month in the Holy Land, and Professor Graystock who was in Greece researching a book. But they missed Dame Enid who'd gone on a walking tour in Wales with a woman friend, and, after August 12th when he pushed off to Scotland to shoot, they missed the inanities of the Lord-Lieutenant. They'd all grown very fond of Henry. Janey Lloyd-Foxe, hampered by two children and a book to finish, seldom showed up. Billy was in Australia making a film for the B.B.C.

For Wesley Emerson, August was a wicket month. He took 8 for 42 against the Australians in the Leeds Test. Venturer basked in his reflected glory.

The letter with the answers to the supplementary questions was dispatched to the IBA at the beginning of September, by which time the franchise wives were getting very fed up. The long summer holidays were slowly grinding to a halt. The smell of molding leaves and bonfires, the sight of huge red suns and dewy cobwebs hanging on the fences, reminded them with a pang that summer was nearly over.

Sarah Stratton, for example, not only had Paul hanging around at home, out of work and grumpily demoralized, but also his ghastly daughters who never stopped implying that Daddy would be Prime Minister now if he had stayed with Mummy.

Valerie Jones was increasingly irritated that Freddie seemed to be spending so much time on the stupid franchise. Completely off gardening since James had failed to immortalize her opening, Valerie had dragged Sharon off to a villa in Portugal for a month.

Monica Baddingham also had, as Cameron would have said, a somewhat "stressful" summer. There had been no discussion between her and Tony about Cameron's defection, beyond the fact that Corinium had lost a megastar and an essential weapon in the franchise battle. Privately Monica realized Tony was utterly devastated.

Being humane and kindly, she felt very sorry for him. It was disappointing that Tony couldn't level with her. Comforting him, they might have grown closer. But at least she listened patiently to his diatribes against Declan and Rupert, and stoically accepted that he would want to sleep with her more than once a week until he found a new mistress.

Much more worrying was that Archie, now seventeen and not due to take his "A" levels until next year, was still enjoying a most unsuitable fling with the ghastly Tracey Makepiece, whom he'd met at the O'Hara New Year's Eve party. Both Monica and Tony were terrified Archie would get her pregnant and be forced into an early marriage.

"Why the hell can't you find a girl of your own class?" roared Tony, forbidding Archie to see her any more. Archie had obviously taken no notice. One morning in early August, putting on Archie's raincoat by mistake, Monica found a letter in Tracey's loopy handwriting: *I will love you dearest, until all the seas run dry.* Archie had promptly been shunted off to Tuscany for three weeks.

Most despondent of all the wives, however, was Maud. No one had fallen in love with her for ages, and Declan, having been totally obsessed with the franchise, and then his Yeats program, was now totally obsessed with both. Not wanting to leave Maud when she was so depressed, apprehensive about going to Ireland with Cameron, Declan tried to persuade Maud to play Yeats' great love, Maud Gonne, in the program, so she could come with them. Terrified of failure, Maud turned him down flat and then detested herself for doing so. It was as though she was deliberately pushing him into an affair with Cameron.

Finally, Caitlin had been home most of the summer, full of teenage moodiness, criticizing everything Maud did, particularly her clothes, which Caitlin claimed were so out of date they should be called "a first world wardrobe." Maud was not amused; she'd always prided herself on being able to go to a party in a pair of Declan's pajamas, with a jeweled comb in her hair, and look marvelous.

One morning toward the end of August Maud read a piece in the *Daily Mail* about Princess Michael entering a new golden age of maturity and confidence. She's the same age as me, thought Maud broodily, and I'm ten years younger than Joan Collins, and look how great she looks. Why am I riddled with self-doubt and about as confident as a mongrel at a dog show?

Having borrowed a hundred pounds and Taggie's new violet

dress, she decided to ignore Declan's bank balance and go into Cotchester and buy some new clothes. I'm over the hill, she thought with a shiver, as she started to put on her makeup.

Cotchester was full of tourists, drifting aimlessly down the High Street, photographing the cathedral and the ancient houses, and the statue of Charles I. By contrast, Monica Baddingham, striding purposefully through the crowds, was like a powerboat chugging through a flotilla of yachts on a windless day. She detested shopping but she needed batteries for her Walkman and there was a new recording of *Don Giovanni* on order which, maddeningly, hadn't arrived, and she had to pick up some scores of *The Merry Widow*.

Every year the West Cotchester Hunt put on a play which was performed to large noisy audiences in November. This year they had decided to be slightly more ambitious and join forces with the Cotchester Operatic Society to put on *The Merry Widow*.

Monica had already been appropriately cast as Valencienne, a virtuous wife. Charles Fairburn had been inappropriately cast as her randy admirer Camille. Bas Baddingham was still dickering over whether to play the male lead, Count Danilo, but as yet the director, Barton Sinclair—ex-Covent Garden no less—was still searching for someone to play Hanna, the Merry Widow. He was holding auditions in Cotchester Town Hall that very day, but was deeply pessimistic that anyone would be beautiful or stylish enough, or have a sufficiently good voice. Luck, however, was on Barton Sinclair's side. Outside the Bar Sinister Monica bumped into Maud.

"How jolly nice," said Monica in her raucous voice as she kissed Maud. "I've been hoping I'd run into you for ages. I wanted to say how wonderful Taggie's been. Completely saved my life cooking for all the hordes this summer. You must be so proud of her."

Maud said, yes, she supposed she was.

"But she's getting too thin," went on Monica. "She used to be so round, soft, and smiling. I hope she's not taking on too much. You, on the other hand, look splendid. How's Declan?"

"Oh, obsessed with the wretched franchise," said Maud fretfully.

"Isn't it a ghastly bore?" sighed Monica. "Tony can't think of anything else. But I don't see why, just because our husbands are on different sides, we can't be friends."

It was very hot in Cotchester High Street. The cool wine- and garlic-scented gloom of the Bar Sinister beckoned.

"Nor do I," said Maud. "Why don't we go in and have lunch?"

"What a good idea," said Monica in excitement. "Ploughman's lunch, and half a pint of cider."

Maud's aims were slightly more ambitious, and they were soon sitting down with Muscadet and crespolini. Her tongue loosened by a third glass. Maud told Monica about Declan's trying to persuade her to play Maud Gonne, and how her nerve had failed. "I couldn't face Cameron screaming at me when I didn't come up to scratch," she confessed. "Her sarcasm could strip furniture, and I've always found it difficult to act in front of Declan."

Monica, at this point, became very thoughtful. She fished in her shopping bag and brought out one of the scores of *The Merry Widow*. On the cover was a painting of a beautiful woman with hair swept up under a big pink hat and a waist in its swirling cyclamen pink dress as slender as her neck. She was raising a glass of champagne in one long purple-gloved hand. Four handsome men with black twirling moustaches were raising their glasses to her in admiring salute.

"Why don't you start with something less ambitious than Maud Gonne?" said Monica. "We're desperate for someone to play the Merry Widow."

"I couldn't," faltered Maud. "It's a very demanding part."

"Nonsense," said Monica briskly. "You'd waltz it."

"What are my two favorite women doing lunching at my restaurant without telling me?" said a voice.

It was Bas, absolutely black from a fortnight's polo in America.

"Bas," said Monica delightedly. "I know I'm not supposed to talk to you either, after the dreadful way you've betrayed Tony, but sit down and help me persuade Maud to audition for Hanna."

Bas needed little persuading. Up to now he'd by-passed Maud in his amorous travels, but she looked stunning today. That violet dress emphasized her white skin and just missed clashing with the gorgeous red hair. Another bottle of Muscadet was ordered.

"Bas is toying with the idea of playing the leading man," said Monica.

"Hopefully it'll lead to other things," said Basil, rubbing one of his long muscular, polo-playing thighs against Maud's as he refilled her glass.

Later, not even allowing her a cup of black coffee to sober her up, Basil and Monica frogmarched Maud down the High Street to the Town Hall where the director, Barton Sinclair, had reached screaming point, having heard ten amateur hopefuls murdering the score.

Up on stage now, the eleventh, a made-up blonde who'd never see fifty again, was crucifying the Vilja song. The pianist was desperately trying to keep in time with her.

"At least you can do better than that," whispered Bas to Maud.

"I can't," muttered Maud in terror. "That's Top G she's missing."

As she tried to bolt, Bas's arm closed around her waist. "Yes you can," he murmured. "Just think of the fun we can have rehearsing together night after night, and it won't be all singing I can tell you."

"Thank you very much," said Barton Sinclair in his chorus-boy drawl.

"I sang the part in 1979," said the blonde, teetering down the steps in her four-inch heels. "It brought the house down."

"Pity you weren't buried under the rubble," muttered Barton. "We'll be in touch. I'll be making a decision at the end of the week," he told her.

"I'm going home," said Maud.

"Could you hear just one more?" said Monica.

Barton Sinclair looked at his watch and sighed: "Do I have to? I was hoping to get the three forty-five back to Paddington."

"It'll be worth getting the next train, I promise you," said Monica. "This is Maud O'Hara. She used to act and sing professionally."

Barton Sinclair straightened his flowered tie, and smoothed his straggly mouse-brown hair.

"You certainly look the part," he said.

"I haven't practiced," bleated Maud, the crespolini and the Muscadet churning inside her.

"Try the same song," said Barton, handing her the score. "Take it slowly, Mike," he added to the pianist.

"You come in on the last quaver of the fourth bar," the pianist told Maud kindly.

Below her, Maud could see their faces: Monica's eager, flushed, and unpainted, Basil's sleek and mahogany, and Barton Sinclair's London nightowl and deathly pale. They seemed infinitely more terrifying than a first-night audience at Covent Garden.

"I can't," she whispered, wringing her sweating hands.

"Go on, darling," said Bas. "We're all on your side."

Off went the pianist. Maud fluffed the opening.

"I'm sorry. Could we start again?"

"Of course," said Barton.

Off went the pianist again, and Maud opened her mouth.

"There once lived a vilja, a fair mountain sprite,
She danced on a hill in the still of the night."

Her voice was sweet, true, and hesitant, but suddenly, as she launched into the main theme, it seemed to soar out glorious and joyful. The four other people in the room felt the hair rising on the backs of their necks.

"A star is reborn," whispered Monica, wiping her eyes.

"I *am* going to have a nice autumn," reflected Basil. "Over forty, they're always so grateful!"

"Vilja, Oh, Vilja, be tender and true," sang Maud, triple pianissimo, *"Love me and I'll die for you."*

For a second there was silence, then her audience burst out clapping and cheering.

"You've got the part," said Barton Sinclair. "The only problem is how much you're going to show up the others."

"Thank you, Barton," said Monica and Basil in unison.

After that they all went back to the Bar Sinister for several more bottles of Muscadet and Barton Sinclair only just made the six forty-five.

Tony and Declan were very apprehensive when they heard the news of such close fraternization between the rival franchise sides. Declan, however, who was going to have to spend the second half of September and much of October in Ireland with Cameron, was principally relieved that Maud was so much happier. The sound of her caroling away upstairs practicing her songs reminded him of the carefree days in Dublin when they were first married. Perhaps, if *The Merry Widow* were a success, she'd have enough confidence to take up acting professionally again.

Caitlin, who had now dyed her custard yellow hair so black it almost looked blue, found her mother's euphoria even more irritating than her previous picky depression, and decided to push off to London for a few days to stay with some schoolfriends. She was going back to school the week after next and might as well have some fun before the prison doors clanged shut again.

She found Taggie in the kitchen fainting over a final notice from the Electricity Board. "I can't think why it's so high."

"Mummy's vibrator's battery-operated, so it can't be that," said Caitlin. "Hullo, darling," she added, hugging Claudius.

"He's in disgrace," sighed Taggie. "He's just eaten one of Mummy's new shoes."

"Good thing; they were gross," said Caitlin. "Every Claud has a silver lining! Can you lend me fifty pounds to go to London?"

"I haven't got it," protested Taggie. "I've just lent Daddy a hundred pounds for a new pair of cords for Ireland."

"At least I'll be gone for nearly a week, so you won't have to feed me," cajoled Caitlin. "So that's worth fifty."

"And we haven't done your trunk yet," wailed Taggie. "You've grown out of everything, you need new Aertex shirts, and both your games' skirts are split."

"Oh, sew them up," said Caitlin airily. "We can't possibly afford new ones if we're so poor."

CHAPTER 36

After a riotous five days in London, Caitlin rolled up at Paddington Station with just enough money for her half-fare home. Her blue-black hair was coaxed upward at the front into a corkscrew. She was wearing peacock feather earrings, a black and white sleeveless T-shirt, a black Lyera mini which just covered her bottom, black tights, and huge black clumpy shoes, all of which belonged to various friends of hers, a great deal of black eye makeup, and messages in magic marker all over her arms.

It was hardly surprising, therefore, that the man at the ticket counter refused to believe she was under sixteen. A most unseemly screaming match ensued, which first amused then irritated the long line of commuters behind Caitlin, who began to worry they might miss their trains home.

"My father is a very very famous man," screamed Caitlin as a last resort, "and he'll get you."

"Don't threaten me, young lady," said the clerk.

"It's people like you who turn liberals like me into racists," screamed Caitlin even louder. "You're just discriminating against me because I'm white. I'll report you to the Race Relations Board."

At that moment Archie Baddingham, on his way home from his three weeks' banishment in Tuscany, reached the head of the neighboring first-class line. Hearing the din, and recognizing Caitlin's shrill Irish accent from New Year's Eve, he bought her a ticket.

"Remember me?" he said, tapping her on the shoulder.

"No, yes," said Caitlin. "You're Archie, aren't you? Can you lend me my fare, this stupid asshole won't believe I'm under sixteen."

"I've got you a ticket," said Archie.

"I can't accept a ticket from you," stormed Caitlin irrationally. "Your father's been absolutely shitty to my father."

"My father's shitty to everyone," said Archie, calmly taking her arm. "Come on, we'd better move it."

They barely caught the train on time, but managed to find two single seats opposite each other.

"I've never traveled first class before," said Caitlin, stretching out on the bright orange seat and squirming her neck luxuriously against the headrest.

Archie looked wonderful, she thought. Like her, he'd shot up and lost weight. He was wearing black jeans, rolled up above black socks and black brogues with a black turtleneck tucked into a western belt with a silver buckle, black crosses in his ears, and a brown suede jacket. His blond hair, washed with soap to remove any shine, was long at the front and cut short at the back and sides. His still slightly rounded face looked thinner because of a suntan almost as dark as his eyes.

"Why are you so disgustingly brown?" asked Caitlin.

"I've just spent three weeks in Tuscany. My parents booted me out there to get over a girl."

"Tracey-on-the-Makepiece."

Archie grinned, making him look even more attractive. "How d'you know that?"

"You were superglued to her at Patrick's twenty-first."

"So I was. Actually, I'm over her, but Dad and Mum thought I wasn't, so I thought I might as well take advantage of a free vacation. Have you been away?"

"We never go anywhere. My parents are always broke." Caitlin gazed out of the window, wondering what to say next.

"What would you like to drink?" asked Archie.

"They got any Malibu?"

"I doubt it."

"Well, vodka and tonic, then. Can I come with you?" The Inter-City, belting toward Bristol, swayed like a drunk as they walked toward the buffet car.

"Of course," said Archie, admiring her narrow waist and slim legs. "I'll buy you some grub as well."

* * *

"Been to a funeral?" said the gay barman, running a lascivious eye over Archie's black legs.

"*Passengers are reminded that it is an offence to serve intoxicating liquor to persons under the age of eighteen,*" read Caitlin loudly, as Archie paid for everything.

"Keep your voice down," hissed Archie.

The journey back to their seat, with each of them carrying white plastic trays of vodkas and tonics, glasses, bacon sandwiches, Mars bars, and bags of potato chips, was much more hazardous. They had no hands to steady themselves against the lurching train.

"Terribly sorry," mumbled Caitlin, going scarlet, as for the third time she cannoned off a commuter back into Archie.

"Who's complaining?" said Archie.

"Thank you so much," said Caitlin as they sped past slow winding rivers, rolling fields, and clumps of yellowing trees. "This bacon sandwich is the best thing I've ever tasted."

"I'm surprised you can say that with Taggie cooking for you," said Archie. "How is she?"

"Bit low. She's hopelessly hooked on Rupert Campbell-Black."

"Won't do her any good," said Archie, pouring out a second vodka and tonic for Caitlin. "He strikes women down like lightning bolts. Anyway, he's bonking my father's ex."

"Cameron Cook," said Caitlin dismissively. "She's a crosspatch, isn't she? I can't see what men see in her. My brother was crazy about her, and now she's gone off to make a film in Ireland with Daddy. I hope they don't end up in bed. People usually do on location, don't they?"

"Dad was mad about her. I was scared-shit he'd leave Mum and marry her," said Archie breaking a Mars bar and giving half to Caitlin. "I dread my parents getting a divorce, in case they marry again and leave all their money to their new children."

Caitlin giggled. "Mine haven't any to leave."

A lot of passengers got out at Didcot, so they practically had the carriage to themselves. As the cooling towers of Didcot power station belched out unearthly white steam against a darkening charcoal gray sky, the gay barman came by with a black plastic bag, gathering up rubbish.

"I want to keep my tonic can," said Caitlin, grabbing it back.

As she put it in her bag, Archie examined the heart-shaped face, the pointed chin, echoed by the widow's peak, the small, beautifully shaped green eyes, the snub nose, the coral pink mouth, sweet now it was no longer set in a sulky petulant line, the blue-black mane parted on the left, which she kept lifting with her fingers and tossing over to the right.

Glancing up, she caught him staring at her and smiled.

"That's it," said Archie wonderingly. "Your braces have vanished."

"So have your zits," said Caitlin.

Archie went pink: "I fancied you the moment I saw you."

They were nearing Cotchester now, dense woods clinging to steep hills on each side of the line giving way to lighted houses.

Archie removed his earrings, putting them in his pocket, because he said his father would only make a fuss. Then blushing again, he forced a tenner into the pocket of Caitlin's clinging Lycra skirt.

"What's this for?" asked Caitlin in amazement. "I owe *you* money."

"For a taxi," said Archie. "My father's chauffeur is meeting me, and if we give you a lift he's bound to sneak to Dad."

"It's just like the Montagues and the Capulets," sighed Caitlin. "I hope we don't end up like Romeo and Juliet."

"I'll call you tomorrow," said Archie, "and hopefully we can fix an evening when all our parents are away."

Opening his bank statement next morning, Archie nearly fainted. To make matters worse, it was his mother's birthday on Friday and he'd promised to buy her the latest recording of *The Flying Dutchman*. He'd been stupid to show off and buy first-class tickets and all that booze.

Archie gazed gloomily at the same page of Aristophanes for twenty minutes, then threw the book across the room. If he hurried he might reach the Bar Sinister before lunch and catch his Uncle Basil before he rushed off to polo or some amorous jaunt.

He found Bas humming the Vilja song from *The Merry Widow* and taking fifty pounds out of his own till.

"Can I have a quiet word?" said Archie.

"You can have several noisy ones if you like," said Bas. "I thought your father had forbidden you to talk to me. Where is Rambo, anyway?"

"In Edinburgh," said Archie. "And please don't pump me."

He admired his uncle, who always had the loudest tweed jackets and the prettiest girls of anyone he knew.

"Have a drink?" said Bas, taking down a bottle of Chambery and two glasses.

"Yes, please. If I work really hard in the kitchen for three days, will you let me sign the bill for dinner for two on Saturday night?"

"Are you bringing Tracey Makepiece?"

"No."

"Good. There are limits. I really was on Tony's side for once on that score. Yes, you can, then."

On Saturday night Taggie's violet dress paid its second visit to the Bar Sinister in ten days—this time with Caitlin inside it. But, with the waist jacked into nothing by a black elastic belt, and the skirt hemmed up from mid-calf to mid-thigh by Taggie, it was almost unrecognizable. Archie, having scrubbed mussels for three days in the kitchen, felt he had really earned his date. Basil was out that evening, but all the waiters were in on the secret and gave Archie and Caitlin a table in an alcove where no one else would see them. Determined to get his wages' worth, Archie ordered a bottle of Dom Perignon and they started off with a wine race, seeing who could drink a half-pint of champagne fastest to get things warmed up. But after that they found that they were so excited by each other's company they weren't very hungry.

"This is the most delicious thing I've ever eaten," said Caitlin as she toyed with foie gras on radicchio. "I can't think why I can't eat more of it."

Archie slowly undressed a giant prawn and dipped it in dill sauce. "Try this."

"Gosh, it's yummy. I wish school food was like this. Nellie Newstead found a used Band-Aid in her shepherd's pie last term. Aren't you dreading going back?"

"Not if you promise to write to me."

Caitlin looked up. God, she's sweet when she smiles, thought Archie.

"Every day if you like," said Caitlin.

"I've looked up the distance between Rugborough and Upland House," said Archie. "It's only about forty miles. A mate of mine's passed his test, so we'll drive over and take you out one Sunday; and it'll be half-term soon."

Archie was wearing a dinner jacket over black baggy trousers and a gray and white shirt over a Sisters of Mercy T-shirt. He looks incredibly cool, thought Caitlin lovingly.

As if in a dream, she watched his sunburnt hand closing over her white one; his palm felt so warm and dry that suddenly she longed for him to touch her all over.

Archie ordered another bottle of champagne.

"You really shouldn't," protested Caitlin. "It's frightfully expensive in restaurants, and I already owe you for my ticket and my taxi."

"You can pay me in kind," said Archie, gently stroking the inside of her wrist. "A pound a kiss. No, I won't be able to afford it, a penny a kiss."

"*Da mi basia mille,*" sighed Caitlin.

"What's that?"

"Catullus. Give me a thousand kisses."

"Are you frightfully clever?"

"Of course, that's why I chose you."

They screamed with laughter; suddenly the stupidest things seemed funny.

"What are we going to do after this?" said Archie, getting out a pack of Sobranie. "Did you say your parents are both away?"

"Daddy's in Edinburgh, probably killing your father, but Mummy might be back from her rehearsal, although she seems to be getting later and later."

"There's no one at home," said Archie. "I'll get them to get us a taxi."

It was only when she got up to walk out of the restaurant that Caitlin realized how drunk she was. It's like InterCity all over again, she told Archie. Only by grabbing her arm did he prevent her cannoning off every table.

He kissed her all the way back to The Falconry. Caitlin, who'd spent three days practicing kissing the palm of her hand, found Archie's mouth a great deal more exciting.

And when they were ensconced on Monica's huge flowered chintz sofa, having carefully removed each other's earrings, Archie discovered that Caitlin's small, incredibly springy white breasts were far more thrilling than Tracey Makepiece's. It was just a question of preferring nectarines to melons. And her waist was so tiny, once he'd removed the black belt, that he was terrified he might snap her in two. But nothing could exceed her enthusiasm.

"I do hope I'm not too pissed to remember every minute of this tomorrow," she said.

"Have you ever been to bed with anyone before?" Archie mumbled into the gel-stiffened straw of her hair.

"Never. Have you?"

"Yes."

"Lots?"

"About two and three-quarters."

"A man of experience," sighed Caitlin in ecstasy.

Undoing a few more buttons, Archie, who was down to his Sisters of Mercy T-shirt now, kissed his way down her shoulder until he was sucking her right nipple. He was also wrestling with his conscience as to whether he ought to take her to bed. He wanted to like mad, but he was pissed enough to botch it, and she was certainly so pissed she might easily regret it in the morning. He had a condom in the breast pocket of his dinner jacket, which was hanging over the chair. But if he got up to get it, it might destroy the mood. But again it was unlikely they'd have an empty house to themselves again for months.

As her little hands slid inside his T-shirt, he found his hand, as if magnetized, creeping up her legs.

"I'm climbing to paradise," he whispered.

The next minute he jumped out of his skin as a great white light shone in at the window.

"Holy shit," said Archie.

"Ooh," squeaked Caitlin in excitement, "it's a close encounter."

"Bloody sight too close!" said Archie. "It's my father back from Edinburgh."

It was too late to make a bolt for it. With lightning presence of mind, Archie turned on a lamp, plugged a tape in the video, pressed twelve on the remote control and did up Caitlin's buttons.

"I'll ring for a taxi as soon as I can and take you home. We'll just have to try and bluff it out."

The next minute James Vereker's new pilot on "Keeping Fit for the Elderly" burst onto the screen.

Tony, fortunately, had been hosting a very successful dinner for the IBA and, after several belts of brandy on the way home, was in a mellow mood. It became even mellower when he found his favorite son in the living room with an enchantingly pretty little brunette. She looked vaguely familiar, but Tony was too vain to put on his glasses and by no stretch of the imagination could it be Tracey Makepiece.

"This is Caitie," said Archie heartily. "I was just going to ring for a taxi to take her home."

"Where does she live?" said Tony.

"Chalford," lied Archie.

"I'll take her," said Tony expansively. "No distance at all. Let's all have a drink."

"Caitie's tired," said Archie desperately.

"She doesn't look it," said Tony, admiring Caitlin's flushed cheeks and glittering green eyes. "There's a bottle of Moët in the fridge."

Shoving Caitlin's belt under a pink and white striped cushion, Archie reluctantly left the room.

"Why are you watching this tape?" asked Tony as a lot of geriatrics with purple faces started doing push-ups.

"I love Corinium's programs," said Caitlin dreamily. "I adore 'Master Dog.' We've got two dogs, one's very thick, one's brilliant. I'm sure she'd win."

"Give me a ring in the office next week," said Tony. "We're always looking for bright dogs."

"I'm going back to school."

"Where d'you go?"

"Upland House."

Better and better, thought Tony in delight; the girl was a lady.

"D'you know my niece, Tonia Martin?"

"Frightful slut," said Caitlin. "She nearly got kicked out last term for having boys in her room. She's got a terrible reputation."

Tony was enchanted. His sister's daughter was always being held up as a paragon of virtue.

"And d'you by any chance know Caro Mckay? Teaches Biology, I think."

"Of course. She teaches me," beamed Caitlin. "Ghastly old dyke. She and Miss Reading live in a two-bedroom house with a spare room." She screamed with laughter. Tony joined in.

Once Caitlin got an audience, there was no stopping her. Archie was torn between hysterical laughter and total panic as she regaled Tony with one scurrilous story after another about the daughters of his friends and colleagues.

After the bottle was finished, Tony insisted on driving her home. The only way Tracey would have got out of the house, reflected Archie, would have been in a hearse.

It was a lovely night. A butter-colored moon was gliding in and out of threatening blue-black clouds, gilding their edges. Mist was rising. There was a smell of dying bonfires and wet leaves.

"What a heavenly car," said Caitlin, playing with the electric windows.

"How long have you known Archie?" asked Tony.

"About nine months. I don't mean to suck up, but I do think you've brought him up well. He's so considerate."

Tony purred. "He is a nice boy. Wish he'd work a bit harder. Have you taken your exams yet?"

"Last term."

"Do well?"

"Very," said Caitlin simply. "You seem more pleased than my mother," she added bitterly a minute later.

Archie's father, she decided, was really nice. Extraordinary how her father and Tag got everything wrong. He was soon saying she might like to come to the Hunt Ball if she could get off school, and even suggested skiing in the Christmas holidays.

"Oh, I'd love to," said Caitlin.

As they neared Penscombe, she noticed the car telephone. "Oh, how lovely, you are lucky. Can I use it?"

"Of course," said Tony.

Without thinking, Caitlin called The Priory. It was two o'clock in the morning and no one answered for ages.

"Hullo," murmured a sleepy voice.

"Taggie darling," said Caitlin, "did I wake you?"

Tony nearly ran into a wild rose bush. Suddenly the temperature in the car dropped below zero.

"What did you say your last name was?" said Tony as Caitlin put back the receiver.

"O'Hara," said Caitlin in a small voice.

"Declan's daughter?"

"Yes."

"What the fuck are you playing at? Did your father put you up to this?"

"Oh, please don't tell him," gasped Caitlin. "He'd be furious."

"Not any more furious than I bloody am," roared Tony. "The little snake! I'll murder Archie when I get home."

"Oh, please don't!" Caitlin, who'd had a great deal too much to drink, burst into tears.

"For Christ's sake," exploded Tony.

"I like you so much," sobbed Caitlin, "and I thought you liked me."

"I do," said Tony in exasperation, handing her his blue polka-dotted handkerchief, reeking of the inevitable Paco Rabane. "I just can't stand your father."

"The fathers have eaten sour grapes," sniffed Caitlin dolefully, "and the children's teeth are set on edge."

"And you're not going to tell Declan that you're going out with Archie?"

"Christ, no," said Caitlin. "I don't want to get butchered in my prime."

Tony did a lot of thinking as he drove home. When he turned on the light in Archie's room, he found him huddled under the duvet, with his pajamas buttoned up to the neck, desperately pretending to be asleep. Not for the first time, however, Tony astounded his son.

"You can go on seeing that girl as long as you try and find out as much as you can about Venturer."

"That's immoral," said Archie, shocked.

"Don't be bloody naive," said Tony brutally. "D'you want Corinium to lose the franchise?"

"No."

"Or for me to forfeit four hundred thousand minimum a year?"

"No," said Archie.

If he was rich, he reflected, he wouldn't have to scrub mussels for three days every time he wanted to take Caitlin out to dinner. One day she would live in The Falconry with him. His father was right, he decided, blood was thicker than water. If Declan didn't get the franchise, he, Archie, would look after Caitlin.

CHAPTER 37

Taggie had a very wearing September. Getting a besotted and reelingly untogether Caitlin packed up and back to Upland House was bad enough, but dispatching Declan to Ireland was even worse.

As the departure date drew nearer, he grew increasingly reluctant to leave Maud or his precious franchise, which was just coming up to the boil.

Maud was plainly reveling in *The Merry Widow*. Declan was glad, but was her euphoria slightly exaggerated? And was it really necessary for her to have a bath and wash her hair before every rehearsal? And when she caroled the words *"All the world's in love with love, and I love you,"* over and over again, who were they really aimed at? As the yellow woods turned gold and the swallows seemed to postpone their departure, and even the huge red suns sank more slowly into Rupert's woods in order to hear Maud's exquisite notes floating down the valley, Declan prayed she wasn't leading her leading man on too much.

Maud herself was much happier after Caitlin had gone back to school, but now it seemed Cameron Cook was always in the house, monopolizing the telephone and Declan. Anyone would think they were going off on a six months' polar expedition rather than three silly weeks on location.

The eve of their departure was full of spats, and now at dusk Declan was in the library firing off last-minute instructions to Freddie, who was just back from Portugal again, and Rupert, who was just off to Virginia for a few days. Between them they would probably run things far more smoothly than Declan. The appalling Professor Graystock had also dropped in, returned from his working holiday in Greece to get ready for the new university year, and was, as usual, swilling Declan's whisky. Dame Enid had just come down from upstairs, after going through Maud's *Merry Widow* score with her and making some extremely helpful suggestions.

"She'll be totally irresistible," Dame Enid told Declan as she accepted a large pink gin.

Cameron sat in a corner going through her lists for tomorrow with half an ear on the meeting. She'd checked that everyone—actors, wardrobe, makeup, and crew—knew where to meet her and Declan at Birmingham Airport; she'd double checked that the air-conditioned bus would be waiting to take them to Sligo by early evening, and that the hotel overlooking the bay would be expecting them for dinner.

Glancing across the room at Rupert, who was gazing moodily out of the window at Claudius chewing a library book, she knew that he was bored. He'd been affectionate recently, but slightly detached; perhaps he always distanced himself before a separation. She hated the thought of him going to Virginia on his own. She couldn't imagine American women leaving him alone.

"Now, you all know that I'm on the end of the telephone," Declan was saying. "By the time I get back we should have the date for our IBA interview. Then we can start having dry-runs. I've booked Hardy Bissett to coach us." He ran his hands through his hair and leaned back in his chair surveying the chaos on his desk.

Rupert turned away from the window. "When d'you reckon Yeats'll be finally in the can?" he said.

"For Chrissake, dumbass," screamed Cameron, "I've told you a hundred times, it's pronounced 'Yates.' "

Declan raised a disapproving eyebrow. Dame Enid was much more up front. "You haven't learned to pronounce the word 'hostile' yet, young lady,'' she snapped, "but you certainly manage to be it most of the time."

"Thank you, Enid. The age of chivalry is not entirely dead," said Rupert lightly, but his face had lost all expression.

Oh, God, thought Cameron, I shouldn't have said that.

"The answer to your question," said Declan to Rupert, "is sometime in December. We'll have to edit and do all the voiceovers when we get back."

"I hope you've got in the story about Yeats cutting his precious fur coat in half because he didn't want to disturb a cat who was sitting on it," said Dame Enid.

"Or the time that he signed a lot of checks 'Yours sincerely, W. B. Yeats,' " said Professor Graystock, determined not to be upstaged. "Or even the story . . ." he began.

Rupert had had enough—fucking intellectuals. He walked out of the library, out of the front door, and down the garden. Migrating arrows of birds were flapping down the valley. There had been a storm at lunchtime; roses were pulping and disintegrating; tobacco plants prostrated themselves like palms before his feet. Beyond the garden, in one of his fields, the grass had been flattened by the deluge, as though a herd of elephants had been having a gang bang.

Half a dozen young steers grazing there had recently been joined by a Guernsey cow and a little chocolate-brown calf, which a grateful neighboring farmer had sent Rupert as an early birthday present. Now he could see the steers pushing the baby calf away and drinking her mother's milk. With her long-legged gawkiness, her big eyes and long fringed eyelashes, the calf reminded him of Taggie. He looked at the mother's pink udder with its four teats. Perhaps Cameron would pronounce them "tates." Fucking intellectual. He'd get the mother and calf moved to a field of their own tomorrow.

Instead of returning to the library, he went around to the kitchen and found Taggie listening to pop music and trying to iron a great pile of Declan's shirts and read a recipe at the same time.

"You're about to scorch that shirt," said Rupert.

Hastily Taggie upended the iron. "You're just the person I wanted to see. Sarah Stratton wants me to do a dinner party for her the week after next, and she's given me this recipe all in French, and I can't make head nor tail of it."

Rupert, who'd had plenty of experience of Sarah's writing, took the piece of paper and reeled off the recipe.

"Oh marvelous! Could you dictate it to me?" said Taggie, grabbing a pencil.

Rupert was about to take the pencil, saying it'd be much quicker if he scribbled it down himself. Then he remembered something he'd read recently about encouraging dyslexics. Very slowly, making sure he didn't get too far ahead, resisting the urge to touch Taggie's white neck, revealed in all its vulnerability as her black ponytail fell sideways, he translated it for her.

"You are brilliant," sighed Taggie as she finished. "No one else could translate it. Daddy doesn't read French, nor Mummy, nor even Cameron."

Suddenly Rupert felt ten feet tall again. What a pity he had to fly to Virginia tomorrow, but he desperately needed a new stallion and he hoped to get in a few days' hunting.

Cameron felt twitchy as she packed. She was still kicking herself for showing Rupert up in front of the others, but she got so uptight before she went on location. At the bottom of her bags she'd packed a book on coping with stepmotherhood. When she came back from Ireland, she was determined to get along better with Marcus and Tab. Wandering into Rupert's dressing room, she found him also packing. He was catching the Concorde in the morning.

"I love you," she said, putting her arms around him. "You will fly out to Ireland when you get back, won't you?"

"Of course," said Rupert, as he hastily flipped a book called *Understanding Dyslexia* under a pile of shirts.

For a man so confident in business matters, Freddie Jones was surprisingly timid in matters of the heart. For months he had longed to call up Lizzie Vereker, but only screwed up the courage the day Declan and Cameron left for Ireland.

"How about lunch today?" he said, wading straight in.

"Where's Valerie?" asked Lizzie.

"In Portugal."

Because she had the curse and a large pimple, dirty hair, hairy legs, and unpainted toe nails, Lizzie said no, she was frantically busy. Then felt absolutely miserable. "What about next week?" she asked hopefully.

"Valerie'll be home," said Freddie.

"Well, call me anyway," said Lizzie.

* * *

All week Lizzie was absentminded. She spilled red wine over a re-
view copy she hadn't reviewed, and which James intended to give
to his mother for a birthday present. On Thursday morning she kept
filling up cups of coffee with cold water and swallowed a heartworm
pill which she'd intended to give to the dog. Perhaps she'd go barking mad. She knew she ought to be working on her new book, but
all she could think about was Freddie. Distracted, one morning, she
walked in the pouring rain down to the lake. A moorhen was summoning her chicks into the rushes with a strange fluted call. The
beeches trailed their red leaves in the raindrop-pitted water. Suddenly Lizzie heard shouting from the French doors. It was Jilly, her
treasure of a nanny, who seemed even more of a treasure when she
said Mr. Jones was on the telephone.

" 'Ullo,'' said Freddie. ''Fort you might like to go for a picnic?''

"But it's pouring,'' said Lizzie joyfully.

"We could 'ave it indoors at Green Lawns.''

"Where's Valerie?''

"At the Nearly New Sale for the Distressed Gentlefolk.''

Lizzie painted her nails, washed her hair, bathed and shaved and
cleaned her ears. Then she rubbed body lotion into every centimeter
of her body.

The only problem was that she had forgotten that the Corinium
Television gardener (one of James's perks) came that morning. He
must have been amazed to see Lizzie emerging so startlingly painted
and scented at midday, to announce that she was off to the Nearly
New Sale and then going on to do some shopping, so would he weed
the main herbaceous border, which she had already thanked him profusely for weeding last week. She'd even called James to tell him she
was going to the sale and to ask if he needed anything in Cotchester.

Lizzie had no intention of going to bed with Freddie that day.
She wouldn't have if she hadn't bought that lovely blue tweed skirt
for a pound at the clothes booth and passed Valerie noisily manning
the produce booth on the way out.

"Look, look,'' cried Lizzie, waving the skirt, ''at my lovely bargain.''

"You'll never get into that!'' said Valerie crushingly. ''That used
to be Sarah Stratton's.''

Valerie was looking very Sloane, Lizzie decided, in a pale blue
cashmere sweater, dark blue stockings, and Gucci shoes, with her
hair drawn off her forehead in a velvet bow.

"Do you know what that absolute swine Tony Baddingham is

threatening to do?'' Valerie went on, lowering her voice. "Build twenty homes on a field next to our grounds. It'll ruin our view. I mean, we *are* designated an area of outstanding natural beauty.''

"He won't get a zoning variance,'' said Lizzie.

"Probably will, with all those bribes he offers. Tell James to absolutely refuse to interview any of the Planning Committee on 'Cotswold Roundup.' So embarrassing when Monica and I are such close friends.''

Valerie's beady eyes fell on Lizzie's purse. "Now what are you going to buy? I'm sure James likes pickled beets. I'll give you a penny off.''

"I'll buy that coffee cake; it looks delicious. How long are you stuck here for?'' asked Lizzie.

"Until four o'clock,'' said Valerie crossly. "Someone has to hold the fort.''

"It's the fort what counts,'' murmured Lizzie.

"I fort you was never coming,'' said Freddie as he opened the door. In the kitchen was a bottle of Dom Perignon on ice and a huge plate of smoked salmon. Freddie had picked Rupert's brains about seducing techniques.

"The ideal picnic,'' sighed Lizzie. "I brought us some coffee cake for dessert.''

They stayed in the kitchen, in case they messed up the cushions balanced on their corners on Valerie's settees.

"I want to see a great deal of you, Mrs. Vereker,'' said Freddie, "but it won't be easy wiv Tony Baddingham, an' Valerie, an' James breaving down our necks.''

"James won't be,'' said Lizzie.

"Where is he at the moment?''

"Inside Sarah Stratton, I should think.''

They both roared with laughter and, for the first time, Lizzie found she didn't mind. She liked everything about Freddie, she decided—the way his eyes turned down at the corners, and his beer belly, and the damp patches under his arms because he was so nervous, and the way he smoked with his cigar between finger and thumb to eke it out.

As a writer, she told herself firmly as Freddie led her upstairs, one has to experience life. All the same she didn't think she would have gone to bed with Freddie on that first day, and certainly not in Valerie's bedroom, if she hadn't found four of her favorite books in the spare room bookshelf, which she'd lent to Valerie when she'd had flu and which Valerie'd sworn she'd given back to Lizzie.

When they got upstairs Freddie initially seemed far more interested in showing off his gadgets—the eight-horsepower Jacuzzi and
the bath which turned on by remote control and regulated the water
from the bed, which was huge and oval, with a great dashboard of
buttons at the head.

"Shall we sleep in it," whispered Lizzie, "or hi-jack it and fly it
to paradise?"

"You do say the loveliest fings," said Freddie, drawing her close.
His paunch slotted in below her splendid breasts, so it was very easy
for them to kiss.

"What music would you like?" asked Freddie.

"Brahms's Second Piano Concerto," said Lizzie.

Next moment, incredibly, it flooded through the room. "I must
have a pee first," said Lizzie, wading through the thick carpeting to
the bathroom.

"I'll get undressed," said Freddie.

Lizzie washed herself with Valerie's washcloth, but not too
much, in case she rubbed away all the lubrication. She wanted Freddie to know how excited she was. For a second she examined the
lips of her labia, just peering out of her bush, like a wrinkled old
tortoise, then shoved them inside. How could men possibly find
women beautiful down there? Would her opening be prettier than
Valerie's, she wondered.

Coming out, she opened the wrong door and nearly went into
the linen closet. Goodness it was tidy, as though it had been laid out
with a T-square. Adultery certainly taught you about other people's
houses. She expected Freddie to be completely undressed by the
time she got back, but he had so much jewelery to remove that she
beat him to it.

"I've dreamed and dreamed of this moment," said Freddie as he
stretched out beside her. "Ever since we first met at that 'unt ball,
eighteen monfs ago. I fort, what a lovely lady."

"I'm so fat," sighed Lizzie.

"You're not," said Freddie. "It's much more fun climbing Everest than the foothills."

Lizzie put her hand on his cock. "And it's so nice to see software
becoming hardware."

"And I'm going to declare this an area of outstanding natural
beauty," said Freddie. Reaching for his glass of champagne on the
bedside table, he emptied it into her bush and proceeded to lick it
all off. After Mousie's fragility, he reflected as he climbed on top of
her, it was like having a wonderfully sturdy cob between your thighs.

"I hope you're using a Condom Perignon," mumbled Lizzie half-laughing and half-crying with pleasure as he entered her.

Brahms's Piano Concerto was her favorite piece of music, but from then on she forgot its existence until the last ecstatic bars of the final Allegretto.

"You're absolutely perfick," whispered Freddie. "You're the big fing in my life now."

"I love you," said Lizzie.

"And I love you," said Freddie.

Afterwards they had another bottle and ate all the coffee cake, and longed to make love again, but decided it was too risky. To establish an alibi, Lizzie then went shopping in Cotchester, so drunk and happy she could hardly get the clothes back on the hangers. Coming out of the drugstore, having bought a huge guilt present of Aramis for James, she heard a car tooting.

Not being vain, she didn't even turn around when it went on tooting, and only did so when Tony Baddingham lowered his electric window and yelled out to her.

Keeping her mouth tight shut so he wouldn't catch the champagne fumes, wondering if he could see the words "adulterer and traitor" branded on her forehead, she edged toward him.

"You're looking great," said Tony smoothly. "Really great. What have you been buying?"

"Scent for James," said Lizzie.

"How very nice," said Tony. "And it isn't even his birthday! You're a good wife, Lizzie. Look forward to seeing you next Saturday."

"Saturday?" said Lizzie, bewildered.

"Sarah Stratton's dinner party," said Tony. "We'll have a good talk then."

Back at Lake House, Lizzie rushed upstairs, washed off all her make-up and scent, removed the nail polish from her toes, and got into her old clothes in case James came home early. Fortunately he was very late, so she was able to watch almost the entire production of *Midsummer Night's Dream* by herself. It was quite magic, and must have won Corinium a lot of Brownie points in the franchise battle. Throughout the performance, Lizzie kept thinking of Freddie, and how cuddly and sweet and kind he'd been, and how she wanted him to make love to her over and over again.

"Funny goings on at Venturer," said James in a pleased voice, pouring himself an uncharacteristic drink the moment he got in. "Evidently Cameron's pushed off to Ireland with Declan, and I've just seen Bas coming out of the Bar Sinister with Maud."

Funny goings on everywhere, thought Lizzie dreamily, what with James and Sarah, and her and Freddie, and Rupert probably still hankering after Taggie. It was as though they'd all been affected by Puck's mischievous witchery like the mortals and Titania in *Midsummer Night's Dream*. James fell asleep the moment his head touched the pillow.

"I am the mistress of a very nice man," wrote Lizzie ecstatically in her diary before she turned out the light.

CHAPTER 38

The first Saturday in October, Taggie overslept. Working late, she hadn't got to bed until four. She was just making a cup of coffee when Wandering Aengus, mewing horribly, padded in with a live field mouse in his mouth.

"Beast," yelled Taggie hurling a dishcloth at him. She missed, but Aengus was so startled he dropped the field mouse, which took refuge under the counter.

Having shut the enraged and growling cat in the pantry, Taggie managed to rescue the mouse with a dustpan and brush and put it in a cardboard box. Dressed in only the briefest nightie and gumboots, she carried the box across the lawn to set it free at the edge of the fields. Very gently she tipped it out, but the poor little thing didn't move; perhaps it had died of shock. Next moment she nearly died too. Coming toward her out of the blue mist across the dew-drenched field on a big, sweating dark-brown horse rode Rupert. As he raised his hat, Taggie put her finger to her lips and showed him the mouse which was still motionless.

"Aengus caught it," she whispered. "D'you think it'll survive?"

Rupert privately thought a quick shove with his boot would put the mouse out of its misery, but, knowing this would upset Taggie, said it might just be frozen with fear, and why didn't they leave it for a bit. Gazing at Taggie's nightgown and gumboots, he asked her if she was going out. Taggie went crimson and said she'd been doing a late dinner party. There was a long pause. Casting desperately around for something to say, Taggie mumbled that it was a nice day.

"Very. I've been cubbing," said Rupert.

"Oh, poor little things," said Taggie in horror. "Did you kill any?"

"No," lied Rupert. "I brought you these," he went on, producing some huge mushrooms out of his riding-coat pocket.

"Oh, aren't they beautiful?" Distracted, Taggie examined their pleated pink undersides, "How really kind. Thank you so much."

Anyone would have thought he'd given her another Fabergé egg, thought Rupert. Stammering furiously, she asked him if he'd like some breakfast.

"I hoped you'd say that. I'll drop off my horse and come back."

Taggie raced upstairs and was appalled to see that her nightie had a huge rip, her eyes were full of sleep, and her mascara was all smudged. Frantically she washed, put on an old pair of black cut-off cords and a dark brown T-shirt and started cooking breakfast. She steeled herself to the possibility that Rupert would get caught up in some drama at home and forget to return; or that Maud, smelling frying bacon, would come down and join them. But he was back in a quarter of an hour with a bottle of champagne and Maud stayed upstairs, perfecting a song called "Jogging in a one-horse gig."

"She really is working at it," said Rupert, edging the bottle open with his thumbs.

"It's wonderful. She's so much happier," said Taggie, thinking how black and luscious the white mushrooms had gone, and tipping most of them onto Rupert's plate.

They had breakfast outside on the peeling white bench. Despite the warmth, the cedars, wellingtonias, and yews flanking the house were already full of orange leaves from the nearby horse chestnuts. Lavender, roses, and evening primroses still bloomed on, bravely waiting for the first frost.

"I've never felt such hot sun in October," said Rupert, taking off his sweater. "With a few more leaves off the trees, I'll be able to see your house again."

"How was America?" asked Taggie, dividing her bacon between Gertrude and Claudius.

"Good," said Rupert, deciding not to mention four magnificent days of fox hunting in Virginia. "I've found a marvelous stallion, and a brood mare for Freddie. Which reminds me, I saw Freddie's red Jaguar parked outside the Verekers' house while "Cotswold Roundup" was on the air last night. If he's going to err and stray, he ought to find a more discreet car."

Taggie giggled. "Lizzie's so nice, isn't she?" she said, breaking a sausage in half for the dogs.

"She certainly deserves some fun. James treats her like an old wheelchair he can fall back into in old age. This breakfast is quite marvelous. Why are you giving all yours to the dogs?"

"I don't usually eat breakfast," mumbled Taggie.

Rupert ran his eyes over her. "You're losing weight. I'll have to start adding molasses and carrots to your oats."

"Jogging in a one-horse gig, any time of night or day," sang Maud from upstairs, *"Careless of the weather, very close together, lovers fall in love that way."*

Rupert raised his eyebrows and filled up Taggie's glass.

Please God, she prayed, make this moment go on forever and ever. The next moment Gertrude had joined them on the bench seat on Taggie's side so Taggie had to move closer to Rupert.

"Well done, Gertrude," said Rupert, grinning. "You really are on my side."

Taggie's heart seemed to be beating completely out of time to Maud's singing. Frantically, she stroked Gertrude.

"Heard from your father?" asked Rupert.

"No," stammered Taggie. "Have you heard from Cameron?"

"Not recently."

There was another long pause. Laughing and watching her, Rupert waited.

"You mustn't worry about Daddy and Cameron being on their own together for so long," Taggie finally blurted out. "I know Daddy's wildly attractive, but he is utterly obsessed with Mummy."

Rupert was about to deny that he was remotely worried about Cameron. Instead he removed a long dark hair from her shoulder and put it in his shirt pocket.

"I dreamed about you last night."

"You did?" said Taggie in amazement. "Was it nice?"

"Lovely, and extremely disturbing." He trailed the back of his fingers down her arm. Taggie quivered and stopped stroking Gertrude.

"It's the last night of the Horse of the Year Show tonight," went on Rupert. "Tabitha's in the final of the mounted games. It's a good evening. Why don't you come with me? We could have dinner afterwards."

Taggie nearly wept. "Sarah Stratton's giving a dinner party. I've got to work."

"Pity," said Rupert lightly.

Gertrude stuck her nose under Taggie's trembling hand, jerking it upwards, urging Taggie to stroke her again. Gertrude and me, thought Rupert.

"The Baddinghams and the Verekers are going, so they'll all talk about the franchise. I'll probably be made to stay in the kitchen," babbled Taggie.

"Well keep your ears open and put a pint of arsenic in Tony's whisky. I'm off to the Tory Party Conference next week," said Rupert, getting into his car. "I'll ring you when I get back. That was a lovely breakfast, thank you. By the way," he added ultra-casually as he drove off, "I hope you noticed I didn't burn my stubble this year."

In a complete daze Taggie finished off the champagne. Rupert had dreamed about her, *and* he'd asked her out, *and* he hadn't burned his stubble. The whole thing was desperately confusing. She ran upstairs and looked out her window. It was true. Instead of charred patches all over the valley, his cornfields were still yellowed by stubble, or reddy-brown after being ploughed up. She couldn't possibly be the reason, but it was so nice of him to say so.

There were so many things she ought to do, picking apples, planting the indoor bulbs, getting in the geraniums. There were large bowls of picked mulberries and blackberries in the fridge waiting to be turned into jam. And she must make some tomato chutney, not to mention painting the bench and mowing the lawn.

Suddenly she heard an enraged mewing from the pantry. She'd forgotten Aengus. She couldn't even get cross that he'd eaten half the turbot mousse she'd made for the first course this evening. At least when she went out to search for the field mouse it had run away.

By the time she reached the Strattons' house she'd sobered up. Paul was still out playing golf. Sarah was in a panic because she wanted everything to be perfect for Tony, her boss, and even more so for James.

"Giving a dinner party is far worse than going on television," she moaned. "Look, I know it sounds horrendously Valerie Jones, but do you mind pretending I've done the cooking tonight, especially the main course, which is a particular favorite of a friend of mine," added Sarah going pink. "If anyone rings, pretend you're our cleaning woman, Mrs. Maggs."

Then, leaving Taggie with a mile-long list of instructions, she drove off to Bath to buy a new dress.

At least everything was tidy, the table set and the house clean. Taggie got out the French recipe Rupert had translated for her. An hour and a half later, she was getting on well. The beef daube was sizzling in the oven, the dessert was in the fridge and just needed whipped cream and sugared violets, and she'd done the vegetables earlier. All she had to do was to make another fish mousse. Perhaps she'd just better double-check the beef.

"Oh, my God," she said aghast as she licked the spoon. She tried again from the other side of the dish, and then the center, where it was even worse. She must have been so distracted by her encounter with Rupert that she'd added a tablespoonful of salt instead of sugar. She tested the sugar in the glass bowl and went green. It was definitely salt.

The beef was quite inedible, absolutely impregnated with salt, and she'd used up all the other ingredients. It was after five and she'd never get to Cotchester in time. She gave a whimper of horror. She'd wrecked Sarah's party and she knew Sarah could be extremely difficult if things didn't go right.

The telephone rang. Oh God, she sobbed, I've got to remember to be Mrs. Maggs. Trembling, she picked up the receiver.

"Hullo," crackled a voice from a car telephone.

"Mrs. Stratton be shopping, thank you very much. Who be you?" mumbled Taggie.

Rupert laughed. "That is the worst Gloucestershire accent I've ever heard. How's it going?"

Taggie burst into tears. "It was James's favorite recipe and she'd supposed to have made it for him," she sobbed.

"Cheer up or you'll cry more salt into the beef," said Rupert calmly. "Get on with the fish mousse. I'll be over in half an hour."

He arrived twenty-five minutes later. He screeched the Aston Martin to a halt in a cloud of dust and nearly tipped Beaver and Blue, who were sitting on the back seat, through the windshield, then he sauntered into the kitchen with a huge casserole dish containing Boeuf Bourguignon for twelve from Luigi's, the local five-star restaurant in Cheltenham.

"Oh, you are lovely," said Taggie, flinging her arms around his neck.

"Hands off! We've no time for dalliance!" said Rupert briskly, as he emptied the Bourguignon into one of Sarah's big bowls and chucked Taggie's salty remnants into Luigi's casserole dish. "Don't tell Paul and Sarah what happened," he added. "Just pretend this is how the recipe turned out. They'll all be too pissed to notice, anyway. I'd better beat it, or she'll be back from shopping and start accusing me of bugging the room."

Still stammering her thanks, Taggie followed him out to the car. An owl was hooting. A semi-circle of orange moon was rising out of the sycamores.

"I can't ever begin to thank you," bleated Taggie.

Rupert pulled her toward him, dropping a kiss on her cheek-bone.

"Oh yes, you can, angel. Just wait till I get back from Black-pool."

The patron saint of cooking guided Taggie that evening. The food was positively ambrosial, and Sarah took all the credit, particularly for Luigi's Boeuf Bourguignon, which was so tender you could cut it with a spoon.

"D'you remember that daube we had at the White Elephant at Painswick?" whispered Sarah to James as they went in to dinner. "Well, I wrote to them for the recipe and I've made it for you tonight."

Putting on his horn-rimmed spectacles to have a closer look across the table, Tony Baddingham decided he hadn't been wrong about Lizzie Vereker. She looked sensational.

The talk during dinner was mostly of "Master Dog" which was edging up on "EastEnders" in the ratings; but they waited until Taggie was safely out of the room to discuss the franchise.

"There are some quite fascinating developments," Tony said tantalizingly, "but I'm not prepared to leak them until November, when it'll be nearer the IBA meetings. And then, my God, Venturer will wish they'd never tried to take us on." He paused as Taggie came in with the salad.

Not that she would have taken anything in that night. In the kitchen she was frantically trying to watch the Horse of the Year Show hoping to catch a glimpse of Rupert. At least she saw Tabitha in the mounted games—utterly adorable and so like Rupert. The finals were just coming up when Sarah summoned Taggie to clear away the dessert.

In the hall after dinner, James felt that Sarah had been so very very caring to go to all that trouble with the daube, that he was foolish enough to be caught by Tony not only kissing her, but putting his hand inside her new silk dress.

On Monday morning Tony summoned James to his office. "I've decided it's time for you to have your own series," he began briskly, "which we'll almost certainly sell to the network."

"That's very good of you, Tony," said James.

"I want to make a series examining all aspects of marriage," went on Tony.

"Finances, dual careers, how much housework should the caring husband do," rattled off James excitedly. "Sex, rows, decorating the house."

"That's right," said Tony. "We could perhaps even introduce children and the pressures they put on a marriage. But basically the whole series will be aimed at couples who are getting behind marriage again, who want to stay with the same person for the rest of their lives. We'll call it 'How to Stay Married.' "

"With the AIDS panic, it'll be a real franchise-grabber," said James excitedly.

"Exactly," said Tony urbanely. "And I want you and a very charming lady not far from your heart to present it."

"I don't even have to guess, Tony," said James warmly, "but d'you really feel she's experienced enough?"

"More important," said Tony, who was enjoying himself, "she's a natural. She's not too obviously glamorous, but she's got just the right kind of lovely warm bubbly personality that'll make couples talk and trigger off a really good audience reaction."

James bowed his head. "I know Sarah will appreciate the very great honor you're bestowing on her, Tony."

"I'm not talking about Sarah, you jerk," said Tony icily. "I mean your wife, Lizzie, and if you value your job, the less you see of Mrs. Stratton over the next three months the better."

Taggie spent the next week dreaming of Rupert. She knew he loved and lived with Cameron, who would be back in a week or so, but she couldn't help herself. On Thursday she watched him on television at the Party Conference making a brilliant speech saying that the Tories must get off their fat backsides and start thinking positively about unemployment and the way it directly affected rioting in the inner cities. Taggie, detecting Declan's influence, felt very proud.

On Friday night a slight distraction was provided by Caitlin coming home for a long weekend, with her black hair dyed white at the front, still utterly besotted with Archie.

"He went into the town and brought eighty cans of beer back in a taxi and smuggled them in and sold them to the other boys on the black market in order to buy me this gorgeous sweater. I haven't taken it off since he sent it to me, so please can you wash it tonight, and my black jeans so I can wear them tomorrow? Archie's taking me out to lunch. What's Mummy doing for the rest of the day?"

"Rehearsing, I think," said Taggie.

Exactly on cue, Maud wandered in, looking radiant. "Hullo, darling, how's school?"

"Ghastly. Anyone with layered hair is being sent home, so I'm going to get mine layered on Monday."

"I've bought some apples," said Maud, waving a large paper bag at Taggie. "They're so cheap in the market."

And they cost nothing in the orchard, thudding on to the grass every two minutes, Taggie wanted to scream. She wanted to murder her mother sometimes.

"That's a nice sweater," said Maud, looking at Caitlin. "Where did you get it?"

"It was a present," said Caitlin. "You will wash it carefully, won't you, Tag? How's *The Merry Widow*?" she asked her mother.

"Oh, exhausting, but fun," said Maud, pouring herself a large whisky. "I-er-thought I might go to the movies with some of the cast tomorrow night," she added casually. "Taggie's cooking. Will you be all right on your own, Caitlin?"

"Brilliant," beamed Caitlin. "Stay out as long as you like. I've got masses of work. Have dinner and make a night of it. I've got to read *Antony and Cleopatra* and write an essay on *Streetcar Named Desire*. I think it's extraordinary that they shut us up in single-sex schools and then assign these amazingly erotic books."

By the time Taggie had cleared up supper and washed and ironed Caitlin's sweater and jeans it was two o'clock in the morning. Admittedly her progress had been slowed up by constantly looking out the window to watch for Rupert's helicopter landing on the lawn, or his car coming up the drive. But there was nothing. Perhaps he'd gone to Ireland to see Cameron after all.

It seemed she'd hardly fallen asleep when she was roused by a hysterical Caitlin. "That bugger Mummy used all the water, so I can't wash my hair or have a bath, and even worse she's gone off in my new sweater and jeans. And now I can't wear it for Archie, and he'll never believe I haven't lost it, like Desdemona's handkerchief. I hate, hate, hate her, bloody old cow, and she's bound to split my jeans."

"I'll run you into Cotchester and buy you something else," said Taggie. "I got paid in cash yesterday."

"It's no good," screamed Caitlin. "I wanted Archie to see me in his sweater. I'll kill her, I'll absolutely kill her."

Nothing Taggie could say would calm her down.

"I'll call Rupert and see if you can have a bath there," said Taggie in the end.

Throat dry, heart thumping, hands drenched in sweat and trembling, Taggie misdialed the number three times in her nervousness. When Rupert didn't answer immediately, she nearly hung up.

"Hullo." He sounded irritable and very sleepy.

"It's Taggie."

"My darling," his voice softened.

"I'm desperately sorry," she began. Then, stammering worse than ever, she explained what had happened, but didn't mention Archie's name. "Could I possibly rush Caitlin over to wash her hair and have a bath?"

"Of course," said Rupert, "as long as we can all have it together."

Rupert hadn't shaved when they arrived. He was wandering around in bare feet, having obviously just put on the white shirt and the black dinner-jacket trousers he'd been wearing last night. He looked bug-eyed.

"I won't stop," mumbled Taggie, desperate not to impose on him. "I'll pick Caitlin up in an hour, OK?"

Rupert pulled her into the house. "Don't be boring. As I'm such a notorious reprobate, you ought to stay and chaperone Caitlin."

Caitlin promptly started raging on about Maud. "Bloody old cow, nicking all the water and my seducing outfit. What does she want with it? I bet she's up to someone, the old tart. It's high time my father came home."

"Cait-lin," remonstrated Taggie, going pink. "Rupert hasn't got all day. I thought you wanted to be ready by twelve. Go and have a bath."

Grinning, Rupert took Caitlin upstairs and showed her where everything was. Taggie glanced at some photographs of Tabitha which were lying on the kitchen table.

"Aren't these gorgeous?" she said, as Rupert came back. "I saw a bit of it on television at Sarah Stratton's, but I missed the final. Did her team win?"

"No, but they came third, and she did well. *Horse and Hound* described her as a 'chip off the old Campbell-Black'; which was nice."

"Marvelous," said Taggie. "Am I in your way?" she asked as Rupert paused on his way to the fridge.

"No, I just like standing behind you. I've got a hangover. Let's have a drink."

"I mustn't," said Taggie, "or I'll make another muddle of cooking tonight."

"Don't say you're working again?" said Rupert, appalled. Taggie nodded dolefully.

"Jesus," said Rupert. "I'd better make a date with you for *next* October."

"I'm so sorry," stammered Taggie, hanging her head, "It's n-not that I wouldn't love to."

"I've got an idea," said Rupert. "My children are coming over this afternoon. Why don't you come out with us for the day tomorrow, and help me entertain them?"

"I'll make a picnic," said Taggie, suddenly excited.

"No, you won't. For once you're not going to cook a thing."

With both Maud and Caitlin plundering her wardrobe, Taggie was at her wit's end as to what to wear. Feeling desperately guilty, with the Electricity Board, the television rental firm, the village shop, and God knows who else baying to be paid, she blew Friday lunchtime's cash wages on a pale gray cashmere turtleneck which brought out the silver-gray in her eyes and clung to her in all the right places. There was no more money, so she'd have to wear her old black cords.

Next morning Maud whizzed off very early to yet another rehearsal. Caitlin, who nobly said she'd dogsit and read *Anthony and Cleopatra*, hustled Taggie out of the house.

"You look delectable. Randy Rupe won't be able to keep his hands off you. Don't hurry back. I'm quite OK on my own—" she smirked wickedly—"or, almost on my own. The Hon Arch will be dropping by *plus tard*. Or Marble Arch, as I call him, now he's lost his suntan."

Tabitha, amid the swirling pack of dogs, answered the door looking belligerent. She was wearing a pink sweater embroidered with blue flowers and a blue puff-ball skirt.

"Hullo," said Taggie in delight. "I recognize *you*; you were on television last Saturday. You were wonderful, and what a beautiful clever pony. He was much the fastest. What's his name?"

"Biscuit," said Tabitha coldly.

"Can I see him?"

"He's at my other house."

"Oh, what a shame. I've brought him some carrots." Taggie rummaged in a carrier bag, "and I've made you some fudge."

"Thank you," said Tab, looking slightly mollified. "Can I have a piece now?"

"I don't see why not. I like your puff-ball skirt. I wanted to get one, but my knees are too knobbly."

"Mummy says hers are, too," said Tab. "Perhaps they're not suitable for grown-ups."

Stroking the dogs, Taggie sat down on one of the stone seats inside the porch.

"What's your name again?" said Tabitha.

"Taggie. It's really Agatha, isn't that awful? Tabitha's so much nicer. My parents call me Tag, sometimes, which sounds just like Tab, doesn't it? I expect when Rupert shouts Tab we'll both go charging into the kitchen to see what he wants and bump into each other in the doorway."

Tabitha stared at her consideringly, and suddenly she smiled.

"And you're nine and a quarter?" said Taggie. "It's awfully young to be in the Mounted Games. Were you the youngest?"

"Yes," said Tab. "If you come back to Warwickshire with us tonight you can see Biscuit. We've got a foal here. Would you like to come and see it?"

"Yes please," said Taggie.

The front door opened; it was Marcus. "Hullo," he said. "Daddy wants to know where you've got to."

"She's talking to me, stupid," said Tab. "She's brought you some fudge."

"Tag," bellowed Rupert from the kitchen, "where are you?"

"Here," said Tab and Tag in unison. Then they both looked at each other and burst out laughing.

Taking Taggie's hand, Tabitha dragged her into the kitchen. "Can she come back to Warwickshire with us this evening and see Biscuit?" said Tabitha.

Rupert, who was drinking black coffee and reading the racing pages of the *Sunday Times*, looked surprised.

"Of course she can. I thought you'd kidnapped her."

"She's brought us fudge, and carrots for Biscuit, and a big bottle of cough medicine," said Tabitha, unpacking the carrier bag.

"It's sloe gin," said Taggie, blushing. "I made it yesterday. You mustn't drink it for three months."

"Thank you, angel," said Rupert, kissing her on the cheek. "I hope I don't have to wait that long for you," he murmured in an undertone.

"Come on Taggie," said Tabitha impatiently. "I thought you wanted to see the foal. This fudge is smashing."

* * *

They had lunch in Cheltenham in an up-market hamburger bar. The children, who insisted on sitting on either side of Taggie, had huge milkshakes. Rupert, who complained he had alcohol shakes, ordered a carafe of red wine.

"That sweater suits you," he said approvingly to Taggie. "How d'you manage to keep it out of Maud's clutches?"

Taggie blushed. "I slept with it under my pillow."

"We're doing a 'Messiah' at the end of term," announced Tabitha, sucking air noisily from the bottom of her milkshake. "There are going to be two trumpets and a drum, and real fathers in the chorus. I'm in the altos."

"D'you like singing?" asked Taggie.

"No. Mrs. Brown takes us. She's just got married. She takes us for history too. She was reading a book called *Improving your Home* in class this week."

"She was reading a book about drains in our class," said Marcus.

"And that's what I pay tuition for," grumbled Rupert. "I wish they'd organize a sponsored walk to Save the Parents."

Having ordered, he looked across at Taggie, who was talking to Marcus about chestnuts.

"We used to roast them slowly to harden them up."

"We soak them in vinegar," said Marcus.

"My sister Caitlin used to put them in the linen closet and they always fell down behind the tank and went moldy. We've got masses at The Priory if you want any more, but I expect you've got hundreds already."

Christ, she's sweet, thought Rupert, noticing the way the gray cashmere molded the full breasts.

"Mary had a little lamb and surprised the midwife," said Tabitha to her father.

"Really," said Rupert absentmindedly.

"Mary had a little lamb and surprised the midwife. It's a joke."

"Ha, ha," said Rupert, filling up Taggie's glass.

"Why d'you always say ha ha and not mean it? Can I have a bag of potato chips?"

"No," said Rupert. "Here's your lunch."

"Can I have punk hair like Cameron?" said Tabitha, picking bits of mushroom out of her salad and putting them around the edge of her plate.

"No."

"Why not?"

"Because I don't like short hair."

"You've got very nice hair," said Marcus to Taggie, blushing scarlet as he bit into his hamburger.

"Yes," agreed Rupert. "She has."

Tabitha gazed dreamily into space. "Mrs. Bodkin must have slept with Mr. Bodkin an awful lot of times."

"What on earth makes you think that?" asked Rupert in amazement.

"She told me she'd had four miscarriages," said Tab.

Taggie didn't dare look at Rupert. She thought she had never been happier in her life. Suddenly the most ordinary things—a hamburger smothered in ketchup, the mural of the village street around the wall, with its milk cart and postman—were illuminated because she was with Rupert and these adorable children.

"Everything all right, Meester Campbell-Black?" asked the Manager.

"Perfect," said Rupert. "Could we have another carafe of red?"

"I would like to congratulate you," went on the Manager, looking around rapturously at Marcus, Tab, and Taggie. "I never knew you had three such beautiful children."

After lunch, they went for a walk in Rupert's woods. It was ridiculously mild. Insects moved leisurely in the rays slanting through the thinning beech trees, like specks of dust caught in the light from a projector. Birds sang drowsily, orange leaves drifted down onto already orange paths. The squirrels, stupefied by the sun, were fooling around on the ground instead of gathering nuts.

"What are you singing at school?" asked Taggie.

" 'Green grow the rushes-oh,' " said Tab.

"I'll sing you three-oh," sang Marcus.

"What is your three-oh?" sang back Tab.

"Three for the rivals, Two, two the lily-white boys, Clothed all in green-o," replied Marcus, his pure treble echoing through the soaring cathedral of beech trunks. Then both children took up the chant:

"One is one and all alone, And ever more shall be so."

"Lovely," sighed Taggie.

"Three for the rivals sounds like Corinium, Venturer, and Mid-West," said Rupert.

He used up a couple of reels of film, then, exhausted after a strenuous week at Blackpool, fell asleep under a chestnut tree, while Taggie played games with the children.

"D'you know," she said, drawing them away down the ride so

they wouldn't wake Rupert, "that every time you catch a falling leaf, you get a happy day. Let's see if we can catch thirty, so we can give Daddy a really happy November when he wakes up."

"Easy peasy," said Tabitha, leaping forward as a yellow syca- more leaf pirouetted through the air toward her, then, caught by a puff of wind, dummied around her and fluttered to the ground.

"It's harder than it looks," panted Marcus, reaching out as a twig of ash leaves floated tantalizingly out of his grasp. "Would those have counted as seven?"

"Not really," said Taggie.

"Bugger," screamed Tab, as she just missed a beech leaf.

"Hush," said Taggie. "We mustn't wake Daddy."

Silently they raced around the wood trying to suppress their screams of joy whenever they managed to catch a leaf. After a par- ticularly piercing yell, when Tab tripped over a bramble root but managed to hang on to a wand of chestnut leaves, Rupert woke up; but he pretended to be asleep. Watching Taggie, gamboling long- legged over the beech leaves, ponytail flying, looking, as the Manager had thought, not a day over fourteen, he was suddenly kneed in the groin with longing.

"Here you are, Daddy," said Tabitha, her hands full of leaves, "a whole happy month for you."

Rupert, who privately thought that the only thing that could make him happy at the moment was a whole month in bed with Taggie, said thank you very much.

"Can we go and see the new Woody Allen film?" asked Tabitha.

Rupert looked at his watch: "It's nearly four o'clock. You'll be very late back." The last thing he wanted to do was to go to the movies.

"We can go on our way home," pleaded Tabitha.

"We've done our homework," said Marcus.

Rupert turned to Taggie who said she'd adore to see it; anything to prolong the day with Rupert.

"I'm going to sit next to Taggie," said Tabitha, seizing her hand.

"I'm going to sit next to her too," said Marcus, taking her other hand.

The Woody Allen film was great, but Taggie hardly took any of it in, she was so aware of Rupert slumped in the seat beyond Tabitha gazing totally unmoved at the screen. How awful for Rupert being left by Helen and losing these heavenly children, living alone by himself in that big house.

"One is one and all alone and ever more shall be so," sang Tabitha as they drove home to Warwickshire.

Taggie felt Rupert's loss far more acutely when she met Helen, who was simply the most beautiful woman she'd ever seen, with huge serious yellow eyes and long red hair drawn back in two combs from her freckled face, and incredibly slim ankles and wrists.

But before she had much time to observe Helen or her husband, Malise, who seemed very old, Taggie was dragged off to the stables by Tabitha to meet Biscuit and Dollop.

Back in the drawing room, she found Helen tapping her beautifully shod foot and looking at the clock, and Rupert standing in front of an unlit fire, holding an empty glass and looking absolutely glazed.

"What would you like to drink?" Malise asked Taggie.

Taggie glanced at Rupert, who almost imperceptibly moved his head in the direction of the door.

"Nothing, thank you very much," she said.

"We must go," said Rupert. "I've got to get this child home."

So the day was to end just like that. Taggie suddenly felt suicidal. Malise, seeming to sense her depression, said, "Helen and I are tremendous fans of your father's. I do hope he gets the franchise. Corinium's programs are absolutely ghastly."

"Oh *The Dream* was excellent the other night," protested Helen. "Marcus said Cameron Cook had something to do with that, Rupert. You must bring her over sometime. I'd love to discuss the production with her. It was a most original interpretation."

Rupert stifled a huge yawn.

"I think Taggie and Rupert want to go, darling," said Malise gently, putting his arm around Helen's shoulders.

The children came to see them off.

"Promise, promise, we can see you next time we come over," said Tabitha, clinging to her like a monkey.

Rupert was very quiet on the drive back to Penscombe after dropping off the children. Taggie, feeling utterly miserable because the day was almost over and the Aston-Martin seemed to be gobbling up the miles, assumed he was merely depressed because his wife and children didn't live with him any more. Rupert, however, for the first time in his life, was battling seriously with his conscience.

Taggie was Declan's teenage daughter; he was committed to Cameron, who was already paranoid about Taggie, and there were deadly serious things like franchises to be won.

Then, in the light from a street-lamp in Cheltenham, he caught sight of Taggie. Everything seemed to turn upwards, her nose, her long sooty eyelashes, her adorably short upper lip, and those beautifully soft breasts, which he'd dreamed of the other night. His conscience lost.

"Would you like some dinner?"

"Oh yes, please," said Taggie joyfully. "If you're sure you're not too tired and I look smart enough?"

"Never, never get smart," said Rupert. "I loathe done-up women."

The White Elephant at Painswick was packed and taking last orders, but still managed to find a corner for Rupert. Taggie fled to the ladies room. All she had in her bag was a defunct mascara wand, a comb, some cologne, and a picture of Claudius. If only she could brush her teeth. She made do with soaking the roller towel, rubbing some soap on it, rubbing her teeth, then rinsing her mouth out with water. Then she de-tangled her hair and put it back in its ponytail.

When she got back to the table, Rupert, realizing she would be totally floored by the French menu, had ordered a bottle of Pouilly Fumé and smoked salmon and scrambled eggs for both of them.

At first they discussed the children.

"I wish they got on better with Cameron," sighed Rupert, "but, being totally unused to children, she makes neither extra beds nor allowances."

It was good that they could talk about Cameron naturally now, thought Taggie, suddenly longing to touch the fan of fine lines at the corner of Rupert's eyes. Perhaps she could become his long-term confidante, and even when he was eighty, he'd come roaring over to The Priory and tell her he'd met some marvelous new fifty-year-old. At least it'd be better than not seeing him.

"Does it still upset you going to the Horse of the Year Show when you're not winning all the cups any more?" she asked tentatively.

"Yes," he said. "That's why I wanted you to come along last week—" he took her hand—"to hold *my* hand. I don't think I realized at the time how desperately I minded giving up. Just stopping overnight after the World Championship, burying myself in politics, refusing to recognize I was suffering from withdrawal symptoms far worse than any junkie. There's so little time to think while you're show jumping. Even on those interminable drives there was always Billy to yak to, or some horse to natter about, always something to look forward to, a prize to be won, someone else's time to be beaten, a girl to be laid. I suppose I never gave myself time to grow up, and when Helen buggered off I blocked that out too."

Still holding her hand, he looked into her loving, infinitely understanding and sympathetic eyes. Christ, he'd never admitted things like this to anyone, not even Billy. Then she asked, "Does it still hurt thinking about Helen?"

Rupert shrugged. "I got bored with hating her, I guess. The only thing that really irks me is that Malise succeeded where I failed. I can't honestly say I've ever made any woman happy, or not for very long."

"You make me very happy," said Taggie gruffly.

For a second they gazed at each other and he watched the color mounting in her cheeks.

"I'd like to try," he said softly. "I'll just pay the bill and we'll go."

As he drove her slowly back to Penscombe Chris de Burgh was singing "Lady in Red" on the car radio. It was such a beautiful night. The moon was hiding behind a vast ebony cloud shaped like a yew tree, tipping its edges with silver; the rest of the pearly gray sky was threaded with stars. A few windows were still lit up in the village like cardboard cut-outs.

Just before he reached the right turn up the long chestnut avenue to Penscombe Court, Rupert slowed the car down almost to a standstill and raised a finger to Taggie's cheek.

"Are you quite sure, angel?"

He could feel her cheekbone rubbing frantically against his finger as she nodded. Totally adrift with love, she had no thought of refusing.

"Fucking hell," howled Rupert, as they drew up outside the house. Parked outside, beside Taggie's car, was a Lotus. In the moonlight it could have been any dark color.

"Cameron," thought Taggie in horror.

But the girl who came out of the front door had thick lustrous hair, as golden yellow as the sycamore leaves swirling across the gravel. It was Sarah Stratton. Sobbing, she threw herself into Rupert's arms.

"I must talk to you."

"I must go," said Taggie.

"No, don't," said Rupert sharply. Then, realizing what he was saying, added, "Well, it is a bit late. We'll check through the rest of those names tomorrow, and we'll tackle the Southern part of the region later in the week."

"Oh, the fucking franchise," screamed Sarah.

Leaving time only to squeeze Taggie's hand and say he'd call her tomorrow, Rupert took Sarah into the drawing room, where she collapsed sobbing on the sofa. The temperature suddenly seemed to have dropped several degrees. The house felt horribly cold and empty without Taggie and the children.

It was a few minutes before he could get any sense out of Sarah. Evidently James Vereker had given her a pink slip.

"Tony ordered him to. He said everyone was gossiping about me and James, and it doesn't do Corinium's reputation any good in a franchise year. Jesus, and when you think of the way he was carrying on with Cameron."

"*Was* is the operative word," said Rupert, pouring Sarah a glass of brandy. "There's no prude like a reformed rake."

"I know James loves me," sobbed Sarah hysterically, "but that shit Tony offered him the carrot of his own thirteen-part series on staying married, and ordered him to do it with Lizzie, so James and the podgy frump have to present a lovey-dovey united front until the franchise is in the bag, and James is going to go along with it."

Hum, thought Rupert. "Well, you'll just have to be a bit more discreet until after December 15th," he said.

"That's what I said, but James is refusing even to have a drink with me. If I talk to him at Corinium, he scuttles off like a daddy longlegs, he won't even gossip during the break in "Roundup." I know he's vain and ambitious, but I love him. I can't live without him." Her voice rose to a shriek.

Slumped on the sofa, in an amber miniskirt, and a saffron yellow sweater, with her tousled tawny hair and her tear-streaked face, Sarah should have been the epitome of desirability. But, comparing her hard, petulant, demanding little face to Taggie's, so sweet, so infinitely kind and gentle, Rupert wondered how the hell he'd ever fancied her.

"I can't live without him," Sarah repeated shrilly. "I'll never get over it."

"I hate to point it out," said Rupert, "but you said exactly the same thing to me after Christmas, and you've got over me pretty thoroughly, and no doubt when Paul thought he ought to do his duty and stay with Winifred you said the same thing to him."

"You can't compare the two," said Sarah furiously. "I've just spent a whole weekend with Paul," she added with a shudder.

"Paul's palled, has he?" said Rupert, topping up her glass.

"I can't stand living with him a moment longer. He won't stop pawing me," wailed Sarah. "And he's so old. I mean he's nineteen years older than me. It was all right when I started working for him. I was twenty and he was thirty-nine and he seemed so wonderfully forceful and dynamic and experienced. But now I'm twenty-nine and he's forty-eight, and his body's going, and he looks all gray and rumpled when he wakes in the morning, and he wears cornplasters and snows dandruff on his suits, and he's always clearing his throat and picking his nose and peering at me over his spectacles." Sarah's voice rose to a screech again as she cataloged his crimes. "I can't stand it."

Mindlessly, Rupert patted her heaving shoulder, as he bleakly worked out that the age gap between him and Taggie was exactly the same, or would be when he was thirty-eight next month.

Gradually Sarah stopped crying. She sat up and rubbed the mascara from under her eyes. "I suppose I'd better seduce Tony, but he's got one cloven hoof in the grave too. You and Cameron are so lucky—being near in age."

It was like a dentist hitting a raw nerve with a high-speed drill. Mercifully he was saved by the telephone. Then the dentist seemed to hit another nerve.

"Christ, I've missed you," said Cameron's seductive rasp. "Sorry I haven't called, but we've been up to here. Perry O'Donovan's such an asshole, and he can't stand Esther McDermott. She's an asshole too, and they've both had such rows with Declan, he's walked off the set twice."

"So it's all going as planned," said Rupert.

As Cameron rattled on about the frustrations of filming, all he could hear was prison doors clanging shut on him.

"So we've managed to finish a day early," she said finally.

"God, what a bore," said Rupert who hadn't been listening.

"Sweetest, this is a terrible line. I said I'll be coming home a day early. Declan and I are flying in tomorrow."

"Great," said Rupert, feeling sick. "I'll come and meet you."

"No, I've got the car at the airport. I'll see you late afternoon, and darling," her voice dropped huskily, "I've been celibate for three weeks. We've got a lot of catching up to do, so cancel any appointments for the rest of the day. I love you."

"Me too," said Rupert automatically.

"Good," said Sarah, as Rupert put down the receiver and went and poured himself a large whisky. "An absolute bastard like you needs an utter bitch like her to keep you in order."

After she'd left, Rupert couldn't face going to bed. He took the dogs into the garden. As they weaved about snuffling and barking after badgers, he looked across the valley. The moon had set; black clouds covered the sky; a chill wind was shepherding beech leaves irritably across the lawn; The Priory was in darkness, except for one light in Taggie's bedroom. Rupert almost wept. He longed to call her now to explain why he wouldn't be calling her tomorrow, or any day after that, but he didn't dare in case he weakened.

He was too old, too shop-soiled, too reprobate. He'd only bring her unhappiness. Besides, Cameron was coming home tomorrow and he couldn't jeopardize the franchise by risking her running back to Tony. It was his fault; he'd gone into the whole thing with his fly open. Not only had the prison door clanged shut, but he could hear a huge key turning forever in the lock.

One is one, and all alone, and ever more shall be so, he thought despairingly.

CHAPTER 39

Across at The Priory, by some lucky chance, a starry-eyed but slightly sheepish Maud rolled in at five to twelve, just in time to take a telephone call from Declan saying he was coming home tomorrow. Cameron would drop him off and, bar fog or airport strikes, he would be with her by twilight.

All next day Taggie waited for Rupert to call, and by some vicious twist of fate, as she cleaned the house and cautiously dusted and vacuumed around the chaos of precious papers in her father's study and put clean sheets on her parents' bed, the telephone rang incessantly. But it was only Archie calling to say goodbye to Caitlin, or members of the cast calling for Maud, or every member of Venturer calling to ask whether Declan was back. Each time, Taggie pounced on the telephone, and each time, like a stray dog dumped bewildered on the highway hoping each passing car might be her master returning, when it wasn't Rupert she slunk back in utter despair. And as the day ebbed, so did her hopes. Once Cameron was home, he wouldn't call.

The weather had changed too, and, as the gray skies closed in on the October afternoon, the black tracery of ivy fretted against the casement windows and sharp bitter winds swept the leaves from the lime walk and drove them in withered heaps along the dry gravel paths. However many sweaters she put on, however much she raced about the house, Taggie was still cold, while upstairs Maud oiled and scented herself for Declan's return, no doubt leaving a horrible mess both in the bathroom and bedroom, which Taggie had just cleaned.

In the kitchen, having put some green tomato chutney on to cook, Taggie was trying to find a place on Caitlin's incredibly skimpy panties to sew a name tape. Caitlin, having dumped papers and magazines on the table, left the orange juice carton out and her scrambled-egg pan unwashed in the sink, and was now peeling an orange.

> *"Give me to drink mandragora,*
> *That I might sleep out this great gap of time*
> *My Archie is away,"*

she moaned. "One day you'll be sewing the name Caitlin Baddingham and a coronet on my undies. Don't you think I'll make a good Lady Baddingham?" She dropped a deep curtsey. "I'm going to sneak out of school next weekend to see him."

"I wouldn't," said Taggie, breaking off a thread with her teeth. "You'll get expelled. Oh, for God's sake," she snapped, as Caitlin dropped her orange peel on the table, "can't you even throw anything in the garbage can?"

"Don't nag," said Caitlin. "When I grow up I'm going to live in a really messy house."

"What happens when you meet a fantastic man at a party and want to bring him back for a cup of coffee afterwards?"

"I'd go to his house," said Caitlin. "How can I live without Archie till next weekend?"

How can I live without Rupert forever? thought Taggie, getting up to give the tomato chutney a stir. She jumped as Gertrude and Claudius rushed in and leapt onto the window seat, bristling furiously. They were followed by Maud in a big fluffy pink towel.

"What on earth are you cooking?" she demanded in outraged tones.

"Tomato chutney," said Taggie, through gritted teeth.

"What a disgusting smell to welcome home your poor father,

and there are cows in the garden doing great splattering cowpats all over the lawn and the paths, which is even worse. They must be Rupert's. Call him up and tell him to take them away."

"You call him," screamed Taggie. "I can't do everything."

"Temper temper," said Maud, exchanging surprised glances with Caitlin. "Well, I certainly haven't got time to call."

Maud flounced off upstairs. Caitlin put a hand on Taggie's shoulder.

"You OK?"

"N-not really."

"Is it Rupert? Did you have a lovely day?"

Taggie nodded. "But Sarah Stratton was waiting for him when we got back, so I came home. He said he'd call, but . . ." Her voice trailed off. She stared at the great congealing brown mass of onions, brown sugar and tomatoes. Her mother was right. It was a repulsive smell.

"I'll call him about the cows," said Caitlin. "That'll remind him."

But when she got through, Rupert was on the other line and the secretary said she'd send the farm manager over at once to remove the cows.

"Rupert's probably terribly busy," said Caitlin consolingly. Then, as the telephone rang, "There, that'll be him now."

"You answer it," gasped Taggie. Please God make it be Rupert, she whispered over and over again into the vat of chutney.

"Hullo, Upland House Bakery. Which tart would you like to fill?" said Caitlin. "Oh Archie, darling, I won't survive either."

She was interrupted by frantic barking. Gertrude and Claudius shot off the window seat, taking the cushions with them, and rushed into the hall as a car crunched on the gravel.

"My father's just got back. He'd lynch me if he knew I was talking to you," said Caitlin hastily. "I'll write tonight. Love you madly. Ciao."

Fighting back the tears, Taggie went out to welcome Declan. He looked wonderful, incredibly suntanned from filming outside and much less tired. He was about to hug her when she was sent flying by Maud, a tornado of Arpège and desire, wearing Taggie's new gray cashmere sweater. Throwing herself on Declan, she buried her face in his chest so that he shouldn't see the guilt flickering in her eyes.

"Darling, you're so brown and handsome," she murmured. "I've missed you every single minute."

Caitlin, lounging in the doorway, whistled.

"When my love swears that she is made of truth,"

she quoted sardonically,

"I do believe her, though I know she lies."

Declan was too delighted to find Maud in such good spirits to take in what Caitlin was saying. "Cameron's outside," he said. "Come and say hullo while I unload the car."

Taggie's heart sank as Cameron came through the door. Like Declan, she looked wonderful. Her face seemed softer, her hair less severe. She was wearing a cream silk shirt tucked into brown suede jodhpurs above tight, shiny brown boots. Either it had been a highly successful shoot or she was obviously over the moon about seeing Rupert again.

Ignoring Taggie and Caitlin, she went straight up to Maud and hugged her. "Ireland was terrific, but we sure missed you. If you'd been playing Maud Gonne, we'd get an Emmy. Declan was such an inspiration."

"Really," said Maud, not altogether enthusiastically.

Taggie, unable to take any more, went out to the car, where she had no difficulty in picking out her father's battered roped-together leather suitcase from Cameron's Louis Vuitton. On the second trip she picked up a couple of carrier bags.

"No," said Cameron sharply, appearing in the doorway. "Those are gifts for Rupert and the kids. I must show you what I got Tabitha, Maud."

She produced a little leather pony, with a girl rider, and bridles and saddles that came off.

"Isn't it neat?"

"Lovely," said Maud without interest.

Cameron had bought a beautifully illustrated book of Irish legends for Marcus, and a pair of gold cuff links for Rupert, which she insisted on showing to Taggie.

"I'll get his crest put on later," she said. Taggie stared at her dumbly.

"Very nice, I'm sure," said Caitlin tartly. Then, looking at Cameron's jodhpurs, "Are you going for a ride?"

"I sure am," said Cameron with a sudden lascivious smile. "After three weeks away I need one, and not on a horse. I'm off, Declan," she yelled into the house, "I'll call you as soon as I know when we can see the rushes."

"Bitch," screamed Caitlin at the departing Lotus. Taggie shook her head. Cameron was the one Rupert belonged to.

Taking a bottle of duty-free whisky, Declan and Maud went up to bed. Taggie also went up to her room and, with trembling hands, tried to hold Caitlin's binoculars still as she looked across the valley to Penscombe Court. Enough leaves had come off the trees now for her to see lights on downstairs in the kitchen and the drawing room. Then, like a firefly lighting up the almost leafless chestnut avenue, she saw Cameron's Lotus storming up Rupert's drive. In an unbearably short time another light went on, which Taggie knew from Tabitha's guided tour of the house yesterday was Rupert's bedroom. No one bothered to draw the curtains.

Taggie collapsed on the bed. What was that expression her father was always quoting? *"The heart transfixed upon the huddled spears."* She knew what it meant now. Two minutes later there was a bang on her door.

"Go away," she groaned.

Caitlin walked in with the dogs, who leaped onto the bed, frantically trying to lick away Taggie's tears.

"You got over Ralphie; you'll get over Rupert," said Caitlin. "Anyway you may not have to. He's got to keep that bitch sweet until after the franchise."

"Bugger the franchise," sobbed Taggie. "What would you do if you saw Archie and some woman in bed?"

"I'd light a cigarette, have a drink and go and stuff my face," said Caitlin. "Look, I hate intruding on your grief, but the tomato chutney smells even more disgusting burning, and, as those carnal beasts won't emerge from their bedroom before morning, I'm afraid you'll have to take me back to Uplift House."

"There's a pauper just behind me and he's treading on my tail," groaned Declan the following morning as, reeling from a hangover and too much sex, he went through the pile of bills and endless requests from charity organizations for his time, his money or "one of his very personal things."

"Why don't you send them all a lock of your hair?" suggested Ursula.

"I'd be bald in a week."

"It's only because you're a household name that people mistakenly assume you're rolling," said Ursula soothingly.

"I'll be a poorhouse-hold name at this rate." Declan winced as he bent down to retrieve an unopened letter that had fallen under the table. "This looks more interesting."

The letter was from the IBA telling Venturer that their interview would be at ten o'clock on November 29th at the IBA headquarters at 80 Brompton Road.

Declan immediately swung into action and called a Venturer meeting the following week. The room over the nightclub in Cheltenham was considered too risky, so a suite was booked in an obscure Bloomsbury Hotel. For security's sake, a large board in the lobby announced in white plastic letters that the O'Hara, Black & Jones Drainage Co. Sales Conference was being held in the Virginia Woolf Suite on the fourth floor. The whole of Venturer turned up except Dame Enid who had a concert in New York, Janey Lloyd-Foxe whose baby was sick, and Bas who had ostensibly been caught up in some crisis at the Bar Sinister.

Cameron took special trouble with her appearance, wearing a new red silk suit with padded shoulders, a very plunging neckline and an extremely short skirt. This was because she was meeting Rupert's best friend, Billy Lloyd-Foxe, for the first time and she was determined to make a good impression. She needn't have worried. Billy came up to her straight away with that famous smile which had been described as "able to beam into millions of homes without the aid of satellite."

"Hullo, gosh, I've been longing to meet you," he said, kissing her. "I'm mad about "Four Men went to Mow." Janey's taped all the episodes for me. It's exactly how Rupe and I used to carry on before we were married. It was just starting in Australia when I left, and being marvelously received."

He was extremely attractive, Cameron decided. His light brown hair had gone grayer and he'd thickened out since his show-jumping days, but he had such a young face, and his turned-down eyes were so merry you didn't notice the broken nose or the doubling chin. He also had a sweetness and an air of life being hilarious. Janey was mad to cheat on him, thought Cameron.

Rupert and he seemed to know each other so well, they slipped into familiarity like a pair of old bedroom slippers, arguing about horses, finishing each other's sentences, howling with laughter at each other's jokes. It was nice to see Rupert happy again, thought Cameron. His fuse had been very short since she got back.

"When you come back to Penscombe, we're bloody well going to start a racing stable," Rupert was saying in an undertone.

"I thought we were going to run a television station," said Billy.

At that moment Declan tapped a large mahogany table in the center of the room and asked everyone to sit down on the row of chairs lined up on the opposite side.

"Where's the bar?" asked Rupert.

"No one's having anything to drink until we've finished," Declan said firmly.

Wesley's face fell. Billy turned pale. "What is this, a concentration camp?"

"Concentration—" Declan smiled thinly—"is what we're after tonight. There's Perrier if anyone wants it."

"Now I know why it's called a dry run," said Billy sulkily. "Come and sit by me," he said to Cameron, patting a chair. "At least I can cheer myself up gazing at your legs."

Billy, Harold White, Seb Burrows, Georgie Baines, and Sally Maples, the children's editor Declan had recruited from Yorkshire Television, then jumped out of their skins when an unknown man in spectacles with a crew cut and a purposeful expression walked in.

"It's all right," said Declan soothingly. "This is Hardy Bissett. He used to work for the IBA and knows exactly what sort of questions they'll ask us at the interview. He's going to drill us over the next few weeks."

"Who's that turgid old crone in the portrait over the mantelpiece?" Billy whispered to Cameron.

"Virginia Woolf," whispered Cameron.

"I'd do anything to keep her from my door!" said Billy. "What did she do for a living—belly dancing?"

"A fine writer," said Professor Graystock reprovingly.

Declan found Hardy a chair beside him on the other side of the table. Then he said, "The IBA meeting, as you all know now, is fixed for November 29th. The good thing is that Corinium's meeting is the afternoon before, so there won't be any problem for those of you who have to go to both meetings."

Everyone jumped again as a fat man waddled into the room wearing a stocking over his head, waving a blue plastic toy gun, saying, "This is a stickup."

Then he peeled the stocking off with a broad grin and said, "Boo!" It was Charles Fairburn.

"Oh, for fuck's sake Charles," exploded Declan. "This is serious."

"By now," he went on "the IBA will have digested our applications, our answers to the supplementary questions, and noted our performance at the public meeting. But have no doubt, the interview on the 29th is key. I'm now going to hand you over to Hardy," said Declan, sitting down, "who'll take you through the dry run."

Hardy Bissett, despite his bristly crew cut, had an air of officialdom which unnerved them all. Getting to his feet, he tapped the table with a pen: "This is exactly the kind of table you'll sit along during the interview, except the IBA table is oval-shaped. Facing you will be the twelve members of the Authority, with Lady Gosling in the center. None of them know much about television. They are worthy public figures, academics, business people. One of them, Mrs. Scott-Menzies, is the ex-Chairman of the Woman's Institute. Another used to run the Post Office. Another is an ex-Labor Minister of Edjucation. Behind them during the meeting will sit half a dozen officials who work for the Authority, who know *all* about television. They do not speak during the interview, but they brief before and advise afterwards, and will be watching you all like hawks."

Billy mopped his brow. "It sounds most alarming," he sighed.

Hardy Bissett continued. "One of the crucial things at the interview is to prove you are not merely a star-studded bunch after a quick buck, but actually capable of forming a workable and amicable team. As you will be sitting in an almost straight line and will not be able to catch each other's eyes, it is also crucial to work out in advance who will field what questions. Freddie perhaps should answer any technical questions, the Bishop should deal with religion, Dame Enid with music, Charles the arts, and so on.

"It is also vital that everyone has his say. One excellent consortium lost the franchise a few years ago because their chairman answered all the questions quite brilliantly, thereby convincing the IBA that they would be too much of a one-man band.

"All right." He clapped his hands together. "To begin with I'll fire questions directly at individuals. Later on in rehearsals we'll get to the stage when I can fire a question in the air, and the appropriate person will leap to answer it. Now remember, the interview will last at least an hour."

"I won't if I don't get a drink," grumbled Billy.

Hardy Bissett turned to Henry Hampshire. "I'm interested to know why as Lord-Lieutenant of Gloucestershire, you decided to join the Venturer consortium?"

For a second, Henry mouthed helplessly like a goldfish. "Because Rupert told me I'd make a fortune," he said.

Everyone screamed with laughter except the Bishop, Declan, and Hardy Bissett.

"This is meant to be a dry run," said Hardy icily. He turned to Wesley. "How d'you intend to retain the cultural traditions of the ethnic minorities in your area, Mr. Emerson?"

Wesley looked blank. "Don't know, man."

Billy wiped his eyes. "This is wonderful," he whispered to Cameron.

Like a terrier, Hardy Bissett caught Billy off guard. "As Venturer's head of sports," he asked sharply, "how d'you intend to revolutionize Corinium's sporting coverage?"

"Er-hum," said Billy helplessly. "Making programs is a bit like sex. I do it all the time, but I never talk about it. Programs are living things, particularly sports," he went on apologetically. "They seem to materialize as you go along."

"Very lucid," said Hardy so sarcastically that Billy went crimson. He then turned to Professor Graystock. "I wonder, Professor, if you might be able to provide us with a more serious answer to the question I asked Wesley?"

The Professor cleared his throat. "At Venturer we would naturally give the ethnic minorities the chance to develop their own programs in their own way," he said in his fulsome drone. "This will keep alive the cultures and traditions which would otherwise be neglected as the minorities become fully integrated into the population."

"Excellent, Professor," said Hardy. He turned to Freddie. "Have you got a definite policy toward industrial relations?"

Rupert got out the *Evening Standard* and surreptitiously started reading his Scorpio horoscope, which was all about career opportunities and staying cool in the face of provocation. Then, because he read Taggie's horoscope as automatically as his own these days, his eyes moved up three places to Cancer.

"As there is a new moon this week, you are probably wondering where the next blow will fall and feel everyone is against you."

Oh the poor little duck, thought Rupert, suddenly overwhelmed with longing and protectiveness. She'd been so adorable the other day. He never dreamed he'd miss her so much.

"Rupert," snapped Cameron. "Hardy wants to know if we've got an employment policy."

"Yes," said Rupert coolly. "We'll employ very good people. We'll pay them extremely well to work, and if they don't we'll tell them to fuck off."

The Bishop and Professor Graystock exchanged pained glances. Declan's bitten fingernails drummed on the table.

"Slightly too simplistic," said Hardy Bissett acidly. "I hope someone else has something a little bit more illuminating to say on the subject."

At the end of half an hour Hardy called a halt.

"That was absolutely appalling," he said bluntly. "Declan, you're fielding too many questions and getting totally carried away by your own blarney. So are you, Bishop." The Bishop turned purple. "You're both far too long-winded. The rest are too short. The object is to put across Venturer's message and make your pitch."

"Christ," said Billy to Rupert "it's like one of those terrible nightmares of being back at school. Who is this fink on my right who talks like a technical manual?"

"Professor Graystock," said Rupert. "Declan brought him in. He's a disgrace."

"We'll have another half-hour session," said Hardy Bissett. "Then we'll have a drink." He turned to Freddie. "Mr. Jones, how did the idea for Venturer originate?"

Freddie scratched his curls.

After that Harold White and Cameron were both excellent on program plans, Georgie was brilliant on advertising, and Seb marvelously bitchy about the newsroom and "Cotswold Roundup."

But at the end Hardy Bissett was just as scathing.

"You've got to sit forward, be eager and positive, bursting with enthusiasm," he said.

"Gimme a drink, then," murmured Billy.

"You've got just over a month to get your act together," said Hardy.

When they'd all got drinks, Declan gave them a brief progress report. "You needn't be too disheartened by our abysmal showing today. Elsewhere things are looking good. The most dramatic bit of news is that Mid-West have pulled out. They can't raise the cash evidently, so their Geography teacher will probably never get to London now." He grinned. "This means it's a two-horse race—just us and Corinium."

Everyone was wildly excited by this information, except Rupert. "Two two the rivals now," he thought bitterly. Why did everything remind him of Taggie?

"I've also heard off the record that the IBA have had at least three thousand letters from local organizations pledging their support for Venturer," Declan went on. "So we're on our way."

"So am I," said Freddie, going toward the door.

Rupert followed him. "Where are you going?"

"To a meetin'," said Freddie, looking shifty.

"With Mrs. Vereker?" said Rupert. "For Christ's sake be careful. Sarah Stratton rolled up at my house in hysterics the other day, saying James had been told to back off and concentrate on Lizzie, as they're going to make this marriage series together."

"I know," said Freddie. "Makes fings very difficult. That's why Lizzie and me's meeting up here."

It was two-thirty in the morning before Declan got home to Penscombe, but he found Taggie still up, laying out apples in an upstairs spare room. With all the bills flooding in, it might be all they had to live on soon.

"How did it go?" she asked.

"Awful, but Hardy Bissett says it's always ghastly to begin with. He'll knock them into shape. Billy Lloyd-Foxe turned up."

"Is he nice?" said Taggie.

"Enchanting," said Declan. "Exactly the right kind of person to calm everyone down. They're all getting incredibly twitchy. Rupert was flip and obstructive the whole way through the meeting. I don't know what's got into him, or how poor Cameron puts up with him."

It was poor Cameron now, reflected Taggie grimly.

"She was fantastic at the meeting," Declan went on with unexpected warmth. "The more I see of her, the better I think she is. In fact all the moles distinguished themselves, even Sally Maples, once she got over her nerves. And Charles keeps everyone's spirits up. And Billy, as I said, just has an enchanting personality, which is bound to endear us to the IBA. I hate to sound over-confident—" he reached over and touched the woodwork—"but if we don't do anything bloody silly between now and December, our chances of getting the franchise must be fucking good."

In the first week in November Tony Baddingham called a press conference. He looked on top of the world, the scarlet poppy in his buttonhole adding just the right note of concerned sobriety to offset the hedonistic effect of a splendid Los Angeles suntan.

He had been in LA, he told the waiting army of reporters and cameramen, to sign up a brilliant new woman program controller who would start in the new year.

"Assuming you win the franchise?" asked ITN.

"There's no doubt about that," said Tony smugly.

"Is she better than Cameron Cook?"

"I have no doubt about that either," said Tony even more smugly.

He went on to say that Corinium had set aside £16 million next year for new programs and pledged to have "an even fresher and more responsible approach to covering the region."

"The old fox is up to something," muttered the reporter from the *Mail on Sunday*. "He didn't get us here just for this crap."

"Why weren't you prepared to face Declan O'Hara on Radio Cotchester?" asked the *Scorpion*.

"Because Corinium prefer to rest on their laurels and not indulge in vulgar abuse and—" Tony lowered his voice, so the journalists had to crane forward to catch what he was saying—"Declan O'Hara might not have been quite so happy to face me had he been aware that I know everything he's been up to."

"Here it comes," said ITN, as Tony very slowly got out a cigar and made a great play of cutting off the end before lighting it.

"Declan O'Hara," he went on slowly, "has been poaching my staff. This summer he enticed Cameron Cook away, but as early as May he had signed my sales director, George Baines, my religious editor, Charles Fairburn, and my finest news reporter, Sebastian Burrows. I'd like also to warn the B.B.C., London Weekend, and Yorkshire Television, that Billy Lloyd-Foxe, Harold White, and Sally Maples—" Tony enunciated the names particularly carefully so all the journalists could get them down—"are also signed up and poised to move to Venturer in the most unlikely event of them winning the franchise."

There was a stunned silence.

"How the hell did you find all this out?" asked the *Mail on Sunday*, almost sent flying by the unseemly dash for the telephones.

"I wouldn't be chief executive of Corinium if I didn't know everything that was going on in my own company," said Tony grimly.

For twenty-four hours Tony left the three Corinium moles to sweat, and the whole Corinium building in a turmoil of rumor and speculation. James Vereker, for one, was absolutely furious. How dare Declan ignore him and sign up Charles who was nothing but a fat drunken fag, or Seb who was infinitely junior to James in the newsroom? Then James's fury turned to pleasure, as he realized that all three moles had their necks in the noose. He even gave several interviews to the newspapers, saying he was utterly disgusted by their disloyal, uncaring behavior, and he felt huge sympathy for Tony Baddingham in his hour of desertion.

James was therefore not the only member of Corinium's staff hanging around the newsroom waiting for fireworks the following morning, after word whistled around the building that Tony had sent for Georgie Baines. Seb was demented with worry, thinking of the loan he'd wheedled out of his bank manager for a new Ferrari. Charles could only take another gulp of claret and think grayly of his five-figure overdraft and the mortgage he'd just taken out on a cottage near Penscombe.

Half an hour later Georgie Baines staggered into the newsroom making agonized faces and clutching his bottom as though he'd just been given twelve of the best. Then, very slowly, he drew the latest Corinium Company Report out of the seat of his trousers, then roared and roared with laughter.

"Tony gave me an absolute bollocking," he told his amazed audience, "said if I have any more dealings with Venturer, he'll sue me for breach of contract, but it's made him realize how much I'm worth to Corinium. So he's doubled my salary, and made me Deputy Managing Director—so you better all behave yourselves, my darlings."

"Oh, how sweet," said Daysee Butler, bursting into tears.

"You're not joining Venturer then?" asked Seb.

"Not for the moment," said Georgie.

Seb was summoned ten minutes later and received more or less the same treatment.

"Tony's sending me to the New York office for six months to get me out of the way," he said. "Then, if I behave myself, I can come back. I suppose it's better than the sack."

"Much, much," said Charles Fairburn, draining his bottle of red. Feeling vastly relieved that he wasn't going to be out on his ear, Charles too obeyed a summons from above.

"Mea culpa," he said in mock seriousness, winking at Miss Madden as he sauntered into Tony's office.

Five minutes later he was back in the newsroom, trembling like a great white blancmange. Everyone stopped their reveling.

"Whatever's the matter?" said Georgie, who'd been tangoing in and out of the desks with Daysee Butler.

"I've been fired," whispered Charles. "On the spot, and he's not giving me any severance pay because I was warned three times."

Over at the B.B.C., at London Weekend, and Yorkshire Television, Billy Lloyd-Foxe, Harold White and Sally Maples, all ashen and trembling and mindful of their overdrafts and their dependants, denied any involvement with Venturer and were all suspended pending further investigation, and warned that the most tenuous contact with Venturer would mean termination.

The story was front page in every paper for several days. Declan and Rupert, as the best-known members of Venturer, were blamed for enticement, which no one minded about very much, and lousy security, which reflected badly on their management skills. Worst of all, Venturer was now left without a sales director, a program controller, a children's editor, a sports editor, and a head of news, until Seb, enraged by the cavalier firing of Charles Fairburn, told Tony to stuff his New York job and quit. This was all very high-minded of Seb, but now meant that Venturer's fast diminishing kitty was faced with paying both his and Charles's salaries. Seb would have no difficulty finding another job, but, at fifty-one and a notorious lush, Charles was far more of a problem.

Venturer, meanwhile, had been thrown into complete pandemonium. On the afternoon of Tony's putsch, Rupert, Freddie, and Declan met at The Priory.

"There must be a countermole, or how could Tony have found out all these things?" said Declan. Freddie, however, was scrabbling under Declan's desk. Then he took Declan's telephone apart.

"Bugged," he said bleakly. "I'll get my men in at once to sweep the room and check all the phones. It's possible the whole place is bugged. They better do your phones as well, Rupe."

Declan was appalled. "But how the hell did his men get in here to bug the telephone? The dogs would frighten anyone away, and there's always someone in the house."

As Taggie was out doing a dinner party in Cheltenham, Declan sent for Maud. "Has anyone called to check the telephones lately?" he asked.

"Yes," said Maud, "someone from British Telecom came last Friday; such a delightful young man. He said his mother's favorite opera was *The Merry Widow*. He heard me rehearsing and made me sing the Vilja song over and over again."

"What was he doing here?" asked Declan wearily.

"His department had been notified that we'd been overcharged, so he was checking all the telephones to see if they were using up too many units," said Maud beaming. "He said they might be able to give us a message refund. I quite forgot to tell you."

Declan put his head in his hands.

"How long was he here?" he groaned.

"About three hours," said Maud.

Rupert and Freddie exchanged glances of horror. If it hadn't been so terrible, it would have been funny.

"That was your bugger," said Rupert.

In an atmosphere of sniping and growing suspicion, each one wondering which of the others had leaked the information to Tony, Venturer carried on preparations for the IBA interview. There were secret communications with Georgie, Billy, Harold, and Sally, arranging that they would join Venturer if and when the franchise was won—it no longer seemed a certainty—but there was no way they could be present at the IBA meeting on November 29th. Night after night without them, therefore, Hardy Bissett fired endless questions at the rest of the consortium, until they were word perfect, and answered almost without thinking. Then he accused them of being too glib.

One evening Charles Fairburn, desperately trying to hide his anxiety about being fired, turned up dressed as Lady Gosling in a gray wig, half-moon spectacles, and hundreds of shawls, and proceeded to lay everyone in the aisles by answering questions in a high soprano until Hardy sharply slapped him down.

But the questions rolled on: "How d'you hope to promote interest in scientific matters in your schedule? What is your attitude about training programs? How will you ensure equal opportunity for women in your company?"

"By screwing every one of them," answered Rupert.

"Don't be bloody flip," yelled Hardy. "You can be funny, but never flip, and, with a female chairman, never never be funny about women."

Rupert was bored and fed up. Why the fuck couldn't they tell the truth, that they just wanted to make good programs and a lot of money, and dispense with all this shit? He was relieved when Cameron and Declan set off to Ireland for a final week's shooting. He needed some space and time to think. He spent most of the week they were away in London on political work and keeping the rattled Venturer backers happy. Outside his office the last of the plane leaves were drifting down, reminding him unbearably of Taggie. He still had the thirty leaves she and the children had given him. They hadn't bought him much bloody happiness. He steeled himself not to call her up, or drop around. He was truly terrified how much he wanted to.

CHAPTER 40

When Rupert didn't take advantage of Cameron's week away to call her, Taggie wanted only to retreat into her turret room in utter despair. But, alas, Monica had asked her to do the food for the opening night party for *The Merry Widow* next Saturday, and when she wasn't cooking and freezing in both senses of the word (now the cold weather had set in, The Priory was absolutely arctic) Taggie was calming down or boosting the morale of an increasingly demanding and nervous Maud. Corinium were showing highlights of the opening night and Maud was counting on Declan getting back from Ireland in time. She couldn't face such an ordeal alone.

In addition the Press were on the prowl for a story. Both Venturer and Corinium consortiums were turning out in force and dinner jackets for opening night. The newly fired Charles Fairburn was playing Monica's lover, Declan's exquisite wife was making her stage comeback, and her leading man was the handsome Bas who was on opposing sides to his loathed brother Tony. With Declan due back from Ireland with Rupert Campbell-Black's live-in lover, who was also Tony's ex, it was clear that there were endless possibilities for fireworks.

The *Merry Widow* dress rehearsal on Friday afternoon was disastrous. The presence of the television crew on a dry run threw the entire cast. Tempers flared, lights dimmed too early, lines were fluffed or forgotten. The television director decided to put two cameras in the dress circle and in the two boxes on either side of the stage, so they wouldn't have to take out any orchestra seats. The technicians stood around yawning, one sound man even fell asleep and snored loudly throughout the second act. James Vereker would be announcing the program.

Over in County Galway Cameron and Declan were at the end of their last day's filming. Declan in a dark blue fisherman's sweater and jeans, his thick black hair lifting in the gentle west wind, was speaking to camera.

"Hallow this spot," he began softly. *"Here once stood the proud white Georgian house that belonged to Lady Gregory. Here for the last thirty years of his life, Yeats spent every summer and most of his winters. That's a long time to put up with not the easiest of house*

guests—" Declan smiled briefly—*"even bearing in mind the number of servants large houses employed in those days. Here in this tranquil, ordered household, Yeats's genius was able to blossom on and on like a rose right into the winter of his days. 'I doubt,' said Yeats, 'if I'd have done much with my life, but for Lady Gregory's firmness and care.' "*

"Cut!" shouted Cameron. "That was excellent. We'll now do close-ups of the copper beech on which he carved his initials, and then straight down to the lake for the last shot. We'd better hurry. The sun'll set in three-quarters of an hour."

Twenty minutes later Declan was standing on the shore of the lake with a huge blood-red sun sinking gradually behind the colored trees and casting a warm glow on his face.

"While Yeats stayed at Coole Park," said Declan, bending down and picking up a pebble and sending it spinning across the still water, *"he wrote his poetry in a room looking toward this lake, a time lovingly remembered in his poem* "The Wild Swans at Coole":

> *"The trees are in their autumn beauty,"*

he began to quote softly,

> *"The woodland paths are dry,*
> *Under the October twilight the water*
> *Mirrors a still sky . . ."*

Oh, that husky, heartbreakingly sexy voice, thought Cameron, feeling the hairs lifting yet again on the back of her neck. They'd been so lucky with the weather too. Enough leaves still hung from the trees to pretend it was October, but one hard frost would have stripped them in a day.

The crew, going out to get plastered at an end-of-shoot party, tried to persuade Declan and Cameron to join them, but because they were both tired and faced a late night at *The Merry Widow* tomorrow, they opted for a quiet dinner at the hotel. Afterwards they sat alone in the bar. Apple logs cracked merrily in the grate, giving off a sweet cider smell. Occasionally the flames flared, lighting up Declan's face, as he sat immersed in the *Galway Post*, his whisky hardly touched.

Cameron was happy to watch him, memorizing every tiny black bristle of stubble, every deeply trenched line on the battered, craggy face. Without seeing the rushes, she knew they had made a great program. Schemes were afoot for other shows, but this first would always be the most exciting. Exploring and luxuriating in each other's talent, she had learned so much from him already. He had more charm than anyone Cameron had ever met.

Tomorrow, she thought, putting another log on the fire, she'd return to Rupert and reality. Or was it unreality, with each of them following their separate career in that huge house with nothing in common except the franchise, only coming together for sex in that huge pink and yellow silk-curtained four-poster.

She wanted to marry Rupert more than anything in the world, to tame and hold such a beautiful man, and have access to all that wealth and privilege. Rupert was her fix, but she was frightened how increasingly she was drawn to Declan. Together they could make an amazing team. He would understand her far better than Rupert, and she would look after him, and sort out his money problems far more efficiently than that parasitic, feckless, hopeless Maud. And what would happen to her and Rupert if they lost the franchise?

Declan looked up and smiled: "I'm neglecting you. How's your drink?"

The barman had wandered off and left the whisky bottle and a jug of water on the table for them.

Cameron was even learning to like whisky without ice; she'd be saying dustbin and petrol soon.

As Declan filled her glass she said, "This time in a month, we'll know if we've won. I was just wondering if there was life after franchise for me and Rupert."

The dark brooding eyes bored into her. "I'd like to think there was. I've grown very fond of you both."

"Honest?" stammered Cameron.

"Honest. Under all that bitching and stridency, you're as soft as thistledown. The only problem is that you may be too good at your job for Rupert. He needs a wife to come home to, not one to come home with."

"A stately homemaker," said Cameron bitterly.

"Partly. He must be the dominant Tom. You'd compete with him, and I'm not sure he could handle you becoming a star."

Then, suddenly, out of the blue, never having mentioned it before, he asked: "Why were you so fucking awful to Patrick?"

Cameron gasped. "I guess I liked him too much. I was scared. And Tony was pathological about any competition. All I cared about then was getting to the top, so I could have the space and freedom

I needed. There was no way a penniless student could be part of my plans.''

"I wish you'd read his play," said Declan.

"And I knew how violently you disapproved of me and Patrick," said Cameron slyly.

"Indeed I did," Declan grinned. "But I know you better now. He'd suit you better than Rupert. And he wouldn't cheat on you."

But it's you I want, thought Cameron, resisting a terrible urge to reach out and touch Declan's hand, and then drag him up the black polished winding stairs to her hard narrow bed.

Wondering if she was crazy to jeopardize what had certainly been their most intimate conversation yet, she said: "Maud cheats on *you* enough."

"Maud," said Declan, topping up his glass, "is a dramaholic. That's why she devours novels, soap operas, and newspapers like a junky. Occasionally her heroine-addiction spreads to real life, and she has to live out one of these romantic plots. It never lasts very long."

"Has she got something going at the moment?"

Declan looked out the window at the moon, peering through the bars of an elder tree like a prisoner. Then he drained half his whisky in one gulp.

"Yes," he said harshly, "Bas."

"Doesn't it crucify you?"

Declan shrugged. "Adultery isn't the only kind of infidelity. I'm unfaithful to her each time I get locked into work. I can't help myself any more than she can. And if you marry someone like Maud you accept the conditions that beautiful people are the blood royal of humanity and not governed by the same rules as ordinary mortals."

"She's not *that* beautiful," protested Cameron, glancing at her own extremely satisfactory reflection in the mirror above the fireplace.

"She is to me," said Declan simply.

Cameron wanted to shake him.

She got up to examine a horse brass, pulling her big black leather belt forward with her thumbs so he could appreciate the slenderness of her waist.

"Have you ever cheated on her?" she muttered into the flames.

"No."

"Have you ever wanted to?" she whispered to his reflection in the mirror.

"Yes," said Declan simply. "All this week."

Cameron stayed motionless by the fire until the heat from the flames became too strong. "Then it wasn't just me?"

"It's going on location," said Declan flatly. "When you create something you both know is special, it seems natural to have some kind of consummation."

"One devoutly to be wished," said Cameron fiercely.

"And ludicrously prevalent in television," said Declan. "It happens on shoots all the time."

"Not like this," pleaded Cameron. Turning, she went up to him. Idly he reached out and fingered the huge low-slung silver buckle of her belt.

"It'd complicate things," he said roughly. "At a time we don't need complications. Maud would disintegrate; I can't afford to fall out with Rupert. I can't afford anything at the moment."

"Don't joke. It's too important," hissed Cameron, moving her legs between his, pressing her groin forward against the palm of his hand. She felt Declan tremble.

"We'd be so good together, let's go upstairs now," she urged. They both jumped as the barman returned.

"Not much wind tonight," he said blithely, "but what there is is blowing terrible hard."

"You look frozen," said Declan. "Sit down and have a drink."

Fuck fuck fuck, or rather no fuck, Cameron screamed inwardly, as the barman collected a glass and sat down between them.

"You'll be being a bit of a writer, Declan," he said. "Did ye know there's another of your kind living not ten minutes from here? Anglo-Irish, name's MacBride."

Declan froze, like a dog hearing a rabbit in the undergrowth. "Dermot MacBride, he lives here?"

"Came in the other night. Said he'd just finished a play, but he didn't think anyone'd be interested. Thought they'd all forgotten him."

"Him!" said Declan incredulously. "Do you forget Ibsen or Arthur Miller? Have you got his address?"

"I've his number," said the barman. "He wanted some manure for his garden."

"Name's familiar," said Cameron.

"The angriest of all the angry young men," said Declan, "and easily the most talented. He made a bomb from his first play, then the second was so venomous and obscene no one would touch it.

He took umbrage and vowed never to write another word. Christ, it's like a new novel from Salinger. Give me the number," he said to the barman, "I'm going to ring him."

"But it's half past eleven," protested Cameron.

Declan was back, ecstatic, ten minutes later. "He'd gone to Dublin. I rang him there. I'm going to see him at eleven tomorrow morning."

"Cutting it a bit fine," said Cameron. "The flight's at one. Maud," she added bitterly, "would totally disintegrate if you missed it."

"I'll see him alone," said Declan. "He's not keen on women. I'll keep a taxi waiting and meet you at the airport."

He put his hand on her head, briefly stroking her hair: "We'd better go to bed, we've got an early start in the morning."

As Saturday wore on, Maud was increasingly in need of Declan. To fill in time, she went to the hairdressers, and even had a manicure, but her hand shook so much the manicurist had trouble getting the polish on. She also bought good luck cards for the rest of the cast, and some champagne in case by some miracle anyone came backstage to see her afterwards.

Arriving at the theater, she gave a gasp of terror at the huge lights on metal stands trained on the main entrance, ready to film the arriving celebrities, and huge cables running from these and from the cameras inside the theater. She felt even sicker at the sight of a make-up trailer, a mobile dressing room, and a double-decker catering bus for the technicians.

Even though the town hall was less than 300 yards from the Corinium Television building, union rules required all these facilities.

Going into her dressing room, Maud gasped again, but this time with delight, because she'd never seen so many flowers—from the family, and Rupert and Cameron, and the Verekers, and the Joneses and the Baddinghams, and so many of her friends in London. There were also scores of good luck cards including a telex from darling Patrick in Brisbane. But so much goodwill made her feel even more nervous. What if she let them all down?

She looked at her watch: five o'clock. She needed twenty minutes alone with the script to absorb the notes Barton had given her yesterday. Then her makeup would take an hour, by which time Declan would be here, and he could do up her dress and her jewelery and they could have a quiet hour together. But, as she tried to concentrate on the script, she was interrupted by the arrival of more and more flowers, and by Monica popping in to see if she was all right, and by Bas who'd brought her a fluffy stuffed black cat which meowed good luck when you pressed it. Maud was enchanted.

"And we've got time to rehearse 'Love Unspoken' just once more," she said.

"Let's rehearse it lying down," said Bas, who was feeling randy.

"Not before a performance," said Maud, shocked. "I couldn't possibly concentrate."

"Well I'm not risking you going down on me with chattering teeth," said Bas. "So I'd better buzz off back to the Bar Sinister and pay the wages. We're doing a roaring pretheater trade."

As Taggie carried great saucepans of chicken Marengo in through the stage door, she could see people gathering in the foyer hoping for cancellations. The advance publicity and the possibility of the audience appearing on television had made it a total sellout.

As she fell over cables and bits of scenery, she could hear, behind every dressing room door, the cast warming up like the record department at Harrods. She felt simply terrified for her mother. Once she'd unloaded the stuff, there wasn't much to do. The desserts were cold. The salads only needed dressing and she had just to put the chicken, the mashed potatoes, and the garlic bread in the oven to heat up.

If the ovens were turned on low during intermission everything would be ready, in case anyone was frightfully hungry, by the final curtain. Thank goodness Monica had provided plenty of people to help serve and clean up. As she came in with the last chocolate meringue cake, the telephone was ringing by the stage door.

"Maud O'Hara," shouted the doorman.

"My mother," said Taggie. "Shall I take it and see if it's urgent?"

It was.

"Maud," said the all-too-familiar, seductive rasp.

"No, it's Taggie."

"Your fucking father's missed the plane."

"Oh, my God, are you sure?"

"'Course I am, I was on it," snapped Cameron. "The next one doesn't land until nine forty-five. I've arranged for a car to pick him up and bring him straight to the theater."

"But M-Mummy'll die. She's been going through our leaking roof with nerves all week."

"Take care of her till we get there," said Cameron. "I've got to change, and then Rupert and I'll be over."

With a sinking heart, Taggie knocked on Maud's door.

"Declan," said a low excited voice.

Maud, wearing only a sliding emerald green towel now, sat at the brilliantly lit mirror, different eyeshadows littering the shelf in front of her, as though a paintbox had been upended. She had just spent forty minutes on her eyes. Huge, gold-green, hypnotic, impossibly seductive, like two separate works of art, they seemed almost too dominant for the heart-shaped, delicately flushed face.

"You look beautiful," said Taggie nervously. "And what wonderful flowers."

"Where's Daddy?" demanded Maud. "He should have been here five minutes ago. Is he parking the car?"

Taggie took a deep breath, and was almost asphyxiated by the heady smell of fuchsias and jasmine. "I'm sorry, he missed the plane," she said. Then, as Maud opened her mouth to scream, "But he'll be here for the end of the last act and the party. He didn't mean to."

Going into hysterical sobs, Maud put her hand up to her eyes and deliberately smeared the makeup all over her face, neck, and shoulders. Taggie winced. It was like seeing the Mona Lisa slashed with a razor.

"I don't believe it," sobbed Maud. "He can't do this to me. The one night I need him. He did it on purpose because he was jealous. He doesn't like me having the limelight." Her voice rose to a screech. "I can't go on, I can't."

Hearing the din, Monica rushed in wearing only her petticoat with one eye made up, demanding what was the matter.

"You *must* go on," she said in a shocked voice. "Don't be so jolly selfish. They're all coming to see you."

"He did it on purpose," screamed Maud, rocking backwards and forwards. "If it had been an act of God like engine trouble or fog I could have forgiven him, or even a crash."

"Oh don't say that," said Taggie, turning pale.

"And you can shut up," yelled Maud. "You and your father are just the same, never think of anything but your bloody work."

"That's jolly unfair," said Monica.

There was something almost obscene about Maud's daubed screaming face and neck, and her bare shoulders and breasts as the towel slipped downwards.

Monica yanked it up around her, tucking it in, as Barton burst in. But neither Monica's rallying exhortations, nor Barton's hair-tearing, nor Charles's jokes could move Maud. Finally they all lost their tempers and shouted at her like some operatic trio admonishing a wrongdoer, and Cameron, who'd heard a great deal too much in praise of

Maud recently, was only too happy to make it a quartet when she arrived.

"For Chrissake, Maud," she screeched, "you can't let the cast and the audience down. Don't be so fucking unprofessional."

"I'm not going on," Maud screamed back. "And why did Declan miss that plane?"

"He went to see . . ." began Cameron, then realizing she couldn't mention Dermot MacBride in front of Monica who might tell Tony, "to see someone very important about the franchise."

It was like a spark from the fire landing in a box of matches. Maud went berserk.

"All he thinks about is his fucking franchise," she screamed, her face a shuddering grotesque colored pulp of rage and misery. Turning on her flowers, she started to tear them apart, pulling off the heads and then the petals and throwing them on the floor.

"Shouldn't we slap her face?" said Cameron longingly.

"Stop it, Maud," said Monica angrily. "That's wanton and destructive."

"I don't care," screamed Maud, ripping apart poor Taggie's yellow roses.

In despair, Taggie went out into the corridor and ran slap into Rupert. Behind him members of the cast and the Corinium television crew were peering out of doors and around corners.

"Where is she?" said Rupert grimly.

"Oh, please. They're all shouting at her. They don't realize how frightened she is."

Rupert paused, weighing options, then, like a wand fleetingly restoring her happiness, he touched Taggie's cheek with his finger: "Go and get a large brandy, angel. I'll calm her down. Shut up the lot of you," he yelled, as he went into the dressing room."

"We'll have to play the understudy," said Barton despairingly.

The floor was entirely carpeted with petals now.

"She won't go on," said Cameron contemptuously.

"I'm not surprised, with you yelling at her," said Rupert. "Get out, everyone." And he slammed the door on them.

Rupert sat down on the bed and pulling Maud into his arms, gently stroking the silken shoulders, letting her cry, until gradually the sobbing and shuddering ceased.

"There," said Rupert encouragingly. "There's a brave girl."

"He wanted me to go to Ireland with them and play Maud Gonne," said Maud in a choked voice.

"I know." Rupert went on stroking her.

"I wanted to do it so badly, but I didn't want to fail again, particularly in front of Cameron. I'm sure she's having an affair with Declan. I kept imagining them meeting secretly after a day's shooting, and discussing how terrible I'd been."

"You're a dick," said Rupert gently.

"Declan fell in love with me the first time he saw me acting. I wanted him to fall in love with me all over again tonight."

"Declan adores you. He's never looked at anyone else."

"Then why isn't he here?" Maud's voice grew shrill again. For a second Rupert thought he'd lost her.

"He went to see Dermot MacBride."

"*The* Dermot MacBride?"

Rupert nodded. "He's written a new play. Declan felt if Venturer could tell the IBA we'd bought an option, it would really give us the edge."

Maud quivered with rage. "I loathe the franchise," she said tonelessly.

"Declan's only obsessed with it because he sees it as the one way he'll get you out of your financial mess. You don't want to sell The Priory, do you?"

Maud shook her head violently: "Could it come to that?"

"It almost has," said Rupert.

"There was a knock on the door.

"I don't want to see anyone," said Maud hysterically.

Rupert wrapped the towel around her again. But it was only Taggie with an enormous brandy for Maud and an equally huge whisky for Rupert.

"Thanks, sweetheart." He took them from her. "Now beat it."

Maud took such a huge gulp that she choked. Rupert didn't tell her that the Press were howling like jackals outside and that, if she didn't go on, the publicity, with both her and Declan letting everyone down, would be devastating for Venturer.

"I'm disappointed," he said idly. "I heard you practicing at The Priory so often. I wanted to hear it for real, and see the others make absolute tits of themselves by comparison. Look, you've had a shock, why not finish that brandy."

There was a long, long pause.

"Better not," said Maud shakily, putting down her glass, "or I'll start forgetting my lines. I'd do better with a drop of oil to get me through all those skylarking bits."

Rupert said nothing, but, reaching for the huge blue tin of

cleansing cream, he took off the lid, gouged out a white blob and very slowly began to smear it over Maud's face, blurring away the ravages.

"How did you know to use that?"

"I've watched enough actresses take their makeup off in my time."

"Most of mine's come off on you," said Maud, suddenly contrite, as she noticed his hopelessly streaked evening shirt.

"Treat it as war paint," said Rupert. "Later I'll be doing battle with Tony."

Docile as a child, Maud let him remove all the smeared makeup: "You won't leave me?"

"I'll stay with you the entire evening, but I have to admit making up your face is beyond even my skills."

Outside, Barton looked at his watch for the hundredth time. It was ten past seven. The press were howling for a decision. The understudy was already changed. If only he could make an announcement that the performance was starting late at least it would keep the audience happy.

"If she weren't going on," said Cameron, "Rupert would have come and told us."

"He was always good with difficult horses," said Bas, who had changed into his costume and was raring to go in and comfort Maud.

As her door opened, everyone surged forward. Coming out, Rupert put a finger to his lips, then made a thumbs up sign: "Has anyone got any eyedrops?"

"Mine are by appointment to the Queen Mother," said Monica, diving into her dressing room to get them. "They jolly well make your eyes sparkle."

CHAPTER 41

Out in the foyer, Tony was now welcoming the Mayor and Mayoress.

"I have to warn you there may be delays," purred Tony happily. "Declan O'Hara, who usually misses the boat, has missed the plane this time and failed to turn up on the night of his poor wife's famous comeback. She's gone to pieces and is refusing to go on, so the understudy is waiting in the wings. I'm afraid one really can't rely on Venturer," he added to Fergus Penney, "but at least we can all pass the time pleasantly enough having a glass of champagne."

Steering them through a door marked *Private*, he found his latest acquisition wearing a new black and gold dress to complement her newly streaked hair and sampling the Bollinger.

"Can I introduce Lizzie Vereker," said Tony warmly. "She and James are hosting our new series 'How to Stay Married.' "

"Norman and I could give you a few tips on that," said the Mayoress. "We're celebrating our forty-fifth next week."

"You must come on Lizzie's program then," said Tony raising his glass. "Cotchester's most distinguished married couple."

I can't bear it, thought Lizzie, allowing her glass to be filled up. In this dress she felt as though she'd been gift wrapped at Harrods. She longed to get out into the foyer and see if Freddie had arrived. Because of James's new uxoriousness and a general tightening up of security, she and Freddie had only managed to talk on the telephone this week.

Outside in the auditorium Sarah Stratton was spinning out the signing of autographs. Anything not to be trapped in the middle of the second row with Paul and thus not able to accost James as he came past.

As the five-minute bell went, Tony glanced at his watch. Seven thirty-five. Bugger, they were hardly going to be late at all. At least they could rely on the understudy to be perfectly awful.

"I think we'd better find our seats," he said.

Charles, wearing pantaloons so tight he felt he was standing inches above the ground, peered through a chink in the thick Prussian-blue velvet curtains, as he and Monica and the chorus, all in evening dress, waited in the wings to go on.

"It's absolutely packed," he reported in a hollow voice. "People are standing at the back and in the side aisles."

Taggie helped Maud pile up her hair with two diamanté combs and zipped her into her slinky black ball dress. Then, leaving Rupert and Bas to do up her jewelery, she slipped into her seat. There were only two empty seats between her and Cameron, but they should have been filled by Declan and Rupert, so the gap seemed wider than the Atlantic. Judging by Cameron's set profile it was obvious that she was seething because Rupert wasn't beside her, particularly as a smirking Tony had just rolled up with the mayor and was sitting directly behind them.

Cameron was seething even more that, after not seeing her for three months, Tony should catch her when she'd only had a few minutes to change and hadn't showered or washed her hair. She was wearing the red velvet jacket which Taggie'd tipped dessert over last year and which didn't evoke very happy memories either. It definitely needed clean hair and very dramatic makeup to carry it off. She felt horribly butch, but at least she didn't look as awful as Taggie, who was wearing a dreadful brown dress that was just the wrong length and made her look completely flat-chested.

There was a gap on Taggie's left too. Where the hell was Caitlin, wondered Taggie. She'd arrived by taxi half an hour ago and, despite promising to behave, had promptly disappeared.

All around, Taggie could hear the roar and sizzle of anticipation as the lights went out and the orchestra started. The cameramen, who'd been forced into dinner jackets by Tony, took up their positions behind their cameras, the soundmen made a final check of the microphones, as Caitlin, apologizing profusely, clambered along an irritated row of people and collapsed panting by Taggie's side.

"Do up the buttons of your shirt," said Taggie furiously. In the row behind, from the other side, having trod on the Mayoress' bunions, the Hon Archie, the bow of his black tie under his left ear, collapsed panting beside Tony.

Next moment Tony's annoyed expression turned to one of apoplexy: "How dare you wear a made-up tie?" he hissed, as the Prussian-blue velvet curtains creaked back on the Pontevedrian Embassy in Paris. The Ambassador was giving a ball, and the guest of honor about to arrive was the Merry Widow.

After a rousing opening number by the chorus, it was Monica's and Charles's turn. Monica, playing the ambassador's beautiful ex-actress wife, couldn't act for toffee. But by tackling the part with the same breezy competence with which she ran charity committees or bathed Labradors, she gave the rest of the cast a much-needed confidence, and Charles looked sweet in his tight pantaloons, swearing eternal and extremely camp devotion.

"My marriage is sacred to me," warbled Monica, to the smirks of the audience, who all knew she was married to Tony.

"If marriage is sacred to you," sang back Charles, lasciviously stroking her bare arm, *"there's not very much I can do,"* to even more smirks from the audience, who nearly all knew Charles was gay. And they liked it even better when his moustache fell off and he nearly split his pantaloons bending over to pick it up.

"What a lot of gold fillings Monica's got," whispered Caitlin to Taggie, "and, waving that baton, Dame Enid looks as though she's playing Stickie with Gertrude. When's Mother Courage coming on?"

"Any minute," said Taggie, who was praying.

Maud, clinging to both Bas's and Rupert's hands, stood shivering like a whippet in the wings. Although her black velvet dress was Turn-of-the-Century in fashion, Basil, for some reason, was dressed as a Regency buck. The longest legs in Gloucestershire were set off by gleaming black boots and pantaloons, the cut of his slate blue coat would have had Beau Brummel in raptures and his sleek black hair had been coaxed forward into Byronic curls. He looked the perfect Georgette Heyer hero.

"You look gorgeous," he whispered to Maud.

"So do you," said Maud, whose teeth were chattering loud enough to provide the castanets in the orchestra.

"You'll be all right," said Rupert, patting her shoulder.

And suddenly she was. There was no more need of Rupert's presence; she was really keen to get on stage. She must gather the audience into the play and say every line exactly right. She was only nervous because she was a young provincial widow, a little shy but heartbreakingly beautiful, about to be launched on Parisian society.

There was a terrific roll of drums, a tantivy of horns, and she glided into the glittering ballroom, standing deliberately under the huge chandelier so all her jewels sparkled and the audience could take in the beauty of her body in the tight black dress, and her pallor which only set off her red lips and her brilliant red hair.

"Gentlemen no more," sang Maud, pianissimo.

"I've never seen the Spring going to a ball before," sang a swooning French aristocrat, played by the bank manager of Lloyds, Cotchester. *"You throw us into ecstasies, lovely lady."*

And for once the words were believable. Now Maud was singing again, the exquisite voice hitting F sharp and clear as a bell.

"Shit," murmured Caitlin. "She's fucking good."

"Oh, thank God," breathed Taggie. "It's going to be all right."

I can't bear it, thought Cameron. She'd dismissed Maud as a sluttish, middle-aged parasite with unfashionably long hair, who dressed like a tramp, and here she was bringing the entire audience to their feet at the end of her first number.

Bas's entrance stepped up the excitement even more. He had a glorious, slightly husky voice and added just the right touch of rakish Latin glamour.

"Shit," said Caitlin again. "Lucky Mummy. He's *dead* attractive."

The sexual tension between Bas and Maud was incredible. Having dispatched all the competition, he was left alone on the stage with Maud at the end of the first act.

"Music so sweet," he crooned softly, dancing around and around her, tempting her into his arms, *"speaks to the heart and the feet."* And finally, triumphantly, he swept her into a waltz.

Elegant, incredibly romantic, they revolved under the chandelier until the curtain came down to a deafening roar of applause and a fusillade of bravoes.

After the first act, even though there was the Vilja song and several big numbers to come, Maud felt nothing but relief. It didn't matter that Declan hadn't turned up. She even sent Rupert back to his seat. She felt totally insulated. She'd been so petrified, and concentrated so hard on getting that first act perfect, that now she felt on automatic pilot. All trace of tears had gone. And although Charles almost stole the show when he bent down to retrieve his moustache yet again and his trousers split to reveal pink boxer shorts covered in pale blue teddy bears, it was Maud's night. When the final curtain came down she was cheered to the rooftops, taking curtain call after curtain call, as the whole audience, even Tony, were on their feet, yelling and clapping.,

Rupert turned to Taggie. "We did it," he said triumphantly.

"No," she said. "You did it."

"Don't cry," said Basil, as he and Maud took their final bows.

"You were better than anyone could have dreamed," said Barton Sinclair, pale beside the made-up actors, as he kissed Maud's hand and, to roars of applause handed her a huge bouquet of flowers that appeared through the curtains.

"I saw *The Merry Widow* in Paris," said Valerie Jones petulantly to Professor Graystock. "It was quite a different opera. But then it was performed by professionals."

"I wouldn't call *Die Lustige Witwe* opera," said the Professor, showing off that he knew the German title, "but I did think Maud O'Hara was marvelously in voice."

Maud rushed back to her dressing room to change out of her gold last-act dress into a blue silk suit she'd bought for the occasion. After that it was bedlam, people pouring in and out, hugging, kissing, and congratulating her. The champagne went in a flash. The press bombarded her with questions, but she was not to be drawn on the subject of Declan. "My husband's in Ireland on business," she said firmly. "He'll be here later."

At the party everyone kept coming up and saying how marvelous she'd been, but she still felt curiously detached, as though nothing could *dent* her now.

She was just going over to thank Rupert once again when she felt a warm hand on her back.

It was Tony. *"Even the ranks of Tuscany could scarce forbear to cheer,"* he said softly. "Couldn't you hear me yelling like a schoolboy?"

"Was it really all right?"

"Stupendous. There wasn't a man in the audience who wasn't madly in love with you. I'm sorry your husband didn't make the grade. But then making the grade has never been one of his specialties, has it?"

"Unfortunately he takes the franchise as seriously as you," said Maud bitterly.

"Ah," said Tony with an evil smile. "But the difference is, he's not going to win."

"Maud, my dear," said Monica, bringing forward a distinguished looking man in a leather jacket with graying hair. "I didn't tell you before, but this is Pascoe Rawlings."

Maud's jaw dropped. Pascoe Rawlings was simply the most powerful theatrical agent in London.

"Were you in the audience?" said Maud.

"And in total raptures," said Pascoe, drawing her out of the shadowy corner and under the naked light bulb hanging in the wings and examining her face carefully. "Yes, close-up you're even better. Look, Jonathan Miller's casting *A Doll's House*. Can you have lunch with me very early next week?"

The party was, in fact, a great success. James spent the evening holding Lizzie in front of him like a riot shield to ward off the advances of Sarah Stratton, and only let her go because he wanted to be introduced to Pascoe Rawlings. The next moment Freddie had whipped Lizzie behind one of the huge cardboard pillars which had stood in the Pontevedrian ballroom.

"This is a pillar of unrespectability," said Lizzie.

"I love you," said Freddie desperately.

"And I love you. James is going to London tomorrow night."

"What time will the children be asleep?"

"By nine," said Lizzie, "even if I have to drug them."

"I'll be there at nine-thirty," said Freddie.

In her mother's dressing room, on a floor of wilting petals, Caitlin lay in Archie's arms and had no need of words.

Taggie spent the evening removing plates, keeping out of Rupert's way, and sticking up for her father. It was not just Tony who thought he'd behaved appallingly.

"So unsupportive," snapped Cameron.

"He ought to have his knuckles rapped," said Monica, "but in a way that storm of grief seemed to enhance her performance."

"I always said you can never trust the Irish," said Valerie Jones.

"D'you think Declan's coming back tonight?" whispered Bas in Maud's ear at midnight, "because if he isn't . . ."

Everyone stopped talking as Tony tapped his glass with a spoon.

"On behalf of Corinium Television," he said suavely, "I'd like to thank our Mayor and Mayoress for being here this evening. I want to congratulate Barton and all the cast of *The Merry Widow* for a truly splendid performance, but most of all I think we should praise Maud O'Hara, who, under the most difficult circumstances"—he smiled at Maud—"was without doubt the star of the evening."

Exactly on cue, Declan walked in. He was deathly pale and still wearing yesterday's jeans and dark blue sweater. But such was his presence that, as usual, he made everyone else seem like pygmies.

Charles Fairburn, who was pissed, gave a very theatrical hiss. "Hullo, Declan dear, I'm surprised you haven't popped up through a trap door in a great puff of sulphur and brimstone."

"Good morning, Declan," drawled Tony, ostentatiously looking at his watch.

Declan ignored him and walked up to Maud.

"I'm desperately sorry, darling," he said. "I hear you were sensational. I knew you would be. There's a reason I'm late, but as I don't like some of the company you're keeping this evening, I'll tell you later. Let's go."

"But she's the guest of honor," said Monica furiously.

Just for a second everyone expected Maud to slap Declan's face. Instead she kissed him.

"Poor darling," she said, "you *must* be tired. Thank you all—" marvelously theatrically, the big star now, she turned slowly around, smiling at everyone in the room — "for a lovely, lovely party."

Then, taking Declan's arm, she followed him off the stage.

Caitlin, who'd just emerged from Maud's dressing room with Archie, shook her head. "I'll never understand that couple," she said.

On the way out Maud and Declan passed Rupert and Cameron. "Rupert saved me," said Maud, ignoring Cameron, whom she had not forgiven for her abuse earlier.

"I know," said Declan, "Taggie told me on the way in."

Briefly he took Rupert aside. "Look, I'm sorry I fucked everything up, but Dermot MacBride insisted I sit down and read the whole play. I didn't realize his mother was from Gloucestershire and the play's all about his childhood just outside Stroud. He's giving it to us, with an option on the next play. I'm going to fix a price with his agent tomorrow. It's a fucking good play."

"It better be," said Rupert icily. "You nearly paid for it with a far higher price than money."

CHAPTER 42

Six days later the Gatherum, which was the neighboring hunt to the West Cotchester, held their hunt ball in Henry Hampshire's beautiful moldering Elizabethan house. This was the last time the two consortiums would meet before their encounters with the IBA next week, and once again the whole place seemed to divide like the Dreyfus case. At one table sat Freddie and Valerie, Henry Hampshire, very much on his best behavior as host and in the presence of his wife, Hermione, Declan and Maud and Rupert and Cameron. Bas was turning up later.

Two tables away sat the Baddinghams, Ginger Johnson and his wife, Georgie Baines, with his long eyelashes cast down, and his wife, Paul and Sarah Stratton, and James and Lizzie Vereker. Although some of the women in both parties exchanged occasional banter and smiles, the men of one side studiously ignored those of the other.

Maud appeared to be the only member of the Venturer party in tearing spirits. The two subsequent performances of *The Merry Widow* on Tuesday and Wednesday had been just as successful. She had had hundreds of letters and telephone calls of congratulations, and yesterday she had lunched with Pascoe Rawlings, who was arranging for her to audition for *A Doll's House*. Tonight she looked stunning with her red-gold hair piled up, and an old-gold taffeta dress which looked suspiciously new, turning her green eyes a tigerish yellow.

Cameron, who'd been editing the Yeats rushes all week, and working hard with Declan on additional program plans to present to the IBA next Friday, looked thin and drawn. She was worried because Declan seemed suddenly distant. There was none of the intimacy they'd achieved in Ireland. Tonight, obviously hating being so near Tony, he was pale and edgy. As the only member of the party in a dinner jacket rather than a red coat, his black lowering presence seemed to accentuate Venturer's gloom and tension.

Cameron was even more worried about Rupert, who had gone increasingly into his shell since she'd come back from Ireland. He also looked desperately tired. The new Socialist majority was so tiny that the Tories were determined to contest it to the full on every vote, which meant endless late night sittings. The interminable IBA rehearsals, even though both Henry and Wesley were word perfect now, were also taking their toll. Even Freddie didn't seem his usual bouncy self. Only Valerie was appallingly unchanged.

"What are you doing, Fred-Fred?" she screeched, as Freddie started crawling around under the priceless Jacobean table.

"Lookin' for bugs."

"You're more likely to find woodworm," said Valerie disapprovingly. "I can't think why Henry and Hermione don't junk all this nasty dark stuff and invest in some decent modern furniture. And have you seen the state of the place?" Valerie had already had a prowl around some of the bedrooms, the long gallery and the grand staircase with its heraldic leopards. "All the plaster's peeling. There's so much damp, and you should have seen the moths flutter out when I touched the drapes in Hermione's bedroom."

"Didn't you realize this is a moth sanctuary?" said Rupert gravely. "You know Henry is Venturer's conservation expert."

Valerie looked at Rupert sharply. She was never sure if he wasn't putting her on.

"Actually I wanted to pick your brains," she said, lowering her voice, "about Fred-Fred's birthday. There was an article in *The Times* yesterday saying the latest thing in the hunting field is to have a brass flask of sherry attached to your saddle."

"Sounds hell," said Rupert with a yawn. "The only think I want attached to my saddle is my bum."

Valerie turned to Cameron. "You're looking a bit washed out. I don't think black's really your color. Why don't you pop into the boutique and buy something nice for all the Christmas functions coming up?"

"What's the difference between a shop and a boutique?" asked Henry, who'd got bored with welcoming people.

"They sell exactly the same stuff, but a boutique is about five times as expensive," said Rupert.

The waitresses were beginning to carry plates of smoked trout down the aisles. Looking around, Rupert noticed the place was absolutely crawling with beautiful, only-too-available women. It was just the sort of evening he once would have reveled in, getting drunk and behaving atrociously, not a cordoned-off four-poster untested. What the hell was the matter with him? He didn't even want to sleep with Cameron any more.

"Where's Taggie?" asked Valerie, picking up her fork. "No, leave your bread roll, Fred-Fred."

"Dog-sitting," said Maud, holding up her glass for more Muscadet. "I don't know what's got into her at the moment, she's so lethargic. I tried to persuade her to come this evening, but she wouldn't. She didn't have a date. When I was her age I had hordes of boys chasing after me."

"When all this franchise business is sorted out, we must all put our heads together and find her a decent guy," said Cameron.

"Don't be fucking silly," snapped Rupert. "You can't find people for people. Taggie's perfectly capable of finding someone herself." He put his fork down, his trout hardly touched, and refusing wine, asked the waiter to bring him a bottle of whisky.

Across at the Corinium table, Sarah Stratton plonked herself down beside James.

"You shouldn't be here," he hissed, giving her the sort of look delphinium growers reserve for slugs. "The High Sheriff's wife is supposed to be sitting there."

"I shifted the place cards," hissed back Sarah. "You don't want to sit next to that old bag."

"But you've totally ruined Monica's placement," said James in outrage. "And that means Tony's got to sit next to the High Sheriff's wife, which he won't like one bit."

"Serve him right for trying to split us up. I love you."

"Keep your voice down." James looked furtively around.

"I'll talk even louder if you don't let me stay. Surely you must have a program in your marriage series on coping with temptation? Well, you can bloody well research it tonight."

* * *

Home at The Priory, Taggie, having dispatched her parents to the ball, was wondering forlornly what to do for the rest of the evening. The only decent movie on television was Italian, and she wouldn't be able to read the subtitles fast enough to get the gist of it. It was a vicious night. The wind was howling around the windows, trying to get in out of the cold. The snow was falling steadily, already lining the window-ledge and bowing down the evergreens. At least there was a nice fire in the little sitting room. Gertrude, Aengus, and Claudius were all stretched out in front of the blaze. The logs came from their woods, or rather it was Rupert's woods now; everything seemed to come back to him.

How will I ever get through my life without him, she thought hopelessly?

She jumped when the telephone rang. It was Bas. "Taggie, babe, you're coming to the ball."

"I can't," squeaked Taggie. "I haven't got anything to wear."

"Fret not, I'll be over in an hour with some frocks."

Bas, naughty as his word, arrived an hour later with a back seat loaded with ball gowns.

"Where did you get them?" asked Taggie incredulously.

"Corinium's wardrobe department," said Bas. "Their security is atrocious."

"This dress is made by B-A-L-Main," spelled out Taggie slowly. "What happens if I put my foot through it?"

"Try the crimson one," said Bas. "It's much the best color for you and at least it won't show up the red wine that's bound to get poured over you."

"It's awfully low-cut," said Taggie dubiously.

Back at the ball, dinner was over and dancing had begun. Valerie, determined to demonstrate her dancing skills, had dragged a reluctant Freddie onto the floor. She was soon bawling him out.

"Can't you concentrate for one minute, Fred-Fred? I said fish tail not telemarque."

Through a swirling herbaceous border of red coats and brilliantly colored dresses, Freddie could see Lizzie in fuchsia pink being humped around the floor by James, who'd at last managed to shake off Sarah.

As they passed Tony sitting at the Corinium table, James deliberately pressed his cheek and his body against Lizzie's.

I can't stand it, thought Lizzie wretchedly. She'd imagined it would be better seeing Freddie tonight than not seeing him at all, but it made everything much, much worse.

Watching across the room, Freddie wanted to punch James on his perfectly straight nose and then whisk Lizzie upstairs onto a moth-infested four-poster and tear off her fuchsia dress and kiss her all over.

"Fred-Fred," screeched Valerie in his ear, "are you tipsy? This is a foxtrot."

Declan danced with Maud. Over his shoulder she glanced at her gold watch. Bas was very late. At the Venturer table it was plain to Cameron, watching Rupert pour another large whisky, that he was deliberately setting out to get drunk. People kept pausing to say hello, but, seeing the set expression on his face and the sinister glitter in his eyes, they didn't stay long. Cameron, acutely conscious of Tony two tables away, talking in lowered tones to Ginger Johnson and watching her every move, tried to talk to Rupert. A slow anger rose in her when he only answered in monosyllables.

Why make it so obvious that you've absolutely no interest in me, she wanted to scream. Was he deliberately goading her to go back to Tony?

"The next dance is definitely mine," said Henry to Cameron.

"Oh, good. Here's Bas at last," said Maud, pinning up a tendril of hair at the back.

"Good Lord," said Henry in wonder, his glass of wine poised halfway to his lips. "What a stunning girl!"

"She is pretty. Most dramatical," said Freddie, putting on his spectacles. "Blimey, it's Taggie."

Rupert swung around and caught his breath. There, undulating across the floor, rouged, lipsticked, her eyes vast and black-lined with kohl, black hair a mass of snakey ringlets, her shoulders, far creamier and lusher than Maud's, rising out of a ruched crimson dress with a bustle, was indeed Taggie. Everyone was turning around to gape at her. Basil, who'd been slowly stalking her for fourteen months, looked beside himself with pride.

Taggie was slightly overwhelmed by the sensation she seemed to be creating. Her only aim was to please Rupert. She wanted to show him that she had at last grown up. But as he stared at her, his face totally unsmiling, her courage failed and she gave the dress a desperate tug upwards. Then, just as she and Bas reached the Venturer table, the band started again.

"Lady in Red," said Basil in delight. "How appropriate." And, taking Taggie's bag from her and dropping it in front of Rupert in a curiously insolent gesture, he swept her onto the floor.

"I can't dance," pleaded Taggie, half-laughing. "I truly, truly can't."

"You can with me," said Bas, putting his hand around her waist. "This is a nice slow one to start with. This song could have been written for you, you are so so beautiful. *'Never seen you looking so lovely as you do tonight,'* he sang, *'never seen you shine so bright.' "*

"I find all this lipstick a bit strange," said Taggie.

"Don't worry, I'll kiss it all off later."

Taggie blushed. He was at least five inches taller than she, and so supple and strong, and with such a Latin sense of rhythm, that Taggie was soon following him perfectly in time.

"You dance beautifully," he said, laying his cheek against her hair.

"I can do it," said Taggie excitedly. "I can really dance."

"The Lady in Red is dancing with me," sang Bas gazing deep into her eyes, *"There's nobody here, just you and me."*

"Lady in Red, Lady in Red," sang Taggie dreamily and tunelessly, not knowing any of the other words. "It is a most gorgeous song."

"And you're the most gorgeous girl," said Basil, French-kissing her shoulder.

Maud was looking extremely wintry. Cameron was watching Rupert. His face was like marble, but the tendons on the back of his hand, which was clenched around his glass, were like underground cables. He never took his eyes off Taggie as she and Bas moved around the floor. Then, suddenly, as the music stopped and Bas bent his otter-sleek head and kissed Taggie on her crimson mouth, his hand tightened on the glass so convulsively that it shattered. Amazingly he didn't cut himself, but there was glass everywhere.

"My Auntie was so superstitious," said Valerie, as a waitress rushed in with a dustpan and brush, "that if she broke something precious she'd rush down to the bottom of the garden and smash two jam jars to break the run of bad luck."

"As Rupert's heart's just been broken as well," said Cameron viciously. "We only need smash one more thing."

"Shut up," snarled Rupert, pouring a slug of whisky into a nearby wine glass.

Declan shot him a warning look. Nor were matters improved by Bas arriving at the table with Taggie.

"Haven't I done well?" he said smugly. "I knew you'd be pleased, Maud darling," he added blithely as he bent down to peck

Maud's gritted cheek. "You were just complaining yesterday Taggie never had any fun."

"You look absolutely perfick," said Freddie.

"Where did that gown come from?" asked Valerie.

"Corinium wardrobe department," said Basil, lobbing Freddie's roll at Georgie Baines at the next table. "Suits her, doesn't it?"

"She looks great," said Declan proudly. "But make sure it isn't bugged."

"All the bug would pick up is the hammering of her heart because she's with me," said Bas, squeezing Taggie's hand.

Taggie glanced shyly across at Rupert, who was now looking at her with complete indifference. Suddenly she felt utterly deflated. Even with every stop pulled out, there was no way she could win him. But there was little time to fret. Next minute a thoroughly over-excited Henry had whisked her off to dance. They were just circling decorously when the band broke into "Rock around the Clock."

"Ha ha ha," said Henry, suddenly galvanized like an over-adren-alized tarantula. "I know this tune. There's life in the old dog yet." And he flung Taggie across the floor with great energy.

Every time he twirled her around he nearly pulled her out of her dress. She frantically tugged it up again. As soon as the band stopped, a young blood swooped and asked her to dance, and then another, and another. Each one took her telephone number and said they'd call her.

Freddie had vanished, ostensibly to fetch Valerie some Perrier, but he'd been away for three-quarters of an hour, and James Vereker could be seen hunting everywhere for Lizzie as he tried to escape from Sarah. Bas claimed another dance with Taggie and persuaded the band to play "Lady in Red" again. As he and Taggie danced past them, all the band stood up in salute to her beauty.

Rupert was three-quarters of the way down his bottle of whisky when he was tapped sharply on the shoulder by one of his more forceful lady constituents.

"I know this isn't the time, but could we have a word about the Swindon-Gloucester highway?"

She had a face the color and texture of corned beef and it was now very close to Rupert's.

"Bugger the highway," he said.

Getting to his feet, leaving her mouthing apoplectically, Rupert reached the dance floor just as Taggie and Bas were coming off. Grabbing Taggie's hand, he dragged her back onto the floor. Alone in the center, they gazed at each other. Slowly Rupert examined the huge, blackened, almost feverish eyes, the trembling ruby mouth, the quivering white breasts hardly covered by the crimson ruching. Adoring the way she looked normally in old clothes, with hardly any makeup, he detested this new grown-up, glamourous Taggie.

"What's the matter?" she stammered, stepping back as though scorched by the disapproval in his eyes. "I hoped you'd l-l-like it."

"You look like a tart," he said viciously, "and as you're with Bas, you're obviously going to behave like one."

Taggie gave a gasp of horror as, turning on his heel, Rupert walked straight back to the table.

"What was that about?" taunted Cameron. "I thought you liked little girls with bust measurements bigger than their IQs."

"I like them better than fucking American smart asses," snarled Rupert.

Spitting with fury, passing heraldic shields, suits of armor and antlers of several kinds of deer, Cameron fled to the ladies room. Rupert was a bastard, an utter asshole. But as she looked at her reflection in the ancient, dusty mirror, which should have flattered her, she couldn't blame him for neglecting her. She looked awful, and the black dress she'd thought so sophisticated and understated had understated her so much she was practically invisible. Why the hell hadn't she worn her suede dress? Savagely she daubed her cheekbones with blusher and emptied the remains of a bottle of Jolie Madame—what a singularly inappropriate name—over her wrists and neck.

Coming out into the long gallery, she saw Tony emerging from behind a suit of armor and went sharply into reverse. He was too quick for her. Grabbing her wrists, he drew her into an alcove behind a huge urn filled with blue hyacinths. She tried to wriggle away, but he was too strong. Oh why did that sweet, heady smell make her almost faint with longing?

"I've missed you," he said, as he regained his breath. "I've never stopped missing you. I need you. Corinium needs you. Come back to us."

"Don't be fucking infantile," hissed Cameron. "After the dirty trick you've pulled on us?"

"I'm going to bury Venturer," he said evilly, "and you'll go under too. You've no idea what I've got up my sleeve."

Cameron tried not to appear fazed: "You'll never get away with it. The IBA knows you're crooked."

"By the time I've finished with Venturer I'll look like a shining white angel."

Drawing her toward him, he slowly fingered her rib cage, then pressed the ball of his hand up against her breast, at the same time running the other hand equally slowly over her bottom. It was an act of assessment, not of lust.

"Dear, dear," he sighed, "you used to have such a beautiful body. Now you could do a commercial for famine relief." The hand still rotated on her bottom. She shuddered, unable to stop the squirming, helpless, revolted longing. Tony always did this to her.

"You're having Rupert trouble. I watched you tonight and last Friday."

Suddenly Cameron realized what the scent of the blue hyacinths reminded her of—the much fainter smell of bluebells in Rupert's woods the first weekend she spent at Penscombe.

"He's got the hots for Taggie O'Hara, hasn't he?" gloated Tony. "Everyone's talking about it."

In the distance the band was belting out "Mac the Knife." It was as though Tony was turning it in her heart.

"Bullshit," she said with a sob, and fled away from him, hearing his laughter following her all down the long gallery. Cameron was so distraught, she didn't see Declan standing in the shadows. Worried about her scrap with Rupert, he'd come looking for her, wanting to comfort and steady her. He was about to call out. The next moment he froze as he saw a man emerging from behind the urn. The glint of his huge signet ring as he smoothed his hair, and the almost orgasmic expression on his face as he passed, made him instantly recognizable.

Declan went straight back to the Venturer table, but found only Maud and Freddie.

"You was so dramatical in *The Merry Widow*," Freddie was saying.

"Was I really?" said Maud, looking very happy.

"What's hup?" said Freddie in alarm as he saw Declan's face. Sitting down, Declan came straight to the point.

"I've just seen Cameron talking to Tony."

"Just saying 'ullo."

"No, it was a long and very intimate conversation. She left him in tears. He looked delighted with himself."

"Shit," said Freddie. "It's Rupert's fault. He's been diabolical to Cameron all evening."

"What's much, much worse is that she and I have been working on the Dermot MacBride deal and the Royal Shakespeare negotiations all week. If she leaks those to him we're stymied."

"I still don't fink she's like that," said Freddie. "They was probably just reminiscing."

"We're off," said a voice.

It was Bas with his arm around a somewhat tearstained Taggie.

"You've only just arrived," said Maud hysterically.

"I know, but we've got somewhere else to go on to," said Bas.

Suddenly there was a shriek of excitement as Henry rode a horse into the ballroom and around the floor, followed by hounds. He had snow on his shoulders and his black hat and all the hounds had snow on their faces and their frantically wagging tails. Everyone came rushing in to cheer them. A hound trotted calmly up to the Corinium table and lifted its leg on the back of Tony's chair.

"Wish that dog was a member of the IBA," said Freddie.

By the time the hounds had gone, Cameron and Rupert were back at the table. Rupert, Declan noticed, had snow on his hair too and was shivering uncontrollably. Maud, too, seemed suddenly terribly upset, particularly when Valerie pointed out how keen Bas seemed on Taggie.

"Much better for him to find someone nearer his age," she said smugly. "Where are they, anyway?"

"Gone," said Declan.

"Where?" asked Rupert, looking up sharply.

"I don't know."

"Get your coat," said Rupert to Cameron.

He was waiting in the hall, glaring at a buffalo whose eyes were as glassy as his own, making no effort to conceal his impatience.

"It's not easy extracting one's coat from underneath a heaving husband and someone else's wife," snapped Cameron.

Outside there were already four inches of snow. As the long dresses of departing guests trailed over the white lawn, flurrying flakes seemed to blur the great house and a party of whooping young bloods, all no doubt with Taggie's telephone number in their breast pockets, engaged in a snowball fight. Cameron felt she had gone back four hundred years.

"I'll drive. You're drunk," she said to Rupert as they reached the car.

Careful, she told herself, as the Aston-Martin slid all over the road, he's reached that pitch of drunkenness that will erupt into violence at any minute. Having been beaten up by Tony, she was terrified of it happening again. But as they drew up outside the front of Penscombe Court, Rupert waited until she got out of the car, then slid across into the driver's seat and set off in a tremendous flurry of snow.

Sobbing uncontrollably, Cameron let herself into the house and, shouting at the dogs to get out of her way, went straight to Rupert's office and started searching. In the bottom drawer of his desk, under the lining paper, she found what she was looking for—that impossibly misspelled and ill-punctuated letter Taggie had written Rupert, thanking him for Claudius, and two photographs of her running in the woods. She stiffened when she saw the second. Rupert's kids were there as well as Taggie. They were holding her hands and laughing. The leaves were flame-red on the beech trees, so it must have been autumn, and Tab was wearing her puff-ball skirt, so it must have been this year. Shit—they all looked so happy. It must have been while she was away in Ireland. That was why Rupert had been so reluctant to have the kids over since, and insisted on taking them out on his own, in case they babbled on about Taggie. That was almost the worst thing, that she had utterly failed with the children, where Taggie had succeeded. Also under the lining paper, which she couldn't interpret, were a pile of faded leaves.

Rupert knew he was far too drunk to drive, but he didn't care. Anyway, he had always jumped horses when he was pissed, with that much more dash and brilliance. Unable to stop himself, he drove straight into Cotchester and parked outside the Bar Sinister. The roofs of the honey-colored houses were completely hidden with snow now. Flakes were landing like huge polar bears, almost obscuring his vision, but not so much that he couldn't see the lights in the apartment above the bar. Bas was plainly at home.

Christ—why had he been such a shit to Taggie? She'd looked so fucking gorgeous and he'd detested it because he wanted to keep her as his little teenager. At the back of his mind he'd expected her to be always there. Rationally he knew he must never make a play for her, that one day she'd find some nice dull kind boy of her own age to take care of her. But he hadn't thought the whole thing through or realized he'd be driven into a maddened frenzy of jealousy because she'd been stolen from under his nose by the second worst rake in the county who was probably expertly initiating her into the pleasures of the flesh at this moment.

He slumped on the steering wheel, groaning. He wanted to break down the door, to kill Bas, to drag Taggie back to The Priory like a father out of a Victorian melodrama. In his misery he didn't even feel the cold. Gradually the snow obscured the entire windshield and he had to turn on the engine to start up the wipers, when suddenly the balcony doors opened and Bas and Taggie came out. She was wearing Bas's red coat. Winding down the window, Rupert could hear her cries of joy at the beauty of the snow. Next moment Bas had gathered up the snow along the balcony rail to make a snowball and handed it to her, but she only managed to chuck it a few yards down the ghostly whitening street.

"Tell you never played cricket at school," said Bas fondly.

Then, drawing her close by the lapels of his coat, he slowly kissed her. They were so preoccupied, they didn't even notice Rupert. Totally sobered up, he drove back to Penscombe.

The rest of the weekend was like the Cold War. Rupert and Cameron were perfectly polite to each other. She worked on the franchise, he was off to Rome on Sunday for a meeting with the International Olympic Committee, but would be home on Wednesday night.

The only time she saw him with his guard down was when she caught a glimpse of him watching a Lassie film in the study. He was clutching Beaver and the tears were running down his cheeks.

C H A P T E R 43

After lunch next day, having scraped the frozen snow off the bird table and fed the birds for the fourth time, Declan had great difficulty getting out of his driveway to visit Freddie. The sanders had been at work on the main roads, but the side lanes were murder. For once the beauty of the black and white landscape held no charms for him. He passed several cars, totally snowed under, which must have been abandoned last night, and a farmer frantically trying to dig out some sheep. The sky was a dull mustard yellow, promising more snow. What would happen if none of the Venturer consortium could get up to London for the IBA meeting? Freddie's driveway had already been lavishly sanded.

He poured Declan a large brandy and took him into his study. The house was blissfully warm after The Priory. Outside, Valerie's garden had never looked more beautiful, totally hidden by snow, the gaudy colors wiped out, the vast rockery transformed into a mini-

Andes, the garden gnomes and the plastic cherubs fluffed out into creatures of fable. Even the serried ranks of hybrid teas had become a white army hoisting up fistfuls of snow. If Valerie moved to the Arctic, reflected Declan, she might become an arbiter of garden taste, a Vita Sackville-North.

Freddie was in terrific spirits, brandishing the *Telegraph* with a piece on the forthcoming franchise struggle.

"It says four incumbent companies are vulnerable and names Corinium as one of them. It also says: *'Venturer, Corinium rival, must be reckoned a considerable creative and management force.'* Then it goes on to say: *'Corinium are strongly challenged, and as a result their shares are selling at a substantial discount to assets.'* "

"I don't understand what that means," said Declan.

"Don't matter. It's good, believe me. We're on our way, boy."

"What are we going to do about Cameron and Tony?"

Freddie chewed on his cigar. "I can't believe she's turned."

"I don't want to, but we still don't know who leaked the names of the other moles to Tony."

"How was she in Ireland?" asked Freddie.

"Wonderful," said Declan wistfully. He was astonished how much seeing her with Tony had upset him.

"We've fought this fight absolutely straight up to now," said Freddie.

"Except for Rupert seducing Cameron in the first place."

"But so much is at stake now," Freddie went on, "that we'd better put a private detective on Tony and get Rupert to slip a tiny bug into Cameron's 'andbag."

The snow was falling again, flakes tumbling down dark against the muddy yellow sky, then getting lost to view as they reached ground level.

"She's got a dozen bags. Rupert's bound to bug the wrong one, and he's off to Rome for three days tomorrow," said Declan.

"OK," said Freddie, stubbing out his cigar and getting to his feet. "We'll start wiv a private detective on Tony. I know an ace one. Leave it wiv me."

Declan sensed that Freddie was anxious to get rid of him. "Where's Valerie?" he asked.

"Visiting her sister in Cheam."

"Do you want to come over for supper?"

Freddie shook his head. "It's not really a night to go out, thanks. I've got an 'ell of a lot of work to do. I keep forgetting I'm the Chief Executive of a public company."

* * *

Committing adultery, Freddie reflected ruefully after Declan had gone, made one tell an 'orrible lot of lies. James Vereker was spending the night in London at another Corinium dry run. Lizzie's nanny was away for the weekend. He must remember to call Valerie before he left, so she wouldn't call and find him not at home.

As he arrived at Lizzie's, he felt glad that the steadily falling snow would cover any tire tracks by morning. Lizzie was looking out for him, so no doorbells should wake the children.

She welcomed him in a primrose yellow silk dressing gown, rosy, warm and Floris-scented from the bath. The lights were low in the bedroom, but a fire burned merrily in the grate. Reflected tongues of flame lasciviously licked the ceiling. Making a mental note to throw away the evidence first thing in the morning, Lizzie said there was a bottle of Moët to be opened. Instead, Freddie opened her silk dressing gown and felt his heart stop. Lizzie was wearing just black high heels and a black corset which pushed up her breasts, molded her waist and stopped just above her damp blonde bush, except for four black garters holding up black fishnet stockings.

"You are the loveliest fing I've ever seen," murmured Freddie. "Come live wiv me, and be my love. Leave it on," he added as Lizzie started unhooking.

Kneeling down, he removed her shoes and, kissing her instep, slowly kissed his way up until he could bury his face in the soft marshmallow of her thighs. Lizzie bent down to take off his sweater and shirt, feeling his stomach muscles tauten as she unbuckled his trouser belt. There was a huge mirror on the ceiling. James adored to watch his own reflection when he made love. Beside his lithe and taut bronzed beauty, Lizzie had always felt like a frump. With Freddie she felt slim and beautiful and wanted to watch the whole thing.

The snow had grown two inches on the window ledge. Freddie had grown several inches and diminished again. The logs had died in the grate before Lizzie leaned up on her elbow, smoothing the red gold curls on his chest.

"I love you," she said softly, so as not to wake him.

Freddie opened an eye. "I meant it when I said come live wiv me and be my love," he said.

The following Tuesday morning James Vereker had a rare and intimate breakfast with his five-year-old daughter Eleanor. Usually James fled the din of little children in the morning and either had his mueslix, prunes, and herbal tea in bed or breakfasted at the

Corinium cafeteria after a workout in the gym. This week he and Lizzie were recording their second program in the series on the way children enrich and restrict a marriage. James had already written his script which began: *"As a caring parent, I . . ."* and was now, in between reading the *Guardian*, doing a little research into fatherhood.

Sebastian, Ellie's brother, who'd already got soaked making a snowman and nearly drowned testing the ice on the lake, was upstairs having his clothes changed by Jilly, the dependable old shoe of a nanny. Lizzie was working. Ellie was eating a boiled egg, dreamily dipping buttered toast into the yolk.

"I hope you'll watch 'Roundup' tonight," James said to her. "We're visiting the zoo and filming a new polar bear cub, which is called James after me."

"I saw Freddie bare the other night," said Ellie dreamily.

"I don't think I know Freddie Bear," said James. "Do the B.B.C. make it, or is it one of ours?"

"I saw Freddie bare," repeated Ellie.

"I heard you," said James patiently. "Is it a new cartoon?"

"No—Freddie bare. He was on the bed with Mummy. They were struggling."

James put down his spoon. "I beg your pardon?"

"I wanted a drink of water, so I went into Mummy's room. Freddie and Mummy were in bed. Freddie was bare, but Mummy was wearing long socks with her bottom hanging out."

James went very red in the face.

"Are you trying to tell me that Mummy was in bed with some-one—er—someone who wasn't Daddy?"

"Yes," beamed Ellie. "Freddie with the big tummy. He's nice, he brings us lollipops."

"You're not to make up wicked fibs," said James furiously. "Jilly!" he yelled. "It's time the children went to school."

Lizzie had the effrontery to giggle when James confronted her.

"It's not funny," thundered James.

"No, it isn't. Oh dear, I hope the poor darling isn't totally put off sex for life."

"Is that all you can say? What about me?"

"Nothing would put you off sex for life," said Lizzie.

"Stop being frivolous. I cannot believe you'd cheat on me with that dreadful, overweight, common little man."

"Freddie is a very nice man," said Lizzie.

"He's totally dishonorable and so are you."

"What about all *your* affairs?"

"They're finished," said James sanctimoniously. "And being in the media one is inevitably the target of certain attentions. Anyway, it's different for men."

"Don't blame Freddie then."

"Freddie," said James, working himself up into a fury, "is a member of the rival consortium. I feel utterly betrayed. And what's this about wearing long socks and your bottom hanging out?"

Lizzie giggled again. "It must have been my fishnet stockings and my corset."

"You dress up like a prostitute! Whatever for?"

"To excite him," said Lizzie simply.

"You never bothered to do that for me," said James indignantly.

Lizzie watched James catch sight of himself in the mirror. Smoothing his hair, he composed his features into an expression suitable for a wronged husband. He's just the wrong husband, she thought.

"I suppose you realize," said James nastily, "Freddie's only been running after you to worm Corinium secrets out of you. I shall have to tell Tony of course. We have to report anything suspicious. I shan't blame you. I'll say being somewhat unsophisticated and unused to male attention, you fell for it."

"I've heard enough," said Lizzie furiously. "Freddie is the most honorable man I've ever met. After you dumped Sarah, because Tony ordered you to clean up your marital act, she went screaming around to Rupert and told him everything."

James winced.

"Rupert was all set to give the story straight to the *News of the World*. It would have been a goody: *'Corinium stud ordered to give up mistress by boss in order to present image of idyllic marriage to viewers and IBA.'* Freddie stopped him. He didn't want mine, or the kids' names, dragged in; said it wasn't fair having them branded as the offspring of an adulterer—and a jerk," she added as an afterthought.

"You uncaring bitch," spluttered James.

"And what is more," continued Lizzie coldly, "if you breathe a word about me and Freddie to anyone, I'm leaving you, and then your silly marriage program's going to look even sillier."

The moment James left the house, Lizzie burst into tears. She was still crying when Jilly got back from the school run. In the end Lizzie told her the whole story.

"I'd no idea poor darling Ellie came into our bedroom that night."

"She'd have screamed if she'd been frightened," said Jilly comfortingly. "She was perfectly happy on the way to school on Monday; only interested in whether the lake would be frozen enough to skate on."

She picked up a table which James had knocked over as he rushed from the room.

"If it comes to a split, I'd like to stay with you. You're the best boss I've ever had, and I love the kids. I don't mind taking a cut in salary if things get hard. There, there, there's no need to start crying again."

Freddie was just going into a board meeting when Lizzie called.

"I'll come and get you."

"No, no," said Lizzie. "We've got to lie low. I don't want to give Tony any ammunition. We'll just have to play safe and not see each other till after December 14th."

"That's over a fortnight," said Freddie aghast.

"Well, we must try, anyway."

Freddie was utterly distracted at the meeting. When an outside director congratulated him on the new billion-pound deal with the Japs, he looked blank. When another informed him that the ex-Chairman, General Walters, had died of a heart attack, Freddie said, "Triffic news. Keep up the good work!"

Outside in the beautifully kept company gardens, the sun, like a huge red Christmas ornament, was setting down the side of a large yew tree. Freddie shivered at the thought that the sun might be setting on his relationship with Lizzie. Then one of his secretaries summoned him from the meeting. There was a call, she said, on his very, very, very private line whose number was only known to Lizzie—and now the private detective. It was the latter calling: he'd seen Tony and Cameron go into the Royal Garden Hotel early that afternoon. They'd spent ninety minutes in the Residents' Lounge. He'd walked through twice and there'd been no one else there.

Freddie's heart sank. He told the detective to keep on tailing Tony and immediately called Declan, who was utterly shattered. They both decided, however, that if Cameron had spilled any more beans, it was too late to muffle Tony now. If she hadn't, she was still too important a trump card with the IBA to be frightened off.

They decided to wait until Rupert returned from Rome tomorrow before tackling her.

* * *

After a restless night, Declan woke up to more snow, and, not wishing to risk either car, walked down to the village shop to get the papers. Yesterday at The Priory, they'd had a power failure and frozen pipes. Today the washing machine and the dryer were kaput, and it was warmer out than in. Three-foot icicles hung from the faulty gutters. The evergreens lining the driveway were bent double by the snow. Every blade of grass edging the road was rimed with frost.

The traffic was crawling so slowly that Declan didn't bother to put the dogs on leashes. Gertrude, a bit lame from the hard ground, still rushed into every garden and barked at the snowmen. Claudius, encountering his first snow, was wild with excitement, plunging into drifts, leaping to catch the snowballs Declan hurled for him. As Declan passed the white church, he sent up a prayer that Venturer might win. On such a beautiful day, one couldn't fail to be optimistic. But as he walked into the village shop Mr. Banks, who was a great newspaper reader, waved *The Times*.

"Lord Baddingham's been blowing his trumpet again."

Declan felt his throat go dry, his stomach churned.

"Page five," went on Mr. Banks, handing the paper to Declan.

"Lord Baddingham set for victory," said the headline. There was a very nice picture, taken from above and at a slight angle to reduce the heavy jowl. Tony was smiling and showing excellent teeth. The interview had been written by a well-known financial journalist.

As he was so confident of retaining the franchise, Tony had told him, he was only too happy to reveal Corinium's plans for next year. They were very happy to welcome three new directors onto the board, all production people, including Ailie Bristoe, who'd just spent three years in Hollywood and who would be Director of Programs. They were also very excited about their new thirteen-part series on marriage which, Tony predicted, would turn James and Lizzie Vereker into big stars.

It was safe enough stuff. Declan sat down on the snow-covered window-ledge outside the shop, obscuring the postcard advertisements for lost gerbils, cleaning women, and second-hand cribs in the window.

Corinium, he read on, had also made arrangements with the Royal Shakespeare to televise special productions of whatever Shakespeare plays children in the area would be studying each year. Then they would offer the videos for sale. They'd also be filming Johnny Friedlander's *Hamlet*, which had been postponed until the summer.

Shit, thought Declan in horror, those were both Cameron's ideas.

But most exciting of all, he read on, was that Corinium had signed up a new play by Stroud-born playwright Dermot MacBride, with an option on the second. There followed a lot of guff about MacBride's towering genius, and how happy Tony was to welcome this lost son of Gloucestershire back into the fold.

"We paid a lot for MacBride," Tony had admitted.

But, as the financial journalist pointed out, the publicity value alone would be worth thousands of pounds to Corinium.

Looking down Declan saw Gertrude and Claudius sitting at his feet, shivering miserably. Slipping and sliding, falling over twice, moaning with rage, Declan ran home to The Priory.

"Look at fucking that!" He brandished *The Times* under Maud's nose.

"Tony's bought Dermot MacBride's play. Cameron must have leaked it."

"I always thought she was untrustworthy," said Maud, who was plucking her eyebrows.

Declan's hands were so cold it took him a long time to dial the number of Dermot MacBride's agent.

"We had a deal. What the fuck are you playing at?"

"The contract hadn't been signed," said the agent defensively. "My duty is to get the best deal for my authors. Tony offered three times as much as you."

"You could have come back to me. I'd have matched his offer."

"He said if I talked to you the deal was off."

"That's the last deal I'll ever do with you," roared Declan.

"Never mind. I'm retiring at Christmas."

Through the window, Declan watched The Priory robin furiously driving a rival robin away from the bird table.

"How did Tony know about our deal?"

"Dunno. He phoned about five yesterday. I spoke to MacBride. We exchanged contracts this morning."

The moment Declan put down the telephone, Freddie called.

"Have you seen the *Cotchester News*? There's a bloody great picture of you an' me, an' Rupert, an' Basil, an' 'Enry—all in our red coats out huntin' wiv big grins on our faces, wiv a caption: *'Do you want these butchers to run your television station?'* "

"That's libelous," howled Declan. "Have you seen *The Times*?"

"Yes," said Freddie grimly. "Unfortunately that's not."

"I'm not waiting for Rupert to get back," said Declan. "I'm going around to have it out with Cameron right now."

But when he got to Penscombe, Mrs. Bodkin told him Cameron

had gone out and wasn't expected back until evening. Guilt, thought Declan in a fury.

Cameron got home around eight that evening. She knew she shouldn't have played truant, but, having brooded agonizingly about Rupert since the hunt ball, she felt she had to get out of the house. The heavy frost had made the white valley look so beautiful that morning. Why should I give up all this without a fight? she had thought. Rupert was an alpha male, he was exceptionally handsome, funny, very rich, clever in a totally different way from herself, and, now that she'd given him six months' intensive training on pleasing a woman rather than automatically pleasing himself, spectacular in bed.

A great believer in positive action, she drove into Cheltenham to the branch headquarters of 'Mind the Step,' a support group for stepparents and stepchildren, which had just opened. Cameron figured the subject would not only make a good program, but might help her love Rupert's children and understand her own tortured relationship with her mother and Mike. She had a long talk with the organizer, who then gave her several names and addresses. Driving around Gloucestershire, Cameron was amazed how many people welcomed her in. At their wits' end, hemmed in by snow and coping with stepchildren at home for several days, they were only too happy to talk to someone.

Listening to the shrill invective, to half-hearted attempts at love, to occasional genuine affection, to grown women blaming their own stepmothers for lack of love, which prevented them in turn loving their own husbands and children, Cameron forgot her own miseries. She decided it would make a marvelous program and was already preselecting the people to interview.

Like Declan on his way to the village shop that morning, she returned to Penscombe with a feeling of optimism. She found messages from Mrs. Bodkin that Rupert had called twice, Freddie three times, and Declan four.

She poured herself a large vodka and tonic and decided to scribble down some ideas for the "Step" program while it was still in her head. Searching for a pen on the kitchen shelf, she found the yellow sachet that had been included with the flowers Tony had sent her after he beat her up, which you were supposed to add to the water to make the flowers last longer. She wished she could sprinkle the sachet on Rupert to prolong their relationship.

With a lurch of apprehension, she heard the dogs barking in the hall. Not Rupert, the welcome wasn't clamourous enough, but it was obviously someone they knew. She went into the hall.

"Declan!" Her face lit up. "Sorry I didn't call back. I've had a great idea for a program."

"On treachery?' asked Declan bleakly. "You're an expert on that subject."

"What are you talking about? Do you want a drink?"

"No thanks." He followed her into the drawing room. "You seen *The Times*?"

"Haven't seen any papers. I've been playing hookey."

Declan picked up *The Times* from the table. It took him ages to find the right page.

"Here." He thrust it at her.

"What a crazy photo of Tony," she said, settling down on the sofa for a good read. "They've made him look almost benign. Oh my God," she whispered a minute later, the laughter vanishing from her face. "I don't believe it. How the fuck did he find out?"

"You tell me."

Something chilling in his tone made her look up in alarm. He had moved close and seemed to tower above her, his legs in the gray trousers rising like two trunks of beech trees, the massive shoulders blocking out the light, and, in his deathly pale face, the implacable ever-watchful eyes of the Inquisitor.

Cameron shivered. "What d'you mean?"

"I saw you plotting with Tony on Friday night."

"He was waiting for me when I came out of the john, for Chrissake."

"So Freddie and I had him followed."

Cameron's eyes flickered.

"You're not going to tell me you and Tony were talking just about cucumber sandwiches for an hour and a half in the Royal Garden yesterday afternoon," said Declan.

Cameron suddenly looked the picture of guilt.

"Sure I saw him. We had tea. I needed advice on, on—"she flushed scarlet—"a personal matter."

"You gave him all our program plans, just as last month you told him the names of all the moles. No doubt he's got lots of other info about Venturer up his pinstriped sleeve for the meeting tomorrow."

Cameron looked furious and terrified now—the hawk cornered by her captor about to strike.

"I didn't tell him anything."

"You bloody liar," thundered Declan. "How long have you been spying for him? Ever since the beginning, since Rupert got his leg-over in Madrid?"

"How could I possibly spy for Tony?" she screamed. "He beat me up, for Chrissake. This"—she waved *The Times* piece at Declan—"sabotages everything we've worked for. Someone else leaked it."

"Why go to London on the worst day of the winter?" snarled Declan.

Blue, the lurcher, who'd been hovering nervously, jumped up on the sofa beside Cameron and, glaring at Declan, started to whine querulously at him. The other dogs licked their lips. Beaver slunk out of the room.

"Blue believes me," pleaded Cameron. "Why the fuck should I come to Ireland, not to mention the program plans, if I was spying for Tony? He's given my old job to Ailie Bristoe."

"That's a front."

"Bullshit," said Cameron furiously. "Is this some kind of a nightmare? Are you back at Corinium? Am I your guest tonight? Where's the fucking thumbscrews and the rack, or do you use electrodes and knee-capping like the fucking IRA?"

Grabbing her arm, Declan yanked her to her feet.

"No one else knew about Dermot MacBride. How much else have you told him?"

Ignoring the low growl from Blue, he started to shake her like a rat.

"You arrogant, pig-headed Irish asshole," yelled Cameron. "Why don't you believe me?"

Maddened because she'd let him down, violent because he felt guilty about wanting her so much, Declan slapped her very hard across the face. The next minute Blue leapt at him, burying his teeth in Declan's arm.

"Leave!" screamed Cameron. "Leave, Blue." Grabbing the dog's collar she tugged him off, then, almost carrying him back onto the sofa beside her, collapsed sobbing into his shaggy coat.

Pulling himself together, Declan lit two cigarettes, but, as he handed one to Cameron, Blue gave another ominous growl.

"It's OK, boy," gasped Cameron.

She wiped her eyes frantically on her sleeve, then took the lighted cigarette. Inhaling deeply, she felt she was drawing the fires of hell into her lungs. Blue struggled up on his front paws and licked her face.

"My only friend," she said tonelessly. "You'd better have a tet-anus shot," she added to Declan.

Massaging his arm, Declan retreated to a respectable distance in front of the empty fireplace.

"OK, what was the personal problem? And why Tony?"

"I know he's a shit, but sometimes I figure he's the only person in the world who cares about me."

"After beating you up?"

Cameron fingered her reddened cheek and shrugged. "Seems to be catching."

"I'm sorry."

Cameron took a deep breath. "I saw Tony because Rupert doesn't love me any more, and I can't handle it."

"Just because he was bloody-minded at the ball," said Declan scornfully. "We're all uptight at the moment."

Cameron's lip was trembling again. "Rupert doesn't give a shit about the franchise. All he cares about is Taggie."

"Taggie," said Declan, flabbergasted. "My Taggie? Are you out of your mind?"

"He saw her when we were in Ireland. In his bottom desk drawer, under the lining paper, he's hidden pictures of her with his kids." Cameron gave a sob. "And he's also kept some totally illiterate thank-you letter she sent him."

Declan was utterly appalled.

"Rupert and Taggie," he growled so furiously that Blue started rumbling back at him, like rival storms across a valley. "I'm not hav-ing that profligate bastard laying a finger on Taggie."

"But it's OK for him to finger me," hissed Cameron. "I'm only a mole."

Earlier that afternoon Rupert had flown in from Rome and gone straight to his office in Whitehall. Ignoring a long list of telephone messages, he signed his letters, gathered up the rest of the mail, made sure he was paired for the Finance debate that evening, and set out for Gloucestershire. Slumped in the corner of a first-class carriage with his hand around a large Scotch, he looked at the snowy land-scape turned electric blue in the twilight. Even in London it wasn't thawing. It had been a wasted visit to Rome. He'd made no contri-bution to the International Olympics Conference. He hadn't been able to sleep, or eat, or think straight, he was so haunted by the image of Taggie and Basil on the Bar Sinister balcony, or of Taggie's gasping with pleasure in Basil's expert embrace.

He tried to concentrate on the *Standard*, but beyond the fact that Corinium shares had unaccountably rocketed, he couldn't take anything in. Sitting opposite, an enchanting blonde was eyeing him with discreet but definite interest. Glancing at her slim knees above very shiny black boots, Rupert reflected that by now, in the old days, he would have bought her a large vodka and tonic and been investigating the prospect of a quick bang at the Station Hotel, Cotchester—if not at Penscombe. What the hell was happening to him?

Unknown to him, Taggie was slumped, shivering and equally miserable, in a second-class carriage on the same train. She'd been doing an early Christmas lunch for some overseas sales reps in Swindon which seemed to go on forever. She always found train trips unnerving, having to read all the strange station names and the platform directions and the train times. Today by mistake she'd got on a train going back to London and had to get off and wait in quite inadequate clothing on Didcot station for half an hour.

Maud had borrowed Taggie's car to buy a new dress for her audition for *A Doll's House* tomorrow. She'd promised to meet Taggie at Cotchester if Taggie called and told her what train she was coming on. But when Taggie had tried to call, there was no answer.

Rupert thought he was dreaming when he saw Taggie ahead of him on the platform at Cotchester. The snakey curls had dropped; she was back to her old ponytail. As she turned to hand in her ticket, under the overhead light bulb he noticed the black shadows under her eyes. Too much sex, he thought savagely.

No one was there to meet her; there were no taxis; the telephone didn't work. Peering out through the square glass panes, Taggie's legs nearly gave way beneath her as she saw Rupert getting into his car. Rushing out into the street, she waved at him. There was a moment of blind hope as she thought he waved back as he stormed past spraying snow all over her, but he was only adjusting his driving mirror. The next minute his car skidded to a halt beside her.

"What the hell are you doing?"

"Trying to find a telephone to ring Mummy," she muttered through furiously chattering teeth.

"Get in," said Rupert. Viciously he punched out the number he knew so well. He let the telephone ring for two minutes. There was no answer.

"Mummy's on the toot as usual," he said. "I'll run you home."

"Oh please don't bother."

"It's not exactly out of my way," he said sarcastically.

The frozen snow twinkled like rhinestones in the moonlight. Once they'd got out of Cotchester onto the country lanes there was only room for single-lane traffic between the huge polar drifts. They didn't speak for a few miles, then, glancing sideways, Rupert saw the tears pouring down her face.

"What the fuck's the matter now?"

"I thought we were friends."

"Then why did you go to bed with Bas?"

"I didn't. I meant to, because I was so miserable about you. I thought if I got some really good experience, you might fancy me a bit, but when it came to the crunch, I couldn't do it. I love you too much."

Rupert stopped the car, pulling into a gateway.

"I'm desperately sorry," sobbed Taggie, groping in her bag for a tissue. "I know it must be boring having every woman you meet in love with you. I didn't want to be one of them. I've tried so hard to get over you. Work doesn't help at all. It's just that you've been so kind looking after us, sorting Mummy out the other night and getting all that food when I spoiled Sarah Stratton's dinner party, and giving me all those lovely things, and buying the woods for far more than they're worth."

"Who told you that?" said Rupert, appalled.

"Ursula did. She saw Daddy's bank statement. It was the only good thing in it. I'm sorry for being such a drip."

Rupert raised clenched fists to his temples in a superhuman effort not to reach out for her. Taggie mistook the gesture for sheer horror at being propositioned by yet another girl.

"I'm sorry."

"For Christ's sake stop apologizing." Rupert started speaking very slowly and deliberately as if he was addressing some loopy foreigner. "Look, it wouldn't work. I'm terribly fond of you, Tag, but I'm far too old. Remember that hamburger bar manager who thought you were my daughter? I've never been faithful to anyone for more than a few weeks, and I'm not going to ruin your life by having a brief fling with you."

"My life's ruined already," sobbed Taggie, who'd soaked one tissue and was desperately searching in her pockets for another.

"You'll get over me," said Rupert, handing her his handkerchief.

"Like that five-bar gate in front of us," said Taggie helplessly.

The Priory was in darkness when they got back.

"Tell your father I'll call him later," said Rupert, cannoning off a low wall in his haste to get away.

Across the valley he could see lights on in his house. He couldn't face Cameron at the moment. Mindlessly he drove back to Cotchester and parked outside Basil's flat.

One look at Rupert's set white face was enough. Bas poured him a large whisky.

"Taggie said there wasn't a leg-over situation."

"There wasn't," said Bas. "Not through lack of trying on my part. She is utterly adorable, but she utterly adores someone else, you lucky sod."

Rupert drained his whisky.

"I'm not going to do anything about her."

"Why ever not?" said Bas incredulously. "It's on a plate."

"I'm too old, shopworn, evil . . ."

"Oh don't be so fucking self-indulgent. All these histrionics and tantrums are just the last frantic struggles of the lassooed bronco. You've never been in love before. It's really very nice, if you stop fighting it. Everyone's got to hang up their condom sometime. Taggie'd be worth it."

"I don't want to talk about it."

"OK," said Bas, filling up their glasses.

"Am I interrupting you?"

"Not excessively. I was just looking at the books. The Bar's had a staggering year, thanks to all those malcontents from Corinium drowning their sorrows and plotting my big brother's downfall. Won't be so good next year, with you and Freddie and Declan running things. They'll all be working so hard, they won't have time for a lunch hour. D'you really think we'll get it?"

" 'Course we will," said Rupert, thinking he really didn't give a fuck anymore.

Bas shook his head. "Tony gave a bloody good interview to *The Times* this morning. Came across as Mr. Caring." He threw the paper in Rupert's direction.

Rupert ignored it. "Did she really say she loved me?"

"Yes, she did, which I find embarrassing, knowing you as I do."

Rupert shook his head in bewilderment.

"It's never, never hit me like this before either. I'm still not going to do anything about it."

Up in London that night the fourteen directors and senior staff of Corinium television had an extremely successful final dry run before their meeting at the IBA the next afternoon. Tony, in a new dark blue pin-striped suit paid for by Corinium, was in coruscating form.

"They can have one drink," he told Ginger Johnson beforehand, "and then not one drop until we've been around the course—and I'm going to grill then."

No one at the meeting tomorrow, he said, was to speak until he'd introduced them. There was now, as a result of recent hiring and firing, a most satisfactory preponderance of ex-production people on the board who would do most of the talking. The money-men, like Ginger and Georgie Baines, who brought in the vast advertising revenue, would keep a low profile. In fact it would be better if the word "profit" were not mentioned at all. All the men had had haircuts.

"No doubt," muttered Sarah Stratton to James Vereker, "there will be a nail inspection in the morning."

Afterwards they all dined wisely but not too well at the Carlton Towers, where they were staying overnight. No shellfish was allowed, nor liqueurs after dinner. Everyone was very impressed with Ailie Bristoe, the new Program Controller, who'd flown over from Hollywood for the occasion, and seemed as beautiful as she was bright. James Vereker thought she looked very caring.

"I'm surprised Tony hasn't put the women in separate hotels," grumbled Sarah, as they were all sent up to bed early.

"Be sure to order a *Scorpion* for tomorrow," was Tony's parting shot. "You'll all find it very interesting reading."

Back in Gloucestershire, Declan finally stormed out of The Priory around ten o'clock, having failed to get a confession out of Cameron. Utterly devastated that he and Freddie could possibly think she was a spy, Cameron was slumped on the sofa, still cuddling Blue when the telephone rang. It was some girl, saying Rupert wouldn't be back until the morning, but he sent his love. There was a terrific din in the background and the girl sounded as though she was phoning from a bar. Bastard, thought Cameron, but she was too proud to ask where he was. As she put the telephone down it rang again.

"Can I speak to Rupert Campbell-Black?"

"He's not here."

"Is that Cameron Cook?"

"This is she."

The voice thickened and became oily as though it was asking for extended credit.

"This is the *Messenger* here. Wondered what you feel about Rupert's memoirs in the *Scorpion*."

"I don't know what you're talking about."

"Rupert's really done it this time. Bloody bad timing on the day before your IBA meeting."

Cameron had had a long day and was not connecting well but gradually it sunk in that Beattie Johnson had finally got her revenge on Rupert by telling all to the *Scorpion*. Not only, according to the *Messenger* reporter, had she produced every kind of salacious detail about her two years with Rupert and the unbelievably kinky things they'd done, but, even worse, revealed intimate details of his sex life with other women, including Helen.

"Oh my God!" whispered Cameron. "Does he mention me?"

"Not yet, sweetheart," said the reporter, who'd already seen and admired Cameron's photograph, "but you may be in Saturday's installment. They're trailing the spread that's going out on Friday, the morning you go to the IBA. It's all about Rupert's affair with Amanda Hamilton, wife of the shadow Foreign Secretary. Very pretty lady, evidently she liked being spanked."

Cameron groaned.

"And there's a particularly damaging bit tomorrow," said the reporter, who was beginning to enjoy himself. "I'll read it."

"I don't want to hear any more," screamed Cameron, slamming down the receiver. It rang again. It was the *Sun*.

"Go away," she screamed.

Immediately she'd put down the receiver, she dialed out.

"Fuck off, all of you," snarled a voice.

"Declan, it's Cameron. Have you heard about Rupert's memoirs?"

"Yes," said Declan, "and I don't know where the fuck to get hold of him."

"Nor do I," sobbed Cameron.

The trucks rumbling along Cotchester High Street woke Rupert the next morning to the worst hangover in recorded history. Moaning, he pulled the blankets over his head. There was a knock on the door.

"Bugger off. I feel terrible."

"You're not going to feel any better when you read this," said Bas, handing him a Fernet Branca and the *Scorpion*, which Rupert read in silence.

"The dirty bitch," he said softly. "She said she'd get me in the end."

It was as though some terrible monster from his past had put a hand up from a manhole and dragged him down into the mire and slime below. He went straight to the bathroom and threw up.

"Lend me a toothbrush, and then a telephone," he said to Bas. He was put straight through to Freddie.

"Look, I've only just seen the *Scorpion*. I'm ringing up to re-sign."

"Don't be daft," said Freddie.

"I've got to. There are two more days to go, and it's bound to get worse. Unless I pull out, there's no way you'll get the franchise."

"Don't be rash, mate. We won't be much good at running a TV station if we can't ride out somefink like this. Got to stick togevver. Come over 'ere and we'll sort out the best plan of action, but you're not resigning."

"Up to me really," said Rupert. "I must see Cameron, and then I'll be over."

Arriving at Penscombe, he found cars parked all the way up his driveway and the gravel in front of the house completely hidden by journalists, photographers, and television crews. Corinium had even had the temerity to send a mobile canteen. Stony-faced, grayer than the trampled snow, Rupert got out of his car.

"Fuck off, the lot of you," he snarled as they all surged forward. "I've got to talk to my lawyer."

"What about the franchise?" asked the *Mail on Sunday*.

"Come on, Rupe," said the *Star*. "Give us a quote. We've waited all fucking night."

"I've got nothing to say. I'll put my dogs on you if you don't beat it." Fighting his way into the house, he slammed the door behind him.

"Well, well, well," said Cameron from halfway up the stairs.

She wore no makeup, her hair was sleeked back from her face which was deathly white.

"I'm sorry," began Rupert.

"Fuck off," screamed Cameron, as a photographer appeared at a side window. Racing downstairs, she drew the curtains.

"Come upstairs," said Rupert.

They went into his bedroom, the set for so much of the action in the first installment of the memoirs. Almost as though the great four-poster would contaminate her, Cameron gave it a wide berth and went over to the fireplace.

"How could you?" she whispered. "Have you told people those sort of things about me?"

"Never, never," said Rupert. Suddenly dizzy, he slumped on the flowered chintz-covered chair in front of Helen's old dressing table. "Beattie was a special case. The thing that turned her on was stories of my screwing other women. She must have had a tape recorder running under the bed the whole time."

Cameron shuddered. "You realize your career's finished? You'll be kicked out of the party. I hope you've already resigned from Venturer. And I suppose Saturday's installment will be all about your touching designs on Taggie O'Hara."

Rupert looked at her incredulously.

"You're in love with her, aren't you?" said Cameron.

Rupert looked across the valley at his white fields. He'd always seen them as arms protecting Taggie. Now they seemed like a great predatory polar bear, crushing The Priory to death.

He turned back to Cameron.

"OK," he said flatly, "I do love her. If I'm honest, I've loved her ever since New Year's Eve, probably long before that. I'm desperately sorry, I know I've dealt you a marked card. I'm much too fond of you to kid you along any longer, just for the sake of the franchise, that you and I are going to end up together."

Cameron opened her mouth to yell at him, but Rupert raised his hand for a second's more silence.

"I didn't know a thing about these memoirs coming out—not that you'd want me anyway after reading them—but I want you to know that I was intending to level with you today about Taggie."

For a second Cameron seemed to sway with frenzy, like a viper about to strike, then she screamed: "You won't get her. Declan knows about it too, and there's no way he'll let you ever get your filthy depraved hands on his daughter."

"I know there isn't," said Rupert. "This"—he picked up the *Scorpion* and wearily dropped it in the wastepaper basket—"has finally done for us."

"Serves you fucking right," yelled Cameron. "I'm getting out of here, and I never want to see you again."

Rushing downstairs out the front door, she kicked and punched her way through the waiting journalists, sending several of them leaping for safety as the Lotus stormed down the driveway.

"Nice quiet girl," said the *Mail on Sunday*, picking himself out of the snow.

Arriving at Green Lawns, Rupert found Freddie and Declan desperately trying to salvage the IBA meeting. As a result of Rupert's memoirs, two of the major financial backers had pulled out and Professor Graystock had resigned. As Rupert went into Freddie's study, the Bishop called.

"I'm afraid in the light of Rupert Campbell-Black's quite appalling revelations, I shall have to withdraw my support for the Venturer bid."

"You can't," said Freddie aghast. "The meeting's tomorrow morning. Your not being there will really tip the scales. I fort the Church of England were supposed to forgive sinners."

"I have to set a good example to my flock," said the Bishop and hung up.

"Lily-livered bastard," said Freddie furiously. "We're well shot of 'im."

"He'd have impressed the IBA," said Declan bleakly, who couldn't look Rupert in the eye. Was it because of Taggie or the memoirs?

"Then I must resign," said Rupert. "It's the only honorable thing to do."

"No, you won't," said Freddie. "It don't add up. Beattie Johnson was a slut, but she 'ad a good 'eart. I don't fink she'd 'ave written those fings wivout considerable financial inducement. Seb Burrows has got nuffink to do at the moment. I'm going to put him onto the story and see what he can dig up. And can't we slap an injunction on the *Scorpion*?"

Rupert shook his head wearily. "I wish we could, but I'm afraid it's all true. Although, it's appallingly slanted. It was never, never meant for publication, but she was such a fucking good listener, and you know I can never resist making people laugh. We were together for two years, for Christ's sake."

"How's Cameron taken it?" asked Declan harshly. "She was in a terrible state last night. Thinks you and she are kaput."

Rupert slumped on the sofa, putting his head in his hands.

"We are. I've just told her."

Declan lost his temper. It was like an earthquake and a volcano erupting at the same time.

"Can't you ever keep your fucking trap shut? First you tell everything to Beattie Johnson, then you have to give Cameron the boot. Don't you realize this'll screw up any final chance we have of getting the franchise? No Bishop, no professor, no financial backing, no Cameron—she'll bolt straight back to Tony and tell him everything she hasn't told him already."

"What d'you mean?" Rupert looked up, the bloodshot eyes suddenly alert.

"Haven't you read *The Times* yet?"

"Bas muttered something about it last night, but I forgot to read it."

"Cameron leaked all our plans to Tony on Tuesday."

"Don't be ridiculous."

"We put a private detective onto Tony. They spent an hour and a half together in the Royal Garden."

"So?" said Rupert. "Cameron's straight, I swear it."

"So do I," said Freddie.

Unshaven, putty-colored, his shirt on its second day, his suit crumpled, Rupert looked so desolate and so ill, slumped on the sofa, that Freddie went over and put a hand on his shoulder.

"Could 'appen to anyone. You'll come out of it."

"Venturer won't. I've fucked it up for all of you."

At that moment Valerie marched in.

"I've read every word of your disgusting memoirs," she screeched. "I don't want you in the house."

"Shut up," snapped Freddie. "He's 'ad enough punishment. Now just bugger off and bring us some black coffee."

Feeling he was such an irritant to Declan, Rupert left soon after that. Holing up in Bas's flat, he spent the rest of a nightmare day on the telephone, trying to resign from the party, from his constituency and from the International Olympics Committee. To his frustration no one would accept. The Leader of the Opposition, for example, was amazingly sanguine:

"Wait until the franchises have been awarded," she said. "That tramp Beattie Johnson took me to the cleaners just before I became leader—slanted the whole interview. Nearly cost me the job. It isn't as though you were married when you were in office. Just hang on a bit."

Malise Gordon, by contrast, was icy cold with rage that Helen's name had been dragged into it.

"I'm not excusing what's happened," said Rupert, "but I was very raw when Helen left me. Beattie lived with me for two years. Naturally I confided in her about my marriage. None of the stuff that's been printed was intended for the memoirs. Will you tell Helen how desperately sorry I am? I did tell Beattie hundreds of good things about her, which she conveniently forgot to put in."

"I'm sure that'll be a great comfort to Helen," said Malise acidly.

"Look, I'm going abroad immediately after the IBA meeting tomorrow," said Rupert. "I won't be back for Christmas. I must see the children before I go."

"I don't think that's at all a good idea," said Malise crushingly, "and I know Helen won't either. Tab's far too young to understand, and I doubt if Marcus will ever speak to you again after the things you said about his mother. The press are howling around the place; your presence would only exacerbate things. Just bugger off and leave us all alone."

"I must explain—" just for a second Rupert's voice faltered— "that whatever's happened, I still love them. For Christ's sake, Malise."

"You can always write," said Malise and hung up.

Rupert sat slumped for a long time. Then he borrowed two hundred pounds in cash from Basil's till, a piece of writing paper and an envelope.

"Darling Taggie," he wrote, *"I'm sorry I was bloody the last two times we met. Of course we're still friends. One day you'll find some nice boy who's worthy of you, and he'll be the luckiest sod in the world. In the meantime could you spend the enclosed on Christmas presents for Marcus and Tab. You'll know instinctively what they'd like. Thank you for everything. God bless you . . . Rupert."*

Shoving the cash and the letter in an envelope, he gave it to Bas to deliver to The Priory.

Toward nightfall, over at Green Lawns, Freddie and Declan were just trying to prevent another backer pulling out when the private detective called on another line. He had something too important to tell them over the telephone. He'd be right over. He turned out, to Declan's surprise, not to be some seedy unfrocked cop in a dirty raincoat, but a delightfully understated, mouse-haired young man with an innocent pink and white face. Nor did he beat about any-one's bush.

"Tony Baddingham spent yesterday afternoon in a Stow-in-the-Wold motel with a woman. I've got pictures of them arriving separately and then leaving together, and exchanging kisses in the parking lot."

He threw the pictures down on the table. Fascinated, Freddie and Declan got up to have a look. In the first photograph the woman had her black coat collar turned up and was wearing a black beret, dark glasses and her hair tied back. In the second, coming out of the motel, her coat was unbuttoned, she was laughing, holding the dark glasses and the beret in one hand, her glorious red hair trailing down her back. In the third, she was kissing Tony in front of Taggie's car.

"Is this some kind of a joke?" hissed Declan.

"I'm afraid not," said the private detective. "I'm awfully sorry, Mr. O'Hara. After they'd gone I talked to the receptionist. She admitted they'd been there several times before. She showed me the register—they'd signed in as Mr. and Mrs. Jones. The girl remembered Mrs. O'Hara because she was so beautiful."

Declan started to shake. It was like seeing the first stroke of the woodcutter's axe going into a great oak tree, thought Freddie.

"But it was Bas, not Tony," muttered Declan.

"Bas must have been a front," said Freddie.

"Look how upset she was the other night when Taggie turned up with Bas," said Declan, frantically trying to convince himself.

"That's because she's jealous of Taggie," said Freddie wisely. "It was only later she got really upset, which was when you told us you'd just seen Cameron with Tony—and she did know all about Dermot MacBride and the Shakespeare plays."

"I don't believe it," muttered Declan. "She wouldn't. I must find her." He stumbled toward the door.

"For Christ's sake drive slowly," warned Freddie.

As Declan walked into The Priory Maud came out of the drawing room with a glass of champagne in her hand. She was wearing a black turtleneck sweater, a black coat, black stockings, black flat shoes, and a black beret on the back of her head. She was very pale, she wore no lipstick, but her skin had a glowing luminosity and her eyes were huge and dreamy. Declan thought she had never looked more beautiful, and suddenly knew she was as guilty as hell.

"Darling—I got it!" she said ecstatically.

"What?"

"The part—Nora—in *A Doll's House*. We start rehearsing immediately after Christmas and they're paying me four hundred a week, so our money worries are over."

How little she knows about anything, thought Declan—how can such a child have done such terrible things?

"Where's Taggie?" he asked.

"Cooking supper, I think. You don't seem very pleased for me, darling."

As if in a dream he led her into the drawing room, shutting the door and then opening it again to let in Claudius and Gertrude. Gertrude had a rawhide bone sticking out of the side of her mouth like a pipe. She could sit there for hours, saliva hanging in festoons. Declan leaned against the door for support, watching Maud put a log on the fire. Despite all Maud's grandiose plans for The Priory, there were still no curtains at the windows which were as black as her clothes.

"How long have you been having an affair with Tony?" he asked almost conversationally.

Maud's face went as blank as a digital clock in a power failure.

"I don't know what you're talking about."

"Don't prevaricate. I've got evidence." Declan threw the photographs down on the sofa. Slowly Maud examined them.

"Rather good, that one." She took a leisurely sip of her champagne. "I might use it as a publicity photograph."

"How long's it been going on?"

"Since September."

"So you told him everything?"

Maud shrugged: "I really don't remember. We found so much to talk about."

This can't be happening to me, thought Declan. I don't feel anything. It's as though we're discussing two characters in a play.

"But why Tony? Bas I can understand, but not—" for the first time he betrayed any emotion—"not that filthy venomous toad."

Maud looked at him for a moment, her hand gently stroking Claudius's ears.

"Because he was kind, because he listened to me, because he was interested in me as a person—not just as a hole between two legs."

Her sudden uncharacteristic coarseness shocked Declan almost more than her betrayal.

"Tony!" he said in amazement, "kind?"

Suddenly Maud flipped. "You're so obsessed with your fucking franchise," she yelled, "you don't know anyone else exists, except when you want to fuck them. You couldn't even forget it for one moment to get back for my opening night, when I really needed you. Christ—I needed you! And then breezing in and ordering me away from my own opening night party.

"I was only fooling around with Tony until then. It was only after that that it got serious. He arranged for me to meet Pascoe Rawlings. He saw that a car delivered me to Pascoe's office last week and brought me back. He fixed for me to be driven to the audition today, and even though he'd got his IBA meeting this afternoon, he still called me this evening to see how I'd got on. You'd even forgotten I was going." She laughed; it was a horrible sound without any merriment. "The great interviewer, so praised for his judgment of character and his consideration to the staff, who doesn't know a thing about his own wife."

"Can't you understand that he's using you?" said Declan slowly. "The only thing that turns Tony on is acquisition. You've just lost us the franchise, and you were going to stand by and let me blame Cameron."

"Serve her right—arrogant little bitch," cried Maud hysterically.

Outside in the hall Taggie could hear her mother's screams getting louder and louder. Oh God, her father didn't need upsetting any more when he had the IBA meeting in the morning. Next moment the drawing room door burst open.

"I'm leaving you," screamed Maud.

"Come back," roared Declan.

"Never." She shot past Taggie and out the front door, banging it so hard the whole hall rattled.

Taggie ran to open it. Outside it was snowing again. She watched Maud drive off in her car, hell for leather, down the driveway.

"What on earth's the matter?" she said, turning to Declan, who was standing as if blasted white by lightning.

"She was the mole."

Taggie gave a gasp. "She couldn't be. She can't have meant to."

"She did," said Declan in a voice of utter despair, "because I neglected her. It's all my fault. I blamed Cameron last night and Rupert today, and just now I blamed her. But through my fucking obsession and hubris I've brought us all down."

CHAPTER 45

For Rupert next morning the Press was crucifixion—ranging from highly moralistic pieces about the chronic Tory failure to keep their noses clean to double-page spreads with pictures charting the rise and fall of the Tory party golden boy. The tabloids had dug up several of Rupert's more bitter exes, who, having done a great deal more than kiss, were now only too happy to tell. The seamiest tabloid of all had a huge front-page headline: *"Campbell-Blackguard,"* above an enchanting picture of Tabitha.

"In the playground of exclusive Bluebell's school (fees £1,500 a term)," ran the copy, *"a little child sobs alone. 'My friends won't play with me anymore.' "*

"This is the final fucking limit," howled Billy Lloyd-Foxe, hurling the *Scorpion* across the room. "I'm coming with you to the IBA."

"The Beeb will fire you if they find out," said Janey who was painting her nails because it was less hassle than cleaning them. "And as I turned down a hundred grand to tell all about our life with Rupert yesterday, and this suit cost nearly as much, I don't think you can afford to."

"I don't care," said Billy. "Rupert's my best friend."

At Freddie's house, the remnants of the Venturer consortium gathered before the meeting. With no Bishop, no Professor, no Cameron, and none of the moles, their numbers were utterly depleted and their bid in tatters. The second day of Rupert's memoirs was even worse, with intimations of under-age school girls. Freddie had spent half the night trying to persuade a demented Declan that they'd got to expose Tony, not just for seducing Maud and bugging their houses, but because Seb was working on excellent evidence that Tony had bribed Beattie Johnson to sing to the rooftops, just when it would be most damaging to Venturer.

But like Wellington at Waterloo refusing to turn the guns on the enemy commandant, Declan refused to let anyone condemn Tony. He didn't want Maud's name dragged into it. He was clearly still suffering from shock. He looked terrible.

"A black ram is tupping my white ewe," he kept saying over and over again, "and it was all my fault."

Rupert, who arrived with Bas, didn't look much better, but at

least he'd got a grip on himself. The meeting had to be got through.
There were people not to be let down, there would be the rest of
his life to mourn for Taggie and probably his children as well. Helen
had called this morning, saying she was applying for a court order
to deny him visitation rights.

Even Henry Hampshire arrived walking wounded, wearing a dark
suit with uncharacteristically flared trousers, and with his leg in a
cast.

"Horse put its foot down a rabbit hole," was all he would say
about it.

"Morning." He went up to Rupert, who was huddled on the sofa
trying to keep down a cup of coffee. "Enjoying your memoirs; great
stuff." He lowered his voice. "I had a crack at Mandy Hamilton myself twenty years ago. God, she was pretty. Might have made more
progress if I'd known she liked having her bottom smacked."

Rupert managed a pale smile. "At least it kept you out of the
papers."

Dame Enid arrived next, resplendent in a pinstriped trouser suit
with an even wider white stripe than Tony's, a bright blue tie, and
an Al Capone hat.

"Stick 'em up, it's a shoot out," said Marti Gluckstein, who came
with her. He was dressed in a lurid green Norfolk Jacket and knick-
erbockers, and sucking on a pipe.

"Did you get that at Valerie's boutique?" said Bas, then hastily
shut up in case Freddie overheard.

"Thought I ought to appear as the country squire," said Marti.
"Where's the Bishop?"

"Pulled out, I'm afraid," said Freddie, handing him and Dame
Enid cups of coffee.

"Good riddance, pompous old fart," said Dame Enid, helping
herself to sugar. "Can't you pull a Rabbi out of a hat to replace him?"
she added to Marti.

Marti smirked. "For you, my dear, anything."

"Crispin Graystock's pulled out too," said Freddie.

"Well, thank God," said Dame Enid philosophically. "Graystock's got complete verbal diarrhea."

"Really feel for you, lad," Marti said. "But everyone regards the
Scorpion as fiction. That Beastly Johnson did me over once. Took
down what I said, but twisted it like barley sugar. What's up with
Declan?"

"Wife trouble," said Rupert.

"Happens at franchise time," said Marti. "When we bid for the

Midlands eight years ago, the wives got so fed up, they were all at it—even mine."

"Only two more to come," said Freddie, trying to cheer up his own and everyone's spirits. "And 'ere they are," he went on, as Seb and Charles came through the door.

"We're going to have a fuller house than you thought," said Charles. "I've just seen Billy, Janey, Harold White, and Sally Maples getting out of a taxi."

Freddie had tears in his eyes as he welcomed them. "You shouldn't have come. It's totally out of order," he said. "I know what you're risking, but I won't say I'm not bloody pleased to see you."

Declan seemed hardly to notice, but Rupert's jaw quilted with muscles when he saw Billy. "You're fucking insane," he said roughly.

"I like lost causes," said Billy cheerfully. "Anyway, I brought you luck at the LA Olympics. And you brought me luck, too. If I hadn't done the commentary for the B.B.C., they'd never have given me a job."

"Which you're about to lose."

As the hands of the clock inched past nine-thirty, they decided that there was no point waiting any longer. Cameron wasn't coming.

"Pity," sighed Hardy Bissett, going around straightening ties. "Now, don't forget, no sniping—solidarity is all. Sit up straight. Burst with enthusiasm. You're bursting a little too much, Janey darling." He did up two buttons of her shirt.

It was still bitterly cold when they set out for the IBA. The snow in the park was the color of dirty seagulls.

Janey's scent was making Rupert feel sick. "Oh look, there's Santa Claus," said Janey, pressing a button to lower the window, as the car swung around The Scotch House into Brompton Road.

"Please Santa," she called out to him, as he marched alongside the car, "will you put a franchise in my stocking?"

"Ho, ho, ho," said Santa Claus, hoisting his sack onto his back and batting his long black eyelashes at Janey. "For a pretty little girl like you, I just might."

"My Christ," said Janey, with a scream of laughter, as he turned right in front of the car and strode purposefully across the road through the revolving doors of the IBA. "It's Georgie Baines."

"I wish I'd thought of that," said Charles petulantly. "I wanted to come as Gwendolyn Gosling again, but I thought I'd better play it straight."

To avoid the Press and preserve the utmost security, the convoy of cars turned left down Lancelot Place and entered the IBA from the back by the underground parking lot. From here their passengers were whisked up to the eighth floor and, although the moles nervously looked for reporters in every dark corner, they were all safely led along the corridor and installed in an empty office.

"I feel like a courtier waiting for an audience with Louis XIV: 'Please don't banish me to my estate in the Loire, Sire,' " said Charles.

"God, I'm nervous," said Henry, mouthing the answers to possible questions.

"I wish I could take in a calculator," said Marti in a hollow voice.

"D'you think they'll shine lights in our faces?" asked Janey.

"They didn't yesterday, but then Corinium has a better track record," said a voice. It was Georgie Baines, who'd shed his Santa Claus disguise and was now wearing a dark suit and fluffing up his dark curls.

Everyone crowded around him in delight.

"Of course! You went in yesterday afternoon with Corinium," said Freddie.

"Wearing a different tie," said Georgie.

"How long were you in there?" asked Seb.

"Exactly an hour," said Georgie.

"What was it like?"

"Falling off a log. Not one difficult question. Tony's star is definitely in the ascendant, that's why *I'm* here. I've always believed rats should desert a rising shit."

"How did you manage to get away?" asked Janey, removing a last bit of white beard from Georgie's chin.

"Tony thinks I'm at Saatchi's."

A female IBA official was trying to organize everyone's entrance into the conference room in a preordained order, so the Authority would know who they were.

"I expected eleven people," she said in bewilderment. "There seem a great many more. I know who you are," she said to Janey, "and you," she said to Rupert, keeping her distance, "and you," she turned to Declan, looking perplexed as though she hardly recognized him.

"Are you the Bishop of Cotchester?" she asked Marti as she consulted her notes. Everyone giggled. "And I wasn't expecting you, Mr. White, or you, Billy, or you, Miss Maples, and certainly not you *again*, Mr. Baines."

"Well we're all here," said Harold White. "We belong to Venturer."

"Have you all got your two photographs?"

Everyone duly produced them.

"Had to go into Woolworths to get it taken," announced Henry. "Never been there before. Rather a lark."

The female official scratched her head in despair: "And where's Cameron Cook?"

"Not coming, nor the Bishop, nor Professor Graystock. They've dropped out," said Freddie. "Nor Wesley Emerson. He's still wiv us, but he's playing in a test match abroad."

"No, I'm not," said a voice deeper than the Caribbean Sea.

It was Wesley in a support Venturer T-shirt. He was greeted with screams of delight. Dame Enid thumped him on the back till he pleaded for mercy.

"How did you manage to get away?"

"Pulled a muscle, man," said Wesley, grinning from ear to ear. "But I haven't slept all night, so I hope there's no tricky questions about ethnic minorities."

Rupert took him aside. "You really are fantastic," he said.

Wesley grinned. "I read all that shit about you, man. Same thing happened to me; thought we ought to show a united front."

"I really think I've got you all sorted out," said the IBA lady. "I'll just check that Lady Gosling's ready."

After that there was a dreadful quarter of an hour wait.

"It's just like standing outside the headmaster's study," said Seb.

"Will you all come in, please?" said the IBA lady.

"Good luck, everyone," said Freddie.

"Remember the old bat who isn't Lady Gosling is Mrs. Menzies-Scott, ex-chairman of the WI," hissed Georgie.

The twelve members of the authority, flanked by six senior staff from the IBA, were already seated along one side of the beautifully polished oval table, as Venturer filed in and took up their places opposite them.

In the center sat Lady Gosling in a thick brown tweed suit and a bottle-green cardigan. Despite the warmth of the room, a thermal vest could be seen peeping above her brown check shirt. Mrs. Menzies-Scott of the WI, who'd been foolish enough to wear a rust angora sweater, had already turned scarlet in the heat. Other members of the panel included such worthies as a Welsh Judge Davies and Lady Barnsley, late of the White Fish Authority, who was alleged to have an orgasm every time she saw a celebrity. Handbag rammed protectively against her groin, she was now gazing at Rupert with a mixture of terror and excitement.

Freddie sat in the middle facing Lady Gosling, flanked by Rupert and Declan. On Rupert's right, as obvious and disfiguring as a lost front tooth, was a space where Cameron should have been. Janey was near the end of the table, with only Henry beyond her, so he could stick out his plaster cast.

Henry was gazing out of the window at Knightsbridge Barracks. "Used to work there," he announced in a loud whisper. "You'd never believe there were squash courts on top."

Lady Gosling, who had not winked at her friend Dame Enid, greeted them with the utmost coolness.

"I'm sorry you were kept waiting so long. It was because of the very considerable changes in the numbers attending. I see all the so-called 'moles' "—one could feel her fastidiously putting quotes around such a slang word—"have decided to show up, despite the threat of dismissal, and we certainly weren't expecting you," she added to Wesley. "We gathered you were playing in a test match."

Wesley gave her the benefit of his heavenly banana-split smile.

"I was, Mrs. Menzies-Scott."

"Gosling," hissed Janey.

"I'm sorry, Mrs. Gosling. I got injured. And coming to this meeting seemed more important. After all, we'll be running a television company for a long long time."

"Hum," said Lady Gosling. "Somewhat hubristic of you. And where are the Bishop and Professor Graystock?"

Freddie cleared his throat.

"Er, they've withdrawn because of a conflict of interests."

"One can understand that," said Lady Gosling heavily.

"And Cameron Cook?"

Freddie opened his mouth.

"I'm here," said a voice behind him. "I'm so sorry, Lady Gosling, my cab ran into another car in the Old Brompton Road."

It was Cameron in her scarlet silk suit, bringing a wonderful warmth and color into the room. She was very pale beneath her blusher, and wearing dark glasses, but totally self-possessed. Sliding into the seat beside Rupert, she very deliberately put a hand over his, then smiling down the row said once again: "I'm so sorry everyone."

"You little beauty," said Freddie under his breath.

* * *

Cameron's arrival seemed to pull Venturer magically together. The first questions were about finance and technical specifications, and initially fielded by Freddie. Then he passed the ball to Rupert, Bas, Lord Smith, Marti, and Georgie Barnes, who'd arrived with a pile of income predictions.

Freddie in fact was the life and soul of the application. A born showman, puffing on his cigar, giving occasional infectious roars of laughter, he exuded honesty, energy, and huge enthusiasm for the task.

Mrs. Menzies-Scott didn't throw Wesley on ethnic minorities, but, seeing him yawning, asked him why he personally wished to oust Corinium as the franchise holder.

"I live in the area, man," drawled Wesley. "I'm absolutely fed up, like everyone else in this consortium, with having to watch such God-awful programs."

Even Lady Gosling surpressed a smile, and asked if the applicant's program plans were based on its view of the characteristics and needs of the franchise area. There was a long pause.

"Almost entirely," said Cameron. "We all know and love and live in the area, so we want to put something back, and give it a regional identity. We want to make friends with the viewers, to make them feel part of one great Venturer family.

"But our approach would be the same if we were pitching for any area in the British Isles. Great television comes from telling people the truth, from entertaining them so well they don't realize they're being educated. We want to make documentaries and dramas that tackle the problems we all face, coping with unemployment, loneliness, adolescence, being in love. Even"—she smiled, testing the age group of the panel—"with the traumas of having one's grandchildren to visit over Christmas." The panel smiled warmly back.

"Cameron can hardly say this for herself," chipped in Charles, "but I'd just like to add that with her and Declan we have a most exciting team. They've been in Ireland making a film on Yeats for Channel 4. I saw the uncut version last week. It is utter magic and will bring Yeats's poetry and the beauty of the Irish countryside to millions of new viewers. It would be nice to think they could do the same for the Cotswold area."

Lady Gosling nodded sagely, noticing, however, that Declan was gazing blankly into space, taking no part in the proceedings.

Everyone drank a great deal of Highland Spring water. Dame Enid and Charles were superb on the arts; Billy charmed all the panel on sports; Janey had some wonderful ideas for women's inter-

ests; Seb made them laugh on news coverage, saying that the Corinium Head of News was so idle, he consulted his opposite number
at the B.B.C. every morning, so they could both cover the same local
events, and there would be absolutely no danger of either of them
being bawled out for scooping the other.

Henry started off brilliantly when Judge Davies asked him about
his involvement in the consortium. He was just waxing lyrical on
capturing the wild life of the area on film, and appearing to scratch
his cast for the third time, when Janey suddenly realized he was
pulling up the cuff of his trousers and reading the whole thing off
his plaster cast.

"Shrews, voles, badgers," ended Henry dropping his trouser-
leg.

"I love badgers," said Lady Barnsley, looking very excited.
"We've got some in our woods."

"Have you really?" said Henry. "So have we, and so has Declan
actually. I passed two big chaps having a fight the other night. They
were so preoccupied, I managed to get really close up."

"Did you really?" said Lady Barnsley.

Lady Gosling, however, had had enough about badgers. She
looked straight at Declan, who was still slumped in his chair totally
unrecognizable from the dazzlingly charismatic, self-confident dem-
agogue who'd laid into Tony Baddingham at the public meeting.

"Who is going to run the company?" she asked him.

"I'm chairman," said Freddie, when Declan didn't answer. "I
intend to devote at least one day a week to Venturer if not more.
'Enry's nonexecutive deputy chairman, Rupert'll handle finance and
administration with Harold. Declan and Cameron will oversee programs. Georgie will be in charge of sales. Charles, Janey, Sally, Billy,
and Seb will all be Heads of various departments. Marti, Bas, Lord
Smiff, Dame Enid, an' Wesley will be nonexecutive directors. But
they'll all act on a consultancy basis, and add to the smooth running
of the company."

"But who is really going to run the company?" persisted Lady
Gosling.

No contribution was clearly forthcoming from Declan, so Rupert
looked at Lady Gosling squarely. "I am," he said.

"I would have thought," said Lady Gosling icily, "that your very
limited business experience doesn't include the creation of new companies. It's a tough skill to acquire."

"When I was twenty-one," snapped Rupert, "I started my own
show-jumping business, which has now developed into a horse-

breeding operation that turns over ten million a year. I'm also an MP, and on top of all this I ran an extremely successful sports ministry for four years. I shall also have the constant and incredibly able advice of all my directors, particularly Harold, who's been in charge of LWT's programs for the last few years."

"The entire board would support Rupert as Chief Executive," said Bas.

All of Venturer murmured their assent except Wesley who was sleeping peacefully.

"He did come on an overnight flight," explained Janey, giving him a nudge.

"Howzat," said Wesley, waking up.

Lady Gosling looked with infinite disapproval from Wesley to Declan, to Rupert to Billy, then up the table to Janey. "Don't you feel there are too many celebrities, too many prima donnas in your consortium? Can you honestly convince us that Venturer will be able to stick effectively together as a team?"

"Yes," said Rupert evenly, once more looking her straight in the eye. "It hasn't been an easy week with my so-called 'memoirs' coming out, but except for the Bishop and the Professor, we're all here, aren't we?".

Lady Gosling dropped her eyes first.

Glancing at the clock on the wall, Cameron could see they'd been in there an hour and a half. Was that a good sign, or did the IBA merely want to prove Venturer's inferiority beyond doubt? Knowing nothing about Maud's affair with Tony, she had also realized there was something seriously wrong with Declan. He hadn't contributed to the discussion at all. By now he ought to be revving up for his final peroration, tearing Corinium limb from limousine, but he was saying nothing.

She looked down the row, at Janey and Billy radiating panache and glamour and high spirits when she knew how desperately broke they were, at Charles who had no future if Venturer went down, at Georgie, Sally, and Harold, who'd certainly jeopardized their careers, at Henry dreaming of bosoms and badgers, at Wesley who'd flown thousands of miles to support them and probably jeopardized his test career as well, at Rupert who, despite the devastating blows that had been dealt him that week, had performed so incredibly bravely, and back to Declan, who had taught her humanity. They were her friends, the people she most wanted to work with.

Lady Gosling looked at her watch, and poured herself a glass of Highland Spring. "Well, we've listened to you all, and studied your bulky application. Has anyone anything else to say?"

There was a long agonizing pause:

"I have," said Cameron, getting to her feet, as slim and brave in her red suit as the young Portia.

"Ladies and Gentlemen, last week at one of the northern television stations a young Head of News hanged himself." She glanced along the row of shocked reproving faces. "Sure, we've all been fed the official story that he had domestic and financial problems. The truth was he couldn't handle all the pressures in the buildup to the franchise awards. He was being so bullied to get so many different lobbies, local worthies, friends of his Managing Director onto his program to impress you, the IBA, so that his lousy bosses could keep their franchise and go on making a fortune. This is a tragedy and a disgrace," went on Cameron fiercely, "and an appalling indictment on the whole IBA and ITV system. We in production should not feel we've got to put on worthy uplifting boring programs every eight years in order to impress you and retain the franchise. We should make good programs all the time."

She turned, pointing to the framed document on the wall, giving the IBA its own coat of arms and motto: "Your motto is *Servire populo*. But you're not serving the people if you're encouraging the companies to make programs that please you, which you feel the people ought to watch, rather than what they want to watch. I worked for Tony Baddingham for four years," she went on bitterly.

"And produced some very good uplifting programs that weren't boring," said Lady Gosling dryly.

Cameron grinned. "Touché." Then instantly she became serious again. "But that was because Tony Baddingham gave me carte-blanche to ride roughshod over all the staff, and also gave me an unlimited budget, while cutting the budgets of all other programs to nothing. Morale at Corinium was and is absolutely rock bottom.

"Declan O'Hara," she looked at Declan, pleading with him to glance up or react in some way, "is one of the all-time greats of television. But when he was at Corinium, he was very nearly broken by Tony, who forced him to interview people of total insignificance, big businessmen, local dignitaries, people whose influence he believed he needed to win the franchise. Fortunately Declan escaped and formed Venturer. I've spent the last two months working with him and learned that you don't need to terrorize people, or reduce them to hanging themselves, to make good programs. Once you've got the authority, if you'll forgive the pun, you get far more out of people by kindness and interest in their welfare."

The Welsh judge put on his spectacles for a better look at Cameron. Really she was a most astonishingly attractive girl. She could read for the Bar, if ever she got fed up with television.

"ITV audience figures are plummeting," went on Cameron accusingly, "because so many of the programs are so awful, and because most of the companies are run by accountants who aren't prepared to take risks any more. Why spend ten million on a serial that may fail, when for peanuts you can buy a quiz from another company?

"Venturer's going to change all that. We're going to revitalize independent television and not only make really good programs right across the board, but also change the scheduling of the whole network so it's based on an exact analysis of what the public wants. We know what difficulties lie ahead. We know we can't produce profitable results if we have to make continually uplifting programs. We'll need your help, understanding and guidance all along the way. I'm sorry, I've gone on too long." She collapsed back into her chair embarrassed.

It was some comfort that Rupert put his hand over hers with real pride.

"Normally your chairman would sum up at this stage, but I think we've all heard quite enough about Venturer's policy from Miss Cook," said Lady Gosling. "Thank you all for coming."

After all the effort it was a very curt dismissal. Feeling utterly despondent, Venturer filed out of the room. Even worse, as they were smuggled out of the underground parking lot they ran smack into the Press, who were out in force clamoring to get a quote from Rupert about the memoirs. Fortunately they concentrated on getting pictures of him and didn't notice the rest of the moles cringing inside the convoy of cars.

For want of anything better to do, they all went back to Freddie's for a wake. On the way there, Janey, Billy, and Freddie told Cameron about Declan and Maud.

"But the IBA ought to be told," stormed Cameron. "Someone's got to wise them up what an absolute bastard Tony is."

"You made a pretty good job of it just now," said Freddie. "And Declan won't hear of it."

As soon as he got to Freddie's, Rupert took Cameron aside.

"Thank you for turning up, sweetheart. You were absolutely marvelous."

Cameron shrugged. "If you can win a gold medal with a dislocated shoulder, I can talk too much with a broken heart."

"Christ, I admire you."

"I'd so much rather you'd loved me," said Cameron sadly.

For a second Rupert lowered her dark glasses, and winced to see how red and swollen from crying her eyes were.

"I'm so sorry, angel. You know you can stay on at Penscombe as long as you like. I won't be there for the next few weeks."

"Where are you going?" asked Cameron, suddenly frantic.

"America, this afternoon. The only hope is to get the hell out of England until the dust settles."

"So you won't be back for Christmas?"

Rupert shook his head wearily. "What Christmas?"

"Or for the IBA verdict on the 15th?"

"The result's a foregone conclusion. Couldn't you feel the tidal waves of disapproval and distaste emanating from those tweed bosoms throughout the interview? We haven't a hope."

"Probably not," said Cameron, glancing at Declan who was now slumped in a chair, shivering uncontrollably with an untouched glass of whisky in his hand. "But Declan's going to need a lot of support in the next few days."

"Not from me," said Rupert bitterly. "The best thing for all the O'Haras would be to have me out of their hair." He looked at his watch. "I'd better be off."

"Can I ask you just one favor?" said Cameron. "Could I possibly keep Blue?"

The doorbell rang and they both jumped thinking it might be Taggie. Freddie's secretary answered it and the next moment a man marched into the room. For a second Cameron thought she was hallucinating, for it seemed as if the old Declan, the forceful confident, aggressive, clear-eyed, suntanned Declan, whom she remembered so clearly that first day he arrived at Corinium, had just walked through the door. Then she realized it was Patrick, thickened out, weathered and bronzed from five months working on a sheep farm. He'd obviously come straight from the airport, and being Patrick, even in a family crisis, had bothered to buy Duty Free whisky and cigarettes. He'd need them both over the next few days.

Near to tears, Declan rose to his feet. Ignoring everyone else in the room, Patrick went over and put his arms around him.

"It's all right, Pa," he said gently, "I called home first. Taggie told me about Mum. It was a terrible thing for her to do, but she had reasons. It'll be all right. It's you she loves. She'll come back.''

He was like the father comforting the child.

''She sabotaged the franchise,'' groaned Declan, ''and it was all my fault.''

''Rubbish,'' said Patrick. ''The responsibility for that lies elsewhere.''

He let go of Declan and turned toward Rupert, his face hardening. ''You deliberately set out to seduce Cameron because you wanted her on Venturer's side, didn't you? Well that's for fucking *her* up.'' The next moment he'd smashed his fist into Rupert's right jaw and, as Rupert reeled sideways, caught totally by surprise, Patrick hit him again on the right eye with his other fist. ''And that's for fucking up Taggie,'' he added, as Rupert crashed to the ground.

In the press over the weekend there was endless speculation as to which of the wronged husbands named in Rupert's memoirs had given him the black eye.

CHAPTER 46

The next two weeks were terrible for Venturer. Deeply guilty that his utter failure to pull himself together at the meeting had finally cost them the franchise, Declan went home to The Priory. Taggie and Patrick made sure he was never alone, as he seemed to sink deeper and deeper into depression, constantly vacillating between loathing Maud for betraying him and longing to have her back. There was no word from her; she seemed to have totally vanished.

Patrick, displaying patience and understanding way beyond his years, spent hours talking to his father: ''Taggie said Mum was absolutely gibbering with terror before *The Merry Widow*. It was such a colossal distance from obscurity back to the limelight. A little amateur production perhaps to you, but to her it wasn't just an extra step to cross the Frogsmore, but a vast leap over a five-hundred-foot-deep ravine. She needed you so desperately to witness her triumph or catch her if she fell.''

''I know,'' groaned Declan. ''Because I always had to fight so hard to keep her, I never realized how much she needed me.''

''And you know she lives any part she plays. In her head she's now become poor bullied Nora in *A Doll's House*, marching out with a slammed door on an insensitive tyrannical husband.

"And finally you musn't underestimate the influence of Tony Baddingham. I know the effect he had on Cameron. He is pure Iago. He only had to point out how brilliant, beautiful, and sexually voracious Cameron was; how you were spending more and more time with her; how could the two of you not be having an affair? You know what an imagination Mum has. This was even more immediate than P. D. James. Imagine, too, the appalling things he must have said about you, and finally the escape from poverty he offered her: new dresses, new jewels, furs, no more overdrawn bank balances or creditors at the gate, even warmth." Patrick shivered. After the Australian summer The Priory central heating left a great deal to be desired. "And he was around all the time, and you were away, or preoccupied with the franchise or Yeats, and Mum was probably turned on because the whole thing was so utterly verboten. All he had to do was to switch on his electric carving knife and turn it in the wound."

Declan winced: "I can understand all that, but deliberately to hand over all our secrets."

"She may not have done," said Patrick. "Taggie was out a lot. Tony probably came to the house. The plans were on your desk. Your writing isn't *that* indecipherable."

"D'you think I should go around to The Falconry and kill him?"

Patrick gave a wintry smile. "I wouldn't. You know how Lady Gosling abhors violence."

Taggie, who was kept enormously busy cooking for parties and filling up people's freezers for Christmas, made heroic attempts to be cheerful, but she worried Patrick far more than Declan. Never one to grumble, she refused to discuss Rupert, but Patrick knew she was bleeding to death inside.

Outside the weather was frantically warmer, the snow thawed in patches, leaving fantastic shapes, a sea horse there, a camel here. All down the valley the streams that tumbled into the Frogsmore were still frozen into dirty gray glaciers. Wandering numbly through the fields with the dogs, Taggie only noticed the flattened tufts of thick tawny grass sticking up through the snow, like the heads of a thousand Ruperts slain in battle.

"To long a sacrifice," quoted Patrick bitterly, thinking too of his own situation, *"can make a stone of the heart."*

* * *

Sunday, December 15th was D day. The form was that from nine
o'clock onwards, in an atmosphere of high drama and secrecy, the
existing Managing Directors of all the commercial television companies would roll up at the IBA in their limos at quarter of an hour
intervals. Driving past the battalions of reporters, photographers, and
camera crews, they would be ushered once again into the building
from the underground parking lot and be whizzed up in the elevator
to yet another empty office. Here, not unlike the suitors in *The Merchant of Venice*, they would be handed a sealed envelope from Lady
Gosling and then be left alone to open it and learn if they had held
onto their franchise, or whether, as in some instances, they had to
merge with their rivals. Allowed a few minutes to digest this information, they would then be summoned to Lady Gosling's office for
a brief word of congratulation or commiseration. Afterwards they
would leave the building by the back door or by the front, having
sworn not to reveal a word of the results to the Press. After all the
existing groups had been seen, the contenders, who hoped to depose
them, would come in one by one and endure the same procedure.

At four-thirty Lady Gosling would call a press conference to an-
nounce the results, which would simultaneously be rushed to the
Stock Exchange and the Home Secretary, who would inform the
Prime Minister.

Tony Baddingham was so certain he had retained the Corinium
franchise that he'd taken a suite overnight at the Hyde Park Hotel.

Expectation had been boosted by front-page forecasts in most
of the Sunday papers of a definite Corinium victory. The Krug was
therefore flowing at a reception for the Press and for all Tony's Corinium supporters, as he left for his twelve o'clock appointment with
the IBA.

Tony was relieved the contenders weren't being seen until the
afternoon. He would need police protection if he met Declan in the
elevator. He preferred to gloat over Venturer's utter humiliation from
a distance.

It was a bitterly cold gray day, with an icy wind. Rather than
walk the two hundred yards from the Hyde Park Hotel to the IBA,
Tony made Percy drive around the park and approach 80 Brompton
Road from South Kensington. Innumerable cameramen and journalists were mingling on the pavement with the Christmas shoppers as
his Rolls drew up.

Never one to resist publicity, Tony decided to go in through the
front door and let Percy take the Rolls around to the parking lot.
There was a frenzy of activity and popping of flashbulbs as he got

out. Tony had always kept a high profile; most of the Press recognized him. Posing for thirty seconds in his Garrick tie and new £500 suit, he told the gray forest of microphones that he didn't believe in jumping the gun, but he was confident, quietly confident, that he'd still be in business that afternoon.

"Arrogant fucker," snarled Declan who was watching ITN at Freddie's house. "Don't talk about guns in my presence, you bastard."

"Don't watch it," said Patrick, switching off the television. "It'll only upset you. You ought to change soon, and have a shave."

"What's the point of looking pretty for a firing squad?"

The door bell rang. Declan started. Why did he pray each time it might be Maud?

"I'll answer it," said Freddie.

Freddie's heart was heavy. He knew there was no hope of Venturer getting the franchise, but he'd tried to keep everyone's spirits up for the last two weeks and tried even harder to be a good husband to Valerie. In return Valerie hadn't even bothered to come up to London today, she so detested failure. But as Freddie peered through the peephole, he felt his heart expand in joy and gratitude, for there, her face as red and purple with cold as a mandrill's bottom, stood Lizzie. Never was a door opened so fast. As he drew her into the house out of the sight of any lurking Press, she fell into his arms.

"You shouldn't be here," he mumbled incoherently.

"I know I shouldn't," said Lizzie, "but James is being so smug, and I couldn't sit around drinking Tony's champagne. I thought it would poison me."

At Tony's house in Rutland Gate, totally oblivious of the franchise affair, with only thought for one another, Caitlin O'Hara and Archie Baddingham met up on the first day of the school vacation.

"Are you sure it's safe," asked Caitlin as they went into Monica's bedroom, "and your father won't come down the chimney like Santa Claus?"

"No, they'll be whooping it up all day at the Hyde Park," said Archie. "And poor Mum will spend her time fending off kisses from ghastly drunken hangers-on like James Vereker. I'm sorry your father hasn't got it."

"It's a shame," said Caitlin. "He worked jolly hard. So did Tag."

"I'll support you," said Archie, putting a bottle of Sancerre and two glasses on his mother's bedside table. "Look, are you sure you want to go through with this?"

Caitlin, who, despite her habitual air of unconcern, was trembling like an earthquake, nodded her head. "I reached the age of consent last week. It's awfully tidy in here." She looked around in amazement. "You ought to see my parents' bedroom. D'you think we ought to put a towel underneath us? It'd be so awful if I bled all over your mother's sheets."

"What time is it?" whispered Archie.

"One forty-five," said Caitlin, looking at the flickering red figures of the digital clock. "Why?"

"I want to remember what time the most important event in my life took place," said Archie, as he unbuttoned her black cardigan.

He looked terrible, thought Taggie, as she brushed Declan's dark blue suit and straightened his tie. The new Harvie and Hudson green and blue striped shirt Cameron had bought him last week in honor of the occasion was already too big. In the last fortnight the thick black hair had become almost entirely silver, and despair and grief had dug even deeper trenches on his forehead and on either side of his mouth.

The clock struck two.

"Car's here, Declan," called Freddie from the hall.

"Good luck," said Taggie, hugging him. "It'll be over in half an hour."

One by one the members of Venturer shook Declan's hand and wished him well. Billy gave him the faded four-leaf clover he'd worn in his boot when he'd won the show-jumping silver medal in Colombia. Henry Hampshire gave him a piece of white heather, foisted on him by a gypsy outside Harrods that morning. Rupert had sent a telex from LA. Everyone waved to Declan as he set off.

"Majestic though in ruin," said Patrick ruefully.

"Not yet," boomed Dame Enid. "Don't be so defeatist, boy."

The media went berserk as Declan's car drew up. It had been a long, cold, somewhat boring day. Not admitted inside the IBA for reasons of security, they had spent their time belting the hundred yards between the front of the building and the back, desperate to get a story. Managing Directors of television companies are enormously powerful but not always very well known men. One camera crew had had the embarrassment of asking their own Chief Executive what television company he worked for. Another crew wasted a lot of film on their own press officer.

But everyone knew Declan. Many of the crews had worked with him, and loved him, and wished he could have won. The Christmas shoppers, battered by the cold and each other, knew him too, and cheered and mobbed him. It took him several minutes to fight his way across Brompton Road and, as he went in through the revolving doors, a fat woman gave him a piece of holly for good luck. Coming the other way was Johnny Abrahams, his old boss at the B.B.C. who'd put in a bid to oust Granada.

"How did you do?" asked Declan.

"They told us to go home," said Johnny despondently.

Declan was taken up in the gray steel elevator to the eighth floor and ushered into a large office which said "Members' Viewing Room" on the door. Inside a lot of maroon chairs were lined up in front of a large screen. The gray telephone in the corner was dead. A smell of turkey drifted down the passage, the aftermath of Lady Gosling's festive lunch. Out the window he could see Knightsbridge and the northeast corner of Harrods, strawberry roan against a sullen gray sky with its colored flags fretted by the ice wind.

He looked down at the piece of holly which still had two red berries. It was nice that all those people had been pleased to see him. Perhaps one day when he'd got this mockery of a franchise behind him, he might work again. He wondered what Maud was doing; probably celebrating at the Hyde Park Hotel with Tony. Directly below him was Lancelot Place. It was ironic that he was the Arthur who'd promised the IBA Camelot, and Tony was the Lancelot who'd stolen his Guinevere. Oh Christ, he groaned, how could he possibly ever do anything in life without her?

"Mr. O'Hara."

Declan started, looking around stupidly. A kind-faced woman in spectacles had walked through the door with a tray full of envelopes and handed a white one and a larger brown one to him.

"Your envelopes. Best of luck."

"Thank you," muttered Declan.

He waited politely until she'd gone, then shoved them in his coat pocket. Like bills, he never believed in opening unpleasant things. Out of the window he saw a group of horses and riders jingling back to the stables at Hyde Park, back to oats and a warm straw bed. Christ, how peaceful to be a horse. And how beautiful they were. He'd have to put The Priory on the market immediately, but he might get a day or two's hunting before he left.

"Mr. O'Hara."

"I'm sorry. I was just leaving."

"Would you come upstairs and have a word with Lady Gosling?"

"Not much point really. Nice of her to bother, though."

"She asked me to collect you," said the bespectacled woman firmly.

Lady Gosling sat in her office, behind a huge desk. The Director General and his deputy sat on the sofa. The room was full of smoke. They'd obviously all had a good lunch.

"Good afternoon, Mr. O'Hara." Lady Gosling rose slightly, holding out her thin freckled hand.

Declan held out his, realized he was still holding the bit of holly, and blushed.

"Rather premature to celebrate," said Lady Gosling dryly. "I should sit down if I were you."

Declan mumbled he would prefer to stand.

"Well," she began sternly. "There were certainly some patchy moments in your bid. Freddie Jones obviously had an exceptional grasp of finance, and Cameron Cook was first class. What a very bright, courageous girl. And, of course, some of your program plans are extremely interesting."

What's she going on about? thought Declan wearily. It was like a condemned man being told that he's got a really sympathetic hangman.

"Some of the publicity, on the other hand, has been perfectly frightful," went on Lady Gosling fiercely. "And your security left a lot to be desired. However, we were impressed by this." She handed Declan some sheets of paper.

At the top of the first were three typewritten lines. It was a little time before Declan's tired eyes could make out what they said.

"We, the undersigned, wish to state we would like to support Declan O'Hara's bid for the Corinium franchise. He makes a kind of television we believe in, and in the brief time he was at Corinium we were all impressed by his utter integrity and kindness to staff at all levels. If his consortium were awarded the franchise we would all like to work for him."

Slowly, slowly, Declan's eyes traveled down the list of names: Georgie Baines, Cyril Peacock, Daysee Butler, Deirdre Kilpatrick, Mike Meadows, then on to PAs, secretaries, production buyers, designers, security men, receptionists, gaffers, producers, riggers, researchers, makeup girls, engineers, floor managers, directors, cafeteria ladies, sound men, vision mixers. He turned the page. The list went on in three columns down to the bottom of the next page, and then down to the bottom of the next and swam before his eyes.

Declan turned toward the window. The horses had all gone in. He pressed his hands to his eyes, his great shoulders shaking.

"That's a most impressive document," said Lady Gosling gently. "I should frame it and look at it if ever you feel low."

Declan turned to her, frantically rubbing his eyes.

"I'm sorry to let them down," he said in a choked voice. "It was good of you to show it to me."

"On the contrary," said Lady Gosling. "You haven't let them down at all. Why don't you open those envelopes."

Still clutching his piece of holly, Declan's hands were trembling so much, he tore the white envelope and had to piece the letter together.

"*Dear Mr. O'Hara,*" he read incredulously, "*We have great pleasure in telling you that the Venturer Consortium has been awarded the Corinium franchise.*"

Declan read the letter three times in silence. Then he opened the brown envelope, which contained contractual details.

"I wouldn't bother to try and absorb those at the moment," chipped in the Director General, also in a slightly unsteady voice, "but it's all good news. Well done."

In silence Declan shook hands with them, then presented the piece of holly to Lady Gosling and walked out of the room. Totally forgetting Freddie's driver waiting in the underground parking lot, he took an elevator to the ground floor. Outside the building the press surged forward.

"How d'yer do, Declan?"

Then, seeing he was fighting back the tears, they divided and let him through as he walked unsteadily off in the direction of Holland Park.

Gathered around the radio, because there was no television news till six o'clock, the Venturer consortium pounced on every bit of news. A great cheer went up when the reporter said that Tony Baddingham had been seen driving away from the building looking stony-faced.

"Perhaps we haven't come to another wake, after all," said Freddie, in amazement. "Let's have a drink anyway."

"Maybe the IBA wants us to merge in some way with Corinium," suggested Cameron.

"Count me out then," said Charles.

They all jumped as the radio crackled.

"The latest news on the franchise front," said the commentator, "is that Declan O'Hara has just come out of the IBA building in tears, so I'm afraid things look bleak for Venturer. He's just walking through the crowds and was last seen heading toward South Kensington subway station like a man in deep shock."

Cameron looked at Patrick. "That's that, then."

"That bugger Baddingham's beaten us after all," said Dame Enid furiously. "I'm bloody well going to tell Gwendolyn Gosling how he enticed Maud away and bribed Beattie Johnson. I don't give a damn what Declan says, we must be able to appeal."

"I don't fink we can," said Freddie wearily. "The decision's final."

"Nothing's final," said Dame Enid briskly.

Taggie went white. "You don't think Daddy will do something silly?"

"Of course not," snapped Cameron, because she had thought the same thing and was frightened too.

Lizzie took Freddie's hand. "I'm so sorry, darling."

Freddie shook his head, near to tears too, unable to speak.

Next minute Freddie's chauffeur called from the car: "I 'eard the bad news on the radio, Mr. J. I've picked up Mr. O'Hara at South Ken."

"Is he OK?" said Freddie.

"Well, he's not making much sense, but I'll bring him back to Holland Park."

Ten minutes later Declan walked into the drawing room. For a second he looked like a thundercloud, so they all knew finally there was absolutely no hope. Then for the first time in weeks, he gave his wicked schoolboy grin: "It's all right, my darlings. We got it."

There was a stunned silence, followed by an explosion of cheering; everyone was hugging each other. Janey burst into tears, so did Charles. Dame Enid and Billy were wiping their eyes.

"Fuckin' 'ell," yelled Freddie, jumping up and down.

"Good Lord," said Henry.

Taggie suddenly found herself hugging Cameron. "We got it," they both screamed simultaneously.

"Are you quite, quite sure?" said Bas incredulously. "Can we see the proof?"

Grinning broadly, Declan got the torn white letter out of his pocket. Everyone crowded around to have a look.

"Bloody hell, it's true," said Janey, giving a whoop of joy and hugging Billy. "We can move back to Penscombe."

"I might keep my cottage after all," said Marti.

"What decided them finally to give it to us?" Cameron asked Declan over the Tarzan howls and the deafening fusillade of champagne corks.

"Mostly you," said Declan, putting an arm around her shoulders. "They thought you were marvelous, and they adored Freddie, but it was everyone," he went on, raising his hand for silence. "It was all of you turning up at the IBA that finally swung it. A case of everyone ventured, everything won. In the end, none but the brave deserved the franchise." He wiped his eyes. "I'm so proud and happy for us all."

Over at Rutland Gate Caitlin lay in Archie's arms.

"Are you sure that was all right," he asked her for the hundredth time, as he stroked her flat white belly.

"Of course it was."

"I love you more than ever. You're so beautiful. Did it hurt very much?"

Caitlin giggled: "One has to suffer to be beautiful. And we've got the whole vacation ahead of us. Have you got masses of work to do?"

"Yes," said Archie.

"So have I. We can do it together."

"Are you hungry? I am. I'll see if there's anything in the kitchen." Archie got up. Naked, still slightly plump, but to Caitlin entirely beautiful, he peered through the curtains. At three-thirty, it was getting dark.

"Holy shit," said Archie. "My mother's just getting out of a taxi."

Frantically Caitlin kicked the bottle under the bed, put the two glasses in the bedside table drawer, dragged on her jeans, her black cardigan and her boots, and shoved her shirt, bra, panties, and socks in her carrier bag. Archie turned off the bedroom lights.

Monica found Archie and Caitlin sitting on either side of an empty fireplace. Caitlin was reading *Country Life* upside-down.

"Hullo, Mummy," said Archie heartily, getting up and kissing her. "I thought you'd be at Dad's celebration piss-up. I was about to join you."

"It's been cancelled," said Monica numbly. "We've lost the franchise."

"What!" exploded Archie. "We couldn't have. All the papers said it was in the bag."

"They were wrong."

"My God, I'm sorry."

Caitlin couldn't take it in. "D'you mean Daddy's got it?" she said slowly.

"I don't know." Monica looked at Caitlin dazedly. "I suppose so."

Still in her fur coat and headscarf, she sat down very suddenly on the sofa, stared at her rough gardening hands, with their huge diamonds, and burst into tears. Archie, who'd only seen his mother cry once, years ago when one of her Labradors had to be put down, was utterly helpless. It was like watching the *Titanic* sink.

"I just feel so sorry for him," sobbed Monica. "I know he's done dreadful, dreadful things, left no stone unturned to try and win the franchise, but he wanted to beat Rupert and Declan so very badly."

Rushing across the room, Caitlin put her arms around Monica.

"I'm so sorry. I'm delighted for Daddy of course, but it's like the Boat Race. Someone's got to win, but it doesn't stop it being horribly, desperately, publicly humiliating for the crew who don't. There, please don't cry. Get her some brandy," she ordered Archie. "Will you be terribly poor?"

"No," gulped Monica, "I don't think so. Tony's got all his other companies. It's just that he minded so much, and it's such a shock. He was so certain."

Struggling to her feet, desperately wiping her eyes, saying she must find a handkerchief, she stumbled off to her bedroom.

Thinking of the unmade bed, Archie and Caitlin looked at each other in horror.

"I must be going senile," gulped Monica when she returned, wiping her eyes and blowing her nose. "I could have sworn I made my bed this morning."

"You've been under a terrific strain," said Caitlin sympathetically. "My father topped up a whisky and soda with milk the other day."

"But I never leave it unmade," whispered Monica. "I can't afford to go to pieces. Tony's going to need so much support."

She made a face like a little girl drinking medicine as she took a gulp of the brandy.

"I'll go and make it for you," said Caitlin. "That'll make you feel better. "Then Archie and I are going to get you some lunch."

In the middle of Venturer's amazed and joyful celebrations, the telephone rang. Dame Enid picked it up. Not bothering to put her hand over the receiver, she yelled: "It's the boring old fart for you, Declan."

"Congratulations, Declan," said the Bishop of Cotchester heartily. "Delighted you've finally got the franchise. With the festive season nearly upon us, I've been pondering much on the nature of forgiveness. I think, on balance, my flock will understand if I overlook Rupert Campbell-Black's lamentable behavior. I would like to reconsider my position vis-à-vis Venturer."

A beatific smile spread over Declan's face: "Flock off," he said, and hung up.

Cameron sat on the sofa cuddling Blue.

"A penny for your thoughts," said Patrick, sitting down beside her. "Although, now you've won the franchise, I suppose they're much more expensive than that."

Cameron grinned: "I was thinking how odd it is to feel so wildly happy when one's heart is breaking."

"It's relief," said Patrick, filling up her glass, "to discover you're going to survive after all."

He glanced across at Taggie who, with a fixed smile on her face, was gathering up glasses like a zombie.

"I'm not sure my sister is."

"What's she got to complain about?" said Cameron bitterly. "Rupert loves her."

"She hasn't got a clue he does," said Patrick, "and he's not going to do anything about it. He's probably at some Hollywood orgy, busy forgetting her, at this moment. Freddie and Pa have been trying to get through to him all evening, but there's no answer."

Cameron looked at her watch.

"It must be breakfast time in LA," she said.

CHAPTER 47

Over in California Rupert was slowly going out of his mind with misery. Leaving England had made everything far, far worse. He couldn't eat or sleep. He must be dying if he didn't even want to drink. All he could do was long for Taggie. He'd never dreamed anything could hurt so much.

"Rupert," said Suzy Erikson, his beautiful hostess, as they breakfasted by the pool, having just come in after an all-night party, "I've been talking to you for twenty minutes, and you haven't heard a single word."

"I know. I'm sorry."

"I've also trailed all the most glamourous women in Hollywood in front of you for the past fortnight and you've paid no attention to any of them."

"I know. I'm sorry about that too."

"Still brooding about your Irish teenager?" said Suzy, plunging a spoon into her melon. "Go home and screw her. It's the only way you'll get her out of your system."

Rupert looked at his cooling cup of coffee. "I can't, I mustn't fuck her up," he repeated dully. "Apart from Billy, she's the only genuinely good person I've ever met."

"That seems rather a good omen," said Suzy. "Billy's the only person you've ever been faithful to, and the only one you haven't fucked up either."

As Rupert got up to prowl up and down the terrace, Suzy thought how much weight he'd lost and how really ill he looked. Having some years ago been desperately in love with him, she'd always longed to see him brought to his knees. But now, so abject was his despair, she could only feel sorry for him.

"I want to look after her," he was saying. "She's the only person who's ever made me want to find a dragon and slay it for her sake, although," he added with a half-smile, "she wouldn't appreciate it. She doesn't like cruelty to animals at all."

"Good thing she didn't know you in the old days," said Suzy. "Have you got a picture?"

Rupert walked back to his chair and extracted a creased snapshot from the inside pocket of his boating jacket, which was hanging over the back of the chair. It was one he'd taken in the woods. Taggie was pink-faced from catching leaves with the children.

"Not a great beauty, is she?" said Suzy with a certain satisfaction. Rupert snatched back the photograph.

"She is," he said icily. "She's the most beautiful girl I've ever seen."

"Hum," said Suzy. "Well, if you think that, you have got her badly."

An extremely tense silence was broken by the telephone.

"Someone called Declan O'Hara for you," said Suzy. "He seems kinda drunk."

Rupert steeled himself for abuse.

"We've got it, we've fucking got it," yelled Declan.

"You what?"

"Not just us—you as well. We've fucking got the franchise."

Judging from the shrieks and whoops, there was the most terrific party going on in the background. Rupert wished, after the initial passionate relief, he could feel more excited and respond appropriately to Declan's almost incoherent ecstasy. Then he talked to Freddie, who was calmer but equally euphoric, and briefly to Cameron who sounded pretty overexcited as well. Then Declan snatched back the telephone.

"Isn't it fucking marvelous? You better come back soon, and we can find out if we know how to run a television company—what's that? Oh Taggie says to wish you a Merry Christmas."

Rupert walked to the edge of the shimmering pale blue pool and looked up at the snowy peaks of the Santa Monica mountains, that rose like one of Taggie's desserts. He wondered if the snow had thawed at Penscombe.

"I'm going home," he said. "I think if I was in the same country as her, it might hurt less."

The journey home was hell. All the stewardesses fluttered around him, plying him with champagne and delicious things to eat which he left untouched. By some ghastly irony, the film was the same Woody Allen which he'd seen with the children and Taggie. He took in as little of it as he had the first time. He tried to sleep, but it was as though he was destined to watch eternal television with Taggie's face on all four channels. He dropped off for a few minutes as the plane flew over Ireland, but dreamed of her and woke in utter desolation to find she wasn't there.

Heathrow at seven-thirty on a raw December morning was still dark.

"Good morning, Mr. Campbell-Black," said the passport man, who didn't even get a nod.

As he waited for his luggage, Rupert watched the carousel going around. It was the last circle of hell, he reflected, for people who never got the person they wanted in life. His heart was so heavy, he'd have to pay excess baggage on it. As he went through the green door at Customs, he thought of all the times in the old days when he'd sauntered through carrying dope or illegal currency in the bottom of his boots. Now he had nothing forbidden to declare but his hopeless love for Taggie.

Once through the barrier, he looked wearily around for his driver, but no one came forward. Christ, that was all he needed. He set off toward the telephones, passing a fleet of people brandishing cards with names on them. Suddenly a particularly large placard caught his eye. On it was painted in huge letters: Roopurt Cambel-Blak. Only one person could spell that badly! He must be going mad. Then below the placard, he saw a pair of very long, very slim legs in familiar faded jeans. The legs were shaking frantically, so was the placard. Rupert, finding too that his legs would hardly hold him up, walked toward it. Very gently he pushed it down, seeing first the mane of black hair, then two silver-gray eyes, then the deathly white face, and the desperately trembling mouth he'd dreamed of kissing for months now.

"Oh Tag," he said despairingly.

"I can't help it," she sobbed. "I'll do anything. I'll drive you around. I'll look after your children. I'll cook, clean your house, muck out your horses, weed your garden. I just want to be near you. I can't bear it any longer."

The next moment the placard crashed to the ground and Rupert had taken her face in his hands, feeling the contrast between the softness of her cheeks and the frantic tension of her jaw. And just to prove to himself she was real, he wonderingly kissed her lips, and her wet salty eyes, and then her forehead.

"I'm such a selfish bastard," he muttered into her hair.

"I'm used to selfish people," sobbed Taggie. "I'd be lost without them."

"And what about the memoirs?" There was so much uncertainty and despair in his voice that Taggie drew slightly away from him. Then she laughed despite her tears. "I couldn't read them. That's one advantage of being dyslexic."

Rupert started to laugh too, and then, taking her in his arms, gave her a kiss that, everyone gathered around said afterwards, should for length and passion have gone straight into the *Guinness Book of Records*.

"I love you," he gasped as he came up for air. "I've never loved anyone like I love you." Then, aware that she was still trembling, added, "It's all right, darling," and suddenly he knew that it was and he'd never let her go again.

Glancing around, Rupert saw they were surrounded by Press. Holding Taggie close, he whispered, "Where's the car?"

"Outside, just through the door."

"We'll make a dash for it."

* * *

On the highway he managed to shake off the reporters, took an exit into some Royal Berkshire countryside and pulled up in a lay-by. Then, removing both their seat belts, he turned to face her, taking her hands.

"I want you to know . . ." it was he who was stammering now ". . . that I only joined the fucking consortium because of you. In fact, I only came back from Gstaad for your rotten brother's twenty-first because I wanted to have a crack at you. I only let myself be interviewed by your father because I thought he'd think me a wimp if I didn't, and I might be able to ingratiate myself with him. I only bought his bloody woods for that ludicrously inflated price because I love you. The only reason I didn't move in on you months ago was because in the one unselfish gesture of my life (and Christ, it was the most difficult), I thought it was unfair to foist my sodding bloody-minded nature on you. No one could have had a more appalling past."

Taggie put up a hand to his lips to halt him. "I don't care about your past," she said shakily. "All I want to be is your future."

It was not long before the car had misted up completely, and Rupert stopped kissing her and wrote, "I adore you. Will you marry me?" on the windshield.

And underneath Taggie wrote, "Yes pleese."

Back on the highway it was light now, and Taggie could see how gray and thin Rupert looked, and how blackly shadowed he was under the eyes.

"I just can't wait to feed you up," she wailed.

Looking ahead, she saw the pallid full moon, which like a sympathetic friend had peered in at different windows of her turret bedroom throughout the night as she paced the floorboards wondering whether or not she should go and meet Rupert. Now, clearly dying to go to bed, the moon kept on bobbing around clumps of trees or above the frozen white downs, as if just managing to keep awake to see how the story ended. Silently, thankfully, Taggie made a joyful thumbs-up sign as the moon finally disappeared from view.

"How did you screw up the courage to come and meet me?" asked Rupert, putting his hand on her thigh as they turned off the highway.

"I went to see the children and gave them your presents yesterday afternoon. I was so desperate, it was the nearest I could get to you. They were so sweet, and Malise and Helen were really nice. They asked me to stay to supper, and after the children went to bed,

I talked to Malise. He said he and Helen had overreacted about the memoirs, and he was sorry, and how happy Helen had made him, and he was thirty years older than her, and he told me to go for it.''

"Really," said Rupert in amazement. "Good old Malise."

"Where are we going?" asked Taggie, snuggling up to him.

"To ask your father's permission. If he won't give it, we'll have to elope, but I don't want it hanging over us."

"You'll have to see Mummy as well."

"She's back!" said Rupert in outrage. "When, for Christ's sake?"

"The day before yesterday, the evening we got the franchise."

"That figures," said Rupert dismissively. "Realized she'd backed the wrong horse."

"No," said Taggie. "She saw Daddy crying on television when he came out of the IBA. You know how emotional he is, and she thought it was from unhappiness because he'd lost it, and felt so sorry for him that she rushed back and turned up at Freddie's house in the middle of the celebrations just after Daddy'd called you in fact. It was so odd. I'm not boring you?" she added quickly.

"You never, never bore me," said Rupert, touching her cheek.

"Well, d'you know what Mummy said when she first saw him? Such a strange remark that I remembered it. She said: 'My Oberon! what visions have I seen. Me thought I was enamoured of an ass.' Patrick says it comes from *Midsummer Night's Dream*. Anyway, they were both crying and fell into each other's arms, and disappeared into Freddie and Valerie's bedroom."

"Pa and Ma for the course," said Rupert, shaking his head.

Taggie giggled. "It was a bit embarrassing. Hordes of press and television people turned up to interview Daddy and photograph him about getting the franchise, and he'd locked himself in with Mummy. So Freddie and Cameron had to field all the questions.

"And then, even worse, Valerie arrived. She'd beetled up from London the moment she'd heard Venturer had won, to get in on the act, and she found everyone plastered, and Freddie kissing Lizzie Vereker on the sofa. So she stormed off to bed, and she couldn't get in because Mummy and Daddy were in there already."

"Christ, we'll never behave like that, will we?" said Rupert putting his hand over hers.

All the same Rupert was surprisingly nervous about confronting his future father-in-law. He needn't have bothered. When he went into the library Declan was poring over all sorts of leaflets for electronic equipment spread out on the table.

"Rupert. Great to see you, good of you to come back so quickly. Come and look at this stuff. We're going to bid for a satellite next."

Rupert took a deep breath. "I actually came back to ask for your daughter's hand in marriage, Declan."

"Have you?" Declan peered over his spectacles at Taggie. "I thought you might. Well she certainly looks happier than she's done for the past nineteen years, so I'd better say yes. We've got a hell of a lot to do here. Can you start work before Christmas?"

"No, I bloody can't. I'm going to be on my honeymoon over Christmas."

"So soon. Can't you wait till the spring and go to Paris? Maud and I went to Paris. I'd better call her and we'll have a drink. Good thing you didn't turn up yesterday, we were all so hungover, you might not have had such a genial reception. Maud!" he yelled up the stairs.

Maud wandered down, looking pretty wretched after her prolonged disappearance, but with plenty of her old insouciance, and embraced them both.

"She's obviously so glad to be home, she wouldn't have minded you marrying the cat," Rupert said to Taggie afterwards.

A bottle of champagne had been opened, when Patrick marched in, looking like a thundercloud.

"I've just heard the news on Radio One," he said coldly. "I suppose none of you has had the decency to tell Cameron."

"Oh dear," said Declan. "I'll call her."

"It's my responsibility. I'll do it," said Rupert.

"I'll do it," said Patrick heavily.

He took the telephone into the living room and dialed the number of Cameron's house in Hamilton Terrace. She took a long time to answer.

"I've just heard," she said in a flat voice.

"It must hurt, I'm very sorry."

"You needn't be," snapped Cameron. "Why should I care if your sister's finally got him, when it's all over between him and me?"

"Still hurts," said Patrick reasonably. "Not much fun seeing someone get a clear round on a horse you were bucked off by. I'll be over later."

"Whatever for?" Cameron's voice was shrill with hostility. "I'm going out."

"You stay where you are."

Cameron collapsed on her bed. She had nowhere to go anyway. She supposed her house belonged to Venturer now. Outside, the shoppers were trailing argumentatively home in the rain, weighed down by Christmas presents. Then, like a frozen pipe that suddenly bursts with a thaw, Cameron, for the first time since Rupert left for America, gave way to tears.

Around five-thirty, when there seemed nothing left to weep out of her system, she tried to pull herself together, took Blue for a quick desolate walk across the water meadows and had a bath. At half-past-six and seven she was interrupted by carol singers. At a quarter past seven she was disturbed by two men with a truck who said they had some stuff to deliver.

"What stuff?" snapped Cameron.

"Six trunks full of books, records, and some clothes."

"Don't be fucking stupid! You've got the wrong house! Take it away!" she screamed.

At that moment Patrick walked purposefully through the door, carrying two squash rackets and a portable typewriter under one arm and a large cat under the other.

"I don't like cats, nor does Blue," snarled Cameron.

"You will," said Patrick soothingly. "Just give me five minutes," he added to the driver, as he pushed Cameron into the sitting room and shut the door behind him.

"What are you playing at, and what's all that shit they're delivering?"

"I'm moving in," said Patrick, putting the cat down. Immediately Blue bounced up to the cat, dropping gracefully down on his front paws, head on one side. The cat hissed, tail like a Christmas tree, and took a fierce swipe at Blue's nose. Blue gave a yelp and retreated between Cameron's legs.

"They'll get used to each other," said Patrick, "just like we will."

"We bloody won't."

"Yes, we will. I love you."

"You can't any more. I've been such a bitch," said Cameron, going very pale. "Anyway, I love Rupert."

"No you don't, or you wouldn't have gone to bed with my father in Ireland."

"I didn't," stammered Cameron.

"Anyway," said Patrick with more than a touch of Declan's arrogance, "as I'm a much younger, more beautiful, more together, about to be much more successful version of my father, it's perfectly logical that you should fall in love with me.''

''You're a toy boy,'' said Cameron as his hands tightened around her waist.

''I'm not. I'm a man of substance. The B.B.C. have just bought my first play and commissioned another.''

Cameron grinned. ''You'd better cancel the contract, and I'll produce them both.''

''Nope,'' said Patrick firmly. ''I never mix business with pleasure, and you, my dear, dear love are only pleasure.''

''I love Rupert,'' wailed Cameron.

''Don't be silly,'' said Patrick, drawing her close to him.

''Well, perhaps I don't,'' said Cameron bewildered, as a few minutes later they were interrupted by a loud knock on the door.

''Can we unload the stuff now, sir?'' said the driver. Then, lowering his voice, he added, ''It's bleedin' cold outside.''

Patrick looked at Cameron questioningly.

''Oh well, I guess you can.''

As the men stomped out to the van, Patrick smiled down at her: ''I just want to check out your availability for the next thousand years,'' he said.

''I've never seen such a change in Taggie,'' said Caitlin to Archie next morning. ''She keeps giggling all the time, and grinning from ear to ear, and she's suddenly got terribly protective. Rupert's been asleep for twenty-four hours in the spare room, and the most amazingly important people have rung up, and she hasn't let any of them talk to him.''

''That's nice,'' said Archie, kissing her. ''They say love hits you with even more of a thunderbolt when you're old.''

Rupert woke to blue skies and birds singing outside, a fire in the grate and total panic inside. He had no idea where he or Taggie was. Then suddenly he became aware of something warm and furry, and realized Gertrude was lying in the small of his back. Slowly the events of yesterday reasserted themselves and he felt so happy he nearly went back to sleep again. Next minute the door opened very cautiously.

''I'm awake,'' said Rupert.

''You did sleep well,'' said Taggie in delight as she put down the breakfast tray.

''Because I felt safe for the first time in my life. Come here.'' Rupert patted the bed, and when he kissed her, she smelled of toothpaste and her mother's scent.

Afterwards he stroked her face incredulously. "I still can't believe I'm going to spend the rest of my life with you."

"Nor I you," sighed Taggie.

Breakfast consisted of homemade apple jelly, croissants, coffee
and orange juice.

"I was going to bring you bacon and eggs," said Taggie, spooning a seed out of the orange juice, "but I thought if you hadn't been
eating, it might be too rich for you."

Then she giggled. "A girl from the *Daily Mail* rang up just now."

"What did she want?" asked Rupert, thinking how wonderfully
it suited her to be so happy.

"She said, 'How did you first meet your fiancé and what was he
doing?' I couldn't say you were playing nude tennis with Sarah Stratton, so I said Basil brought you around for a drink. And the Leader
of the Opposition rung twice. Evidently the Government's fallen and
there's going to be an election. She wants you to ring her urgently.
I said you were asleep."

Rupert's eyes gleamed. "I've got a feeling you're going to be far,
far more use to me than I ever dreamed. We'd better get married at
once. I'm allergic to the word fiancée."

"I certainly can't spell it," said Taggie.

Later, downstairs, they discussed marriage plans.

"I suppose it'll have to be Cotchester Registry office," said Maud,
who was thinking about her wardrobe.

"I got married in a registry office the first time around," said
Rupert. "As it's the real thing this time—" he raised Taggie's hand to
his lips and kissed it—"we thought we might get married in church.
I'm sure we can find some trendy parson in London who won't mind
my being divorced."

"I've got a better idea," said Declan, reaching for his telephone
book.

"Tabitha's going to be a bridesmaid," said Taggie to Caitlin.
"Would you like to be one too?"

"Only if I can wear jeans," said Caitlin.

Declan, having for once dialed the right number, was put straight
through to the Bishop of Cotchester. He immediately apologized for
being so shirty on the telephone the other day and wondered
whether the Bishop would reconsider coming on to the Venturer
Board after all.

After some huffing and puffing about having to take a stand over
Rupert Campbell-Black's disgusting memoirs, the Bishop said he

would be delighted, and wrote down the date of the first board meeting in January.

"There's just one other thing," said Declan. "My daughter, Taggie, is getting married and her one wish is to be married by you in Cotchester Cathedral."

Taggie turned crimson. "It isn't true," she squeaked, looking at Rupert who had started to laugh.

The Bishop once again told Declan that he'd be delighted. He'd become extremely fond of Taggie in the past year.

"Just the simplest service," said Declan. "Only family and very close friends and, of course, all our Venturer supporters."

"Splendid, splendid," said the Bishop. "And who is the very, very lucky young man?"

"Well, I'm just coming to that," said Declan.

ABOUT THE AUTHOR

Jilly Cooper is a novelist and journalist whose credits include some thirty-two books. Her previous novel, *Riders*, was a #1 British bestseller, as was *The Common Years*, Jilly's delightful chronicle of life with her family, dogs, and neighbors in London. For over thirteen years, she entertained readers of the *London Sunday Times* with her humorous columns, which have been published in five collections. Jilly has been married to publisher Leo Cooper for twenty-seven years. They have two children, Felix and Emily, five cats, and two dogs, and live in the Cotswold area of Gloucestershire. She is at work on her next novel, a sizzler about the international world of polo.